PULSE

ALSO BY MICHAEL HARVEY

Brighton

The Governor's Wife

The Innocence Game

We All Fall Down

The Third Rail

The Fifth Floor

The Chicago Way

PULSE

A NOVEL

MICHAEL HARVEY

BLOOMSBURY PUBLISHING
LONDON • OXFORD • NEW YORK • NEW DELHI • SYDNEY

BLOOMSBURY PUBLISHING
Bloomsbury Publishing Plc
50 Bedford Square, London, WC1B 3DP, UK

BLOOMSBURY, BLOOMSBURY PUBLISHING and
the Diana logo are trademarks of Bloomsbury Publishing Plc

First published in Great Britain 2018

Designed by Paul Russell Szafranski
Frontispiece art © Rio Nindyawan / Arts Vector / Shutterstock

A catalogue record for this book is available from the British Library

ISBN: HB: 978-1-4088-9536-8; TPB: 978-1-4088-9531-1;
eBook: 978-1-4088-9534-4

2 4 6 8 10 9 7 5 3 1

Printed and bound in Great Britain
by CPI Group (UK) Ltd, Croydon CR0 4YY

MIX
Paper from
responsible sources
FSC
www.fsc.org   FSC® C013604

To find out more about our authors and books visit
www.bloomsbury.com and sign up for our newsletters

Human madness is oftentimes a cunning and most feline thing. When you think it fled, it may have but become transfigured into some still subtler form.

MOBY-DICK
Herman Melville

PART I
1970

1

HEAVY HANDS pull him from a skim of sleep, a blind scramble for the door handle and the backseat of the car, vinyl rough on his face as he's dragged across it. He wriggles like bait on a hook, cold air pimpling bare skin, the mouth of the trunk grinning wide and deep. And then he's dropped inside, a blur of features flashing at the edge of the frame before the lid slams shut and the voices recede and he huddles against a spare tire, smelling the cold rubber and grease, retreating into the womb while the radio gets turned up and the voices rise and fall, bubbles of laughter giving way to a gentle rocking in the springs, low moans in rhythm, building.

He hears his mother's sigh, long and circling down, whispering her pleasure, whispering her sadness, whispering her fear, whispering apologies to the son she'd never see again. A second voice breaks the surface, a man's, muscular and pulsing, calling Daniel's mother by her first name as he wraps his hands around her throat and claims her life.

"Easy now, Violet." The man speaks like he strangles, in smooth, velvet strokes. "Little more, little more. That's it. Now, down you go."

And then it grows still. A rattle of keys and the dry cough of an engine. The car begins to roll, picking up speed as it tumbles forward.

Daniel pulls up his legs and kicks at the wall of the trunk with both feet. As the car goes airborne, the eight-year-old is birthed all over again, this time into the backseat of a '58 Buick.

———

Daniel Fitzsimmons opened his eyes and scanned the bumpy terrain of the schoolyard, the fall of the gulley that led to the street, faces in the windows of a bus as it toiled past. When you're different, really different, you know it. You wear it like a second skin, one you'd give anything to slip even if just for a moment. But you can't. You're inside the game and the game's inside you and it runs your head and messes with your mind and there's no way back, no way forward, no map to "normal." No matter what anyone tells you. At least not in this life.

He'd known all this before he was ever capable of knowing. It worked in his blood like a fever, surging and ebbing, keeping him off-balance, at odds, adrift in a sea of shifting depths. Then his mother died. And no one suspected the truth but him. No one ever would. And now he was ten.

He'd never been much of a talker. After the crash and the hospital and the rest of it, his world shrank to a single point—just him and his brother. Barely a word for well-meaning foster parents, cow-eyed teachers and counselors. Not a scrap for any of the kids in any of the schools. It wasn't a surprise then that he had no friends. And if you had no friends on a schoolyard in Dorchester, you sure as hell had enemies.

Joey Watts was older. Thirteen, fourteen. Big, dumb as a hog, hard in the chin and eyes. Suspicious, greedy, scared of the world, and pure bully. He came up behind Daniel as he sheltered against a wall, waiting for the bell that would take them into class. Daniel could feel the bully's approach, tracking it in his head in some way he didn't yet understand. Watts stopped a few feet away, measuring. Then he stepped forward and popped Daniel's cap off his head. Watts snickered. Three of his pals were watching and snickered as well.

"Freak," the bully said.

"Fitzsimmons the freak," his friends echoed.

Daniel bent for the black-and-gold Bruins cap. His hand found a rock, hard and smooth, shaped to a purpose. Daniel gripped it and felt its curve while something stirred in his chest, something ancient and evil, blessed and sublime. The young warrior in him wanted to strike out even as the old man within counseled patience. The enemy still lay hidden, not yet ready to be named.

Daniel let the rock slip from his fingers and picked up the cap. As he straightened, Watts lashed out again, catching Daniel in the ribs with a boot. He fell forward, pulping his face against the pavement and splitting his lip to the meat. He tasted blood rich in his mouth and heard his mind whisper as it whirred, spinning fast, stopping at the nexus of a certain time and a certain place. The pale sun shifted behind some clouds and the air grew bitter. Daniel wiped his face and raised his eyes to his tormentor, piercing him to his essence, fixing him to his fate.

"You drowned her. You didn't mean it. You were just being mean. But you did it."

In a stroke, Daniel had slipped inside Joey Watts, two now one. He saw the bully as a boy, in the summer of his eleventh year, standing nipple deep in the cold waters of the Quincy quarry, pushing down on the head of nine-year-old Jeannie Jameson.

Daniel watched her mouth fill as she went under for the last time, felt the grim thrill that coursed through Watts's body as the little grub thrashed and kicked and her life streamed away in a string of tiny bubbles. And then everything blurred, a final fingernail scratching the back of Watts's wrist before her limbs went soft and sloppy and sank.

"You watched them try to revive her on the rocks," Daniel said. "And then you left with your pals."

He reached out to touch Watts, but the boy reared back, nostrils flaring, a wild look in his eyes. And then he ran, the others with him. No shame was so great they couldn't bear, anything to be distant from those eyes and the god-awful truth that lived therein.

Twenty years distant, Joey Watts would climb over a railing on the upper deck of the Tobin Bridge during rush hour, take one look at the pale-ribbed water below, and jump like a motherfucker. In his studio apartment, the cops would find a woman dead in a bathtub along with a note about Jeannie Jameson and that summer day at the quarry. They'd also find Daniel's initials scrawled all over the walls. No one would ever make heads or tails out of that part of it. No one ever could.

The playground in Dorchester was empty; the wind stilled. A bell tolled, calling Daniel to class. By the time he slipped into his seat, he'd chalked up the whole thing with Joey Watts to his imagination. The lead in his belly, however, told a different tale. Whatever had taken hold of him was still there, submerged in the blood, waiting.

Six years later, it would resurface.

2

1976

THE APARTMENT was above the Rathskeller, a Kenmore Square dive known to the locals as the Rat. If he'd been older, the name might have given him pause, but Daniel was all of sixteen and the price was right. So he pulled the index card off the window, tucked it in his gym bag, and trudged up a staircase decorated with trash that looked like it had blown in off the street. At the top of the stairs was a plain wooden door with no name, no mailbox, and no doorknob. Daniel banged on it with the heel of his hand only to hear an audible click as the door swung in.

The apartment was a surprise—old-school Victorian with waxed floors that smelled like cut lemons and heavy, double-pane windows framed in their original woodwork and finished with brass fittings. A clock ticked away the time on a wall, its hands reading ten o'clock even though it was well past two in the afternoon. Nearby a silvered cat with one eye of cobalt blue and the other glassy white stared out from a shelf. The cat flexed his long back and leaped through a ribbon of sunlight, landing noiselessly on a desk before winding his way through stacks of paper and disappearing behind a pile of books. An old-fashioned turf fire smoldered in a blackened fireplace. The reeky smell mingled with a hint of pipe smoke, giving the room the feel of Galway or Mayo circa 1880. A shabby couch and soft leather chair completed the picture, huddling for warmth around the hearth while a table to one side held the fixings for tea and coffee.

Daniel moved tentatively to the center of the room. He was as awkward as a teenager got, tall and scrawny with pale oversized features, a scattering of acne, and long brown hair curling at the ends and trailing out over a hooded gray sweatshirt that had BOSTON LATIN printed across the front in boxy purple letters. He turned once in a circle, taking in the layout before drifting over to the desk and picking a piece of paper off one of the many stacks.

"Can I help you?"

Daniel could have stood in the room until day gave way to night and never noticed the person who spoke. So perfectly had he painted himself into the contours of the wall he was leaning against that it wasn't until he moved before the boy could actually put form to voice. Or, rather, shadow to voice.

"The door was open." Daniel pulled out the index card with pieces of Scotch tape stuck on each corner. "I'm here for the room."

The shadow moved like, well, a shadow. The voice seemed to be everywhere. "Your name?"

"Daniel. Daniel Fitzsimmons."

"Irish?"

"Yes. Does that matter?"

"Course not. Take a seat." An open hand directed Daniel to a chair. He sat while his host moved behind the big desk and settled, steepling his fingers and holding the tips to his lips. By the muted light of the window, Daniel got his first good look at the man. If he'd been more self-aware, or not *so* self-aware, Daniel might have noticed the man's eyes, pulling energy from whatever they touched, or the skin around the edges of his face, like butter someone had smoothed over with a knife.

"My name is Simon Lane," the man said. "But you can call me Simon."

"Okay."

Simon gestured impatiently at the index card Daniel still held in his hand. He slid it across and watched two veins that crisscrossed in the man's forehead.

"You want the room?"

"If it's still available."

"I wouldn't have left the card up if it weren't. Hmmm, maybe you won't do."

"Do for what?"

"You go to Latin School."

It was more of a statement than question so Daniel didn't respond.

"Not as old as I'd like." Again more statement than question, but this time inviting a response.

"I'm eighteen."

Simon held up a finger, crooked at the middle knuckle. "Lie."

"Seventeen."

"Won't do. Won't do at all."

"I'm sixteen. I know, it's young."

"To a person who dies at fifteen, it's an eternity. Did you think I wouldn't give you the room because of your age?"

"I wasn't sure."

"Are you a runaway? No, of course not." Simon nodded at Daniel's sweatshirt. "Where is Latin School, by the way?"

Daniel pointed vaguely out the window. "In the Fens. Avenue Louis Pasteur."

"Yes. And what year was it founded?"

"Sixteen thirty-five."

"And what book must every sixie read? And when you answer, please preface by explaining to me what a sixie is."

"A sixie is a seventh grader at Latin. He's got six years to go before he graduates. And the book we all have to read is called *Breeder of Democracy*. It's the history of Latin School."

"Boring as sin, right?"

Daniel nodded.

"See, your bona fides is established. Not a runaway. Just a local seeking a place to sleep. The rent is fine?"

The room had been advertised at fifty dollars a month. Incredibly cheap.

"The rent's great."

"Yes, it would be. Any questions for me?"

"How old are you?"

"I thought you'd ask to see the room."

"That, too."

"I'm twenty-three years older than you, Daniel. Give or take." Simon opened a desk drawer, then another, mumbling to himself as he rummaged. Daniel half expected him to come out with a runny candlestick, holding it aloft like some moth-eaten character from a Dickens novel. Instead, it was a flashlight.

"Out here by the windows isn't bad, but once we get into the hallway, the lights are hit or miss. Come on." Simon led the way toward a kitchenette tucked into the back of the room. There was a sink, a stove, a refrigerator, and a butcher-block countertop with two stools. Daniel saw a couple of plates and mugs in an open cabinet.

"Do you cook?"

Daniel shook his head.

"The refrigerator's there if you want to use it. Just leave me some space."

They reached a door cut into the wall next to the sink. It opened to a long, narrow hallway that smelled of damp. Simon snapped a light switch up and down to no avail. "I'll fix that." He clicked on the flashlight and moved it along the passage. At the far end were two more doors.

"Those are my rooms. I work in one and sleep in the other." Simon pointed at each door with the light. "You're at the other end. Bathroom's between us. This way."

For fifty bucks a month, Daniel didn't expect much, and he wasn't disappointed. Bed, dresser, mirror, and a tiny window that looked out onto the redbrick face of a building across the alley.

"All right?" Simon poked the light at Daniel, who held up his hand and squinted.

"Does the electricity work in here?"

Simon grunted and reached up to pull on a cord. A naked bulb dropped on a wire from the ceiling cast a wavering glow over the room.

"How's that?"

"Great."

"So you want it?"

Daniel shrugged. Of course he wanted it. They made their way back to the main room and took their seats again at the desk.

Daniel noticed white threads running wild through Simon's dark head of hair.

"Where's your stuff?" he said.

"I don't have much. Maybe I can bring it over later?"

"Fine." Simon produced an envelope from the top drawer. "Two keys. The gold opens the door downstairs. Usually you can just push it in, but sometimes the lock works. The silver opens the front door to the apartment."

"There's no doorknob."

"Just push that one in as well. Don't look so horrified. I've got a deadbolt on the thing."

"How do I leave?"

"There's a little handle on the inside. Works fine. You thinking of moving in tonight?"

"Probably. When do you need the rent?"

Simon waved at the notion. "Whenever. I'll get a bulb for the hall. You want tea? Good. Let's sit over here."

Simon directed Daniel to a seat on the couch next to the fireplace and walked back to the kitchenette, where he filled a kettle with water. The man was tall, big hands, knotted muscle for forearms. Not someone who worked out a lot, but possessing a natural strength that would serve him well should he ever need it. He put the kettle on a burner and returned to the main room, settling in the easy chair and once again studying Daniel over tented fingers.

"I work mostly at night in the rooms you saw at the end of the hall. That's my private area, just as your room is private. We'll share this common space. Fair enough?"

"Sure. If you don't mind me asking, what do you do? For work, I mean?"

"I'm a professor at Harvard. Well, I used to teach there. Theoretical physics."

"I'm taking physics now."

A dry smile flitted across Simon's lips. "You like science?"

"I guess. What's that?"

To one side of the fireplace was a small easel with a sketchpad on it and some pencils. Simon brought the pad over.

"I dabble. Chalk, pencil, the occasional acrylic. This is a beach at night. It's half finished."

The sky was the color of pitch, with a moon dipped in red and hanging low, casting pale bars of light across wet sand and sheening the hard, black water. A tarred road wound up from the beach, dotted with snarled trees and tufts of dark weeds. Vague white lumps grew out from the road here and there like soft tumors. The sketch still needed to be shaped and left Daniel uneasy. He was happy to hand it back to its owner.

"It's not very good," Simon said.

"I like it."

"Really?"

"Kind of creepy, but maybe that's what you're going for?"

"Maybe. If you want, I'll give you a look when it's done." Simon flipped the pad to a blank page and returned it to the easel. The kettle had begun to whistle. He went back to the kitchen and fixed them each a cup. Daniel's was the way he liked it, strong with milk and three sugars. He took a sip and set the cup down on a low table next to a folded copy of the *Boston Globe*. Simon moved the *Globe* to one side and picked up a copy of the *Harvard Crimson* that was tucked underneath. The article he showed Daniel was from last summer, a preseason piece about the Crimson's All-Ivy running back, Harry Fitzsimmons.

"That your brother, Daniel?"

"How did you know?"

Simon blew on his tea and took a sip. "There's a resemblance."

"Really?"

"More than you think. I assume you don't play football?"

"Too skinny."

"Still, you're an athlete. I'd guess runner. Long distance, maybe? Mile in the spring, cross-country in the fall?"

"You haven't been reading about me in the papers."

"It's your shoes." Simon nodded at Daniel's running shoes, blue nylon with yellow laces and white racing stripes down the sides. "Tigers. Japanese racing flats. Bad sneakers, but great if you're a runner."

"You're not supposed to wear them as sneakers."

"Exactly. Then there's your body type. All legs and lungs. You're not as good at longer distances, but the strength will come. And then you'll be very good, if you want that."

Daniel returned the paper to the table. "I like to run."

"But not race? Compete?"

"I didn't say that."

"Hmm." Another sip of tea.

"Tell me about theoretical physics."

Outside, a spasm of rain drummed against the windows and was gone. Simon put down his cup and pulled a pipe from his pocket. "You mind?"

Daniel shook his head.

"Love a good pipe. This one's a Dunhill Bulldog. Here, you can see the markings on the bowl." Simon turned the pipe over. On the underside were stamped the words:

DUNHILL   MADE IN

SHELL BRIAR   ENGLAND4

"What does the '4' mean?" Daniel said.

"That's how Dunhill dates their pipes. The baseline for this series is 1960. Add on whatever number is stamped there and you have the year the pipe was made."

"So this one's from 1964?"

Simon winked as he packed the bowl and lit it with a wooden match. When he had it going to his satisfaction, he sat back again and took a couple of puffs. "Beautiful draw." His mumbles were lost in a layer of smoke and the scent of ripe berries. Daniel didn't mind a bit and allowed his mind to float. There was a banging on the stairs below and then it grew quiet again. Simon's voice cut through the fog.

"What were we talking about?"

"Theoretical physics."

"Of course."

"Do you have a specialty?"

"Most of my work's in the field of quantum mechanics."

"The study of subatomic particles."

Simon pulled the pipe from his mouth and pointed the stem at Daniel. "They teach you that at Latin School?"

"I read it somewhere."

"I study the quantum state. Specifically, I focus on a phenomenon known as entanglement. Ever heard of that?"

"No."

"Einstein first flagged it in the 1930s. Called it 'spooky.'"

"Is it? Spooky, I mean?"

"Hell, yes." Simon leaned forward so his long face was bathed in licks of red from the fire, except for the circles around his eyes, which were black with white at the very center. It should have been frightening, but Daniel felt entirely at home, as if he'd been in the room with the smell of tobacco and old books, the glow of the turf and windows closed to the weather outside for most, if not all, of his sixteen years. That was how Daniel felt as he took another sip of his tea and wriggled his toes in his Tigers and waited to hear about the professor's research.

"Imagine," Simon said, pausing to issue a stream of smoke from one side of his mouth, "that you have a charged electron isolated in this room, sitting on this very table between us, and another electron sitting on the edge of the Milky Way, a hundred thousand light-years away."

"Okay."

"Now, imagine that the two particles are entangled—that is, in an entangled state."

"What does that mean?"

"Hell of a question. Let's think of it this way. If I rotate the electron sitting on this table, say, a half turn to the left"—Simon used a thumb and forefinger to spin his imaginary electron—"its entangled companion will turn that exact same amount to the right." Simon sat back to gauge the effect of his words.

"So the two particles are communicating?"

"No. Well, yes and no. That's the spooky part. In our hypothetical, if the two electrons were actually communicating, even if they were communicating at the speed of light, it would still take a hundred thousand years for that signal to travel across the galaxy, correct?"

Daniel nodded.

"In an entangled state, however, the change between the particles happens instantaneously."

"So the signal is traveling faster than the speed of light?"

"It would appear that way. And your Latin School physics tells you what?"

"That's impossible."

"Precisely."

"Then what's happening?"

"No one's sure. What we do know is this—for the period of time that our two particles are entangled, they move in concert regardless of the distance between them, as if they were two parts of the same body. For all intents and purposes, they are."

"Are what?"

"One and the same."

"Even though they're on opposite sides of the galaxy?"

"You've studied Einstein's special theory of relativity."

"$E = mc^2$."

"Mass converted into energy, the two being essentially interchangeable. I suspect, and I'm not alone, that entanglement is more of the same, except at a level and in a world we don't fully perceive or understand."

"A world? You mean some other world?"

"The universe isn't about the lumps of matter we can see, Daniel." Simon shook his head, trailing more smoke from his mouth and narrow, probing nose. "Stars, planets, animals, people, rocks. Abhorrent, obvious things. No, the universe is about everything we can't see—energy. Beams of the stuff running through everything that is, connecting all creation in an infinite number of impossible ways. Ways that violate what we know, or thought we knew, about the physical world. That's the piano one has to play if one wants to understand quantum mechanics. That's the piano I play, and entanglement is merely the opening chord in the symphony, the first glimmer of what lies underneath. And there's so much underneath. You take Latin?"

"Everyone at Latin School takes Latin."

"The word *conscire*. Translation?"

"'To know.'"

"Literal meaning?"

"'Scio' and 'con.' To know with."

"And it's where we get our word *consciousness?*"

"If you say so."

"Pull out your dictionary and look it up. *Conscire*, 'to know with,' provides the root concept for our idea of *consciousness*."

"I'm not sure where you're headed."

"It's right there in the word. The very act of human consciousness is a communal effort, a shared experience. To know *with* someone. In fact, I contend it would be entirely impossible for a human being to be 'conscious' as we understand the term without at least one other sentient being at the other end to record that fact."

"Because the signal would have no recipient?"

"The signal. That's exactly right. Human consciousness is nothing more or less than a signal, a pulse of energy, and entanglement describes the process by which that energy is transmitted, received, and sometimes manipulated."

"Manipulated how?"

"Einstein again. Energy cannot be destroyed. Either it is transformed into some other state or it gets passed along. You feel anger, you feel hatred, fear, envy. You must learn, we all must learn, to change it into something productive. If not, it will fester and spread, infecting everything and everyone it touches."

"Can you prove any of this?"

"You sound like you don't believe me."

Daniel shrugged. "I thought science was supposed to be all about proof."

"Have you ever heard of Einstein's thought experiments?"

"No."

"He was your age, sixteen, when he first started thinking about chasing a beam of light. He'd sit in his high school physics class and imagine riding up alongside it. If such a thing were possible, Einstein thought, surely the light would appear to be at rest, frozen in time. Later, he'd say it was his first insight into what would become the special theory of relativity."

"I'm no Einstein."

"The point is there was no blackboard in the beginning. No long strings of numbers. No concrete proof. Just a young man and his willingness to open himself up to the tension of the universe and everything it holds. The easy and the difficult. The light and the dark. The good and the evil that lies within it."

For the first time in a long time, Daniel thought about the playground in Dorchester and the feeling when he'd slipped inside Joey Watts's skin. And then Joey was there, sitting in the room along with Jeannie Jameson, dripping water and smelling of the quarry, staring at Daniel with her slack mouth and her fish eyes.

"What is it?" Simon was peering at him through a lazy circle of smoke. A smile sharpened the edges of his lips.

"Nothing."

Simon nodded and puffed, the mutter of Kenmore Square traffic distant in the street below. When the apartment buzzer rang, it was sharp and raw, scattering Daniel's soggy childhood pals and nearly knocking him off the couch. Simon padded over to the front window.

"Oh, hell." He slammed the window open and leaned out. "I told you tomorrow. Hang on." Simon went back behind his desk.

"Maybe I should go get my stuff," Daniel said.

Simon looked up. "Sorry, it's this student. He dropped out of Harvard and is heading back to California. Guy's nuts for computers. Stays up all night writing source code. You know any-thing about that? Never mind. I told him I'd give him something to play with. You say you'll be back tonight?"

"If that's okay?"

"Sure, sure. Listen, tell this guy to come up when you go downstairs. Name's Gates."

Daniel started to respond, but Simon was already deep in a notebook, making some calculations. From a bottom drawer, he'd pulled out a small black box with a blue X taped across the top. Simon looked up from his work and noticed Daniel staring at it.

"Prototype for a portable computer. I call it a laptop. You ever heard of internetworking?"

Daniel shook his head.

"Right now, it's just a few universities connecting on main-frames. But this thing"—Simon tapped the top of the black box—"this is the game changer. Of course, it's child's play compared to what we were talking about, but Gates asked if he could take a look. You got your keys?"

Daniel nodded, but Simon was gone again, popping open his prototype and typing on what looked like a keyboard. Daniel left the apartment, walking back down the stairs slowly. Gates's first name was Bill. He was grad-student thin with horn-rimmed glasses and a wild mop of ginger hair. He offered a friendly if cu-rious smile and brushed past as Daniel told him to go up. Then Daniel was alone on the street.

—

He jogged across Commonwealth Avenue and cut through the Kenmore Square bus shelter. On the corner a man was grilling hot dogs at a stand painted mustard yellow. Business was good, the line five deep, customers with bills in hand, shifting back and forth in the cold, going up on their tiptoes to get a look at the dogs cooking shoulder to shoulder with thick links of Italian sausage and German bratwurst. Next to the stand sat a spaniel mix at full attention, back muscles aquiver, head tracking the cook's every move, a long drool of saliva swan diving off his lower jaw toward the pavement.

Daniel closed his eyes and thought about his new roomie, the slightly crazy, slightly scary professor from Harvard. Maybe they were all wack jobs in Cambridge. Or maybe it was just physics. No wonder Daniel liked the stuff. He smiled to himself and breathed through his nose, exhaling as a door in his mind swung open. He found himself untethered, adrift in a cream of fog, dark shapes zooming up and whispering past. Ahead a light flickered and grew, dissolving the fog to a thin mist. It was Albert Einstein, Albert the teenager, skimming his way toward Daniel across a surf of colors and numbers, grinning and waving as he rode his beam of light to his destiny. Daniel moved closer, looking up at young Einstein, who held out his hand. Daniel reached for it and fell, weightless, nameless, tipping head over heels into a space devoid of form. Einstein was gone, his beam of light transformed into a ripe, juicy sausage, dripping golden fat and oozing smoke and heat.

Hot dog.

Sausage.

No, hot dog.

No, sausage.

Daniel sat at the bottom of a well, a dog's-eye view, staring up at the man from the stand as the man stared down, something pinched between his fingers. It smelled like gristle and grease and meat. Glorious, wonderful, amazing meat. The prospect of it moved through Daniel like a current, wiggling his body from head to toe and back again. Then the man tossed the scrap into the air, and Daniel rose as it fell, jaws snapping, saliva streaming, belly in full growl.

He opened his eyes. To one side of the hot dog stand the spaniel's butt was up, tail waving as he feasted on leavings the cook had thrown his way. Otherwise, nothing had changed. Unless everything had. He circled closer, scratching the dog between the ears and running a hand across his flank. The dog paid no attention, but a woman in line did. She was staring at Daniel kind of funny, like maybe he'd been barking or howling or foaming at the mouth or something. He flashed a quick smile and hurried down the block.

On the next corner stood New England Music City. Daniel stopped in front of the plateglass windows and stared at the Andy Warhol cover for *Sticky Fingers*. Next to the album was a pair of dice and the sheet music for "Brown Sugar." Beyond that, the most beautiful girl he'd ever seen in his life or any other. When she smiled, all thoughts of Einstein, Simon Lane, and a dog's life went right out the window. Daniel waved and hustled inside.

3

LIKE MOST things in the city, South Boston was all about geography. The place was surrounded on three sides by water and hermetically sealed on the fourth by six lanes of expressway. A virtual island in a city full of them, Southie was the cousin who drank all the beer at your wedding, threw up in the punch bowl, and tried to fuck your sister for good measure on the way out. No one wandered into the place by accident. You were there cuz you grew up there or you knew someone. And that someone you knew better know the guys you were talking to. And they better be on good terms. Sort of like hitting the trifecta at Suffolk Downs, except if your horse didn't come in, there was likely to be a pack of crazy fucks trying to cave your roof in with a piece of pipe or a hockey stick. And that was if you were white and Irish and looked the part. If you were black, well, black people didn't actually go into South Boston, not unless they were under federal order and sitting in the back of a yellow school bus. And wasn't that just fun as fuck.

William Barkley Jones hit his blinker and hung a left. He didn't give a good goddamn what anyone did or didn't do in South Boston, or anywhere else for that matter. He was a black man with a badge and a gun. He was also six-five and north of two and a half bills. If the I.R.A. wanted to go to war, so be it.

Barkley parked on D Street and watched as his partner came out of a corner grocery store. Tommy Dillon was five-nine and a buck sixty soaking wet. Still, he had the strut, the swagger, the *I'm from Southie and if you don't like it, fucking try me* attitude that defined his life and wrote the moment and manner of his death in windswept strokes of gray. But that was for another day. Today, Tommy was sipping coffee from a Styrofoam cup and carrying a paper plate wrapped in tinfoil. He climbed in the passenger's side along with the smell of breakfast.

"Cocksucker bookie had a stroke last week. Can't get outta bed."

"So you're taking him scrambled eggs?"

"And chopped-up bits of sausage. Prick's a hundred and fucking six. Gums this shit down for dinner. Say a prayer he chokes."

Barkley chuckled and started up the car.

"You think it's funny?"

"More like humiliating." Barkley swept away from the curb. "How much you owe?"

"You sound like Katie."

"How much?"

"A hondo. Bet the Pats last week. Took it right up the ass."

Barkley grunted and tapped his fingers on the steering wheel.

"What?"

"You know you got the monkey, Tommy." Barkley's partner had spent six months in rehab a year back. Gambling, booze. The department didn't know about the coke. If they had, they probably would have shit-canned him, but Barkley covered. And Tommy's wife, Katie, nursed him through the rest. Tommy thought he was out the other side. Barkley wondered if it wasn't past time to look for a new partner.

"Jesus, B. It's a hundred bucks and a plate of eggs."

"If that's all it is . . ."

"That's all it is. Come on. He's in the South End."

They cruised a block that looked just like the last four—three-deckers, two families, all jammed up one against the other. Irish everywhere, mayonnaise faces playing hockey in the street, sitting on the front steps, hanging on the corner, big eyes, hard eyes, flat eyes, gypsy eyes, pointing at Barkley, one little fuck giving him the finger as the big-shouldered car cruised past.

"Assholes," Tommy said.

"Forget it." Barkley blew through a red light and turned onto Dorchester Street. The city was in its third year of forced busing; the protests that started outside high schools in Charlestown and South Boston had metastasized into a pitched battle between a federal judge determined to integrate Boston's public schools and the city's white working class, just as determined to protect their turf and not be told what to do with their kids by the government . . . or anyone else. Last spring Bostonians watched, some in horror, some in grim satisfaction, as a gang of white kids attacked a black man outside city hall, charging at him with the pointed end of an American flag. A photographer from the *Herald* caught the moment and splashed it across the front page. A couple of weeks later, some black kids in Roxbury pulled a white guy from his car and cracked his skull open with a paving stone. A crowd chanted "Let him die" while the cops arrived and EMTs loaded the guy into an ambulance. As the summer of 1976 ground on, the city burned in a blaze of its own making. Residents stuck to their block. Those who did wander into the wrong neighborhood kept their car doors locked and, if they were smart, didn't stop for nothing until they were back on safe ground. For Barkley and Tommy, it didn't really matter. They were homicide detectives and business was good—people killing other people for all kinds of fucked-up reasons. And a bunch of kids going to school in yellow buses didn't change one stroke of that.

"Check it out." Tommy pointed at a blue police bus packed with staties stitched up in their best riot gear. A second and third bus rolled right behind the first as kids began to pour into the streets, congregating in angry knots of muscle and moving in packs.

"What do you think?" Barkley said.

"Gotta be the high school."

"You wanna take a look?"

"Like I don't have enough fucking heartache? Let's go see my book."

Barkley shrugged and wheeled the car onto West Broadway. A mile later, they shot under the expressway and into the South End.

——

They found a spot on Albany Street, across from a Chinese restaurant called Hom's. A dirty rain slanted across the windshield and was gone as quick as it had arrived. Barkley nodded at a thick silver watch that hung loose on his partner's wrist.

"New?"

Tommy smiled and adjusted the bauble. "Nice, right? Check it out. The band is inlaid with turquoise."

"Katie give it to you?"

"Pawnshop. She likes it, though."

"How long you gonna be?"

"Ten minutes. Fifteen, tops."

"Don't forget your dinner." Barkley grinned and held out the paper plate of scrambled eggs, still covered in tinfoil. Tommy gave him the finger, grabbed the plate, and jogged across the street, disappearing into a fenced-off salvage yard jammed up next to a garage with a sign overhead that read STEVENS AUTO SUPPLY. Barkley switched on the radio and turned up the volume.

WRKO. DJ Mike Addams talking a mile a minute about the lowdown on the hoedown tonight at who the fuck knew where. Fifty-cent drink specials, except for the ladies. They drank free. Barkley switched off the noise and gazed out the window. The South End was a study in urban rot, gently putrefying from the inside out. Halfway down the block a flophouse advertised rooms for seven bucks a week. Next to it was a bar with a 'Gansett sign in the window and no name on the front. On the other side of the bar, a soup kitchen where the boozers could refuel for their next bender.

The door to Hom's swung open and an Asian woman popped out. She was carrying a bag of food in one hand and dragging a young girl with the other. The woman wore a cloth coat and black galoshes with metal buckles. The kid shuffled along in green boots with yellow heels.

Barkley watched as the pair picked their way around a string of trash cans and on down the block. He wasn't the only one. A whisper of a man hung in a doorway, smoking a cigarette and shivering in a jean jacket. He let the woman and child go past, then tossed his cigarette and followed. The woman ducked into a three-decker that looked like it was about to topple into the street. The man went right in after her. Barkley cursed his luck and got out of the car.

Someone had propped open the front door to the building with a chunk of cement. Barkley brushed his hand across his gun. Domestics, loud parties, dogs barking, cat up a fucking tree. It was always the most mundane, penny-ante, bullshit things that got cops shot. He shouldered open the door. To his left, a skylight striped a narrow staircase in prison bars of gray. Straight ahead, the girl with the green-and-yellow boots sat on a small bench, tongue curled between her teeth, working hard with crayons on a coloring book. Barkley squatted down so he was eye level and put a finger to his lips.

"Where's your mom?"

The girl widened her eyes and chewed on the end of a Crayola.

"She in there?" Barkley pointed at a door behind the girl, who nodded.

"That man take her in?"

Her face clouded. Barkley told the girl to stay put and sidled up to the door. He could hear a low bubble of sound that resolved into voices growing louder, more urgent. A man screamed something in what sounded like Chinese. Barkley glanced at the girl, pulled his gun, and pushed inside.

The room looked like it might have once been a garage. Cement floor, high roof with large overhead lights fixed to a double set of steel girders. On one side of the room six dingy Asian men were crowded around a table covered in pai gow tiles and cash, mostly fifties and hundreds. Five of the men were seated. The sixth, the one who had screamed, was standing up, still screaming in Chinese and shaking a golden metal cup over his head. With a final oath, he slammed the cup on the table just as Barkley came through the door. Tiles and money went flying and some dice tumbled out of the cup. No one, however, was watching where they landed. Why bother with that shit when there was a massive black man sticking a gun in your face?

"Hey, what you want?"

The woman with the buckle boots was smoking a pink cigarette and chewing on an egg roll. The man in the jean jacket sat next to her at an angle. He had a fork full of what looked like chow mein raised to his mouth and a healthy length of noodle hanging from his lower lip. In front of them was a table packed with more cash and a pile of papers. The money was wrapped in rubber bands and organized into neat stacks. Barkley flashed his badge at the woman and lowered his piece.

"Is this your little girl?" Barkley nodded at the girl, who was standing wide-eyed on the threshold. The woman barked something and the girl scurried in, disappearing behind the woman so all Barkley could see were the child's eyes, peeking out from the crook of the woman's arm.

"Bark, what the fuck?" Tommy popped out of a back room, wiping his fingers with a paper towel. "That's Tian Chen." Tommy pointed to the man eating the chow mein. "And his wife."

"Yolanda." The woman offered a limp hand. Her smile looked like an empty pocket.

"Tell them not to leave the kid outside."

"Don't leave the kid outside. They don't speak much English, B."

Barkley holstered his gun and left. Tommy followed.

"Bark."

"Chen's your bookie?"

"I told you my book had a stroke. He's holed up in the back. Yolanda and Chen run the dice and card games. Actually, Yolanda runs them. Real fucking ball-breaker, too."

"So you go in through the salvage yard?"

"Cut down the alley and came in the back."

Barkley paused at the front door to the building. "Lot of cloak-and-dagger for a hundred-dollar bet, Tommy."

"I told you they run the pai gow games in here. Piles of cash lying around and these fuckers are paranoid as shit."

Barkley started to leave. Tommy grabbed him by the shoulder. "It's nothing, B. A hondo. Go back and check with Yolanda."

Barkley walked off. He was pissed at his partner and felt stupid about pulling the piece. More the latter than the former, but Tommy didn't need to know that. A pickup struggled down the street, grinding its gears and belching flourishes of black smoke. Barkley squinted at the machine smell of oil and turned his head just as a woman came out of the Chinese restaurant, her arms full of packages. Barkley veered to avoid her, but she dipped right into his path and the two bumped shoulders. He reached for the woman's elbow as she started to topple into the gutter. She was weightless, hollowed out in the way incredibly old people get even though she was no more than thirty. Barkley noted her hands, marbled in blue, and her fingers, one decorated with a silver ring enameled in red and encrusted with diamonds in the shape of a rose.

The woman slid her hand along Barkley's wrist and gripped it, sending a hot wire up his arm and pulling him in. Her face was Western, smooth and unlined, cheeks touched with powder that smelled like the notes spinning off an old jazz record on a phonograph in a picture hanging on a wall. Then she unhooded her eyes. And Barkley's world exploded.

The concussion was silent, short-circuiting the sparks of conscious thought that arced in his brain while snatching him clean off his feet. He fell through hanging mists of pink and white, bouncing off the plateglass window of the restaurant before landing face-first on the pavement. Except it wasn't pavement anymore. It was wood, old and buckled, rotting and warped, smelling of the sea and salt and hobbled with hard round nails that bit into his cheek. Barkley opened his eyes and recognized the long wobbly run of a pier on Boston's waterfront. Below he could see the harbor, slicked with circles of oil and mottled in lumps of gray and green. The water began to bubble and then something popped to the surface. Bloated, spread-eagled, and floating on its belly, the body sagged like a half-deflated balloon. A wave swept under the pier, banging the naked corpse off a piling and rolling it over and over. In the churn Barkley spotted bits and pieces of what had once been a person—elbow, earlobe, a flash of bleached thigh leading to an ankle rubbed raw where it had slipped its tether of chains and anchor of cinder blocks. A seagull blew in sideways, circling the corpse before perching on the meat part of the shoulder. The gull stared at Barkley with a fierce black eye as its claws worked the slack flesh in small, worried circles. The bird took flight again, pushing the corpse so it rolled once more in the wash and settled faceup, lolling and bobbing merrily in the lumpy water. Barkley watched as the corpse's blue lips curled into a perfect bow and its eyelids shot open.

"Hey, Bark, what the fuck you looking at?" Tommy Dillon winked as his arm stretched out of the harbor like a bleached rubber band, snaking up a piling and across the pier. Five mossy fingers wrapped around Barkley's wrist and pulled him over the side, headfirst toward the broken sea where his partner lay in wait, jaws agape, tongue curled, eager to feed, eager to swallow him whole.

Barkley recoiled, head popping off the brick facade of the

restaurant. He was back on the pavement in front of Hom's, sitting up while Tommy looked at him all kinds of funny.

"B, you all right?"

Barkley felt for a lump on the back of his head and let Tommy help him to his feet.

"Where's the woman?" Barkley scanned up and down the block.

"What woman?"

"There was a woman coming out of the restaurant." Barkley pointed toward a CLOSED sign in the window.

"They closed up twenty minutes ago, B. I seen you fall."

"Yeah?"

"Looked like you tripped or something. Hit your head pretty good off the side of the building."

"There was a woman."

Tommy shrugged. "What say we go grab a coffee or something?"

They made their way across the street to the car. Tommy wanted to drive. Barkley told him to go fuck himself and took a hard look at the street as he sat behind the wheel.

"We going?" Tommy said.

"You think I'm crazy."

"We're all crazy, B. It's just your day today. Come on. There's a place with good pie two blocks over."

Dispatch popped on the radio. Tommy took down the details as Barkley listened, a dead finger prickling the skin of his soul. Sure as fuck, someone had just pulled a body out of Boston Harbor. He started up the car and spun the wheel into traffic. But it was Fate who was driving. And they were all just along for the ride.

4

SHE WAS standing in the ROCK aisle. Albums from artists beginning A–M ran down one side, N–Z down the other. As he got closer Daniel could smell the soap on her skin, see the moisture on her cheek and lashes.

"You're wet," he said.

"Got caught in the rain." Grace Nguyen swung her long mane of hair, catching it with both hands and piling it atop her head. "I've got to get this mop cut."

"I like it."

"Short or long?"

"Just leave it the way it is."

"Easy for you to say. You don't have to brush it and wash it and deal with it." She let the hair drop past her shoulders and clasped his arm, pulling him over to the "S" section, where she found the new Stevie Wonder, *Songs in the Key of Life*.

"They should have him in the 'W's," Daniel said. "Anyway, you like him more than I do."

"Seriously? Stevie Wonder?" Grace widened her eyes in mock horror.

"He's awesome, but I like Bruce. *Born to Run*. And the Stones."

"The Stones. Always the Stones."

"There's nothing purer in rock and roll than the first twenty seconds of 'Jumping Jack Flash.'"

"Oh my God. Let me guess, you saw *Sticky Fingers* in the window?"

"What else you gonna put in the window? We don't have the money to buy anything anyway."

"Yeah, but if we did . . . it'd be Stevie every time." Grace slid the album back in its slot and Daniel swore the minute he got the money scraped together he was gonna buy a bunch of Stevie Wonder albums, wrap them up, and watch her open them. Then they'd listen to the whole stack and he'd tell her Stevie was great but not the best and listen to her explain how he knew nothing about music and she hardly knew why she wasted her time.

"Did you stay for seventh period?" he said.

"Zzzzz." Grace closed her eyes and rested her cheek on folded hands. "Total snore. We're supposed to finish 'Book 1' by the end of next week."

Like Daniel, Grace was a sophomore at Latin School. They had a lot of classes together, including Latin, where they were in the middle of translating Ovid's *Metamorphoses*.

"Did anyone notice I wasn't there?" Daniel said.

"No, but Hamilton said there's gonna be a test. You wanna get something to eat?"

"Can't. Gotta go for a run."

They spent most days together after school bumming around Kenmore Square. For Daniel, it didn't matter where they went or what they did. He was with her and whatever came next was more than enough. So they'd hit the record store, grab a cheeseburger at Charlie's, rummage through the bins at Supersocks, or just sit on the curb and people-watch. Kenmore Square was great for that—a lot of drifters and panhandlers, hippies and Hare Krishnas mixed in with students, wannabe musicians, and artists living in cheap apartments up and down Beacon Street.

In the summer the show moved to the other side of the Pike and Fenway Park. They'd walk down Lansdowne and sit against the wall outside Gate C. Sully was always there. The scalper from Charlestown wore jeans and a white T-shirt with a pack of cigarettes rolled up old-school in his sleeve. He'd hold his tickets low by his side, making no attempt to get the attention of fans as they floated past. Cool worked better than fine in Boston and the regulars went out of their way to find him, whisper in his ear, and shove money in his hands as if Sully's reserved grandstand were somehow better than the guy selling on the next corner. Daniel and Grace were never looking for tickets, but that didn't stop people from dropping extras in their laps. Sometimes they went in if it was a good game. Usually they just gave them to Sully.

One afternoon they met a kid from Somerville named Dapper. He worked on the grounds crew and asked if they wanted to get into a Yankees game the next night. Grace was on it in a blink. Two hours before game time, they met him outside a service gate Daniel had never noticed before. Dapper shoved a couple of dark green slickers at them and said to put them on, tugging the hood up over Grace's head and tightening the string under her chin. They followed him into the belly of the park, dipping beneath the grandstand, staying quiet and small as Dapper nodded and bullshitted with ushers and concession guys who were stocking up on peanuts and rolling in kegs. He led them down a set of stairs and along a cramped corridor,

then up another set. They surfaced in a gangway that opened
to a rectangle of light and the baseball cathedral that was a
half-empty Fenway Park at twilight. Dapper stashed them in a
corner behind some buckets and rakes while he and the rest of
the grounds crew got the field ready. The crew knew who they
were with and were fine with it. Dapper told them everyone got
a turn sneaking in someone during the season and this was his
night. Daniel wondered why Dapper would use his free pass on
a couple of kids he barely knew, but then Sherm Feller came over
the loudspeaker.

Ladies and gentlemen, boys and girls, welcome to Fenway Park . . .

After Sherm, everything spun into another dimension. Daniel
felt the weight, the buzz, the Friday night jazz of thirty-thousand
plus—first dates, last dates, fathers with sons, guys flashing eyes
at girls, loners with their transistors and scorecards, kids like
Daniel and Grace, except with tickets and parents and all the
rest. They gathered like supplicants, row after row rising up into
the night—field box, grandstand, bleachers, kids hanging off the
Canadian Club sign in the outfield—welling until they filled the
precious and finely cut chalice that was Fenway to overflow, their
ferocity and their angst pouring out of the stands, bent toward
the destruction and ruin of the hated and hateful Yankees.

Daniel turned his eyes toward the jeweled perfection of the
diamond and found himself lost in it—the green of the outfield,
bases blindingly white, the soft red skin of the infield. Daniel
was sure he could curl up in the hollow of shortstop and never
wake up. And then Tiant strolled out of the dugout. Luis grabbed
the rosin off the slope of the mound, bouncing the bag across
the back of his knuckles before pounding it back to the ground.
He started in on his warm-ups, chewing on a cud of tobacco as

he threw, kicking at the dirt in front of the mound like a Cuban *toro*. Yastrzemski lobbed grounders across the infield. Closest to Daniel, Rico Petrocelli stood by third, chatting casually with the ump as everything swirled in colors around them. A warm breeze pumped up the gangway, recirculating all the Fenway smells—cigar smoke soaked in draft beer, roasted peanuts in the shell, Fenway franks and Gulden's mustard. A wrapper floated on the slipstream, dancing past Daniel, brushing the edge of the tarp and tumbling toward the infield. The ump talking to Petrocelli saw it out of the corner of his eye and snagged it with his right hand, jamming it into his back pocket without ever breaking stride in the confab with Rico.

Tiant had finished warming up and the ball was tossed around the diamond. Mickey Rivers strode to the plate, Sherm Feller taking a good thirty seconds to announce Mick the Quick's arrival as the crowd rose to its feet. Petrocelli kicked the third-base bag and looked directly at Daniel, touching the brim of his cap and pointing a finger before grabbing a handful of dirt and turning back toward home. Daniel's heart jumped three sizes in his chest. He turned to Grace to ask if she'd seen Rico see him. No Grace. Tiant cut loose. Strike one. In the lee of the crowd's roar came the boom of an usher's voice. He was pointing at Grace, who'd wandered away and was leaning over a small gate that opened onto the field. Even worse, the hood had slipped off her head. Dapper looked back at Daniel as if he were responsible. Daniel had visions of them all being tossed into the deepest, darkest Fenway Park dungeon the Yawkey family could find. Then Grace smiled, a nuclear weapon for sure, and the old usher just melted, right there in the field box section. He waved her back and mimed for her to put the hood back on and tie it tight. She did, tucking beside Daniel and squeezing his hand, thrilling him, thrilling her, probably thrilling the heck out of the usher.

Later, after the Sox had won one-zip on a Tiant three-hitter, after they'd thanked Dapper a dozen times and said good-bye, they walked across Lansdowne to a warehouse that sometimes left a side door open when the janitors were cleaning at night. It was ajar and Daniel and Grace slipped in, running quiet as a couple of Fenway mice up seven flights to the roof and crawling into their usual spot between two huge AC units. Fenway's lights were mostly off, but the moon hung rich and buttery over the park, bathing them in a healing light that gave texture and movement to their postmortem. They went over every moment, laughing at Grace with the usher, talking four or five times about Rico and his nod to Daniel (Grace said she'd seen it—how could she miss it!), sitting quietly and sharing without ever having to say a word. They were two aliens in this world—Grace, a refugee from Vietnam, arriving on a boat five years ago, the only English speaker in her family and a picture-perfect one at that, warm, open, brilliant, and kept at arm's length by the blinding whiteness of the world around her; Daniel, a refugee of another kind, no parents, foster homes, and huge chunks of his life already gone AWOL. His brother had football, Harry's fluency with the game easing his passage. Daniel had no such passport. What he did have was his mind in all its strangeness. And Grace. They had each other and wasn't that a hell of a thing. He studied her in the moonlight that drenched the rooftop and suddenly saw what Dapper from Somerville had seen, why he'd given them the cook's tour of Fenway. Daniel's friend was more than a friend. She was on the cusp of becoming a beautiful young woman. And so the world shifted on its axis and, from that night on, things got a little more complicated, a little more sudden.

"You gonna tell me why you skipped out?" Grace said, snapping him from his reverie as she pulled out another Stevie Wonder album, took a look, and replaced it just as quickly.

"No reason. Just had to take care of something."

She raised her hands and wiggled her fingers on either side of her face. "Oooh, big mystery."

"Hilarious."

"Just kidding. If you don't want to tell me, that's cool."

Daniel's secret pushed him a little closer. "If I tell you, will you promise to keep quiet?"

"Really? You have to ask?"

Why was he hesitating? Of course he was gonna tell her. It was Grace.

"I just rented a room above the Rat."

"Across the street?"

"Second floor. Looks right out over the square."

"Wow. Does your brother know?"

"Gonna meet him after my run. He won't like it, but we've got no choice. If school finds out I'm living in Cambridge . . ."

"They won't find out."

"Still . . ."

"Hey, I think it's great."

"Yeah, it's pretty cool. The guy who lives there is a prof from Harvard. Giving me the room for fifty bucks a month."

Grace whistled.

"I know. Dirt cheap, right? And the place is actually not half bad."

"When can I come over?"

"Tomorrow, maybe. Once I get settled and stuff."

Grace sighed. "My life is soooo boring."

"What are you gonna do this afternoon?"

"I don't know. Go home and work on Ovid, I guess. Call me tonight if you can. We'll go over what you missed in class."

"I'm probably gonna be moving in."

"So jealous."

"Yeah, right." He reached for another album. *Station to Station* by David Bowie. Grace reached at the same time and their fingertips touched. He felt a tingle up his arm while a single star shot across the yawning chasm of his consciousness. He knew it was her. Not him thinking of her, not him pretending to be her, but her, Grace Nguyen, living inside his head. Entangled. She rubbed the edge of her finger against his and the star shivered before exploding into countless particles of spinning light that fell in lovely streams all around him.

"Daniel?"

"What?"

He dared a look into her eyes and saw a thousand different doors that opened to a thousand different rooms and he wanted to explore each in turn. Then she leaned in just the perfect amount, at the perfect angle, in the perfect moment, and kissed him. Perfectly. Right there in the aisle of Music City.

"Why did you do that?" His voice was hoarse and choked with he had no idea what. Grace giggled.

"I don't know. Felt like it, I guess. Why? Was it that bad?"

Daniel shook his head and she touched his arm, her fingers so much finer than his. "Has anyone ever kissed you, Daniel?"

A middle-aged woman saved him, shooting them a murderous look and a "Shhh" from the CLASSICAL aisle. Grace waved at the lady, who sniffed and went back to perusing Bach.

"Probably a cat lover," Daniel said, and they both laughed hysterically for no reason at all.

"I gotta go," Grace said, pulling back but not before pushing a lock of hair behind his ear. "You're very sweet, Daniel."

"Just what a guy wants to hear."

"Shut up and tell your brother about the apartment."

"I will."

"Good. And call me if you can." She walked toward the front of the store, stopping behind the Bach lady to swipe at her back and give her a mock meow. Daniel laughed as the woman turned to see what was going on. Grace booted it down the aisle and out the door.

He watched as she wound her way through the afternoon crowd, stopping once to look back and see if he was still there. Daniel waved. She waved back and disappeared into the subway. Daniel pulled the sheet music for "Brown Sugar" from the front window, then put it back and went over to a case where they kept stacks of sheet music and lyrics. He found Stevie Wonder's "Higher Ground" and took it to the register. Daniel had a quarter for the bus and another seventy-five cents for something to eat. The lyrics cost two dollars, but the kid who worked there knew Daniel and gave him a deal. He took his purchase into the men's room and locked the door. Carefully, he folded up the sheet and placed it at the bottom of his gym bag. Then he changed into a pair of running pants and a long-sleeved Bruins shirt made of lightweight mesh. He pulled on a hat and stuffed an extra pair of socks into his pocket. He'd use them as gloves while he ran. The clerk kept the gym bag with his clothes and the lyrics behind the counter. He'd done it before and had a face Daniel trusted.

Outside he shook his legs and arms loose. A clock on an insurance building across the street read 3:46. He began to run west toward BU's campus and the river. In the first half-dozen strides, all the awkwardness of adolescence disappeared, and the man Daniel would become emerged. Inside his head, however, he was still a teenager and for the first mile all he thought about was Grace Nguyen, his first "real" kiss, and whether or not he'd stacked the deck to get it.

5

THE DEAD man lying on the pier looked nothing like Tommy Dillon. Thank fucking God.

The corpse was long, young, and well muscled. Hispanic, clad in white sweatpants and a long-sleeved BU sweatshirt. The fishermen who'd found him said he'd gotten hung up on a line from one of their lobster pots. They were huddled at the far end of the dock, a clump of yellow and orange slickers giving their statements to a couple of uniforms. Three forensics guys were working on the body. Barkley told them to take a break, leaving the scene to the two detectives. They circled like the jackals they'd become for longer than they'd known.

"How much time in the water?" Barkley said.

"Tech says not more than a couple of hours." Tommy squatted by the head and stared into the corpse's ear for some godforsaken Tommy reason. "Hispanic, for sure. Maybe twenty-five."

"No pockets," Barkley said. "No ID."

Tommy grumbled and stood up, one knee popping with the effort.

"What's that?" Barkley pointed to a rip in the sweatshirt.

"Pulled him in with a gaff." Tommy rolled the body onto

one side with the toe of his boot. The corpse grinned, a trickle of seawater coming from the side of his mouth and a horseshoe crab crawling out from inside his shirt.

"Two in the head," Tommy said.

Barkley walked around and took a look. Two small-caliber holes drilled into the curve of the skull just above the spine. "Twenty-two?"

"Be my guess." Tommy let the body flop back onto the deck. The sun had sunk down into the harbor and light was going fast.

"What do you think?" Barkley said.

"I think he's a drug dealer, probably an illegal. We'll spend the better part of two weeks beating the bushes and get no-where. Then we'll shove it into the cold pile with the rest of 'em."

"Love your job, don't you, Tommy?"

They'd been working crime scenes for eight years running. Barkley was the alpha. Did most of the interviews, handled the press, took the heat from the brass if there was any coming down. As for Tommy, he was good at two things. First, he knew the streets better than any cop in the city. His home turf, Dorchester, Mattapan, Charlestown, North End, South End, Allston-Brighton. Tommy had contacts everywhere. And he always came up with a name. Barkley never asked what Tommy promised, or to whom. Looking back, maybe he should have, but he never did. The other thing Tommy was good at was records. Turn him loose in a room full of files and he was a happy fucking camper. Worked fast and, again, did what he did best—sniffed out names, addresses, leads.

"I'll get going on an ID tomorrow. You want to talk to the guys from the boat?"

"Why not?"

Tommy started over to the uniforms. Barkley stopped him.

"About earlier. When I fell."

"I didn't see no woman, B. You just tripped is all."

"When I was out, I had a vision or a dream or some fucking thing."

"Oh, yeah?" Tommy seemed a little anxious and a little amused. But that's how Tommy seemed with most things.

"I thought I was down here, on the docks. A body came up out of the water. Tied up in chains and shit."

"Fuck me. Look anything like our Juan Doe?"

Not really, Barkley thought. *As a matter of fact, it looked like you, Tommy, your scarier-than-shit face floating in a burp of seawater. How's that, partner? Pretty fucking funny, huh?*

"Bark, you hear me?"

"I didn't see the face, Tommy, but, no, I don't think it was our guy."

"I told you, B. It's the job. Every time I close my eyes at night, the creeping Jesus motherfuckers crawl all over me, up my ass, tickle the balls, right down my fucking throat."

"And you say you got no demons."

"Let's go the No Name. Get a bowl of chowder."

"We gotta talk to the fishermen."

"Chowder, B. Then the rest."

Barkley nodded for his partner to take the lead and watched him walk down the pier, stopping once to joke with one of the forensics guys. Barkley followed quietly in his wake.

6

HARRY FITZSIMMONS put his fist in the mud and leaned forward, weight perfectly balanced in a three-point stance. His lungs were on fire and his legs felt like lead. Push through. One more. Now. Harry shot forward, keeping low for the first few strides then letting his body rise as he accelerated. The wind pushed at his back, sweeping off the river, lifting as he went. He flew past ten yards, then twenty, floating now, breath and body one, moving in perfect sync. It wasn't until the last twenty that he started to tie up, thighs cramping a touch, lungs spent. The final ten yards were all about form. Lift the legs, pump the arms, lean through the finish. As he crossed the goal line, he popped the stopwatch wrapped in his fist.

"What are you doing them in?" Pat Costello was sitting a few rows up in the end zone seats at Harvard Stadium. Not that Harry had a problem hearing him. Costello coached Harvard's defensive backs. Like most football coaches, his normal tone of voice started at bellow and only deepened from there. Harry raised a hand and bent at the waist, sucking in air as Costello made his way down to the field. He took the watch from Harry and gave it a look.

"Not bad. How many did you do?"

"Two sets of ten at sixty. Before that, forty-yarders." Harry's words came in fits and starts, his breath steaming in the November chill.

"You lift?"

"Couple hours."

"Damn." Costello handed back the watch as Harry straightened, breathing nearly back to normal. He didn't know Costello all that well but had heard good things. The two men took their time, walking across the broken turf toward the players' tunnel. At six two with his buzz cut, brushed wire on top shaved down to bone on the sides, Harry towered over the former Syracuse corner.

"You know the season's over, Fitzsimmons. I mean, you got the memo."

The Crimson had played their final game last weekend, a win over Yale and a second-place finish in the Ivy League. Harry was a shoo-in for All-Ivy. There was even talk of honorable mention All-American.

"Just don't want to lose the edge, Coach, especially with the cardio. Once you lose it, it's a bitch to get back."

"Yeah, well, it's good to unwind as well. You ready for exams?"

"I should be good." Harry was carrying a 3.8 average and everyone in the program knew it.

"All right, then. Why don't you call it a day? Grab a shower and go home."

"Actually, I told someone I'd meet them here."

Costello grinned. "Girl?"

"My brother, Daniel."

"Didn't know you had a brother."

"He's a sophomore at Latin. After my mom died, we stayed together."

Costello slackened his pace. "Must have been rough."

"We got through it okay."

"Where you living now?"

"I got a place off-campus with Prescott."

"Prescott?" The coach shook his head. Neil Prescott was a backup running back and full-time tool.

"He had a spare bedroom and didn't mind Daniel so it all worked out."

They came to the mouth of the tunnel and stopped. Costello leaned back with his shoulders and jiggled a set of keys in his pocket. "What do the Fitzsimmons brothers got going for Thanksgiving?"

Harry shrugged. The truth was they had no plans. Prescott was supposed to be heading home, so the apartment would be empty. They'd probably get a pizza and watch football.

"Why don't you come out to the house? We do a big thing. Fifty, sixty people. Lots of food and beer. Tag football game. More of it on the tube. I got five kids, one of whom has your jersey, by the way, and would love to get it signed."

"Thanks, Coach, but we'll probably just bachelor it at the apartment. I don't get to see Danny much with practice and school and everything."

"You sure?"

"Yeah, but thanks. Bring that jersey in and I'll sign it for your son."

"I will. And let me know if you change your mind."

"Will do, Coach."

Harry watched Costello disappear up the tunnel, then took

a seat in the stands, tipping his head back and soaking in the emptiness of the stadium. There wasn't anything about football Harry didn't love. Sweat in the summer. Snow and ice in the winter. Cut grass and mud. The snap of the chinstrap and taste of the mouthpiece. Feel of the pads when they got worked in just right. The thrill of hitting and being hit. But mostly Harry loved the locker room. He wasn't a big talker, preferring to lead by example. And he did lead, always first to accept the challenge, first to hold himself accountable whether he deserved it or not. For Harry it was about the team, something bigger than him, bigger than all of them. He'd never found anything else quite like it and knew he probably never would.

He got up from his seat and walked back across the field, pausing for a final look before heading up the tunnel and out of the stadium. Traffic from Soldiers Field Road swept by in a line to his left. Beyond that was the Charles River, slate gray with crests creaming white. Harry worked his way across a patchwork of practice fields. His limbs hung loose in their sockets and there was the pleasant tingling of fatigue settling in his bones. He found a spot in the grass and stretched his legs out in front of him, wind freezing the sweat in his hair and prickling his scalp. He bent forward slowly at the waist, feeling the pull in his hamstrings. All the while he kept an eye focused on a bend in the river.

Daniel appeared as a tiny black wedge. He looked like he was barely moving, but Harry knew that was a lie. He'd run with Daniel many times, but only once in a race—a three-miler in Watertown when Daniel was thirteen. They went out with the lead pack, college runners and older. Harry stayed with the group for the first mile then told Daniel he was going to dial it back.

As he dropped off the pace, he stole a look at his kid brother. His face was a mask, no pain, no fatigue, no acknowledgment of Harry's imminent demise. Daniel came in third that day. The next week he started running for Latin as an eighth grader. His times were good enough to qualify for the state cross-country finals, but Daniel never seemed interested in any of that. He'd show up for some meets. Skip others. It drove his coach crazy.

He was closer now so Harry could make out some details. His little brother was wearing a Bruins jersey and a black watch cap with white socks covering his hands. He wore blue-and-white running shoes that flashed as he went, the only indication of how quickly he was moving. Daniel disappeared for a moment, then popped up again, slipping through an open gate and stopping just inside it. He pulled the socks off his hands as Harry approached.

"How far did you go?" Harry said.

"Five, six."

"Why don't you wear gloves?"

"Don't like 'em."

"They make them now for running. Superlight."

Daniel shrugged. His cheeks were stained red and his hair was sopping with sweat when he took off his hat. Otherwise, you'd never know he'd gone for a run. And a hard one at that.

"You work out?" Daniel said.

"Yeah. One of my coaches invited us for Thanksgiving." Harry waited but knew Daniel wouldn't entertain the notion of going. "I told him we were gonna hang at the apartment."

"You can go if you want."

"Hell, no. Besides, we got football games to watch." They began to walk. Harry had an old Saab he'd parked near Harvard's field house. They'd drive back to the apartment. Harry would take a shower first. By the time Daniel got done, Harry would be working on dinner.

"I found a place today," Daniel said.

"A place for what?"

"My own place."

Harry stopped walking. "That's not gonna happen, Daniel."

"Already done. Fifty a month in Kenmore Square."

"What is it? A cardboard box?"

"This guy lives above the Rat. He's got an extra room."

"You're serious?"

"I'm sick of being a mooch."

"You're not."

"I am. Sleeping on the floor of your bedroom. You're gonna have girls . . ."

"I don't have a girl. Besides, that doesn't matter."

"I know it doesn't matter to you, but what about me? I feel like a jerk."

"You're sixteen. You can't be living on your own."

"Yeah, right."

Of course he could live on his own. Daniel could do whatever he wanted. He already had. And they both knew it.

"Who is this guy?" Harry said.

"Actually, he's a professor right here."

"At Harvard? What's his name?"

"Lane. Simon Lane."

"Never heard of him."

"I think he's on sabbatical or something. Teaches physics. Anyway, it's all set. I'm moving my stuff tonight."

"Tonight?"

"Sooner the better. If school finds out I live in Cambridge, it's gonna be a problem."

Boston Latin School was part of the public school system and thus free—provided you lived in the city. Harry had gone to Latin before Daniel, but that didn't really matter. If the school discovered Daniel was living in Cambridge, they could charge him thousands of dollars in tuition. Or maybe just throw him out altogether.

"No one's gonna find out," Harry said.

"You don't know that. And don't tell me you don't get girls. If you're a football player at Harvard and you're breathing, you're gonna get girls. Even a guy who looks like you."

Harry feinted a left. Daniel ducked away, smirking. They walked some more.

"You hate all this, don't you?" Harry said.

"All what?"

Harry raised his eyes toward the stadium, a black bowl outlined against a sky of hard silver. "Harvard, football. All the stuff that goes with all that."

"You know I don't."

"No?"

"I couldn't be prouder of you, Harry. And I couldn't love anyone more than I love you." Daniel shrugged as if that was just as obvious as the breath that moved between them.

"But it's not for you?"

"What's not for me? Your life? Of course not. Your life's yours and my life's mine. But my brother's special. And it's not cuz he's smart or plays football for Harvard. He was special long before that."

"Yeah?"

"The rest of it's just stuff, Harry. Comes and goes, you know? So you're okay with the apartment?"

"I want to see it. And I still want to hear from you every day."

"Sure."

"How you gonna get over there?"

"Red Line. Green Line. Fifteen minutes."

"I'll drive you."

"No, you won't. I'm taking the T. Once I get moved in, you can come over and check it out. Okay?"

"Let's go home and eat."

They walked the rest of the way in silence, the older brother with his head down, younger watching the first, each frozen in the other's echo on the muddy stain of grass. And then they stepped onto the hardtop of the parking lot and the slack tightened, time spinning forward again as Harry found his car and Daniel walked around to the passenger's side. Inside, the windows fogged with their collected breath. Daniel wiped the glass with his sleeve while Harry worked the wipers and they both waited for the heater to kick in. At the apartment Harry made dinner—burgers and tater tots. In the other room his little brother packed his things.

7

IT WAS past nine before they finished on the dock, almost ten when they turned down Tommy's block. There were still plenty of kids out. A handful leaned on their sticks and watched resentfully as the detectives cruised through the middle of their street hockey game. By the time they'd parked, the game had resumed. Pools of light illuminated the action, the frantic chatter of wood against blacktop filling the night.

"Pricks out here twenty-four fucking seven," Tommy said. "Think they're all Bobby Orr or something."

"You were probably the same way."

"My ass." Tommy lived on G Street, a block and a half from where he grew up. Southie bred and buttered. Like a lot of folks born here, the neighborhood was beginning and end. Cradle to coffin. Nothing better, nothing worse. And Tommy wouldn't have it any other way. Not that he ever really had a choice.

"I'll get rolling on Juan Doe first thing tomorrow, B."

"Where you thinking of starting?"

"Run Juan's prints. Make some calls to a few guys I know down at the waterfront."

"You think someone seen him down there?"

Tommy shrugged. "Could be."

Barkley watched a kid rip a wrist shot toward a goal marked out by a pair of Timberlands. The orange ball was blocked by the kid in the goal. There was a scramble for the rebound and someone scored, the ball scooting just inside one of the boots and halfway down the street. Cheers, yelling, one kid pushing another as a third chased the ball. The game rumbled on.

"Sorry again about today," Barkley said. "Must have been the knock on the head or something."

"Don't worry about it. I told you, I believe in all that vision shit."

"You're Irish. You got no choice."

Tommy skimmed him a look. "I ever tell you about the fairy rings they got over there? Don't say nothing."

"I didn't say shit."

"You were thinking it."

Barkley nodded toward Tommy's three-decker, slumping peacefully at the corner. "Is Katie waiting for you?"

"The fairy ring's a pack of mushrooms growing in a circle in a field. Back in the old country, they think it's enchanted."

"You're fucking enchanted."

"Listen to me, B. If you walk into one of these things, these rings, you can't ever get out. You're in there forever, running in circles while the demons chase you."

"Demons?"

"Your demons, the ones you make out of nothing, the ones that live inside your dreams, except now they're flesh and blood and bone. Turned loose to drive you shithouse crazy." Tommy's eyes shone with the telling and Barkley thought about the booze and the cocaine and the gambling and figured it was all lit by the same quenchless fire.

"Go on inside, Tommy. Katie's waiting."

"Come in for a pop. She'd love to see you."

On cue the door to the apartment opened, and Katie Dillon appeared on the stoop. Tommy's wife was tiny, maybe five three, and Southie tough. First team all-scholastic point guard in high school, she'd gotten a full ride to play hoops at B.C. The summer of her senior year she met Tommy and decided to defer for a year. That Christmas they got married. Eight months later, the twins arrived. One dream dead, another begun. She still looked young and college fresh, a beauty who'd maybe lost her way, wandering through Southie in her hip-hugger jeans, Converse sneaks, and hooded B.C. sweatshirt. One of the hockey players yelled at her as she crossed the street and Katie waved. Then she was there, leaning through the window with her brown hair in messy curls and hard-as-diamond smile.

"Someone's gonna call the cops on you two. Hey, Bark."

She pressed her cheek against his, letting him feel the flutter of her eyelashes as he smelled her life—Ivory soap and hot water, kids scrubbed fresh, the makings of dinner, all the small, warm moments that bubbled and beat in her blood. Tommy leaned over and touched a hand to the steering wheel.

"Hey, babe. I was just trying to get him to come in."

"It's late," Barkley said. "And I'm beat."

Katie stepped back, cocking her hip and resting her eyes on her husband. "Let the man go home, Tommy. Besides, the girls just woke up and I need you to get them back down."

"How old are they now?" Barkley said.

"Nearly seven. I know, can you believe it? Molly's a terror. Maggie, of course, is an angel."

"Just a quick one, B," Tommy said. "You can stick your head in and see the girls."

"How about we figure out a night for dinner?" Katie said.

"Bark can come over and I'll cook. Open up a bottle of wine and we can all catch up."

"Done," Barkley said.

"Awesome. And if you want to bring someone . . ." She smiled with her eyes and leaned in again to give him a quick kiss on the cheek. "Great seeing you, Bark."

"I'll be there in five," Tommy said.

Katie made her way back across the street. The two men watched until she disappeared inside.

"Best part of my life," Tommy said.

"You got that right. What about tomorrow? You driving?"

"Supposed to pick up the car in the morning."

"Call me if it's not ready. Now, go see your wife. And don't forget to hug your kids."

Tommy bumped Barkley's fist and climbed out of the car. Katie met him on the stoop, letting her husband go inside and then leaning against the doorframe, smiling at Barkley and lifting a lonely hand his way. He popped the horn and waited until she'd gone in before starting up the car. Fuck the Irish pricks with their hockey sticks and shaved heads, painter's pants and shamrock tats. The real danger in South Boston was right here. Flesh and blood. Katie fucking Dillon. Shit.

He pulled away from the curb, laying on the horn and watching all the wannabe Bobby Orrs scatter. It was too late for Carson so he'd sit up in his apartment and watch one of those detective movies. Hoped it was a Columbo. He wouldn't think about today. Fucking lie. Of course he would. Think about today, then think about the fire escape outside his window. His own private fairy ring, whispering with his own personal pack of demons. Barkley pressed down on the gas, sparks flying as old thoughts ran ahead and were lost in the night.

8

DANIEL CLIMBED out of the Kenmore T station at a little after ten. A trio of girls was huddled by the front door to the Rat. Wrapped in leather and jingling rings on every finger, they smoked their cigarettes and chattered brightly, shaking out spikes of hair dyed in pastel swirls of color and flashing pale smiles at one another in the steam and the hard light. A bouncer checked their IDs and collected the cover, adding the bills to a fold of money he kept under his jacket. The girls descended into the ragged mouth of the Rat while Daniel negotiated the front steps to his new place, a garbage bag with everything he owned thrown over his shoulder and his brother's sad smile floating just ahead. The good-byes had been hard, but Daniel would see Harry soon enough. He'd promised. And Harry always kept his promises.

Daniel's key turned easily in the outer lock. He walked up the interior set of stairs, thought about knocking, then let himself in. The apartment was dark and cold. Daniel dumped his bag by the door and fumbled along the wall until he found a light switch. He could have sworn the place was empty, but there was Simon, ghost again, sitting behind his desk, packing another pipe, this one small and flat with a perforated metal bowl.

"Sorry, I didn't see you," Daniel said.

Simon fired up the pipe and launched a gentle spiral of smoke. "I was watching you cross the street." He gestured to the bag of clothes. "Is this all you have?"

"Pretty much."

"Must be nice to be that free. You want to take it back to your room?"

"Sure." Daniel took a seat on the couch and placed the bag between his knees. "What kind of tobacco is that?"

"You trying to be funny?"

"Sort of."

"It's pot. If you're not all right with that, I can go up to the roof."

"It's fine."

"Good. It's cold on the roof."

"How do you know I don't smoke myself?"

Simon didn't bother to answer, reaching over with a long arm and cracking one of the windows. "Did you tell your brother you were moving out?"

"Yes."

"What did he say?"

"He didn't want me to go."

"And already you miss him."

"I know, sounds stupid."

"Not at all." Simon checked the bowl of his pipe and knocked the contents into an ashtray. He slipped the pipe into his desk along with a thick plastic bag that Daniel assumed held his weed.

"I tried what you talked about," Daniel said.

"What's that?"

"The entanglement thing."

"It's not a toy, you know."

Daniel thought about the hot-dog stand and the spaniel with the wagging tail. "Does it work with animals?"

Simon smirked. "Is that what you really want to talk about?"

"There's a girl."

"Always is."

"What does that mean?"

"You'll find out. Let me guess. You like her and tried to use what we spoke about to get her to like you back."

"I just wanted to see if there'd be any effect."

"But the effect you wanted was for her to like you back."

"I don't know."

"You don't know." Simon shook his head. "Fine. So what happened?"

"We talked. I concentrated like you talked about."

"Directed your thoughts. Focused them."

"Yes."

The cat appeared out of nowhere, a sliver blade flashing up onto a bookshelf as Simon's voice sharpened and tightened. "Tell me, what did it feel like?"

"I guess it felt like I was pushing something."

"And you felt resistance?"

"Resistance?"

"From the other side? Like you were actually pushing against a physical object?"

Daniel tried to summon up the moment when he touched Grace's mind. "Yes, I think so. For a second, anyway."

"And then what?"

"And then she kissed me."

Simon leaned back, brushing the side of his desk with his fingers and magically producing another pipe, the Dunhill from this afternoon. Daniel watched as he packed it and lit a match, flames leaping across the pulled-down bones of his face. When he had it going, Simon plucked the pipe from between long, thin lips. "This is regular tobacco."

"I told you, it's fine with me."

"Go put your clothes away. I'll make some tea."

When Daniel returned, Simon was sitting in his chair by the fireplace. There was a fire in the grate and a pot set on a table.

"Help yourself."

Daniel poured himself a cup of green tea and sat on the couch. The overhead light had been extinguished and the glow from the fire cast shadows that reached across the floor. Daniel took a sip and felt the warmth on his feet.

"You're happy about the girl," Simon said.

"Are you asking or telling me?"

"It's a responsibility, you know."

"What's that?"

"Entanglement. I'm assuming you now believe what I told you?"

"Maybe."

"You felt something?"

"I told you I did."

"Why do you think I'm sharing all this with you?"

Daniel shrugged.

"You think I'm boasting?"

"I didn't say that."

"You didn't have to. Of course that would be the assumption. In this case, however, you're wrong. I told you about entanglement for a very specific reason. I know a little bit about you."

The tea went cold in Daniel's mouth, and he could feel the cup and saucer grow heavy in his hands.

"Relax, Daniel. Remember when I told you about internet-working."

Daniel nodded.

"Well, it allows me, among other things, to research people. There will be much more information available in the future, of course, but if you know what you're doing, it's a place to start."

Daniel put his cup down. Simon's face was cast in darkness, but he could see the smooth curve of his forearm in the flickering light as he held the bowl of his pipe and the soft glow as he puffed and the twist of his smoky exhale as it lifted and wreathed around them.

"How could you have researched me? I didn't even know I was going to come here until I saw the sign on your front door."

Simon's shadow nodded on the far wall, but the man said nothing. Daniel continued to think out loud.

"You knew I was going to come here?"

"In a way."

"Are you saying you pushed me here? Entangled me? Is that possible?"

Simon dipped his face into their shared light. "I read about your brother in the newspaper, but I knew about you before that. Hospital records. Letters. A couple of phone calls. Don't leave, Daniel. What happened to you makes you who you are. Makes you perfect for this. If you truly felt something today, you know that to be true."

Daniel was standing, staring down at the wooden floorboards, striped in ribbons of moonlight from the windows.

"Stay, Daniel. Find out about the rest."

Daniel found himself sitting again. Simon offered, and Daniel allowed him to refill his cup with the fragrant tea. Then they began.

"The first rule is this." Simon held up a finger. "I will never lie to you. And I'll do everything I can to keep you out of harm's way."

"Who would want to harm me?"

"You already know the answer to that. What time do you leave for school tomorrow?"

"It's a shorter commute from here. I'll probably leave about seven."

"You have your appointment."

He knew about that. How did he know about that?

"You think this is about pushing other people," Simon said. "Affecting their behavior. Control."

"Isn't it?"

"You think I can sit here and concentrate and get you to do whatever I want?"

"I'm in this apartment, aren't I?"

"Only because you wanted to be. Entanglement is a two-way street, Daniel. You won't be able to affect every person you meet. Others will be an open book. At times you might not even have a choice in the matter. The point is this. You'll be pushed even as you push someone else. Take on another's pain while you unearth your own. It's part of the price paid for opening up oneself. In fact, I suspect it's the whole point."

"I'm not following you."

"Once we get past the power trip, the ego trip that seduces with the idea we might be able to affect someone else's actions, it inevitably comes back to us. Who's willing to peel away the layers of himself and evolve? Who isn't? Who lives, who dies? Darwin, of course, had it right all along."

"So you're saying I can't make someone do something?"

"Probably not against their will, no. When you feel that push, it's just you bumping up against them, allowing them to feel what was already there, maybe learn a little about themselves. Maybe learn something they don't want to know."

"Is this thing dangerous?"

The room filled with a soft hiss as Simon drew on his pipe and the tobacco glowed and crackled and burned.

"Of course it's fucking dangerous. Now, go get some sleep."

—

Daniel crawled between a set of unfamiliar sheets, resigned to a night of staring at the ceiling and listening for strange sounds. Almost immediately, however, reality began to fray, his mind melting, body sloping down the slippery hallways of his dreams. Nurses came. Nurses went. Doctors stood at one end of an impossibly long bed, arguing over shadows on an x-ray before turning to stare at their patient. Words dripped down into his consciousness—

HEAD TRAUMA, COMA, DISASSOCIATION

Some wanted to stimulate his cerebral cortex. Others preferred to let him sleep. Let him heal. The others held sway and so Daniel lay in his coffin, in the absolute zero cold of his mind, watching as they fed him through clear tubes, emptied his bowels, and pored over their endless medical tests.

He was eight years old, buried alive in a coma, and entirely alone. Well, not entirely. Harry sat at the foot of his bed during the day. And then there was Daniel's special visitor. He came late at night, when the ward was dark and the only sounds were the drowsy beeps of machines that charted the pump and push of heart and lungs. Larry Rosen worked as an orderly at Boston City Hospital. Curly black hair, narrow-shouldered, crooked and skinny, with a protruding Adam's apple that was creased in the middle and teeth that crowded up into the front of his mouth. On the first night he dragged a chair close and studied Daniel as he slept. On the second night he played with Daniel's face, lifting an eyelid and opening his mouth, giggling furiously while Daniel sat up high in a corner of the room and watched. On the third night Rosen brought out the needle. The orderly took his time, toothy grin washed in moonlight, eyes hungry for any hint of pain as the steel sank into the pocket of Daniel's hip. Rosen got nothing for his trouble, not even a flicker as the needle pierced muscle, fascia, and bone. The next night he was back. And the night after. Different-size needles. Different parts of Daniel's body. Never a twitch along the expanse of skin. Never a murmur on Daniel's lips. Still, the eight-year-old watched everything Larry Rosen did. Watched and took notes.

Daniel felt his eyes flutter and open. He was back in the narrow bedroom above Kenmore Square, the fire inside his head dimmed to a scalpel's edge of light that reached across the wooden floor toward the foot of the bed. He'd closed the door before going to sleep, but now it stood ajar and something was crawling hot and funny on his skin, feeling here and there at the soft parts of his face. Daniel dared not move, dared not look directly at the door, and when he finally did there was nothing to see but an exhale of air stirring the golden fill from the corridor.

He stole out of bed and into the hall. Daniel was committed now and didn't think about it, lest he think better and jump back under the covers. At the end of the hallway the door to Simon's workroom was cracked an inch. Daniel made a pretense of knocking even as he pushed in. A cold slab of mirror hung on one wall and he jumped at his own startled reflection, mobile skin stretched over a rack of bones, brown hair wild and tufted, fists clenched on either side, his attempt at ferocity more likely to elicit sympathy than fear. Such was the lot of a sixteen-year-old, or at least this sixteen-year-old.

He moved around the cage of a room, dominated by a large desk scraped clean of paper, book, and pen. A window gazed out over Kenmore Square, empty at three in the morning and shivering under twitching sheets of rain. A breeze, fresh and wet and full of the night, drifted across his feet and up the legs of his Latin School sweats. The draft was coming from beneath a door that connected this first room to Simon's bedroom. Again, Daniel didn't pause. Simon's bed had not been slept in and the only window was flung open, the storm tugging at the shades and casting a fine spray of mist across the floor. Daniel moved closer and saw a boot print limned in wet drops of silver on the sill. He climbed out onto the fire escape.

The weather was fiercer than he'd imagined, a rake of wind pushing him to the iron railing where he stared down at the roof of a green VW bus and a skull-cracking expanse of sidewalk. The squall pivoted again, turning his shoulders and pulling him back toward the building. Simon was standing in the storm's blind spot, waiting. He seized Daniel by the shirt, sucking him close and lifting him clear so he dangled out over the city. Daniel looked down at his legs, bicycling in midair, then back at Simon, who tossed him into the night.

I never seen you looking so bad my funky one
You tell me that your superfine mind has come undone

Daniel dropped headfirst, Steely Dan ribboning his brain as he split the roof of the VW and plunged through a translucent pool of water—layers of warm salty greens, fading to blues, fading to blacks. He fell until there was nowhere left to fall, and then he floated, unable to speak, unable to think, unable to see his hand in front of his face. He was in the place where thoughts got shredded and Plato went to die, the place where the unconscious found its shape and its form. Moon-skinned demons with eyes on stalks and heart-shaped tears. Snakes in circles, feeding on themselves as they fed on one another. Clocks running around and around like a Chuck Berry song gone mad. And Daniel. He felt his heartbeat in his tongue and wondered what it might be like to consider. To ponder. To choose. From somewhere below a watery lamp was lit. Daniel dove, the current fierce and cold, fighting him as something inside impelled, pushed him onward, willed him to be. The last ten feet were a mad, blind struggle. And then Daniel reached for the light, ripping the sheets off his face and sitting straight up in bed.

For a moment, he imagined he was alone in his bedroom, safe in his cocoon of darkness, listening to the black drumbeat of rain outside and tasting the intimacy of all that lived within it. Then he saw him. Simon was standing by the room's only window, long face bathed in wet blues and wetter whites.

"You were screaming."

"Sorry, just a bad dream."

"Do you dream a lot?" His voice lived on the end of a string, swinging free in the night, measured and even like a ticking watch.

"It was nothing."

"Dreams are windows, Daniel. Windows into streams of time."

"I'm not sure I know what you mean."

Outside the storm tightened, lashing against the cracked New England brick and rattling all around the apartment. Simon leaned forward, allowing a brushstroke of light to play across his face. "Have you ever heard of something called 'deep time'?"

"No. Should I?"

Simon shrugged. "Get some rest. We can talk later." And then he left, closing the door behind him so it clicked.

Daniel lay back in the darkness, trying to determine where his dreams ended and his bedroom began. It was all a woolly jumble, his brain sodden with sleep. Daniel's last thoughts were that the whole thing was a trick and the stuff he imagined at night would look far different in the skeptical light of day. He wanted above all to open his eyes, just to make doubly certain his door was still shut. Then he was gone, tumbling into the abyss, this time failing to stir until morning.

9

FAIRY RINGS.

Barkley cracked an eye, letting the fevered carousel of his dreams slow to a stop. His alarm clock showed five minutes to seven, which meant he'd gotten four and a half hours of sleep. Plenty.

The black-and-white TV was still on in the kitchen, but Columbo was long gone, cigars smoked, case solved, bad guy in cuffs. Barkley snapped off the set and filled a kettle with water. He liked his coffee hot and strong in the morning. Black with two sugars.

He drank that first cup like he always did, sitting at the kitchen table, eyes fastened on a pair of boots he kept by the stove. When he finished, he washed out the cup and put it on the sideboard to dry. Then he pulled on the boots, lacing them tight, and shrugged into an overcoat he kept on a hook sunk into the wall.

Next to the kitchen was a pantry with a window that let onto a fire escape. Barkley cranked open the window and stepped out. His apartment was on the sixth floor of a walk-up overlooking Sullivan Square in Charlestown. The building was old and tired and the fire escape creaked under his weight as he moved to the center of the grated floor and peered through the cold iron at the concrete below. Then he began to jump. Two hundred fifty pounds, cracking hard, cracking mean, cracking fast. The rods that anchored the fire escape shifted in their moorings, separating a good six inches from the brick face of the building as the fire escape bucked and swayed. Barkley planted his palms against the exterior wall and started to rock. The building groaned in its bones and scrapes of red rust floated in the air. Still, the goddamn thing held.

Barkley sat down on the windowsill and pulled out a pack of Marlboros, lighting up the one he allowed himself every morning and staring out at the dark buildings and bright sky. By his boot was a small container of potting soil. Barkley dug in a thumb, breaking through the frozen crust and turning up the bones of old ghosts. Twelve years ago they'd lived wrapped in a cloud on the top floor of a Roxbury tenement. He was just out of school. Unformed clay. She was everything anyone could ever be and never feared it ending. People like her never did. That's why they had people like him. He'd told her to stay off the fire escape. More than once. But he'd never nailed the window shut, had he? And Jess loved her flowers. She kept a half-dozen different kinds all around the apartment, potted plants stuck in every available chink of light. She told him the apartment was magic, how the sun flooded their space and the rain dripped off the roof in cold, clean streams, all of it conspiring to feed their life and their love, sanctifying, purifying, keeping them safe and whole. She told him morning sun was best. And nowhere was it better than in the east-facing window off their kitchen, the one that let onto the fire escape.

He'd even bought nails, long silver ones, and a hammer. They were sitting in a drawer on that Sunday morning in June while Barkley slept in. He smelled the flowers first, hints of them floating through the apartment. He recalled smiling in his sleep. He thought about that smile often, the luxury of it, the arrogance of it, and wondered if he hadn't been so lazy. So fucking lazy. The scent of the flowers lived on a breeze and the breeze came from the kitchen. She'd opened the window. And if the window was open, she was out on the fire escape. Feeling the magic. Living in its light.

Barkley jumped from their bed just as the first bolt sheared. Caught the tail end of her scream as he reached the window. He might have called her name as she fell, a carousel of bolts and broken steel, plants and clods of dirt and Jess in the middle, staring up at him, reaching for him, telling him with her eyes that it would be all right and don't be angry, don't withdraw, don't let it fester, don't let in the wolf. Don't, don't, don't. Then she turned to face the pavement, extending her hands as if they could somehow break the fall.

He ran down six flights and found her, fine traces of potting soil patterned on her cheek and throat, a scattering of blossoms all around, still fragrant, no longer magic. He covered her body with his and groaned into the earth, wanting nothing more than for it to swallow them whole, leave them to lie together and feel everything or molder. A couple of neighbors came out and stared, then the police and an ambulance. It wasn't until three days after the funeral that they told him about his unborn daughter, eight weeks along. Then his education was complete and the circle closed itself.

Barkley promised himself he'd never live in the ghetto again.

White-people buildings only. They might not look him in the eye and cross to the other side of the street when they did see him, but white folks were also less likely to die for nothing. And he'd had enough of that. Or so he thought—until he picked up the badge and gun and became a merchant of death, until he moved into the oldest building he could find in the white person's world, until he started playing Russian roulette with his ghosts on yet another creaky fire escape.

He took a pull on his cigarette and flicked the butt into the breeze. Then he stepped back through the window and hung up his coat. Boots back in their spot by the stove. He took a long shower, letting the water run as hot as he could stand, and got dressed—brown suit with a soft stripe, blue shirt, and mocha tie. Barkley shined his shoes slowly, nagged by a feeling that this day wouldn't be like every other. Today was a day to lay traps for one's demons. And see what the fuck was what.

10

HARRY FITZSIMMONS picked his way through the early morning bead sellers and bookshops, sidestepping a long-haired guy
strumming a guitar in front of the Coop and a couple of girls in
low-slung bell-bottoms buying postcards off a rack. The chunky
smell of weed was already hanging thick over Harvard Square,
mingling with a waft of cheap beer as the front door to the
Wursthaus burped open and a Puerto Rican in a white apron
popped out, lugging a crate full of empties. Next door every stool
in the Tasty was taken, locals scarfing down two eggs, home
fries, and white toast for a buck and a half. And that included
coffee.

Harry jogged across the street and bought a *Rolling Stone* at
the Out of Town newsstand. A fleet of commuters swept past,
two or three breaking off like fighter planes to buy their papers
before disappearing into the wooden shack that marked the open
mouth of the Red Line. Harry rolled up his magazine and tucked
it in his back pocket, dodging between a couple of cars stopped at
a light and angling for a set of wrought-iron gates. Harry enjoyed
Harvard Square, a collection of odds and ends that marched to
its own beat, a talisman of what was hip and what was about

to be, even if it never was. Harvard Square, however, was not Harvard. Maybe its schizophrenic stepchild, or some demented relation, but not the pristine, unsullied image most folks had of America's premier university. To get that, to feel that, to smell that, one needed to dip into the oldest part of the past, the adult drinking tea in the parlor—Harvard Yard.

He entered off Peabody Street, slipping inside Johnston Gate and past the freshman dorms—Mass Hall where the president of Harvard had his office, Weld where JFK once slept, Wigg in all its various and sundry forms, a handful of others, each with its own history and rites of passage for its wet-behind-the-ears, wide-eyed residents. Harry ventured a little deeper, doubling back through the Old Yard and into the beating heart of the place—also known as Tercentenary Theatre. For him, this would always be the best part of Harvard and the only place, besides the football field, where he felt at peace. Along one side of the quadrangle was University Hall, its white granite defiant among a forest of Georgian brick. Across from it crouched Sever, impossibly heavy with its round bay windows, hipped roof, and whispering archways. Closing off either end of Tercentenary were the twin idols of religion and reason. Memorial Church seemed almost quaint, like a poor relation invited to peal its bells in celebration of its soaring cousin, the Widener Library.

One of the world's great libraries, the Widener had never been accused of being subtle, boasting a sweeping run of unnaturally broad steps ending in a row of Corinthian columns fronting a building made of brick the color of blood. Inside, the library housed more than three million volumes spread out over fifty-seven miles of shelving. Even better, no one working there had a clue as to where anything might be shelved and the only obvious sign in the place was one that read EXIT over the front door. The thinking was, if you were smart enough (or lucky enough or connected enough or rich enough) to get into Harvard, you sure as hell should be able to find a book on your own. And if the book you were looking for happened to be a copy of the Gutenberg Bible? Well, you'd come to the right place. There were only forty-seven such copies in the world and, of course, the Widener had one of them. One night a would-be robber tried to steal Harvard's Gutenberg. He was found the next morning facedown and unconscious after he slipped trying to shimmy down a rope hung from one of the library's upper windows. The burglar got a cracked skull for his trouble. The two-volume, seventy-pound bible emerged without a scratch. The message for all those wannabe book thieves out there: Don't fuck with Harvard lest the gods themselves smite ye down.

Harry found a seat near the top of the library steps and looked out over the Yard, still dozing in the early morning chill. Thanksgiving break didn't start until next Tuesday, but a lot of students were already clearing out. Harry didn't mind a bit. He closed his eyes and dropped his head back, letting the winter sun warm his face. Most of the jock types at Harvard went for collared polos and khakis, topsiders in the spring and duck boots in the fall. Harry was wearing a beat-up leather jacket with ripped jeans tucked into a pair of paratroop boots he'd bought at an army surplus store.

"Who you waiting on?"

"Go away." Harry spoke without opening his eyes. Jesus Sanchez wasn't having it. Harry shaded his face and watched the man everyone called "Zeus" climb the final few steps, his massive

stride one of the few things on campus that was a match for the
Widener's staircase. Zeus had barely taken a seat when a woman
called out and waved. The woman's name was Suzanne and hell
yes, she was going to be at the Oxford Ale House this afternoon
for happy hour. Were Zeus and his pals going to be there? Good,
she'd look for them. Zeus watched until she disappeared from
sight.

"You know who that is?"

"I bet you're gonna tell me."

"Hot, that's who that is. Hot as hell." Zeus swung his keg of
a head around. "Dude, she'd love someone like you."

"Yeah, right."

"Women love that rebel shit. By the way, I'd bleach the hair."

"No way."

"Why not? The season's over. Bleach it pure fucking white.
You'd look like Bowie."

"Let Bowie look like Bowie. You been running?"

Zeus was wearing a maroon practice jersey and plain gray
bottoms. His black hair was wrung with sweat and he had a towel
wrapped around his neck. "Three miles along the river."

Harry held out his fist. Zeus touched it.

"Had to get rid of the poison. Too many beers at Wursthaus
last night. Then we went over to Eliot."

"Eliot. What were you doing over there?"

Eliot House was "more Harvard than Harvard"—full of blue
bloods who liked to drink G&Ts, talk about their families' money,
and laugh up their sleeves at everyone who wasn't them. Of
course they had the best parties with the best women and everyone secretly wanted to live there.

"That's what I was thinking," Zeus said. "What the fuck am

I doing here? You know what, though? They're not bad guys. Told me I should think about transferring next year."

The backup offensive tackle should have been an afterthought at a place like Eliot, a poor Hispanic kid from Hyde Park who'd wheedled his way into Harvard cuz he had some heft and could play football, not spectacularly well but good enough for the Ivies. Still, there was something about Zeus, an oozing brand of charisma that was hard to nail down and even harder to resist. Whether he was hanging with the crew who cut the grass at the stadium or the Saltonstalls from Eliot, Zeus had a way of making people feel good about themselves, drawing them in even as he kept them at a distance. Harry figured Zeus was the first natural-born politician he'd ever met.

"Met a nice woman last night, Harry."

"At Eliot?"

"The Wursthaus, but then she came over with us. Premed at Tufts. Hot."

Harry snuck a glance. With his baker's belly, old man jowls, and receding hairline, Zeus didn't remind anyone of Paul Newman. Still, the women were as helpless against the man's powers of persuasion as anyone else.

"That's great, Zeus. I'd like to meet her."

"Really?"

"Sure. You gonna be okay for exams?"

Zeus was majoring in finance, with an eye toward Harvard's B-school. Long shot? Maybe. Then again, it was Zeus, so maybe not.

"Stats is a bitch," he said. "Otherwise, I'm good."

"Let me know if you need help."

"How about tonight?"

"I already told you."

"You need to go, Harry."

It was an unofficial tradition among the football players. Every year at the end of the season a handful of them piled into a car (sometimes cars) and headed down to Boston's Combat Zone. They'd park on Washington, crack the windows, and watch the action. The girls would come over and flirt, maybe drink a beer with the college kids, even do a little business in the alley if anyone had the cash.

"You know I work down there," Harry said. For the past year and a half, he'd been volunteering at Boston's Pine Street Inn. The first few months it was handing out coffee and sandwiches from the basement of a dark, damp building in Chinatown. Pretty soon he was tagging along with a couple of social workers as they ventured into the Zone, passing out pamphlets on venereal disease and strips of condoms. If the girls didn't know him by name, they'd probably know his face.

"Be an hour. Two, tops. Drink some beers, whistle at the girls, and we're out." Zeus cocked his head and gave Harry his best hangdog look. Harry knew he was being worked but didn't mind it. That was the genius of Zeus. Harry sometimes wondered what the guy was like when he wasn't onstage, when he wasn't working it.

"We don't get out of the car," Harry said.

"What do you think? I wanna get my dick sucked in an alley by some toothless grandma? We're tourists. Windows up, doors locked, enjoy the show. You wanna grab breakfast?"

"Tasty?"

"Let's go."

Zeus got up first and started down the Widener's front steps.

Harry hung back. Maybe it was his little brother leaving the apartment, maybe it was something else, but a sudden melancholy had stolen over him, like it was all happening too fast and the best of it had already passed him by. He took a last look out over the Yard and inhaled, wanting nothing more than to put the morning in a bottle and take it with him. Then Zeus yelled and waved an arm. Harry exhaled and followed his best friend down the steps.

11

DANIEL SAT near the back of the bus and felt the two bottles in his pocket. One contained clear capsules, a tiny snowfall of white powder heaped up in each. The other was filled with multicolored tablets, reds and oranges and purples that always reminded him of Flintstone vitamins. Except they weren't. They were dream chasers.

Twice a month, Daniel visited the clinic where his doctor asked the same questions. How did he feel? Sad? Glad? Angry? Anxious? Describe, if he could, his color wheel of emotion. When he talked, which wasn't often, Daniel told the doctor he couldn't feel a thing. That was a lie. He felt everything. His feelings, hers, the people down the corridor sitting in the waiting room. Every-one's. And it weighed on him, rendered him numb.

He cracked the window and closed his eyes, letting the wind pucker his cheeks. The bus groaned to a stop and spit out a few passengers, then picked up speed as it slipped back into traffic. Daniel glanced around to see if anyone was watching. All he saw were the backs of newspapers. No one watched anyone on the Brookline Avenue bus at seven in the morning. It was a living, breathing hearse, rolling down the street in a velvet green fog.

Daniel pulled out the two bottles of pills and held them tight in his lap. He hadn't told the doc about his dreams from last night. She would have loved them. And why not? Dreams were the red meat of the mind. And these were prime cuts. A tumble of images so fast and so fresh and so real they threatened to break through the skin of sleep and burst into some unhinged mutation of reality.

Terrifying. Fascinating. And entirely his.

Daniel unscrewed the top of the Flintstone bottle and slowly tipped it upside down, watching Wilma and Fred and Barney bounce off the side of the bus and disappear under its spinning rubber wheels. Then he did the same with the capsules, laying a lovely trail of dream chasers down Brookline Avenue for anyone who might care to follow.

—

He got off at Longwood Avenue, walking the half mile or so to Avenue Louis Pasteur. There was a line of buses outside Latin School, belching smoke and burping out dozens of kids who streamed up the steps and through the front doors. Daniel made his way down the row, searching for the charter from Dorchester and not finding it. He sat on the curb to wait. Five minutes, ten. Finally, it hit the corner, driver fat and white, face lobster red with concentration, lips mouthing a string of silent curses while the yellow bus slammed to the bottom of a pothole and struggled to hold the turn. Daniel stood up as the charter slid to a stop, brakes grinding in protest, and the door opened. The driver studied Daniel with whiskey eyes that blinked once then disappeared behind a wall of kids, all elbows and fists, fighting to get off first like the bus was gonna blow up or something. The Dorchester charter ran through Dot and Roxbury, snaking through the South End and Chinatown at the tail end of its route. Most of the kids on the bus hailed from neighborhoods like Fields Corner, Savin Hill, and Dudley Square. Some had parents who gave a shit. Plenty didn't. Still, they were on the bus every morning. And that said something.

Grace was one of the last to get off. Ben Jacob was just ahead of her. Daniel had first met Ben on the charter two years ago when they were in the eighth grade. Ben lived in Milton and his parents were both doctors. Later, Daniel would discover Ben could have gotten a ride every day from his dad, but he wanted to take the charter. So his father dropped him off at a stop in the city and he rode in. That first day Ben was sitting in a seat across from Daniel when another kid, Billy Shine, got on. Shine was a fullback on the football team and a grade-A asshole. He took one look at Ben and ripped him out of his seat. The side of Ben's face hit a metal pole in the middle of the aisle, and he fell into the well for the back steps. A couple of kids snickered. Most just pushed past to grab whatever seats were left.

Ben was on his hands and knees gathering up books and papers when Daniel knelt down to help him. "Fuckin' hebe" rang down from somewhere behind them, a titter of nervous laughter following. Ben pinned a black yarmulke back on his mop of hair and settled himself on the top step. His glasses were broken, so he got out a roll of electric tape and began to mend them. Shine sat ten feet away, gazing out the window. Daniel joined Ben on the step, turning and staring as hard as he could at Shine, challenging, daring him to make eye contact. He knew Shine wouldn't mess with him because of Harry, who was still at Latin and a senior. If Shine did come after him, that was all right, too. Daniel had never been afraid of a beating. In the end, Shine did what bullies usually do when someone pushes back, even a little. He looked around for easier pickings. It would be another six months before Daniel actually talked to Ben, but Daniel always felt good about that first day. Ben would have, too, if he'd ever noticed. But that was Ben.

"Hey, Daniel." Ben gave up a high five, bumping a large brown briefcase against Daniel's legs and adjusting his glasses.

"Hey, Ben."

Grace crowded close by Ben's shoulder. "You didn't call."

"Sorry," Daniel said. "I got busy."

Grace wanted to hear about the apartment, but Daniel shook his head and the three of them started walking.

"You have all your lines translated?" Grace said.

Daniel hadn't done any of his homework and would just have to hope he didn't get called on.

"I can help," Ben said. He was in advanced Latin and Greek. Basically, Ben knew Virgil better than Virgil. He was also the kind of guy who'd help anyone who asked and never make a big deal out of it.

"Thanks," Daniel said, stopping about halfway up the front steps of the high school. "Where are you first period?"

"Study hall, but I'm working as a door monitor. One of the side doors near the gym. How about you?"

Daniel pointed at himself and Grace. "We got study hall, too. Working in the English Department."

"Let's go." Grace tugged at Daniel's sleeve. Most of the kids had already filtered into school. Ben was looking anxiously across the street.

"What is it?" Daniel said.

Ben poked his chin toward the hulking outline of Boston English. The second-oldest high school in the city, English dated back to 1821. Unlike Latin School, English was not an exam school and had a student population that was more than ninety percent black. Two weeks ago, a kid from English was beaten up outside a drugstore on Huntington Avenue. Three days later, two Latin School kids were mugged in the Fens. One of the Latin School kids got slashed in the side with a knife and showed off the wound to twenty or so students in the bathroom. Last week, more than a hundred English students massed on the street shared by the two schools. Daniel watched from the windows like everyone else as one of the kids from English climbed up on a car and the students started to chant. As quickly as it started, however, the thing lost its momentum, the crowd breaking up into smaller groups and drifting away. Pretty soon the block was quiet again. But the time bomb was ticking and everyone knew it.

"Nothing's gonna happen," Daniel said, while Grace continued to nudge.

"You don't sound like you believe it," Ben said.

"You worried about being on the door?"

"Heck no."

Ben weighed a hundred pounds on a good day and had never thrown a punch, or anything else, in anger in his life. As door monitor he'd be Latin School's first line of defense should something happen. Not the best of plans—in fact, probably the worst—but it was what they had. The three friends ran up the steps and ducked inside just as the bell for homeroom rang.

12

THE TASTY'S early morning rush had subsided for the moment, allowing them to spread out at one end of the counter. Harry took a sip of coffee and stared out the window at traffic, listening idly as Zeus ordered four eggs scrambled and a side of toast. The counterman asked Harry what he wanted. He got an English muffin just to be polite, then put down his mug and rubbed a hand over his scalp. The counterman must have thought that was some sort of signal because he hustled over with the pot and gave them both a refill.

"He thinks you're from fucking Mars," Zeus said.

"It's Harvard Square. The guy sees all kinds coming through the door."

"Yeah, but none of them made first team All-Ivy."

Harry laughed.

"You think he doesn't know who you are?"

"Save it."

"I'm serious. People know you, Harry. And that means something."

Zeus's mountain of eggs took less time to cook than they did to crack. Harry watched as the big tackle pulled across the salt and pepper shakers and began to season his food.

"What's bugging you?" Harry said.

"Nothing."

"Come on."

"You should be careful, that's all."

"Careful of what? I got a couple of mentions in the *Globe*. Big deal."

"Folks notice. That's all I'm saying."

"I don't get it. One minute you're telling me to be careful, then you're dragging me down to the Zone."

"Different."

"How so?"

"Cuz it's one night and I'll be there."

"And you're gonna look after me?"

"I'm always looking after you, bro. Always." Zeus shoveled a forkful of eggs onto a piece of toast and folded it into his mouth, washing it down with a mouthful of coffee. "Hey, look, it's your asshole roomie."

Harry followed Zeus's gaze out the front window. Neil Prescott stood in the shadow of the Red Line stop, talking to a woman Harry didn't recognize, probably trying to get her number with an eye toward getting her drunk and into his bed.

"Guy's a tool," Harry said.

"Hence the moniker—asshole roomie. Fuck, he's coming over."

Most students at Harvard lived on campus. Prescott was a junior who couldn't. Harry wasn't privy to all the details, but there was a rumor of gambling during his freshman year. And something about a fifteen-year-old he'd knocked up. Prescott's dad and grandfather were both Harvard men, both football players, so it all got handled. Harry didn't really care. Prescott had an apartment near campus with an empty bedroom. And Harry had Daniel. So they struck their deal. Harry watched as Prescott made his way across the street and into the diner. He slid onto a stool next to Zeus but turned his attention immediately to Harry.

"What's up, Fitzsimmons?" Prescott called everyone by their last name.

"Just hangin'."

"You sleep in the apartment last night?"

Harry nodded. He knew Prescott had been out all night and was dying to share details of his latest conquest. Again, Harry wasn't interested.

"I left you a note back at the place," he said. "My brother moved out."

Prescott didn't give a shit. As long as the rent got paid Harry could do what he liked. Zeus was a different story.

"Moved out? Kid's in fucking high school." Zeus had only met Daniel once, but it didn't matter. Daniel was a Fitzsimmons, and that meant family.

"Technically, he's supposed to live in Boston to attend Latin School," Harry said. "So he found a room in Kenmore Square. Says he's renting from a Harvard prof. Simon Lane?"

"Never heard of him," Zeus said. Prescott shook his head.

"You working out?" Prescott nodded at Zeus's sweats.

"Little morning jog."

"How about you?" Prescott glanced at Harry. Prescott had been a hot-shit running back in high school, but the speed hadn't translated to college. Still, he was a jock in his head and that horse died hard, if at all.

"Lifted yesterday. Did some cardio."

Prescott nodded like he was the guy who kept track of that stuff.

"Just talking about tonight," Zeus said.

"You in, superstar?" It'd be like Prescott to make a big deal if Harry said no.

"Yeah, I'm in."

"Awesome. I'm driving. Sanchez, you're getting your dick sucked. Fitzsimmons, who the fuck knows?"

The door to the Tasty opened and two women walked in. Behind them was a tall, middle-aged man, tightly wound through the neck and shoulders, the tension releasing in a shock of curly hair. The man's eyes widened a touch when he saw the three of them sitting at the counter. Prescott raised his hand.

"Nick, over here. You guys know Nick Toney?"

Nick Toney was a photographer, one of those high-end guys with exhibitions at universities and places like the Museum of Fine Arts. For some reason Prescott loved photography and had all kinds of fancy-ass equipment lying around the apartment. Toney had come over one night to talk to him about some gear. Harry hadn't been there, but Prescott told him Toney's advice was simple. Stop buying cameras and start taking pictures. Harry liked that.

"How you guys doing?" Toney slid in next to Harry as Prescott made the introductions. Zeus grunted through a mouthful of eggs. Harry shook the man's hand.

"Nice to meet you, sir."

"Do me a favor and drop the 'sir.' You're Neil's roommate?"

"Yes, sir. I mean, Nick."

"I feel like I know you from somewhere?"

Harry shrugged. "I don't think so."

"No?" Toney cocked his head and offered up his best doorman's grin, teeth white and straight and strong.

"You probably seen him in the paper," Zeus said. "First team, All-Ivy."

"Whoa. Superstar."

"Hardly." Harry felt the burn at the back of his neck and in his cheeks.

"He's the modest type," Prescott said, buttering a piece of Zeus's toast and enjoying the hell out of Harry's discomfort.

"Nothing wrong with being modest," Toney said. "Still, that's a hell of a thing, Harry."

"Thanks."

"You guys headed home for Turkey Day?"

"Staying in town," Harry said. "Me and my brother are just gonna hang around the apartment."

Toney raised his chin and let his eyes drop over to Zeus.

"Probably head home."

"We were just talking about tonight," Prescott said. "Thinking about going down to the Zone." Prescott looked expectantly at Toney, who shifted his shoulders and grinned uneasily.

"Nick does a lot of shooting down there," Prescott said.

"Actually, I've got some studio space. I do portraits of the girls when they're not working. Try to document their lives."

"I volunteer in Chinatown," Harry said. "We do a lot of outreach in the Zone."

Toney shot a finger at Harry. "Maybe that's where I've seen you."

"Could be. You probably get a lot of college guys down there."

"College, high school. Businessmen, tourists. Perverts, priests, fuckers older than dirt. All kinds, my friend. All kinds." The counterman came by with a coffee for the photographer. Toney stirred in some sugar and took a measured sip. "Something I don't understand. Football players from Harvard, right? World by the balls. So why in the fuck would you wanna go down the Zone? I mean, to me, it makes no sense."

"It's sort of an end-of-the-season tradition," Harry said, feeling as stupid as he sounded and trying to figure out how and why he was explaining something he wanted no part of.

"Not a nice place, Harry, but you already know that."

"It's just a night."

"It's always just a night. I mean, what else can it be, right? Anyway, I'll give you a free piece of advice. Take it for what it's worth." Toney dropped his voice a notch as the three Harvard boys leaned in. "I know most of the girls who work down there. I know the guys who run the girls. No offense, but they live for a crew like you. Drunk, horny as shit." Toney rubbed a finger and thumb together. "Plenty of cashish. Girls will pick your pocket, pimps roll you in an alley. And that's just the start. So what you gotta do is play it smart. Stay together. In the bars, on the street. Together. Do that and you'll be fine. All right?"

They nodded. Toney made eye contact with each in turn, lingering on Harry, taking note of the ripped-up clothes and the rest of it. "It's always the crazy-looking fucks that wind up being the most responsible. Am I wrong?"

"I don't think we should be going if that's what you're asking."

"But you'll keep an eye out?"

"Yes, sir. Sorry, Nick."

"Good. I feel better. Come on, Neil. If you want me to take a look at those lenses, we better get moving. Later, boys."

Toney threw down enough money to pay for everyone. Then he and Prescott left.

"Guy acts like he knows us," Zeus said.

"Probably just seen a lot of idiots like us."

Zeus shrugged.

"What is it?"

"Been thinking 'bout tonight. Maybe it's not such a great idea."

"Now you come around. Christ, what did Toney say that I didn't?"

"I don't know. Nothing."

"Well, we gotta go now. Otherwise, I'll have to listen to asshole roomie. Anyway, Toney's right. If we stay together, it's not a problem. You done?"

Zeus nodded and they both got up.

"What time we supposed to meet?" Harry said.

"Seven o'clock. Prescott wants to grab dinner first."

"Don't worry, Zeus. Like you said, an hour. Two, tops, and we're out of there." Harry patted the big tackle on the shoulder. "Besides, I got you watching my back."

13

KIDS EVERYWHERE, sprinting up and down stairs, yelling at each other in the halls, slamming lockers, dropping books, everyone rushing to beat the bell. Grace led the way, tackling the main staircase two steps at a time. A door opened and they caught a glimpse of the school's auditorium. Benjamin Franklin, Samuel Adams, and Ralph Waldo Emerson were just a few of the names carved into the white frieze that ran around the room. Daniel remembered staring up at them the first time he sat in the auditorium. Their headmaster, William Keating, told the class of five hundred seventh graders to take a good look at the student to his left and his right. "Two of you won't be graduating with a Latin School diploma," Keating assured them with a grin that was more predator than educator. After all, *Sumus Primi* and all that. So let the games begin.

Grace had slipped just ahead, taking a corner at the top of the stairs. Daniel sprinted up the last flight, Ben sharp on his heels. They caught up to her just as she hit homeroom. One kid had his head on his desk and was dead asleep. Two others played football with a bus pass, sliding the plastic disk across the width of the table and trying to get it to hang over the edge without falling off. If one of them scored, he got to kick an extra point by flicking the disk with his fingers while the other kid held his hands together and made a goalpost.

"Haverly is out sick." One of the table football players spoke without ever taking his eyes off the game. "No homeroom today."

The three of them walked back into the hallway. Eddie Spaulding was chewing on a plastic straw and sitting in a chair, balanced on its two rear legs and tilted back against the wall.

"Bookworm." Eddie was a senior, starting running back and safety on the football team. The hype had him pegged as a star in college, but Daniel thought high school might be as good as it got. For some unfathomable reason, Eddie had opted to study ancient Greek and it quickly became his bane. In other words, Ben was his best friend.

"Hey, Eddie." Ben didn't seem to care about the nickname Eddie had given him. Maybe he was oblivious, or, again, maybe just Ben.

Eddie tipped forward so all four legs of his chair were on the floor. "Haverly's out today."

"They told us," Grace said. "What are you doing out here?"

Eddie's eyes moved from Grace to Daniel before settling again on Ben.

"Let me guess," Grace said. "You need help?"

"It's the fucking *Iliad*. I was up until three in the morning and got nowhere."

"We're in the middle of 'Book Six,'" Ben said. "Hector and Andromache." He plopped down on the floor and opened his briefcase. Eddie Spaulding began to pull books out of a canvas bag he'd stashed by his feet. First came a copy of the *Iliad* in the original Greek, then a Greek dictionary followed by a spiral note-book with a few lines of English translation scribbled in it. The fourth book was smaller, bound in red with its title written in tiny script on the spine.

"What's that?" Daniel said.

"It's a trot," Grace said. "Gives you Greek on one page and English on the other."

Daniel picked up the book and flipped it open. He'd heard of them but never actually seen one. "Wow."

"Don't get so excited," Eddie said. "DiCara can smell a trot a mile away."

"That's true," Ben said. "Most of the teachers here can tell if you're using a translation aid. Besides, Eddie, you don't need it."

"Because I have you?" Eddie grinned as the bell rang, signaling two minutes until the start of first period.

"Because you're smart." Ben tapped his temple. "It's just a matter of sticking with it. Remember what DiCara said about the grain of sand trapped in an oyster."

"It doesn't become a pearl overnight."

"It takes time and diligence. Just like football."

"Yeah, yeah, that's pissa. Just help me with a couple of spots." Eddie pointed to a line in the Greek text. Ben took a look.

"ἐϋκνήμιδες Ἀχαιοὶ. It means 'strong-greaved Achaeans.'"

"That's what the trot says. Gimme another word."

"'Well-greaved.'"

"What the fuck are greaves?"

"They're like shin pads for hockey. The Greeks wore them during battle."

Eddie looked up from his scribbles. "You're kidding?"

"It's an epithet. Homer uses them throughout the poem. Most people think it was a mnemonic device as well as a way to keep the lines in meter."

"Can I say shin guards?"

"No, Eddie. Say 'greaved.' 'Well-greaved.' That will get you by."

Eddie scribbled some more and fretted. "Shit, I got a lot more."

"I'm on door duty by the gym for first period."

Grace shook her head. "Ben? Seriously?"

"Come by and we'll go over the rest of it."

"You'll give me the lines?" Eddie said.

"Only after we go over them."

The bell rang again. One minute to first period.

"Thanks, Bookworm. Sorry, I mean Ben. I'll come by." Spaulding stood up, giving Grace a longer glance than Daniel would have liked before drifting around the corner. Ben picked up his briefcase and took off running in the opposite direction, the words floating back over his shoulder.

"I like to help people, Grace. It's what I'm good at."

"Guess he told you." Daniel elbowed Grace in the ribs and followed Ben, the three of them skidding to a halt in the stairwell.

"You know they have asbestos in this place?" Ben pointed to an insulated pipe running across the ceiling and a burst of white filament feathering into fine strands. "I read an article that says it's toxic."

"Forget about the asbestos," Grace said, touching Ben's sleeve. "Just keep your door closed and locked."

"You think something's going to happen?"

"Better safe than sorry."

The bell rang a final time, this one longer and louder, indicating the beginning of first period. Grace and Daniel watched as Ben tumbled down the stairs. Then they hustled up a flight, slipping into the English Department just as Mr. Rozner stepped out of the teachers' lounge, reading the *New York Times* and sipping a cup of coffee.

Daniel and Grace buried themselves at the back of the department, the familiar smells of copying fluid and textbooks saturating the air around them. Grace got to work shelving copies of *David Copperfield*. Daniel reviewed a stencil of next month's schedule for the department and snapped it onto the ink-filled drum of the mimeograph machine. He'd just begun to turn out copies when Rozner came in. Usually the head of the English Department wandered back to their work area for a brief chat. Today, however, he went straight to his desk. Then Daniel heard something he'd never heard in his three months of working there—the sound of a television.

—

Mr. Rozner was tucked into his tiny desk, half-moon glasses pushed down his nose, riveted to a small black-and-white perched atop an annotated edition of William Shakespeare's complete works. Daniel cleared his throat and rustled up against a stack of books. Rozner half turned.

"You were late. Both of you were."

"Sorry, sir." Daniel felt Grace bump up behind him. "The buses were running slow today."

Rozner dumped a spoonful of Cremora into his coffee and took a sip. "Not surprising. Not surprising at all."

Daniel could feel Grace stiffen even though she wasn't actually touching him. Rozner was old-school and had that effect on everyone who worked for him. In class he was supposed to be even worse.

"Nguyen."

"Yes, sir."

"Go see Professor Lonergan in Room 311. He's got a book I need you to pick up."

Grace left without a word. Rozner went back to watching television. On the tiny screen, a fist of a woman stood at a microphone. The sound was too low for Daniel to make out the words, but he could see her pale face and red-lipped mouth opened wide to accommodate whatever was coming out of it. The camera panned back to reveal the crowd. They covered City Hall Plaza, filling the redbrick and concrete tiers all the way to the Government Center T stop. Handmade signs of varying designs and shapes waved up and down, back and forth. NO BUSING. RESIST. EAST BOSTON AGAINST FORCED BUSING. Rozner turned down the sound all the way. They listened in the quiet as footsteps passed in the hall. Sheets of dust drifted in yellow light falling from a cracked porcelain fixture that hung off the wall. The light was newly born but already seemed old beyond knowing. Daniel wondered if other students had labored beneath it, generation after generation, making their copies while mapping their futures in their heads.

"You're Harry Fitzsimmons's brother?"

Daniel jumped. Rozner was watching him closely. Daniel had no idea what he'd seen. "Yes, sir."

"How's he doing at Harvard?"

"Pretty well."

"I remember about that. Your mother and all."

"I was eight."

"Yes, well, I heard about it. Later, of course. What's Harry now?"

"A sophomore, sir."

"A sophomore?" Rozner pulled off his glasses and rubbed his

hands over his face. His Shakespeare class was a rite of passage for juniors and seniors, his command of the material and attention to detail the stuff of Latin School legend. This morning, however, Rozner seemed far more man than myth, deep red lines creased down both sides of his nose, his white head of hair slightly mussed on top and at the sides.

"Do we have you working here for the whole year?"

"That's up to you, sir. I'd prefer the whole year."

Rozner gestured to the straight-backed chair beside his desk. "Sit down."

Daniel did.

"You know what Latin School does, Fitzsimmons?"

"Gives you a good education."

"It does a hell of a lot more than that."

"Yes, sir."

"It gives you a chance. Something you might not ever have otherwise. You realize how fragile that is?"

"Fragile?"

"Yes, fragile." Rozner nodded at the silent images flashing across his TV screen. "What you see there is the genie let out of the bottle. I thought it might tire itself out."

"But it's not?"

"I'm afraid not." Rozner straightened his shoulders and sat up. "Latin School provides the opportunity, but it's up to you to make something of it. Do you understand?"

"Yes, sir."

"Good. That's good." The head of Latin School's English Department ran his hands quietly over his hair as if to compose himself and replaced his glasses, the black edges of the frames fitting neatly into the grooves in his nose they'd carved there.

Then he cleared his throat and began to shuffle through a stack of blue books piled up on his desk. "There's some notices that need to be copied and sent out. They're on the table beside the mimeograph."

Daniel found the stencils right where Rozner said he would. He clipped the first one to the large steel cylinder on the mimeograph and began to crank. Rozner sat at his desk and read, the veins in his cheeks threaded with color, thick fingers working as he cut and slashed his way through the blue books. They didn't exchange another word for the rest of the period. When the bell rang, Rozner came over and checked Daniel's copies. He made a couple of notations on a sheet, nodded, and moved to the door. Grace was standing there.

"I didn't tell you to get lost for the period," Rozner said.

"I'm sorry, sir. Mr. Lonergan couldn't find the book. And then the headmaster came in and wanted to talk. And then . . ."

There was a sudden rumbling from somewhere in the bowels of the building, followed by a boom like an explosion, then a second. Rozner rushed into the hall as teachers and students poked their heads from classrooms. Word spread quickly. Boston English had gone off again. And now they were coming across the street to liberate their Latin School brethren.

14

DANIEL RAN to a set of windows overlooking Avenue Louis Pasteur, wedging out a spot for himself and Grace among the chattering students and peering down into the street. A steady stream of bodies poured out of English, flowing down the block and up the steps of Latin School. The crowd cleared space around the front door while a steel pole was stripped of its stop sign and passed overhead. The first rank of kids, all twitch and itch, lined up the pole and started to ram it against the door. The crowd cheered with each blow, none of which seemed to have much effect on the door. Inside Latin School, however, it was a different story. Some of the students were scared. Some wanted to get out on the street and bust heads. A rock flew through the air, falling short of its mark. The second broke a first-floor window, sending the crowd on the street into hysterics. The kids on the pole redoubled their efforts. Grace punched Daniel in the shoulder and pointed. A section of the mob had broken off and was running down the far side of the building.

"They're headed to the gym," Grace said.

"Ben."

They flew down one flight, then a second. The sound of

banging echoed up the stairwell. Grace and Daniel turned the corner together and found Ben hanging on to a set of push bars as the door he was supposed to protect bowed and buckled under the weight of the assault. Daniel could hear screams and swears through the door. "Jew boy. We gonna fuck you up."

Daniel grabbed on to the push bars. His friend's shirt was torn at the shoulder.

"Did they hurt you?" Daniel said.

"No, but I barely got the thing closed."

Someone outside was talking about liberating the white man. There was a lot of laughter and the doors bowed outward again. A hand reached through to grip the inside of the frame and a shoulder followed, wedging the doors open. Ben pointed to a Koho hockey stick by his feet. The shoulder had been joined by a head as Ben's door gave birth to a smiling teenager explaining to them how much he was looking forward to kicking some Latin School ass. Grace picked up the Koho and popped the butt end off the kid's forehead. Then she tomahawked down with a two-hander. The kid fell away and the doors slammed shut again. She slid the stick between the two inside handles, securing the doors for the moment.

"Holy shit." Ben's eyes goggled out of his head as he absorbed her handiwork.

"I know, right?" Grace held her hand over her mouth and started to giggle. Just then there was another massive boom and the hockey stick snapped like kindling.

"What do we do now?" Grace said.

Daniel pulled her back as the doors blew out, light shafting the dark gray of the stairwell. A hand yanked Ben outside, leaving behind nothing except his scream. Eddie Spaulding appeared at the top of the steps. He paused for a moment, then rushed down the stairs and plowed into the mob after Ben. Daniel followed him through the gap.

———

Daniel tripped over something and stumbled down a short flight of steps, scraping his chin and hitting his nose before winding up face-first in the dirt. He was on the edge of a rough field that ran down one side of Latin School. To his right was an empty parking lot, to his left thirty to forty kids enveloped in a rising din of fists and curses and shoves and elbows. At the very center of the mass was Eddie, an attacker on his back and a second hanging off his arm as Ben kicked and clawed to stay by the football player's side. Daniel pulled himself to his feet and dove in. His fist cracked off the side of a skull with no apparent effect. He swung again, this time connecting and hearing the crunch of what might have been bone or tooth or both. Someone screamed in his ear and pulled his hair as he fell to his knees. A blow glanced off his cheek and someone bit his shoulder. There was no pain in any of it, his blood spiked with adrenaline as a tangle of bodies threated to crush him. He rolled to one side and watched the pile of arms and legs tumble past, windmilling across the field until it slammed into the side of a green Dumpster.

For a moment the space cleared and the action seemed to slow. Eddie Spaulding had Ben behind him, safe for now between the Dumpster and the building as a half-dozen kids circled. Eddie had blood and snot bubbling from one nostril. A swipe of fingernails had scraped his cheek. He caught Daniel's eye and raised his chin. Daniel turned just as a tree branch swung out of the sun. It clipped him on the shoulder, freezing one side of his body as he fell. The kid swinging the branch wasn't much bigger than Daniel, the weight of the limb carrying him ass over teakettle past Daniel and into the dirt. Daniel was about to get up and jump on the kid's back when he felt a second presence behind him. Another kid, more man than kid, stepped forward, stopping within arm's reach and looking down at Daniel. His forehead was heavy and thick; his eyes sunk deep in his skull. He was wrapped in a long leather coat with gray sweats and black winter boots and held his hands loose and quiet by his sides. The man-child wore a white do-rag with short dreads poking out from underneath, and a silver tooth hung from a chain around his neck. He smiled at Daniel, who saw the gap where the tooth should have been and felt a chill as his mind went off script, reaching out and pushing up against his soon-to-be attacker's.

Almost immediately Daniel felt them entangle.

The man-child was twelve when his "uncle" hit him with the hammer—broken pieces of teeth and gums and blood all over the cracked kitchen table and linoleum floor. That night the man-child sat in a locked closet under a set of stairs, sucking on a wet towel and listening to the thumping and bumping until it was quiet. Then he forced the lock and slipped through the kitchen. They were in his mother's bedroom, wrapped in a sheet and the foul smell of their sex. The man-child raised the hammer, clean light from the hallway catching its heft. He saw the gleam of their eyes as they rumbled out of their sleep and opened their mouths but never screamed. And then the hammer fell and skulls cracked in the red moonlight and bone and brains leaked all over the man-child's bare feet. No one had ever heard the story because no one had ever told it. But Daniel knew it now, felt it pumping in his blood, a pulsing, living cord of tissue and flesh and feeling and memory, a flowing back and forth that Daniel wanted to cut off but couldn't. Cuz he'd entangled when he shouldn't have and now they were one.

"I'm sorry," Daniel said.

The man-child blinked and Daniel felt the weight of the gun hidden deep inside the man-child's leather coat. Daniel watched in his mind as the man-child pulled it free in a smooth, practiced fashion. The first bullet struck Daniel square in the throat, blood bubbling up into the back of his mouth and spilling over his chest. The second caught him in the shoulder, turning him as the final bullet ripped through his left cheek and roofed in his skull. Daniel fell forward, striking the ground with a dull thud and rolling onto his back so he was staring up at the white blue of the sky as his soul swirled down and away to whatever place went the souls of young boys who spent the coin of their lives foolishly and thoughtlessly and recklessly and reckoned the world would stand still as they fell when nothing could be further from the truth. Daniel saw all that in the wink of a moment as the mind of the man with the silver tooth yawned wider and Daniel peeked over the edge at the twisted ribbons of smoke blowing through the breach. Then he leaped, hanging on to the man-child's right arm before he ever had a chance to pull his gun, ripping at the man's coat, clawing at the weapon still tucked inside.

"Motherfucker." The man-child pivoted, Daniel clinging like a terrier, his weight peeling the leather coat back from the man's body and dislodging the gun. It flew through the air, still dark with fury as a brace of sirens sounded and three cop cars rolled into Latin School's back lot. The man-child with the tooth around his neck shook free of Daniel and felt for the gun against his ribs. He cursed when he realized it wasn't there and looked around wildly for it. Then he ran, quicker than anyone could ever have imagined, taking Death with him, leaving an ugly, rippling scar behind.

Daniel was still on his knees as the squad cars rolled up, chasing what remained of the mob across the bumpy field toward Avenue Louis Pasteur. Eddie and Ben were gone. Daniel had no idea where. He struggled to his feet and ran crookedly toward the steps and the side door Ben had been tasked to protect. He'd just reached the first step when he heard something he thought he knew—the soft sounds of a woman's struggle. In a stray panel of light Daniel could just make out a couple of backs, three backs, huddled on the far side of the Dumpster. They hadn't run like the others and the air rippled and danced around them. Daniel went up on his tiptoes, changing the angle enough to catch a glimpse of a red sneaker attached to a long leg. It was a girl's sneaker, Grace's sneaker, trapped beneath the hump-backed monster.

Daniel opened his mouth to scream, but heard only a high shriek, torn from his lips and borne away in the tumult. He began to run, taking one step, then a second. He felt his foot gouge the earth, pulling up clods of dirt and rocks. Daniel looked down as his legs narrowed, his feet, first one, then the other, curving into hard yellow talons. Feathers sprouted from his shoulders and traveled down his arms until they covered his fingers in fine, swirling ruffles. His bones hollowed and the breeze at his back coarsened, lifting him as he took a third step, then a fourth, and then he no longer touched the earth.

Daniel soared high overhead, flapping his wings in long,

powerful strokes and peering down at the three sets of gray shoulders huddled over Grace. One turned and looked up, fleshed hood slipping off a bald head to reveal pulpy red eyes, a hooked beak, and the thick tongue of a vulture rattling in a hiss. Daniel angled back against the breeze and settled on a corner of Latin School's roof, almost directly above them. He could hear Grace's fear—thin music that pierced his skull to cracking and filled the air with its tremble. Daniel spread his wings again and dove, the cold slipstreaming over sinew and muscle. He clenched and unclenched his talons and sharpened his eyes as he dropped through the sky, hunting for a soft spot among the scavengers. Then he was back on the ground, back in his own skin, falling on Grace's attackers like hell's hammer with fists and teeth and spit and screams. They ran as one, overwhelmed by the fury without ever considering the size and strength, or lack thereof, of their foe. Daniel watched them go, nostrils laid back, sucking in air while one leg shook and there was nothing he could do about it. Grace was huddled tiny against the wall, fully clothed with her knees under her chin and her hands locked around her legs.

"They didn't do anything." She was looking straight ahead, voice stripped and tender and raw.

"I know."

"They didn't."

"It's okay, Grace."

"Don't tell me what's okay." She tried to get to her feet but stumbled and collapsed back against the wall. Daniel sat down beside her and touched her arm.

"You wanna talk to the cops or something?"

She shook her head. "They didn't do anything, Daniel."

"Grace . . ."

"They tried or they would have tried, but you stopped them." She leaned over and kissed him quickly on the cheek, touching a soft spot under his eye. "Tell Ben and the other guy I said thanks as well."

"Why don't we go inside and see the nurse . . ."

"I just wanna go home."

"All right."

"Maybe we can meet tonight. Nine o'clock at the fish tank?"

Daniel nodded. She gave him a hug and stood up, making no sound as she crept down the side of the building, holding on to the brick wall for balance, and then slipping through the back lot to the street.

He sat back and let the chemicals percolate in his blood. He was coming off it now, whatever "it" was, and fatigue was setting in. The moments, real and imagined, rampaged through his head, rippling in staccato bursts of color and sound. It all seemed slightly off-kilter, out of control. Daniel wondered about the meds he'd refused to take and dug his nails into his palms just to feel the bite. That was when he saw the beaded grip of the gun sticking out from under the Dumpster. He pulled it toward him with his foot and stretched his legs out, covering the gun with his thigh as the sirens whooped and someone on a megaphone told the crowds at the front of the school to disperse or they'd be arrested. Close by came the crackle of a walkie-talkie and the crunch of footsteps on cold gravel. The cops were circling back, putting together the pieces of the brawl. They'd want to talk to him for sure, but only if they found him.

Daniel picked up the gun, surprisingly snug in his palm, and stuffed it in his pocket. Then he crawled toward the door, duck-walking as he got closer to keep the Dumpster between himself and the cops. When he got close enough, he took a deep breath, paused for a second, and ran into the building. He expected to hear a cop yelling for him to stop, but there was nothing. Daniel went down to his locker and stashed the gun behind a text on Cicero's Catiline Orations. Then he wandered back to the school's main entrance. Kids filled the hallways, chattering excitedly about what had happened, the accounts growing wilder by the minute. Daniel hung on the edge of the conversation and listened. Eddie was the hero who'd saved Ben the bookworm. No one mentioned Grace. No one mentioned a gun. No one mentioned a student transforming into a bird of prey.

Daniel went into a bathroom and touched his face in the mirror. The images came ripe and unbidden. Claw and beak. His body morphing, lifting, soaring. He closed his eyes and tipped his head back as the headmaster's voice crackled over the intercom. Classes were canceled for the day; buses would be waiting outside. Daniel took his time washing his hands and walked slowly back to his locker. He pushed the gun he'd found down to the bottom of his bag and covered it up. Then he threw the bag over his shoulder and left by the same side door where he'd found Grace and fought his battle. The cops were still there, but they had bigger problems. It was just past eleven in the morning and a little more than a mile back to his new home.

He'd walk it. Unless he flew.

15

TOMMY DILLON skimmed the surface of the Tobin Bridge at eighty miles an hour, flipping through stations, hopping and popping from blues to jazz to Elvis. He settled on Bowie's "Starman" and picked up the garage bill stuck in his console. Three hundred fifty bucks for what? Tommy pressed down on the accelerator. Piece of shit still had no pickup. He flew off the end of the bridge, sparks flying as he scraped bottom, and sipped from a paper cup filled with ice and Coke and a hit of fine, dark rum. Tommy called it taking the edge off.

He glanced down at the directions he'd printed on the inside of his wrist. Five-mile bomb down Route 1, then another mile or so once he got off. The Stones came on the radio. Tommy turned it up and started slaloming in and out of afternoon traffic, humming to himself as he hunted for gaps, then jumping into the breakdown lane and punching it. A piece-of-shit Vega tried to squeeze him into the guardrail. Tommy laid on the horn and flipped him off, laughing like a motherfucker and loving it.

He peeled off the expressway in Revere, took a quick suck on the rum and Coke as he squeezed between two trucks, and pulled into a fenced-in parking lot behind an old cement factory. Fucking drama with this guy. Tommy could have met the prick in Faneuil Hall and it would have been just as good. He killed the engine and watched two men climb out of a puke-green Monte Carlo. The one Tommy knew was wrapped in a leather duster coat and wore biker boots with run-down heels. A Mexican was just behind him. Both stood with their backs to the sun and their legs spread, like it was the fucking OK Corral or something.

Not a problem.

Tommy made his way across the lot with a bow in his legs and a roll in his gait. John fucking Wayne, taking his John fucking Wayne time. The Mex was hard around the eyes, but nervous. He wore a brown corduroy jacket bunched at the shoulders and had a gun in his pocket.

"Tommy, you know Rafa?" The man in the duster was nothing to Tommy. A means to an end. Another route through the sewer.

"Get rid of him," Tommy said.

The Mexican grinned, white teeth flashing, and mumbled something in Spanish.

"What'd he say?"

"He says he's seen you around. Says they call you *ardilla*. Means 'the little squirrel.'" The man in the duster thought that was funny as all fuck. Tommy pulled out his gun and whistled a slug by the ear of the Mex, who hugged the ground and looked like he might just piss himself.

"Hey, hey, hey." The man in the duster spread his hands. The Mex raised his eyes off the gravel, his piece in his fist. Maybe he was gonna shoot someone in the ankle.

"I ain't in the fucking mood," Tommy said, putting his gun away and bringing himself back to heel.

The man in the duster nodded at the Mex, who scrambled

to his feet and walked backward to the Monte, never taking his eyes off Tommy as he climbed in the front seat.

"Why am I out here?"

"Fucking relax, Tommy. Jesus, it was a joke."

"I'm fine."

"Fine, my ass. What's the problem?"

"Nothin'. Cases piling up. Partner's nervous as a fucking cat. Yesterday we pulled your guy out of the harbor."

"Afraid I can't help you with that one."

"No shit. So why am I here?"

The man in the duster led Tommy back behind the Monte. Tommy toodled his fingers at the Mex as he went by, then stood back as the man in the duster cranked open the trunk. The inside was layered with fat bags of cocaine. Tommy moved closer, lip twitching, one hand resting on the rubber lining of the trunk, the other running smooth and light over his gun grip.

"You know I work Homicide?"

"Fuck Homicide. For you, this right here is forever money. Your wife, your kids. Game changer."

"Got the wrong guy."

"Do I?"

"If you think I'm gonna help you move this much product, absolutely."

The man in the duster slammed down the lid of the trunk, nearly catching Tommy's fingers. "Who said anything about moving product? I don't let users—sorry, former users—anywhere near that end. No offense, but it's bad for business."

"Then what do you want?"

"Small job, but it's gotta be done right. Everything goes well, you and I are done. And you get the taste."

"Why the fuck am I so lucky?"

"You have the skills for the job. Plus I'm getting out of the business and don't need any more cops in my Rolodex. Let's sit up front and talk. I think you're gonna like this."

They pulled the Mex out of the car and told him to take a walk. Where? Who the fuck knows cuz there was nowhere to walk. Still, the Mex went. Then the man in the duster sat behind the wheel of the Monte, Tommy beside him, listening as the man told him about the job. Tommy tried to keep it all in his head and wanted to take notes but knew that wasn't allowed. Mostly, though, he thought about the money. And when he wasn't thinking about the money, he was smiling and nodding at the man in the duster and imagining taking out his gun and decorating the inside of the car with the cocksucker's brains. Then he'd hunt down the Mex. *Ardilla, my fucking ass.*

Tommy never got another look at the product. When they finished, he shook hands and hopped in his car. This time he put the bubble on the roof and did a buck ten across the Tobin, amazed at all he had to do and wondering where he could get something to eat, while another part of his brain admired the sudden balls his car was showing. Fucking grease monkey might have actually done something after all.

Tommy buried the needle. Up ahead dusk was falling, and the city loomed.

16

DANIEL RAN loose-limbed along the path, footsteps soundless as he went. Evening traffic zipped past on his right, bullets of pure light reflected in long ripples across a glass canyon of buildings. He slipped under the BU Bridge and followed the bend of the Charles, the humped backs of old New England brownstones replacing sleek steel on the other side of Storrow Drive. Daniel slowed, then stopped in front of an apartment building three stories high and taking up two city lots. Someone had ripped out the building's guts and installed floor-to-ceiling windows, affording the occupants a sculpted view of downtown. He settled in a shelter of trees and stared up at the building's top floor. The fish tank was long and deep, an illuminated collection of blues and whites and pinks floating free in the night. Daniel slitted his eyes until he could just see his fish, slippery streaks of copper and silver cutting paths in their invisible prison. He sank into the pattern of color and swirl, sitting still against the tree, hearing her approach long before she arrived, footsteps caught between the thin scream of cars and the ceaseless murmur of the river. Daniel turned as she reached to touch his shoulder. Grace pulled her hand back, eyes painted in patches of light from the moving night.

"You scared me," she said.

"I told you I'd be here."

"Yes, but how did you know . . . Never mind."

"You wanna sit?"

She took a seat beside him on the bare ground. He could feel her warmth even though it was November and they were both bundled against the cold pushing in from the harbor.

"How are your fish?" She'd been here before. No one else had. Not even Harry.

"I think they're hungry."

"They sure are pretty. Like a painting."

They sat together, watching the fish do their fish thing.

"I'm sorry about this morning," Daniel said.

"I told you it was fine."

He snuck a look across. "Did you tell your parents?"

He'd never been to the walk-up in Chinatown where Grace lived. She'd explained once that her father didn't like "round eyes" and made a pair of circles with her fingers that she held up to her face. Daniel had laughed at the joke and they'd ignored the rest. It was Boston, after all, and that's just how the world was.

"They don't need to know," she said.

"Why not?"

"Nothing happened, Daniel."

"Okay."

"Did you tell your brother?"

"I haven't talked to him yet."

"Do you think other people saw? People from school, I mean?"

"I don't know. Ben won't say anything."

"No, Ben won't say anything."

"Eddie Spaulding won't either. He's actually a pretty good guy."

"If you say so. Was it on the news?"

"I doubt it."

"Good."

He reached over and covered her gloved hand with his. Their shoulders touched. "Hey."

She angled her face toward him and he could see peach fuzz lying against the smooth of her cheek. Her mind was running at a low hum, a perfect sphere spinning in a perfect circle just at the end of his reach. All he had to do was flick a finger and that perfect rotation would stutter, wobble for a moment, then resettle, except not the same now. He remembered what Simon had said about being careful. He was probably right, but what harm could it do, the two of them alone, here by the river?

"You should have worn a hat," he said.

She pushed at a lank piece of hair that hung over one eye, then shoved her hands back in her pockets, moving a fraction so their shoulders were no longer touching. "I'm all right."

He pulled off his Patriots stocking hat and put it on her head. She resisted at first, then let him adjust it until he could see Pat Patriot's face. They watched Daniel's fish some more. A gray squirrel with bright black eyes joined them for a while and left. Daniel knew she'd have to go soon as well.

"Are you hurt?" She peeled off a glove and reached out to touch a bruise and some scraping under his eye.

"I'm good. And don't call me scrappy."

"I won't." She took a closer look, probing gently with her forefinger.

"It's just a scratch," Daniel said, wincing a bit and wondering if she'd seen the gun, wondering if he should tell her about his hallucination during the brawl, wondering about dreams hung in flesh and a parade of pills bouncing under the wheels of a bus and on down the street.

"There's something I need to tell you," he said.

"You want your hat back?"

"Funny."

"It's not about today, is it?"

"No."

"Go ahead, then."

So he told her about Simon and his theories on entanglement. And how Daniel had used it on her in the record store. She put her hand over her mouth and laughed and he thought she'd never stop.

"You're saying you 'pushed' me? Is that the term you use?"

"Entangled, pushed. Yes."

"You pushed me in Music City?"

"Yes."

"You touched my mind and willed me to kiss you?"

"Yes, yes."

"So you're a mind reader?"

"No, it's not that."

"Mind control?"

Daniel shook his head. "It's more like we were two and then we were one. And, in that moment, things changed. Not necessarily cuz I planned it or anything. Just cuz that's how it was."

"I don't think so."

"Trust me."

"Daniel, I've been thinking about kissing you for a month and a half."

He popped his head back. "Seriously?"

"Sort of."

"That's just it. Everyone 'sort of' thinks about things, but you acted on it. Right in the moment."

"And that was because of you?"

"Could be."

"Okay, let's say I believe you, which I don't for even a second. Is this an apology?"

"More like a confession. I mean, it was just a kiss."

"Hmmm."

"What?" He edged closer, studying the curve of her face while an unconscious part of him thrilled at her nearness.

"Maybe there was something."

"Really? In the record store?"

"Maybe. I mean, I *had* thought about kissing you, just to see what it was like. I think we're better as friends, though. Don't you?"

Pain. Not as piercing as he'd imagined, but still. Daniel shoved it to one side for now. "Tell me what you felt."

"Well, it was like a click." Grace snapped her fingers.

"A click?"

"Something clicked and I just decided to plant one."

"That was it?"

"Yes, a click in my head and a warm pulse in my stomach, like I was going to do something fun and great and I shouldn't think about it because it felt so right and it might not always feel that way."

"All that in the click, huh?"

"And the warm feeling. Don't forget the warm feeling, Daniel. It was actually wonderful."

He sat back. "Wow."

"Wow is right. Fifty years from now, if I'm still alive, I'm pretty sure I'll remember it all, the record store and the kiss. A little touch of forever that blossomed right here." She pressed the spot over his heart. "So if you 'pushed,' whatever that means in your quantum physics world, then thank you." Grace leaned in as easy as that and kissed him again, dry and precious and fleeting on the lips. "Besides, maybe it was me who was pushing, maybe I'm pushing you right now. So there."

She stuck out her tongue and they laughed at the crazy talk that maybe neither thought was crazy at all. And then she took his hand and wrapped it in hers while the fish flew through the night in streaks of color and the cold river ran on behind them in a ceaseless current of conscience and memory.

"Tell me about your professor," she finally said.

Daniel felt the shift, something in his gut stirring and stretching, blinking itself awake. "What about him?"

"You don't think it's strange he talks to you about all this stuff?"

"It's part of his work as a physicist."

"And what are you? One of his lab rats?"

Daniel thought about his dreams, one living within the other. And Simon watching. "He's all right, Grace."

"He's changing you."

She was as wrong as she was right. There was a narrowing in Daniel's soul. At first he'd thought it was just part of growing up. But maybe it was something more. Maybe Simon was his watchman, lifting a spear in warning at an approaching storm. Or maybe the warning was meant for someone else. He touched the back of her hand.

"How are you getting home?"

"Green Line to Boylston. Then I walk."

"I should go with you."

"It's not even ten."

"You sure?"

"I'm fine, Daniel. I mean, what happened today was awful, but they didn't get anywhere and I'm tough and it's over. Okay?"

"Okay."

"What are you gonna do?"

"I don't know. Finish my run, I guess."

"Call me tomorrow. And don't run all night, crazy."

He watched her walk up the bare path to a footbridge that crossed over Storrow. She was halfway across when a squat, dark figure appeared behind her and quickly closed the gap. Daniel crept to his feet and began to run. He was about to yell when the dark figure paused, then retraced his steps across the footbridge and came down on Daniel's side, walking quickly in the opposite direction while Daniel stood in the shadows. When he looked up at the bridge again, Grace was gone.

Daniel thought about following, catching up with her, and riding the T back to Chinatown. But she'd hate that and he didn't want to ruin what had already happened. So he struck off in the opposite direction, jogging lightly along the path, keeping the river on his left and downtown just out of reach. He should have called Harry and told him about the fight at school. He would have wanted to come over and talk about it. Maybe they'd have gone on a run together, Harry beside him right now, matching him stride for stride.

Daniel picked up his pace as the wind turned, hard and black in his face. He thought some more about Harry, about the man following Grace and the brawl again. He thought about Grace behind the Dumpster, her lonely red sneaker sticking out and the feeling as Daniel sprouted feathers, grew claws, and took wing, all of it realer than real if only in his head. A foul odor walked off the turning river and he could taste that thing again, slick in his throat, alive and crawling blind in his belly. He knew what his doctor would say. PTSD, she'd call it. Post-traumatic stress disorder. Daniel preferred a simpler name. Terror. Free-floating and looking for a home.

He willed his heart to slow as he pounded along the path, shooting over another of the small footbridges spanning Storrow and dropping into a tangle of narrow streets that made up the Back Bay. A car nearly clipped him at a corner, the driver laying on the horn and rolling down his window to let loose a string of curses. Daniel kept going. Up ahead the Boston Common lay fallow, like a black, unplowed sea.

17

THE NAKED i was in full swing. In the front room, a dancer named Inga hung off a pole, Red Sox pasties on her nipples and zipper scars running underneath both breasts. No matter. They lined up at the low bar that wrapped around the stage and filled up the small tables, heavy eyes drinking in the show while they sipped their ten-dollar drinks and smoked their cigarettes and never said a word to each other, most barely aware of anything other than the scent of the woman above them and the swing of her hips. At one end of the bar, a bald man in a checked suit waved a bill between two fingers, hoping to catch Inga's attention. Beside him, his pal breathed into a paper bag between sips of his 7 and 7. Women drifted through the back of the lounge, working lurkers at the door—talking, laughing, flirting, touching, pushing them to buy a drink, then coaxing their fish into an alley outside where maybe there was a blowjob waiting, or maybe a pimp with a knife. Over the intercom the manager announced in his best Fenway Park voice that Desiree would be starting her show in the Pussy Galore in ten minutes. The Pussy Galore was the Naked i's back room. Not much bigger than a bathroom, it sometimes held fifty patrons, pressed up against one another and gazing at women even more past their sell-by dates than Inga. The guy with the paper bag lurched to his feet and headed toward the back bar. One of the lurkers grabbed his spot and ordered a drink.

Harry was sitting at a table near the door. The promise about staying in the car had lasted twenty minutes. Harry was surprised it took that long. A girl who knew him from his volunteer work brought him a club soda on the house. Zeus sat to one side, drinking a Bud that had cost him nine bucks. Neil Prescott had his back to Harry, eyes glued to the stage. He'd opted for a rum and Coke, a bargain at twelve-fifty. They'd started their night at the Harvard Club. Eaten dinner there, cardboard chicken and rubber rice, and drank three pitchers of beer. Zeus had done most of the drinking. Prescott seemed content to sip at the watered-down draft while Harry ordered a ginger ale. A couple of alums had stopped by to talk football. They'd gone on for a while and Harry thought the night might begin and end right there. But Zeus had his eye on the clock and told the alums they had people they needed to meet. That was partly true. There was a vague plan to meet other members of the team somewhere in the Zone. Exactly where and when remained a mystery, but the Zone wasn't that big and Zeus seemed certain everyone would somehow find one another.

It was just ten when they walked out of the club. A couple of women followed, asking where they were going, complaining that Zeus had promised to buy them a drink. Harry pulled his pals away and herded them down the block. *Stay together.* The photographer Toney's words rolled around in his head looking for something to bump up against. Zeus wasn't feeling any pain and wanted to take a stroll. They skirted past the Pilgrim

Theater and then the Brompton Arms, a rent-by-the-hour hotel perched precariously at the corner of Washington and LaGrange streets. Women came out of the alleys, swarming like sucker fish to a herd of fat, slow sperm whales. Harry knew a lot of the faces, but none of them seemed to care. He was a potential john now and this was business. One of the girls slipped her arm around Prescott and pulled him down LaGrange. Another ran her hand up the inside of Zeus's leg and asked how big he was. Harry wasn't having it. The girls swore and one tried to kick him with the spike of her heel as he dragged his friends back toward Washington and the safety of the car. Prescott was driving and jumped in front. There was a cooler of beer beside him so Harry and Zeus got in the back.

"What the fuck, Harry?"

"Shut up."

"What did we come down here for? Neil, gimme a beer."

Prescott pulled a can of Schlitz out of the ice and handed it back. Zeus popped it and took a hit, all the while continuing to berate Harry for taking them off LaGrange. Harry ignored the noise. Zeus had been right this morning when he'd described the Zone. They were little more than tourists down here, staring out the window at the wildlife prowling past. Harry's job was to make sure no one got bit. Or dropped their pants in an alley no matter how much they had to drink.

"Where are the other guys?" Prescott said.

"No idea." Zeus took another hit on his beer, tapped Harry on the knee, and winked. "Hey, Neil. Check her out."

"Yo." Prescott knocked on the windshield at a black woman in a tight leather dress. She blew him a kiss. Prescott went off on how hot she was and what he'd do to her if he ever got a chance.

Harry recognized the woman from his volunteer work and didn't have the heart to tell Prescott his "she" was a "he."

"Let's hang here for a bit," Zeus said. "If the rest of those guys are around, they'll come by."

Prescott thought that was a good idea and grabbed another beer out of the cooler. A couple more women appeared out of the smoke and the cold and the night. Zeus rolled down the back window halfway so one of them could lean in. Harry could smell her perfume but couldn't get a good look at her face. Zeus mumbled something. Prescott caught Harry's eye in the rearview mirror and mugged silently. There was another woman now, walking across the street with her eye on the car. Prescott cracked his window as she approached. Beside Harry, Zeus had pushed his window all the way down. Harry could see long fingers, nails painted orange, and a thin wrist flashing gold bracelets. Up front, the woman with an eye for Prescott had disappeared. Zeus shifted his weight, blocking Harry's view entirely as he talked in a low voice to the woman. Harry caught Prescott's eyes again in the rearview mirror and was about to suggest they go when there was a sudden movement beside him. He turned just in time to see the woman's silhouette as she disappeared down the block. Zeus was swearing and struggling with the handle on the door.

"She took my wallet. Fucking bitch took my wallet."

Harry grabbed at his friend. "Wait."

The sleeve of Zeus's coat ripped through Harry's fingers and the big tackle was gone, running hard after the woman. Prescott fumbled for his door handle. Harry gripped his shoulder.

"Stay with the car. You understand me?"

Prescott nodded, eyes wide and weak. Harry climbed out. Someone was watching from a doorway and pointed. The guy was drunk and cheered Harry like he was running the marathon. Half a block ahead, he could see Zeus turn down LaGrange. Harry took the same corner just as his friend ducked into an alley. Harry hesitated, then started back toward the car. He'd get Prescott and they'd go together. Easier that way. Safer. Someone called out. He turned and saw a woman standing in the middle of LaGrange. She was long and willowy and wrapped in a short leather coat. She started to raise her hand when the door to a club called Good Time Charlie's kicked open and a thick man stumbled out. He grabbed blindly at the woman, who stepped back, white light from inside the club catching her profile before the door slammed shut again. The woman slipped from the man's grip and ran into the same alley Zeus had gone down. Harry followed.

As he hit the mouth of the alley, he heard the dying chatter of heels on asphalt, then nothing. Harry called out for Zeus but got no answer. Blank windows stretched up both sides of the passage, the occasional lamp casting light here and there. A green door loomed on his left. Harry tried it. Locked. He could make out a Dumpster about halfway down one side and a string of garbage cans down the other. Harry crept forward, hissing for Zeus. He was about to start running again when he caught a flicker of movement. The man was crouched in a tight space between the Dumpster and the wall. He came at Harry from behind, swinging a blade that flashed in a yellow seam of light. Harry heard himself yell and caught the man's elbow as the blade swung. It sliced in just below Harry's rib cage, nicking the corner of his intestines and starting a flow of blood into his abdominal cavity. Harry felt the warm leak as his legs turned to slush and the back of his head hit the wall. Harry's pulse was hammering, mind racing, wondering how, why, what. His attacker tripped and stumbled forward, looming over Harry, who caught a glimpse of gritted teeth and the shine of skin. A silver tooth dangled from the man's neck. Then there was the knife again, at the top of its arc, poised to swing.

—

Daniel plunged through the layered darkness of the Boston Common. A necklace of streets surrounded it, embroidering the edges in soft yellow while the golden dome of the State House hung steep and chaste overhead like some secular confessor god. Daniel accelerated up a hill, not knowing where he was headed but certain he was desperately behind. He ducked between a set of park benches and paused on the edge of a wide field.

Daniel could feel his heart beat in his blood, the flex and ripple in his legs even as his arms began to lengthen, fingers cracking and thickening into scaled pads of flesh, nails extending and hardening into yellow claws. Fur grew in ridges along his back, tawny orange with stripes of ebony running up his shoulders and around eyes that were sulfurous yellow with wet orbs of black in the very center. Daniel dropped to all fours and sprang forward, tearing up the earth as he powered across the field. He could smell the sourness of his breath and felt his teeth curve in his jaw, white whiskers bristling like wire in the November cold. He slowed, padding silently past Park Street Station—fully grown now, a Bengal tiger staring out at the passing cars and the fuzzy lights and the tender city.

Daniel began to move again, gliding past a kiddie pool and over another rise, night vision aglow, picking up the heat of a man bundled on a bench. There was the smell of liquor and cigarette smoke and stale popcorn. Daniel sped on, feeling the brush of spiked tops across his belly as he jumped an iron fence. He was in a graveyard, the ancient tombstones cut hard by moonlight, set down in ragged rows like a rotting set of teeth. Daniel wove between them, tail flicking. Two strides and he was back over the fence, racing the curve of a walking path, Boylston Street cresting just ahead. He paused for a moment, rubbing his flank against a tree, enjoying the scratch of the bark on his hide and the smell of the earth in his nose. Then he stepped out of the Boston Common and back onto the street, back into his own body.

Daniel had no memory of his run through the park, at least not on two feet, yet here he was. He looked down at his running shoes, Tigers of course, soaking wet and caked in mud. He took off his hat and shook the light sweat out of his hair. An image of Grace filled his head, followed by a black face with a silver tooth on a chain, swinging free off his neck as he reached for his gun. Harry rose up, Harry somewhere in the city, clutching at minutes, seconds, moments as they slipped through his fingers.

Daniel sprinted the rest of the way up Boylston to the intersection of Tremont. Half a block away, a squad car lit up its flashers and accelerated, the cry of its siren spiking his blood and freezing all thought. The squad fishtailed around a van stopped at the light and disappeared down Tremont. Daniel followed, diving into the fragrant, yellow heart of Chinatown, the Combat Zone waiting just beyond.

—

Harry raised his arm as the blade fell, tearing at the sleeve of his jacket before scraping off the brick behind him. He was on one knee and came up hard, hammering a right under his attacker's ribs, driving him back against the iron spine of the Dumpster. The black kid grunted and slumped halfway to the ground, his knife clattering onto the hardtop. Harry reached, but the kid was closer. He had the knife in his left hand, swiping low this time, catching nothing but air. The kid's eyes were moving and Harry could see the clock ticking in his head.

"You got thirty seconds," Harry said. "After that the cops are here and you're done."

The kid responded with another swipe of the knife, wider now, wilder. A drunk stumbled against a garbage can somewhere, the noise rattling through the maze of concrete and brick.

"I'll tell them I didn't get a look," Harry said. "But you got to go. Right fucking now."

The kid's eyes slalomed from side to side, weighing, measuring, deciding. He slipped the knife into his pocket and disappeared down the alley. Just like that, Harry was alone. He slumped back against the Dumpster, legs splayed, hand over his stomach, feeling his abdominal muscles twitch and the thin flow of blood between his fingers. Harry tipped his chin up and stared at the wall of faceless windows scaling up both sides of the alley. Jimmy Stewart and *Rear Window*. That's what it reminded him of. If Grace Kelly came walking down the alley, it might even be worth it. He chuckled and felt his eyes flutter. The cold was in his bones now as the adrenaline drained away. Shock wasn't far behind. He lifted his shirt and checked the wound, not more than an inch or so, angry and red. He could feel the blood leaking inside, but it was slowing, clotting, stopping. Harry would live. He was certain of that. And he'd keep his promise to the black kid. A soft scuff of shoes. Someone approaching. Didn't sound like Grace

Kelly, but Harry wasn't complaining. Whoever it was stopped on the far side of the Dumpster.

"Over here." Harry's voice was that of an old man, not much more than a croak. Then the person stood over him, backlit by the glow from a streetlamp.

"I'm hurt," Harry said, and held out his hand. His savior crouched, withdrawing a long sinew of silver from under a coat. This time there was no doubt, the steel driving deep into Harry's belly, pinning him to the wall behind him. Once, twice, three times, the steel flashed. Then his attacker was gone and Harry lay flat on the pavement, blood bubbling out of the fresh holes with every pump of his heart. He turned his head, eyes clinging to each precious piece of life around him. He noticed the rough rub of the alley next to his cheek, the grit of dirt, and the crooked rubber wheel of the Dumpster six inches from his nose. J.J. ALBUS & SONS was stamped on the wheel's metal caster and Harry wondered what J.J. looked like, what manner of man he might be. One with glasses and a fine, even temperament, Harry guessed. His eyes reached for the far wall. He studied the strata of brick, taking apart each grain of sand that made up the mortar mix, puzzling over its composition and the men who worked with it one summer's day—months, years, decades ago. He saw a hot dog wrapper just beyond his reach and would have given what little was left of his life if there had been writing on it. A rat scuttled out from between two garbage cans and sat by his ear, whiskers twitching, eyes calculating. Harry moved two of his fingers in greeting. The rat lifted a paw, scratched its face, and scuttled off. Better things to do, no doubt.

Harry took a final look around, inhaling every particle of the alley, feeling the energy of "being" as it sparked and flickered and hummed all around him. He could see clearly now the infra-structure that he'd always known without ever knowing, the cosmic glue, the light, the pure, effortless grace that bound and transformed and breathed life into inanimate lumps of clay we called "things"—people, buildings, cars, flowers, dogs, cats, rats and the garbage they picked through. He saw it all, entangled in a shifting, eternal, breathtaking pulse of light and dark, good and evil, birth and decay and birth again. And he knew, just as sure as he knew he was on the point of his own death, that Daniel was close by, that Daniel was coming, that they'd never really be apart again. Harry called out his brother's name as he closed his eyes and breathed his last, falling forward into the web of seam-less light, into the warmth, enveloping, embracing, taking him home. A place he'd never been before. A place from which he'd never leave.

18

FACES FLOATED past, painted eyes and curled lips, gums, teeth, and folds of flesh hanging loose from cheeks and under chins, all of it caught in harsh stripes of light. Daniel turned away, stumbling down one alley, then a second. In the close, sticky confines of the Combat Zone, he was forced to slow down. A door kicked open and a tide of human refuse flushed out, men, women, high heels and perfume, hard leather shoes and liquor, pushing him one way, pulling another. Someone asked if the kid was looking for a blowjob. Laughter. "Maybe a handy Andy. Denise, whaddaya say?" More laughter. Daniel was scraped up against the side of a building and left stranded as the tide drained off.

Terror blinked in his belly, opening its filmy eyes again, sinking its fangs into his liver. Daniel fell to his knees and got sick, the vomit splashing up in his face before being carried by a trickle of water to a small grated drain and the sewer that ran rank beneath the city. He stretched out flat on his stomach, cheek against a rough cobble, and wondered what he was doing here, if the docs were right after all, if he was losing his mind, if he'd opened a door to something that would swallow him whole. He thought about Harry as the thing inside bit again, this time taking a chunk of his spine. Daniel shivered and groaned and struggled to his knees.

Breadcrumbs of noise. Gruff voices giving directions, a high-pitched protest, someone cursing, the whine of a walkie-talkie. A door opened to Daniel's right, and a wrinkled Asian face ghosted into view. Daniel tried to ask a question, but the door slammed shut. The noise was getting louder, the voices closer. A curtain moved in a window above him. A man leaned out, forearms on the sill, and gawked at something in the adjacent alley. He ducked from the window and returned with a camera, snapping away at whatever he'd spied below. Daniel got to his feet and took a final corner so he was almost directly beneath the window. A black man was kneeling beside a Dumpster. He turned and fixed Daniel with a hollow stare.

"Who the fuck are you?" The black man was dressed in a dark overcoat and had a gold badge hanging shiny around his neck. "How the fuck did this kid get in here?"

There were more sounds, heavy footsteps pounding toward them. The man climbed to his feet and moved to greet the newcomers. As he did, Daniel got a glimpse of what he'd been bent over. And then Daniel screamed, high and dry like an animal caught in a trap, willing to trade a limb for his life. Or his brother's. The black man with the badge knew that scream, had heard it before, and dove. Too late. Daniel had Harry in his arms, still screaming, mingling tears with his brother's blood, thick and dark and warm as it frothed and flowed from the hidden wounds. Three cops had him now, too many hands tearing at him, dragging him off Harry and trapping him in a corner. The black man shoved his face in Daniel's and asked a bunch of questions, but Daniel didn't hear any of them. All he did was scream and scrape at the flesh on his arms and the flesh on his face. He screamed while they cuffed him, screamed while they dragged him down the alley, screamed while they muscled him through the crowd of pimps and hookers and johns and hustlers who'd massed behind the police tape to see what sort of entertainment the night held, screamed while they threw him in the back of the cruiser still covered in blood, screamed while they drove him away. Then it was quiet and the people on LaGrange Street talked among themselves, agreeing this was a fine show and when were they going to bring out the body.

—

In the alley a cold, black rain began to fall in earnest. Barkley and Tommy were huddled under an umbrella while a couple of forensics guys worked on the corpse. Barkley pulled Harry's Harvard ID out of his wallet and showed it to Tommy. They exchanged a look and told the forensics guys to go get coffee. Then Barkley crouched on his haunches and studied Harry's face, comparing it with the ID. Behind him Tommy was on the radio, calling for more backup and cursing their luck.

PART II

19

BARKLEY NEEDED coffee. They had a pot, filters, and silver bags of the stuff stashed in a corner of the squad room, but he had neither the patience nor the palate for fresh-brewed. With a soft grunt he got up and walked down the hall to a vending machine not far from the front desk. He dropped in a quarter and selected COFFEE-BLACK. There was a whirring sound, then the good stuff began to hiss into a cardboard cup with a smiley face on it. He took the coffee back to his desk and settled before the typewriter. It was already loaded with a blank police report and four layers of colored carbons. Barkley had just typed 3:15 A.M. in the box where it said TIME when Tommy hit the door.

"Bark . . ."

"Typing, Tommy."

"It's the kid."

"You wanna do the typing, Tommy?"

"He's a problem. And no, I don't wanna do the typing."

Barkley looked up. "You get him clean?"

"He won't clean. Won't leave the fucking room."

"Where you got him?"

"Number one."

Tommy stepped aside as Barkley swept past and down the hall to holding room number one. Barkley stopped at the door and turned. "We heard anything from the press?"

Tommy shook his head. "How long you think before they turn up?"

"Hard to say. Prick from the *Herald* already had Fitzsimmons's name at the scene. He'll get here first. After that, it's the bigger prick from the *Globe*. And then the cameras."

"We gonna have to talk to 'em?" Tough guy that he was, Tommy hated the press. Pretty much shrank back into the skin of a ten-year-old anytime he got near a hot mike.

"Sure as shit they're gonna want my black face out there."

"Sorry, B."

"Ain't your fault. Now, listen, this kid here, he's gotta be gone before any of that starts."

"So we either arrest him or turn him loose."

"Arrest him? For what? You got an ID yet?"

"Nothing in his pockets. Actually, he's got no pockets. Looks like he was running."

"Did he give a name?"

"All the kid did was scream. Thank Christ he's stopped that."

Barkley pushed open the door. The kid was curled up in a corner, knees tucked under his chin, skinny arms wrapped around his shins. He wasn't wearing a shirt and his chest was smeared with Ivy League blood.

"You wanna take a seat?" Barkley turned one of the two chairs in the room toward the kid and sat in the other. Tommy leaned against the doorframe and folded his arms across his chest. The kid looked at both men, got up, and took the seat.

"You want something to eat?" Barkley said. "Something to drink? How about we take you into the bathroom and let you clean up?"

The kid shook his head.

Barkley had forgotten his coffee so he folded his hands on the tiny table wedged between them. The kid was gripping the shit out of both sides of his chair and rocking back and forth. His eyes were glued to the floor.

"What's your name, son?"

"Daniel."

Bingo. That wasn't so fucking hard.

"Daniel what?"

"Fitzsimmons."

The kid's last name crushed the room to the size of a closet. Barkley felt the familiar weight in his chest. Tommy shifted in his boots.

"My name's Barkley Jones. I'm a detective with the Boston PD." Barkley threw a thumb over his shoulder. "The other guy who's been helping you is my partner, Tommy Dillon. We're gonna need to ask you a few questions."

"Go ahead."

"Are you related to Harry Fitzsimmons?"

"He's my brother."

"I'm sorry, Daniel, but your brother's dead."

The kid rocked a little faster. "I already knew that."

"You sure you don't want some water or something? Go get him some water, Tommy." Barkley heard his partner leave and pulled the chair an inch closer. "Can we talk for a second, Daniel? Just me and you."

"Sure."

"Thank you." Barkley's voice was a clean river running over smooth stone. Most of the people he questioned called it hypnotic, soothing, comforting even. Whatever it was, it worked. People liked to talk to Barkley, unload their secrets, bare their souls.

"I'm sorry about Harry."

Nothing. That was all right. Barkley knew there was plenty bubbling underneath. So he'd talk. And he'd wait. Sorta like fishing.

"My partner tells me you were running."

"I was."

"You run a lot?"

The kid shrugged.

"How did you wind up in the alley, Daniel? Did you plan to meet Harry there?"

Why the fuck would you meet your brother in the middle of the night, in an alley in the Combat Zone, Daniel? Tell me that.

"Harry had no idea I was gonna be down in the Zone."

"But you knew he was gonna be there?"

Daniel shook his head. Barkley sat back. Cocksucker. Tommy came back in and set a Styrofoam cup of water on the table. Barkley waited until he returned to his spot by the door.

"Now, Daniel . . ."

"Who was he with?"

"We don't know . . ."

"Who was he with?" The kid rocked a little faster in the chair.

"A couple of his pals from the football team, best we can tell."

The kid stopped rocking and leaned in, eyes locked like fucking lasers on Barkley until a spot behind the detective's temple grew warm and started to throb. Barkley broke off, severing the connection with a subtle shift of his shoulders.

"Let's get back to the alley, Daniel. Why were you down there?"

"I told you. I went for a run."

"In the middle of the night?"

"I run at night all the time. I like it."

"You on a team?" Tommy's voice carried in a higher pitch that popped and pinged off the concrete walls.

"I run track for my high school. Sometimes, anyway."

"Where do you go to school?" Barkley said.

"Boston Latin."

Good, Barkley thought. *Good.* "You live with your parents?"

"They're dead. I live with Harry."

"How about relatives? Family in the area?"

"No one."

"Okay. We can get someone to take you home when we're through here."

"I'd like to go now."

"Tell you what. Help me with the alley and we're done."

"Maybe you should be thinking about finding the guy who killed my brother."

"Hey . . ." Tommy came off the wall. Barkley held out a hand.

"I hear you, son. Believe me, I fucking hear you. And if it was up to us, we'd drag the prick in here, give you a gun, and let you empty it in his skull. But it ain't up to us. And that ain't never gonna happen. And you're smart enough to know that, so I'm gonna ask again. How and why were you in the alley?"

"I told you. I was running along the river when I got a feeling Harry was in trouble. And I had to help him."

"A feeling?"

"Very strong."

"And you knew exactly where to go?"

"You wouldn't understand, but, yes, I did. I knew exactly where to go. At least until I got into the alleys. I lost it a little there and then I heard all the noise and I knew I was gonna turn a corner and find Harry, just like I found him." Daniel's eyes turned up again, yellow light glancing off the patterned black of his pupils. The pain that lived there sprang from love. Barkley knew that pain. It was the kind that fed on people's souls and had no use for tomorrow.

"You should get some sleep, son. And we've got a lot of paperwork to get through." Barkley scraped his chair against the floor as he stood. "Detective Dillon can arrange a lift home."

The kid didn't move.

"Daniel?"

"I'm guessing you don't want me talking to any reporters."

"Now that you mention it . . ."

"Not a problem. But you gotta do something for me."

Barkley sat back down. "And what would that be?"

—

The partners had identical desks, gunmetal gray, pushed together in a corner so they were sectioned off from the rest of the squad room. Barkley was tilted back in a swivel chair with his feet up. Tommy was drinking coffee from a thermos and eating a sandwich that had come wrapped in wax paper.

"Where did you get that?" Barkley said.

"Katie made it. Meatloaf with ketchup. You want a bite?"

Barkley held up a hand.

"Hungry as a motherfucker." Tommy chewed as he talked. "Ate around seven. Still starving."

"Where'd you go?"

"Fast food. Crap."

Barkley had been at his desk, filling out pain-in-the-ass paperwork when the call came in on the Fitzsimmons kid. Tommy had been doing his thing, beating the bushes on the guy they'd pulled out of the harbor.

"You get anything on the John Doe?" Barkley said.

"You mean Juan Doe. Didn't get shit. Something else came up, though."

Tommy's voice rippled across the empty squad room, stirring the chemicals in Barkley's brain. He looked up from the report he'd been reading. "We need to talk about it?"

"Got a dead kid from Harvard sitting in our laps. What do you think?"

"You sure?"

"It'll keep."

Barkley nodded and made a mental note to circle back to whatever it was that was bugging his partner. He flipped the report shut and eased his feet off the desk. "Okay, let's talk about our football player. What are we thinking?"

"Left word for people down the Zone. Should hear something soon."

"Yeah?"

"Why not? Probably some fucking street punk, sees Fitzsimmons wandering around in the alley. Figures he'll roll him."

"But Fitzsimmons fights back?"

"Exactly." Tommy took another bite of his sandwich and put it back on the wax paper he'd spread out on a corner of his desk. "You got a napkin?"

Barkley found a stack in a drawer with some Chinese take-out menus and tossed them over. Tommy wiped a lick of ketchup off his mouth. Barkley waited. Tommy wasn't as quick at putting things together, but when he did, it usually held up.

"So they fight?" Barkley said.

"Fitzsimmons is a football player. Young, tough. He's not gonna roll over even if he is an Ivy Leaguer. Maybe especially cuz he's an Ivy Leaguer. So, yeah, they fight. Fitzsimmons figures it's a fistfight. Takes a couple of swings, but our boy says 'Fuck that' and pulls out the knife."

"He's playing for keeps."

Tommy nodded. "Fitzsimmons probably never saw it. Blade in the gut, down he goes, and the guy books. My point is, whoever he is, he's a fucking punk, which means people are gonna be willing to give him up."

"And what if our guy's black?"

"What if he is?"

"Shitstorm, Tommy."

"We've handled worse. Either way, I'll get us a name by the end of the day. Tomorrow, at the latest. Just promise me one thing."

"No cameras in your face?"

"Fucking hey."

"Tell me about the Harvard guys."

"We already went over that."

"Tell me again."

Tommy sighed and pulled out a black leather notebook. They had stacks of the things, Tommy usually scribbling while Barkley conducted his interviews.

"Neil Prescott and Jesus Sanchez. Nickname Zeus. Both football players. Both say they were at the Naked i with Fitzsimmons. Came out of the club a little juiced, walked around a bit, then back to the car on Washington. Sanchez and Fitzsimmons are in the backseat."

"Prescott's up front with the cooler."

"Right. A girl comes by and starts chatting 'em up. At some point she reaches in and grabs Sanchez's wallet. Runs down La-Grange and Sanchez follows. According to him, it all happened real quick."

"Fitzsimmons is still in the back?"

"He tells Prescott to stay with the car, then goes after Sanchez. Prescott says it might have been ten, twenty seconds between Sanchez leaving and Fitzsimmons following."

"Okay," Barkley said. "Then what?"

"Sanchez says he ran after the girl. Thought he saw her take off down an alley and followed. Never knew Fitzsimmons was following him. Says he went down two or three more intersecting alleys . . . there's a shitload of them back there . . . then found his way back down Washington to the car. Best we can figure, by then Fitzsimmons was already dead."

"How about the yelling?"

"Fuck, B, you did the interviews. You know all this shit."

"Just tell me."

Tommy flipped through the notebook some more, then tossed it on the desk and produced a second. "I haven't typed any of this up yet."

"That's okay."

"All right, here it is. Prescott says Fitzsimmons yelled at Sanchez when he got out of the car."

"When who got out?"

"Sanchez. Fitzsimmons yelled at him to stop. Then Fitzsimmons yelled again as he ran down the street."

"Prescott doesn't know what he said?"

"That's right. Says it might have been Sanchez's name. He's not sure. Sanchez says he never heard a thing."

"How many beers did they have?"

"Sanchez says he had a few. Both of them say Fitzsimmons didn't drink."

"So he wasn't necessarily an easy mark in the alley?"

"The punk who did him wouldn't know that. Sees the kid wandering around. What else is he gonna think? My theory's still good, B."

"What do we got on the girl who pinched the wallet?"

"Caucasian. Sanchez says she had blond hair and might have been wearing heels. Not much, but we got people working it. They'll turn her up."

"Good." Barkley put his fingertips together and talked over the top of them. "What did you think of the little brother?"

"Felt sorry for the poor bastard."

They'd finished with Daniel Fitzsimmons just over an hour ago. His price for not speaking to reporters was a final visit to see his brother. Barkley wasn't a hundred percent on the request, but he didn't want the kid talking to the press either. So he made a couple of calls and told them to hold off on releasing the body to the morgue. Then they'd packed Daniel off to Boston City Hospital where he'd get to say his good-byes.

"Why was the kid in the alley?" Barkley said.

Tommy shrugged and flipped his notebook shut. He'd finished his sandwich and drained what was left of the thermos into a plastic cup. "Who knows? Maybe he just had a feeling like he said."

"You believe that?"

"You really don't get feelings? Intuition?"

"You're not gonna start on the fairy rings again?"

"Fuck you, Bark."

They shared a cop's smile, passed between partners who'd known each other too long and too well to have it any other way.

"Let me tell you a story," Tommy said.

"I was hoping."

"One night I'm off duty, drinking with some pals at the Tap."

"Southie's chapter of the KKK."

Tommy extended his middle finger and kept talking. "I have a few and decide I better not drive. So I leave my car parked in front of the bar and grab a ride home from one of my buddies. Katie makes me something to eat and I'm fucking comatose by ten. Right?"

"Right."

"So two thirty in the morning, I sit straight up in the bed like someone greased the fucking Pesky pole and shoved it right up my ass. Katie jumps up with me—it's like we're sharing the same brain or something, except we're most definitely fucking not—and thinks I think someone's in the house. I'm swearing a blue streak. 'Fuck, fuck, fuck.' She's asking what's the matter and I tell her our car's been stolen. Tell her I left it parked in front of the bar and the fuckers just busted out a window, popped the ignition, and are joyriding around like a bunch of cocksuckers who need to get their roof caved. 'Fuck, fuck, fuck,' I say, and put on my socks and go downstairs into the kitchen. Katie follows me down and asks how I know the car's gone if I left it at the bar. I tell her I just do, but not to worry. Car's a piece of shit, go back to bed, we'll deal with it in the morning. She thinks I'm fucking Looney Tunes and goes back upstairs. I sit up in the kitchen, phone on the table in front of me. I sit there and I drink my coffee and I stare at the thing, not wondering *if* it will ring, just waiting for it. Fifteen minutes later, boom. It's a uniform calling from Station Six. Wants to know if I own a '65 Bonneville. Says they found the thing torched and dumped in a lot off Emerson. Windows busted out, ignition popped. Not a surprise to me. Not a bit. Cuz I knew. When I woke up, I just knew it was gone. How did I know? No idea. But I knew, Bark. Abso-fucking-lutely, I knew."

"So you're telling me you believe the kid?"

"What did I say yesterday? Not everything has to have a reasonable explanation, B. Some things just are."

"You wanna put that in our report?"

"The kid didn't kill his big brother, run off, and then come back to scream and wail over the body. That make more sense to you?"

"No."

"All right, then."

Barkley leaned his forearms on his desk and rolled the still mostly blank police report up and down in the typewriter. As usual, Tommy had a point. At the end of the day life was a blind free fall and no one could tell you when or where or how you were gonna hit the pavement. Just that at some point, sure as fuck, you'd hit it.

"Listen, I'm not saying you're wrong . . ."

"You can't buy in, B. You'd like to, but you just can't."

"I like facts, Tommy. Keeps me warm at night."

"Well, the fact is this kid was in the alley. And there's no getting around that."

"How about him wanting to see the body?"

Tommy shrugged. "It's fine. Besides, they said they'd watch him."

Barkley grumbled to himself, then checked a watch that wasn't on his wrist. "What time you got?"

"Just past five. Why?"

"Nothing. While we're waiting for one of your sources to call, why don't you do me a favor and dig in to some files."

"What do you want?"

"Daniel Fitzsimmons. And Harry. Police reports, newspaper clips, school records, whatever you can find. Just for the hell of it."

A door slammed somewhere and loud voices drifted back from the front of the station house. A skinny uniform named Guilfoyle stuck his head in.

"Yeah?" Barkley didn't like anyone from the outside hanging around when they discussed the guts of a case. That included cops he didn't know who worked the front desk.

"You guys caught the thing tonight in the Zone?"

"What is it?" Tommy said.

"There's a guy out front. Says he's a photographer. Lives right over the alley where the thing happened."

Barkley felt himself sit up in his chair. "What's he want?"

"Wants to talk to you guys. Says he got pictures of the killer. I'm not a detective or nothing, but I thought that might be something you'd be interested in."

Guilfoyle had a wiseass grin on his ugly face, but Barkley didn't give a fuck. He could have kissed him.

"Where'd you put him, Guilfoyle?"

"Down the hall in Room Three. Locked the door just in case the fucker changes his mind."

—

"So you take naked pictures for a living?"

"We're gonna do that, huh?"

Tommy Dillon smiled hard and toothy behind a blue screen of smoke. He'd wanted to take the lead on questioning the photographer. Unusual, but Barkley didn't mind. Best he could tell, it was all headed to the same place.

"I got a studio, top floor of the Brompton."

"You mean Hooker Central."

The photographer's name was Nick Toney. He was middle-aged, long and angular in that starving-artist, hippie-freak, I-might-be-banging-your-teenage-daughter sort of way some guys just had, even if most of them turned out to be harmless.

"Look, I take pictures of the girls, but it's art. 'Decisive moment' type stuff, you know?"

"Why don't you show us what you got?" Barkley said.

"I'm gonna, but why's this guy giving me a hard time?"

"No idea. You two know each other?"

"Only like I know every other fucking skeeze-ball down there," Tommy said. "Giving fifteen-year-olds a skinful so they can take their picture, then get their dicks sucked."

"Hey . . ." Toney got up out of his chair. Guy didn't look like he was gonna start swinging, but he might just leave and Barkley couldn't have that.

"Whoa, whoa, whoa, Tommy. Sit down, Mr. Toney."

"I don't have to listen to this crap . . ."

"Give us a second, okay?"

Toney held up his hands but sat back down to his cigarette. Barkley and Tommy stepped into the hall.

"Guy's full of shit," Tommy said.

"You don't know that. What the fuck's eating you?"

"Nothing."

"We seen a million of these guys, Tommy."

"Yeah, but now I got the twins in school. I know that's bullshit . . ."

"It ain't bullshit."

"Every day, I kiss 'em good-bye and smile and watch 'em go off and think to myself it's a fucking sewer."

"The girls have lots of years, Tommy. And they got you and Katie. And they got me."

"I hear you. First fucking grade, right?"

"Wait till some poor bastard shows up for the prom."

Tommy laughed, the tension draining from his voice. "Come on, let's go in and I'll apologize."

Barkley shook his head. "Go home. Make your kids breakfast and grab some sleep. I'll take care of this."

"You sure?"

"Yeah."

"I'll pull some of them files before I go."

"Don't worry about it. I'm gonna crash on a cot in the back after I talk to this guy."

"What about the reporters?"

"I'll talk to 'em at some point. Why don't I swing by the house this afternoon? We can pick up the pieces then."

"Thanks, B."

"Tell Katie I said hey. And give those girls a kiss for me."

Barkley watched Tommy go down the hall and wondered again if it wasn't time to start looking for a new partner. Tommy was like a brother, but maybe that was the problem. He shook his head and walked back into the interrogation room. Toney took a final drag and crushed the remains of his cigarette into an ashtray.

"Your buddy head out?"

"He's been at it all night. Listen, I'm sorry . . ."

"Not a problem."

"Let's start over. You want some coffee? Something to eat?"

"I'm good."

"There's a bakery around the corner. Guy opens at five. Beautiful blueberry muffins. Still hot and everything."

"I'm good."

"All right." Barkley pulled out a chair and sat down again. "Tell me about your photography."

"What do you want to know?"

"Whatever you want to tell me."

Toney shrugged. "It's not like your pal said. No skin mags, nothing like that. I had an exhibit at the Museum of Fine Arts, for Chrissakes. I'll send you the pamphlet."

"Any girls from the street in the exhibit?"

"The girls *were* the exhibit. People love it. Living on the edge and all that stuff. That's why I have the studio down there. I live like they live. So they trust me. They open up."

"Yeah?"

"Lot of pain, Detective. Lot of pain."

"You got the photos, Mr. Toney?"

"Right here." Toney opened his jacket. He had a manila envelope tucked against the flat of his stomach. "Before I show them to you . . ."

"What is it?"

"I was listening to the radio on the way over here. Heard the name of the kid who got killed."

"Harry Fitzsimmons."

"Yeah. Football player from Harvard. That's all they gave out."

"What about him?"

"I knew him."

Barkley felt the skin under his left eye pucker. "How's that?"

"I knew him. Not well, but I actually saw the kid yesterday morning. Early. Him and his buddies were at a diner in Harvard Square."

"Small world."

"You think I didn't think that?"

"Relax, Mr. Toney. Stuff like this happens all the time."

"Yeah?"

"More than you imagine. You get any names?"

"Of what? His buddies?"

Barkley nodded.

"Neil Prescott was one kid. He's into cameras. I was helping him pick out some lenses. You know, make a buck or two."

Barkley wrote on a pad of paper—tight, coiled lines of cursive. "So you know Prescott?"

"Just through the cameras. How do you know him?"

"Have you spoken to Prescott?"

"When? Since this happened?" Toney shook his head.

"Okay, go ahead."

"The other kid he was with was named Sanchez. Zeus was

the first name, I think. Something like that. They told me they might be headed down the Zone. Few beers, some laughs. Fuck me, I shoulda stopped 'em."

"Not your fault, Mr. Toney."

"Still feels like shit, you know?"

Barkley stopped writing and flipped the pad over. "Let's see the photos."

Toney pushed across the envelope. Barkley took out the photos and laid them down in a row on the table.

"Tell me what I'm looking at."

"I snapped these from my window."

"Overlooking the alley?"

"I heard some yelling and running so I looked down and seen the two of them. Black kid and a white kid."

"Definitely black?"

Toney touched one of the pictures. "You tell me."

"Go ahead."

"These two are circling each other. Looks like a fistfight. I got cameras everywhere in the place, so I grab one."

"You said it was a studio. You live there or something?"

"I got a pullout bed I make up in the back. As you can imagine, a lot of my work down there is at night."

"Sure, sure. So you see these two. You yell down, tell 'em to stop?"

"You know how many fights I see in that alley every week?"

Barkley shrugged like *What's a guy to do*. At the end of the day that was why people went to the Zone. To sit in the shadows and watch. "Go ahead, Mr. Toney."

"So I see them down there and I just pop off the shots. Bang, bang, bang."

There were five photos in all. The first two showed a white man with his back to the camera faced off against a black man. The pair were shoved up next to a Dumpster almost directly beneath Toney. In the third and fourth shots, the white man was on one knee, the black man swinging his arm down, a knife clearly visible in his right hand. In the last photo the white man's shoulders were turned toward the camera, one arm obscuring his face, the rest of his body lost in the thick back and shoulders of his attacker.

"Did you know it was Fitzsimmons?" Barkley said.

Toney shook his head. "I only saw what I saw through the viewfinder. Whole thing lasted less than ten seconds. As I snapped the last one, I did yell something."

"Why then?"

"Dunno. Guess I registered the knife. Anyway, the black guy just took off running. I leaned out and saw the white kid was holding his side up against the Dumpster so I went into the hall and started yelling for help."

"And?"

"You can yell a long time in that building and never see a soul."

"You call the police?"

"My phone's out so I ran down two flights to a pay phone and called from there. By the time I got back to my apartment, there were people in the alley trying to help the kid, so I popped off some more shots. Then you guys showed up."

"Why didn't you come down when we were on scene?"

"I could talk to some cops or go in the darkroom and develop film. Which would you rather I did?"

"Fair enough." Barkley tapped the face of the black man,

caught in a random bloom of light. "I assume you don't know this guy?"

"I'd only be guessing."

"Welcome to the world of police work, Mr. Toney."

"I think the pictures are enough, don't you?"

Barkley turned the photo over and stood up.

"You know I could have sold these for some coin to the *Herald*."

"I appreciate that. Give me five minutes and we'll get you a ride home." Barkley collected the photos and left the room. There was a young uniform standing in the hall outside.

"Couple newspaper guys are up front."

"What's your name?"

"Charlie. Charlie Herbert."

"Charlie, take this guy out the back and make sure the press doesn't get a sniff."

"Yes, sir."

Barkley scribbled out a few lines on a piece of paper and tucked it in the uniform's hand.

"What's this?"

"Name and address of the guy in that room. After you drop him off, I want you to call down to the phone company. See if his line's in service. If it's out, find out when and what's the problem. All right?"

"Yes, sir."

"Get going, Charlie. And remember, no press, especially the cameras."

Herbert went into the room. Barkley walked down to the can. He washed his hands and face and quick shined his shoes with a paper towel. Then he ran a hand over the top of his tight

Afro and wiped the fatigue out of his eyes. Barkley adjusted the knot in his tie and gave himself a final look in the mirror. Shit. Sidney Poitier had nothing on him. Richard Roundtree, neither. He left the bathroom, swinging both arms loose and easy as he strode down the hall to meet the press.

20

DANIEL SAT on a bench in the basement of Boston City Hospital and stared at the entrance to the tunnel. He'd spent six months here as an eight-year-old and knew there was a passageway that burrowed under Albany Street, connecting Boston City to the morgue. Now he was staring down its mouth, gaping wide and stinking of urine. A woman approached, pushing a sheeted body on a gurney. She considered Daniel with the disconnected eyes of a prison guard before ducking into the tunnel and quickly sinking from sight. Daniel thought about Heracles and his trip to Hades, Cerberus and the river Styx. Was there something of Charon in the woman's flat-paneled gaze, the coin already in her pocket, slipped from under the tongue of the Bostonian lying perfectly still and perfectly dead under the woman's starched sheet? Daniel wondered why he wondered such things and fig- ured he was in shock. Probably had been since the alley. And now he was here.

They'd given him a long-sleeved T-shirt at the police station. It was cheap and anonymous and itched his neck, but it covered up some of the blood and that was good. The attendant who'd set him on the bench and told him not to move appeared on the horizon. He carried a uniform appropriate to the setting and task—blue scrubs, gloves, even a mask. *Why the mask?* Daniel wondered, but slipped it around his neck, pulled on the scrubs, and followed the attendant to one of several doors cut at regular intervals down both sides of the hallway. The attendant opened it and stepped aside. Daniel had told the cops he wanted to go in alone, but they said that was impossible. The attendant would wait by the door. Daniel had fifteen minutes.

He circled the room, clinging to the plastered walls like he was afraid the floor might tilt and suck him into its center. Light arced from an overhead lamp, spitting shards that glanced off the steel legs and grooved runnels of the examining table. A plastic bucket of water and a sponge sat on a stool next to the table. Daniel moved toward it.

The air felt cold and stuck to his skin. He picked up the sponge and plunged it into the bucket, feeling it swell as it soaked up the warm water. Daniel washed his arms to the elbows, then his face and neck. He stripped to the waist and scrubbed his brother's blood off his chest, water streaming down the contours of his body and forming puddles at his feet. The attendant was watching but never moved from his post by the door. Daniel let himself look at Harry for the first time, face framed over the top of the sheet, feet out the other end, knobby lumps of flesh. Here was the prime of life, everything ahead and about to happen, decaying from the inside out. Daniel could feel it nest in his belly, smell it on his skin, cloying and impossible to scrape off no matter how many buckets of water they brought, no matter how many times he scrubbed.

He plunged the sponge into the bucket and squeezed it dry. Then he started. Daniel washed his brother's arms and hands first, running fingers along the small joints. He dabbed at Harry's face—eyelids, nose, cheeks, all cold to the touch, frosted in death. Daniel ran the sponge across Harry's stubbled scalp and watched the water sluice down his face and catch on his lips. They'd already processed the body for evidence and examined the wounds, photographed them, measured them, touched them. All that remained was the coroner and his tools—knives, saws, and rib cutters. They'd gut Harry, weigh whatever needed to be weighed, bag whatever needed to be bagged. And so on.

Daniel let the sponge fall from his hand and slumped to the floor, pressing his face up against the dark glass of his soul.

Two boys sit on a subway car, snaking somewhere beneath the tangled city. Daniel is just nine and wears a blue hospital bracelet around his left wrist. Harry is twelve and pulls out a folding knife to cut the bracelet. Daniel watches it fall to the floor of the streetcar. The driver calls out his stops in a voice that bleeds through a tinny speaker—Government Center, Park Street, Boylston, Arlington. People shuffle on; people shuffle off. Furrowed faces, Boston eyes, features carved from hard wax melting into soapy smiles when they see the two boys together. Daniel had emerged from his coma a week ago. That morning someone from the state arrived with a pile of paperwork and his ticket out. Harry insisted the brothers be allowed to take the T to the group home where they'd stay until something better came along. Harry's demand provoked a flurry of meetings, but the brothers didn't give a damn. In the end, they got their way.

The train rumbles out of Arlington and Harry looks down as Daniel looks up. He can see Harry thinking, even at that age, literally see his brother's thoughts as they whirl and hiss and sort and shape into words.

"I love you most," Harry says as the streetcar creaks around a

curve and comes to a stop in the breathing darkness. Daniel smiles. It's the game their mother used to play on the T when she was wearing her high heels and her dress made of shiny silver scales, when she was cooked in a cake of makeup and rouge and lipstick, when she was dropping the boys off at the apartment of a woman they called their aunt but really wasn't. Mom always started. Daniel always went next. Now, his mom was gone. But the game runs on.

"No, I love you most," Daniel says.

"I love you most."

"I love you most." Daniel's voice feels small as sin and big as fear. He digs into his brother's shoulder as the overhead lights in the car flicker and they start to move again.

"I love you most, bud. I'll always love you most, and that's all there is to it." Harry draws him close and holds him, not giving a damn what anyone on the Green Line thinks cuz that's Harry.

"I love you most," Daniel mumbles.

"Nope, I love you . . ."

They rumble through Copley that way, then Auditorium, and, finally, Kenmore. The two boys get off the streetcar, still playing their game, the "I love you"s more like a string of prayer beads now or a meditation, each boy lost in his thoughts, their thoughts the same while the ghost of their mother dodges their footsteps and touches their cheeks. And so it went. And so it goes.

Daniel opened his eyes, the chemical air of the room dry at the back of his throat. The attendant was gone, nothing there but an empty chair and a wedge of yellow gleaming wicked beneath a crack in the door. Daniel knew where the attendant was—outside in the alley, in the early morning blush, enmeshed in a web of pulse and shadow, sharing a cigarette with a woman who worked in the hospital. The man was married, but Daniel could still feel his desire for her, hot and slick and blind and desperate. Daniel got to his feet and stood over Harry, hovering close enough that he could have felt a breath stirring on his brother's lips. Or maybe a word.

"You loved me most," Daniel said. "And we both know it." He climbed onto the table and curled up next to the sheeted body, drifting among the soft lights, words and memories sparking and dying in his head. When he finally left the room, he knew better than to look back. In the hallway he took a seat on the floor and hardly breathed, mumbling "I love you most" and wrapping himself in his new life, stitched as it was from the sins of the past.

The attendant returned from his smoke and they walked silently to the reception area, neither looking at the other. Daniel took off the scrubs and tossed them in a bin. Then he was on the flat sidewalk, head back, staring at the curved lines of the building outlined in a predawn light streamed with pinks and purples and rivers of black. The great aloneness was coming, a crushing wave that would only grow as he ran.

Daniel turned and started down the street. At the end of the block, two cops waited in a car.

21

THEY DROPPED him in the middle of Kenmore Square at a little after six. Two men and a woman were sleeping in the shelter of the bus station. One of the men was using his backpack as a pillow while the woman rested her head against his side. The other guy was bundled up in a camo jacket on a wooden bench, his nose pressed against a concrete pillar. Two more packs were stowed under the bench along with a guitar case and a tiny dog that looked like Toto. Daniel watched while an MBTA driver with a thick Italian face walked over and kicked one of the guys in the head. The guy rolled onto his back so his soft belly was exposed. The driver kicked him again, this time in the ribs, and left. The woman got busy organizing their things while Camo Jacket smoked a cigarette. Eventually, the trio cinched up their packs and picked their way through the square, Toto happily at their heels.

Daniel took his time climbing the stairs to his apartment. He sensed the space was empty even before he pushed in the door and lingered on the threshold, smelling the cold char of the fireplace, noticing the slant of morning light across the books on the shelves, listening to the pad of cat's feet on rubbed planks of wood.

He walked back to his room and sat on the bed. Daniel knew

he should sleep and knew he wouldn't. In the tiny bathroom across the hall he showered, turning on the water as hot as it would go and standing under the spray and steam. He found a pair of scissors in the medicine cabinet and hacked at his hair until the floor around him was covered with curling piles of locks. Back in his room he changed into fresh clothes. The gun he'd found outside Latin School was still at the bottom of his book bag. He pulled it out and gripped it, pointing it at himself in the mirror. The gun knew death. Daniel could feel the knowing in his hand and it comforted him—something found even as everything else was lost. He stuffed the gun back underneath his books and returned to the front room, stretching out on the couch and closing his eyes. Harry lived in the space between thoughts, filling the void with grief that swelled and streamed like a heavy sea. When Daniel opened his eyes again, his face stared back at him from the ceiling, curling a lip before turning away.

He got up and cracked a window, then circled the room in a prowl, picking up various objects and putting them down. Simon's desk was its usual mess, which was why he almost missed the envelope set in the very center, *DANIEL* scrawled across the front in slanting lines of lead. He tore open the envelope and took out the single sheet inside.

ON THE ROOF IF YOU WANT TO TALK. SIMON

—

It took him ten minutes to find the staircase that twisted to the roof. Simon was sitting on a stool at the eastern edge of the building, staring out over the city with a sketch pad on his easel and colored pencils strewn at his feet like tiny licks of light. He was bundled up in a long coat and spoke without turning.

"A father has a dream. In it his wife is strangled by their infant son. The father has had these dreams his entire life and, one way or another, they always come true. So he becomes convinced this horrible thing will happen. One night while his wife is sleeping, the father leans into the crib with a hatchet and hacks off his son's hands at the wrists. The father goes to prison. The woman remarries and has another son, who strangles her one night in her sleep when she's deep into her seventies. Meanwhile, the father spends his life locked in a cell while the son he made a cripple visits him every Sunday and is the only person there when they wheel him out in a coffin."

"What's the point?"

"I know about Harry. I'm sorry."

"I was with the police all night."

Simon nodded but still didn't turn his head. Daniel took a seat on a wall that ran along the edge of the roof. From where he sat he couldn't see the sketch Simon had been working on and wondered if that was by design.

"He was killed in an alley in the Combat Zone. I wound up down there myself. I wasn't really sure how, but I knew where to go and knew what I'd find."

"I'm sure the police were curious about that."

"They asked some questions."

Simon slipped the sketch into a sewn leather case he kept by his feet and zipped it up. Then he swung around on his stool, the case laid across his lap. "Did you tell them about the gun?"

"What gun?"

Simon dismissed the response with a shrug.

"Have you been through my stuff?"

"Do you believe that?"

"No."

"Good. And, no, I haven't been through your belongings."

"You don't think I could have stopped what was going to happen to Harry?"

"I think that's what Harry would tell you."

"How do you know about the gun?"

"There are two major sources of energy in this world. Any idea what they are?"

Daniel shook his head.

"Love and hate. People think of them as feelings or emotions, but they're actually physical, tangible, measurable forces. In fact, they provide the foundation for everything they seem to oppose."

"Oppose?"

"Math, technology, logic, reason—they all live in the tension between these two. When you get into an entangled state . . . and you were in an entangled state when you found your brother, no doubt about that . . . when you're in that state, you're enmeshed in their paradox, trading on the physical energy of one or the other."

"I didn't feel hatred. I don't feel hatred."

"No? Why the gun?"

Daniel felt the lie he'd told like a dark rain in his chest.

"It's all right, Daniel. In fact, it's inevitable." Simon swept a long arm across the tatter of Boston's skyline. "The energy exists whether you understand its nature or not. It's what holds all this together—from the structure of the atom to the architecture of the universe, the blood that pumps in our veins and the infinity of a single kiss, everything you see, everything you don't, humming along faster than the speed of light, binding and pulling, usually at the same time. Some people cast it as a battle between good and evil, but those are moral, subjective measures. Relative only to each other."

"And you're talking about something that's absolute?"

"I'm talking about science. The reality is we're just beginning to see the first glimpses of how it all works."

"Which is how?"

Simon shrugged. "Imperfectly, like everything else in Nature. Sometimes hate is the answer. The need to separate and split things apart. The need to fight, to rage, to use that elemental bloodlust to accomplish one's goal. Sometimes it's love. Sometimes when we hate, we spin out a yarn of love somewhere else. And when we truly love, it nurtures hate. The truth is both can wound and both can kill. They just leave very different marks."

"Harry was pure love. At least for me."

"I believe you."

Daniel looked down into the guts of Kenmore Square, curled gray snakes of cars and buses clogging the streets, people on foot filling the gaps between.

"I used to do all my calculations, the higher math stuff, on white sheets of paper," Simon said. "Used a black pencil, strong, thick lead. Then one day I stopped."

"Using the pencil?"

"Doing the math. Harvard didn't like it, but fuck Harvard, right? Have you checked me out with them yet?"

"Should I?"

"You probably have better things to do."

"I was just thinking everything never seemed so random."

"The person who killed your brother will be delivered to you, Daniel. His life will be in your hands. That's what the gun is for."

"Did you know Harry was going to die?"

Simon considered him with a sadness that threatened to break him in two.

"What is it?" Daniel said.

"Do you like the girl?"

"What girl?"

Simon pointed. "The girl."

Grace was sitting on the steps of Music City, a hand shading her eyes, looking hard at the roof.

22

THE MATTRESS just wasn't made for two-fifty-plus pounds of detective. Barkley cursed and rolled onto his back, searching for a halfway comfortable spot. The mattress read his mind and shoved a metal spring up his spine. Message fucking received. He sat up and reached for his watch, nestled in his suit coat, which was folded in a neat bundle. It was just nine. He'd gotten two hours of solid sleep, not great but it would have to do.

Barkley stood and stretched, his reach filling the converted storage room from stem to stern. The first stories would be out by now. He could feel them circulating through Boston's bloodstream. He'd wanted to limit his presser to details about the victim. His boss was all about covering the department's collective ass, insisting specifics about Toney's photos be included so the city could see the Boston PD was on the fucking job. In the end, they'd compromised. Barkley didn't mention the pictures but did confirm they had a suspect—young, black, and in the wind. Now, the shitstorm.

Barkley walked into the squad room and plucked a newspaper off the nearest desk. The *Herald*'s headline was an inch high, in bold, black type.

HARVARD FOOTBALL PLAYER SLAIN IN THE COMBAT ZONE

BLACK SUSPECT STILL AT LARGE

The department could try to downplay the racial angle all it wanted, but the press knew. And the public knew. In Boston, three years into the death march that had become forced busing, the Athens of America was bleeding, black and white and bigotry all over. Throw in Harvard and the stew of emotions that institution stirred up and the Fitzsimmons murder was big news. Letting a black detective run point on the investigation? Hell, that was just icing on the cake.

Barkley dropped the paper back onto the desk and went into the bathroom. He washed his hands and face, then got a cup of coffee from his machine. A couple of detectives gave him a shout as he made his way to his desk, but Barkley didn't play well with others. No wonder they paired him with Dillon. He'd told Tommy to go home, but Barkley knew that wasn't gonna happen. His partner was pure hunting dog. Barkley had given him a scent and Tommy was gonna scare up a couple of bones before he called it quits. So it was no big surprise when Barkley found a stack of files on his desk—background on Harry Fitzsimmons and the younger brother. A folder on top caught Barkley's eye. Tommy had taped a piece of paper to the front and scrawled on it in big fucking Tommy letters.

READ THIS ONE FIRST

Barkley took a sip of coffee and pulled across the file. It was an accident report from 1968. The name of the sole fatality was typed on the first page. Violet Anne Fitzsimmons, aged twenty-nine. The only witness, her eight-year-old son, Daniel Patrick.

Barkley took another sip of coffee and cracked the file. A half hour later he picked up the phone and called out to the uniform who'd helped him with Toney. Charlie Herbert had dropped off the photographer at his place and was working on running down his phone records.

"Good. Do me a favor. Pull anything you can find on Violet Fitzsimmons. Lemme give you some details." Barkley talked to Herbert for another ten minutes, then hung up. An hour later he was hip deep in Violet's life, Herbert coming in and out with the occasional tidbit. And there were tidbits. Barkley pulled across the phone and dialed a number.

"McShane."

He smiled at her voice—the best kind of smile cuz it happened before he ever realized it. Catherine McShane was the county's medical examiner. A graduate of Holy Cross and Johns Hopkins medical school, the good Irish girl from Milton had returned home as the freshly minted ME a couple of years back. Barkley had worked with her on a handful of cases. He'd also asked her out for a drink and, surprisingly, she'd accepted. The drink had turned into dinner, then a stroll through a soft summer night to her flat in the Back Bay. He'd promised to call, meant to call. That was almost six months ago.

"Hey, Cat."

"Detective Jones. How can I help?"

Why hadn't he called this woman? The truth was he'd had a great time. Almost enough to forget he was big and black and scary as hell and she was straight masterpiece beautiful, face full of perfect lines and pleasing angles, the result of generations of money and careful breeding. It was easy to say that shouldn't matter, but this was Boston and the only black people Barkley ever saw at a Celtics game were playing ball. Double down on that for Fenway Park and all points in between. Maybe that was why he'd bailed. Or maybe he was just like every other guy. Running scared.

"I owe you a call, Cat. I'm sorry."

"There's no need to apologize."

"Sure there is."

"You realize I could have picked up the phone?"

"Never thought of that."

"What a surprise. I like you, Bark. Like talking to you. I just don't want to date you. And it's got nothing to do with color."

"Did I say that?"

"You're not nearly as hard to read as you think. The truth is you're not ready to date anyone. Not now, at least."

"How do you figure?"

"I just do. If I'm wrong, so be it. But I'm not."

She'd pinned him like a butterfly to a mounting board. Ready for dissection. Barkley needed to do something quick before she pulled out the magnifying glass and tweezers.

"So you don't hate me?"

"Jesus Christ."

"What?"

"Are you listening? You're my friend. And that doesn't shake easy, at least not for me. Besides, you're gonna need all the help you can get."

"That bad, huh?"

"The radio just described you as the high-profile black detective investigating the stabbing death of a white football player from Harvard. Might as well make it easy on everyone and turn yourself in as his killer."

"Shit."

"Rolling downhill. And then some."

"How you doing with him?"

"Another couple of hours and I should have the basics. Toxicology's gonna be a while."

"Talk to me on this one first, all right?"

"You know how I operate. Your eyes only."

"Thanks, Cat."

"Not a problem. That it?"

Barkley ran a finger across the dog-eared pages of Violet Fitzsimmons's file. "I'm looking at an old case. Nineteen sixty-eight. Deceased's car jumped a seawall near a beach in Dorchester. Fire department found her in the front seat. Eight-year-old son was with her and survived."

"Deceased's name was Violet Fitzsimmons. Your victim's mother."

"How'd you know that?"

"What do you think, we're a bunch of idiots over here?"

"I've always thought of you as ghouls with long, sharp knives."

"Funny. We like to do a little background on our high-profile cases. When we ran Harry Fitzsimmons's name, the mom popped up. I assume the boy in the crash is Harry's younger brother?"

"Name's Daniel."

"I saw that in the report. So what's bothering you?"

"It says she went through the windshield. Suffered several blunt force injuries consistent with the crash, but none of them were fatal."

"So?"

"The cause of death was listed as asphyxiation. I also noticed she suffered a fractured hyoid bone."

"Where you headed, Detective?"

"When I see fractured hyoid, I think manual strangulation."

"Do you really?"

"I do."

"It can happen in other ways."

"Like a car crash?"

"Why not? Probably slammed her throat against the steering wheel."

"You ever seen that?"

"No, but that doesn't mean it couldn't happen."

"You saw the fingerprint?"

"I told you I reviewed the file."

Forensics had pulled a single bloody print off the hollow of Violet Fitzsimmons's neck, a fourteen-point match to eight-year-old Daniel's thumb.

"What do you think about that?" Barkley said.

"As I recall, the boy said something about trying to resuscitate his mom."

"By choking her?"

"He was eight, Bark. What does this have to do with your case?"

"It also says in the report they found him wandering away from the car covered in his mother's blood."

"He was in shock. He'd just crawled over her dead body to get out of the wreck."

"And the time he spent in the hospital?"

"I'm not an expert, but I'd guess some form of post-traumatic stress disorder."

"English, please."

"They're seeing a lot of it in soldiers coming back from 'Nam. The boy's mind couldn't take what had happened so he withdrew.

You'd have to ask his doctors, but I've read about cases where people sat in a room and stared at the wall for the better part of a year."

"From what I understand, this kid slipped into a coma."

"Not unheard of, especially if he suffered physical trauma from the crash."

"So he couldn't have been faking it."

"Seriously?"

"Would he remember anything about the accident, aftermath?"

"Might not. That's the whole point. The mind is trying to protect itself from something it can't handle. What does any of this have to do with your murder?"

"Daniel's sixteen now and stumbled into the alley last night as we were working on his brother."

"Did he see the body?"

"Hell, yeah."

"Wow."

"I'm assuming that's not a good 'wow.'"

"Again, I'm no psychiatrist, but I'd guess that could trigger a lot of bad things."

Barkley was suddenly very happy he hadn't told Cat about letting Daniel visit his brother's body at Boston City. "What kind of things?"

"I don't know. Flashbacks, hyperarousal, withdrawal . . ."

"What the Christ is hyperarousal?"

"Inability to sleep or focus, irritability sometimes escalating to irrational, self-destructive behavior, aggressiveness, violence, delusions. Can go a lot of different ways."

"All right. Thanks."

"You don't seriously believe this boy tried to strangle his mother?"

"Not really. It's just the pieces. I see them lying there in the file and can't help trying to fit 'em together."

"You want me to dig a little deeper on Daniel?"

"Can you do that?"

"Wasn't that your goal all along?"

"Mostly I was just hoping you'd take the call."

"I'll poke around and see if anyone remembers anything." Cat paused like she was writing something down. "Meantime, I've done my preliminary exam and there's one thing that's a little curious about your victim. I mean, there might be more, but there's one thing right off the bat that bothers me."

"Go ahead."

"The wounds. Did you notice anything?"

"Yeah. They were fatal."

"When we examined them, it was obvious he was attacked with two different weapons."

Barkley pulled his feet off his desk and sat up in his chair. "How do you know that?"

"Easy. There's a slash mark on the sleeve of his coat and what appears to be a related wound to the abdomen."

"Consistent with a knife attack?"

"Yes, but the abdomen wound was not fatal. What killed your football player were three puncture wounds. All driven in just under the rib cage, two exiting in the back."

"Shit."

"Yes. These wounds are small and square, tightly packed together."

"What are you saying?"

"There's no way they were made by a knife, certainly not the same knife that slashed him in the stomach. Whoever killed Harry Fitzsimmons got very close. And made no mistake."

"You're telling me this wasn't an alley fight?"

"I'm telling you this guy was gutted and put on a spit. Maybe that's what alley fights have come to these days, but you'd know better than I. I'll call you when I have more. And Bark?"

"Still here."

"If he's not already, make sure Daniel Fitzsimmons gets himself to a therapist."

Barkley hung up and thumbed through the file on the old car crash. There was one additional item he hadn't shared with Cat McShane, something he'd unearthed when they ran their check on Violet. She was a working girl, busted for solicitation and misdemeanor drug possession a half-dozen times. Maybe that was fucked up. Then again, one of her kids had gone to Harvard. The other was at Latin School. God bless her, Violet must have been doing something right. Barkley shoved the file in a drawer just as the phone rang. On the other end of the line was his captain. They'd IDed the black man in Nick Toney's photo. Surprise, fucking surprise, he had a record.

23

DANIEL COULD feel Grace's pull as he walked through Kenmore Square. He kept his head down, eyes averted, gingerly but inevitably entering her orbit. And then he was there, crumbling into her arms on the steps of Music City, burying himself in the smell of her skin, stripping himself of himself.

"Let it out," she breathed, a whisper as ancient as the grief he felt, one that stirred the leaves of death and carried the seeds of something else, something women seemed to understand and embrace so much better and finer than men ever could. Maybe it was healing, maybe it was just acceptance. But Grace understood it. And so she comforted him and he could feel her edge, just a fraction, from young girl to young woman. And part of him marveled at such a thing even as the rest of him heaved in choking, shuddering gasps.

"How did you know?" he finally said. Did it matter how she knew? No, but the mind asked its questions to keep itself busy. Keep itself in the game.

"My dad heard it on the news."

"So you came over?"

"Was that okay?"

He nodded, wiping his nose on his sleeve and producing another spate of tears that filmed his cheeks and salted his lips. "Fuck." Daniel never swore, but he was tired and stretched and dangerously out of control and couldn't have that.

"Why didn't you come up?" He pointed vaguely toward his building.

"I don't know. Just figured I'd wait."

"Did you see us on the roof?"

"I thought it was you. You wanna walk?"

Moving seemed like a good idea so he nodded and they got up.

"What time is it?" he said.

She pointed to the clock on the insurance building. "Nine thirty-two."

Nine thirty-two. Harry had been dead how long? Daniel tried to do the sums, but the numbers wouldn't line up in his head. He wondered if they'd burned the body yet. "Let's walk to school."

"You sure?"

"You think people will know?"

"Probably." She reached out and touched the ragged line he'd chopped across his head. "You cut your hair."

"Yeah." He'd brought his book bag and slung it over his shoulder. "Come on. We can get there by third period."

They crossed the street and started up Brookline Avenue, over a bridge that spanned the Mass Pike. The Green Monster loomed on their left. Daniel noticed a baseball trapped at the base of the stiff, twisted netting and wondered if they'd leave it there all winter. And if they did, would it still be there in the spring? Maybe he'd come by every day and check. Maybe he'd be there when it fell.

"You sure you wanna go in?" Grace said.

He wasn't sure, but his feet seemed to have a mind of their own. And so he led the way as they slipped over the bridge and dipped down past Fenway.

"I was there last night," he said. "In the alley where it happened. Spent all night at the police station, then went down to see the body."

Grace didn't ask for more. She hadn't asked for what she'd gotten. Daniel continued, anyway, because it felt like it scrubbed at something inside.

"The police wanted to know how I got down where Harry was, but I couldn't explain it."

"You couldn't explain it cuz you didn't want to, or you couldn't explain it cuz you couldn't explain it?"

"The second one. I don't know how I got there, but I did. And I saw in my head what I was gonna find."

"You saw like a picture?"

"More like a color or a feeling. But I knew it was Harry. And I was hoping . . ."

"You thought you could save him?"

Daniel shook his head. "Don't think it works that way."

She skimmed him a fresh look and for the first time he saw that maybe, just maybe, she was a little afraid of him. They walked another block.

"You hungry?" Grace pointed to a Dunkin' Donuts on the corner of Brookline and Boylston. They went in and got a couple of plain crullers, sitting at a counter by the front window and staring out at traffic streaming through the intersection.

"He knew I loved him," Daniel said. "Harry knew that."

Grace made a small sound in her throat. Daniel felt her fingers brush his.

"Let's not talk about it anymore," he said.

"Okay."

His cruller had just come out of the deep fryer. There was a fine crunchy crust on the outside and it was warm and soft in the middle. He ate it slowly and, for the first time since the alley, allowed himself a respite, a moment where he enjoyed something of this world.

"Want mine?" Grace said.

Daniel shook his head and tugged a napkin from the dispenser.

"The guy you live with . . . the professor?"

"Simon."

"Are you gonna stay there?"

"For now, I guess. Why?"

Grace turned so their knees were touching. "What do you know about him?"

"I told you what I knew."

"I get feelings, too, Daniel."

"Everyone gets feelings."

"I mean something more, like what you described in the record store." She read the disbelief in his face. "Doesn't matter what you think."

"I didn't say anything."

"Have you ever thought maybe this professor is entangling *you*? Manipulating *you*?"

"Why would he do that?"

"Good question. Did you tell the police about the gun?"

Daniel felt his face grow hot and pink. "What gun?"

"The one you picked up outside of school yesterday. People see, Daniel. People know. Okay, people guess. *I* know." Her eyes moved to his book bag on the counter. "Is it in there?"

He put a hand on the bag and noticed the small muscles in his forearm as he moved his fingers.

She blew a puff of air from her perfect lips. "You know they have a suspect?"

"Who told you that?"

"My dad. I guess it's all over Chinatown."

"Do you have a name?"

"I don't. And if I did, I'd tell you to leave it to the police."

She was growing older even as he watched, body ripening, eyes deepening, her coltish movements becoming a study in poise and polish. He saw her standing at the back of a church, in a white dress with orange flowers in her hair and scent on her cheeks, a wedge of sun warming her face and turning it a dozen shades of golden. Her life flashed past in a series of flip cards—quiet nights on the couch, movies and popcorn as the snow piled up outside, summers and sun-brewed tea, puppies, children, cookouts, a husband, partner, friend. Love. Bubbling, endless, overflowing. And so it went to the end of her days. And then it was done and Grace moved on, one of ten thousand lives she'd lead and a special one at that. It was all as it should be, but only if he was part of none of it. Love and hate, pain and perfection, one tugged at the thread of the other and life unraveled.

"I never told you about my mom."

"What do you want to tell me?"

"She died in a car crash when I was a kid."

Grace didn't offer any condolences because he didn't need any. He needed to talk. So she took his hand and listened.

"We'd sit up in an apartment we had downtown. I was seven or eight and would lie in her bed, watching in the mirror as she put on makeup." Daniel remembered lifting his nose and the smell of her powder, sweetening the thick clouds of cigarette smoke. Coffee cups kissed with lipstick crowded together on the vanity as he ran up and down a short set of stairs, getting her this, bringing her that. A hiss of silk as she stood up in her slip, figure long in the mirror, and asked how she looked and he'd stare at her face and she'd smile in the glass and kiss him and tell him he was so perfect and don't ever change. Then she'd put on her dress and he'd zip it up and he'd thread a needle if she needed it because her eyes were no good for that and he'd watch as the rings and earrings came out and went on. When she was ready, she'd kiss him again on the cheek and tell him he'd be okay and if he wasn't he could go to the lady who lived downstairs or the Chinaman on the corner. Then she'd look at herself a final time in the mirror, that hint of something else always tugging at her lips, as if she was waiting, begging, for someone to tell her to stay. But no one ever did. And so she'd go.

"I'd watch her from the window, then sit up as the streetlights came on and wait for Harry. He wouldn't get home until late from football. We'd go down in the street and play catch." Laces spinning, perfect spirals in the night, a kiss of leather as the ball hit soft in his hands and he cradled it close to his body. Harry at the other end, smiling as Daniel threw the ball back, covering only half the distance and a wobble at that. They'd sit on the curb or a bench and talk while the sweat cooled on Daniel's neck. Sometimes, they talked about football. Sometimes, it was their mother. Sometimes, it was her "dates." Once Harry asked if Daniel remembered their dad. Daniel shook his head. He could feel his brother's angst rubbing and stretching and searching for a home and he never told their mother about those conversations. Not because Harry asked him to keep quiet, but just because Daniel knew. And now he told Grace because she was everything that was left.

"I'll help you, Daniel. But in my own way."

"What do you think I want to do?"

"Let's talk outside." She waited until they were back on the sidewalk before speaking again. "If I'm wrong, just tell me. You want to find Harry's killer. Right now. Today."

She'd spoken the words and he felt better, like it was real and normal and just the next thing.

"Yes, that's exactly what I want."

"But not the gun, Daniel."

"You don't think he's gonna have one?"

"Not the gun."

He pulled the heavy revolver from his bag and handed it to her. She turned it over quickly in her hands and shoved it in her coat pocket. Then they walked down Brookline Avenue in silence. Not perfect silence, but the words they said sounded wooden and hollow and meant nothing compared to what had already been said and left unsaid. Just before they hit Avenue Louis Pasteur, Daniel stopped and turned.

"It can't happen like this."

"Then how?"

"I don't know, but the gun's part of it."

She shook her head but took out the revolver. Whatever had been set in motion was running now, free and easy, and would be as it was meant to be, regardless of what they said or did or felt or didn't. So Daniel shoved the gun back in his bag and they walked the rest of the way down Avenue Louis Pasteur. As they hit the front steps of the school, Grace took his hand.

24

THEY WENT in a side door and down to the basement to wait for the end of the period. Eddie Spaulding was sitting on the floor in the hallway, eating a Hoodsie with a wooden spoon and reading CliffsNotes for Albert Camus's *The Stranger.* He fixed Grace with his golden gaze. She didn't give him a second look as they ducked into the cafeteria. A couple of women were setting up for lunch at a long steam table, carrying out pans heavy with Salisbury steak and industrial-strength mac and cheese, all of it arriving in clouds of white steam. Nearby a man with a face like an old bucket pushed a long-handled broom across the cement floor. Grace headed to the bathroom. Daniel sat on a bench at one of the narrow tables. The swinging doors to the cafeteria squeaked once and Spaulding walked in. He took a seat across from Daniel, propping up one sneaker and flexing his wrist as he spoke.

"I heard about your brother. I'm sorry."

Daniel ducked his eyes, hiding from his pain like any animal would. "Thanks."

"Great football player. Looked out for me when I was on jayvee."

"Sounds like Harry."

"He was a stand-up guy, Daniel. Real fucking deal."

Daniel was sure that meant a lot to Eddie Spaulding, but it didn't mean jack to him. He wanted his fucking brother back. Could Spaulding do that? No. And it didn't matter how many nice things people said.

"Ever tell you I lost a brother?" Spaulding's words were clipped and perfectly shaped. Daniel shook his head and waited for more.

"We live in Old Colony. Me and my mom."

Old Colony was a housing project in Southie. Daniel had never been there.

"Terry got hit by a drunk driver. I know the guy, but no one ever did nothing."

"How old was he?"

"My brother? Eleven and a half. I was ten."

Daniel thought about the almighty Eddie Spaulding, sitting in a one-bedroom box with his mom, both of them staring at a class photo of the dead kid who wasn't there and was always there. The man with the broom came down again to work their area. They let him sweep and didn't say another word until he'd left.

"You talk to the cops yet?" Eddie had cut his voice.

"Last night."

"The guy who killed Terry's still around. I know exactly where he lives."

"That must be tough."

"People in the projects still talk about it to this very fucking day. Wonder why I never went after the guy. Some of them think I'm a pussy. No one says it to my face, but I know that's what they think. Latin School, college boy. Didn't stick up for his dead brother. Pussy."

Daniel played with a seam on his book bag and felt the barrel of the gun through the fabric. "What do you think?"

"I think I want to get my mom the fuck out of the projects. My brother never gave a shit about school, but he wanted it for me. Told everyone I was gonna be starting for Harvard. He was gonna sit in the stands for Harvard-Yale. Not happening with my grades, but that's all right. Still gonna try the fuck out of whatever they put in front of me."

The zombie with the broom rotated through again. Eddie stood up. "You know they're looking for you?"

"Who's that?"

"Headmaster's office. Sent out word first thing this morning. Anyway, I gotta get."

"Thanks, Eddie."

Spaulding nodded. It was what you did if you were a certain kind of guy. You passed along what you knew to someone who was drowning. Maybe the other guy drowned anyway. Maybe you drowned together, but at least you tried. Grace came back from the bathroom just in time to see the star running back leave.

"What did he want?"

"Just being a friend."

"Really?"

"In his own Spaulding way. He's worried I might be out for blood as well."

"Are you?"

"I'm not gonna sit by, Grace. Not again."

"What does that mean?"

Daniel was about to respond when the cafeteria doors squeaked and Boston Latin School's headmaster stepped through. Daniel had never seen the great and powerful William Keating outside of the assembly hall and had a difficult time imagining him in a place as dingy and common as the school cafeteria. But there he was, blue three-piece suit, red tie, and black oxfords that shined like mirrors. Grace put a soft hand on the strap of Daniel's bag.

"Want me to take that?"

Daniel shrugged her off and stood up, his face etched in hard grooves of light.

—

They settled by a tall set of windows overlooking the front steps of Latin School. Daniel was in the middle of the loose triangle, Latin School's headmaster, William Keating, on his left, the president of Harvard University on his right.

"This is Lawrence Trent," Keating said.

"How are you, Daniel?" Trent wore a dark silk suit that made a hissing sound when he offered his hand.

"Fine, sir."

Keating got up, muttering to himself and looking for something on his desk. He returned to his chair with a sigh that whistled through his teeth. "I'm sorry, Daniel. So very, very sorry."

"Thank you, sir."

"Such a senseless tragedy. We didn't know if you'd be in today."

"I was with the police until early this morning but couldn't really sleep."

The word *police* caused Keating's shoulders to jump and Trent to blink. Harvard would be under the microscope for letting a bunch of its players loose in the Combat Zone. The fact that they were mostly white and entirely privileged while a lot of the girls on the street were black didn't help anyone, especially the guys from Cambridge.

"Have you given any thought to the funeral?" Trent said.

"There won't be any service. Harry will be cremated as soon as they finish with the body."

Keating's jaw dropped a full inch. Trent gave Daniel a lacerating smile.

"Do you think that's wise? There are many people at the university who would like to pay their respects."

"It's what my brother would have wanted. Besides, it's already done."

"Of course." Trent paused as if to gather momentum. "There are a few things about Harry we want to make sure get mentioned. First, of course, to you, and then to the public at large."

Daniel might be broken and bleeding and naked. Harry, beyond caring. All of that, however, needed to be weighed against how Harvard came out of this. And so Trent hammered on.

"Your brother was only on campus for a short time, yet he made an indelible impact on everyone he met. Harry was a brilliant student, a leader on and off the football field, and, most important, a young man of the utmost integrity, utmost character. He enriched everyone he touched and represented the very best of Harvard. We offer our condolences and join in your grief."

"Thanks."

"We want to remember Harry." Trent pulled a piece of paper from his pocket and fixed a set of reading glasses he kept on a cord to his treacherously long Beacon Hill nose. "And to that end, the Board of Fellows has decided to establish a full, four-year scholarship in your brother's name. It will be awarded each year to a graduate from the Boston Latin School. The recipient will be chosen by a committee of Harvard and Latin School alumni, chaired by the sitting president and headmaster of the schools, respectively. Criteria for the scholarship will be leadership, academic prowess, athletic ability, outstanding character, and service to the community. The scholarship will be fully endowed in perpetuity by the university and serve as a testament to the life and character of Harry Fitzsimmons." Trent folded up the paper and dropped the glasses to his chest. "We want this to be something special, Daniel. Awarded to an outstanding student from the city who might otherwise not have the means."

"That's great," Daniel said.

Trent lifted a patrician finger. "There's one more thing. We'd like to start the scholarship with your graduating class and we'd love for you to be the first recipient."

Daniel glanced at Keating, who had a smile slathered across his face like a smear of Irish butter. "Your academic record is outstanding, Daniel. Everyone here knows what kind of a person you are. And everything you've overcome. Frankly, we can't think of a better recipient."

Trent reached for Daniel's hand. "Daniel, I'm thrilled to offer you a place in our freshman class upon graduation from Latin School. I suspect you'll make a great Harvard man."

"Thanks," Daniel said, "but I'm not interested in going to Harvard. I mean, it's a wonderful school and all, but it's just not for me. Not with Harry having gone there and everything."

Trent smiled and nodded, still pumping Daniel's hand as if that might force-feed some sense into the boy. "Why don't you take some time and think about it?"

"I don't need to."

"Take it anyway. Please. We'll announce the scholarship next week. See where things go from there. William."

Both men rose from their chairs and walked out into the hallway for a private chat about the moron who'd just turned down a free ride to Harvard. Daniel stole a look across the flat expanse of the headmaster's desk. Behind it was an open door that led to a small, interior office. Daniel could see a row of pictures running down one wall and a man sitting in a chair just inside the door. Actually, he could see the man's cuffed pant leg and a brown shoe, heel tapping impatiently against the nub of carpet. Keating returned from seeing Trent out and sat down again.

"Well, Daniel."

"I know you want me to take the scholarship."

"Let's talk about it when things are a little more settled."

"Let's not. Tell Harvard I'll go to their press conference and sing their praises, but only if they award the thing to Eddie Spaulding."

"Spaulding?"

"That's it. He gets the first scholarship when he graduates at the end of the year and we never had this conversation. Now, why don't you go ahead and bring in the cop."

"Excuse me?"

"You have a cop stashed in the office next door. I recognize his shoe."

Keating narrowed his eyes and all the bonhomie was gone, if there had ever been any bonhomie in the first place. He ducked into the other room and returned with the black detective from the alley. The headmaster left without another word, closing the door behind him as he went. The cop took the seat Harvard's president had been keeping warm and smiled.

"Hey, Daniel. Remember me?"

"Detective Jones."

"Call me Barkley. That was a nice thing you did just now."

"Eddie will do a lot more with it than I ever could."

"I'll take your word on that. Thing is, I don't give a shit about Harvard or Eddie."

"No?"

The detective leaned forward, pressing his palms together and touching the tips of his fingers to his lips. "Let's talk about the gun."

—

He should have known better. Grace had told him as much. People see things. People know. And if people know, cops like Barkley know. It's how they make a living.

"Why didn't you tell me about it at the station?"

"About what?"

"Not gonna work, Daniel. Not gonna work at all. Have you been to bed?"

"I slept a little."

"There was a fight here yesterday. You were in the middle of it."

"What does that have to do with Harry?"

"Several people say they saw a gun. At one point you had your hands on it."

"I was in a fight, sure, but I didn't see any gun."

"Daniel . . ."

"I'm sure you've been in fights, Detective. It's crazy."

"There were at least two students hiding in the gym. They told the cops you knocked it out of the guy's hands."

"What guy?"

"Doesn't matter. You don't remember any of this?"

"I remember fighting a black kid. Had a silver tooth hanging around his neck."

Barkley took out a ballpoint pen and began to write in a notebook.

"He was bigger than me so I grabbed his arm. He threw me around like I was nothing. I remember being on the ground, this kid coming after me when the cops showed up. The kid ran and that was it."

"Was a girl attacked?"

"A friend of mine. A couple of other kids grabbed her, but she got away."

"What's her name?"

"I'd rather not say. What's any of this got to do with my brother?"

The detective stopped writing and looked up.

"She doesn't know anything. If she did, I'd tell you."

Barkley clicked the pen a couple of times with his thumb. "Would you?"

"Yes, I would."

"So you didn't see a gun?"

Daniel shook his head. Barkley's eyes flicked to the bag at Daniel's feet, then settled back on the boy.

"Why would I lie?" Daniel said.

"Maybe cuz you're thinking of doing something stupid."

"I'm not stupid, Detective."

"We have a suspect in Harry's death. We're looking for him right now."

A knocking came from pipes buried deep inside the walls, a scent creeping up from the building's ancient heating vents. It was the smell of dry powder, his mother's talced fingers reaching into the back of their old Buick and pulling his lungs from his chest, smiling and squeezing the pale pink sponges until all the air had bled out and Daniel was lying flat on the car seat, dead but alive, breathing yet unable to strike a breath while the detective sat in the front, feet up on the dash, and took notes. Daniel began to wheeze and cough like an old man, the sound harsh and rasping in his ears. Barkley reached over and patted him on the back.

"You all right?"

"I'm fine."

"You want me to get you some water or something?"

"What do you know about my mother, Detective?"

"I was just about to ask you the same thing."

25

SHE WAS standing on the corner of Washington and Essex, wearing a short yellow jacket with tassels, a tight blue skirt, and a floppy hat that hid one side of her face. A skinny Asian kid squatted on a box in front of her, working polish into her stiletto heels and buffing them to a high shine. The kid wore thin wool gloves with the fingers cut out and talked nonstop as he worked. The woman checked her makeup in a compact while keeping one eye on the street. Daniel slouched past, invisible to both of them.

Grace was waiting at the King of Pizza. It was a storefront shop set up in the heart of the Combat Zone with maybe the best slices in the city. Grace was parked at a counter by the front window, sipping a Coke.

"How did you know I'd come?" Daniel said.

"I didn't."

She'd taped a note to his locker telling him to meet her after he got done with Keating. She was right. Going into school today had been a bad idea. So he'd stuck the note in his pocket and headed out to meet her.

"You want something?" Grace pointed to a couple slices of pepperoni on a paper plate.

"Not hungry."

She pushed across a slice and Daniel took a bite.

"What did they want?" Grace plucked a pepperoni off the other slice, then picked it up and nibbled.

"They just wanted to talk about Harry. Make sure I was all right."

Outside the woman in the hat had finished getting her shoes shined and was talking to a tall man wrapped in a camel hair coat with a roll of dark fur around the neck. Daniel couldn't make out the words, but he could tell the woman was angry. She stood on the corner with her hip cocked and finger raised, waving it in the man's face then jabbing it in his chest. The man didn't seem to notice the woman until he did, catching her flush on the jaw with the back of his hand. She bounced off the side of a building that housed fifty-cent peep shows and would have fallen into the gutter, but the tall man caught her by the elbow, holding her up so he could plant a platform heel in the small of her back. The woman skidded on her hands and knees, snapping a stiletto and banging off the side of a parked car. The tall man followed her into the street, taking off his belt and wrapping it around his knuckles. A cab flashed past, swerving around the two of them and laying on the horn. The kid with the shine box materialized out of nowhere, slipping between man and woman, laughing and joking, forcing the man to make eye contact while the woman struggled to her feet and wobbled toward the King of Pizza. She stopped in front of the window and put on her shoe with the broken heel, then walked lopsided to the far end of the block. Across the street, the tall man had put his belt back on and was smoking a brown cigarette, one foot up on the shine box as the Asian kid worked his polish and talked his magic.

"We probably should've met somewhere else," Grace said.

"It's fine."

"Was it far from here?"

Daniel flicked a finger in the general direction of the alley where Harry had died some twelve hours earlier.

"Let's just go."

"I already saw the body, Grace. Can't be anything worse." Daniel picked up the slice in both hands, then put it down again. Grace watched.

"You live close?" he said.

"Five minutes. My dad doesn't want me coming in here. He's always driving past. Checking."

"I don't blame him."

"The girls are actually really nice. Besides, no one bothers me."

Daniel considered the shine of her skin and clean lines of her face and thought, *Not yet*. She turned so their knees were touching.

"There's something I want to tell you."

"What's that?"

"If I tell you, you have to promise you won't do anything crazy."

"You mean with the gun?"

Her smile flickered like a lightbulb that was loose in its socket. Her eyes fastened on Daniel's book bag. "Is it still in there?"

"What do you want to tell me?"

"Harry's killer was a student from English. A guy named Walter Price. At least that's what I heard."

Walter Price. The name thrummed through his body and hummed hot in his brain. Daniel did his best to sound casual. "You know him?"

"My dad says he's a big black kid who hangs around down here. Says he's a drug dealer or a pimp, but someone else said he's just a wannabe. Anyway, the police are supposed to be looking for him."

"What does he look like?"

"I told you. Big, black. That's all I know."

"So you've never actually seen him?"

"My dad says I have, but I'm not sure. Everyone thinks it was a robbery, Daniel. Just a freak thing. I'm so sorry."

"Why did you tell me?"

"If the situation was reversed, what would you have done?"

"Told you."

"Exactly."

"But you're worried about the gun?"

"I'm not worried you'll use it."

"Then what?"

"Yesterday you were talking about energy."

"Simon was talking about energy."

"Well, I think he's right. Everything has an energy—people, places . . ."

"Even guns."

"Especially guns. If you want to find the guy who killed your brother, be there when the cops arrest him, tell him what you think, whatever, that's fine. I'll even help you. But lose the gun first."

"There was a cop in Keating's office today. He was asking about it as well."

"The gun's gonna kill you, Daniel. At least it could. That's what I'm trying to say."

A car pulled to the curb and laid on the horn. In the driver's seat was a square-faced Asian man with white teeth and a black buzz cut.

"Your dad?" Daniel said.

"Shit."

It was the first time he'd ever heard Grace curse and he knew he'd always remember it.

"I gotta go." She pulled him away from the window so her father couldn't see and took his face in her hands to kiss him. Not the sweet, storybook kiss from the record store. That was a lifetime ago, when they were still kids and anything was possible. This one was wet and sloppy and reeked of desperation, her mouth opening and tongue pushing through his teeth as she flattened him against a wall next to the ladies' room. Their time together was running thin and Grace felt it as much as he did. Maybe more. She nipped at his ear and whispered, "I'm so sorry." Then she ran out the door to the waiting car.

Her father glared at Daniel as the ancient Ford crawled across King of Pizza's plateglass window and was gone. Daniel rubbed his lips with the back of his hand and listened to his heart bump in his chest. He was suddenly ravenous and ordered another slice. He'd just gotten back to his seat when a tall man with curly brown hair and eyes the color of gravy slipped onto the stool beside him.

"You mind?"

Daniel shrugged and took a bite.

"Good slice, huh?"

Daniel remembered his warning to Grace. This was a place full of predators. And they didn't discriminate between male and female when it came to whom they preyed upon.

"Just leave me alone, okay?"

"What are you doing down here?"

Daniel grabbed his book bag and got up to go. The man reached out and gripped his forearm. Daniel tried to break free, but the man was surprisingly strong. Daniel thought about Simon, about men with layers.

"I wasn't gonna hurt you, kid. You know what, fuck it."

The man let Daniel go, turning on his stool and crossing one leg over the other. A small Italian with quick hands and a round face was behind the counter, throwing cheese on a pie. The man with the curly hair seemed to see him for the first time.

"Mr. Sal, how you doing?"

Mr. Sal looked up with four teeth and a full smile, nodding and talking while continuing to work on his pie. "Hey, Signor Nick. You wanna slice?"

"I'm good, thanks."

Daniel sat back down on his stool. After all, it was the middle of the afternoon and they were in a pizza shop.

"What do you want?"

The man turned, surprised at first but getting past it quickly. "You're looking for information on the college kid, the one that was killed last night."

"You heard us talking?"

"You and the girl? Sure, but I knew anyway."

"Yeah, right."

"I saw you last night. You came down the alley and ran right into it. Started screaming and the cops grabbed you."

Daniel let his mind spin through the images—black buildings with windows lit up like cats' eyes in the smoky darkness, the crunch of a cop's boot, Harry collapsed in a corner, face empty, gutted.

"Name's Nick Toney." The man held out his hand. His skin

was cool and dry, the wrinkles of his palm fitting neatly into Daniel's.

"I know, you think I'm some kind of freak, but I'm not. Mr. Sal . . ." Toney looked back toward the counter. "Am I some kind of freak?"

Mr. Sal looked up again from his pie. "That's Mr. Nick. Good man. Caan."

"Thank you." Toney turned back to Daniel. "He thinks I look like James Caan. I don't see it either, but what the hell. You mind if I smoke?" Toney already had his cigarettes out and lit up, pulling a piece of tobacco off his tongue and studying it before flicking it away with the flat of his thumb.

"The man who was killed was my brother."

"Shit." Toney lapsed into silence, shaking his head and staring at the capped toe of his shoe while he drew on the cigarette and exhaled.

"My name's Daniel."

"Daniel. Okay, good. I'm sorry, Daniel. I made a mistake and I'm gonna go."

"You had something to tell me."

"Did I?" Toney let more smoke drift from his nose, then dropped the butt to the floor, twisting it into the yellowed linoleum. Daniel stared at the inner black of the man's left eye and thought about trying to go inside.

"My brother's dead, Mr. Toney, and nothing's gonna change that. If you have something to say, just say it."

Toney wet his lips. "You know a detective named Jones? Big black guy?"

"How do you know him?"

"Talked to him very early this morning."

"Why?"

"I'm a photographer. Got a studio on the top floor of the Brompton Arms. Looks right over the alley where you wound up last night."

Daniel summoned up the face he'd seen in the window above the alley. The man with the camera. "You took pictures of the murder."

"How'd you know that?"

"I saw you with the camera. Did you give them to the police?"

"Cops are looking for the guy right now, Daniel."

His name rolled off the photographer's tongue in a way that made the air prickle, but that was just the vibe you got in the Combat Zone when you were sixteen and swimming upstream, a gun in your bag and the idea of killing a man running like a rat through the maze in your head.

"Can I see them?"

"Probably not a great idea."

"Please."

Toney sighed and stared at the traffic on Washington, looking for all the world like a man who wished he'd kept his mouth shut.

—

The studio had six windows, four looking out to the street, two staring straight down into the alley where Harry had died. Toney pulled the shades on all of them, flicking on a set of overhead lights and directing Daniel to a seat at a long worktable. He listened as Toney rummaged around in the back. Three lengths of wire were strung across the room. Attached to each were what looked like work prints. Finished photos hung on the walls. Almost all the shots were of women, most of them taken in the studio or at night on the street. Toney returned from the back with a couple more prints.

"Sorry for the mess." He pushed aside the remains of a Greek salad and a couple half-eaten chunks of gray meat.

"What kind of photos do you shoot?"

"I document lives. Girls, pimps, whatever catches my eye. Last night I was working with a fifteen-year-old girl. Runaway from Minnesota."

Toney pointed to a trio of pictures clipped to one of the wires. Daniel got up and took a look. The girl reminded him of Twiggy, except even skinnier and grimmer around the eyes. Honest, unflinching, a black-and-white study in the perfection of corruption.

"See this one." Toney had come up behind Daniel, plucking one of the few color shots off the wire and holding it under the light. The print shivered in his hand.

"Who is she?" Daniel said.

"Pretty, right?"

The woman was older, straight brown hair, hollow green eyes. Toney had caught her at a street corner in the morning, just as she turned and before she'd had time to armor up.

"Her name's Elena Benson. Haven't seen her in over a year. Happens a lot down here. Anyway, the reason I was looking out the window was because I thought she was down in the alley. Just a minute or two before your brother. I yelled at her, but she was close to LaGrange and couldn't hear me."

"What's her name?"

"I told you. Elena. Elena Benson. She wasn't there when Harry died, Daniel. I'm not sure she was ever there." Toney clipped the photo back on the wire. "Let's sit down."

Toney took a seat and placed one of the photos he'd brought out from the back facedown on the table. "Before I show you anything, there's something you need to know."

"What's that?"

"I actually met your brother yesterday morning. Just a chance thing in Harvard Square. I can't say I knew him, but it still kind of shook me."

"Is that why I'm here?"

"I don't know. Maybe. I saw you sitting there with the girl and you looked like you'd had your guts kicked out . . ." Toney's voice trailed off to nothing.

"It's all right, Mr. Toney."

"What's all right?"

"You feel like you're part of what happened to Harry, maybe even a little responsible, but you're not."

Toney nodded and drummed his fingers on the table. Daniel's eyes were fixed on the blank back of the print. Toney rubbed a thumb along its border.

"I cropped it so you can only see the killer."

"Thank you."

Toney flipped over the photo. Harry's attacker was perfectly caught in a fracture of street light, staring directly up at the unblinking lens. If this was Walter Price, Daniel knew him. He'd fought with him outside of Latin School yesterday and had his gun stuffed at the bottom of his bag.

"You recognize him," Toney said.

"Why do you say that?"

"It's written all over. Don't worry. I ain't gonna tell no one."

"He's a student at Boston English. I go to Latin. It's right across the street so I've seen him around. Name's Walter Price."

Toney turned the photo around and gave it a hard look. "No shit?"

"You know him as well," Daniel said.

"I didn't have the name but, yeah, I've seen him down here from time to time."

"You know where he is."

Toney turned the photo facedown again and laid his hands flat over it. "I might know where he'd go if he was scared."

"Did you tell the police?"

"Nah."

"Why not?"

Toney shrugged. "Down here you depend on a lot of people for access. Part of the deal is I look the other way on some things. Otherwise, it's just no good."

"You gave them your photos."

"Maybe that's where the line is for me. Besides, I went down there at five in the morning. Made sure no one saw me coming or going."

"Give me the address, Mr. Toney."

"Go home, son. Bury your brother and let the cops handle it."

Daniel pointed his chin at the print. "Can I at least keep that?"

Toney kicked it across the table with a finger. "Go ahead, then."

Daniel unzipped his book bag and slid the picture inside. Then he pulled out Walter Price's revolver.

"Give me the address or I swear I'll put a bullet in your head."

After Toney got done laughing, he told Daniel to put the

goddamn gun away. The photographer opened the shades to the front windows and cracked them each an inch. Then he got a couple of ice-cold bottles of Coke from a small fridge. As the city whispered in the street below and the sun worked its way across the sky, the two of them talked.

"I can't give you the exact address," Toney said.

"Why not?"

"Does the phrase 'lambs to the slaughter' mean anything to you?"

"You think I'm gonna go busting in there and start shooting?"

"I think you'll go busting in there and get yourself shot, but what's the difference? Truth is I don't have an exact address."

"I don't believe you."

"Tell someone who gives a fuck. Best I can do is put you on the same block. After that, you're gonna have to wait for the cops. Take it or leave it."

Daniel took it. After he'd left, Toney pulled the shades, turned off the lights, and sat in the dark, wondering like hell if he'd done the right thing.

26

BARKLEY PULLED up in front of Tommy Dillon's apartment at a little after three. He unfolded his six-foot five-inch frame slowly from the front seat, well aware of the four kids arranged on the stoop across the street. Barkley let them get a good look at the piece on his hip as he walked past, listening for the trail of Irish whispers that followed like soft blessings all the way to his partner's front door.

Katie Dillon answered on the first knock, pulling him close for a hug and pressing her body against his. "God, that feels good." She leaned back a fraction to get a look at his face. "Come on in."

They walked into the living room. Barkley stopped near a table full of photos. Tommy with Katie. Katie with Tommy. Both of them with the twins.

"Tommy said you guys are on the Harvard thing."

"That's the rumor."

"It was on the news all morning, Bark. *You* were on the news all morning."

He picked up a photo of Katie playing hoops back in the day. "I hear you have a sweet jumper. Or should I say 'had.'"

She took the photo from him and put it back on the table. "I'm serious."

"So am I."

"Why's it always you two who catch these ones?"

"Which ones you talking about?"

"You know what I mean. White kid, black suspect."

"Black cop, white partner."

"It's just a boatload of stress, Bark. Tommy, me, the girls. All the way around. You know what I'm saying?"

"There's the big dog." Tommy came rolling down the hall, hair still wet from the shower. He tossed Barkley a can of Bud.

"Am I supposed to open this now?"

"I'll take it." Tommy gave him the other can he had in his hand and popped the first. A froth of foam bubbled out of the top. Tommy drank it off and plopped down in an easy chair. "Take a load off, brother."

Barkley sat across from Tommy on the couch. Katie took a seat between them.

"Smells good in here," Barkley said.

"Homemade spaghetti and meatballs." Tommy pointed to a crush of take-out bags in a wire basket by the door. "My wife says I need to eat better."

"She's right."

"This from a guy who eats beans out of a can."

"You got time for a plate?" Katie said.

Barkley held up a hand. "Grabbed something before I came over."

"Don't believe it," Tommy said. "He slept at the station. Breakfast was probably a Zagnut bar."

"Hey, you didn't go home like I told you."

"I was home by eight thirty, nine. Got five good hours, plus a little extra." Tommy grinned at Katie and yo-yoed his knees back and forth. Katie colored but didn't move from her chair.

"We got some things to run down, Tommy."

"K was just telling me. How'd we get a suspect?"

Barkley glanced at Katie, who got up neatly. "I've got sauce on the stove. Bark, we're still gonna set a date for dinner?"

"You got it."

"Thanks, babe." Tommy spoke without ever taking his eyes off Barkley. They waited until she'd left.

"The photographer."

"Toney?"

"He's got a studio looking right over the alley." Barkley pulled one of Toney's photos from his pocket. Tommy turned on a lamp and studied it under the light.

"Fucking hey."

"Dumbass luck."

"We catch all the shit when things go sideways. Don't be afraid to take a bow."

"Ever hear of a kid named Walter Price?"

Tommy shook his head and tapped the picture with his finger. "This him?"

"Looks like it. Student at English. Part-times as a hustler down the Zone. Got a sheet. Girls, dope, ragtime shit."

"Lemme guess. He's in the wind?"

Barkley nodded.

Tommy handed back the photo. "I'll have an address for us by the end of the day."

"That's what I want to hear."

"Just lemme say good-bye to the girls." Tommy got up, draining his beer and tossing the empty in the basket.

"Hold on a sec." Barkley waved his partner back to his chair.

Tommy sat, one heel rapping a beat on the wooden floor. This was his thing, like letting a bloodhound off the leash. "Yeah?"

"Relax."

"I'm good."

"Fuck you're good. You look like you want to lift your leg and take a piss in the corner. How's Katie doing?"

"She's fine. Why?"

"Nothing. Let's talk about the file you left on Violet Fitzsimmons."

"Fucked up, right? Guy's mother dies in a car crash and then the kid himself gets offed."

"Did you read through the file?"

"Quick look."

"You know she was a hooker?"

Tommy popped his head back. "The mom?"

"Was raising both boys while she was working."

"Probably kept 'em for the welfare chit. Any dad listed on the kids' birth certificates?"

"Nope. The one we talked to last night was in the car with her when she crashed."

"No shit."

"Eight years old. They found him walking down the beach in a daze. Then he slips into some sort of coma."

"That was in the file?"

"Finding these things does you no good, Tommy. Not unless you read 'em."

"And if I did that, why in the fuck would we keep you around? Where's all this headed, B?"

"Don't know for sure. Just bugs me. I mean, what are the chances he's in the crash and then this happens? And why was he down in that alley?"

"Know what I think?"

"What's that?"

"Best thing we can do for that kid is find the cocksucker who killed his brother."

"Yeah."

Tommy got up. "Let me say good-bye to the girls and we'll roll."

He disappeared down the hall. Barkley hadn't told him about Daniel's print, traced in blood and pulled off his mother's throat. Or about Barkley's trip to Latin School. He'd asked Daniel about the accident. And the print. Daniel said he couldn't remember a thing. Barkley hadn't bought it. And then there was the quiet way the kid looked at him, like he knew Barkley's heart and every mark life had left upon it.

He got up and walked into the kitchen. Katie was chopping garlic. Meatballs and sauce simmered in a pan.

"Smells good."

"You should stay."

"Can't."

"I know, you're all so goddamned busy." She swept the garlic into the pan and cracked a second clove with the flat of her knife.

"What's the problem, Katie?"

She glanced at the connecting door that led to the hallway.

"He's with the girls," Barkley said.

She walked around him and shut the door, putting her back up against it. "He's on that shit again."

"What? Blow?"

"I don't think he ever got off."

"My ass. He went through a six-month program."

"You know Tommy. All the Irish bullshit comes out when he needs it. He'd have those counselors eating out of his hand."

"What makes you think he's using?"

Katie pulled a baggie from her pocket. "How much is that?"

Barkley held the baggie up to a trickle of sunlight bleeding through a tiny window over the sink. "Quarter gram, maybe a half."

"I don't know what that is, Bark. I don't know what that is, but I can't have it in my house. Shit, I'm gonna start bawling, great."

There was a sound from somewhere. Katie cracked the door, pushing the hair back from her face and yelling down the hall, "What are you looking for?"

"Never mind," Tommy said. "I got it. Tell Bark I'll be there in a minute."

She nudged the door shut and returned to the stove, wiping at her eyes with the heel of her hand and reaching up into a cabinet for a can of whole tomatoes. She was wearing a long-sleeved Celtics shirt that rode up to reveal an ugly purple welt running along her arm just above the elbow. Barkley touched her wrist and turned the arm gently.

"What's that?"

She tugged herself free.

"Is he fucking hitting you?"

Katie lifted her chin, Irish heat baked into cracked eyes, two red spots marking her cheeks. "You know better."

"Do I?"

"We were arguing and he grabbed me. I bruise easy. Makes it look a lot worse than it is." She reached to adjust a burner on the stove, brushing her hip against his thigh. He sensed the pulse of her blood sync with his and remembered the feel of her flesh, the way she moved above him, her amazing hips and the small sounds she made as he rocked inside her and filled her. It'd be three years Christmas. They'd separated, her and Tommy, both of them confiding in Barkley, both convinced it was so fucking done. Not that it should have mattered, not that it did matter. She showed up at Barkley's apartment one night. The snow was falling, first of the year, perfect and white, making everything blurry and soft in a city known for none of that. She didn't want to talk about Tommy. Just a Christmas drink with a friend. He never saw it coming. If he had, he'd have run like a hound from hell. Not that he regretted it. That was the best part and by far the worst. He couldn't ever have Katie Dillon for his own. They both knew it even as they lay together in his bed, with the moonlight tiptoeing through the window and the snow falling in great drifts across the rooftops of Charlestown. And so every touch was a first, every kiss, their last. Hours slipped past in a moment and moments would have to last a lifetime. Six months later, she was back with Tommy. At his partner's insistence, Barkley met them for a drink at a bar near Fenway called Copperfield's. She hugged Barkley and said she was happy. But he could read her eyes and knew what was there and knew she was reading the same thing in his eyes. Meanwhile, Tommy watched both of them, tickled as all fuck cuz his life had been Scotch-taped back together and desperate to move on before anyone looked too close. And now this. The tiny-as-shit kitchen, her, Tommy in the back with the twins. The bag of dope.

"Who's he running with, Katie?"

"I dunno."

"Where's he getting his stuff?"

"That ain't hard. Walk a block in this neighborhood and

you'll find someone who'll sell you pretty much whatever you can dream up."

"You scared?"

Katie shook her head. "I told you. Tommy would never hurt me. Not for real."

"The twins?"

"Exception to the rule." She reached behind her back and picked up a curved knife from the counter. "He'd cut me for those two. Wouldn't think twice about you, either."

Tread in the hall. Katie put down the knife and slipped her hands to Barkley's hips, sliding past and kicking the door open as Tommy turned the corner.

"Something smells good." He lifted his nose to the air. "You sure we ain't got time, boss?"

Barkley shook his head. Tommy had his service weapon clipped to his belt. He pulled his faded leather jacket off a hook and gave Katie a kiss, goosing her as they broke their clinch.

"See, Bark, girl can still move. Am I driving?"

"I'll drive."

"Be careful," Katie said, turning back to her stove. The two cops rumbled down the hall and left.

—

Barkley's car had a half-dozen eggs splattered across the side panel and windows. Tommy wanted to roust the little pricks. Barkley told him to climb in.

"I'll get the cocksuckers," Tommy said as Barkley turned on his wipers and squirted fluid across the windshield.

"Forget it. Where we headed?"

"Left at the end of the block."

Barkley started to roll. He figured they'd start in the Zone, but Tommy was taking them deeper into the neighborhood.

"You going local on this?"

Tommy shrugged. He was a million miles away now, playing with the silver-and-turquoise watch on his wrist, staring out the window as ciphers slipped past. Names, faces, connections only he could see. "Left here."

Barkley hung the left. "I talked to the ME this morning."

"What'd that bitch have to say?"

Tommy actually liked Cat, but talking that way about women made him feel like a big man. Barkley didn't give a damn. All he wanted was an address.

"She was going on about the wound patterns on Fitzsimmons. Said there were two different types. The first was nonlethal, in the belly. Made by a knife like the one in the picture. And then there were the wounds that killed him. Three of 'em, all deep puncture wounds."

"How deep?"

"Ran the kid right through."

"Not with the knife?"

"ME says no way."

Tommy let that sit for a minute. "Does it really matter? One knife, another knife. I mean, who gives a fuck? We got the photo. Let's just grab this guy and call it a day. Right here."

Barkley pulled up to a single-story wooden shack painted pure black for some godforsaken reason only someone from Southie would understand. A Schlitz sign hung off a rusted piece of pipe; green neon tubes spelled out THE IRISH TAP in the only working window. Barkley nodded toward the front door. "What are we gonna find in here?"

"People talk, B. Even in Southie, people love to fucking talk."

Tommy popped his door and got out, then stuck his head back in. "Do me a favor."

"What's that?"

"When we get inside, order a beer and sit right in front. Fucking bartender will love it."

27

A COUPLE of smoke hounds were set up at the far end of the bar, fluorescent skin, yellow teeth, eyes like two sets of pissholes in the snow. One of them hacked into his sleeve and spit into a paper cup while the other rounded his mouth into an "O" and popped out a parade of smoke rings that floated through layers of runny light toward the ceiling where they joined the rest of the ghosts drinking in the rafters. Tommy touched Barkley on the shoulder and nodded to a booth at the back of the place. Two women were staring out of the gloom like a pair of feral cats. Tommy headed their way with a cigarette angled between his teeth and a fresh bottle of Bud. Barkley watched his partner go, then settled on a stool directly behind the taps. The snow-capped barkeep had skinny legs, no ass, and the swollen belly they gave out as the door prize for a lifetime of drinking. He poured Barkley a thin draft and reached up to turn on a TV slotted over the register.

The Eyewitness News update led with Harry Fitzsimmons's murder. What else? Three guys played pinball beside a window boarded up with cardboard Schlitz cases. Closer to the TV another threesome looked to be fresh off the job—arms, neck, and hair splattered in smears of whitewash. Barkley had never met a painter who wasn't a drunk and was guessing this crew to be no different. The detective winced inwardly as his face popped up on the TV, assuring the city that the Boston PD was on the job and the unidentified assailant, a young black male, would be apprehended soon enough.

One of the painters, the thickest of the bunch, pointed at Barkley's face on the screen. "We lose one monkey, we send another one out to look for it. What the fuck?"

The painter had salt-and-pepper hair and a fox face that creased into a smile as he lifted a bottle of beer to his lips and slitted his eyes toward Barkley. His pal snickered nervously beside him while the third guy, by far the youngest of the crew, slinked off to the jukebox.

"What do you think, Willie?" Salt and Pepper yelled. "Hey, Willie, whaddaya think?"

The old bartender took his time walking back toward the painters, wiping the counter with a rag as he went. "Why don't you take your business down the street?"

"You barring me?"

"I didn't say that."

"Then what?"

The barkeep didn't need a scrape in his joint, especially not with a Boston cop. "You boys have had enough. Go home and get some dinner."

Salt and Pepper ignored him, draining a shot that was sitting on the bar, then heading over to the jukebox where the youngster was picking out some tunes. Barkley glanced toward the back. Tommy was huddled up with the women. Overhead the speakers cranked out the Stones' "Monkey Man"—Nicky Hopkins on piano, Keith on the slide. Salt and Pepper put his bottle of beer to his lips and offered up his best Jagger, lip-synching about a fleabit peanut monkey and again slipping his eyes toward the big, black Boston cop.

In an earlier life, Barkley would have already been picking bits of the guy's teeth out of his knuckles. Fucking maturity. Sometimes it really sucked. He threw down a five and got up to go. Didn't even get halfway to the front door.

"You know who this is?" Salt and Pepper grabbed his baby-faced drinking buddy by the back of the shirt like he was a fish he'd just pulled out of the surf at Castle Island.

"Afraid not." Barkley cracked a hard grin and kept moving toward the door.

"This here's Billy Randall."

Barkley knew the name. Six months ago, Randall had been standing next to the guy who'd attacked a black man with an American flag during an antibusing rally at Government Center. A photographer from the *Herald* caught the moment. Two days later, it was national news.

"That ain't Randall," Barkley said, taking a step closer and brushing the gun on his hip with the tips of his fingers.

"He was there, though." Salt and Pepper shifted his story just as easy as that cuz that's how liars worked, especially when they were bigots. "Stood right behind Randall. Didn't you, Timmer?"

Timmer nodded and looked like he wanted nothing better than to crawl back to his barstool and be left the fuck alone. Barkley could have told Timmer what was gonna happen if he stayed in Southie. He'd always be the kid who was standing behind the kid who was standing next to the kid who went after the smoke with the American flag and got his face on the cover of the *Herald*,

Newsweek, and who the fuck knows what else. He'd never have to buy another beer in the neighborhood. And he'd never have a life beyond it.

"Sorry, boys, I don't have the time for your happy horseshit today. Now, go back to the bar and sit the fuck down before I lose my patience."

Barkley turned and headed for the door. His fingers had just brushed the curve of the knob when someone's head hit something hard and flat. Barkley knew it wasn't gonna be good and turned anyway. Tommy had been listening. Fuck, yeah, he'd been listening. And now he had Salt and Pepper pegged up against a wooden post that held up one end of the sorry-ass, saggy-ass bar. Tommy had a hand gripped around Salt and Pepper's fleshy throat. In the other hand, Tommy held a small, sharp blade that was pressed against Salt and Pepper's cheek.

"This one bothering you, B?"

"Forget it, Tommy."

Barkley's partner pressed the knife in, drawing a line of bright blood. "I don't *fucking* think so."

The three guys from the pinball machine came up behind Tommy. Two of them had bottles in their hands. The bartender pulled a billy club from underneath the taps. Barkley drew his gun.

"Tommy?" Barkley could see the crazy circling in his partner's eyes. "Not worth it, bud."

Tommy moved his knife from the cheek to just inside the left nostril. Salt and Pepper whimpered a little in the back of his throat. No one else moved.

"I go inch and a half and you never breathe out of this side again. Six months of rehab, plastic surgery, and you look like a fucking freak the rest of your life. Trust me, brother."

"Tommy."

"I know this guy, B. Fucking puke always running his mouth."

Maybe Tommy knew the guy. Maybe he knew his brother. Or his cousin. Or maybe Tommy bumped into him once at the grocery store. Didn't matter cuz no one manufactured rage like Tommy. He adjusted the knife.

"This here's an inch. You could live with this one. Still need surgery, but you could live with it. Might even help your looks. What do you think, Bark? Could you see this boy sucking some cock up the Brompton?" Tommy leaned close and dropped his voice. "That there's a *Boston* cop, motherfucker. And my partner. You know what that means?"

Salt and Pepper had lifted his chin as high as it would go. Anything to get away from Tommy's knife. "I understand."

"You understand what?"

"I understand, sir."

Barkley holstered his weapon and moved closer, kicking at a couple of plastic cups on the floor.

"Fucking cunts," Tommy said.

Barkley touched the knot of muscle that was his partner's shoulder. Tommy slowly withdrew the knife. Salt and Pepper came down off his tiptoes. The bartender dropped his club. Everyone exhaled. Quicker than the grin of a deformed freak show walking the streets of Southie with a scar that told everyone everything they needed to know, Tommy flicked the blade and laid open Salt and Pepper's nose. Blood geysered as the painter screamed and tried to hold his face together. Tommy snapped the knife shut and slid it back in his pocket. Barkley's gun was out again, covering their exit. Five minutes later, they were driving through a warren of side streets. Tommy had his

elbow out the window, smoking a menthol cigarette and enjoying the cold air.

"No one's gonna say shit, B."

"Yeah?"

"Took a quarter inch. Half, tops. I call it the Chinatown cut."
Tommy laughed at his joke and streamed smoke out the window.

"Not funny, Tommy."

"Seriously, two, three stitches, tiny little scar, no big deal.
What the fuck, man's calling you a monkey. I'm supposed to sit
there and take that?"

"We better not get a call."

"What did I tell ya? Ain't gonna be no call. Now, listen, I got
a line on our boy."

Barkley bumped through an intersection just as the light
went red. "Go ahead."

"Word is he's headed to the Bury."

"Who we getting this from?"

"Couple of broads I know buy from him."

"They sure?"

"They'd already heard rumors this guy was good for it."

"No shit."

"Price is a bottom-feeder. No one wants to help him. No
one likes seeing the Harvard kid dead. Bad for business, bad all
around."

"So you got an address?"

Tommy launched his cigarette butt with a flick of his finger
and rolled up the window. "I told you he's headed to the Bury.
One of the girls is gonna call with an address. Hang a louie."

Barkley took the left and two rights. They pulled up in front
of Tommy's three-decker.

"Your source calling you at home?"

"Why not? You wanna come in and wait?"

"Nah, I gotta hit it. What time's the call coming in?"

"If it's happening tonight, it'll be in the next hour or so. Otherwise, tomorrow. Where can I get hold of you?"

"Try the station. If I'm not there, leave a message."

Tommy started to get out of the car and stopped. "I know what Katie told you."

"How's that?"

"I know what she told you in the kitchen."

Barkley pulled the bag of coke from his pocket and dropped it on the dashboard. "Says she found it in the house."

"And what do you say?"

"What do I say? I say, 'What the fuck?'"

"That it?"

"You know how it works. One of us got a problem, we deal with it. No one else. Just us."

Tommy picked up the baggie, holding it between a thumb and forefinger. "I got a bunch more inside."

"Fucking great."

"Signed 'em out of Evidence last week. Cleared it with the captain and everything."

"Why don't I know?"

"Told him you did. Figured I'd catch you up later."

Barkley believed him. The story could be checked easy enough so what was the point in lying?

"Why you needing a bunch of blow, Tommy?"

"Sweetens the pot. Some of these lowlifes, you give 'em a toot and they're your best pal. Start talking and don't know when to stop."

"I never seen anyone cop to a homicide cuz he got fixed up with a couple lines of blow."

"Maybe it ain't about a homicide."

Barkley killed the engine and turned so he was facing his partner. "Let me guess. This is the other thing you wanted to talk about before."

Tommy nodded, eyes roaming around the car, searching for someplace safe to land. Barkley waited.

"Talking product, B. High-grade shit. Trunks full of it."

"And how'd you get hooked into that?"

"I'm an ex-junkie. I know this fucking world."

"Which is why you're the last person who should be working it."

Tommy offered up his best *Is what it fucking is* look. Barkley sighed and massaged his temple with the side of his thumb. "Who else knows about it?"

"No one knows shit. We clear the Harvard thing, then I need another week or so. After that, I bring you in and we decide what to do."

"We got options?"

"This is forever money, B." Tommy held up a hand. "Listen first. I'm not saying you need to be bent or nothing like that. In fact, we make the fucking bust. But maybe we think about breaking off a piece. Just this once. Stash the money somewhere for a couple of years, then pack it in. Early retirement, place in Florida, California, big-ass boat, some fucking thing."

"Tommy, the Irish sailor."

Dillon laughed like hell. "Can't you see it? Listen, I don't wanna talk about this now. Not with the Harvard kid and everything. Just think about it. And if it's no, it's no. We move on. Not a problem. But think about it. Okay?"

What choice did he have? Tommy was Tommy was Tommy. Hopefully he didn't get himself killed in the process. And then there was the money. Barkley would be lying if he said he wasn't wondering how much money his partner thought qualified as "forever."

"How'd you know Katie told me about the baggie?"

"When I came back into the kitchen, there was something between the two of you. Mostly her, but you were acting a little funny. That's right, B, even you give it away, so fucking watch it." Tommy grinned that easy, crazy, spinning Tommy grin. "Just kidding. I was short a bag. She seen one I must have left out and grabbed it. All made sense then."

Barkley grunted and turned over the engine.

"We good?" Tommy said.

"Next time, fucking tell me. And tell your wife. She's worried sick."

"Will do. And we talk about the other thing later?"

"We'll talk."

Tommy got out of the car and stuck his head back in. "You don't wanna come in? Homemade spaghetti and meatballs."

"Rain check. And talk to your wife."

Tommy slammed the door and banged on the roof as the car pulled away. Barkley drove until he found the expressway and jumped on. The pint of Jack he kept in the glovie was out and sitting against his thigh. By the time he circled back to the station, he'd knocked back an inch and a half and Tommy had left his message. No address on Price tonight. Tomorrow, for sure. Probably just as well.

Cat McShane's preliminary autopsy report sat on the corner of his desk. Barkley tucked it under his arm and headed out again. There was a dive called Early's where no one knew he was a cop and no one cared he was black. He walked the five blocks and planted himself on a stool, the ghosts he was trying so hard to ignore settling all around. One of them grinned just like Tommy and thudded a sack full of coins on the bar.

"Forever money," he said.

Barkley toasted the phantom motherfucker with a water glass full of whiskey and drained it.

28

CAT McSHANE kept herself busy counting ceiling tiles. When she finished with those, she started on the slats in the venetian blinds. She was halfway down the second window when the door opened and Boston City Hospital's assistant superintendent walked in. Ruth Davis was thirty years older than Cat and everything about her seemed lovely. Straight spine, perfect posture, gray hair cut in fashionable layers, and a designer suit that hugged her exceedingly neat frame. Davis didn't say a word, keeping her shoulders square to Cat as she ran a finger along the edge of her desk, then found the wall and finally her chair. It was only after she was seated that Cat realized the woman was blind. Or as good as.

"Cataracts." Davis blinked a pair of milky whites from behind silver-rimmed glasses.

"How bad?"

"Left one's ninety percent gone. Other's a little better. They've tried a half-dozen procedures, but it's at the end now."

"I'm sorry."

"I can still see shapes, which is probably more than I deserve. Ruth Davis, by the way." The woman didn't offer her hand.

"Cat McShane."

"I've heard good things."

"Thanks."

"My fault for not arranging something sooner."

"Please, we're all busy."

"Yes, but we're both women. And there aren't a lot of us in Boston's medical community. At least not in jobs where we can make a difference."

She was right, of course. Cat knew her position as medical examiner came with a larger set of responsibilities. It was just that the whole thing was still new and she needed to get her own house in order before thinking about the bigger picture. Ruth Davis wasn't interested in excuses. Women from her generation typically weren't.

"My assistant says you wanted information on a case."

"Daniel Fitzsimmons."

Davis opened a drawer to her left and pulled out a file. "I usually have a member of my staff go through any paperwork and get me up to speed."

"Usually?"

"It wasn't necessary here." Davis nudged the file across the desk. It was thick enough, although perhaps not quite as thick as Cat expected.

"Were you one of Daniel's doctors?"

Davis shook her head. "I'm an internist. Was. They're putting me out to pasture at the end of the year, although really it happened a long time ago." She smiled vaguely. "I remember Daniel well enough. Just a slip of a thing. Looked so small in that big bed."

"Do you recall anything unusual about the case?"

"He was eight years old, had suffered some sort of head trauma as the result of the car accident, was initially conscious and lapsed into a coma on the way to the hospital."

"Who was his doctor?"

A small twitch ticked the corner of Davis's mouth. "George Peters. Head of neurology here for decades. One of the best."

"I assume he's no longer on staff?"

"Passed away five years ago. May I ask why all the interest?"

"Daniel's involved in a criminal case. He's not implicated, but he has been subjected to a certain amount of emotional trauma."

"Are you talking about his brother?"

"You knew Harry Fitzsimmons?"

"He was Daniel's only visitor during his time here. Three times a week he'd show up and sit at the foot of the bed. Stay for hours at a time. I heard about his death on the news. Such a waste."

"Yes."

"I guess I'm still not clear on how Daniel's time here might fit in?"

"I'm not sure either. The detective working the case is a friend and asked me to take a look."

"I see."

"Without revealing too much, I think the police are concerned the trauma of Harry's death might somehow provoke a reaction in Daniel. A little strange, I know."

"Lots of strange in the world. And lots of strange in Daniel's time here."

"How so?"

Davis peeled back her lips, revealing long teeth and a glimpse of the predator the woman must have once been. "My door's closed?"

Cat glanced behind her. "Yes."

"Good. There's no record of what I'm about to tell you anywhere so don't bother looking. And don't bother asking anyone here about it. Agreed?"

"Sure."

"George Peters and I were close. Probably not hard to tell, right?"

"I saw a twitch."

"Really?"

"It was either hate or love. I tend to root for the latter."

"He was married, but I was still young enough up here." Davis tapped her temple with a skinny finger. "Bottom line is I didn't give a damn."

"And now?"

"Even less. If it's real, you'll never regret it. And will pay any price. But who wants to hear about an old lady's love life?"

"I don't mind."

"Yeah, right. George was a talent. He had an unerring instinct when it came to diagnosis and an extraordinary sense of compassion for his patients. Daniel's case troubled him like few others."

"How so?"

Davis raised her chin a fraction and Cat caught a brief glimpse of a pair of gray irises swimming furiously beneath the skim of white. "What you'll find in the file is a fairly standard recitation of Daniel's admission, an initial examination, and subsequent patient assessment."

"And?"

"George could never pinpoint the actual nature of Daniel's

head injury. He ordered x-rays and conducted periodic brain scans during the entire time the boy was unconscious. If you look through the data, you'll find low-level brain activity typically associated with a coma."

"But?"

"Let's take a walk." Davis got up quickly, slipping into a black coat that hung on a hook behind her. She took four measured strides to the door and waited for Cat to open it. Then she touched Cat's sleeve and pointed to an elevator almost directly across the hall.

"Seventh floor."

Neither woman spoke as the elevator climbed. On the seventh floor, Ruth directed Cat to an empty room overlooking an alley. The bed had been stripped of its linens and the room smelled of dust and death.

"This was Daniel's room," Davis said. "You see the door on the far side of the bed? It leads to the roof."

"The roof?"

"I'll explain when we get there."

Cat took them through the door and up a run of rough metal steps. The roof was flat and covered in a dull sheen of tar that had cracked and webbed in a dozen different directions. Cat jammed her hands in the pockets of her trench coat. "Why are we up here, Ruth?"

"Walk me over to the edge."

Cat felt a twist in her gut but did as the woman asked. The facade of the building was ancient. Cat touched a brick with her foot and watched it crumble, loose chunks tumbling into the alley below. Davis's hand slipped to the small of Cat's back, grabbing at the belt on her coat.

"Watch it."

The old woman had a strong grip and it was all Cat could do to break free, nearly pitching herself over the edge in the process. She circled to her left, keeping Davis at arm's length.

"Nervous, Ms. McShane?"

"Should I be?"

"You're wondering what was missing from Daniel's file."

"If you want to tell me something, that's great. If not . . ."

"The brain scans. The real ones. They're not in there."

"Why?"

Davis raised one hand in front of her face and began to surf it up and down. "Daniel's brain was fluctuating wildly the entire time he was here. High-level activity for a period of time, subsiding to levels you'd expect to find in someone who was comatose, then more spikes. George finally figured out the pattern. Three hours on, six off. Over and over and over again."

"What did Peters think?"

"This was 1968, remember."

"So what?"

"It was the first time I'd ever heard anyone use the term 'computer.' George explained how the machines processed information at amazing rates. Talked about 'work cycles' and 'batch processing.' Said that's what Daniel appeared to be doing. As you can probably tell, none of it made any sense to me."

"How was it Daniel remained unconscious if his brain was so active?"

"George never figured that out. He tried several times to rouse Daniel during the active cycles but got nowhere. Then one day we walked into the room and the boy was sitting up in bed, wide awake, looking for his breakfast."

"And Peters never included any of this in the boy's history?"

"He thought Daniel might be studied if the medical community got hold of the scans. Made out to be a freak show. My overall feeling was he was protecting Daniel. Can't be sure, but that would have been George."

"I assume no one ever told Daniel about the scans?"

"The boy hardly spoke. And when he did, he could only recall bits and pieces of the accident and, of course, nothing from his time in the coma. We left it that way."

"Thanks, Ruth. I'm not sure any of this is relevant to Harry's death, but I appreciate it." Cat touched the old woman at the elbow, turning her toward the door and the stairs feeding down into the building.

"I didn't say we were done."

"No?"

"Daniel woke up on the morning of March first, 1969. He was discharged four days later. The morning of March fifth. Harry picked him up."

"All right."

"Forty minutes after they left, a security guard found one of our attendants in the alley below. He jumped off this roof, from just about the spot where you're standing."

Cat couldn't help but peek again. The air between the buildings was swirling and dark and full of echoes. Ruth Davis's voice lived in her ear.

"The attendant's name was Lawrence Rosen. He'd never actually been part of the team that worked on Daniel's case, but George had his suspicions."

"Are you saying this guy might have been bothering Daniel?"

"After Rosen's death, a couple of employees came to George and claimed Rosen used to visit Daniel at night. George had examined Daniel before his discharge. There was no obvious evidence of molestation or other physical contact, but the staff members were insistent. They said Rosen was obsessed with the boy."

"What about the morning Rosen jumped?"

"Best we could tell, Rosen was last seen on the seventh floor, near Daniel's room, roughly an hour before Daniel was discharged."

"Was Daniel in his room?"

"For about a half hour, yes."

"So the two could have been alone, in a room with a door that led to this roof?"

"Unlikely, but possible."

"Why unlikely?"

"There was a steady stream of people coming in and out that morning. Daniel had been here six months so there was a lot of do. A lot of folks involved."

"Did anyone see Rosen alive after Daniel was discharged?"

Davis shook her head. "The next time anyone saw him, Rosen was dead in the alley. George was in charge of the hospital's inquiry and made sure the death was classified as a suicide. Then we forgot about the whole thing."

"Why tell me?"

"I don't know. I guess I thought if there was a chance Daniel was involved in another death . . ."

"The police don't think he killed Harry."

"I'm glad to hear it."

"Did you really think that was a possibility?"

"As I said, I hardly knew Daniel. A handful of conversations before he was discharged."

"And yet you seem afraid of him."

"Do I?"

"Do you think he killed Rosen?"

"Did he come up onto the roof with Rosen and push him off? No."

"Then what?"

"Have you ever met Daniel?"

"No."

"George thought he might possess the ability to influence people, affect their behavior. Perhaps even unwittingly."

"How?"

"I don't know. By talking to them, thinking about them. George was never clear."

"So you're saying Daniel walked your attendant off this roof without ever leaving his bed?"

"You don't believe it?"

"Of course not. Do you?"

"There was something there. Something heavy . . ."

"Heavy?"

"When Daniel looked at you, really focused, there was a heaviness inside your skull. I remember it quite distinctly, almost like you were falling asleep or being pulled into a rip current, one that was very fast and very deep." Davis tipped her face up again, raising blind eyes to a broken sky. "I'm sorry. It all sounds strange, I know."

"I appreciate your taking the time."

"Please remember I'll deny any of this to the police. Or anyone else, for that matter."

"Daniel's not a suspect."

"Good. I'm cold. Let's go downstairs and find some lunch."

Ruth Davis turned on her heel and walked directly to the

door that led downstairs. Maybe she'd been able to see the whole time. Maybe she was familiar with the route. Maybe she was just guessing. Fifteen minutes later, the two women were being shown to a table at Maison Robert. Cat excused herself and found a pay phone. She dropped in some coins and dialed a number.

29

BARKLEY SWIPED at the phone, knocking the entire thing off his nightstand. Whoever had called was now talking a blue streak to the bedroom rug. Barkley uncoiled an arm, feeling along the floor until he found the receiver and lifted it to his ear.

"Yeah."

The talker had been replaced by a dial tone. Good riddance. Barkley replaced the receiver and felt around again until he located a box of Chinese takeout. He'd closed Early's, then gone to an all-night place in Cambridge called Aku Aku and gotten his regular, 13-A with extra pork strips and hot mustard. Barkley chewed on a cold egg roll as he trudged down the hallway. In the kitchen he found a couple trays of ice and dumped them into a sink full of water. Barkley buried his head in the basin, letting the cold burn his brain for a full minute before resurfacing like an orca, blowing water and groping for a towel. He sat at the kitchen table and dripped, consoling himself with the idea he didn't get drunk very often. All the alkies he'd ever known had told themselves that on their way to a lifetime of bad coffee in Styrofoam cups and AA meetings with a bunch of other miserable, dried-out motherfuckers counting their dubious blessings while inwardly jonesing for one more run at a hip flask full of the good old days. Barkley put on the kettle and made himself a cup of instant, letting the hot black liquid sear his throat and water his eyes.

The phone rang again. Jesus H. Christ. He picked up in the hall. It was Charlie Herbert. According to Ma Bell, the phone in Nick Toney's studio had been out for the past ten days. And yes, there was a pay phone in the hall two floors below. The photographer was telling the truth. Barkley wasn't surprised. He thanked Herbert and tried to hang up, but the uniform wasn't done. It was past noon and people at the station were wondering where Barkley and his partner might be. Barkley carefully explained they were working a murder and people should go fuck themselves. Herbert was going on about the captain and the media when Barkley cut the line, leaving the receiver off the hook.

He poured himself a second cup of coffee and settled in the living room with Cat McShane's autopsy report. Tucked inside the front cover was a photo of the puncture wounds that killed Harry Fitzsimmons. There were three of them on the left side of the football player's chest. A second photo showed a close-up of the two exit wounds in his back. Cat wasn't kidding. The kid had been put on a spit and gutted. Barkley took a sip of coffee. He kind of liked working hungover. Calmed his brain. Next he'd be wanting a slug of rum with his morning shower. Barkley gave the report a quick skim. The punctures that had killed Fitzsimmons entered his body at a slightly downward angle, indicating the killer was most likely standing over his victim. Barkley thought about that for a minute, the killer taking down Fitzsimmons with a knife to the belly, then pulling out a second weapon to finish him. Didn't make a ton of sense, but murders rarely did.

He read for another hour, scribbling thoughts in one of his black notebooks as he went. When he was done, he arranged the autopsy report and notebook on a table by the front door where they'd be easy to find. If anyone wanted to follow up, more power to them.

In the kitchen he sat at the table and stared at his boots and coat. He could hear the whispers coming from his fire escape and knew this would be the day. He could see the anchor rods shearing, the mass of bars and bolts shivering and creaking in the breeze, then slowly pulling away from the building. He was falling now, no present, no future, the past sloughing off like old skin. It would happen today. His last ride. About fucking time, too.

He pulled on the boots and coat and stepped out, hearing the brittle metal groan and speak and sing its seduction. He found his spot on the windowsill and sat there, picking up his potting soil for the last time, sinking his thumb through the hard crust and finding soft earth below. Barkley pulled out his smokes and lit up. It was like his vision had been enhanced, allowing him to see all the seams in the grated floor, silent fractures in the iron, how the whole thing hung together, how it would all come apart. He was in Tommy's fairy ring now. And there was no getting out. Who would ever want to?

Barkley took a pull on his cigarette and blew out a fine blue haze. She moved through it like an ocean tide, taking no form he could later recall, sitting close enough so he could smell the powdered scent of jasmine. It was the woman from Hom's. Of course it was. She gestured for a cigarette and lit up, the red enamel of her ring winking and flashing as years slipped past and decades followed. Barkley realized he could see right through her and watched smoke run like a river down her throat and swirl in her chest. Then she exhaled, tendrils of pure light, crimson and yellow and orange and green, curling and blooming with flowers, wrapping around the bars of the fire escape, creeping up the side of the building and rushing toward the pavement below. The woman flicked her cigarette into the ether and glanced at Barkley with her liquid eyes. No concussion this time. No uncovering. She was simply here, sitting with him in the bottom of the hole he'd dug for himself, holding time as she held his hand, telling him it was every bit as real as unreal and that if he dared to believe, dared to let go, the soul he grieved for every moment of every day would be his and he'd be hers. They'd be nothing. And so much more. But only if. And then the woman was gone. And Barkley was alone again, in the cold on the fire escape, listening to the wind sing and the iron creak.

He stepped back through the window to find the hammer from that day twelve years ago sitting on the kitchen table. Alongside it were a half-dozen silver nails. Barkley would have sworn the hammer hadn't been there before, but who was present to listen? Who was present to grieve? So he took his time, driving fresh nails into old wood, feeling each bite and then testing to make sure the window in his pantry was pegged shut. Fuck the landlord. And fuck the fire hazard, too.

He took a long shower, scrubbing himself with soap and letting the scurf slick off his body and down the drain. He'd left his car downtown because of the drink, so it was the Orange Line today. The train arrived on a rush of warm wind and grease. He stood near the door, hanging on to a strap and turning his mind again to the case because what else was there now? Maybe Tommy had called in with an address for Walter Price. Barkley hoped so. Like any good homicide detective, he didn't want to dig any deeper than he had to. But there were things in the case that bothered him—small things, big things, things with roots. Barkley knew all about roots. And how they could strangle the life out of a man.

30

THE FLECKED and formless beast stood in the doorway of a skin show, sloping slabs for shoulders and a bull neck, fleshed nose split in the middle and small, pink eyes needling down the block. She was leaning against a lamppost, tall and gawky, young, potent without knowing it. She wore a short jacket that shined. Under it, a sheer white dress with Daffy Duck and Tweety Bird printed all over in bright blossoms of color. The girl scuffed her shoe on the pavement and tossed her head. The wind shifted and the beast scented blood. He lifted a pinch of cigarette to his lips, then tossed the butt into the gutter and stepped out of the doorway. They talked for less than a minute, the girl pulling away once before settling, the man slipping a hand to the small of her back and gesturing for her to go first.

Barkley watched as they crossed the street and disappeared into the Brompton Arms. Like most things in the Combat Zone, the Brompton would be whatever you wanted it to be. A mouse of a man worked a small desk in the lobby, renting rooms on the first two floors by the half hour. The middle floors were let month to month, mostly to girls and pimps. The top floor was where the photographer Toney had his studio. Barkley got out of his car, hard shoes scratching as he followed the couple up the Brompton's short run of steps. He thought about going inside but settled for copying down the names on a row of doorbells set into a panel by the front door. Then he checked his watch and walked back to the street.

Next door to the Brompton, someone had shoehorned in a greasy Greek joint called Five Faces. Barkley ordered a Coke from a young woman with a lazy eye. He was the only customer in the place and watched while a smooth-skinned man with thin fingers and a bent nose worked a long knife over a shank of lamb.

"Gyros."

He grinned and offered a curling piece to Barkley, who took a pass. The counterman shrugged and popped the lamb in his mouth, then set about fixing chunks of broiled meat onto metal skewers. The place smelled like fried onions with more than a hint of decaying rat. Barkley figured they had one or two fat ones caught in a trap somewhere and was glad he'd passed on the food.

He took a booth by the window, sipping his soft drink and nursing a mild hangover while he flipped through a stack of photos. There'd been no word from Tommy. Barkley had called the house, but no one picked up. He'd thought about heading over but didn't see the point. His partner said he'd turn up an address; Barkley just needed to give him some leash. Besides, there were enough loose ends that needed tying up. He looked out the window as Neil Prescott got out of a cab. The kid from Harvard hustled across the street.

"Thanks for coming down."

"No problem." Prescott took a seat across from the detective. He was bundled up in a pearl gray topcoat with a cashmere scarf and a blue Oxford button-down underneath. Barkley didn't think he'd ever seen anyone who looked so young.

"You want a Coke? Something to eat?"

Prescott shook his head and kept his hands clasped tightly on the table. Barkley let him sit. He'd taken statements from Prescott and his buddy, Jesus Sanchez, on the night Harry Fitzsimmons was murdered. Barkley usually liked to do follow-ups at the station, but he wanted to get another look at the block and Prescott seemed okay with meeting here.

"Bother you being back?"

Prescott shrugged. Why should it bother him?

"Ever been down here before that night?"

"First and last."

"I bet." Barkley pulled out a notebook. "Mind if I take notes?"

"Go ahead."

Barkley turned to a fresh page and wrote down the time and date. "We wanted to meet with Sanchez as well, but I couldn't get hold of him."

"Zeus? He lives in Kirkland."

Barkley wrote down the name. "Is that a dorm?"

"We call them houses, but, yeah, same thing. I stopped in before I came down here, but he wasn't around."

"Any idea where he might be?"

Another shrug. "A couple of guys saw him around noon. Said he might have taken off."

"Taken off?"

"He was pretty shook up. We both were. Thanksgiving break's coming up, so he might have cut out early."

"You think he headed home?"

"Zeus is from Hyde Park. You could check. Knowing Zeus, he might have just gotten in his car and drove."

Barkley made a couple more notes. "Okay."

"He wouldn't have left if he thought you still needed him."

"Sure."

"Zeus was tight with Harry. A lot closer than me."

"How you doing with everything?"

"I'm fine. Well, as fine as . . . whatever. You know what, Detective, I'd just like to get this over with."

One buddy dead. Another, out of pocket. Barkley couldn't blame him.

"Harry lived with you?"

"I told you guys. He rented out the other bedroom. Couple blocks from campus."

"Did you know his little brother, Daniel?"

"Saw him once or twice. He was bunking in with Harry. I think he had a sleeping bag or something on the floor."

"Ever talk to him?"

"Like I said, Harry and I didn't hang out much. The night in the Zone was Zeus's idea. Said it was part of playing football at Harvard."

Barkley had already heard about the football players' ideas on team building and didn't really give a shit. "Daniel still living at the apartment?"

"He moved out last week. Harry wasn't happy about it, but I guess the kid found another place to stay."

"Any idea where he's living now?"

Prescott shook his head. Barkley scribbled a little more. "Okay if I send some officers over to look through Harry's stuff?"

"You won't find anything."

"Why do you say that?"

"Harry was a straight shooter. Didn't drink, smoke, chase women. He only went with us cuz Zeus pushed it."

"Part of the team-bonding thing?"

"He was big on that stuff. Probably why he took off after Zeus. Harry would have figured it was the right thing to do."

Barkley flipped his notebook shut. "Mind if we take a walk?"

"I heard on the radio you guys have a suspect?"

"We have someone we need to speak with."

"How so fast?"

Barkley shrugged. "People down here like to rat each other out. Keeps us in business."

The kid nodded like he knew, and Barkley let him pretend. "Ready?"

Darkness was dropping over the Combat Zone, the seedy blocks along Washington transformed into a valley of blinking sin. Barkley and Prescott walked together, past hard-core bookstores and strip-bar sleaze, rap booths that smelled like latex and jerk-off peep shows, triple-feature movies with titles like *Spiked Heels and Black Tights*, *The Depraved*, and *Flesh Gordon*. Barkley stopped outside the Pilgrim Theater. The front door creaked open, letting out a waft of boozy music and a thin black man who was a dead ringer for Diana Ross. He gave Barkley a glance before drifting across the street, where he leaned against a building and dug a spiked heel into the wall.

"That a guy?" Prescott said.

"Does it matter? Now, where, exactly, was your car parked?"

"Right about here."

"You sure?"

"I remember seeing the pizza joint." Prescott pointed in the general direction of King of Pizza.

"And the woman who grabbed your buddy's wallet?"

Prescott pointed. "Came from over there."

"Where exactly?"

"I don't know."

"You didn't get a good look at her?"

"No."

"But she walked right past you?"

"She must have. Look, there were a lot of people floating by, a lot of scenery, you know?"

"I understand. It would just help if we could find the girl."

"Zeus said she had blond hair. Came in quick, grabbed the wallet, and ran."

"Is that how you remember it?"

"All I know is there was a commotion, Zeus yelling and then he was gone. Harry told me to stay with the car and took off after him."

"I ask cuz usually the girls will stop and talk for a while. It's only if they see no one in the car is buying that one of them might try for a wallet."

"All I can tell you is what I saw."

"Sanchez. He's a running back?"

"I'm a running back. Zeus is an offensive lineman."

"Not too fast, huh?"

"Excuse me?"

"I was just thinking a football player should be able to run down a working girl. On top of everything else, she's probably in heels. Know what I'm saying?"

"Zeus isn't real quick. And if she was gonna lift a wallet, she probably wasn't wearing heels, right?"

Barkley winked and shot Prescott with his index finger. "Fucking Harvard education. Come on."

They walked back down Washington and stopped at the corner of LaGrange, a half block from the alley where Harry Fitzsimmons was killed.

"Sanchez and Harry ran down here?"

"Yeah."

"And the next time you saw them was when?"

"Not until Zeus came back down the street. Then we heard the yelling."

Barkley pointed his chin toward the alley. "Mind if we take a peek?"

"Why?"

"I just want to see the layout again. Helps me sometimes."

"I'd prefer not to. I mean, I will if you really think it's important . . ."

"Forget it. We've got more than enough for now." Barkley stuck out his hand and the two men shook.

"Can I ask you something?" Prescott said.

"Go ahead."

"No one ever told us how he died."

"Harry was stabbed."

"I know, but . . ."

"You wanna know if he suffered?"

"I guess, yeah."

Barkley shook his head and lied. "ME says it was quick."

Prescott nodded but didn't say anything.

"You need a lift?"

"I'm good."

"Had your fill of cops, huh?"

"Something like that."

"I don't blame you. Enjoy the break."

Barkley watched the Harvard kid walk off. Then he un-snapped the strap on his holster and started down LaGrange. Someone was tucked behind a collection of trash cans pushed up against the side of the Brompton Arms. Whoever it was had been watching and listening to every drop of his conversation with Prescott. Barkley cleared the cans and pivoted, pinning the eavesdropper up against the building.

"Fuck, man, that hurts."

"It's supposed to hurt." Barkley leaned against one of the cans until a ninety-pound Asian kid popped out the other side. He was wearing white painter's pants, a jean jacket, and high-top red Cons with one of the soles pulled away from the bottom so his sock was peeking through. Barkley waited until he stopped rolling and planted a shoe on his chest.

"You wanna tell me why you're so interested in police business?"

"Come on, man. Get off me. Police brutality, police brutality."

The cries were met with a collective yawn from the Zone. Barkley removed his foot and helped the kid up.

"What's your name?"

"Kenny Soo." The kid pointed to a wooden box, its contents spilled out across the narrow street. "You need a shine?"

"I need you to tell me why you're so interested in my conversations."

"I was here the night of the murder. Saw it all."

"You saw what?"

Kenny Soo's eyes danced. He thought he had Barkley hooked and maybe he did.

"I work the corner." Soo pointed vaguely. "See everyone come and go. Everyone."

"Tell me what you saw."

"Girls. They come out before the night shows start. Get their heels polished."

Barkley hadn't thought about that. Now that he did, it made sense. Soo dropped his eyes to Barkley's thirty-dollar Florsheims.

"I did them this morning," Barkley said.

"You need it bad, boss."

"Next time. Who else do you see out here?"

"Johns, pimps." Soo tapped his head with his finger. "Crazy people."

"Bet you see plenty of that."

"Plenty." A thin bruise ran along Soo's jawline, collecting in various shades of purple and yellow under his left eye and filling the white around the iris with bright red blood.

"Who beat you up, Kenny?"

"Asshole pimp. A girl I know gonna give him the drip."

"Good for you."

Soo smiled clean and white and Barkley thought he might very well grow up to be a vicious little fuck. Smart, too. Barkley pulled out his photos.

"You wanna help?"

Soo rubbed his thumb and forefinger together.

Barkley chuckled. "Come here." He found an empty doorway and laid out his pictures. Soo squatted with his elbows on his knees and his chin in his palms.

"Smoke?" Soo held out his hand, two fingers extended in a twitch. Barkley lit a cigarette and gave it to him. The kid smoked while he studied.

"You recognize anyone?"

Soo looked up, neon glitter reflecting off the sharp angles of his face. "How much?"

Barkley toed one of the photos. "Tell me what you know?"

"I was a block away when the murder happened." Soo pointed at the picture of Harry Fitzsimmons taken from Harvard's freshman face book.

"You saw him?"

"I'm on the street all day, boss. All night. Remember lots of faces."

"And you saw him?"

"He and his pals were in the Naked i."

"His pals?"

"These two." Kenny touched photos of Sanchez and Prescott. "Big man on campus, just another dick down here. Ha, ha. They were drunk, I think. Which one's dead?"

Barkley nudged Harry's photo. Kenny took a final suck on his cigarette and flicked the butt away, letting smoke drift from both nostrils. "Too bad." If Neil Prescott was a pup, this kid was fourteen going on forty.

"What else did you see?"

"Seen him." Soo tapped a mug shot of Walter Price, taken a year and a half ago when he was popped for possession. "He was out all night. Walking up and down. Talking to lots of girls."

"And you've seen him before?"

"Many times. Grade-A asshole. Number ten." Soo held up ten fingers.

"Where were you when the murder happened?"

"I told you. Block away. Two blocks away. Lot of yelling, police cars. I come running down."

Barkley noticed Soo's English went in and out, becoming a little more fractured as he got excited. Or maybe it was just a game he was playing. Barkley bent down and picked up the photo of Price. "So you didn't actually see this guy near the alley?"

"No."

"Did you see any of these other guys running down into the alley?"

"Too far. I only got there when the police showed up."

Barkley pulled out a twenty and slipped it into the hungry curl of Soo's palm. "Thanks, Kenny."

"That's it?"

"What else can you do for me?"

"Eyes and ears, boss. Eyes and ears."

Barkley pulled out another twenty and wrapped it around his business card. "All right. You see these guys, especially number-ten asshole, you give me a call."

"Yes, boss."

"Don't approach him. Just call."

"Yes, boss."

"Okay, Kenny. I gotta get going."

"What about him?" Soo nodded at the only photo left in Barkley's makeshift lineup. It was a shot of Daniel Fitzsimmons taken from his first year on Latin School's track team.

"You know him?"

"He here yesterday. I noticed cuz he was with beautiful Asian girl." Kenny rolled his eyes. "I think I love her."

"This kid was here? Where?"

"King of Pizza. Talked with the girl. Then he talked to Mr. Toney."

"Toney?"

"Photographer. Lives upstairs." Soo lifted his chin toward the back side of the Brompton.

"Fuck me."

Soo thought that was funny as shit. Barkley, not so much. He gave Kenny another twenty and watched him leave, the sole of his sneaker flapping against the pavement as he went. After that, LaGrange grew quiet. Barkley ducked into the alley where Harry Fitzsimmons had died, finding the exact spot and crouching so he was eye level with the bloodstains, dark smears on brick running crooked into each other and down across the pavement. He imagined the football player staring at the breathing holes in his chest, wondering how they got there, then scanning the alley, every inch of it precious while his life leaked away and Death came calling. A footstep cracked on LaGrange, the murmur of voices, then a woman's laugh that dissolved to a hum.

Barkley walked out to the street, stopping at the Brompton again to lean on Toney's buzzer. No answer. He found a pay phone bolted to the side of a building on Washington and called Tommy, who didn't bother with a hello.

"Where are you?"

"Combat Zone. Why?"

"I'm getting us an address. Gotta be tonight or we might not get him at all."

"I'll pick you up at your place."

"What did you find in the Zone?"

"It'll keep. What time?"

"Swing by around ten."

Barkley hung up and dropped two more dimes. Cat McShane picked up on the first ring.

"It is alive."

"Funny. I got your report on the autopsy. Thanks."

"You don't sound happy."

"My partner's got a line on our suspect."

"And yet . . ."

"I don't know. Something's bothering me."

"Join the crowd. I went over to Boston City today. Talked to a doctor about Daniel Fitzsimmons."

"I'm listening."

Cat told him about Daniel's missing brain scans, her climb to the roof, and Lawrence Rosen's leap off it.

"You telling me you think Daniel Fitzsimmons was responsible for that?"

"No. Rosen committed suicide."

"So what's your point?"

"You asked me to look into Daniel's case. This is what I found."

"What if I told you Daniel was sitting in my skull right now, sitting there and watching my every thought?"

"I'd say you have an overactive imagination."

"He's been down the Combat Zone, Cat. Asking questions."

"Why?"

"Because he wants to find his brother's killer before we do. He wants to find him and he wants to kill him."

31

FRANKLIN PARK is five hundred acres of urban parkland spread across three of Boston's roughest neighborhoods—Jamaica Plain, Dorchester, and Roxbury. Daniel ducked into the park off Williams Street on the J.P. side. He knew the ground as well as anyone. He'd first run Franklin's cross-country course as a freshman, coming out of nowhere to win the city title over a leaf-blown course in late October. His strategy that day had been to lie back for the first mile then accelerate over a hill called Bear Cage. After that, it was a two-man race between him and an Asian kid from Boston Tech. Daniel put away the kid from Tech on a winding stretch of wooded trail called the Wilderness. Daniel was in the Wilderness again, trees sloping all around him in the moonlight. Franklin Park was dangerous at three in the afternoon. Daniel assumed it was worse at night, even though he'd never met anyone stupid enough to find out.

He ran like a runner, easily, silkily, along the park's dim thread of a trail. He was dressed in black from head to foot with dark socks over his hands and black tape covering the white flashing on his Tigers. Daniel kept his hood pulled up over his head and could feel the weight of Walter Price's revolver strapped to the inside of his calf. He slipped off the trail about thirty yards in, accelerating as he went, blood surging, breath growing rank in the closeness of the woods. A warm current buzzed over his skin; bright bits of tinsel light flickered and flared at the edges of his vision. Daniel ducked to avoid a tree branch and felt his jawbone lengthen while his ears stood up and sharpened to points. A bristle of hair covered his cheeks and ran like a flame down his spine and along his flanks, his coat stiff and gray to the edge of blue, his eyes lasers of emerald and his tongue, thick and red and long and rich as it unrolled between a fanged set of teeth. Daniel dropped his muzzle, now fully formed, close to the ground, a lone wolf scenting the earth, making his map. The wind shifted and he could smell his own spoor and it comforted him. Another shift and there was something else to taste—ape, zebra, lion. The human part of Daniel's brain told him it was only the Franklin Park Zoo, even as hackles rose on his back and his jaws glistened with fresh ropes of saliva.

Daniel began to run again, measured strides cutting tight and fast through the woods. He stopped just inside the tree line, making a small circle then dropping to his belly, swinging his head from side to side as he crept forward, stopping at the edge of an open field. There was something else out there, some fresh scent in the night that wasn't coming from the zoo. Daniel buried his muzzle between his paws and covered himself in dirt, rolling around to get as much of the earth smell on himself as possible. Then he lay up against a bush and waited.

It took only a minute or so for the first to reveal himself, creeping along the tree line to Daniel's left. The hyena carried a ridge of orange fur along his humped back, haunches spotted in black, long curved snout sniffing at wisps of purple moonlight.

Daniel sought out the second animal and quickly found him, a pair of burnt yellow eyes buried in a baseball field a hundred yards away. There was a third somewhere behind and to the right, but he wouldn't matter. Not if Daniel moved quickly.

The hyena to his left scratched at an ear, then raised his snout and gave a short coughing sound like a laugh. His buddy in center field offered a low grunt in return. Daniel took off. The laugher was first to give chase, barrel of a body folding and unfolding in a V as he pumped his short legs and cut a swath close to the ground. Among the trees the calculation might have been otherwise, but Daniel was moving across open ground now, the smooth, long strides of a gray wolf easily outpacing his rival. On Daniel's right, however, it was a different story. The hyena closing from center field had an angle and knew how to use it. Daniel watched his back, a flexing whip of orange and black as the hyena moved to cut off Daniel and flush him back toward the woods. Daniel shifted imperceptibly, taking a straighter path then flaring out again, creating just enough space before turning to face his pursuer. The hyena was coming full bore, head down, muzzle streaming, claws extended. Blind. Daniel caught the animal clean, sinking teeth into a fleshy shoulder, scissoring his jaws and feeling the crunch of ligament and bone as the hyena went limp. Daniel immediately released, watching the hyena roll over so his spotted belly was exposed for a moment before he regained his feet and scurried off, tail tucked, limping into the darkness.

Daniel knew he only had moments and sped the rest of the way across the field toward vapor puffs of street light. He ducked into the trees, gliding silently among the bent oaks that bordered the perimeter of the park, listening as his pursuers called to one another in the night and turned this way and that, hot to pick up his trail. He stepped out of the park at Seaver Street and kept running, on two feet now, into the heart of Roxbury. At the corner he snuck a quick look back. Three kids were maybe a hundred yards up the block, standing in the middle of the street, staring down at him but not pursuing. They wore black jackets with slashes of orange on the sleeves and orange lettering across the front. Daniel took off at a run up Blue Hill Avenue.

—

When he finally stopped, he was in an alley. He slumped down between two trash barrels and pulled slowly at the socks he'd wrapped over his hands. One knuckle was smashed and his right pinkie finger was swollen and bloody. Daniel winced as he flexed the hand and noticed his sweatshirt was slashed at the shoulder as if someone had attacked him with a knife. He pulled off the shirt and T-shirt underneath, shivering and checking to see if he had any more injuries. Then he slipped the layers back on and stood up.

His hold on reality might be greasy, but Daniel knew he had to keep moving. Simon had made it clear he couldn't push into everyone's head. But if he did get entangled with someone—like he was with Walter Price—the connection seemed more or less permanent. It might wax and wane like a radio station that went in and out as you worked the dial, but it was always there if he just focused. And trusted. Daniel began to jog down the alley, picking up the pace as a police siren unwound and a pack of dogs answered, barking hard and angry against the night.

A mile later, he was sitting up against a chain-link fence and studying an arthritic three-decker. Price was somewhere inside. Daniel could feel his mind, fissured with heat, tongues of flame running fast and blue in the cracks. Fear? Hell, yeah. Price knew he was being hunted by half the cops in the city and knew it was just a matter of time. Remorse for killing Harry? Daniel couldn't find a drop. He loosened the gun he'd strapped to his ankle and noticed the shake in his hand. It was the terror of beginning, the finality of a first step. He'd made the decision to take another man's life. And now it was time.

Daniel climbed to his feet. The three-decker swayed above him, grinning like a skeleton in the night. He cut across the alley and up the back steps. One floor, two floors, three. The windows on the top were boarded up, the only door blown wide open. He stepped inside what had once been a kitchen. Crooked bars of light ran through the slats lighting up graffiti spray painted in wild slashes of black and green. Daniel followed one strand diagonally across a wall but couldn't make heads or tails of it. His foot knocked against something round. An empty bottle of Wild Irish Rose rolled in a small circle and stopped.

Daniel crept to the doorway and a narrow hallway that fed into the black belly of the apartment. He slumped to the floor and sought out Price's mind again, but there was nothing now. Snuffed. Daniel laid down the gun and flexed his hand, feeling the pain flare in his knuckles, down his fingers, and under his nails. He thought again about his run through the park. Part of him was terrified at whatever it was that was happening to him. The rest thought he might be seeing more than less, if only he'd trust it. On cue, a pair of eyes blinked to life at the far end of the hall. Then a second set. The scrabble of long claws on wood was followed by a whisper of air as something charged. Daniel reached for the gun but already knew he was too late. And then they fell upon him.

32

BARKLEY PULLED to the corner and watched his partner climb in. Tommy had barely closed the door before they were pushing away from the curb.

"What the fuck, B. Let me get in, for Chrissakes."

"You got an address for our boy?"

"Course I got an address."

Barkley crested a hill that ran down toward the water. "He still in Roxbury?"

"Dudley Square. What's the matter?"

"Nothing." Barkley hit his blinker and took a right.

"I told you it might take a day or so. The captain on our case?"

"We just need to make a collar."

"We will. Tonight."

"The kid's been down the Combat Zone."

"What kid?"

"Harry Fitzsimmons's brother, Daniel."

"How do you know that?"

"Someone saw him. Said he was talking to the photographer."

"How'd the kid find him?"

"Who the fuck knows? Hang around down there long enough and you meet every weirdo and asshole pervert in the world."

"I thought the photographer was all right."

"He is, but you know what I mean."

Carson Beach rolled past on the left. Barkley could just see the dark line of sand. Beyond it, waves curling white under the still moonlight.

"Relax," Tommy said. "So what if he talked to this guy. He's a fucking kid. Besides, the photographer . . . Toney's his name?"

Barkley nodded.

"Toney doesn't know where Price is."

"He's down the Zone. He could have heard something."

"And you think he'd tell the kid?"

"Maybe he thinks there'd be no harm in it."

"That's my point. What's a fucking kid gonna do?"

"I'm pretty sure he's got a gun, Tommy." Barkley told his partner about his visit to Latin School and the handgun that had gone missing during the brawl.

"And the kid was involved in the fight?"

"The kid was involved in the fight. From what the head-master told me, he could have easily grabbed the piece."

"Did you ask him?"

"Says he never saw a gun."

"And we don't believe him?"

"Here's my thought. Daniel's in the car when his mom dies. He's eight years old and can't do a fucking thing about it. But it eats at him. Maybe he doesn't know it eats at him, but it does. And then big brother's murdered. Butchered in an alley and again Daniel draws a front-row seat. This time, though, the kid's sixteen and not gonna let it pass. No fucking way."

"You think he's hunting Price?"

"We just need to get there first."

Tommy rubbed his lower lip and stared out the window. Barkley flicked on the radio. Gladys Knight was singing "Midnight Train to Georgia." There was something about Gladys that dug deep in his belly. Maybe it was three generations of Alabama slaves, people he'd never met, voices he somehow knew as well as his own, their blood in every note and every line of Gladys's music. Up ahead there was a dark tangle of traffic at K Circle. Barkley flicked on his siren and the cars parted. He accelerated, pounding over the expressway and down the oil-slicked roads of Dorchester, toward the smoke and lights of Roxbury.

—

Barkley was driving a low-slung, midnight-blue snarl of a Camaro. He pulled the car to the curb directly across from the address Tommy had given him. If Price was in there, they didn't have time for subtlety. Truth be told, it had never been their strong suit anyway.

The Camaro had barely rolled to a stop before Tommy tumbled out the door. He had his gun low by his side and ran in a crouch across the street. Barkley followed, .38 still on his hip as he flattened himself against the side of the three-decker. The place looked deserted, most of the windows boarded up with a couple of lights burning here and there. Tommy nodded at a set of stairs that accessed the three-decker's back porches. They'd agreed to start on the top floor, work room by room and stay together. Hopefully, Price was alone. And hopefully he didn't do anything stupid. Halfway up the second flight, Barkley's flashlight caught a smear of blood on the banister.

"The kid?" Tommy said.

"Could be." Barkley pulled his gun. "Go ahead."

On the third floor Tommy stepped through an open door into a kitchen. There were boards on the windows and curling trails of graffiti, exhales of glitter and smoke covering the walls from ceiling to floor. Tommy held his gun in two hands in front of his chest. Barkley had his piece in his right hand, the flash in his left.

"Easy now, bud."

Tommy nodded and took a half breath before ducking out of the kitchen and into a connecting hallway. Barkley leaned against the doorframe, stirring the darkness with his light. Tommy started to creep along one wall; Barkley hugged the other. A third of the way down, they found another door that opened to a staircase diving into the bowels of the building. Tommy wanted to take a look. Barkley nodded and watched as his partner disappeared. So much for sticking together.

Barkley clicked off his light and continued down the hall, aware of the old floorboards wincing under his tread and Gladys, back now, crooning low and smooth and sweet and wet in the deepest part of his brain where nothing lived but the stuff that spanned time and memory and never knew death. He came to the end of the corridor and an open space, cold with a current of something heavy that tugged at his legs, prickling the skin on his thighs and tickling his balls. He was tempted to click on his flash but knew Gladys would stop singing if he did and he wanted her in his head. His foot nudged up against the wooden bump of the threshold and he stepped across it. The wall to his left moved away from him, telling him the room was probably an oval. And big. Barkley could feel its depth and the height of the ceiling and wondered how and why they made a room so big in this neighborhood. Then he remembered Roxbury used to be a wealthy neighborhood, home to Boston's Jewish population thirty, forty years back. He thought of this even as another voice, the cop voice, told him he had a gun in his hand and should pay the fuck attention to what was or wasn't in the fucking room and a third voice told him Gladys had quit singing and that probably wasn't good.

He stopped near a window, boarded up tight so just tiny rivers of light leaked through. Tommy's lecture on instinct crawled out from under a rock in his brain and Barkley knew before he could know what was about to happen. Not the exact play-by-play, but he had the gist all right. Fuck, yeah, he had the gist. The detective backed up until he felt the crumble of plaster against his back and pointed his gun toward whatever was staring at him in the darkness. He made words in his mouth but no sound came out as whatever it was charged. He should have fired, could have fired, but something stayed his trigger finger. Then they were on him. Furnace breath, slit-back nostrils, and flashing teeth slick with saliva. The gun clattered from his fingers and skidded across the floor. After that, the only sound was the tearing of clothes and working of jaws as the two beasts fought silently over their prey.

33

TOMMY DILLON was in a common stairwell that circled to the bottom of the building. He ignored the second- and first-floor apartments, heading straight for a door that led to the basement. Tommy didn't try to hide his approach, pounding down a broken set of steps and stepping around an old coal bin fixed under a boarded-up chute. Against one wall sat a coffin filled to the brim with car batteries and resting on a pair of runnerless rocking chairs. Beside it stood a six-foot cigar-store Indian wearing a Tribe cap. Tommy took a quick look at both and kept moving.

The tiny room bled out to a long passage covered in a chunky layer of dirt and trash. Tommy picked through the strata, trying to determine who'd been where and when. He found a McDonald's bag and fresh burger wrappers stuffed into a crack in the wall. On the ground nearby was a half-melted cup of ice. Bingo. At the end of the corridor he leaned lightly against a final door and listened. Like any cop who'd been around awhile, he knew the layout of these old three-deckers and knew the door probably led to the building's boiler room. And a dead end. He shouldered his way in, smelling the rankness of stale water and scanning right to left with his weapon. Walter Price was in the far corner, huddled against a hunk of scrap iron that might have once been a furnace. Tommy could see his hollow eyes, dancing in the dark like a couple of question marks, and the blued steel of a gun, stretched out and pointed square at the detective's chest.

"Drop it," Tommy said, and took a step forward.

—

"Someone cut their vocal cords." The boy sat between the two beasts, one lying with his massive head in the boy's lap, the other sitting upright, jaws open, tongue hung like a fresh offering between a wet set of teeth. Neither had taken their eyes off Barkley, sitting still as a stone against the wall some ten feet away.

"You know what they are?" Barkley said.

"Big."

"They're called Presa Canarios, Daniel. Great dogs if they're trained properly."

"And if they're not?"

"What do you think? Make pit bulls look like puppies. They just gonna stare at me the whole time?"

Daniel looked down at the dog's head in his lap and the dog looked back and Barkley saw worlds upon worlds spinning in the compass of the boy's gaze.

"They don't trust humans," he said.

"But they trust you?"

"I listen."

Daniel had placed Barkley's flashlight on the floor so it threw out a pale canopy of light between them. The detective's gun was close by the boy's side. Barkley moved to get up. He could see the Presas tense, smooth muscle quivering under tight coats of skin.

"Just because they didn't hurt you doesn't mean they won't," Daniel said.

Barkley sat again. The dogs collapsed back into their bones, listening to the hum of the boy's thoughts and watching the huge black man like he was their next meal.

"I can't stay here, Daniel. You know that."

"Walter Price didn't kill Harry."

The boy knew Price's name. Barkley wasn't surprised. "You're wrong."

"Whatever you think you see, you don't. And whatever you don't see can hurt you."

"What the Christ does that mean?"

Daniel pulled out a second gun he kept somewhere behind him and put it next to Barkley's.

"He's in the basement. The dogs led me there."

"But you didn't shoot him. Why's that?"

Daniel stroked a shelf of bone between the Presa's eyes. "You think I killed my mother."

Barkley felt a tingling somewhere deep in his skull. The dogs' ears stood up.

"Tell me about her, Daniel."

"Why do you care?"

"Maybe I'm playing a hunch."

The boy slid a small object across the floor. It spun as it skittered, a ring, red enamel, encrusted with diamonds in the shape of a rose. "She was wearing that when she died."

Barkley stared at the ring but didn't touch it.

"Pick it up, Detective."

"Where did you get that?"

"I told you. My mom was wearing it when she died. Pick it up."

Barkley shook his head. The boy's gaze narrowed and the Presas muscled up, one climbing to his feet, nostrils flared, breath bubbling low in his throat.

"I know about the fire escape, Detective. I've seen Jess fall."

"Fuck off, Daniel."

The other Presa was up now, straining to get at Barkley, held fast by an invisible chain fashioned by the boy. He flicked his finger and the dog charged, scuttling close and stopping an inch or two from the detective's face. Barkley could feel the Presa's hot exhaust on his neck and kept his eyes averted.

"You gonna let them tear me up, go ahead and get on with it."

Daniel lifted his chin as the dog retreated and Barkley felt his hand close over the ring. He was there, sitting in his kitchen on the top floor of the Roxbury tenement, windows flung open to the city, a summer breeze billowing sheer white curtains across the room in lovely, liquid streams. He could see Jess through the lacy mesh. She was at the stove, making pancakes and shimmying to a song Barkley couldn't hear but knew was Gladys cuz what else could it be. And then he saw who was helping with the batter. Long limbs, soft curls like her mom. She turned, warm and supple in the morning sun, and Barkley saw she had her dad's smile. And then he couldn't see anymore. Not because he couldn't. But because he couldn't. And so he released the ring and the boy was back, crouched close in the darkness.

"My mother says you're damaged. Says you need time to heal."

"Does she really?"

"Yes, but that's probably not gonna happen tonight." Daniel picked up the ring, putting Barkley's gun in its place. "You need to go."

"In a minute."

"Go. Your partner's in trouble." Daniel turned and left, one dog in the lead, the other following.

Barkley clipped the gun back on his hip, grabbed the flashlight, and climbed to his feet. Already what he'd seen was fading, the threads of a fever dream trailing off into the mist. Maybe it was for the best. Or maybe we tell ourselves what it is we need to hear.

He'd just reached the top of the stairs when he heard the first shot.

34

DANIEL SLIPPED down the alley. To his right was a fenced-in yard full of cold metal—engine blocks and steel frames, hunks of pipe and chains and random pieces of scrap, all of it painted in lashings of white and purple light. A howl of wind swept down off the roofs and the Presas froze. The one Daniel thought of as the leader leaped the high fence in one movement. The other followed before the first hit the ground. Daniel listened for some sound of their passage and heard nothing but the night. The Presas did their own bidding and that was as it was.

He started to walk again, coming to the place where the alley joined the street. A mustard-colored Caddy with a white vinyl roof swept around a bend, cruising past before stopping and backing up. A car full of black men in Boston got watched everywhere it went. Except in the Bury. Here they did the watching.

Daniel could hear the thump of a bass line as a window rolled down. He still had Walter Price's gun tucked under his sweatshirt. His hand drifted toward it as one of the Caddy's heavy doors rocked open. Then the Presas were back—the first vaulting a ragged row of bushes and circling Daniel before placing himself between the boy and the car; the other crossing in front of the Caddy and sitting in the street, just beyond the reach of the car's headlights. Daniel could hear voices arguing. A man leaned out of the rear window and pointed a gun at the dog in front of Daniel. The Presa stood up and waited, aware of death and unconcerned, brave as only a dog can be. The front door swung closed and the gun disappeared. Then the Caddy was gone, disappearing in a taste of oil and smoke.

Daniel knelt and put his forehead to the Presa's, feeling the simplicity of his needs, the nakedness of his wants, life shorn of artifice and full of all its raw, elemental power. It should have been terrifying, but Daniel craved it and celebrated it and tried to understand something he knew before he could ever remember and would never fully know again until he'd passed beyond all understanding.

He walked the rest of the way down the block, one dog ahead, the other leaning up against him. Around the corner a second car waited, this one a silver BMW. Grace stepped from the passenger's side, and Daniel realized for once and forever that it wasn't going to be a teenage romance, no lovestruck, star-crossed, thunderbolt Romeo and Juliet deal. Wouldn't be a slow ripening either. They wouldn't find each other again and again—friends in high school, then dating in college, breaking up, realizing the mutual error of their ways and circling back to each other, this time for good. She'd never bear him children. They'd never grow old. Nope, this was it. Her stepping from the car and standing in an ugly stab of street light, urging him to hurry while the wind tugged and she pushed her hair back behind her ear. Him running, the dogs peeling away and disappearing as quickly as they'd appeared while he climbed into the car. Her never asking why, never asking how, never asking who, just turning and staring at him over the back of the seat as the years and decades and lifetimes flowed past and nothing ever changed as everything moved underneath and around them and they played their part and spoke their lines over and over. He was sixteen, falling in love and getting his heart broken all at once, for the first time and the last. And there was nothing to be done, save miss her for a million moments in the space of a breath and know he'd do anything for it. Again and again.

"You okay?"

Daniel glanced at the driver. "I'm fine, Ben. You didn't have to come."

Ben Jacob's intelligent eyes stared at Daniel from the rear-view mirror. "What else did I have to do?" He'd grabbed his father's car and driven it into Roxbury in the ass end of a winter's night and Daniel would never be able to thank him enough. But Grace would. Daniel could see that, too, just as clearly as the other. For a second he fought it. Then the idea found its place in his heart and he loved both of them for what they were and where they were going, but mostly because they were here when no one else was. Ben put the car in gear.

"The police are in there." Daniel nodded and all three watched the three-decker as it slipped past.

"Did they arrest someone?" Ben said.

"I don't know. I think it's complicated." Daniel turned to Grace. "How did you know I was here?"

"I told you. I get feelings, too."

"We followed you," Ben said. "Lost you in Franklin Park, but Grace said to cruise Dudley Square. And here you are."

Grace put out her hand and Daniel placed Walter Price's revolver in it. She took a quick look. So did Ben as he drove. Then Grace stuck it in the glove compartment.

"The police are gonna be looking for that," Daniel said. "Maybe me as well."

"I don't think they'll be looking in the backseat of a BMW driven by a sixteen-year-old Jewish kid from the 'burbs." Ben's grin lit up the mirror.

"Probably not."

"All right, then. Keep your head down and lock the door. Grace, how the hell do I get out of here?"

35

BARKLEY HIT the bottom of the stairs as the echo of another shot thumped off the walls. He thought about calling it in but just kept moving, through a small room and down a tight corridor. At the very end a door stood ajar. Barkley didn't hesitate. In the Bury hesitation only got you dead. He ducked low and shouldered through, the walnut grip of the Smith & Wesson slick and rough at the same time in his hand. Tommy Dillon was planted in the middle of the room, legs spread slightly, right arm extended as he fired a final time into the crumpled body of a young black man. Tommy dropped his arm to his side, service weapon hanging from his fingertips. Barkley moved in a slow circle, his gun not pointed at his partner but not holstered either. He waited until Tommy could see him before speaking.

"Hey, bud."

"I came in and he took the shot."

"How many did you fire?"

A small rise and drop in the shoulders. "Dunno. Five, maybe."

Meaning he had one left. Barkley took a step closer. "I'm gonna need to take the weapon."

Tommy looked down at the gun in his hand and tossed it near

Barkley's feet. There was a second piece by the body. A .25-caliber Baby Browning. Looked like a toy. Barkley checked the magazine, then searched the pockets of the kid until he found a license. Walter Joseph Price. Nineteen years old and very much dead.

"We should call it in." Tommy's face played flat in the tinfoil light.

"Tell me what happened."

"Just did."

"Ain't gonna fly, bud."

"No?"

"Not unless I back it up. So tell it to me straight and make it the truth."

"You fucking serious, B? After all we done?"

"He fired once, Tommy. You put five in his chest. The last from about two feet away after the man was dead."

"You seen what he done to that kid."

"Tell me what happened."

"Just what I said. He fired. I put him down." Tommy was still wired, breath hissing through narrow slits in his nose. "Gimme his gun."

"Why?"

"Why you think? We pop off a few more rounds. Make it look like the fucking OK Corral. No one's gonna care, B. Gimme the piece." Tommy held out his hand as something stirred in the reptilian part of Barkley's brain and he knew this guy could kill him, right here in the fucking cellar. And it wouldn't even be a surprise. Outside there was noise in the alley. Someone had heard the shots. Tommy flicked his fingers impatiently.

"Give me the fucking gun, B. You call it in and deal with the locals."

Barkley handed over the service weapon and the Browning. Then he left the cellar. Somewhere in the distance, he could hear the winding scream of a siren. Closer, much closer, the pop, pop, pop of a pistol as Tommy Dillon staged his one-man shooting war.

PART III

PART III

36

4:54 A.M.

GRACE SAT in the curve of the doorway, staring at the black face of the apartment building, a lonesome rectangle of canary yellow floating in the middle of the second floor. It was the third night she'd been out there. The third night she'd watched Simon Lane pacing against the darkness. He paused in the eye of the window and Grace felt the pressure of his gaze. He couldn't possibly see her tucked up in the alcove that marked the entrance to Music City. Could he?

She shrank back against the rough cement and ran her fingertips over the architecture of his mind. The thing was a puzzle, a gleaming hall of mirrors riveted with narrow staircases, some leading up, some plunging down, one circling back on another, and everywhere she looked, Grace saw only herself. Was she truly inside his head, or he in hers? Was there a difference between the two?

Grace closed her eyes and lifted her chin, the better to drink in the morning air. She hadn't seen Daniel, hadn't spoken to him since the night in Roxbury more than a week ago. Still, she could feel his presence and knew he was sleeping somewhere inside the apartment. The idea soothed her. Calmed her. Grace's eyes flicked open. The window was empty, the front door to the building swinging wide on its hinges. Simon floated down the steps, gliding to a stop under a streetlight. She could see him clearly, wrapped in a long swath of coat with a red scarf and black watch cap tugged down over his face. He took out a pipe and knocked it on his heel. Then he filled and lit it, streaming a crest of smoke that circled his head as he looked directly at her. The clock on the insurance building clicked over to 5:07. He turned and walked away, sliding down Beacon Street, deeper into the oiled joints of the city. Grace stepped from her hiding place. He'd known about her all along. And now he was telling her to follow. It was the price she'd pay for Daniel's safety.

And so she went.

He moved incredibly fast, a gritty wind funneling him down Beacon, his thoughts reduced to a mumble in her head as she tried to keep up. He was twenty yards ahead when, without warning, he dipped into a side street. Grace sprinted to the corner and stared down an empty block sealed off at the end by a tumble of stone standing big-shouldered against a growing sky. The building looked like an old New England meetinghouse or church, bounded by a black fence and flanked by iron-gray trees with sinuous branches that grew into the sides of the structure and overhung the roof.

Grace paused at the gate and listened. The silence ran wild in her blood, pounding at her temples and dilating the soft veins in her throat. The only marker on the building was a year, 1789, carved into a lintel set over the wooden door. Grace tugged at the door's handle. To her dismay and relief, the thing was locked.

She sat in a finger of street light, one step down from the top, and stared out at silken skeins—fear, desire, anxiety, confusion—flitting in and out of the trees, flying up into the branches and back across the courtyard. The smell of pipe smoke arrived on the ragged edge of a breeze, then a melody of thumps as something landed lightly behind her.

The big cat took his time, circling in and out of sight, drifting a silvered tail across Grace's cheek before coming up on the other side and angling close enough so she could hear the muzzled breathing that might have been a purr and might have been a growl. The cat's face was cut close to the bone, one eye a dry, unblinking blue, the other bleached and blind to the world. Grace watched the cat's black and white whiskers tremor as he kneaded meaty paws, shoulder muscles tensing and bunching and working. The cat peeled back his lips, if cats had lips—Grace knew nothing about cats, except she knew after tonight she'd never have one—and showed his teeth, licking the side of her face with a coarse tongue. For the first time, Grace noticed the others—five, ten, twenty sets of eyes assembled from bits and pieces of darkness and arranged in receding circles around her, watching their leader as he jumped onto a stone railing and switched his tail. The word *subtle* came to mind, like the cat had decided to play with Grace before snapping her neck and feeding her to his friends. Then something whispered in the trees and the cat leaped without warning, bared claws hunting for anything soft, anything breathing, anything flesh, anything Grace.

She screamed and ducked, the cat flying past, tumbling and rolling down the steps in that elegant way cats always seem to fall. Somewhere at the end of a narrow tunnel was the gate and the street. Grace ran for it, felines coiling and closing on all sides, swiping and hissing as she fled. And then she was down the block and around the corner, sprinting through the empty city. Up ahead, Kenmore Square beckoned and teased and laughed at Grace's fears and Grace's foolishness. Behind her, pipe smoke eddied and swirled and she could taste it following in her wake.

37

THE PUBLIC Gardens were mostly empty, Bostonians reduced to scuffs of gray as they hurried through the Arlington Street gate. Fat clouds scudded overhead, greased by a soft wind and sullen with the promise of winter rain. Barkley sipped his drink from the safety of a window seat in the bar at the Ritz. Cat McShane sat across from him, looking like she was in her own private Bogart movie as she toyed with the stem of the cherry atop her ginger ale. They'd given it to her in a tall glass loaded with crushed ice. Cat pointed her eyes at Barkley's tumbler, short, squat, and full of mind-numbing scotch.

"Are we going to eat, or is it that kind of thing?"

He'd bought meatballs and sauce in the North End. A bottle of Chianti. Cannolis from Bova's. Figured they'd have dinner at his place. Afterward, maybe a walk in the neighborhood. Forget about the day and live for the night. Just him and Cat. Then the hearing happened, and Barkley decided to drink his lunch instead.

"You go ahead and order," he said.

The DA's office had set up Tommy Dillon at a conference table ten feet away while one of their prosecutors ran out the dog, then the pony, then the dog again just for good measure. Afterward, there'd been a meeting in another room and then the official finding. Tommy was cleared of any wrongdoing in the shooting death of Walter Price. Pending some paperwork, he'd be back on the street by the end of the day.

"They read your report into the record," Barkley said.

Cat nodded as a waiter came over and dropped off a menu. "I did my job, Bark." He lifted a finger to speak, but Cat wasn't done. "Full autopsy, detailed wound descriptions, entry and exit angles. It's all there."

"You saw my statement?"

"Of course."

"And?"

"And what?"

"Come on, Cat."

"Come on nothing."

Barkley drained his drink and got a fresh one. Cat ordered half of a chicken salad sandwich and picked around the edges. Outside, the world exploded in cannon bursts of white as the sky broke into ripe, fleshy pieces and an unseasonably warm storm lashed against the windows.

"Between you and me . . ." Barkley said.

"Here we go . . ."

"Between you and me, what do you really think happened?"

"I know what happened. Anyone who looks at the file is going to know what happened."

"What happened?"

"There was a 'gun fight'"—Cat made quotation marks with her fingers—"between your partner and a young black man, now deceased. At close range, maybe ten, fifteen feet. The black man was hit five times, once in the shoulder, four closely grouped in the chest. The decedent somehow managed to squeeze off four shots before he died, and your partner, due undoubtedly to a second act of the Almighty, wasn't hit by any of them. Come on, Bark."

"Say it."

"Fine. Tommy Dillon executed that kid. Then he made it look like there was an exchange of gunfire. Maybe you helped him. Maybe you went along after the fact. I don't know. More important, no one cares."

"Why didn't you put any of that in your report?"

Cat laughed and suddenly looked older than she'd ever want. And just as suddenly Barkley's stomach turned sour with the whiskey and he hated the job more than ever for what it did to people.

"I'm not stupid, Bark." Cat pushed her plate of food away. "If the DA wants to put the pieces together, let him. But he won't and we both know it. Forget about this. Once the rain lets up, we'll go for a walk. Catch a movie or something. After, I can make us dinner at my place."

Barkley shook his head.

"I don't think any less of you, Bark. In fact, I think more of you."

"Great."

"Price was going to wind up dead one way or the other. Hung by his belt in a holding cell, shanked in the yard. I mean, was this any worse?"

"So I did the right thing?"

"You did the cop thing."

A flock of pigeons flew up in his head, blotting out their

conversation, leaving behind nothing but Daniel Fitzsimmons, flanked on either side by his dogs, staring down at Barkley as he sat in a cold hole. Daniel had a shovel in his hands and began to backfill, the dirt hitting Barkley's skin and catching in his eyes and teeth.

"Bark?"

"Yeah."

"How's Dillon doing?"

"I'm sure he's fine."

Today was the first time he'd seen his partner since the night of the shooting. Tommy had been put on paid leave, the department requiring the two detectives not communicate until after the hearing. Well, they'd had their hearing. And now his partner was back.

"Chains, Cat."

"What?"

"That's what this job is. Chains with thick iron cuffs."

"Bark . . ."

"The chains don't seem like nothing at first. Hell, they're a badge of honor. But then they begin to weigh on you, every step you take they get heavier." He ordered another drink even though he hadn't finished the one in front of him. "You're in the job long enough, you're gonna get jammed up, slipped between the jaws of a vise, screwed in so goddamn tight you can't move, can't breathe. You can say it's never gonna happen to you and you'll believe it. Right up until it happens."

"Bark . . ."

"Seven years ago last month. You can look it up."

"Look up what?"

"Me and Tommy were on a case. Murder suspect we thought

might be holed up in Columbia Point. Apartment's on the fourth floor and the elevator's out. So up the stairs we go. I'm in the lead, gun out. There's a noise somewhere above us. I look up the open stairwell just as someone tries to drop an AC unit on my head. Tommy pushes me and the fucking thing tears at the sleeve of my coat as it pisses by. No shit, it would have killed me."

"That's what partners do, B. That's why you guys look out for each other. All the way down the line."

"Someone taught you good, Cat. Who was that? Never mind, lemme finish. Tommy pushes me. Like I said, if he doesn't the fucking window unit probably takes me right over the railing and down three stories. Instead, I bounce off the wall and my gun accidentally discharges. The shot ricochets in the stairwell, catches a guy who's peeking out from behind a door a floor below us." Barkley pulled down the collar of his best dress shirt with two fingers. "Right under the collarbone. Goes straight through and explodes his heart. Dead before I can get to him. And it didn't take me long. The wife is there, baby in her arms, staring at me as her husband bleeds his good-byes from the mouth and I lay him down and the woman starts to scream. And now the baby is the one looking at me. But what's the difference, right? Then the old woman comes out."

"The old woman?"

"Dead guy's mother. Lives with them. Or they live with her. She comes out and picks up her son and cradles his head and carries him into the apartment. This guy was big, six feet plus, but she carries him like he's nothing. Tommy and I follow. There's all kinds of hell breaking loose. Chatter on the radio. We still have a suspect in the building. And it's Columbia Point. Half the projects gonna strap up and come gunning for us."

"What happened?"

"What always happens. We called for backup. Some cruisers rolled, some SWAT guys, and we got the fuck out of Dodge. Two weeks of shit followed, lootings, a half-dozen more shootings in the first couple days. They put my face out there as the shooter cuz I was black, but that didn't mean nothing. Far as the projects were concerned, I was blue. That's what mattered. Thing just boiled and raged and thrashed and killed until it died like it always does."

"So you owe Tommy?"

"More ways than one. I fucked up, Cat. The story I just told you was a lie. Not all of it. Just the important part, which, by the way, is the very best way to lie. Yeah, the window unit came down and, yeah, it almost took my head off. Tommy pushed me up against the wall, but my gun didn't accidentally discharge. I saw the fucker who dumped the unit on me peeking out at us from a doorway a couple floors up. So I took the shot. Stupid, right? Enclosed stairwell, no sign of a weapon, no imminent threat. Just some asshole playing games. But I'm shook, I'm scared, I'm pissed. Mostly the last. So I pop off the shot. Just one. It catches a railing, deflects down, and kills the guy one floor below just like I described. That's what really happened. And you know what it would have meant if I'd told that story?"

"I don't know, Bark."

"Like hell you don't know. Man one. Fifteen to twenty-five, minimum. But Tommy steps up. Tells me exactly what to say, exactly how to say it. You'd think I'd know, but your brain freezes when you're in the vise like that. At least mine did. So Tommy gives me the play-by-play and then he testifies at the hearing. All lies, just like me today. I walk and everything fades to background noise. We're back on the job the following week. I look at the guy and I love him. Cuz I owe him. And so right fucking there was the first link in the chain. The strongest link, the one that mattered. And today was the last."

"The last?"

"You want a drink, or am I doing this solo?"

"I think we should go." Cat started to get up.

"You know what else is bugging me?"

"The fact that I'm offering you my virtue and you're shrugging it off?"

"Harry Fitzsimmons's wounds. The two different types of wounds."

"They don't make sense."

"Bet your ass they don't make sense. Did you just offer me your virginity?"

"Is this 1958? Are you Richard Zimmerman from high school chemistry? Pay the bill and let's go."

———

The storm had blown out of the city as quickly as it had arrived, leaving the Public Garden little more than a carpet of mud. Still the walk was nice, with the weight of the trees overhead and the careful paths and rain washing everything clean. Barkley found a section from the *Globe* in a trash can and spread it out on a bench. Cat seemed dubious but sat down anyway.

"It's always quiet here."

"Yeah."

"Go ahead, Bark."

"Huh?"

"You wanted to ask about the wounds on Fitzsimmons."

"It's not just that. None of it makes sense."

"None of what?"

"The girl who grabbed the wallet. Where is she? Why didn't she stop at the car and talk to them longer before going for the leather? How was it that Walter Price was just waiting for Harry in the alley?"

"Every case has holes. I don't need to tell you that."

"The wounds. Why does Price use two different weapons? Why didn't Fitzsimmons fight back?"

"He did fight back. Price stabbed him. Hell, you've got a picture of it."

"I do."

Cat pulled a folder from her bag.

"What's that?"

"What you asked for." She dropped the folder in his lap. Barkley flipped it open. Inside was a photo of Violet Fitzsimmons, taken three months before she died. It was the woman he'd bumped into as she came out of Hom's Chinese restaurant in the South End, the woman who'd held his hand on the fire escape. Barkley drank in the liquid eyes and mobile mouth, the smooth, unlined face. Underneath the photo was a one-page inventory report from the car crash that killed her. Among Violet's personal possessions was a ring—red enamel encrusted with a dozen diamonds in the shape of a rose.

Barkley flipped the folder shut. Cat caught his eyes. "What is it?"

"Do you believe in God?"

She pursed her lips.

"Never mind."

"The 'god' I grew up with is too small to be real. At least for me."

"But there *is* something out there?"

She slipped a hand to his chest. "Or in here."

"Or both?"

"Or both. Why are you asking?"

"I believe in facts. Evidence. At least I always did."

"And now?"

"I think I might have been wrong. And I wonder what I'm gonna have to answer for."

Cat picked up the folder and considered the face of Violet Fitzsimmons. "Know what I think?"

"No idea."

"I think maybe you've seen a ghost."

"So you think I'm nuts."

"Hardly. Doing what I do, I've seen a few myself. And some of them can be quite wonderful."

Barkley grinned despite himself and felt the tension slip from his shoulders. Talking with Cat didn't change a thing, except everything. She let him pull her in, nuzzling her head against his shoulder and fitting her body to his, breathing softly and deeply and letting her eyes close. For a moment they were a couple and the world was full of possibility. Then a small man with a crooked face rolled out of the hanging mist, ringing a bell and setting up his sausage and peppers stand just inside the Arlington Street gate. He popped open a red umbrella and started roasting hunks of meat over a grill. Barkley chuckled lightly.

"Someone should tell that guy it's December."

Cat lifted her head and frowned.

"What?"

"Why do I think I'm gonna regret this?"

"What is it?"

"Evidence." She pointed to a row of metal rods the man had hanging on a piece of wire over the grill. "Right there."

"Where?"

"The skewers he's using for the meat. I mean, there's a million of these guys around the city, I understand that."

"But . . ."

"I'm betting any one of those would match up perfectly to Harry Fitzsimmons's wounds."

Somewhere a husband drank whiskey in a living room while a wife held ice to her face and fingered a knife in the kitchen drawer. A man picked through a pile of bills, listening to the landlord's tread a floor above and thinking about the cash she kept in a shoebox under the bed. A teenager stared at the top floor of a hotel, picturing his girl inside, hard at work on her old boyfriend. The seeds of homicide blew across the city of Boston, 24/7, finding fertile soil almost wherever they landed. For Barkley, however, there was only one. Until there wasn't. And a piece he was hoping he'd never find had just dropped into place.

"How certain are you?"

"I'd need to measure the wounds and compare them against anything you brought me, but I'm pretty confident. Yeah, the more I think about it, I'm sure."

"Did you drive?"

"Why?"

"We'll take my car."

—

They went less than a mile, parking a block away. Cat waited in the front seat with the doors locked as Barkley jogged down

Washington Street, returning with two white paper bags, bottoms already soaked through with grease. The logo on one of the bags read FIVE FACES.

"I'm not gonna eat that," Cat said, pointing to the order of shish kebab Barkley held in his hand.

He used a napkin to pull off the hunks of sweaty chicken and held up the naked metal skewer. "All I need you to do is measure."

Cat made a face. "I don't have a tape measure."

Barkley reached across to the glove compartment and took one out. From the backseat he dredged up a stack of files, rummaging until he found the one on Harry Fitzsimmons.

"You keep it in your car?"

"Bits and pieces. Your report's in here with details on the wounds."

Cat shook her head and covered her lap with a couple of napkins. She laid the skewer across them. "This won't be exact."

"Just ballpark it."

Cat stretched the tape measure.

"I owe you," Barkley said. "How about Jimmy's?"

Cat smirked, made a couple of measurements, and snapped the tape shut. "These would work."

"You sure?"

"I'm using a tape measure in the front seat of your car. No, I'm not sure. Why's that Asian kid staring at us?"

Barkley glanced across the street. Kenny Soo stood in the exhale of an alley. Barkley raised a hand. Soo waved him across.

"Cat . . ."

"I can walk back."

Barkley pulled out some bills. "Jump a cab."

"It's a ten-minute walk." She held up the skewer. "You want me to get a little more precise with this?"

"Can we keep it between us?"

She wrapped the thin piece of metal in one of the napkins and slipped it in her bag.

"You don't like this?" he said.

"I don't see the point. The guy who killed Harry Fitzsimmons is dead. Your partner shot him."

"The night of Fitzsimmons's murder Tommy was out on a case. We got the call on the body and arrived at the alley in separate cars. Tommy got there first."

"So what?"

"Tommy told me he ate fast food that night. The next day I was over to his place. There was takeout in the trash." Barkley held up the bag of Five Faces. "Fucking guy loves his shish kebab."

Cat McShane didn't have to lose bottom to know when the water was getting deep. "Call me, Bark. And I've never been to Jimmy's so don't think I won't hold you to it."

She leaned across and kissed him, running a nail across the stubble on his cheek before climbing out. Soo waved at her. Cat shook her head and waved back. Barkley watched in the rearview mirror until she turned the corner. Then he got out. Soo was sitting on the curb, smiling like a shit-eating motherfucker who thought for sure he was about to get paid.

38

DANIEL FOUND her picking through Led Zeppelin albums. "Really?"

Grace turned, hair tumbling about her shoulders like a dark waterfall of silk. "I can do some Led Zep."

"Yeah, right."

"How did you know I was here?"

"I woke up around eleven, looked out the window, and there you were, sitting on the steps, watching the rain fall."

"You think it's stopped for good?"

"Hard to say."

Grace held a copy of *Physical Graffiti*. Daniel took the album from her, scanned the back, and returned it to its spot in Music City's collection.

"What are you doing, Grace?"

"What are you doing? Besides sleeping all day?"

He'd gone off the grid after Roxbury. Grace and Ben had rung his doorbell, but Daniel wasn't in the mood.

"You ever coming back to school?" she said.

"I think I'm done."

"Smart, Daniel. Real smart."

"The police killed that guy."

"No kidding."

The *Globe* and *Herald* had both tried to track him down, looking for a reaction to the shooting death of Walter Price. The newspaper guys didn't get any further than anyone else. Unlike Grace, however, they gave up a lot easier.

"How's your roommate?"

"You've been out here most nights, you tell me."

Her face warmed at the edges and Daniel could smell something new on her skin.

"He walks your apartment, Daniel. Sometimes all night."

"I know."

"While you sleep."

"So what?"

"So it's weird." Grace picked up another album, this time *Houses of the Holy*, and pretended to give it a look before putting it back. She'd aged five years in a week and he thought there was something more physical, more knowing about her. The idea of Ben rose up in Daniel's mind. Him with her. Her with him, scraping long nails across his shoulders as she whispered his name.

"I know about Ben," Daniel said.

Her cheeks flushed and the air grew close. "It's not what you think."

"How about we go outside and sit?"

They left the record store, settling on the steps. It was Saturday and Kenmore Square felt sluggish, like it was still groggy from Thanksgiving and not quite ready for Christmas.

"I pushed him," Grace said, lifting her chin toward the blank windows of Daniel's apartment. "At least I tried."

"Simon?"

"I was sitting right here, staring up at the window, watching him pace. Guess I couldn't help myself."

"Do me a favor and leave it alone."

"Is that what you want?"

"I saw Walter Price that night in the cellar. Had a chance to shoot him myself."

"I knew you never would."

"He didn't kill Harry. Otherwise, I would have pulled the trigger."

"You can lie to yourself, Daniel, but that's all it is."

He knocked her knee with his and held her hand loosely, tracing a finger across the flutter at her wrist, watching the color wash from her face.

"We're gonna be fine," she said.

That was another lie, but only he knew for sure. So he let it pass and waited for her to tell him what she'd come to say.

"I followed your roommate."

"Did he see you?"

"I don't think so."

"Did he see you?"

"No. It was the middle of the night and I could barely keep up."

"Good. So where did he go?"

39

IT HAD stormed off and on all afternoon, the sky grumbling in a drizzle of purples and blacks. The artistic soul, however, would not be denied. And so Zeus Sanchez watched from the window as a couple of men painted silhouettes of strippers on the side of the building. Sanchez followed the line of dancing women to an electric sign lying flat on the bed of a pickup. Three more men had set up a pulley and winch on the roof while a fourth ran a wire through two iron loops on the top of the sign and turned his thumb up. Sanchez read the block letters as the sign started to rise—KING ARTHUR'S MOTEL AND LOUNGE.

The Old Line Boarding House in Chelsea had been sold a few months back. Along with a new name, the owners were going to put in a bar and a couple of stripper poles downstairs. They'd keep the rooms upstairs, but now they'd rent them out by the hour. As far as he knew, Sanchez was the only guest left in the place. He hadn't paid for his room, never saw anyone else downstairs or in the hallway. There'd just been the key in an envelope, an address, and instructions. Three rings on the phone told him when it was time to eat. He'd troop downstairs and find his meal laid out on a table by the front door. When he was finished, he'd head back upstairs and stay there. If he didn't, they'd know and the deal would be off. At least that's what the instructions said and Sanchez had no reason to doubt it.

He walked over to the dresser and felt the weight of the envelope in his hand. He pulled out the cash and counted it, then counted again and put it away. He'd brought a transistor radio to keep up with the news. He wasn't sure if they knew about that and maybe he didn't give a fuck. He'd been scared at first, but things were changing. He was beginning to see the seams in their plan, cracks where before there'd been nothing. Was there risk? Sure. But he'd grown up immigrant poor and hungry as fuck. Plus he was a Harvard kid. Chances were he saw more than most.

The rain had returned in driving sheets. Sanchez was thinking about heading back to the window to watch the strippers as they washed off the side of the building when he heard a footfall. Three days and it was the first hint of another person in the place. Sanchez reached under the mattress and pulled out the Saturday night special he'd bought for twenty-five bucks with money from the envelope. He pointed the gun at the doorknob and watched it turn. Fucker wasn't knocking. And he had a key. Sanchez's finger tightened on the trigger as the door opened.

"You look like crap," Sanchez said, voice neutral and strong.

"Put it down."

"As soon as you tell me what's going on."

The visitor stepped inside. When you came right down to it, short of pulling the trigger, the kid from Harvard didn't really have a plan. So he dropped his gun hand as the visitor walked around the room, tugging down shades and acting like he owned the place, which he pretty much did. He sat down on the bed and the two began to talk. Actually, the visitor talked. Sanchez nodded a lot and listened.

40

RAIN BATTERED the windows, making a sharp sound before sliding off into infinity. Barkley paused at the top of the stairs, Kenny Soo on his shoulder. The detective put a finger to his lips. Soo was a statue even when he wasn't and shot Barkley a look that said *Let's get on with it*. Barkley led the way, easing across the hall to Nick Toney's studio. He gave the door a light knock, then tried the knob. Locked. Barkley motioned Soo back toward the stairwell and sized up the jamb for one of his size thirteens. Soo touched the detective's shoulder and shook his head. He crab walked around Barkley and crouched by the lock. From a pocket the little prick produced a leather case with a set of steel picks. Thirty seconds later, the door popped open. Soo was already inside. Barkley pulled his gun and followed.

They'd talked downstairs, sitting on the curb as trash blew down the street and the first drops of rain picked at their shoulders and hair. Soo had called the station three days earlier with some information. Barkley had been tied up with Tommy's hearing and never got the message. Now Soo wanted to pass along what he knew. And get paid.

"Kenny . . ." Barkley moved through the darkened photography studio toward a suite of rooms in the back. He found Soo in a small office with a cot in the corner. Soo was rummaging through a set of desk drawers.

"Stay here and shut up." Barkley threw Soo into a chair and checked out the other two rooms. One was a bathroom, complete with a claw-foot tub. The other looked like it might be Toney's darkroom. Barkley grabbed Soo on his way back to the main space. He sat Soo at a long table and flipped open the Fitzsimmons murder file.

"Let's go over what you told me again."

"Okay, boss." Soo sat with his hands folded like he was in third grade. Barkley couldn't figure out the kid and didn't really have the time. He pulled out Harvard's student photo of Zeus Sanchez. "This guy's name is Sanchez. Jesus Sanchez."

Soo nodded, eyes moving from the photo to Barkley and back again. "I told you downstairs. He's the guy."

"Go through it again, Kenny."

"Middle of the afternoon, three days ago." Soo held up two fingers. "He was in Five Faces."

Barkley's balls had tightened when Soo first mentioned Five Faces. Now the detective watched as Soo examined the photo a second time.

"I need you to make sure, Kenny."

"I'm sure. Pay me, motherfucker." Soo grinned and pushed the photo away. Barkley counted out three twenties.

"Pay as we go. Now, what else?"

"He was worried. Major-league worried. Sat in the shop for an hour before the other guy showed up."

"And you've never seen the other guy?"

Soo shook his head. Barkley pulled out a photo of Neil Prescott, as well as the picture of Daniel Fitzsimmons.

"Neither of these two?"

"Come on, man."

"He was a white guy, right?"

"Yeah, but older."

"And not Toney?"

"No way. I haven't seen Toney for a week."

"But Sanchez came up here? With the other guy?"

"I told you. They talked for a while in Five Faces, then they walked next door to the Brompton. I don't know if they came up here."

"Where else would they have gone?"

Soo made a pumping motion with his fist. "Boom boom. Lots of girls live here, boss."

"How long were they in the building?"

"Two hours, maybe."

"And you never saw Toney? Before or since?"

Soo glanced around the room. Outside, the weather couldn't make up its mind, bulleting against the glass one minute, then fading to nothing. "You think he's dead?"

Toney's studio had been emptied. No camera equipment, no photos, just a few strands of wire running the width of the place.

"I don't know, Kenny. You didn't see anyone moving shit out of here?"

"No."

"And you usually see Toney a lot?"

"Every day, in and out."

"Okay. I got some things I gotta do."

"Can I help?"

Barkley didn't want Soo around but figured it was better to keep him close. "Sure. How about I deputize you?"

Barkley pulled on a pair of latex gloves and gave a pair to Soo. Then he got up and began to walk the perimeter. It took the rest of the afternoon and a good part of the evening, but he finally found what he was looking for in the bathroom. Soo had been on his shoulder the entire time, watching what Barkley watched, squatting where Barkley squatted. Now he studied the detective's face.

"What is it?"

Barkley was peering down into the tub. He reached in and ran a finger around the drain.

"Boss?"

"I think that's blood, Kenny."

"Think?"

"It's blood."

"Toney's dead?"

For the first time since they'd met, Soo sounded like a scared kid. Barkley led the way back to the main room.

"Sit down, Kenny."

Barkley made a show of going through the Fitzsimmons murder file a second time, pulling a thick stack of photos from the alley. He picked out five shots and spread them in front of Soo. "These are pictures we took of the crowd on the night of the murder." There were dozens of faces, smudges of color pinned back behind yellow police tape. "Sometimes a killer likes to get a look at his handiwork. So he comes back and watches."

Soo nodded but didn't take his eyes off the photos.

"Take your time." Barkley felt the building's prickly radiator heat laying down sweat and grime in the lines of his neck. "If you don't see the guy who was with Sanchez . . ."

"There he is."

Soo jabbed at one of the photos. Barkley had only been interested in one photo and only one person in it. Kenny Soo had nailed it.

"You sure?"

"He was with Sanchez in Five Faces. Ten out of ten."

Barkley studied the picture of Tommy Dillon, wrapped in a gray overcoat and peering over his shoulder at the camera. Then Barkley restacked the photos and put them back in the file. He locked the door on his way out and called into the station from a pay phone. He gave Toney's address to Charlie Herbert and told him to seal the room. Barkley didn't offer an explanation. Just seal the room and wait until he called. After he hung up, he gave Soo five more twenties and said there'd be another hondo coming if the kid did three things.

"Whatever, boss."

"First, keep your mouth shut."

Soo nodded.

"Second, stay out of Toney's place. Third, let me know if anyone else shows up looking to get in. Besides the cops, that is."

"And what if Toney shows up?"

"Toney ain't gonna be showing up, son. But if he does, you can give me a call."

Soo rubbed his fingers together. "More money?"

"Why not?"

41

BARKLEY UNWRAPPED his sandwich and inhaled. Roast beef, sliced paper thin and piled high on a pillow-soft onion roll, a slice of white cheese, slightly melted, and slathers of barbecue sauce. Barkley ate half of it in one go and looked out the scarred windows of Buzzy's Roast Beef. He'd been driving around most of the night, figuring the angles, weighing the odds, writing his obituary in his head. All in all, it read better than he expected. A couple of college kids slipped out from behind the Red Line station, stumbling across the street and heading in the general direction of the Charles Street Jail. Buzzy's lived in the shadow of Boston's oldest lockup, providing an endless source of fun and amusement for a parade of drunks with a hankering for beef. Some sandwich shops gave their children crayons and paper to scribble on. Buzzy's offered its own life-size jail, replete with barbed wire, searchlights, and a twenty-foot-high brick wall.

Barkley watched as the drunken duo surveyed the outside of the jail, pacing first one way, then the other. Finally they found their spot and went to work, one guy giving the other ten fingers in an attempt to spider-man up and over the wall. Their efforts ended with the first kid folding back into the gutter and the would-be climber falling face-first onto the pavement. He bounced back up, both of them laughing and pushing and punch-ing each other as they staggered the final few feet to Buzzy's.

Ah, the magic of booze.

The pair each ordered a roast beef sandwich and a knish from the guy behind the counter. Barkley took his food to the far end of the place where a pay phone hung on the wall. He crunched down on an onion ring, wiped the grease off his fin-gers, and dropped money into the phone. Cat McShane picked up on the third ring.

"Whoever this is, it had better be good."

"It's me."

"What time is it?"

"Almost four."

"Jesus Christ."

"I'm down at Buzzy's."

"Where?"

"Buzzy's. By the jail. I needed a sandwich."

"So you spend the night in the Combat Zone, then head over to Buzzy's and gorge. How very original."

"I'm working, Cat."

"And I'm sleeping. What do you want?"

"I need you to go over to the address we were at today."

"Five Faces? I told you, the skewers you gave me matched. There's not much more I can do."

"The hotel next door. Place called the Brompton Arms." Bark-ley gave her the address. "You'll find a cop on the top floor guard-ing a door. I told him to expect you. Go inside. There's a bathroom in the back."

"Is this someone's apartment?"

"It's a photography studio. Go into the bathroom and test the tub for blood."

"Your guy can do that. Just spray some Luminol around."

"I don't want him in there. No one but you."

Cat didn't respond.

"If you don't want to do it, I understand."

"I need to know more."

He told her about Kenny Soo and how he'd spotted Zeus Sanchez at Five Faces with a stranger, how the two of them had paid a visit to the Brompton.

"And this studio belongs to someone connected to the Fitzsimmons murder?"

"The guy who took the snaps in the alley. A photographer named Nick Toney."

"What's the name of the student again?"

"Sanchez. Zeus Sanchez. He was the one who got his wallet clipped."

"So Harry Fitzsimmons went down the alley chasing him?"

"Yeah. We took a statement from Sanchez that night, then he dropped off the radar. The way things shook out, it didn't seem important."

"And now you have questions?"

"Soo was able to pick out the guy who was with Sanchez at Five Faces."

"And how did he do that?"

"I showed him a photo."

"Your partner."

"How'd you guess?"

"It's in your voice, Bark. Like a fucking bell."

"Why would Tommy be talking to Sanchez after the Price shooting? And why would they go up and see Toney?"

"You asking me?"

"Been driving around all night asking myself."

"Tommy Dillon has already murdered one kid, Bark. And you looked the other way. Now, you're worried it's not over. And you're worried you're gonna get sucked in even deeper."

"I think he killed Nick Toney."

"Christ."

"I want to make sure I know what I know."

"Then what?"

"You said it. This is a cop thing. And that's how it'll go down."

"Listen . . ."

"I understand, Cat. You don't owe me anything."

"Give me a number where I can call you."

He gave her the number of the pay phone.

"I'll ring back when I have something."

"How long?"

"An hour, two tops. Eat another sandwich and think about how much you're gonna owe me."

Cat hung up. Barkley picked at his onion rings and sipped at a Coke. The two drunks were outside again, throwing pieces of their sandwiches over the wall of the jail and into the yard. Ninety minutes later, Buzzy's was empty when the pay phone rang. The counterman gave Barkley a look like *It sure as shit isn't for me.* The detective picked up and listened. He left money on the counter and found his Camaro where he'd left it, parked illegally in front of the Beacon Hill Pub. A college kid was swaying back and forth as he pissed on one of Barkley's tires. He shooed the kid away and fired up the engine. The sky was just starting to lighten as he headed for the expressway.

42

DANIEL WOKE up and walked into the kitchen. A cantaloupe was sitting on the counter, ripe and round and firm. He took up the knife that lay beside it and worked quickly, cutting first lengthwise, then across. He ate the fruit in large chunks, letting the flesh explode in his mouth and the juice run over his teeth, lips, and down his chin. When he was done, he picked up the knife again, holding it in his left hand as he started down the hallway. The doors to both of Simon's rooms stood wide open. That had never happened before and Daniel hesitated before going in. Simon's workroom looked much like it did in Daniel's dream. A long table, bare of even a scrap of paper, and a chair pushed in neatly as if the owner had washed his hands of the whole thing and wasn't planning on coming back. In the bedroom the mattress had been stripped and the only closet was empty. Daniel climbed the stairs to the roof. No easel, no colored pencils, no sign of Simon anywhere.

Daniel went back downstairs and sat behind the big desk in the main room. From the window, he could see an MBTA worker in one of the lanes of the bus station. The man nudged a cigarette from a pack and lit it, shaking his head at something while he shuffled his feet in the gray morning light. A bus rolled in and the station man stepped aside, acknowledging the driver with a jut of his chin. He had a newspaper stuck in his back pocket and pulled it out as he crossed the street, heading toward Charlie's Diner and breakfast—two eggs, toast, and home fries for a buck nineteen.

Daniel turned from the window. Grace had told him she'd followed Simon to a building that looked like a church. She hadn't wanted Daniel to go but knew he was beyond that now and would do what he would. So she'd avoided his eyes and given him the address, telling him to go in the early morning if he must go at all. It was just seven when he pulled on his coat and headed out.

—

An oculus was cut into the dome of the roof, fresh light spilling and pooling onto the floor, revealing every scrape in the stone, the wearing that comes from generations of feet shuffled one step at a time. Daniel walked the circle, careful not to touch its edge, content to live in the shadows that otherwise filled the space.

He knew he was being watched and waited while his eyes adjusted to the darkness. A gilded angel grinned from the rafters, studying with its Mona Lisa smile. Simon was sheltered in the alcove just below. Their eyes caught and Daniel saw a fighter plane scream, slashes of sun setting its wings ablaze as they tipped and dove. A tree bent over a river, white blossoms dropping from its branches while a circle of silent ripples fled outward. The two images twisted and bled until the wash from the plane and the chop across the water were one in Daniel's head.

Simon beckoned with two fingers. "This way."

He stayed just out of reach, salt on his tongue and in his words, leading Daniel to a room just off the main area. There was a desk with a lamp, a phone, an adding machine, and a spread of newspapers. A sleeping bag was rolled up in one corner and a fireplace was cut into the wall. Simon pulled two coffees from a plain white bag.

"It's black, but there's cream and sugar there." Simon took the top off his coffee, which turned out to be tea. He dunked the bag a couple of times and tossed it into a wastebasket as he settled behind the desk. Daniel sat in the only chair left.

"How are you feeling?" Simon said, blowing on his tea before trying it.

"What is this place?"

"Used to be a church. Puritan, Anglican, Catholic. Now, the Buddhists are giving it a go."

"You got a key or something?"

"I've got a key. They let me come in and think. Sometimes I sit in the sunlight."

Daniel pulled across his coffee but didn't take a sip. "I know you've been in the apartment at night."

"Yes."

"Why don't you come around during the day?"

"Why don't you come out at night?"

"Forget it."

From outside came the muffle of traffic. Simon set his tea on the desk and gave the cup a quarter turn. "In quantum physics there's a principle we call 'decoherence.' It says that the act of looking at or measuring particles in an entangled state will actually cause that state to collapse and cease to exist."

"So?"

"So to get around that, we take our measurements indirectly, with eyes averted, if you will."

"Is that what you've been doing with me?"

"In a sense. You needed space, Daniel. So I gave it to you."

"And now?"

"And now perhaps it's time to risk a more direct approach." Simon opened up a drawer and pulled out two files. One was red, the other green. He picked up the first and balanced it on the flat of his palm. "The autopsy report on your brother."

"And the other?"

"Your mother. Where would you like to start?"

Daniel picked up the green file. Simon stayed his hand. "Let me walk you through it."

Sometimes he referred to the file. Other times, he just sat back and talked and Daniel knew he'd been there, somewhere along the empty highway of beach, watching, studying, keeping score. Simon paused when he came to the part about how Daniel's mother died, why she died, the play-by-play of events that led to that moment. It was a tricky passage and Daniel wanted to take the corners at high speed.

"Who was in the car with her?"

"You mean who put you in the trunk?"

"How do you know so much?"

"I don't know any more than you."

"Afterward I was in a hospital."

Simon pulled out his pipe and took his time lighting it. "Boston City. You lapsed into a coma."

"There was a man there when I woke up. On the day I was discharged, he jumped off a roof."

"You wanted him dead. Just like part of you wanted your mother dead." Simon waited for a challenge that never came. He drew on the pipe and continued. "Coincidentally, they both died. And now, you're wondering if you . . . what's the term you use?"

"Pushed."

"Yes. If you pushed them. I already told you it doesn't work that way. The man jumped because he wanted to. All you did was applaud. As for your mother, you know what you know."

"I saw who was with her on the beach."

"Really?"

Daniel could sense the first bit of tightening around Simon's eyes.

"There are flashes. A glimpse of something as he slammed the trunk."

"What if I told you what happened to her was for the best?"

"I'd tell you to go fuck yourself."

Simon smiled, a sentient thing that stole over his face and was gone. He put down his pipe and picked up the autopsy report on Harry. "The police never told you about the different types of wounds your brother suffered?"

"No."

Simon tossed the file back on the desk. "You hungry?"

Daniel shook his head.

"Me neither." Simon opened up another, deeper drawer and pulled out a bag. It had a Five Faces logo on the side.

"I know that place," Daniel said.

Simon unwrapped an order of beef shish kebab. The meat looked cold and was thick with grease. He pulled the pieces off with his fingers, holding the skewer by one end.

"Open up the autopsy file, Daniel. Page seven, there's some highlighted language."

Daniel read while Simon talked. When he was done, he sat back and watched as Daniel's belly and bowels turned to water.

"You think that killed my brother?"

"One like it, yes."

"And you know who did it?"

"As I said, I know as much as you do."

"How did you get these reports?"

"I told you about computers, internetworking. It will be commonplace in the future to do what I do. For now, it's not." Simon brushed his fingers across the spread of files. "Why do you think I'm sharing all this?"

"No idea."

"Why do you think you see the animals?"

"I became one myself."

"Yes, in the Boston Common. Then, in Franklin Park with the hyenas. And, of course, the first time, at Latin School. Why?"

"I don't know. Guess I'm hallucinating."

Simon turned up his nose at the notion.

"Then what?"

"The animals helped to crack your world open. Create the room necessary for change."

"What sort of change?"

Simon pressed his lips together, and the room seemed to dim. "Remember when I asked if you knew about 'deep time'?"

"Yes."

"It's a term more and more scientists are using to explain spans of time that otherwise seem incomprehensible. The earth, for example, is roughly four and a half billion years old. Does that mean anything to you?"

Daniel shrugged.

"Exactly. An impossible concept for most of us to grasp. But consider a metaphor." Simon snapped his fingers and a thin blue light flickered to life, a laser running in a line from the inside of his eye to the tip of his outstretched finger. "Are you still with me?"

Daniel would have gasped, except he knew if he did the light would disappear and, right now, that was the last thing he wanted. So he just nodded.

"Good. One of my colleagues has suggested we think about the earth's age as the equivalent of the old measure of the English yard—that is, the distance from the king's nose to the tip of his finger." Simon wiggled his outstretched index finger. "If we were to accept that premise, then the entirety of human history—the entirety, mind you—would be represented by the nail's edge on the very end of that finger. One tickle with a file and mankind is toast. Erased from all existence. That's how old the earth is . . . and how insignificant we are in the grand scheme of things." Simon dropped his arm and the blue light vanished.

"I get it," Daniel said, just to say something.

Simon shook his head. "You get nothing. What I've given you is an example of *horizontal* deep time. Interesting, sure, but on its best day little more than a tunnel into the past. What truly matters is something I like to call *vertical* deep time." He leaned closer so Daniel could see the swirl in his eyes. "As an object approaches the speed of light, time slows to a crawl. If we could actually travel at the speed of light, time would stand still."

"But that's impossible."

"Is it? I suspect deep time doesn't just stretch back into history, Daniel. I believe it can also drill down into each passing moment, freezing reality and peeling it back, exposing all its dimensions and all its layers. Kind of like when you dream."

"Except you're not?"

"Except you're not."

"Is deep time tied into entanglement?"

Simon's smile was a flicker of curling flame. "Everything in the universe is connected, every person, every animal, every plant, everything, living or not. Not just spatially, but temporally. All things exist at the same time, all measures of yourself, all that's ever been and ever will be, flows continually like water from a spigot. And all at the speed of light. That's what we feel even if we don't understand. That's what we see even if we don't recognize."

Simon got up and walked over to the hearth, squatting to light a match. The fire blazed quickly, unnaturally, filling the room with its heat. He rubbed his hands together and took a seat against the opposite wall, pulling his knees tight to his chest as his face dissolved into shadow.

"It's the ghost in the mirror. The chill when you walk into an empty house. It's déjà vu, premonition, that tingle of 'clicking' with someone new as if you've known her all your life. People come up with all sorts of names, but what they're really seeing is a crack in the wall, a glimpse, a glimmer of the eternal we're all enmeshed in."

"Entangled."

"You're uniquely able to exist, persist in the great fields of connectivity. You can access them, navigate them. Maintain that space and actually live in it. It's a gift, Daniel. Nothing else."

"It didn't save my brother."

"Every man must one day stretch out his hand. Harry understood that."

"You talk like you knew him."

"I did. And I knew he had to die."

Daniel flinched, head turning as the fire in the hearth cracked like a gunshot. When he turned back, Simon was gone. On the floor where he'd been sitting was his leather case full of sketches. Daniel pulled out the top sketch, the one Simon had shown him on that first day at the apartment, except now it was finished. A piece of coastline—trees, a seawall, and a black road twisting down to a flat slab of beach. Daniel knew the place. And knew what it was he must do.

43

BARKLEY WAS parked on G Street, listening to the radio and watching all the crazy Irish fucks, asleep in their crazy Irish fuck beds. Except one. There was a light burning in Tommy Dillon's living room. Barkley was about to open the door when a set of headlights swept past. A station wagon trimmed in wood pulled up in front of the three-decker and a thick-legged woman got out. Katie Dillon met her on the porch. Katie was wrapped up in a robe and wore a pair of baby blue slippers. The other woman was bundled in a parka and kept it zipped to her throat. The two women seemed anxious, eyes sweeping the street as they talked. Serious talk between serious women. Women with a problem. Katie disappeared inside and returned a minute later, handing the other woman something and hugging her.

Barkley waited until the station wagon had turned the corner, then waited another couple of minutes, listening to Eddie Andelman talk about Norm Cook, the C's first-round draft pick, and how he sucked the big one. Barkley kicked out of the car and made his way across the street. The door opened before he could knock. Then he was inside, in the dark and the warmth, the scent of the house that was a home even with all the rest of it.

She closed the door behind him and turned so he could see her face.

"He hit you."

Katie put a finger to her lips and led him down the hall to the bedroom.

"Where is he?"

"The girls are sleeping."

"Where is he?"

"I dunno."

"Let me see."

She let him turn her face into the light. The right side had ripened to a rich shade of plum and was already swollen, like someone had slipped a soft egg under the skin. Her left eye was partially shut, the white in the lower half clotted with blood.

"My neighbor's coming over."

Barkley let go of her chin. "I just saw her. In the wagon?"

Katie nodded. "Loretta Sweeney. She's gonna take the girls. Could you help get them into the car? I don't want them to see me . . ." She lifted her hands to her face and crumbled a bit at the edges.

"I'll get them."

There was a small knock.

"That's her," Katie said. "I told her to come around to the kitchen."

"Stay here."

"Just tell them it's a sleepover. Loretta will explain the rest."

Barkley went to the back door and let in the woman he'd seen in the wagon. If Loretta Sweeney was surprised to see a massive black man in the Dillons' kitchen at seven in the morning, she didn't let on.

"The kids?"

He led her down the hall and stood in the doorway as she gently woke first Molly, then Maggie. She left them in their pajamas, bundling them into heavy coats and sweeping them, stiff legged and still half asleep, down the hall. One of them, Barkley thought it was Maggie, finally seemed to realize what was going on when the door opened and the cold air hit her.

"Where's Mom?"

Loretta smoothed Maggie's hair with thick, blunt fingers and kissed the top of her head. "She and your daddy have to take care of some things this morning. So you're gonna stay with me. Okay?"

"What about school?"

"No school today. We'll sleep late, watch some TV. Maybe make cupcakes. What do you say?"

"Who's that?" Maggie pointed at Barkley, who squatted so he was eye level with the two girls.

"I work with your dad. You've seen me."

The twins nodded but didn't seem certain. Who could blame them?

"You go on now, okay? Your mom will pick you up this afternoon."

"Can we have cocoa?" That was Molly, finally coming around.

"Sure," Barkley said.

"And marshmallows?" Maggie was in on the game.

"Why not?"

"And cinnamon toast with butter?" Molly, again.

Barkley smiled and nodded, kissing each of the girls on the top of the head. And then they left, Loretta giving him a final, flat look before closing the door. Southie might be a closed book to the rest of the world, but they looked out for their own. And that wasn't something you could say about most places.

Barkley went back down the hall. Katie had been listening. She stepped into the bedroom and sat at a small table and mirror. She was barefoot now, dressed in a thin nightgown and not yet thirty, but Barkley could already see the gentle sag in her breasts, a hint of loose flesh under her arms. When she looked up at him in the mirror, her reflection was that of a woman who'd put in the miles, wrinkles carved around stiff eyes, a hardness at the corners of her mouth.

"I look a wreck."

"Like hell."

"I'm sorry, Bark. Fuck."

"Let's get a better look at your face."

He found a shallow pan and filled it. She fussed, but he made her sit still and soaked a washcloth in the warm, soapy water. Barkley didn't do a lot of gentle things and felt his pulse quicken and the spit in his mouth turn to dust as he dabbed at his partner's palm print tattooed in long red welts across the side of his wife's face. At first touch Katie winced and closed her eyes. His second touch caused her to shiver from the inside out. The third broke her wide open. Blood mingled with water, mingled with tears, mingled with life and ran down her face in a sticky, brave-as-fuck mess.

"It's okay, Katie."

It wasn't okay, would never be okay. She began to cry harder, quieter, fiercer, and Barkley could feel her strength, running generations deep and woman strong, stronger than him, stronger than her husband, stronger than any man could fathom.

"Tell me what happened."

She looked up, eyes fierce now, drenched in life for all its sadness and all its thankless bullshit.

"Tell me."

A tear rolled down one cheek. He caught it with a fingertip
and she stroked the side of his hand, turning so he could feel the
rub of her skin. She kissed his hand and took it in hers, hungry
butterfly kisses along its length before slipping it slowly inside
her nightgown so he could feel the fullness there and her nipple
rise and grow hard.

"Katie . . ."

"Don't fucking talk."

"But . . ."

"No, Bark. Fuck, no." She pulled him down, pulled him close,
opening her mouth as she kissed him, moving now, rising to her
feet, pushing her body against his, pinning him against the wall,
running her hands along his back, free inside his shirt. He heard
himself moan lightly as she tugged at his belt, then slipped inside
and gripped him, staring at him through her damaged eye as she
began to stroke.

"K—"

"Shut up." She slid to her knees, never breaking eye contact,
and took him in her mouth. Then they were on the bed, her on
the bottom, then somehow on top, her nightgown floating away
as she began to move, leaning back so he could see the line of
her body, feel the rhythm of her hips, the grind of her pelvis.
Barkley rolled his eyes back in his head and let himself fill her,
deep-rooted now, joined as one in mind and flesh, if only for this
moment in time and this moment was everything that ever was
and ever would be. And then the front door opened.

She never said a word, just slipped off him in one impossibly graceful movement, switching off the overhead so all that was left was a night-light by her feet and their breath stoking the darkness between them. Footsteps came from the front of the apartment, one, two, three. Whoever it was, and Barkley sure as fuck had a good idea who it might be, made his way to the kitchen, where he started to yell.

"Katie. Fucking Katie."

Tommy Dillon didn't sound drunk, but he didn't have to be. It was five steps from the kitchen to the bedroom. Maybe seven on a good day, which this clearly wasn't. Barkley was on his feet by the second stride. Katie had pushed the door shut and for the first time Barkley noticed the small latch—a dangling hook with an eye socket for when they wanted to keep the kids out. Tommy kept coming down the hall. Three strides, four. Katie was still naked, the curves of her body soft in the fuzzy glow coming from near her feet. She put a finger to her lips and slipped the hook on. Five strides, six. Tommy pulled at the knob.

"Fucking shit."

Barkley watched the hook bounce in the eyelet. Up, down. Up, down. If it stayed in place, maybe he wouldn't wind up shooting his partner. If it didn't . . . Barkley backed away from the door, eyes fixed on that goddamn hook as it danced. He'd gotten dressed somehow. Somehow pulled his gun and held it in his right hand. Katie motioned with her eyes toward a closet. Barkley ducked inside and closed the door until it was open just a crack. In one motion, the beautiful poetry of an all-state point guard maybe a half step past her prime, Katie slipped on her nightgown and called out to her husband, voice doused with the perfect amount of sleep.

"What the Christ do you want?"

Tommy's reply came from a bedroom down the hall. "Where are the girls?"

More footsteps, another wrench on the door and the heroic latch. "Katie, let me the fuck in. Now."

Still she took her time, pulling on her robe, cinching it and running hands through her hair. "Jesus, I sent them over to Loretta's. Hold on."

"Why do you got the fucking door locked . . ."

"Quit pulling at the thing and I'll open it."

Tommy stopped tugging, and Katie slipped the latch free. Then he was in the room, shoulders and back filling Barkley's vision.

"Why did you lock the door?"

"Cuz I felt like it."

The blow came quick and flat, practiced and mean, the back of his hand slashing across the side of her cheek, lifting Katie onto the bed, where she banged off the headboard and wound up on her knees, hands in fists clutching the bedsheets.

"I'm sorry," Tommy said.

"Fuck you."

"I said I was sorry."

Fresh marks mingled with the not-so-old and there was a tickle of blood on her lip. Katie licked at it, then wiped at it with her hand. "You wanna know why I locked the door?"

"Katie . . ."

"You wanna know why I sent the kids away? You wanna let them see their mom like this? Is that what you fucking want, Tommy?"

He moved toward her.

"Touch me again and I swear you'll have to kill me."

Tommy stopped in his tracks. "K—"

"I fucking mean it."

He sank to the floor, elbows on his knees, head in his hands, curling up into less than nothing as he started to cry, wet, heaving, choking sobs dredged up from some place of pain that made Barkley wonder even more about his partner and how deep a hole he'd dug himself. Katie crawled off the bed, making small animal sounds in her throat as she settled close by her husband, taking his head in her lap and kissing the tears and salt off his face, stroking his cheeks and his temples, closing his eyes with her fingers and staring across the room at Barkley in the closet. For all his years in interrogation rooms, talking to every lowlife, psychotic motherfucker Boston had to offer, Barkley couldn't read a word of what was going on inside the woman's head. She lifted her husband's face and framed it in her strong, perfect hands. She kissed him and held him, all gentle now. He mumbled his apologies and tried to touch her cheek, but she wouldn't let him. She walked him back to the bed, undressing him as they went, and made love to him amid the warm wrinkles of the sheets Barkley had felt against his own skin. He watched and knew it was how it had to be because the relationship was a prison and an addiction and would always be for her no matter what might follow. And when it was done and Tommy had stopped crying and grown again from child to man, he told her he had to leave. And she didn't try to stop him, kissing him like it was the last time, in front of the dressing table where Barkley could watch in the reflection of the mirror if he chose, and then Tommy left, taking his gun with him. Katie sat quietly at the table as Barkley came out of the closet.

"If you're gonna follow him, you better get a move on." Her

eyes were soulless, skyless windows, drained of everything now so all that was left was her. And she'd never been lovelier. Barkley turned to go.

"Bark."

He stopped, knowing better than to look back.

"You gonna kill him?"

"Why would I do that?"

"The girls need a dad, Bark."

He left the room, striding down the hall to the front door. He gambled Tommy was headed for the expressway and picked him up just as he hit the ramp. Barkley stayed four or five car lengths back. His partner was in the left lane, cooking at ninety miles plus. Wherever he was going, Tommy Dillon was in a hurry.

44

THEY JUMPED off the expressway in Chelsea, bumping along Williams Street, then Beacham. On one side was a span of railroad tracks. Along the other, a string of truck bays sitting behind high fences and covered in layers of Chelsea grit and Mystic River grime. Barkley tucked behind a delivery truck with a huge head of lettuce and a bunch of baby lettuces painted on its side. He rolled down the window, smelling the sharpness of garlic mingled with the root smell of turnip and wondered where Tommy was headed. They drove for another mile, then the road hooked left, curling past the main entrance to the New England Produce Center. Fifty yards beyond the gate, Tommy eased into a lot. Barkley kept going, slumping down in his seat as he passed a two-story building with a couple of eight-foot-high naked women painted in dancing whitewash along the building's face. It looked like someone had started to paint a third but gave up after half a head, one breast, and an elbow. Barkley drove another quarter mile and turned around, pulling into a gas station and parking so he had a view of the building and lot. Tommy was still behind the wheel, not moving, not doing a thing.

It was another half hour before he got out, hands stuffed in the pockets of his black leather jacket. Barkley looked for the gun on Tommy's hip, but it wasn't there. He hunched his shoulders as he walked, past the twitchy dancing girls and behind the building. Ten minutes later, he appeared on the other side and went back to his car, opening the passenger's-side door and getting in. A semi rolled past, this one featuring a row of smiling tomatoes that looked more like Mexican women than tomatoes, complete with rounded hips, straw hats, and plump red breasts. The semi slowed, then stopped, idling in the middle of the road and blocking Barkley's view. The driver hung there for a couple of minutes, pumping his air brakes a half-dozen times, then rolled again, heading straight for the gates of the produce center. Behind the semi, the front seat of Tommy's car was empty.

Barkley got out and jogged across Beacham, cutting behind the building and coming up on the other side. He crouched beside a Dumpster fifty feet away and squinted against the glare of the sun, rising to his left and reflecting off the flat glass of the second-floor windows. A bank of clouds drifted overhead, cutting the glare for a moment, and Barkley blinked. The first set of windows at the back of the building looked empty. The second-floor window at the front corner, however, was a different story. Barkley could clearly make out the outline of a person sitting in a chair, staring down at the street below. There was something odd about the figure, the shift of the shoulders, the way the head nodded forward. Barkley threaded his way along the edge of the lot until he was almost directly across from the window. The solitary figure was a dark blotch, not moving as the sun peeked out again, bathing the scene in a shiv of morning light, revealing everything Barkley had thought, everything he'd feared.

He pulled his gun and began to run, past the window, around

the corner, and through the front door. To his left was an old staircase winding up to the building's second floor. Barkley took the steps two at a time, bursting through a blue door at the top. The first thing he saw was the back of Tommy Dillon's jacket, faded leather wrapped around a torso rigged to the chair with a couple turns of rope.

"Tommy . . ."

Barkley holstered his gun and took three strides across the room, lifting the body's head and staring into the blank eyes of another dead kid from Harvard. Barkley cut Zeus Sanchez from the chair and laid him out on the floor, checking in vain for a pulse while taking note of the bluish tinge to his lips, damp hair, and absence of any visible wounds. He leaned forward to close the kid's eyes just as Tommy Dillon fired from a doorway. That would have been it, should have been it, Barkley's skull popped like one of the overripe melons sitting at the ass end of the truck bays across the street. But Barkley's lean had saved him, the bullet burying itself in a hunk of drywall an inch or so above the detective's head.

Tommy fired a second and third time, except Barkley was moving now, hugging the wall, giving his partner no angle as he closed the space between them. Tommy Dillon was nothing if not tough, and tough guys could never pass up a fistfight, even when they were giving away six inches plus and over a hundred pounds. So Barkley was ready when his partner charged, roaring like the crazy fuck he was, spitting another bullet and hitting nothing. Barkley caught Tommy's weight easily, tossing him like a sack of Vidalia onions. Tommy hit the wall, spine first, gun clattering across the floor. Barkley kicked it away and waited as Tommy climbed to his feet. He lunged again, hands curled like hooks, hunting for Barkley's eyes. Barkley stepped to one side and loaded up with a short right, dropping his partner, who hit his head on a radiator and didn't move.

Barkley rubbed his knuckles and swore, picking up the gun and pocketing it. Then he stripped Tommy's leather jacket off Sanchez, grabbed him by the heels, and dragged him into the hall. In an adjoining bathroom was a tub with a puddle of water near the drain. Barkley returned to the front and cuffed Tommy to the chair. Barkley found a second chair and sat in it, watching Tommy not breathe, wondering whether he'd killed the fuck. All things considered, that might be for the best. Just then Tommy groaned and lifted his head. Barkley pointed the throwaway piece his partner had tried to shoot him with at his partner's nose and waited.

"You never could punch for shit," Tommy said.

"How's the head? I'm guessing you got a concussion."

"Like it matters."

Barkley shrugged. "How do you want it?"

"Clean. Fast. Don't wanna be no fucking vegetable, pissing on myself and drooling and all that shit."

"I got you."

"You'll make up something for Katie?"

Barkley nodded, breaking eye contact for the first time.

"I know you was boning her, Bark. Fuck, I knew all along."

"You were broken up."

"Exactly. Hell, I was proud of it, you wanna know the truth."

Barkley didn't wanna know the truth. At least not that kind. "Why Sanchez?"

"Where is he?"

Barkley rolled his eyes toward the hallway.

"He's no fucking saint, B. He set up Fitzsimmons. Whole thing was a setup."

"There was no girl grabbing Sanchez's wallet?"

"I sent one of 'em by to duck her head in the car. He was supposed to raise holy hell and then run down the street after her."

"Why?"

"Sanchez said Fitzsimmons would follow. All-for-one, stand-up guy and all that college crap. Big fucking game."

"But why?"

"They wanted Fitzsimmons in the alley."

"Who's they?"

"Can't go there, B. Might come back on Katie, the girls."

Barkley tried a different tack. "What did they have on Sanchez?"

"What do you think? He liked to gamble. Owed money to the wrong people. At first they were pushing him to shave points on a couple of Harvard games, but the kid never got off the fucking bench. Then this came up. Sanchez thought they just wanted to roll Fitzsimmons, grab his wallet or something."

"How about you?"

"You had it sniffed out from the jump. I never really got off nothing. Dope, booze, betting, all that shit. By the time I got halfway straight, the fuckers owned me, balls and all."

"Let me guess. Trunks full of blow and forever money."

"For Katie and the girls, B. You, too."

"All I gotta do is unlock the cuffs."

They both knew that wasn't gonna happen. Even if there'd been no bodies, Barkley wasn't ever gonna get rich skimming money off drug dealers. Would he have looked the other way if

Tommy had broken off his piece? Maybe. But not now. Not with the bodies and all the rest.

"You hired Walter Price," Barkley said.

"Laid it out for him, chapter and fucking verse. Gave him the knife, for Chrissakes. Then he doesn't finish the job."

"So you did?"

Tommy smiled weakly. "I know what you're thinking. We weren't together that night, so I could have been down in the alley and done Fitzsimmons. Didn't happen that way."

"How did it happen?"

"Already told you, B. Not going there."

Barkley nodded in the general direction of the bathroom. "Why kill Sanchez?"

"Fucking guy went off the grid. When he finally surfaced, he wanted to meet. So I had him hole up here."

"He wanted to get paid."

"Worse. Conscience. He's torn up, talking about coming clean. I brought him some dinner. A burger and some fries."

"You put something in the food."

"He went night-night. Woke up at the bottom of the tub."

"And Price?"

"He was a dead man once he took the job."

A truck rumbled past, grinding its gears before accelerating and fading to nothing. Their time was coming to its end now and the air felt sodden and heavy.

"You gonna look after Katie? The girls?"

"You know I will."

Tommy pointed with his chin at his handcuffed wrists. "Take off the watch."

Barkley unclasped the silver-and-turquoise timepiece, weighing it in his hand.

"Pulled that off Juan Doe right after I popped him. Don't look at me like that. Guy was moving product like the rest of 'em. Got his hand caught in the cookie jar and paid the price." Tommy gave a half shrug. "Another one you can pull out of the cold pile."

"That it?"

"I got a file."

"What kind of file?"

"Bunch of stuff on the guy you shot over at Columbia Point."

"Were you gonna blackmail me, Tommy?"

"Insurance, B, that's all. It's in my locker at the bottom, under a pile of shit. Take it, keep it, burn it. Whatever."

"What else?"

"It's not about the Harvard kid. Not anymore."

"I know. It's about Daniel Fitzsimmons."

"You were always too smart for this job. Look after my family, B. And don't fuck this up."

Barkley raised the gun. "Open your mouth. I'll roof it and count to three. You won't feel a thing."

Tommy nodded and closed his eyes, mumbling soft crumbles of long-lost prayers and rocking lightly in the chair. Slowly his mouth yawned open, a string of saliva connecting an upper molar to a lower, all of it soon to be so much rubble. Barkley jammed the gun in deep. There was no shake in Tommy. Barkley gave the prick full marks for that.

"You ready?"

A nod.

"One, two . . ." Barkley pulled on the trigger and the back half of Tommy Dillon's head exploded, whatever was left of his consciousness sliding down the far wall in a slick mess of tissue and bone. Barkley uncuffed his partner's wrists and got up carefully, checking his shoes and clothes for splatter, then standing over the body and taking note of the details. Not that it mattered. The report was already written in his head. Cat wouldn't buy a word, but she'd go along because she was part of it now and that's what people did.

He walked to the door and stopped, taking a final look at Tommy, slumped back in the chair, not a fucking care in the world. Barkley felt a sudden softening inside, old soil being turned over, something new pushing up from underneath. It scared him and shook him and he turned away, shielding himself with the curve of his shoulder as he reached for the doorknob. Outside the hallway was empty; a cruel breeze blew up the stairs.

NO ONE said a word on the drive in. Grace sat in front next to Ben. Daniel sat in the back. There was separation between them now, a parting that was as real as it was inevitable. Ben turned on the radio. Grace's gaze found Daniel's as Aerosmith hammered a couple of lines from "Last Child." They pulled into a gas station just off Neponset Avenue. The station had a steady stream of morning traffic at the pumps and a small convenience store next door where folks could get their coffee and the paper. Grace got out almost before the car stopped, swinging a small green pack across her shoulders. Daniel touched Ben's sleeve and caught his eyes before climbing out.

"In another life," Ben said. Daniel nodded and picked up a gym bag. Grace was already walking.

It was a half mile to the underpass with the whistle of the expressway above it, another quarter mile along a road made of black cinders and bordered by a low seawall winding down to the beach. They didn't talk, each content to match the other's stride and let the concussion wash over as a car or truck zipped past. Daniel ducked into the underpass first, leading Grace through the dark passage to a small hut on the other side. M.D.C. used it in the summer to store gear for the nonexistent lifeguards who patrolled the beach.

The hut was locked up tight, but one of the windows was busted out. Daniel shimmied through and opened the door. A second door cut into the opposite wall fed back to the road and down to the beach. They sat on the floor, with the smell of the ocean all around them. Grace opened her pack and took out some bread, a rind of cheese, and an apple. She sliced the apple with a small knife and cut off a piece of cheese, laying it all on a white towel with a blue stripe down the side. They drank water and ate, neither really wanting to start. When they were done eating, Grace folded up the towel and put all the food away. Then she bent her legs and wrapped her arms around her shins, setting her chin on her knees and staring across at him.

"What?" Daniel said.

"What's in there?" Her eyes moved to the gym bag.

"A gift." He pulled the bag over and opened it. Inside were three of Simon's sketches, rolled up one into the other. He'd left behind seven altogether. The first had brought Daniel here—a perfect rendering of the road and beach that ran just past the hut in which they were sitting. The other six laid out the life of Grace Nguyen, decade by decade. One was a colored pencil sketch of a football game, Grace huddled against Ben, the wind staining her cheeks as the crowd rose and roared around them; next, a chalk pastel of her wedding day, she and Ben cradled in a cocoon of flowers and light; an ink drawing, loose-limbed, of a family around a picnic table, splatters of ice cream and frosting, the sun ripening as they smiled in their youth and celebrated their son's fifth birthday; back to pencil, this time thicker lead, stronger strokes, catching the sweep of leaves across a college campus as

Grace walked with a young woman who was her echo, the only difference the lines around Grace's eyes and threads of gray in her hair; the fifth was acrylic on paper, a dirt and pebble road spiraling into dusk, a cottage at the end of the path with a single light burning in a window; and the last, just a few elegant lines on vellum, Grace, old, willowy, a shadow walking alone through a graveyard.

"Simon did them," Daniel said, and pushed the sketches toward her. He'd only brought the first three. The others he'd burned, except for the map. That he'd left for another.

"It's your life," he said. "Or at least part of it . . ."

Her eyes flared in the dim light of the hut. "How many?"

Daniel held up two fingers. "A boy and girl. They'll be strong and they'll be good."

She nodded.

"You'll live long and full with him because he's true and he loves you."

"That's what the drawings tell you?"

"Yes."

"And you believe that?"

It was an impossible question with the cruelest of answers. So Daniel said nothing at all.

She moved closer, inching imperceptibly along the floor then stopping as if she'd hit a wall. "Tell me about this place."

A seagull soared in his head, black eye blinking like the shutter on a camera. Click. A stretch of hard-packed sand. Click. The moving, shifting sea. Click. Daniel's mother, openmouthed for eternity as the front wheel of her upturned car spun slowly.

"This was where my mom died. Flipped her car over the wall outside and down onto the beach. I was with her."

"In the car?"

For a moment he thought he might tell her what he'd never told anyone, about being locked in the trunk of a 1958 Buick, listening as his mother was slowly strangled. Then he looked into Grace's open face and knew that was a conversation that could never be. "The doctors said I should have died. Sometimes I wish I had."

"I don't."

"Good."

"So why are we here?"

"I'm here because I have no choice. You're here for the sketches." He nodded at the drawings. "Take them and go."

"I'll go when I'm ready." Defiance packaged in a sad, sweet, braver-than-hell smile.

"Thank you."

"For what?"

After the accident, Daniel's world consisted of him and Harry. It was a mute existence. Muffled in stone. And then Grace came along.

"Just thank you."

"You think you know how our story ends, Daniel, but maybe you're wrong."

"Maybe."

"Who are you meeting?"

"I'm not sure."

"Let me come with. Together we can . . ."

He reached across and touched a finger to her lips. She kissed it and pressed his palm against the silk of her skin. He remembered their first kiss inside Music City. That was magic and neither of them wanted to ruin everything they had. Not so close to the end. So she got to her feet, tucking a small object in his hand, then packing up the sketches and making her way to the door that led back to the underpass, Ben Jacob, and the rest of her life.

Daniel stayed where he was, listening to the thump of the ocean and the dying hum in his head. He stood up and walked to the door opposite the one Grace had taken, twisting the knob just as the sky cracked, veins of fire sparking and running wild under a purple skin of sky. He stepped out into a freshening wind and watched a squadron of gray birds with white undersides wheel toward the storm that was slashing a path across the harbor. Daniel started to walk, slowly at first, down the black road toward the beach. In his hand was the object Grace had given him—a small, silver tape recorder. Daniel pressed RECORD and slipped it in his pocket.

46

BARKLEY DROVE through what was once Chelsea's rag shop district. Three years ago it had burned to the stumps, leaving behind cold piles of rubble and choking layers of ash that whipped and swirled across a graveyard of forgotten blocks. The city had begun its rebuild. Like most things in Chelsea, however, it was gonna take a while. Barkley pulled into a lot and watched a half-dozen cats scatter, taking up residence in the grinning husk of a building where they whisked their tails and licked their paws and watched Barkley's every move. Fair enough.

He pushed back the Camaro's bucket seat and summoned his freshly dead partner. It was the flat pint of Jack, however, that answered. He popped the glovie and pulled it out, catching a whiff of himself in the rearview mirror as the bottle lifted and the whiskey tickled his lower lip. Maybe it was how all cops were after a while. Bottles and secrets stashed everywhere, cheap insurance against a colleague or cold comfort when the dead swam up, asking their questions with their dull eyes and freezer-burn smiles. Why should he be any different?

Barkley cranked down the window and dumped the liquor, tossing the bottle into a field already winking with broken bits of glass. The Fitzsimmons file sat on the floor of the car. He picked it up. His notes on Daniel were clipped to a drawing of the alley where the body was found. The boy had given them Harry's Cambridge apartment as his address, but the two cops who'd driven him to Boston City had dropped him off at an apartment in Kenmore Square. The address was scribbled in pencil on the second page of Barkley's notes. 528 COMMONWEALTH AVE. He copied it down and wondered if anyone had heard the shot that took Tommy Dillon's life. They'd call Katie first thing. She'd play the role of grieving cop widow to a T. Then it would be his turn.

He slouched down low in the seat. The softening he'd felt standing over Tommy's body was still there, except now it had become a yielding, a great breaking up inside. The mottled ice that had encased his soul for so long was cracking, an uncharted river feeding up from somewhere, bubbling to the surface in gushes of warm, white water. Barkley had killed his partner because he'd loved him. That was the truth of it and it filled him to overflow, healing him even as he grieved.

He risked another look in the rearview mirror. She was there, weighing with her quicksilver eyes. He couldn't help but grin and Violet Fitzsimmons grinned back, lips frozen in a half curl, eyes flashing one last time before hardening into a pair of pale blue stones. Barkley whipped his head around, quick as that, only to discover the seat empty. If she'd been there, and she had, she was gone now, flown into his heart, mingled in his blood, one with his spirit. He didn't understand why, couldn't fathom how, but he didn't need to. Like his dead partner said—some things just were.

Barkley cranked the seat forward and started up the car, feeling the steering wheel alive under his hands as he weaved through the tangle of cats and rolled onto the blacktop, nose pointed toward downtown and Kenmore Square.

—

He pulled up in front of the Rathskeller and slipped a police placard on the dashboard. The two cops who'd driven Daniel said there was only one apartment above the bar. Barkley pushed a buzzer at the top of the steps and got no answer. The door was open so he went inside and walked up a second flight to the front door of the apartment. He knocked once, heavy and hard, then took a step back and put his boot in it, splintering the jamb as the door kicked in.

The place looked deserted. Barkley walked over to a desk by the window and did a quick check of the drawers. Nothing. Toward the rear of the apartment he found a hallway that led to a small bedroom. This was where Daniel had slept. There was no sign of him, no clothes or other belongings, not a stray wrinkle in the sheets because there were no sheets. Still, Barkley knew this was the boy's room. And he'd been here not too long ago.

At the other end of the hall was a pair of doors. The first opened to a room with a large drafting table facing a window. The second door led to another bedroom. Placed neatly on the bed was a pencil sketch. Barkley picked it up and knew two things immediately. Whoever left the drawing had wanted it found. And whoever it was, he'd probably already killed the boy.

47

THE ROCK picked up speed as it fell through time and space, soaking up the blood of an English battlefield, men on horses and in the mud, gutted on steel pikes and trampled underfoot, screaming and biting and raging as each whirled down to his death; a plain at Somme, thousands in trenches, the unburied rotting in the long graves they'd dug for themselves as the smell of gunpowder and mustard gas hung and twitched in the air; black smoke and soot from the chimneys of Auschwitz, Dachau, and Buchenwald. The faces of Holodomor and Armenia. Backward the rock spun, even as it spun forward—Genghis Khan taking a million heads a day; more blood, winding rivers dark and clotted on the sandy floor of the Colosseum; a string of crosses on a hill; Cain striking down Abel while a mother birthed a child. All hung in the balance as the rock turned ever faster, forward now, closer, hurtling through the cathedral of the heavens. Hitler, Stalin, Pol Pot, Amin. A book depository in Dallas, a balcony in Memphis, a hotel kitchen in Los Angeles.

Daniel raised his eyes and saw the rock dropping through the massing thunderheads. It turned once more and landed at his feet. He picked it up. Cold to the touch, it carried no judgment, no memory. Just ahead the wind lifted off the water, parting the storm and revealing a man standing with his back to Daniel, shoulders angled, clad in a long duster coat that hugged his body in slick folds. Daniel walked forward, rain slicing, peeling off his old skin, leaving him naked as a newborn. And then the man turned.

"I'm surprised you picked this place," Nick Toney said.

"I didn't pick anything."

"I followed you and the other two in the car. But I already knew where you were headed." Toney shifted his weight, slipping his hands into the pockets of his coat as the wind skirted the shoreline and the storm circled back out into the harbor. "It's good you didn't bring the girl."

"She's gone."

"I'd give you my word I won't harm her, but what's the point? Better if you just look for yourself."

Daniel frowned.

"You like to look inside people's skulls. Go ahead. See if I intend to kill her."

Daniel licked his lips, tasting pennies at the back of his throat. "You killed my mother."

"My wife."

"You killed my brother."

"My son."

"And now you're here to kill me."

Hungry smile. "We're the only family we have left."

Daniel lifted the rock in his hand and felt his father's mind swing open, sweeping him back into the trunk of the Buick and slamming the lid, fusing the three of them—father, mother, and son—in an endless loop of shame and fear and death. Daniel knew it had always been so and wondered why he'd ever thought it could be different.

"I only met your brother twice," Toney said. "The first time was on the day your mother died. She said she never told him who his dad was, but I didn't believe a word of it. Anyway, I stopped by her place and we made plans for that night. Harry was in the next room, eleven or twelve but already like a little adult, the way he watched me, keeping fucking score. She said she was gonna drop him off with a friend, but the friend didn't want to take you. So your mom said she'd figure something out. Course she didn't and there you were sleeping in the backseat of the car when I showed up that night. But it was Harry who bugged me. What the fuck did he hear? What the fuck did he know? It was like a little bird pecking away inside my skull, fucking pebble in my shoe. Still, it didn't have to be that way."

"Shut up."

"Next time I saw him was on the day he died, at the diner in Harvard Square. Sure as shit there was that jump in his eye. He didn't realize it yet, but he would. I could already see that." Toney grinned. "That's right, Daniel. I can look inside people's heads just like you. Where the fuck you think you got it from?"

"It's called entanglement."

"Call it whatever you want. I could see he'd recognized me at some level and it was just a matter of time before he pieced it together. Once he figured out I was who I was, it was a short step to putting me with her that night. Not a chance I could take."

"So you set up the alley?"

"I hired someone. He hired the black kid who fucked it up."

"And you finished it?"

"Had to. When the cops search my place, they'll find just

enough of my blood to write me off as dead. The guy I hired will take the fall for all of it."

"Why did you let me live?"

"You were what? Seven? Eight? Too young to remember shit. Besides, you never saw me in your mom's apartment. Never got a look at me when you went in the trunk."

"How about later?"

"You were tough climbing out of that fucking car. Hell, I was proud of you. Then when I finally met you, I figured you might actually go kill the black kid for me. Seemed fitting. Me killing your brother, you helping clean up the mess. So I gave you a nudge. Fed you the address in the Bury and waited."

"Maybe I'm not the killer you thought I was."

"You're worse."

Daniel felt his fingers tighten and the rock start to hum in his hand. His father could feel it, too.

"Your mother was a cunt, Daniel. Great piece of ass, but once she got her hooks in, pure fucking cunt." Toney cocked his head. "You feeling it yet? Want to have a go at the old man? Here, let me help." He dropped to his knees in the wet sand and made furrows with his fingers. Then he put the slurry to his nose and inhaled, closing his eyes and tipping his face to the sky. "Go ahead, son. Close the circle."

Daniel raised the rock over his head and became one with it. Perfect symmetry, perfect balance. Then he brought it down to his side and dropped it on the beach.

One eye popped open. "No, huh?" Toney climbed to his feet and picked up the rock, weighing it in his hand before hurling it into the surf, where the sea sucked it under. Daniel felt his father's DNA wrapped inside his, and wrapped inside that, rotting at the core of himself, the memory of his mother and all he'd wished he could have done for her, for Harry. He turned off the recorder in his pocket.

"Don't put my body in the water."

His father pulled a pistol from under his coat, black and huge and gleaming with grease in the winking eye of the storm. He touched it to Daniel's forehead as Daniel sank to his knees and closed his eyes, waiting for the flat bang that would mark his passage under the archway we all must pass through on our way to whatever waited beyond. When it came, Daniel felt nothing, except the release of his soul and the meaty thump of flesh against earth. He opened his eyes to see his father staring back at him, loose-jawed, dark blood pooling and soaking into the hungry sand from the back of a blown-out skull. Simon stepped around Daniel, picking up Toney's gun and taking a quick look at his handiwork. Then he came back, crouching between the body and Daniel, touching his cheek.

"You all right?"

Daniel nodded. Simon helped him to his feet and they walked a few yards, sitting on the edge of the seawall that marked the beginning of the road that led up to the hut. Daniel felt a shiver in the air and stared at his father's body, still sprawled where it fell. "I wanted to kill him, but it wasn't in me."

"You had the rock in your hand and chose to drop it. You knelt and pressed your head to the muzzle. That changes everything."

"He's still dead."

"And you think it's murder?"

"That's what the police will tell you."

"Reality has its own plasticity, Daniel. Warm, alive, capable of being molded and shaped."

"This isn't one of your sketches. And a bullet to the head isn't some string of numbers on a blackboard."

Simon pulled out Toney's gun and another, carrying both down to the water and throwing them in. He walked back slowly, taking a seat across from Daniel, positioning himself so he was blocking any view of the body. "What is it you'd like to know?"

"Nothing. Just leave me alone."

Simon picked up a stick and began to draw in the sand. "Remember I told you about entanglement, that it works temporally as well as spatially, that all measures of yourself exist at the same time, in the same space."

Daniel fixed on the swell of the sea and the waves, one after another, covering everything that came before.

"This planet will quickly become a smaller place, the gap between the few that have and the billions that don't growing wider and wider. Hatred will see its opportunity, stoking the fires while religion takes hold, evil, black, divisive religion, the worst kind, carried like a virus on the back of the technology we've spoken about.

"Our leaders will be leaderless, old wounds of race reopening and bleeding all over again. Money and greed will hold sway, everyone grabbing what they can as the politics of hatred spur us forward through an ever-telescoping window of time. Until finally it all falls apart, the center collapsing and the rest with it."

Simon tossed the stick away. Daniel glanced down at a tangle of lines that looked like two towers.

"I'm more or less a messenger," Simon said. "A harbinger of what's to be. Or what might be."

"And me?"

"You're connective tissue, a way for many to be one. But only if you're free."

"Free from what?"

"You lived her death, Daniel. Right here on this beach. You looked in her eyes and stroked her face and sobbed and prayed and watched your mother choke on her own blood. And then you walked away, mourning as only a child can mourn, but knowing also, in the quietest rooms of your soul, that you were rid of her. Rid of the shame you'd felt for how she lived. Rid of her pain and her suffering. Her anxiety and her touch. Her needs, her limitations, her shackles, her sores, her all-consuming fears. And even deeper, in a room you never visit, a room you might not even know exists, you were happy. No more watching as 'dates' came and went, no more listening while you lay in your bed. No more trying, desperately trying, to make it all smooth, to fix what was so unfair, so far beyond the reach of a child. And when the darkness came after the crash, you welcomed that. And when you awoke, it was just you and Harry."

"Harry's dead."

"You said it yourself. Your brother was that rarest of things, pure love. His heart beats within you now. As does your mother's." Simon pointed a finger back toward the unseen body. "There's only ever been two choices, Daniel. Bury yourself deeper or dig your way out."

"How? By killing him?"

"By deciding not to."

"He was my father."

"And mine as well." Simon winked and in that wink Daniel saw himself, twenty years in the future, fifty years in the past, a hundred years forward and another hundred back and he knew he didn't understand, but knew he didn't need to. The circle never explained itself. It just was.

Simon wiped the sand smooth with his foot. He was wearing a pair of Tiger racing flats, identical to Daniel's right down to the yellow laces, but battered and torn from decades of use.

"Bad sneakers?" Daniel said.

"But great for a run." Simon grinned and opened his palm. Daniel traced the creases there. His own. Flesh and blood. Bone and sinew. Real and not. Then he watched as Simon went softly, stepping carefully in the footprints he'd already made. A gray wave crested, blowing a spray of salt and brine across Daniel's vision as it crashed ashore. When he wiped his eyes, the beach was empty, sea and sky woven into a seamless, stillborn haze. A gull cried, dipping its wings as it skimmed the edge of the water before flicking away.

High up on the ridge, a car with a blue bubble on its roof rolled into view. A black man got out and slammed the door, the sound echoing in the well where water met land. Daniel watched as the detective named Barkley made his way down the road of cinders to where Daniel sat. The detective stopped at the body, crouching over it in much the same way he'd crouched over Harry in the alley, like a predator picking over the bones of his latest meal. Daniel crept forward as Barkley turned.

"Stay there, son." The detective had a radio in his hand and was calling for an ambulance. Daniel shuffled to his left, suddenly anxious for a last look at his father. Nick Toney was sitting up, shaking his head and rubbing his neck. No splintered skull, no blood, no corpse. Toney was alive. Groggy, but very much alive. Daniel slumped to the sand as Barkley's radio crackled and the sun split a mass of thunderheads, bathing the three of them in a slant of eternal, eclipsing light.

48

MIKE RIPP drew on his cigarette and exhaled, smoke boiling up into the circle of a fan that beat overhead. "Walk me through the beach again."

Barkley grimaced. They'd been at it most of the day. Cat Mc-Shane had come in for the last half hour. Otherwise, just Barkley and the assistant DA for Suffolk County. No one else wanted any part of the sad tale they were cooking up. Who the fuck could blame 'em?

"I went through it three times, Ripper. You got all the statements. Nothing's gonna change."

"Once I sign off, it's my ass, too. Correct?"

Barkley nodded.

"All right, then. Give it to me again. Just the bare bones." Ripp was like that. Nice guy, but a survivor. Smart, tough, with a keen understanding of the slushy world and shitbag people homicide investigators dealt with on a daily basis. Ripp would work with you on the facts. But if things went south and it was you or him, you'd best believe it was gonna be you.

"I got out of the car and saw the two of them on the beach."

"Daniel Fitzsimmons and the guy we're calling his father?"

Barkley nodded. "Daniel was sitting on the seawall. Toney

was lying on his side. I marked it all up on one of the maps."
Barkley pointed vaguely toward a wreck of files strewn across the
conference table. Ripp didn't give a fuck about Barkley's drawings and kept his hound-dog, smoke-filled prosecutor's eyes fixed
on the detective.

"Toney wasn't moving when you first saw him?"

"Not until I got closer."

"How close?"

"Had the gun out and was maybe ten feet away when he first
moved. I holstered my piece, checked his vitals, and helped him
to a sitting position."

"Where was the boy?"

"Behind me. Starts to come closer and I tell him to stay
where he is. He sees Toney and passes out."

"Passes out?"

"Falls to his knees, then down for the count. Backup comes
in and goes to work on him. I cuff Toney and we stick them both
in ambulances."

"Why cuff Toney?"

"At that point I had reason to suspect him in at least two
murders. Turns out I was right."

Ripp took another drag and crushed out his cigarette, blinking against the smoke and carefully pushing away the full ashtray like he wanted nothing to do with it and how the fuck did it
get there in the first place.

"Beach doesn't matter," Barkley said. "We got the confession."

"Famous last words, fucko. Give me the boy's story again."

"He insisted Toney was dead."

"Didn't he see him alive? Ten fucking feet away?"

"That's why he fainted. Swore he watched Toney get popped
in the head."

"And the boy claims the gun was fired by this mysterious Simon?"

"Simon Lane. Daniel says he rented a room from him. Claims Simon was down on the beach and shot Toney at point-blank range."

"Because Toney was gonna shoot Daniel?"

"That's what the boy said, yes."

"And we found no guns anywhere, on anybody?"

Barkley shook his head.

"Nor did we find any Simon?"

"Had both ends of the beach blocked off, as well as the road. If anyone was there, we would have picked him up."

Ripp leaned back, ham hands locked behind his head, heft of his belly testing the springs in his chair. "Maybe he went for a swim? Maybe we should be looking for him at the bottom of the harbor? What do ya think?" The assistant DA chuckled, a luxuriously smoky sound that jiggled his cheeks and punched a hole in the balloon that was Barkley's carefully constructed tale. "Sorry, Bark. If I don't laugh at some of this shit, I might as well take a gun and blow my own fucking brains out."

Cat McShane cleared her throat. "I think someone should offer some context for the boy."

Ripp raised an eyebrow. "You an expert in this area?"

"No, but I am a doctor. And I've talked at length to the mental health professionals who interviewed Daniel. You have their reports. They're all in agreement."

"I'm listening."

"The boy saw his mother killed when he was a child. Years later he sees his brother murdered. He's admitted to not taking his meds and, as a result, suffered a series of hallucinations."

"You mean his stories about the animals?" Ripp said.

"Yes. He's experienced a number of breaks with reality over the past month or so, culminating with what he thinks he saw on the beach. As far as he's concerned, that *is* his reality."

"And you think I think he's lying?"

"I just want to provide some context."

"Thank you, Doctor." Ripp glanced at Barkley.

"There's no record of a Simon Lane ever teaching at Harvard," the detective said. "And the room Daniel claims to have rented from him has been vacant for more than a year. We think the kid must have been squatting in there. Brought in some furniture, whole fucking nine yards."

"So, what you're telling me, what you're both telling me, is there's no way, six months from now, after we put this thing to bed and my name's all over it, there's no fucking way asshole Simon Lane is gonna pop up with some fucked-up story about who knows what?"

"I don't see it, Mike."

Ripp glanced at Cat.

"He lives in Daniel's head. Nowhere else."

The prosecutor grunted and rubbed his lower lip with his thumb. Barkley had seen him do the same thing in the courtroom, usually as a signal to the jury that he was about to shift gears.

"Let's say I accept your version for the moment. Explain to me what did happen to Toney. EMTs found a small puncture wound on his neck. Fast-acting barbiturate in his system. Are we saying the kid did that?"

"We searched his person," Barkley said. "Searched the beach. No evidence of a syringe, needle. Nothing."

"He was seeing a doctor every other week. Not a stretch to think he might have lifted something."

"Like I said, we found nothing on the beach."

"What does Toney say?"

"He and Daniel were talking. And then the world went black. Says Daniel's hands were empty."

"Why does Toney say he was down there?"

"Just wanted to talk to his son."

"And now?"

"Doesn't want anything to do with the kid. Says he's haunted."

"Haunted?"

"That's what he says."

"Fucking beautiful." Ripp did a little dance in his chair, using his feet to pull himself closer to the table, then picking up a set of papers and weighing them in his hand. "Asshole confessed to killing Violet Fitzsimmons in '68, as well as his son, Harry. Correct?"

"He had no choice."

"Because of the tape recorder Daniel had in his pocket?"

"It cuts in and out, but there's plenty there. And everything Toney said on the tape fits with the case we were developing."

"You and your partner?"

"Yes."

Ripp dropped the confession back onto the table. "Let's talk about that for a minute."

This was what the meeting was really about. The dead cop in the room and how it was gonna play.

"You and Dillon suspected Toney of running a drug operation out of the Combat Zone?"

"We didn't have all the pieces, but that was the idea."

"And Dillon was working on one of Toney's alleged accomplices. The other Harvard kid, Sanchez."

"Tommy tracked Sanchez to Chelsea while I went after Toney."

"That's how you two divvied up the case?"

"Tommy had the address in Chelsea. Must have walked in on them drowning Sanchez."

"Them?"

"We believe Sanchez was getting cold feet and thinking about going to the police. Toney sent someone over to kill him."

"Toney admit that?"

"He's not gonna cop to anything that's not on the tape. What we know for sure is there was a shoot-out and Tommy got hit."

"Five times?" Ripp held up five accusing fingers and glanced at Cat for confirmation.

"Three in the chest. One in the arm, one in the head. It's all in my report."

"Yeah, well, that's a hell of a good thing, Doc, since no one from my office actually got a look at Dillon's body."

"My mistake," Barkley said. "Tommy's wife wanted the body cremated. I thought we had everything we needed and gave the go-ahead."

"Seems like your partner should be in line for some kind of medal."

"You want to recommend that, Mike?"

"I want to be up in Vermont, in some fucking lodge, skiing all day and sitting by the fire at night, getting shitty on good booze and thinking about all the assholes down here, stuck in meetings discussing fucked-up cases like this one with lying sack-of-shit detectives. But that's not you, right, Bark?"

"Tommy had two little girls. We'd like to make sure they get taken care of."

"So give 'em the benny package and fuck the medal is what you're saying."

"Fuck it all, Counselor. Or not. Your call."

Ripp wrinkled his nose at all the bad smells they'd laid out on the table and flipped a hand like he was sweeping out the trash. "Toney takes the fall on the two. Put the rest of it to bed."

Barkley and Cat got up as one, heads down, eyes averted, anxious for the deed to be done and it all to be gone. Ripp, however, wasn't finished.

"One more thing, Detective. Daniel Fitzsimmons."

"What about him?"

"You left out a few details he offered up on Simon Lane."

"Most of that was just psychobabble . . ."

"Simon Lane wasn't just a guy he rented a room from. According to Daniel, Lane was, is, some future version of himself."

"Not exactly a future version," Cat said. "Daniel believes it all runs simultaneously."

"I don't know what the fuck that means, Doc, and, more important, I don't care. The bottom line is this kid thinks Lane's real and that he and Lane are actually the same fucking person. Correct?"

"Correct," Barkley said.

"So the kid's soft as puppy shit."

Barkley opened his mouth to respond when Cat jumped in. "He just needs to stay on his meds. Along with the counseling."

Ripp pulled out a loose sheet of paper. "You ever think about that name, Doc?"

"Excuse me?"

"Simon Lane." Ripp scribbled off a couple of lines and turned the sheet around so Cat could read it.

S-I-M-O-N L-A-N-E

F-I-T-Z-S-I-M-M-O-N-S D-A-N-I-E-L

"It's an anagram for Daniel Fitzsimmons," Ripp said. "Last name becomes first, first becomes last."

"Actually, it's an imperfect anagram, Counselor. Several letters missing in both names."

"So you think it's a coincidence?"

Cat shrugged and pushed the paper across to Barkley, who glanced at it and kicked it back to Ripp.

"What do you want, Mike?"

"Only one question that matters."

"Yeah?"

"Do we need to worry about him?"

49

HE COULD feel their weight in the empty apartment—cops, detectives, evidence techs, all fingers and flashbulbs, notebooks and eye rolls, dusting, measuring, conjecturing. They'd all been looking for some trace of Simon Lane. And finding nothing. Daniel cracked a window and took a seat at the desk. They'd removed every stick of furniture in the apartment except the desk. Barkley told him it was just too big to get through the door. No one could figure out how it had gotten there in the first place. Daniel brushed his hand across the handle on one of the drawers. It was smeared with fingerprint powder and he felt the silk rub between his fingertips. The man who owned the apartment was named Stephen Maas. He was eighty-eight, lived in California, and had never heard of Simon Lane. As far as Maas was concerned, the flat was empty. Had been empty for a year and a half. How about Harvard? No professor named Simon Lane. No student. Not even a onetime visitor on a sign-in sheet. Ghosts. Crickets. The wind in the trees. Or so the police said.

Daniel wandered down the hall to his old room and sat cross-legged on the floor. At the end of the day, what could they really charge him with? Being delusional? Maybe. But he hadn't committed any real crime. And even if he had, Barkley knew better. Daniel felt the bottle of pills in his pocket. All new meds. All new doctors. These ones kept track. Appointments, three times a week. Monthly physicals. Blood work. They'd watch him. Keep his brain on a nice, low simmer. Maybe he'd take up drawing. Wouldn't that be fun? Someone smiled in the corner of the room, long teeth and gums, gone as quickly as Daniel could turn his head. No matter.

He walked out to the main room and sat again at the desk. Barkley had given him an hour alone. They were probably watching through the windows. Of course they were. He thought about Grace. She'd sworn up and down to the police that Simon Lane existed, except she'd never actually met him. Closest she came was a silhouette in a window, a shadow smoking a pipe on a street corner. And what was that? What was anything? Daniel pulled the pills from his pocket and shook out a couple, swallowing them dry as his eyes watered and his head fuzzed. He'd keep his distance from Grace. Like any respectable madman would. All in all, he was lucky to have the time he'd had. Friendships. Memories. He'd parcel them out like crumbs in the hungry days and years and decades ahead. He and Simon, alive inside his skull if nowhere else.

Daniel closed his eyes and got down to business. His mind was a river, running wild and fast, swelling against the crumbling banks of reality. Daniel dove into the flow, down into the cracks and seams where nothing lived but noise so loud it was quiet. He searched until he found the door and a passageway, wide and dry and rising. Daniel walked until he climbed, a set of stone steps cut into a wall and a second door that opened to the apartment and the same room where he sat. Simon lived in the iron grip of a shadow, the smile Daniel had glimpsed in his bedroom now attached to its owner. Simon beckoned and Daniel drifted closer. The smell of berries was strong, Simon's tobacco pouch open on the desk and oozing fragrance. He pulled out a pinch with one hand, fingers of the other disappearing down the side of the desk and reappearing with his precious pipe. Simon filled it carefully, tamping down the bowl then striking a wooden match as flesh burned and reality stripped itself to its bones before collapsing in a pile of ash.

Daniel opened his eyes. He was standing now, in the same spot where Simon had stood. Daniel's hand rested on the same edge, his fingers crawling of their own accord across the same two feet of desk before slipping down the side. Daniel felt a seam in the wood. He should have been astonished but wasn't. The seam led to a small depression. Daniel sensed the tension of a spring underneath and pressed. A flat ledge flipped open. On it was the pipe. Daniel picked it up and put it to his nose, tasting berries again on his tongue. He turned the pipe upside down and found the Dunhill markings and the number "4" Simon had shown him on that first day.

Daniel sat down, hands moving over the pipe as he pondered. Barkley had questioned him closely about the puncture mark they'd found on Nick Toney's neck. At one point, they'd even searched him. Daniel had nothing for them except the story of the gun that never existed, a murder that never happened, and a dead man who was his father and still very much alive. The pipe separated in his hands, stem twisting free of the bowl and a small slip of parchment sliding out. Daniel felt his heart in his fingertips, forty-five beats a minute, as he unrolled the tinder-dry paper. Three tiny darts, razor-sharp and gleaming silver, dropped into the palm of his hand. He slid one into the hollowed-out stem, put the stem to his lips and blew. The dart popped out on a burp of air, streaking across five feet and burying itself in the wall. Daniel couldn't help but grin and pulled the dart, putting it, along with the other two, back in the stem and reassembling the pipe. Maybe Simon had left the Dunhill for Daniel. Maybe Daniel had left it for himself. Maybe it was a distinction without a difference. Two beings entangled, one with the other, collapsing time, collapsing space, collapsing reality until they were one. Hadn't that been the point all along?

Daniel stuck the pipe in his pocket as Aerosmith's "Walk This Way" strutted in off the street. He let the music wash over him and felt the sun fragile on his face. A breeze tickled the back of his neck. It was the cat, fur shimmering a hundred shades of silver as he leaped through a timeless throw of light and landed neatly in the middle of the room. Daniel made a small motion with his hand and the cat orbited closer, marking out a slow, wide circle before jumping onto the desk and wrapping himself in a tight ball. Daniel ran his fingers across the animal's knotted flank and listened to his purr as the light outside flickered and failed. Then Daniel laid his head down and the two slept as one. When he awoke, it was night and the fireplace was lit. Harry sat on the floor nearby.

"I love you most," he said.

Daniel shook his head. "I love you most."

Harry shrugged and they both laughed. Daniel got up and took a seat beside his older brother. They talked as the stars chased themselves across the sky and the moon doused itself in the sun. And their conversation knew no beginning and had no end.

NOTES AND ACKNOWLEDGMENTS

If you're a nonscientist like me and would like to learn more about the world of quantum mechanics, Brian Greene's *The Elegant Universe* is a great place to start. For the evolving relationship between quantum physics and spirituality, I would suggest *The Universe in a Single Atom* by the Dalai Lama; *The Divine Dance* by Franciscan priest and spiritual leader Richard Rohr; and *The Quantum and the Lotus*, a conversation between Matthieu Ricard, a molecular biologist and Buddhist monk, and Trinh Thuan, an astrophysicist at Caltech. For a deeper dive, treat yourself to anything by Pema Chödrön, Eckhart Tolle, Thomas Merton, and any number of books by Father Rohr, who also runs the Center for Action and Contemplation in Albuquerque, New Mexico. All of these writers provided critical background and context for this novel. All are profound thinkers and essential voices in this most uncertain of times.

And then there's Daniel's shape-shifting. My favorite Latin poet was (and is) Ovid. My favorite poem? A tie between *The Iliad* and *Metamorphoses*. If you haven't read the latter, pick it up. It's fun and funny. Timeless and timely. It's a study in the human psyche—how we hide from the world, and particularly from ourselves.

The murder of Harry Fitzsimmons, while entirely an account of fiction, was inspired, in part, by the 1976 murder of Andy Puopolo in Boston's Combat Zone. I won't go into all the details of the actual crime, but Andy's tragic passing had a big impact on the city and still resonates to this day. At the time of his death, I was a student at Boston Latin School, where Andy had graduated four years earlier. I didn't know Andy, but I remember the pall it cast over the school. For many of us, Andy represented the future in all its infinite possibility. He was also a sudden reminder of how fragile life can be and how everything can (and does) change in a moment. As I said, Harry's death is pure fiction. None of the details or characters in the novel are drawn from or based on anything in real life. At the end of the day, however, I'd like to think there's a little bit of Andy in Harry. A little bit of the eternal nature of hope, the pristine wonder of youth, and the immutable power of love. If we can reflect on those simple principles and make them part of our DNA, that's probably a pretty good thing.

Thanks to my editor, Zach Wagman, and everyone at Ecco for believing in this book. Thanks to my agent, David Gernert, and to Garnett Kilberg Cohen for her early read and wonderful editorial eye. Thanks to all the independent booksellers who are responsible for getting my novels, as well as those of other writers, into the hands of countless readers. And, of course, thanks to you, the reader. As always, it's a privilege and an honor.

Thanks, finally, to my family and friends, and especially to my wife, Mary Frances. Love you.

ABOUT THE AUTHOR

MICHAEL HARVEY is the author of seven previous novels, including *Brighton* and *The Chicago Way*. He's also a journalist and documentarian whose work has won multiple news Emmys, two Primetime Emmy nominations, and an Academy Award nomination. Raised in Boston, he now lives in Chicago.

THUNDERER

JULIAN STOCKWIN

THUNDERER

HODDER &
STOUGHTON

First published in Great Britain in 2021 by Hodder & Stoughton
An Hachette UK company

1

Copyright © Julian Stockwin 2021

The right of Julian Stockwin to be identified as the
Author of the Work has been asserted by him in accordance
with the Copyright, Designs and Patents Act 1988.

A CIP catalogue record for this title is available from the British Library

Hardback ISBN 978 1 473 69884 0
Trade Paperback ISBN 978 1 473 69883 3
eBook ISBN 978 1 473 69885 7

Typeset in Garamond MT by
Palimpsest Book Production Ltd, Falkirk, Stirlingshire

Printed and bound in Great Britain by Clays Ltd, Elcograf S.p.A.

Hodder & Stoughton policy is to use papers that are natural, renewable
and recyclable products and made from wood grown in sustainable forests.
The logging and manufacturing processes are expected to conform to
the environmental regulations of the country of origin.

Hodder & Stoughton Ltd
Carmelite House
50 Victoria Embankment
London EC4Y 0DZ

www.hodder.co.uk

'The men are not yet created that can stand against British seamen when properly disciplined & led'
Admiral Sir John Jervis, Earl St Vincent

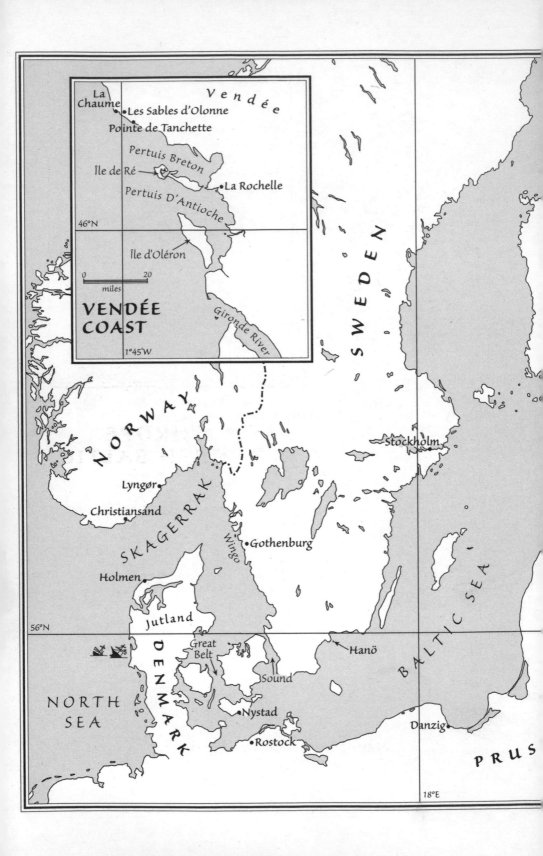

Vendée

La
Chaume
Les Sables d'Olonne
Pointe de Tanchette

Pertuis Breton
Île de Ré
La Rochelle
Pertuis D'Antioche

46°N

Île d'Oléron

0   20
miles

VENDÉE
COAST

1°45'W

Gironde River

SWEDEN

NORWAY

Stockholm

Lyngør
Christiansand

SKAGERRAK

Wingo
Gothenburg

Holmen

BALTIC SEA

Jutland

56°N

Great
Belt
Hanö

DENMARK

Sound

NORTH
SEA

Nystad

Danzig

Rostock

PRUS

18°E

INNER LEADS

Gunboats

58°38'N   Podargus

Najaden

Thunderer

Lyngør

Calypso

0   0.5
nautical miles

SKAGGERAK

LYNGØR   9°008'E

FINLAND

Åbo

GULF OF FINLAND

Kronstadt

St Petersburg

EUROPE
(NORTH BALTIC)

N
W   E
S

0   100
miles

LIVONIA

Riga

RUSSIA

COURLAND

Moscow

Tilsit

Borodino

Smolensk

Vilna

Grodno

Napoleon's advance on Moscow

Dramatis Personae

indicates fictional character

*Sir Thomas Kydd   captain of HMS *Thunderer*
*Nicholas Renzi   Earl of Farndon, former confidential secretary to Kydd

Thunderer, ship's company

*Allen	accounts clerk
*Binard	Kydd's manservant
*Boxall	captain's coxswain
*Briggs	third lieutenant
*Craddock	Kydd's confidential secretary
*Forbin	midshipman
*Franks	writer
*Gubb	purser
*Hare	captain of marines
*Hobbs	sailing master
*Lawlor	gunner
*Luscombe	Kydd's servant
*Lyell	former captain of *Thunderer*

*Mayne	fourth lieutenant
*Opie	boatswain
*Roscoe	first lieutenant
*Sadler	surgeon
*Smale	second lieutenant
*Tucker	petty officer

Others

*Anneke	Dutch agent
Arakcheyev	Russian general opposed to Speransky
Bagration	marshal of Russian army
Baste	French admiral commanding Boulogne flotilla
Berthier	French grand marshal and chief of Imperial Staff
Castlereagh	British secretary of state for foreign affairs
*Cecilia	Kydd's sister, Countess of Farndon, Renzi's wife
*Congalton	high-ranking member of British secret service
Croker	first secretary to the Admiralty
Davis	captain, *Blake*
De Tolly	Russian army commander opposing Napoleon
*Denisov	minor Russian noble
Dewey	port admiral, Plymouth
Duroc	Bonaparte's grand equerry
Everard	captain, *Jason*
*Faulknor	relieving captain, *Tyger*
*Fookes	MP, a.k.a. Prinker
*Houghton	rear admiral, Rochefort squadron
Hoby	adjutant general, Royal Marines

Holm	captain, *Najaden*
Hoskyns	commander, *Daphne*
Junot	French general, invader of Portugal
Kutuzov	grand marshal and commander of combined Russian forces
*Lebedev	Russian academician
Lord Liverpool	prime minister of Great Britain
Lord Eldon	lord chancellor
Lord Keith	commander-in-chief, Channel Squadron
MacDonald	French marshal laying siege to Riga
Melville	first lord of the Admiralty
Montand	Mecklenberg grand marshal under Napoleon
*Moreau	colonel of engineers in Bonaparte's invasion army
Moubray	captain, *Montagu*
Murat	King of Naples and marshal under Bonaparte
Pelleton	long-serving general in Bonaparte's army
Perceval	prime minister of Britain, who was assassinated
*Persephone, Lady Kydd	Kydd's wife
Robillard	lieutenant-in-command, *Podargus*
*Rochambeau	staff officer, corps of *ingénieur géographe* in Bonaparte's army
Rostopchin	governor of Moscow
Ryder	home secretary
Savary	chief of secret police under Bonaparte
Speransky	Russian statesman overthrown for his liberal views
Strickland	port admiral, Portsmouth

Talleyrand	French diplomat known for his cynical and devious moves
Todd	quartermaster, *Podargus*
Ushakov	general at Borodino
*Vonskoy	Russian exile in London
*Youlden	master, *Success o' Bristol* merchantman

Chapter 1

Spring 1812, England

On the last stretch of road to his Devon estate, the balmy weather, the vaulting blue of the sky and the smell of sun-touched woodlands complemented the vista. With rising feeling, Captain Sir Thomas Kydd RN gripped the side of the swaying trap as it took a steep, sweeping corner – and there ahead was Knowle Manor. The vehicle swung through the gates and came to a stop before the ancient front door, but not before he'd caught the flash of a face at an upstairs window.

Lady Persephone Kydd ran down to her husband in delight, embracing him as though they'd been parted for months, yet they'd returned to England just days before. She'd accompanied him on his last voyage and taken residence in Sicily while *Tyger* had stormed the Adriatic.

'How was the Admiralty, my darling?' she managed breathlessly.

'Welcoming above the ordinary, Seph,' he replied, with a chuckle, 'the whole crew main anxious to meet the victor of

Lissa.' A squadron of British frigates had confronted a French fleet twice its size in the Adriatic and prevailed in the tradition of Nelson – an action that had caught the public imagination.

Tyger was now lying in Portsmouth awaiting survey of her wounds and, having reported to the Admiralty, Kydd looked forward to a well-deserved leave until called to London again.

Persephone's hand slipped into his, her smile dazzling, and his heart swelled with happiness. He paid off the driver, who gave a sketchy salute as the horse clopped away.

Kydd took his fill of the old mansion, its mullioned windows and quaint chimneys, the garden a riot of colour, with neat flowerbeds and canes in immaculate condition. He strolled along in a haze of contentment while he heard how the riding school had fared while she'd been abroad – quite ably, it seemed – how much progress there had been on the orangery – disappointing but understandable given the soft soil; and about the re-flooring of the dairy – nearly done.

'It'll be all about the village that you've returned,' she said proudly. 'I've a notion there'll be entertainments to show you off to the Cornwood and Ugborough folk, if not all the tribes to Exeter.'

Kydd squeezed her hand. 'I'll do my duty right enough,' he said softly, knowing how much she would enjoy the village gaiety. 'Um, you haven't word of a visitor arriving at all?' he added, in an offhand tone.

'Oh?' Persephone replied, puzzled. 'No one dares disturb the sea-hero at his rest, I believe.'

So, it had been too much to expect. His confidential secretary Edward Dillon was no longer with him, executed by a French firing squad. His place had been taken by a remarkable individual, Lucius Cavendish Henry Craddock, a Balkan refugee of English origins, who had been a merchant banker in Radonice. The man had lost everything, his home, his business and his family, his wife and children burned alive in the ravages of war. He'd found refuge in *Tyger*, and Kydd had taken to him, with his calm, worldly-wise perspectives even while in the extremity of his suffering. But did he have any right to expect him to continue in the position? The prospects for a captain's secretary in a man-o'-war were far inferior to those he might expect ashore.

Craddock had journeyed to Manchester to show himself alive and well to his relatives and no doubt had been offered a position in the family business more in keeping with his talents.

Meanwhile, Kydd was in no hurry to return aboard *Tyger*. While there was no crippling injury to his command she had been much scarred by shot-strike, which would take some time to heal. His competent first lieutenant, Bowden, would ensure that this was done and it had been a thoughtful gesture of the first lord at the Admiralty to direct that repair be carried out in Plymouth instead of Portsmouth, which enabled him to take his rest at Knowle Manor. And it would be most agreeable to discuss with Persephone how the size-able prize money to come from his cruise of depredation should be spent.

Several days later a corpulent major of the South Devon Militia in full regalia, accompanied by two troopers, rode up desiring Kydd to review a march-past of the other valiant defenders of this vital part of the coast. The public, he added proudly, would be sure to take the liveliest interest since salutes by a detachment of the Artillery Volunteers and their guns might be expected.

Kydd had readily agreed: he had a deep respect for the

3

stirring pageantry the English knew how to display to the fullest. And Persephone would be proudly by his side.

It proved a popular affair. Folk flocked to the Wembury barracks, its parade ground on cliffs overlooking the sea, and thrilled to the colour and spectacle. Kydd addressed the soldiery from his dais in stout seamanlike terms. Then came a crash and the reek of powder-smoke as the little six-pounders made their salute. A civic occasion followed. Combe Tavy took it in good part when Ivybridge claimed a dinner in honour of the hero on account of its commodious church hall, close by Glanville's corn mill, into which the town council and other notables could be squeezed.

Kydd and Persephone were ushered to their seats in the crowded room. It took waiters an eternity to jostle their way along with salvers, the contents cooling rapidly. From outside came the raucous jollity of lesser mortals enjoying an ox-roast and West Country ale. Kydd knew where he would rather be. When he glanced at a perspiring Lady Kydd he guessed she would too.

In the following days he visited his tenants and heard how the harvest had failed for the second year in succession. And late rains had flooded the lower Erme causing considerable damage to the Flete priory. Other happenings had to be prised out of the good country folk, who felt that such could not possibly engage the interest of one who had faced the enemy in far places and triumphed.

The settled rustic rhythms of Devon reached out to Kydd and he felt them work on his soul, the cares and troubles falling away as each day passed into the next.

Then a letter arrived. In it, to his surprise and pleasure, he was advised that he could look forward to the style and title of baronet in public recognition of his valour and service to the Crown in the late engagement. 'Captain Sir Thomas Kydd, RN, Bart' would be his signature on documents from now on, and among other prerogatives, he would take precedence before any other knight in ceremonial occasions. Persephone glowed with pride: her husband had achieved greater honour than any in her family, and her still-cool parents must now render him due respect and esteem.

One evening after dinner, as velvet darkness stole in, Persephone broke into his thoughts. 'Darling,' she opened, in an odd voice, 'shall we go outside? I've heard that the comet is growing in spectacle and must portend something of significance. I want us to be together in witness.'

'Why, if that is your desire, my love.'

The 'Great Comet' had first appeared some months earlier, and while men of science were declaring it to be the brightest event in the heavens this age, the more superstitious were foretelling cosmic doom and an earthly disaster.

They moved out to the front lawn and gazed upwards at the star-field. The comet had grown in length: Kydd estimated it, with its curved tail, to be at least ten degrees long. It was a wondrous thing – an intrusion into the ordered celestial regularity from regions that lay beyond the stars.

'I shall remember this night as long as I live, Thomas,' she said softly.

'That something of great portent will happen shortly?' he teased.

'Yes,' she answered simply, and held him at arm's length. 'For this night will I always treasure as when I told you . . . my news.'

'Seph?' He caught his breath.

'Yes, my darling,' she breathed, her eyes still on the

splendour in the heavens. 'There'll soon be another in our lives to love and cherish.'

From that moment his existence changed for ever. A child – a young Kydd, one who would bear his name and his title. A baronet passed on his honour and, while not an aristocrat with a seat in the House of Lords, his newborn, should he be a boy, in the fullness of time could claim a knighthood by right. He would inherit Knowle Manor and whatever riches resulted from his recent and future prizes. To go on to who knew what in the years to come . . .

It required him to re-orient his place in the dimensions of life, and the days passed in blissful happiness.

Chapter 2

The trap's grinding wheels sounded above the morning birdsong and the breeze and, to Kydd's delight, he saw his visitor was Craddock. The man cut quite a different figure from before: mature and dignified, he now had a Spanish-style beard to hide the scars of the flames, his grey-tinged sable hair styled in the new Romantic mode. He wore taste-fully cut plain clothes of the kind more to be seen around the London stock exchange, and his eyes had lost their pain-filled dullness: they were now sharp and alert.

'I hope I do not inconvenience, sir?' he asked quietly, remaining in his seat.

'Not at all, dear fellow!' Kydd said warmly. 'Do alight – we've a guest room waiting. That is, if you're—'

'So kind in you, Sir Thomas. I only came to enquire if—'

'Nonsense! You shall stay a space and take glory in the Devonshire countryside with us.' He beckoned his estate steward. 'Appleby, a hand with Mr Craddock's trap.'

Later, with both settled in comfortable armchairs, Kydd heard of his long journey north to Manchester and reunion with his kindred for the first time in nine years. There had been astonishment and relief at his deliverance, shock and sorrow at his loss. As Kydd had guessed, a position had been suggested, a partnership in one of the family's Baltic concerns, but Craddock had declined it. 'You spurned the offer? I find that a singular decision, Mr Craddock.'

'Harry, please.'

'What will you now, then, Harry?'

'Should you still have need for a private secretary it would be my honour and pleasure to serve you again in that capacity.'

Kydd couldn't hold back a smile but quickly smothered it. 'Well, in all decency, I should point out that your prospects—'

'My dear sir, as to that, I took the precaution before leaving of making due enquiry of your inestimable first lieutenant, Mr Bowden.'

'Oh! What did he say about me, pray?'

'You have no more loyal and devoted officer on board the good ship *Tyger*. His assessment, however, was truthful and revealing, you may believe. He told me that your run as a frigate captain has been long and meritorious but must end at some point. Beyond that there is little likelihood of a ship, for even as a senior captain you have no interest at work for you in the Admiralty, and with the seas swept clean of Bonaparte's fleets, frigates are, these days, where distinction and prizes are won. My prospects therefore are slender.'

Kydd chose his words carefully. 'Mr Craddock – Harry. If it is your loyalty to me as your rescuer that impels you to make the offer, then do stand disabused. Your services while in the Adriatic have been a more than adequate return and—'

'Thomas . . . may I?'

'Certainly, old fellow,' Kydd said warmly.

'I know enough of your character to believe you would extend your kindness to any unfortunate you might find in my position and this is not the reason for my offer. It is that while in *Tyger* I found I took to the life – the direct speaking and mutual respect I saw among high and low in our little floating town, the consideration of one for another, the joining together in common purpose against the foe, the lack of dissembling. I confess myself in no haste to return to the usual run of shore folk.'

'Then you are right welcome to the post, dear fellow. But there is the matter of remuneration, your entitlement. The post is personal to me and is no concern or obligation upon the Navy Board to meet the expense and therefore I regret that—'

'My good sir, please accept that my motives for applying are not of the customary nature. While you have command of *Tyger* it will be my pleasure to continue upon the sea life, and when that is regrettably past, well, I shall then consult my situation. Meanwhile there are offices I can perform that I'm sanguine shall prove of utility to you more in a private capacity – as your man of business, might I be permitted to say, or perhaps by way of secretary-in-confidence.'

'This I can believe,' Kydd said, with feeling, 'but again, any fee associated—'

'There will be no fee. Only . . . the liberty of calling you my friend.'

'Harry – you have it.'

'Then if you'll allow me . . .'

Craddock was back promptly, bearing a crusted bottle. 'In Manchester there's a fine cellar for shining occasions and if this is not one then I fail to see what is. Shall we?'

Persephone, sensing a line had been crossed, joined them and together they toasted the hour in the finest Armagnac.

They heard more of Craddock's past and his departure from the family merchant-banking concern at the age of twenty to plough his own furrow in the rapidly emerging

markets of the Balkans. His adventures in the Barbary king-
doms of North Africa and the ancient cities of Turkey and
the Levant enthralled them . . . and then the advent of the
French revolutionaries.

Chapter 3

The letter's superscription was very odd: 'Colonel Sir Thomas Kydd, Royal Navy'. Either it was the work of a madman or one so removed from the ways of the navy as to believe the captain of a ship was in fact a colonel. But it was elegant creamy paper, and when Kydd turned it over the seal was unmistakably that of the office of the first lord of the Admiralty.

He opened it carefully as Persephone looked on. This was indeed a mystery: the acidulous first secretary to the Admiralty, Croker, would never allow such a blunder in his office.

It quickly became clear. The missive was a note of congratulation from their lordships at his appointment as colonel of marines, a purely ceremonial position but one that indicated his standing after the action in the Adriatic. Enclosed was an invitation to a dinner in his honour at Mansion House from General Hoby, adjutant general, Royal Marines, and the most senior of that clan in the country.

'Ah. I cannot pretend but that this is well timed. *Tyger* is near complete of her repairs and – save your presence, my dear – I've a yen to take in a mort of sea air after all my pampering. This gives me a chance to make my number with the Admiralty that I'm now enabled to await their orders for sea.'

Lady Kydd, in respect of her condition, would remain at Knowle Manor, content to know that her husband was accompanied by his devoted valet, Tysoe, and Craddock, and would be back before long.

The dinner was a fine event, the guests mingling delightedly with the hero of the hour who, it was said, would be back to sea shortly.

Kydd's speech was well received and the largely professional gathering offered interesting conversation. At the brandy and cigars, he heard the views of the adjutant general that the supremacy of the navy at sea had made opportunities for the ambitious Royal Marines officer now scarce and exceptional. Across the table an army colonel pointed out that consolidating an empire consisted in the main of dusty parade-ground drills in far-flung territories while waiting for an enemy who never came. And this was without the consolation to be had by a Royal Marine in a ship making port back in England: he knew some troopers in India who'd been there continuously for above a dozen years.

Kydd was tempted to make the observation that much of the lack of career distinctions stemmed from the fact that, unlike the navy, whose ships were to be found across the entire globe, the only part of the world in which land forces could in any way be termed active was the Peninsula. There, Wellington had quartered his valuable battalions behind the invulnerable lines of the Torres Vedras, and was not seeking distinction in open battle.

At one point there was general puzzlement at the fuming of the Americans over some imagined slight to honour, but the consensus was that this would not be any cause for armed intervention, let alone war. More concerning was the effect of Bonaparte's Continental System in locking off his entire realm. From the Atlantic to the Baltic, the North Sea to the Mediterranean, trade of any kind with the British was forbidden. Britannia's funding of the war, however, had always been grounded on a healthy commerce with her traditional partners.

A single word could best describe the situation in which the world was finding itself after so many years of war: stalemate. Napoleon Bonaparte was confined to the Continent, raging like a lion in a cage, and, even with his giant armies, unable to break out. On the other hand, with command of the sea, Britain was helping herself to an empire – but was a helpless spectator to events in Europe. And at any point in these parlous times the state of affairs could worsen and plunge Britain headlong into catastrophe.

The conversations died. These conundrums had been chewed over endlessly in wardrooms and nothing had changed the essence of what lay behind them all. With Bonaparte victorious wherever on land he marched, it would be the continuation of a wearisome war as far ahead as any could foresee. Other topics were equally dismal: the bad harvests, economic dislocation from steam engines and such, and the growth, like cancer, of new industrial towns across ancient lands.

With the evening drawing to a close, Kydd made a light bow to General Hoby, gave his thanks for the dinner, and bade him farewell. Others too, rose, leaving him with Craddock, while he waited for his cloak and sword to depart. Craddock had proved the ideal companion: cultured, elegant and with exquisite manners, he'd allowed Kydd to hold forth while his restrained contributions were interesting and to the point.

It was after midnight but Kydd felt restless. 'Shall we call at my club for a snorter before we turn in? There's people I'd like you to meet, Harry.'

It was raining by the time they reached the smoke-grimed Portland stone edifice that was Brooks's Club and entered its august portals.

'Tiger, dear fellow!' one passing member called to him, beaming with pleasure. 'So good to see you unharmed by your late encounter.'

Kydd crossed to shake the prime minister's hand. 'Quite untouched, Grenville. But Craddock here has good enough reason to curse the French.'

After a polite exchange they found a pair of armchairs and prepared to appreciate a particularly flowery cognac, unperturbed by the joyous shouts from a nearby gambling room.

Kydd learned more of his new friend. A more than fair judge of a good brandy, his life at the convergence of the wine trades of France, Italy and the more sombre German vintages from the north had him well placed to advise Kydd on the stocking of his cellar at Knowle Manor. They were pondering what might best grace the cabin stores of *Tyger* when they noticed the raucous hullabaloo from the gamblers had died away. Suddenly a wash of voices sounded as a cluster of figures issued out, led by a plump gentleman in outlandishly extravagant costume waving a chicken leg. His florid features lit up with pleasure when he spied Kydd.

'Yo ho ho, and it's Tiger, as they're not wrong!' The chicken leg was flung aside as the Prince Regent of Great Britain and Ireland advanced to greet him.

'Your Royal Highness,' Kydd replied, rising quickly and bowing.

'A right fine drubbing, I heard.'

'We gave 'em pause to regret their impudence, I believe, sir.' It had not been so long before that he'd made acquaintance of the mercurial prince, who'd been taken with what he saw as Kydd's salty and direct ways. After the illness of his father, the King, he'd become regent and the highest in the kingdom.

'Might I present to you Mr Lucius Craddock, sir – he it was I rescued from the Adriatic in particularly distressing circumstances and now swears to serve me as long as he may.'

'Craddock.' There was a keen look of appraisal and the gaze shifted quickly back to Kydd. 'Do I hear their lordships have rendered their appreciation in proper manner?'

'I believe they have, sir. Know that I'm now not only a baronet but a colonel in the Royal Marines.'

'A colonel only?' The eyebrows contracted in vexation. 'Surely to be raised to a general is more to be expected.'

'It's all I might ask at my humble station,' Kydd said modestly.

'Nonsense! Still in your old ship? A species of frigate, isn't she?'

'Yes, sir.'

'There you are, then! The rascals should give you a ship worthy of your deeds, Tiger! A big one! If you can smite the tyrant with a tiddler, then what commotion can you not stir up with a ship o' size?'

'No, no, sir,' Kydd said hastily. 'Believe that I'm most content with my brave barky.'

'Ha! They'll be taking care of their favourites, I'll be bound. Well, this is to say they picked a wrong 'un in me, dammit. I'll see you into one of 'em, never doubt it.'

Alarmed, Kydd blurted, 'Sir, I'm happy with my present command, you must accept. I'm—'

'Rubbish, Tiger! I'm not accounted king-in-waiting for

nothing. Leave it to me. Should I have to sink the whole pootling crew you'll have your mighty ship-o'-war. Trust me!'

Lost for words Kydd could only bow deeply.

'Have to go now, Tiger. Five hundred on the table and I'm down a gallows deal more. But I won't forget, you may depend on it.'

Chapter 4

Plymouth Hoe, Devon

The vantage point overlooking the harbour was always at its best in the warmth of early summer, with couples promenading arm in arm, children playing, and old folk taking the sun, enjoying their view over a glittering sea where so much of England's history had unfolded.

Kydd had come to these grassy slopes in times past to ease his spirits and today was no exception. While Persephone and their cook, Mrs Appleby, took to the shops he paced along as if it were a quarterdeck before an action that demanded thought above the usual.

The Prince Regent had not forgotten. Just when Kydd had believed himself safe, a terse Admiralty letter had arrived, couched in words almost rude in their abruptness. He was forthwith relieved of the command of HM Frigate *Tyger* in favour of the officer named, to take effect on the date specified, some four days later. No mention of why or honeyed phrases of duty done, or any reference to a ship-of-the-line or, in fact, any further employment. It was personally signed by Yorke, first lord of the Admiralty, and therefore it was useless to complain or appeal. No other communication had been forthcoming. He was grounded solidly 'on the beach' with no ship and no prospect of one.

Was this a political gesture, a spiteful lashing out by Admiral Sidney Smith after his role in putting down the Sicilian plot had been overshadowed by Kydd's victory at Lissa? Probably not. The eccentric had lost most of his friends and influence in high places. Another? There were plenty of serving admirals envious of his fame and willing to take steps to bring this to an ignominious end but they would need extraordinary influence to persuade the strait-laced Yorke.

In the Plymouth port admiral's office Kydd had found they'd already been duly informed, and were preparing to continue the commission of the famous frigate under her new captain with never a blink of an eye to show they'd noticed the change.

It had all the hallmarks of an Admiralty affronted by what they would have seen as Kydd's blatant attempt to claw his way to the quarterdeck of a ship-of-the-line by invoking interest at an incontestable level, the Prince Regent of Great Britain. This would explain what amounted to his near-instant dismissal from *Tyger* and silence on the subject of any other command. And it would be an unanswerable reply to the interfering prince that no ship of a kind suitable for his hero was available at the present time, with the unspoken reality that there never would be.

In something between grief and panic he'd come to realise that his sea career was over. Even the days left to him in the ship he'd taken from mutiny to triumph were to be spent in a dockyard under repair, after which he must finally retire with his memories to the land. It was unbearable to know that the heave of a deck under his feet and the majesty of the deep-sea realm in all its mystery and allure were now firmly rooted in the past.

He'd thought about coming out fighting, harnessing the public respect and admiration so gratifyingly on show recently, not to mention the well of professional esteem he'd earned among his peers. The urge was savage and primeval but doomed. He had no highly placed friends who were in a position within the Admiralty to spearhead a fight-back in a public spectacle that would put their own promotions in jeopardy. Without someone to speak up for him in the councils of the great, things must inevitably take their course.

He'd quietly revealed the situation to Bowden, who after recovering, suggested taking *Tyger* to sea, her repairs so near complete, and rejoin in the Mediterranean as though the letter had arrived too late. But Kydd's visit to the port admiral's office would prove he'd taken receipt.

A stunned, shocked silence had descended on the ship and then a growing hubbub. Before long a stream of petitioners was knocking at his door. They were all after the same thing, something it was not in his power to grant, a circumstance that wrung him with misery for its being so doubly unjust. The sailing master, Joyce, with his peg-leg; Lieutenant Brice, now so firmly on the rung of advancement; gunner's mate Stirk, and his shipmates who'd been with Kydd since his own fore-mast days; Boatswain Herne, now grey and with the dignity of age, whom Kydd had seen climb *Tyger*'s rigging at Lissa in a storm of fire and shot. And the two midshipmen, bewildered and cast down, looking to find that what they'd heard wasn't so.

All had come to be recognised as a follower. It was a humane and effective gesture, the understanding that men long-serving under a captain they trusted would go on to form the core of an efficient and loyal ship's company in another ship. Any number of valued hands recognised as followers could go with their captain in this way, even up to an entire complement.

But there was a hard and fast rule that the procedure could not be considered a move but more in the nature of an exchange. For every follower going into a ship, that captain must provide a replacement crew member from the new ship to go back to the old. But Kydd did not have a new ship – and therefore no followers could be allowed him. *Tyger* would put to sea under her new captain with her company unchanged. The crew Kydd had forged from dishonour through uncountable perils of sea and enemy to form a ferocious instrument of war would be his to care for and lead in all *Tyger*'s adventures to come.

The relieving captain, Faulknor, had arrived promptly, accepting Kydd's distant welcome with ill-disguised delight, his translation from a workaday frigate in the North Sea Squadron to command of the most famous frigate of the day as sudden and unexpected as Kydd's loss of it. He'd gone through the necessary musters and handover routines as rapidly as was decently possible, clearly in awe of his situation but a seasoned captain himself, nevertheless wary and correct.

He'd been given the honour at the farewell dinner of sitting on Kydd's right hand, the familiar faces on either side pale, unbelieving. The meal passed off heavily, jokes of the usual kind falling flat for no one could put a reason to the extraordinary events, still less account for their legendary captain's lack of a future. Their parting gift – a silver hunter – was handed to him with a mumbled valediction. His reply was equally stilted. And then it was over.

Persephone had not attended, unable to face being witness

to Kydd's grief, but she was there by the dockyard landing the next day when *Tyger*'s officers and warrant officers had pulled Kydd ashore in his barge. She caught sight of tears in the eyes of more than one as they glided in to the jetty with a final toss of the oars, captain's coxswain Halgren making a faultless alongside, the last thing he could do for his captain.

All stood, removing their hats and standing motionless as Kydd stumbled away, up and around the corner where he broke down in her arms.

His last ties with the past were severed later that day when his effects were landed, and he'd asked Tysoe for his advice on their storage. His faithful manservant then asked that after these many years he be given release from service. Kydd had sadly agreed, promising an annuity for his loyal devotion that would allow him to see out his years in comfort back in Jamaica.

He hadn't the heart to go to London to petition for a ship, as he had those years ago, and instead sent a pleading letter asking that his recent service to the Crown be recognised with another command, but he held out little expectation.

And then, from this summer vista, he saw the saddest sight imaginable. To the right, emerging from the Hamoaze, instantly recognisable to any who knew her, was *Tyger*. Outward bound for Bermuda.

He gulped and watched for the hours it took in the light airs to dip her topgallants beneath the horizon, once staying about for the run to the Atlantic – was that a sadly clumsy mainsail haul? Probably Faulknor taking his time in a ship new to him. In her, men were securing for sea, the first dog-watchmen would be closing up, and in the first heaves of an open-ocean swell, the gunroom preparing for supper.

Chapter 5

Less than a week later Kydd heard again from their lord-ships, a remarkably short time in the Admiralty's universe.

He'd lost his dear *Tyger*, his frigate and his being, but incredibly he was not to be cast ashore. Despite all his fears a no-doubt-reluctant Admiralty had found him a ship. And not any ship but the one that was most certainly needed on the long and stony path to admiral – a battleship!

These behemoths were at the pinnacle of naval command. Standing in the line-of-battle to withstand the worst the enemy could throw against them, they were the true wooden walls of England, and every action they fought would resound down the ages. In foreign parts the battleship was an unanswerable demonstration of the might of the Royal Navy to all who dared try to wrest sovereignty of the seas from Great Britain.

The captain of such a ship was a hallowed being, privy to plots and strategies at the highest, attended by ceremony and arcane prostrations. Above all, he stood alone as its lord and master, overseer of the greatest artillery batteries to be found on any battlefield, the monster guns carried on several gun-decks fore and aft in dreadful array. He, Tom Kydd, wigmaker of Guildford, had achieved the peak of naval command: a ship-of-the-line.

He clutched the paper for long minutes, gripped by the moment. Then stark reality set in. The cold distancing of Yorke and the absence of platitudes showed that the Admiralty had been compelled to concede to the Prince Regent's desire. The enjoinder that he should take command of HMS *Thunderer*, 74, was a skilful move. She was old. In fact she'd been with the fleet since before the French wars had begun in 1793. Kydd knew that she'd seen blockade duty off the French coast for years and would probably be weary, dispirited and drab. Neatly, the Admiralty were ensuring that the dashing frigate captain of popular imagination was getting the 'promotion' he deserved, a battleship, but at the same time ensuring he could never again range the ocean as a free spirit, or fly at a moment's notice to some distant sea to win yet more laurels in lonely splendour.

Now it was to be part of a standing fleet, with all others around him under the eye and direction of an admiral or commander-in-chief whose desires it was his to concern himself with, whose orders took supremacy over all others. Even to the fundamentals of how to fight – the hallowed Fighting Instructions that governed everything from in what manner to alter course as a line, to the details of signal procedures. There was no more room for initiative, for on-the-spot risk-taking, for daring thrusts deep into enemy waters, simply the duty to exist and thereby contain the enemy.

The chances of fame and distinction were swallowed in being only one of a larger whole, saving that if it came to a mighty fleet action it would be another matter entirely. But the likelihood of such a glorious clash was unlikely, given Bonaparte's reluctance to risk another Trafalgar. Kydd's fate, therefore, was precisely what was wanted: to slide swiftly and gracefully into obscurity with an equally rapid fading from the public consciousness.

It didn't have to be that way. At the moment he was the lauded victor of Lissa, one of the shining band of frigate captains who had made a name for themselves throughout the land. Why should he not now rest on his fame, graciously accept the plaudits and slip into history as one of the select band of immortals who had won imperishable glory on the quarterdeck of his own ship?

To continue in a ship-of-the-line would gain him little more and would have its own risk. The more he considered the situation, the bleaker he felt. He knew he was a natural frigate seaman with the qualities, professional and personal, that were required for such a command. Quite different and equally demanding qualities were needed for a sail-of-the-line: the possession of diplomacy, a cooler head and broader perspectives. What if he didn't have them, if in one or more he proved lacking, leading to a blunder of significance in the larger picture? Offending an ally, failing to see a strategical objective above a tactical, misreading a move by the commander-in-chief at the wrong time? Whatever else, he would be thought unfit for the position and honour of captain of a ship-of-the-line, a failure, and would be quietly retired.

It had happened to others, generally accepted as not their particular fault but rather an unfortunate lack in the requisite skills at that level. But, still, accounted a failure, never to be employed at sea again.

Better he didn't take the risk.

And there was the realisation that he was no longer making decisions for himself, or even for Persephone, but for his unborn child. Would it grow up in adulation for the father who had won such renown in his trusty frigate or would it look upon one known as a hero in a small ship but a derisory failure in a more powerful one?

However, there was a passing but definite possibility he could one day become an admiral. Some with origins before the mast had already achieved this: Captain Cook, Benbow, Mitchell – even the notorious Bligh. Should he throw away any chance he had for fear of failing?

Command of a ship-of-the-line was a necessary milestone on the way. Therefore it all reduced to a simple question: did he want to become an admiral badly enough to risk everything?

Craddock's view was that, in his ignorance of the politics of what was happening, anything he could contribute might be misleading. But Persephone was of one mind: 'Dearest Thomas – know that I'd infinitely rather be married to one who reaches for the stars and falls than one who never tries for fret of disappointment.'

He'd take the gamble.

Chapter 6

When HMS *Thunderer* put into Plymouth Sound, Kydd was at Knowle Manor bearing a hand with the glassing in of the orangery.

A message came from the dockyard informing him that the vessel was moored in Cawsand Bay, the usual anchorage for the bigger ships touching port only. His orders required him to assume command at once, wasting no time to rejoin the blockade squadron off Brest.

Early the next day, he took leave of Persephone and told Craddock he would send for him when the time was suitable. All his anxious fretting, his thoughts and worry over the weeks were now to become reality. He was about to step forward to claim his ship, his destiny.

Kydd had never served in a 74, apart from the ancient *Trajan* out in the Caribbean and that had been as a humble able seaman. Others he'd seen only from afar. He felt a surge of tension at the sight of the bulk and majesty of a full-blooded man-o'-war of the breed as the dockyard hoy rounded Picklecombe Point to open the broad bay. *Thunderer* was lying to a single bower anchor, her black hull relieved only by the line of a varnished wale along each gun-deck, enabling closed gun-ports with their black outside to reveal the fearsome 'Nelson chequer' now almost universally adopted by the fleet.

Her masts were varnished, her spars black and her sails entirely struck. He was curious to see whether, after some hours at anchor, her shrouds had been set up properly with no unsightly bights, the yards squared across and no Irish pennants showing from aloft. There were no concerns there – the first lieutenant and boatswain were doing their jobs – but he'd seen something else.

'Take me around, just the once,' he asked, slipping across a coin, his eyes fixed on the big ship. The lower gun-ports had nettings rigged below them and he watched as a long-boat emerged under her stern: *Thunderer* was taking precautions against desertion. Probably a wise measure, but was this notice of what awaited him after the indulgence of a crack frigate with an all-volunteer crew?

He saw as well, with a stab of pleasure, the massive two tiers of stern windows denoting a 74-gun ship. The upper one, his, had the traditional open captain's walk. And as they rounded the stern closer to, he took in the elaborate and ornate carving, particularly in the supports to the quarter gallery. She'd been constructed before the war when the old eighteenth-century decorative practices had not given way to the plain austerity of wartime builds. In fact, this captain had gone to some lengths to maintain her looks with gilding and point-work in red, green and white on varnish, these days an unusual and pleasing sight.

At her bows was the figurehead, a fierce Jove with a quiver of thunderbolts, one of which he was hurling at the imaginary enemy ahead. It was full-size and extended from the elaborate scroll-work at the beakhead nearly down to the waterline at her forefoot. She might be elderly but was far from drab, and Kydd's spirits rose.

'Take us in.'

As Kydd was in plain clothes in deference to a possibly undistinguished commander, it was necessary to hail the quarterdeck. After a discreet pause, they hooked on at the main chains and Kydd hauled himself aboard briskly. Stepping over the bulwark to the wailing of a single pipe he instantly saw there was no side-party, or welcoming group of officers. Around the deck men stopped what they were doing to stare. No doubt they knew who he was but were making no effort. This was the bare minimum ceremony entitlement for any naval officer.

In a sea-worn uniform an officer stepped over to greet him. Older and of slender build, the man's hard face was set. 'Captain Lyell, *Thunderer*,' he snapped, offering a brief handshake. 'Captain Kydd?'

Something in Kydd rebelled. 'Sir Thomas Kydd, late *Tyger*, frigate.'

'But not her captain at this time.'

'No.'

'Which is why you're greeted in the proper form.' The voice was husky, the manner almost aggressive.

Kydd was taken aback at the man's hostility. Some on deck had not moved since he'd come aboard, agog at the exchange. What was going on?

'Come to take the ship,' Lyell continued darkly.

'Er, my orders are—'

'Shall we step aft?'

Kydd took in that *Thunderer* was in a remarkable state of neatness and fastidious attention. This was a captain who cared for his ship. Unlike a frigate, in a ship-of-the-line the captain's quarters were situated aft on the quarterdeck,

28

forming a poop-deck above for the handling of sail and signals. In this ship its entry was in gleaming dark wood – not stained and varnished but French-polished to a lustrous gleam, as was the interior.

Two chairs were set out beyond the table and, without taking his eyes off Kydd, Lyell sat in one with a brief gesture to Kydd to take the other.

A steward hovered but was brusquely dismissed, and the old captain impatiently leaned forward. 'Sir, allow me to make my position clear beyond any misunderstanding.'

Kydd was puzzled, unable to account for his attitude.

'I believe your actions, sir, are those of a poltroon and unworthy of any in His Majesty's Navy who desires to be known as a sea officer and gentleman.'

Kydd swallowed. 'I beg your pardon?'

'Interests and patronage are not unknown in the service but to seek to further your position by currying favour at court before all others is – is . . .'

So that was it. 'Sir. I'll have you know that it was neither my wish nor my supplication that impelled the Prince Regent to act as he did, which was prompted only by an incident that brought us together in the past. At no point did I attempt to—'

'Do spare me your justifications and excuses, sir. I have a duty laid upon me to yield command of *Thunderer* to you and I shall faithfully carry it out. Do you choose to begin the handover now?'

So Lyell was to be counted among those who believed he was thick with Prinny, the notorious rake now in effect wearing the Crown of Great Britain. Yet at the same time it didn't explain the bitterness, the personal animosity.

'I do. Your books of account, sir?'

'Mr Allen!' Lyell barked. A man in old-fashioned black

coat, breeches and spectacles entered gingerly, clearly primed for business. 'Monthly muster.'

Kydd knew that more naval officers had ended their careers running a-foul of the Navy Board in respect of their accounts than ever suffered from shipwreck and had made it his business to be acquainted with each one. 'I always find the open list to be more useful, don't you?' he came back. This was the original from which the muster-clerk received his information.

Lyell glowered, but nodded to the man.

Then followed the usual general accounts, slop book, sick book and others. There were also the more arcane ones – the latest report of surveys of provisions, an account of casks shaken, backstays shifted, and the all-important purser's certificate. There were so many ways to falsify and cheat, but Kydd made a show of inspecting vouchers and returns, receipts and expenses, knowing, however, that to do a proper job it would be necessary to match them with their accounting in the books, an impossibly lengthy task.

'Very good,' he said at last. He couldn't spot any shortcomings and was prepared to sign for these. Next would be the higher level: the order book, which listed every written order either issued by this captain to one under him or received from those above him. Then there were the letter books, copies of every communication entering or leaving the ship and giving a priceless picture of the efficiency or otherwise of the ship in staying on top of the ebb and flow of events of every kind. With the return of sailing qualities and the ship's log to date in the commission with various remarks and notes they would form Kydd's reading for the foreseeable future.

'The standing officers?' These were warrant officers who remained in the ship even when out of commission.

Boatswain, gunner, carpenter, each with a little empire down in the orlop and having within his charge stores worth a substantial amount and needing meticulous accounting – and for which he himself was ultimately responsible.

Their books were found and slapped down before Kydd, who was conscious of Lyell's smouldering resentment. He nevertheless took his time, sighting pages at random to check for consistency, for diligent and regular entries. They seemed in order but only a formal muster would establish their veracity.

The morning was wearing on but Lyell gave no indication of wanting to call a spell in their pains. It wasn't until the hands were piped to their noon meal that a natural break was offered. It gave Kydd a chance to look surreptitiously around the great cabin and take in where he would have his being in the future. It was of impressive size, with a stateliness in keeping with the ship, which he noticed was quite unmoving in the slight chop in the bay that would have had his frigate snubbing restlessly at her anchor. Around the walls the paintings, miniatures and wistful sea vistas spoke, in their amateurishness, of a loving hand. There was no requirement to step around furniture as was necessary in *Tyger*. The chairs, table and fitments were tasteful but neither extravagant nor out of keeping with the dignified age of *Thunderer*. However, there was no going over to explore the stern walk or the size of the bed-place.

'She's sea kindly?' Kydd asked.

'Your sea qualities are there. The first lieutenant will offer an opinion and the sailing master will give you his views at a later time,' Lyell said stiffly. 'You'll pardon, but I've much to attend to. I take it you're satisfied in the article of accounts?'

'I'd like to take a sight of the condition of the standing

rigging, if you please.' It would give him more than a few clues about how *Thunderer* was keeping the seas.

'You may, but not in my company. As I mentioned before, my time is spoken for, sir.'

'Then I'd like to speak with your officers in turn if this does not inconvenience.'

'It does. Their services I will require until I quit the ship.'

Kydd bit back a response to this pettiness, then asked, 'And when will that be, Captain?'

There was a deliberate pause. 'I will land at eleven forenoon the day following tomorrow.'

'And until then?'

'No doubt I will pass you when you board after that time.' Still the malice, hostility.

The formalities of a handover were largely completed. It might have been a congenial time to chat together over old times and adventures in *Thunderer*, but Kydd was being banished from the ship until the very last moment.

Chapter 7

Two days later Kydd arrived at the Stonehouse steps, within sight of Barn Pool over the Hamoaze. It seemed so long ago that he'd moored his first command there, the little brig-sloop *Teazer*. Now he was about to take charge of one of the grand line-of-battle ships that had so often passed him in stately array without even noticing him.

Dressed in full fig, sword, knightly sash and star, he ignored the stares of passing seamen and dockyard workers. Senior officers were normally accompanied by their retinue of lieutenants, coxswain and others, but he was standing alone.

From Stonehouse Kydd couldn't see *Thunderer* moored past Mount Edgcumbe. He could only assume Lyell would leave at eleven but it was probable he'd land here, relatively private compared to the busy Millbay docks.

At a little over half past the hour a boat rounded Devil's Point with a naval officer visible in its stern sheets. It was Lyell, but the boat was a wherry, not a ship's boat, let alone a captain's barge.

Kydd fell back to allow Lyell to step out. The man affected not to notice him, paying off the waterman. With none to meet him, he stalked, face set, past Kydd without a single backward glance.

The wherry lost no time in taking Kydd aboard. 'Busy time f'r *Thunderer*, this forenoon,' the man at the oars said gruffly, watching Lyell with his eyebrows raised. 'Had his gear shifted earlier. Yez wants a boat for your'n, y'r honour?'

'No, thank you,' Kydd replied. That would be the job of a ship's boat. Settling down aft, he casually swept aside his cloak to allow his uniform insignia to be clearly visible. This time, there would be no ignoring who he was.

In mounting excitement, and with not a little trepidation, his eyes sought out the vision of his ship past the undistinguished point, his command. It would either make his career or break him. But, whatever the future held, there was no robbing the moment of its dignity, its consequence in his life. A battleship: his to reign over from the breathtaking and solitary height of senior post-captain.

And there she was! A massive, almost monumental sight, the sunshine picking out the gold leaf and rosin-enriched varnish, and the lazy swirl of her ensign aft and jack forward, both larger than whole sails in *Tyger*.

'Lay alongside,' he ordered, making an effort to bring his features to an appropriate severity. In the splendour of his full-dress uniform he came up the side, met once again by a single boatswain's call and no side-party. He was still not a captain until he'd read himself in, declared publicly the contents of his commission, whose parchment crackled reassuringly at his breast.

A group of officers waited on the other side of the deck, watching him carefully. Punctiliously, Kydd doffed his cocked hat aft in recognition of the quarterdeck and again to the officers, who returned the gesture. One detached from the group. 'Roscoe, first lieutenant,' he growled, with a brief bow.

The single most important person to Kydd in *Thunderer*'s company. A surprisingly young individual, but with hard, direct eyes and a well-toned body.

'Captain Sir Thomas Kydd. Appointed captain of this vessel. If you'll clear lower deck of the hands, Mr Roscoe?'

Kydd kept to himself, pacing slowly and expressionless while first one, then several boatswain's calls pealed out, fore and aft and at the hatchways, summoning *Thunderer*'s company to the upper decks to meet their captain.

As they mustered, a sea of men looked aft, every one a stranger, yet still an individual, possessing character and skills that on blockade he would have ample time to get to know. Some were blank-faced, others suspicious. A few showed frank curiosity. They would inhabit the same circumscribed sea world as he, would follow him into action or . . .

'Ship's company mustered, sir.'

There was nothing to be learned from Roscoe's neutral growl and Kydd drew out his commission. In a measured bellow he announced to the silent mass that he was appointed by the Admiralty to rule over them as lord and master with powers not to be seen outside an Oriental despot's realm. His very word would send them against slashing blade and roar of cannon. And under the Articles of War he could punish or court-martial any as he chose.

'Carry on, please.'

'Aye aye, sir.' Still the hard-featured, expressionless restraint from his chief lieutenant. But he was captain now and he'd make it his business to discover what ailed the man.

'I'll be aft and I desire that each of my officers in turn will present himself to me privately, yourself in ten minutes. We have five officers?'

'Four.'

*   *   *

35

The great cabin was near stripped of living appointments. All but the cabin-width table, one lonely upright chair and a nondescript armchair were left, the deck exposed with its black and white chequer and all lanthorns removed. Kydd burned with resentment. The least Lyell could have done was give warning of his small-minded action.

He flicked open the door to the bed-place. It was of princely size and he remembered that in a ship-of-the-line he should call it a stateroom. At least a cot was hanging there, though without any bedding, and a large chest with drawers dominated the forward bulkhead. Apart from that, the wash-place beyond was bare of basin, jugs and the usual gear. In its emptiness the compartment seemed filled with the lethal blackness of the two guns standing out in stark solidity, with which he would be sharing his sleeping space.

Furious, Kydd whirled about and went to the after end of the great cabin, to a pleasing decorative and well-lit screen with a door to each side. He opened one, stepping out into the six-foot recess of his stern walk and an outstanding view of the open sea and the shoreline. A warm early-summer breeze wafted in and he felt better, even as the row-guard boat slid into his vision below, progressing languidly past. He let the prospect enter his soul for a few minutes, then went back inside. A wave of desolation returned, and with it, the bleak realisation that he knew not a single person aboard. Not even a Tysoe: if Lyell had left his manservant he would certainly have been awaiting Kydd. As it was, even if he sent for his baggage there would be none to stow it and settle him in. Until he got a measure of *Thunderer* and her company he must take care of himself.

Laying his cloak, cocked hat and sword on the cot he prepared to receive his first visitor.

The knocks on the door were firm and just two in number.

'Come!'

Roscoe entered, his hat under his arm. Undeniably hand-some, dark hair in curls but swept to a discreet queue, he carried himself lithely and with presence.

'Do be seated, Lieutenant,' Kydd said mildly, indicating the upright chair. He was sitting in the armchair – awkwardly, for it was too small for his broad frame.

His first lieutenant's expression was difficult to make out – if anything there was a touch of defiance.

'You've seen some sea time, I'd say.'

'Sir.'

'Well?'

'Midshipman in *Indefatigable* 44, Captain Pellew. *Barfleur* 90, Captain Elphinstone. Fifth lieutenant in the same, fourth into *Canopus* 80, Captain James.' As though apologising he went on, 'And lieutenant into *Raven* brig-sloop, before making third into *Thunderer* in 1804, where I remained until made first in 1810.'

There was interest at work here. All except *Raven* were well known for active and distinguished service under pre-eminent captains. It was curious that he'd not claimed participation in any famous action. And that he'd served so long in *Thunderer*: there'd been fine captains and actions in that time, including Calder's before Trafalgar, then the great battle itself, and more since, such as the Dardanelles expedition, with the fiery Talbot in command.

What it added up to was disquieting. This long-serving *Thunderer* lieutenant had achieved the pinnacle – premier of a ship-of-the-line – and could expect advancement in the wake of his captain's elevation. Why was he not a follower? Not up to the job? Come to think of it, none of the other officers had moved along with the old captain into his new appointment. Had there been bad blood?

'You had no inclination to follow Captain Lyell, I take it,' Kydd said evenly.

There was a flash almost of contempt, which he let go without comment and waited for his reply.

'You don't know Captain Lyell.' The tone was flat, disdainful.

'No.'

'May I speak freely?'

'As it shall be respectful to your captain, Mr Roscoe.' The lack of even one 'sir' and the sullen mood grated on Kydd.

'Then know that, through no fault of his, Captain Lyell has been denied an action of distinction these last two years he's been in command of this ship. Instead of abandoning ambition and hope, he resolved to bring her to the forefront, the best and brightest in the squadron even as the old lady is one of many years and scars. He's a fine captain and I for one doff my hat to him.'

'But not to follow . . .'

Roscoe breathed deeply, his nostrils flaring. 'You said as I might speak freely. I will. His reward for these years? Their lordships gave him two weeks to be off the ship, that a favourite at court might be obliged.'

Kydd's lips thinned dangerously. 'I'd put a reef in your tongue if I were you, sir.'

'Not until I've said my piece. He's gone now – but not to a ship as we can therefore be followers. He has nothing. He goes to half-pay, and without patronage, no expectation of ever getting to sea again. No estate, no fortune – his wife in her grave these last seven years. He's to live with his sisters, all hope gone now. And . . . and all to—'

'Enough,' Kydd snarled, leaning forward. 'Stow your jabber! As a first luff your judgement's all to hooey. Have you thought that as owner of a first-rank fighting frigate it was my idea to be thrown into a scowbunking blockader near as old as I am?'

He regretted it immediately but it was too late. He tried to make amends. 'She's a grand old thing, I grant you, but I hail from a different breed entirely. A frigate!'

That didn't help matters. The real problem was that Lyell had not gone on to promotion as flag-captain or even the captain of a first-rate under an admiral and taken all his followers, including Roscoe, with him. For their loyalty to the old captain, they were now stranded in the ship in which they'd spent years serving in the trust that when Lyell moved up so would they.

Roscoe, sitting bolt upright heard him out, then sank back slowly. 'A frigate. Ah, yes – and if you think your ways are ours, then I pity us all.'

'I find your attitude, sir, impolite, disrespectful and unacceptable in a first lieutenant,' Kydd rapped. 'I'll ignore it the once, given your . . . disappointments. I won't tolerate it further – understand?'

'Sir.'

'And if you so wish it, I shall make it my business to allow you to make your departure from this ship as soon as you may.' He didn't know if he had the power to do this, but if Roscoe had such strong feelings that he'd behave so before a new captain it would be better for both of them if he went.

The eyes flickered but there was no other response.

'In that case you may remain in post – but only as you deserve it. The efficiency and well-being of this ship as part of the squadron off Brest is my prime objective and you, as my right-hand man, are crucial in this. If you fail, I will have no regrets in having you removed. After I see the last officer

39

we shall meet again, when you'll inform me of the state of the ship, its manning and immediate needs. You may go.' Roscoe rose with exaggerated dignity, gave a short bow and made to leave.

'Oh, and send a boat to bring off my baggage, if you please.'

It contained his clothing, writing materials, undress uniform, items of personal grooming. As a matter of priority he had to find another Tysoe, but from where was not immediately evident. Nor was it clear how, before they sailed, he would find time to go ashore and collect items to furnish his living spaces.

After Roscoe had gone he leaned back in his chair. In a way the man had reason to resent Kydd's presence. The perceived court-dictated imposition on *Thunderer* had caused a stumbling block to promotions. And the superseding of Lyell had produced an injustice Kydd regretted, particularly after his own recent fear that he was about to share the same fate.

'Smale, sir. Second luff.'

Kydd hadn't heard the knock and the apologetic voice that announced the second lieutenant. 'Enter.'

A shorter, affable individual came in to present himself. Fair-haired, running a little to corpulence, his air of confidence heartened Kydd, who noted the faultlessly turned-out uniform and lace cuffs that reminded him of Lieutenant Dacres in his first command, *Teazer*.

'I'll know your sea experience, sir.'

'Oh. Joined up as mid in 1801 in the old *Theseus* under Bligh the Second and saw out the rest of the war in *Blackbird*, cutter. After Amiens it was . . .'

Kydd heard it through, a pedestrian career considerably helped along by Earl St Vincent in whose eyes, it seemed,

Smale could do no wrong. This Bligh was the second in the Navy List – perhaps six by that name were serving at the moment.

At the end Kydd asked, curious, 'Tell me, do you get along well with the first lieutenant, Mr Smale?'

Taken by surprise he hesitated. 'Oh, well, yes, I suppose so.'

'Does this mean you agree that Captain Lyell was ill-served by my appointing to *Thunderer*?'

Smale stared at him. 'Er, these things happen, um, as the needs and conditions of service demand.'

Kydd had his judgement of the man. He would trim to the wind wherever it blew. The man was well connected, a safeguard against unfortunate circumstances, so it was easy to gauge his motives.

'Do ask the third to attend me.'

Briggs was different again. Wary but controlled, he answered Kydd's questions carefully and with due thought. Again, long service in *Thunderer*. Something about his bearing, though, reached out to Kydd. Was it because of the cruel twist that had had him as passed lieutenant caught by the peace of Amiens and cast out of his ship still a midshipman? A harsh fate without even the half-pay that came with confirmation in the rank. He'd dealt with that by shipping out as able seaman in a merchantman to Canada and there, ironically, had been press-ganged by a brig-sloop at the sudden outbreak of the war with Napoleon.

He'd been aboard until, as invasion loomed, the ship had been recalled to England where the commander of the sloop, recognising his worth and qualifications, had set him on the quarterdeck as a midshipman once more. Moving quickly, he'd been confirmed as lieutenant and seen a thankless existence on the Toulon blockade. A wounding at Cagliari had had the inevitable effect of delaying his further progress through the ranks. He'd been in the ship some three years now.

Thunderer's fourth lieutenant, Mayne, was, again, different from the others. Fair-haired and of slight build, his was a recent appointment as midshipman from another sail-of-the-line in the same squadron. He had an air of resentment, no pressing desire to shine at this, the start of his presumably chosen course in life. Answering in monosyllables, sometimes averting his gaze, he gave Kydd no cause for confidence in him as an officer.

Contradicting what he'd told the first lieutenant, he decided next to make acquaintance with the warrant officers. These would be of long service, and he must rely on them to maintain and operate *Thunderer* as a ship of war, able to stand effectively in the line of battle.

The boatswain, Opie, was one of the old breed of seamen, lined but muscular, holding himself obstinately, challenging almost, his voice powerful and deep. Kydd suspected he'd be barely literate but would stand for nothing and be obeyed instantly. He need have no uneasiness about this man.

Sailing Master Hobbs was probably the oldest man in the ship. His service was long and varied. From a fore-and-aft rigged cutter through a stint in the Transport Service and surveying under the legendary Hurd, he'd been seeing out what was assumed to be his last active sea post in *Thunderer*. Kydd knew the type – utterly reliable and knowledgeable. At the same time he would not be a risk-taker, his comfort in retirement his to wreck.

Another of the old school was *Thunderer*'s gunner, Lawlor. Unsmiling and deliberate, he chose his words with care. Just what was needed in one who was to take charge of whole decks of guns, the largest in the navy, with magazines fore and aft that could, in a fraction of a second's carelessness, detonate the ship and everyone aboard. His responsibilities were also the custody and accounting of stores in value many times a sailor's wages for life.

The carpenter, Upcot, a garrulous and fidgety man, did not stay long. He lived among his workshop and stores right forward in the bows deep in the orlop, and Kydd would seldom see him.

It was a different story with Sadler, the surgeon. Supercilious and aloof, he seemed to think his time in *Thunderer* was a penance for some medical sin and his patients a lower form of life. Should *Thunderer* ever be caught up in a fleet action Kydd could only pity those who went under his knife.

'Sir – sir!' A face peered around the door.

'Who are you, pray?' The individual had what appeared to be a permanent frown of agitation but his dress was that of an officer.

'Gubb, Sir Thomas, Jonathan Gubb, purser of this ship.' The recently promulgated uniform regulations bestowed a new respectability on the breed.

'Do you require to see me?'

'At your earliest convenience, Sir Thomas.'

'Very well, Mr Gubb. I'll send for you before the end of day.' A thought struck. 'As you may have noticed, I have no manservant or other. Can you oblige with a recommendation?'

'Um, this is an unusual request, sir, but I'll do my best.'

'And another thing. Later I shall need a sighting of the ship's books. Do tell the ship's clerk to oblige me.'

'Mr Allen? I'm afraid he's no longer with us, sir.'

'Not in the ship?' Kydd was astonished. 'But the regulations clearly state that—'

'Yes, sir. That all ship's books shall remain with the ship in the event of a change in command. The books are here, sir, but the clerk is not.'

'Then how the devil can I—'

'Discharged sick to Stonehouse hospital. By order Captain Lyell,' the purser said woodenly.

Had Lyell engineered his removal in pique?

To prepare to sail soon for the French coast Kydd needed an up-to-date state-and-condition of the ship, account of provisions and so forth to give him a picture of her sea endurance. He'd signed for them, but this was to their existence, not contents. Dillon would have had these unobtrusively out and available to him but he didn't have Dillon any more.

He swore, then remembered himself and dismissed the purser to give himself time to think.

He put off the first lieutenant once again and loudly demanded the presence of the midshipman who'd been in *Thunderer* the longest.

The lad who appeared was struck dumb by the summons, having to decide between appearing at once on command or borrowing gear to make himself presentable. He'd made the former choice, assuming Kydd would want punctuality before appearance.

'F-Forbin, sir,' he stammered, shifting from one foot to the other, a lanky youth of about seventeen.

'Forbin. I have a duty for you,' Kydd said sternly.

'Sir?' Whatever were the rumours about the famous frigate captain taking over their ship, clearly they would now grow in the telling.

'Until I say otherwise you shall take station on me all day, stand fast the silent hours. All other duties are hereby suspended. Clear?'

'Aye aye, sir.'

'Then duty the first. Take a boat crewed by trusties ashore and at this address call on the lady now staying there. This

44

will be Lady Kydd, my wife.' He pulled out his new fob watch and consulted it. 'She is to feed you a cold pie while she prepares to return with you to *Thunderer* for a quick visit. Understood?'

Chapter 8

With the line of command from himself through the layers of service to a decent noonday meal being broken by the absence of a manservant, a sullen purser's steward was set to rousing out a bite while Kydd waited for Persephone.

'Sweet love!' she breathed, when shown to his cabin. 'What has happened?'

'Naught but the previous captain venting his spite, so as you can see I'm in mortal need of cabin fitments. Can you make purchase of the needful?'

Practical and never to be discouraged, with the help of the carpenter and his folding rule, Persephone soon had her list and stepped ashore.

Gubb was not having success in finding a suitable manservant within the ship's company so Kydd demanded a man from the pompous captain of marines, Hare, who expected his summons to have a more martial purpose. A stolid, unspeaking corporal was the result and he was set to collecting Kydd's baggage and stowing it in the stateroom.

Finally able to see Roscoe, Kydd discovered the true state

of *Thunderer*. Two-thirds of provisions had been expended and she was in need of wood and water. And there were other matters: a sprung main topgallant yard needing replacement, the main hatch gratings stove in at one point, the chain-pump's leather valves in want of changing.

But the chief need was for men.

'Established complement 640, we've 591 on the muster book. Six run so far, a good few left as are "King's hard bargains", useless and—'

'Yes. Fifty hands wanting – this is a grievous shortage. When I've the time I'll step ashore and see the port admiral about some pressed men.'

'Aye, sir.' Roscoe's smile was wintry.

'Meanwhile, get Lambhay moving with our resupply, the gunner to report to me in detail his standings. I've every intention of sailing within four days, Mr Roscoe. Carry on, if you please.'

Until he could get his quarters squared away he couldn't rest so he decided to make first acquaintance with his ship. 'Forbin!' he blared. The youth had taken to skulking in the lobby in readiness and appeared promptly. 'With me, younker.' Kydd was in comfortable sea rig and, his cocked hat significantly under his arm to indicate an unofficial presence, they stepped off.

The captain's domain was the raised portion at the after end of the quarterdeck. From aft, going forward, was his great cabin, followed by his private quarters to starboard. On the other side was the lobby, or coach, which acted as the ship's office and workplace for administration. At this point, the half-deck, a door led to the open quarterdeck at the mizzen-mast, the ship's wheel and binnacle close ahead with, amidships, gratings to the upper deck next below.

The main ladderway was centred, broad and spacious for rapid climbing in action from below, and further forward, beyond the main-mast, was the open space over which the boats were stowed.

Seamen paused in their work at seeing the new captain on the prowl, but resumed industriously at a glance from Kydd. He stood still for a moment, then pointed to a petty officer driving men at some task, all of whom wavered on seeing him. 'Who's that?'

'Oh, sir, that's Tucker, captain of the foretop.'

Kydd called him over and the man loped across warily. Out of the hearing of his men Kydd accused, 'You're using a stonachie to start those men. I'll not have that aboard *Thunderer*, you hear me?'

It was more than a year since the Admiralty had forbidden the use of a rope's end on unresisting seamen but Kydd had never seen the point of it, believing it not needed for men doing their best, and building animosity and indignation in others.

The quarterdeck was connected to the fo'c'sle by gangways each side, a large open space over-topped by bare spars between: the boat stowage. Down through it Kydd could see the guns of the deck below. He had no need to look up into the rigging as he went: all ship-rigged vessels were similar, and except for size, *Thunderer*'s was no different from any other – three masts: mizzen, main and fore. On each was the main sail, the course, with a topsail above it, topgallant higher and royal the highest of all. The baffling maze of ropes from aloft was the operating machinery of each yard and nearly identical on each mast.

It was the scale that was different: the main-mast was near four feet through, a 'made mast' constructed from a number of timbers strapped together, a monstrous-sized piece that soared belligerently up to the fighting tops with topmasts beyond. It supported acres of sail.

The fo'c'sle was deserted, with hands preparing to store ship. Kydd was able to examine where the seamen took their ease, the jeer-bitts where lines were belayed, and gratings where the upwelling warmth of the galley stove from the deck below would be welcomed. The squared-off forward end reminded him of the times as a young sailor in seas the world over he'd laughed and sung with his shipmates into the starlit night, or sat with his tie-mate Nicholas Renzi exchanging the favour of plaiting each other's queues. Renzi was no longer at sea, having married Kydd's sister, Cecilia, and taken up his ancestral seat as the Earl of Farndon.

Moving down the corner ladder, they arrived at the upper deck, the highest deck that ran uninterrupted the length of the ship. It had guns ranged in an unbroken row into the distance on both sides, each the calibre of *Tyger*'s main armament. With the fourteen nine-pounders on the quarterdeck and another four on the fo'c'sle the impression was of indomitable might.

Forward was the fore-mast, and abaft was the complexity of the galley, its black-metal Brodie stove dominating, the cook and his mates energetically at work. Looking aft, past the centre-line gratings, hatches and ladderways, Kydd could make out the sweep of gleaming dark wood that was the wardroom bulkhead. 'I'll make visit there later,' he growled, and clattered down the ladder to the deck below – the lower deck, which mounted the battleship's biggest guns, the awe-inspiring three-ton thirty-two-pounders firing shot that could pierce three feet of solid oak at a mile range. A musket burned an ounce or two of powder but these beasts filled the air with rolling smoke from a ten-pound charge with a fierce bellow heard miles away. Broadsides from *Thunderer* would bring a devastating storm of ruin to an enemy, but in the thick of an action these spaces would be a near imitation of hell itself.

But the lower deck had another reality. It was for the seamen's rest, their sleep. Unlike the upper deck, which was open to the sky amidships with the boats on their spars, and therefore swept by the elements, it was completely enclosed, preserving warmth and dryness for the hundreds of hammocks crammed within it at night. Their messes would be rigged between the guns and a meal taken after their grog when the events of the day would be chewed over in their refuge and sanctuary. There was little doubt as to what would be the subject tonight.

He glanced down. The decks were spotless, the sides lime-washed to reflect light through the gun-ports, the racks of utensils hoisted out of the way. Next to them were ditty-bags where seamen kept possessions that meant a lot to them. The petty officers' messes were canvas-shrouded for privacy.

Kydd had no need to investigate in detail. He'd started his sea life with the seamen in a mess precisely the same and knew what to expect. What was becoming increasingly obvious was that in this ship the people had been cared for, their quarters clean and bright. This would be down to the first lieutenant under the captain's direction. Whatever Lyell and Roscoe's shortcomings he had to respect them in this regard.

The entire after end of the ship was partitioned off. This formed the gunroom, where warrant officers, midshipmen, various clerks and obscure functionaries took their meals and found their rest. Unlike in a frigate, where the gunroom also messed those from the quarterdeck, a ship-of-the-line boasted a wardroom where, with the exception of the purser and surgeon, the inhabitants were all officers.

Not wishing to trespass on these spaces for the moment, Kydd turned forward.

On impulse he crossed to the ship's massive side and bent to feel about below the lower gun-port sill where the deck met the hull at a waterway, the spirketting. He rapped it hard and it returned a reassuringly solid ring. This was satisfying, for it told of a sound hull. He'd never forget his first night at sea, in the old 98-gun *Duke William*, a sailor pointing out its spirketting as druxy timber, white-speckled spongy wood that seemed to make his whole wooden world suddenly shaky and precarious, about to fall apart before plunging for ever into the depths. *Thunderer* was old but apparently still in good shape.

As he paced slowly aft, men scurried away at his presence, leaving him to take in the spectacle of the massive bulk of the main capstan and the spacious main ladderway. It was so broad it was set parallel to the ship's side rather than across. Past another half-dozen guns, planted fair and square in the centre, were the huge riding bitts that now took the battle-ship's twenty-inch anchor cable about them before it led forward to the hawse and out to the anchor, fathoms below.

Intruding into this warlike setting was the homely sight of animals – a few goats, some sheep, two pigs. They were securely penned within a manger: meat on the hoof while enduring months at sea on blockade. In *Tyger* they had no need for such, for their adventures usually took them to parts of the world where fresh meat was easily obtainable, but *Thunderer* had to maintain herself on a hostile coast or go without. He'd noticed two chicken coops on the poop and more discreetly on the fo'c'sle, the eggs a treat for the officers.

The deck below was the last, the orlop. Below the waterline, it was the dark empire of boatswain, carpenter and gunner, their stores and equipment. The purser would make issue from his quarters and the surgeon hold daily muster of the sick list. In the middle were the cable-tiers where the great length of the anchor cable was coiled. There were also the fish room, the carpenter's wings, the lady's hole – but these could all wait.

'Very well. I'll return now. The midshipmen's berth another time.'

Kydd felt better after his brief foray into the inner world of his ship, even if it must have caused consternation in the various realms he'd trespassed on. The impression he'd gained was of an elderly but well-kept vessel, graceful even, her appointments near palatial compared to a frigate's. With the immense gun-power that was his to wield, it was a most respectable command. Any difficulties lying in wait for him would be human, not *Thunderer*'s.

Chapter 9

Later that afternoon the articles Persephone had found made their way aboard: a compact writing desk that fitted snugly against the forward bulkhead, a handsome long side-board ready to stow his elegant entertaining glassware and china, with a matching pair of leather-bound armchairs. A discreet parcel turned out to be his cot bedding while another held a carefully packed trio of Cornish jugs and a gimballed mirror for his wash-place. A hurriedly scrawled note assured him that more was on its way, including cabin stores, which she was taking time to choose, given that *Thunderer* would be away for so long.

His living spaces were taking on warmth and personality. His servant, the veteran corporal of marines, patiently moved the furnishings and fitments about until he was satisfied, then left Kydd to address the dismaying pile of papers that the purser had brought for him. He worked into the evening, trying to achieve a sense of order, but without someone like Dillon to bring about a regularity of concerns it was heavy going.

As the boatswain's calls squealed out the end of the day

fore and aft he was ready to retire, his cot beckoning with the promise of softness and slumber. But as he lay in the unfamiliar darkness, sleep wouldn't come. As with every ship, sounds in the night were individual, disturbing until their source had been identified. The peculiar rhythm of creaks deep within her that followed a swell down the length of the hull had to be learned and absorbed before it could take its place in the subliminal background of consciousness.

His thoughts rushed on. He'd noticed that the men at work, striking down provisions and necessaries, were surly, bleak-featured. They'd served for months on blockade and were almost within touching distance of England, home and beauty but, like prisoners in a gaol, were being kept and guarded from their rightful freedoms ashore. Their duty now was to take aboard stores that would only extend their exile. In a few days *Thunderer* would put to sea and all this would be a bitter memory.

He rolled over restlessly. How was he to win them over? The officers had been aboard for years and were accustomed to a way that was not his, employing the people in smartening the ship as a means of giving point to their existence.

His thoughts turned to the officers and in particular his first lieutenant. In all probability he'd be obliged to get rid of him. The moral courage he'd shown when speaking of what he saw as the injustice to Lyell would be better displayed in deciding a course of action in battle. But how much chance was there of that? On blockade Roscoe's attitude would leave them both in a corrosive state of confrontation.

Smale promoted to first would be a feather-weight premier, waiting out his patron's advancing him. The third, Briggs, had the makings but was wasted in a ship-of-the-line, and his fourth lieutenant, Mayne, gave every sign of being useless and bitter with his lot.

Melancholy entered Kydd's soul at the thought of what lay ahead. Instead of being here, he could be in Persephone's arms, enjoying a bucolic idyll with all the comforts a retired baronet could expect.

But he'd been through it all so many times and with the same result. If she wanted him to try, damn it, he would!

Chapter 10

'What's our state now?' Kydd asked Roscoe, the next morning, after the hands had turned to.

Without raising his eyes from the activity about the main hatch, the first lieutenant answered, 'Ah, a matter for the purser, I believe. And he's failed to report to me our condition so far this forenoon.'

Kydd held back a retort and sent for the purser. 'Our state of provisioning, Mr Gubb?'

'Oh, I can't tell you, can't tell you, I say,' he babbled. 'Altogether such a rush. No ship's clerk and the master is quarrelling with the bosun about the stowage, and I'm at my wit's end to know where the victuals are being struck down that my steward can take their reckoning.'

'Sort it out for him, Mr Roscoe,' Kydd snapped. 'I'll not tolerate delays. I'm stepping ashore to see the admiral concerning our departure and do not desire to disappoint him.'

Kydd didn't know the newly installed port admiral, Dewey, but he was not left long to discover his views.

'Your first command of a sail-of-the-line, I believe, Sir Thomas.'

'Aye, sir.'

'As desired by His Royal Highness, I've heard,' he went on, in a tight voice.

'No, sir, that is not at all why—'

'Don't take that tone with me, sir! We're all men of the world. We can see for ourselves how many ducks make five! If you've secured the attention of the court to advance yourself, then that is your business. Don't expect the admiration and respect of the service should you choose to indulge in such an unseamanlike manoeuvre.'

'Sir. I must protest at your—'

'You're reporting your ship in all respects ready for sea then, Captain?' Dewey leaned forward, his eyes boring into Kydd's.

'I'm unable to do that, sir.'

'Oh?'

'On assuming command I'm told by my premier that we're short above fifty men. I seek your help in making this good before I sail.'

'What do you expect me to do?' Dewey asked silkily.

Kydd swallowed his pride at having to beg. 'Your standing press, sir. Should you release to me a substantial number, I would be obliged.'

'I have none. There's your answer.'

'None?'

'No seamen worth the name. Possibly I could find some landmen but I've my doubts.' There was a triumphant finality in his manner.

'Then, sir, I ask permission to sleep out of my ship,' he said woodenly. Just one last night with Persephone before he left to meet his fate.

'Certainly not, sir. You've admitted to me your ship is far from ready for sea. How do you suppose this will aid your purpose? Hey? Hey?'

Controlling his rage, Kydd stamped out of the Mount Wise headquarters. Clutching the satchel of orders and communications destined for the commander-in-chief off Brest, he headed back to his boat. As he calmed, though, he felt his anger turn to a cold determination: he would be the one to come out of all this colours flying. Be damned to it if he didn't.

'Ah, Mr Opie,' he said breezily, as he stepped on to the quarterdeck. 'Just the man I hoped to see.'

The powerfully built boatswain loped forward, in his hand a hank of small stuff, line used for working a fine whipping over a splice, and a marline-spike clutched in a tattooed claw-like hand. 'Sir?'

'I thought I'd take a look at the barky's standing rigging.'

The big man gave a shy smile and touched his shapeless seaman's hat. 'All a-taunto, I think ye'll find, Sir Thomas.' He looked past him in an unsettling manner, which Kydd was about to remark on when he noticed that the boatswain's left eye had the milkiness of the unseeing he'd last glimpsed in Nelson.

Going to the mizzen shrouds Kydd nimbly leaped from the deck to reach above the seizings at the deadeyes. He peered into the strands and saw past the grey weathered exterior the heartening blackness of Stockholm tar deep within. As he came down he stopped at one of the upper deadeyes and bent to smell. This time it was the comforting stink of rancid butter. The boatswain was seeing the lanyards were free to ease through the carved holes of the deadeye to ensure an equal strain on all parts.

Dropping to the deck he met the questioning expression with a pleased grin and walked forward, testing the tautness of a stay here, a pendant there. At the fore-mast Kydd swung himself up and around on to the shrouds leading up to the massive fighting top. As he mounted he noticed Opie respectfully one rung behind, keeping him well within view.

Kydd tested the ratlines for their security and positioning. 'You've rattled them down?' he asked pointedly. To have the thinner lines crossing the thick shrouds at right angles to form a ladder to the tops, all neatly parallel with the waterline, gave confidence underfoot to men racing aloft and, besides, was a mark of a smart ship.

'I always does, first thing after the hook kisses mud, sir.'

Without the first lieutenant chasing him, Kydd mused. Opie and *Thunderer*'s captain would get along.

Chapter 11

Storing appeared to be satisfactorily under way and there was no point in standing over the men while they worked. Sighing, Kydd returned to his papers. On the way into his sanctum he noticed the locked cabin on his right, the departed ship's clerk's, and a thought took shape.

He had now a reasonably good grasp of *Thunderer*'s layout below decks and it was crowded. Her 'establishment' when taken into service in the balmy days of peace was for so many sea and marine officers, so many warrant officers and other important persons. Each was given a place to call his own. And then with war came an inexorable increase in these numbers. If he wanted to bring his confidential secretary aboard, there was no cabin for him. The only spare was that of the non-existent second Royal Marine lieutenant but this was situated deep in the noisome orlop and was the smallest. If he wanted Craddock in *Thunderer* he needed to find something like the ship's clerk's accommodation.

Sooner or later a replacement clerk would be found who would claim his cabin, which was where it was so that the captain could call on his services at any time. That was exactly what he needed from Craddock.

A seductive idea took shape. He could have his confidential secretary on the establishment and therefore on the ship's books, and thus perfectly entitled to a fine cabin if he was at the same time a ship's clerk. Craddock would be introduced as his secretary, never as a clerk, the real work to be done by a writer, which he was allowed by his position.

In one stroke he would have trumped Lyell's spiteful robbing him of a critical cog in the wheel of operations and at the same time have at his side a secretary and friend.

If Craddock accepted.

By rights he must mess down in the gunroom with the warrant officers and midshipmen, perceived as less than an officer. A ship's clerk was responsible to the purser. The post was considered preparation for an appointment by the Admiralty as a purser. And the incumbent would be held to the dire provisions of the Articles of War.

Craddock would probably weather better than most the long days and weeks of boredom on blockade but was he up to enduring the misery of long gales and Biscay bluster that were the Brest squadron's eternal lot? Had Kydd the right to subject him to that? There would be no going back on the commitment. If he agreed, the next time he could hope to touch land would be in exactly the same place in some months' time.

Kydd penned a swift note asking him to visit; when he came aboard he would lay it all before him and leave the decision his to make.

Craddock arrived by return. He was dressed thoughtfully in a well-cut black frock-coat, and such was his presence, the Spanish beard, the maturity, that it was the officer-of-the-watch who stood at the great cabin door to announce him.

Kydd rose, unable to suppress a broad smile. 'Welcome aboard, Mr Craddock! Never more welcome, I'm bound to say.'

'My pleasure and honour, Captain.' He looked about him, clearly impressed. 'And into such august surroundings as I've never encountered before. A magnificent vessel of such size and circumstance, if I be allowed to remark it.'

'*Thunderer*? A smart enough man-o'-war I'd be obliged to agree. But she comes with more than my fair share of grief and trouble.' He caught himself. 'But I'm neglecting my guest. Do sit.'

'Your guest? I was rather hoping to appear in quite another capacity,' Craddock said meaningfully.

'Ah, yes. Your post as confidential secretary.' Kydd found some papers to riffle. 'Er, dear fellow. This I can heartily assure you is yours, should you wish it. But first my conscience demands I lay before you some . . . unavoidable inconveniences that will be encountered.'

If he'd ever had any doubts concerning Craddock's character and qualities they were rapidly disposed of. The notional post of ship's clerk as a device for securing both a cabin and access to his friend brought ready agreement, and the happy observation that, being on the ship's books, he was entitled to an official share of prize money. And after Kydd explained the domestic hierarchy, he quite saw the necessity of falling in with the society of the gunroom.

'Shall we see then your quarters?' Kydd enquired, finding the key.

The little cabin was as he expected, stripped of personal effects. Piles of books and packs of files were heaped untidily on the long desk that occupied the after side of the cabin. The rest was bare, pitilessly illuminated by a single window, picking out a diminutive bare cot folded against the forward bulkhead. 'We'll soon have it shipshape for you, dear fellow, never fear.' Even if he had to do it himself.

In his mind Kydd was already seeing how Craddock would have his existence. This would be his private place, for work or leisure. He would dine with Kydd for breakfast and most days for dinner. During the day, when Kydd desired his attendance, he was within easy call. If Craddock needed him he was readily available, and if others wanted to see their captain they'd have first to consult him. It would work out, just as it had with Dillon.

As for his relations with *Thunderer*'s crew, the age-old custom of the sea was that any oddity of manner or appearance would never be made subject of remark or humour unless deserved. That Craddock was patently a gentleman, highly unusual in a warlike company, and equally clearly Kydd's close confidant and friend, would in the course of things be accepted in much the same way as the captain's coxswain was not challenged on what he'd witnessed from his privileged situation.

Fortunately the purser, distracted by overwork, simply took the captain's word for it that his new confidential secretary had kindly agreed to discharge the function of ship's clerk until a new one had been provided. All that was required was his brightest writer to act the assistant to Mr Craddock, both to turn to the next morning. One was found, the sick Allen's bookkeeper, profoundly relieved that order was to be restored.

'I'll leave you to it, Mr Craddock,' Kydd said, smothering his deep sigh of relief. 'Send for your baggage and we'll square away your quarters before evening gun tonight.'

Chapter 12

A dockyard hoy hailed with the news that their press-gang harvest was aboard. Kydd tried not to show eagerness and watched from his quarter-gallery, the round balcony projecting out from the corners of the sternwork. At sea it would conveniently allow him to peer up to the set of the sails.

He left it to Roscoe. Only a dozen or so and, judging from their appearance and clumsy attempts at the side-steps, all useless lubbers. He quietly despaired. It wasn't meant to be like this, the commanding of the most powerful class of ship in the navy, the glorious pinnacle of a sea career. If he—

'Come!' He could recognise Roscoe's knock now, firm and only two.

'Sir, to acquaint you we've eleven hands, now rated and sent below.'

'How many bounty men?' Theoretically these were volunteers.

'One.'

'Any seamen among 'em?' He tried to sound approachable, but the lieutenant remained inflexible and unsmiling.

'No.'

'So we're now north of six hundred complement.'

'Not so – we lost four waisters during the night sharing a pig's bladder to shore.'

'Oh, bad luck, Mr Roscoe,' he responded, determined not to be provoked. 'How's the storing?'

'Two days.'

Kydd was taken by surprise. 'Only two? Well done, Mr Roscoe. That includes watering?'

'Of course.'

He swallowed his anger. If this attitude continued it would infect all in the wardroom, and *Thunderer* would be near unmanageable at sea and against the enemy. 'Very well. Carry on, please.'

The marine corporal excused himself, hefting in more cabin stores, which he was temporarily stowing in the stateroom. As a manservant he was adequate, but his idea of caring and arranging was solid, square and military, and he was never about when Kydd wanted him. Kydd wished Tysoe, his previous man's man, all the best for his retirement but how he missed him at this moment.

But now with a date for sea it was possible to make plans for the cleansing and liberating feel of the open ocean where cares and worries took their rightful place.

Feeling brighter, he went to see how Craddock was getting along. The snug cabin was well on its way to rights, gear stowed tightly but handily and the desk with its proper complement of pen-rests and inkwells. Every nook and cranny was exploited, resulting in an effect of extreme order.

'A right handsome home, Mr Craddock,' Kydd said, leaning in carefully for there was room only for Craddock and his writer.

'And workplace, Captain.' Craddock held up a much-thumbed book. 'And my bedtime reading spoken for by this tome lent to me by my doughty assistant, William – that is to say, William Franks, writer.'

The lad touched his forehead nervously.

Kydd took the book – it had an interminable title ending with '. . . and complete instructions in the duty of a captain's clerk,' author one R. Liddel, late purser of *Monarch* 74 in His Majesty's Service. 'Fascinating,' he murmured, and looked up to catch Craddock's conspiratorial smile.

Chapter 13

As he lay awake in his cot Kydd gave thought to the morrow. He'd always made it a practice on the first night outward bound to bring everyone together in fellowship at a dinner, to welcome new faces, to discover anew the particular brotherhood of the wardroom, of the sea. Why shouldn't he make it a day earlier, to mark the quitting of the land?

Lyell hadn't had the means to support his own chef and had shared the officers' cook. Was the man up to an appropriate meal? He couldn't enjoy his last night ashore with Persephone but here was a way of spending it with her and at the same time introducing her to his new command. She'd be invited – and Craddock, to allow the afterguard to make his acquaintance.

As it turned out, the officers' cook, Tyler, was much in favour of a banquet. It would stretch his professional skills and allow him to make the most of the steadiness of the harbour calms. What did the good captain have in mind?

Heartened, Kydd told him to conjure up what he felt able to provide, given the numbers, and to furnish him with a list of ingredients he required. He would send ashore for them in good time for their preparation. The list arrived promptly and he had it landed with Persephone's invitation.

Another five men were taken in, worthless landmen. The hold completed stowage, hatches were replaced, and one by one the gunner, then the boatswain and others reported their needs satisfied and stores aboard.

He dared to believe *Thunderer* would put to sea very shortly.

The Blue Peter made its way to the masthead, the flag of blue containing an inner white square indicating to the anchorage that the ship was about to sail.

Shortly before midday Persephone's acceptance came, along with her last gift to him. One Josiah Luscombe, a young, fresh-faced man of about twenty was ushered in with a letter of introduction. It informed Kydd that Luscombe had lately been in the employ of the squire of Cornwood. On hearing of Kydd's need for a valet he'd let it be known that he would be honoured if Sir Thomas would consider him for the post. Although he had no experience of life at sea he'd been in service in a distinguished estate since childhood.

Kydd didn't worry about details. Persephone wouldn't have put him forward unless he had the makings for the post and she knew how much he needed a manservant.

Luscombe was a serious young man, trying to hide his anxiety but holding himself with dignity. Soft-spoken, he moved gracefully and had a quiet presence with natural intelligence showing through. Kydd felt they'd get along.

'You must know that the sea life is hard for everyone,' Kydd began, and stopped. Luscombe would find it out for himself before long. 'You have your dunnage with you?'

At his blank look he added, 'That is, your sea baggage?'

He nodded and Kydd briskly welcomed him aboard. 'You've the rest of the day to find your way around.' He summoned two of the first-class volunteers. 'Stay with Mr Luscombe, take him around the ship and show him the important things he needs to know.'

They left and he got on with his work.

Later that afternoon he summoned the marine servant, gravely thanked him for his assistance and, handing him a small reward, released him.

When Luscombe and the volunteers returned, he asked, 'Well, young man, how do you like *Thunderer*?'

'A very big ship, Sir Thomas.' The eyes were round.

'What did you see, then?'

'Oh, you have three masts and many guns. And not forgetting the front one lying down with the statue underneath.'

'Our figurehead.'

'Yes, Sir Thomas. And the steering wheel and chicken coops and—'

'Where does the purser issue his provisions, pray?'

'P-purser?'

'And where is my dinner cooked?'

'Um . . .'

Kydd rounded on the volunteers. 'This is not what I asked, you scoundrels. Luscombe is to be shown what he needs to know, not what is grand or interesting. I suggest he visits where people mess, sleep and eat, and where gear is stowed. No tricks or pranks, take him away again and return him before four bells. Remember, at sea he's to be in charge of you and will give me due report on you both. Compree?'

After that he'd get his cabin stores properly packed away and his personal tackle in some sort of order.

Craddock joined him for the noonday meal and Kydd heard how much the naval system closely resembled shore-side clerking practices of earlier in the last century and how he felt quite at home with the arcane methods.

'The first sentence in Mr Liddel's volume, "The Duty of the Ship's Clerk is in the first Place, to keep all the Books necessary for passing the Captain's Accounts", is repeated above twenty times throughout. Your books will be passed, that I can solemnly assure you, Thomas.'

'I'm glad to hear it. Do you desire then to share in Queen Anne's gift?'

'Er . . .?'

'That's a sum of money awarded over and above the monthly twopence when my accounts are passed.'

'Oh – and if they're not?'

'Dire consequences that I will not dwell upon.'

With this Craddock rose to leave with a smile but Kydd waved him down. 'I need you, Harry. Tonight I'm to host a grand dinner for all the officers and a species of table plan will be required that satisfies honour and position. Will you . . .?'

The table had already been made ready, its cunning leaves manipulated to produce a twelve-place setting. But the seating arrangements took longer than expected as Kydd unburdened himself about each person as their cards were shuffled around the table – and then the purser's steward came demanding crockery, silver and his dining ornaments.

With a rush of warmth he saw Persephone's choice of green and gold service would make its first outing and it would be with her present. In the future he would always associate it with her, no matter the occasion. The pieces of silver he'd acquired over the years would do their duty now in a different ship, in loftier surroundings, but with their memories for him of a simpler, more carefree existence.

Luscombe appeared, still dazed by his experiences, and was put to work on the decorations, while Kydd made himself available to the stream of those reporting ready for sea, Roscoe included.

'The tide will be right for tomorrow forenoon,' Kydd said neutrally. 'We'll weigh at eleven I believe, take advantage of this nor'-westerly while we can. Gives you time to lay along the gear without you need disturb the hands about their breakfast.'

'We're still short forty men.'

'And we're getting no more from the press or any other. This is your affair, Mr Roscoe. I need the ship manned in all respects even if we leave every other gun less one hand.'

It was hard on the fellow but to cover shortcomings in the manning, however grave, was one of the crosses the first lieutenant of any ship must bear. The eyes narrowed. Then he turned on his heel and left.

Kydd was not going to be dismayed. This evening he'd do his best to pull his officers together, talk to them, encourage them to enjoy themselves over a superb repast and possibly some jollity to conclude. If he couldn't, a future of endless sea-time in their company would be wretched.

Persephone came aboard an hour early, observed by a curious watch-on-deck who noticed her seaman-like mounting of the ship's side.

In the stateroom Kydd's full-dress uniform with its gold lace, star and sash, was being tugged into shape by Luscombe, who discreetly left when she entered.

She beamed. 'My darling! You do look so handsome. I'm sure there are quantities of ladies whose heads would be quite turned by your appearance.'

'A fine fellow, Luscombe,' Kydd told her. The young man was taking it very seriously and this evening he would wait at table in the naval manner, standing behind his captain to attend to his wants as the meal progressed.

She looked about, pleased with the changes that had been wrought in such a short time. Little touches that Kydd would not have thought of, pictures and hangings, the near Persian luxury of the cot and the now resplendent wash-place, fully equipped with masculine articles of toilet.

Chapter 14

Craddock apologetically invited himself into Kydd's private quarters, the great cabin imminently to fill with guests. 'The first of many, I trust,' he murmured to Kydd. His dress was perfectly the gentleman's.

Luscombe entered nervously to announce that guests had begun arriving and Kydd went into the splendidly appointed great cabin to welcome them, accompanied by Persephone with the table plan.

'To the forrard end opposite me, Mr Mayne,' Kydd instructed his fourth lieutenant. 'You're Mr Vice tonight, in course.'

One by one the officers made their way in, efficiently placed by Lady Kydd. With all seated, Kydd took the other end before the stern-gallery. On his right hand was Persephone, next to her Roscoe. On his other side, he had placed Hare, the officious captain of marines, in his dramatic scarlet and gold full-dress. On Kydd's left sat Craddock, then the second and third lieutenants. The further end of the table was occupied on the right by the master and purser, and on the left by the lieutenant of marines and the surgeon.

The servants leaned forward to fill their glasses, a disconcertingly expensive Vouvray sec, dry, acidic, but sparkling with zest. 'Gentlemen, I'd be obliged for your opinion of this wine. It may be Gallic but should be fine enough for all that.'

It was a quiet, even sombre table that raised glasses and sipped cautiously. Was this a test by their captain, known among the highest society in the land?

No one spoke.

'Come, come, gentlemen! It's not, as who should say, an indifferent potion. Mr Vice?'

Being so addressed before every one of his seniors, Mayne jerked alert. 'Oh, well, in my taste it seems a mite tart for a champagne,' he attempted.

No one seemed inclined to contradict him as Kydd looked about the table hopefully. 'Is there nobody a judge of wine in *Thunderer*, then?' He turned to Roscoe, who had put his glass down, barely tasted. 'Sir?'

'I agree, but perhaps this is not a champagne.'

Every face turned to Kydd but before he could respond, Smale, the second lieutenant, held up his glass before the light. 'And if I'm not adrift in my bearings we're muzzling a rather fine Vouvray – and the Arbois grape, not your common chenin blanc?'

'Well said, Mr Smale,' Kydd told him. Next to him Craddock murmured something, and Smale smiled, a smug expression just under control. 'So we enjoy it as we may. Drink up, gentlemen, I believe our first course is on the way.'

Still the heavy silence, broken only occasionally by a soft exchange here and there.

'Rather a noble tipple, I vow,' Persephone said, rather more loudly than was indicated, and made much of sampling further. Kydd knew that she had chosen the bottles from the

Knowle Manor cellar, as were others to make their appearance later.

'Do you not feel so . . . Mr Roscoe, is it not?' she said sweetly, to the stiff-faced lieutenant on her right, laying her hand lightly on his arm.

'A fine wine, yes, m' lady.'

Kydd hid a smile. The polite address had been extracted from him by her patrician bearing and striking looks. 'Er, gentlemen, if I might have your attention? In derogation of my duty I have failed to introduce all of you to my guests.' He gave a mock apologetic grin. 'Here on my right hand is my charming wife, the Lady Kydd, who has importuned me shamefully to be here tonight, desiring so much to meet you all.'

She nodded shyly left and right.

'While here on my other hand is a gentleman you will come to know more in the future. He is my confidential secretary, Mr Lucius Craddock. He kindly stepped forward at the last moment to agree to discharge the function of ship's clerk until we are provided with another. I might point out that he has lately served with me in my previous ship, *Tyger*, so you may understand he is no stranger to war in all its forms.'

He paused, watching their faces. In the main it was a studied blankness but he knew the message had been passed. This was the captain's friend, an evident gentleman but, with the exception of the purser, he had no function aboard that intersected with theirs.

The first course of dishes was carried in. A veal fricandeau, chine of mutton, forced lamb's ears, more. The red wine, a silky smooth Margaux, had Luscombe hesitating as to whose glass he should fill first: the grand lady's or his fearsome captain's.

There were murmurs of appreciation but none of the whole-hearted acclaim that viands of this quality would have received in *Tyger*.

'Wine with you, Mr Roscoe,' Kydd urged, drawing the officer's glass to him. 'You're enjoying your meal?'

'Thank you, yes.' The eyes remained cold and distant, the sips at his glass careful, controlled.

Anger surged in Kydd once more. Was this the man who would stand by him on his quarterdeck in battle, whom he could trust to send on a cutting-out expedition?

'Tell me, Mr Roscoe,' Persephone cut in, 'what's your opinion of the state of the war as it stands?'

Kydd left them to it, hearing from Craddock how the nobs in Manchester set about entertaining themselves at a civic occasion, and then it was the second course: oyster patties, woodcock, pork griskins and others equally admirable in their presentation, yet still the gathering had not begun to warm. More wines appeared, but the low hum of guarded conversation was resolutely unchanging.

One thing he'd planned on doing when the affair had got more lively was to take advantage of their presence together and make some kind of commencement of commission address. This moment was probably as good as any.

'Gentlemen! Your attention, please.'

The talking stopped as if cut off with a knife. Faces turned to him, wary, cautious, blank.

'I shall be brief, the third course is still to come and there's brandy and cigars to follow.' He smiled winningly. 'But all I wished to say is how honoured I am to be given command of *Thunderer*, holder of above the ordinary number of honours of battle in her distinguished career.' He went on in similar vein and saw one or two expressions ease.

'I've spent nearly my whole time at sea in frigates, and by

that I mean in the service of the fleet as well as independent cruises. What I learned there I can say in one: that we could do our small part. But it is upon the battleships, the princes of the sea, that England depends as her true wooden walls. And I know to my cost what it is to face the outcome when, perhaps in unfortunate circumstances, the enemy gets past them to the open ocean. Where *Thunderer* is concerned this will never happen.'

There were frowns now, one or two raised eyebrows.

'*Thunderer* will do more than succeed at her purpose – she will excel!' He allowed his voice to harden. 'Different ships, different long-splices. Some captains are known for riding hard on sail-handling, others a smart appearance, more still for signals and manoeuvres. In fair warning you should know that for me it can only be . . . gunnery! A ship exists to prevail over another. She does this by virtue of her superior powers of destruction. I don't need to remind you that a reloading time half that of the enemy is precisely the same as possessing double the number of guns. HMS *Thunderer* of 148 guns! I like the sound of that, gentlemen.'

Expressions were set. So this was the flavour of what lay ahead. Gun drill at all hours.

'You'll know what to expect, then, so I bid you enjoy the rest of this fine repast while you may.' He sat down to a polite scatter of applause, which quickly relapsed into the same joyless reticence.

Kydd was aware of its cause. With perceived injustice done to Lyell, and as a wardroom serving together for years, they had closed ranks against him with Roscoe as their leader. No one was inclined to be the first to break.

And the expensive dinner he'd conjured had not had the effect he wanted: a thaw in relations. It was probably being seen as yet another courtly feast by one whose daily fare must always be something like this. It could even be possible that they believed he would lord it over them, that being his accustomed style of life.

The final course came and with it some choice dessert wines. Kydd sensed Persephone had caught the mood and was despairing. There was Roscoe with his monosyllabic replies and the captain of marines with ponderous anecdotes of times past. Craddock was being monopolised by Smale. Kydd, caught in the middle, was finding himself gazing about inanely without a conversational partner.

At an awkward break in the general conversation, Persephone challenged the first lieutenant. 'Sir, surely a big ship like *Thunderer* has a fiddler at its capstan.'

Taken aback, Roscoe hesitated. Briggs leaned across and mouthed, 'Watkins, fo'c'sle division.'

'Oh, yes. We do have one, m' lady.'

'Then would it be too much to ask the gentleman to oblige me by lending me his violin?'

After a dumbfounded marine returned with it, Persephone stood and took position behind Kydd. 'Not so many know that your captain – my husband – has a very fine singing voice.' Kydd looked up in embarrassment as she went on, 'And tonight you shall hear him!'

She plucked the strings and made one or two adjustments in the tuning, then addressed them: 'This is a piece with which I accompanied him when first we met at a country estate. Do forgive my playing as it's been a long time since I picked up an instrument. I shall feel well rewarded if you do join in, gentlemen.'

Tucking the violin under her chin, she played a few experimental notes and Kydd rose, his embarrassment falling away to be replaced by a special feeling of warmth towards her.

At his nod she launched into the piece, strongly and gaily.

His voice, now well accustomed to command, had deepened over the years from a pleasant baritone into something closer to a bass. To the astonishment of all they heard him launch into the salty, driving strains of the sailors' favourite, 'Spanish Ladies', letting its well-known cadences fill the cabin.

He gestured to the table, urging them to join in the full-throated refrain:

> *We'll rant and we'll roar like true British sailors,*
> *We'll rant and we'll rave across the salt seas;*
> *Till we strike soundings in the Channel of Old England,*
> *From Ushant to Scilly 'tis thirty-four leagues . . .*

One or two began mouthing the words but from most it was a discomfiting mumble, trying to avoid each other's eye. Kydd persevered, thundering out the verses, Persephone now adding lively embellishments that would do credit to any seasoned sea fiddler.

> *We hove our ship to, with the wind at sou' west, boys*
> *We hove our ship to, for to take soundings clear,*
> *In fifty-five fathoms with a fine sandy bottom,*
> *We filled our main tops'l, up Channel did we steer . . .*

The song progressed past the familiar sea-marks – the Deadman, Rame's Head, Start Point, Portland, right on to the Downs. Then it was the triumphant final stanza:

> *Now let every man take up his full bumper,*
> *Let every man take up his full bowl;*
> *For we will be jolly, and drown melancholy*
> *With a health to each jovial and true-hearted soul!*

At its conclusion there was a timid scatter of applause. Still standing, Kydd looked about. 'Do we have another who will entertain us? Anyone? Mr Roscoe, there must be a song in you!'

The man shook his head and calmly took another taste of his wine.

'You disappoint me, sir. How about you, Mr Smale?'

'Sir, after our storing ship I've a raw throat, I fear.'

'So *Thunderer* must be accounted a ship of Philistines.' Kydd snorted theatrically.

In his full-dress with its daunting amounts of gold lace and star of knighthood he knew he cut an imposing figure. Was it that they felt he had no right to act out of part, to confuse the issue? That his it was to sit back in regal splendour and himself be entertained – and, if this was his taste, by a jolly jack tar sent for to perform? And to have his impeccably well-brought-up and presumably aristocratic wife sawing away on the fiddle was surely demeaning.

It was going to be a hard beat to windward to reach an understanding with this crew, let alone gain their trust and loyalty.

And they put to sea tomorrow.

'If you'll excuse me, gentlemen.' The surgeon got to his feet and gave a jerky half-bow in Kydd's direction. 'I've a patient I must attend to.' He left awkwardly.

'Yes, Mr Gubb?'

The purser stood nervously and stuttered, 'The ship sails tomorrow. I have my reservations about the gunner's stores and . . . and . . .'

Did they think that this was just the beginning of some bacchanal, an evening of riot and song into the early hours like some frolic of high society?

Kydd's face set. The evening was effectively over – ruined

by a company whose idea of welcoming a new captain was to set their faces against him.

'Oh, my dear,' Persephone said loudly, 'I do really feel it time for me to retire. Is my boat ready?'

'Of course, my love.' He nodded to Briggs, who left to make it so, then turned to the silent gathering and said lightly, 'And if any so desire, there is an excellent cognac and cigars to be had.'

He shepherded her out and on to the deck, now shrouded in warm summer dusk. She looked up at him, her features wreathed in love and concern. 'My sweet darling, my love,' she began, her voice husky and troubled.

'Dearest,' he answered softly, caressing her hair – but he was forbidden to sleep out of his ship and found himself lost for words.

Seizing both his hands she gazed at him deeply. 'Thomas. I'm frightened. This ship . . . *Thunderer*. It – it's too big, too cold, a hostile stranger, you might say. And it doesn't like you or want you. I'm fearful. I worry it'll not rest until it's seen the end of you, my love.' Tears glistened and where she held him hurt with its intensity. 'You will take special care of yourself, darling? You're everything there is in this world that's sweet and true and . . . and . . .'

The tears began to flow, quite unlike any time previously when they'd parted before a foreign commission, however dire its prospects. Then, she'd always bravely seen him go without an unseemly display. Her farewell now affected him more than he cared to admit.

Briggs appeared quietly and waited.

Kydd crushed her to him, careless of the watch-on-deck. 'Goodbye, my love – and take heart. Remember, I'm the captain.'

She pulled herself together and, with a single wave, followed Briggs.

Chapter 15

'Yes, Mr Roscoe, I do wish it.'

'For me to take the ship out?'

'That's what I said. Have you an objection?'

They stood together on the quarterdeck. Around them the bustle of preparations for putting to sea were well advanced: ropes and falls faked out and laid clear for running, boats stowed, the lower boom and its Jacob's ladder brought in.

'No objection.'

For Kydd it addressed two matters in one. He would get to see what stuff Roscoe was made of and also be relieved of the perils of taking charge of a strange ship in not particularly advantageous weather. The wind was light and fluky, the very worst for winning clear of the land. A robust, reliable breeze was much more to be desired and he had no wish to make a fool of himself before the entire ship's company.

'How else in the short term might I see demonstrated what my premier can do? To trust or not to trust in the future, that is my question.' He gazed directly at Roscoe and was gratified when he dropped his eyes, then moved off to stand alone some yards away.

'You have the ship, sir,' Kydd called over meaningfully.

It left him able to take his measure of proceedings on deck, which his experiences in a frigate left him well able to do. A ship-of-the-line and frigate, three-masted ship rig both, shared most of the operating procedures and gear, with differences only in scale and the speed with which things happened.

Most of the effort now would be out of sight on the lower deck. There, at the capstan, something like two hundred men and boys would be readying, flexing their bodies and standing by for the brutal task of bringing in the anchor. Cable nearly two feet around, weighing as much as a full-grown man every fathom or two and with a three-ton anchor hanging from its end made for a muscle-searing ordeal.

Roscoe had to know precisely the right moment to have sail set abroad. If too early, before the anchor was tripped from the ground, it would put intolerable strain on the cable and the men at the capstan. If left too late, the ship would be carried helpless on to the rock-strewn Rame.

Then, too, the arrangement and timing of making sail would be critical. To employ the staysails, all fore-and-aft rigged, to pay off to leeward before setting the square sails was easier, but needed more time and sea-room. On the other hand the more sure casting under square sail always began with a significant degree of sternway before a ship could take up on the appropriate tack and stretch out.

He would see.

The fo'c'sle party were closed up, tackles laid out, and at each mast topmen stood ready at the base, the sailing master waiting patiently near the group at the conn.

Time passed. In a frigate it was possible to sense slight shudders transmitted through the hull as the anchor came in, reassurance that the ground tackle was not caught up in any way. In *Thunderer* there was not the slightest sign and Roscoe stood rigid, his gaze clamped on the cluster of fo'c'slemen. A hand-flag continually showed the direction of the anchor cable while it gradually shortened as the slack came in. Several times he tore his gaze away to sniff at the wind, a light south-westerly. Then, lifting his speaking trumpet, he blared down the deck, 'Topmen aloft, prepare to cast to starb'd under tops'ls and courses.'

Kydd nodded. The ship was catching the breeze in her upperworks, considerably higher than in a frigate, and ignoring the other influence, the swirling current. Her bows pointed directly at the rocky heights of the headland and he could see that the inevitable sternway of a cast under square sail would prove the more useful.

The flag was nearly up and down, *Thunderer* was directly above her anchor. A particularly back-breaking effort at the capstan – the heavy heave – was now being called on below to release the giant hook from the seabed.

Roscoe leaned forward, tense. Then faintly, down the deck, came the triumphant cry, 'Thick and dry for weighing!' The anchor had been tripped and now hung freely down.

This point in unmooring, termed 'anchors a-weigh', was a decisive moment for it meant that *Thunderer* was now legally at sea. But it also signified that the ship was free to be driven by wind or tide, and sail had to be set without delay.

Orders volleyed out – fore topsail to be loosed and backed, main and mizzen topsails sheeted in to the opposite side and hands to clap on braces for some rapid work.

So far, so good.

The big ship imperceptibly gathered sternway, and as this strengthened, with doubled helmsmen struggling to hold her, she began a sheer to pass through the eye of the wind and at the same time put her head to seaward.

In a way Kydd would not have been sorry to see some kind of blunder, a human mistake on Roscoe's part, but when the fore had been braced around and courses were set, he could see he'd called it at precisely the right time. Their sternway lessened and, after a heart-stopping pause, a chuckle of water under her forefoot indicated that she was safely under sail and outward bound.

Forward, the dripping black of the anchor broke surface and the fo'c'slemen bent to cat and fish it before too much way was on the ship, while everywhere a hive of activity was securing the ship for sea.

Thunderer was on her way to war.

'A satisfactory evolution, Mr Roscoe,' Kydd told him.

The man merely glanced sideways once.

'As will allow you to set sea watches.'

His gaze locked with Kydd's for a heartbeat before he turned and went forward.

Taking a last sight of the safely approaching Penlee Point, beyond which was the massive Rame Head, Kydd could see nothing to stop him leaving the deck to the officer-of-the-watch, Briggs, and he retired to his cabin.

Luscombe helped him off with his coat and Kydd fumbled for his worn and comfortable sea-going one. He was about to return to the quarterdeck when his eye fell on the screen door. Impulsively he crossed to it and found himself on the holy ground of the stern gallery, the entire width of the ship, beautiful carvings on all sides and a fretworked rail at its after edge. He stood for a moment, held by the spectacle granted to him alone in the ship. It was of a gentle wake roiling astern and the peculiar sensation of the sea and land slipping back on either side, a perspective he'd never experienced before. It provoked a surge of emotion, the age-old elation of putting out into the vast wastes of ocean and the adventures lying in wait – but at the same time, all he held dear in this world was out of sight now and he was leaving it indefinitely for who knew what fate.

He took it in for a little while longer, then retreated into the great cabin.

'Hello, Harry.'

Craddock rose from his chair in embarrassment. 'Oh, the sentry said you were here but when I entered . . .'

'I was enjoying the view from my stern walk. Do join me.'

They stood together, wordless, as Penlee slid past and merged into anonymity with the Devon countryside, then into a blue-grey haze of land fading into the distance. Kydd's senses told him that Briggs was making directly south, close-hauled on the starboard tack with a slight Atlantic swell coming in abeam, and for the first time the distinctive symphony of creaks and groans that were *Thunderer*'s unique response to the sea were evident.

'Well, old fellow, how are you settling in?'

Craddock considered for a space, then answered, 'As no one knows me or where I've sprung from, shall we say tolerably well?'

'You're not sure.'

'The midshipmen generally leave me alone but the warrant officers I feel are wanting in common courtesy to a newcomer.'

'Oh?' Kydd growled.

'Nothing of an aggressive nature but rather more of a sniff and ignore. A trifle wounding in the circumstances.'

It would be hard going for an intelligent creature, little or no conversation except with the child-like midshipmen, and having one's social and bodily being in with the old, bold sea masters and their often narrow views.

'Let me think on it,' Kydd murmured.

Luscombe hovered, unsure what to do next.

'See the cook, if you please, and let him know I'd like to have my dinner at one bell after midday, as the men take theirs.' The officers generally came together for a meal at about two, but Kydd liked to have his at an hour when there'd be useful time left in the afternoon for work. 'You'll join me, Harry?'

'I will, with pleasure.'

They were interrupted by the firm double knock that announced the first lieutenant.

'Sea watches set, Mr Briggs and larbowlines closed up for the forenoon.' With a single side-glance at Craddock he went on with his recitation of the state of the ship.

'Thank you, Mr Roscoe.'

He turned to go but Kydd called him back. 'Mr Roscoe. Another matter, less connected with the ship, more concerning her citizens.'

At least it brought raised eyebrows.

'You being president of the wardroom mess. You'll know that Mr Craddock here as my confidential secretary is out of the goodness of his heart as well temporarily discharging the function of ship's clerk.'

'I'm aware of it.'

'And that he is a distinguished gentleman, not to be thought one comfortable with the company to be obtained in a gunroom mess. Might the wardroom consider him suitable for honorary membership, upon payment of a full subscription in course?'

'I rather doubt it,' Roscoe retorted.

'Oh? One would imagine Mr Craddock to be a valued member. Pray why not?'

'There are no precedents that I've heard that allow a ship's clerk and fore-mast hand be granted fellowship of the wardroom of a ship-of-the-line. Further, it would undoubtedly be viewed as a blatant attempt to secure for a favourite a greater prize-money share than he'd otherwise be entitled to.'

'Favourite? I resent the implication, sir!' Kydd said hotly. 'Friend, yes. Favoured above all others, no!'

'Nonetheless, I believe it not unknown in the sea service for gentlemen – no doubt for reasons of their own – to take anonymous refuge in a ship-of-war. It will be pointed out that as they must needs berth with the men, why not your, er, gentleman?'

'Mr Craddock? Sir, if you knew the one fourth of what he's gone through when—'

'Captain Kydd,' Craddock interrupted calmly. 'Sir, do not vex yourself on my account. I will mess in the gunroom – the nature's gentlemen there are pure in spirit if not in speech and I shall find my place.'

There was little Kydd could do and Roscoe knew it. He was president of the wardroom mess and held powers of moral and social discipline in addition to oversight of the catering and wine books. If he objected to Kydd's humane suggestion then Kydd was powerless, for the wardroom was their own to regulate and run without interference.

That in the past he'd been able to secure the privilege for his particular friend Renzi was only because a frigate's society was much smaller and tighter, which had allowed Renzi, somewhat illegally, to claim it as a captain's secretary. In a battleship's wardroom it was all big ships and regulations, and he couldn't ask it.

'Is that all, Captain?'

Kydd bit back a retort, then said, 'Mr Craddock will mess in the gunroom. Carry on, Mr Roscoe.'

Chapter 16

A ship-of-the-line is a quite different beast from a frigate, Craddock mused, as he went below for his meal the following day, past strangers without count, rows of vast guns, expanses of deck that in other circumstances could do service as a ballroom. Above all there was a feeling of massive bulk, of indomitable strength, so different from the light and almost nervous movements of a frigate, with its emphasis on finer lines and speed. It would take a little getting used to.

He couldn't blame Kydd for not winning him a place in the wardroom against the immovable mass of crusted tradition, so valued in the Royal Navy. Still, he would see Kydd regularly to their mutual intellectual benefit, and in the meantime would keep up an appearance in the gunroom, with its concentration of sea elders.

It was midday and he joined those bellying up to the gunroom table for their meal, easing himself in beside one of the master's mates. The dining appointments were robust but plain, well scrubbed and neat: two gunroom servants to bring the mess-kids of stew and bread – in its barge still soft tommy so soon after leaving port.

A chipped crockery bowl and pewter spoon were provided and he tried to make light conversation with the master's mate while awaiting his turn. The gunner, the unsmiling Lawlor, sat in state at the end of the table, glowering until his serve of stew, with the best lumps of mutton, was dished out. On one side of him was the oaken bulk of Opie, the boatswain, on the other the wiry form of Upcot, the carpenter, who were in some kind of amiable disagreement. Further down sat three master's mates with a youngster at the opposite end allowed the privilege of eating with them in return for running errands.

Presumably the half-dozen midshipmen berthed in the orlop below would take their victuals when their betters had eaten.

'Free the slide then, y' idlers,' the carpenter threw down the table in ill-tempered impatience. The butter dish was obediently pushed up to Craddock and conversations resumed. The master's mate next to him seemed to have no larger vocabulary than grunted monosyllables and the one opposite refused to catch his eye. As he was seated at the furthest remove, there was only the ship's boy to talk to and his anxious attention was reserved for the seniors at the other end.

At last the mess-kid arrived at him and from its hollow depths a few wooden ladles' worth of stew and bones were scraped and slopped into his bowl, the penalty for being last. Craddock burned. It wasn't so much that his food portion was so miserly but that this was the third time it had happened. It would never have occurred if he was recognised as a full member of the mess and able to claim his fair whack. He was still waiting for his blackjack, the leather tankard used for beer. Everyone else had theirs in front of them.

He pushed away the bowl and stood up. 'Mr Lawlor, I feel

I must point out that I believe I'm hardly done by in the article of food and claim your intercession.' The rest of the table stopped eating in frank astonishment.

The gunner barely glanced up from the spooning of his gravy. 'It's talkin' again.' He glanced at the boatswain. 'Bull, tell him to siddown and get on with it. This'n is all he's goin' to get.'

Opie swivelled around to see Craddock with his one good eye and took in the miserable serving. 'An' he's got a case, Nobby,' he rumbled. 'The thin end o' the scran every time.'

'So? He's a clerk, ain't he? Does no work as a man would call it.' He put down his spoon. 'Hey, you, Pedro.'

Pedro? The Spanish beard, of course. 'Mr Lawlor?'

'Claim dismissed, mate.'

The table resumed its noise and chatter and Craddock hesitated then sat down. The master's mate opposite gave a sly smile and found something technical to engage his neighbour. He thought he detected a shadow of sympathy in Opie but it was a closed community and he was the despised outsider.

Chapter 17

That evening Kydd was alone. It would not help Craddock just now for the captain in front of the others to invite him to dine, but he missed his company. In *Tyger* the first night at sea would be marked by noise and jollity but that was not to be in *Thunderer*. In palatial splendour he would take his victuals on his own, lord of all he surveyed but master of precious little. He could give orders as he liked but to direct men's minds and allegiance was not within his power, only his persuasion.

He tried to read an improving book on the possible developments the war could take but flung it aside in despair. He crossed to the stern walk and stood gazing out into the gathering dusk where the land was disappearing as the officer-of-the-watch made his offing and with it his last tenuous hold on the life he'd come to cherish.

Irritated with himself, he went back to the great cabin. Luscombe had lit the lamps in their sconces and he sat in his chair, awaiting supper. The pipe 'down hammocks' would turn the mess-deck into a dense sea of swaying canvas when the men had finished their grog and supper.

He would end with a nightcap and then he would be ready to turn in.

The pipe duly pealed, and Kydd heard the usual thunder of hundreds of feet as seamen took down their hammocks from the nettings on deck and flung themselves below. But after some minutes his supper had still not arrived. He waited, becoming more annoyed: he knew the officers would be well into their own with the cheer and joviality of old friends finishing their day.

Eventually Luscombe appeared, flustered and pale-faced, bearing a tray.

'Where have you been, pray?' Kydd asked, frowning.

'Oh, s-sir, the cook said as how you have yours after he's done for the officers. And as we're now at sea the galley fire is out . . .' He trailed off.

The captain to be served after the officers? Clearly they were taking advantage of the young innocent, and in any event the galley fire was always doused for the silent hours so a cold collation was all that was to be expected. If he made a fuss it would go hard on the lad and he would spare him that. 'Ah. Then what do we have tonight?'

The covers came off. Cheese and bread. Ship's issue cheese sliced into near transparent thinness, four slices of cask beef similarly treated, all garnished with an unidentifiable sprig of greenery. And a delicate silver goblet containing some kind of thin gruel.

He began to eat. It was no fault of his servant that the victuals were so poor. In the morning he would discipline the pranksters. Kydd was tempted to send for wine to take away the taste of the musty cheese but he did not feel like drinking. 'Well, young man, how are you taking to a life at sea?' he asked genially, finishing the humble repast.

Luscombe blinked and avoided his eye. 'Not as I'd fancied it afore,' he mumbled.

'Oh? Then what can this be?'

'Er . . .'

'Speak up, lad!'

'They . . . they jest and laugh at me for a Johnny Newcome and won't tell me how to do things. And make me do their washing as well as yours, and—'

'Laundry is not in your duty and they know it, the low shicers.' He stopped himself – he couldn't interfere here either. He was as powerless as ever. They were showing contempt for their captain by taking it out on the young man, and unless Kydd could deal with the larger issue it would go on.

'Well, never mind, Luscombe. This is the tradition of the sea, as I suffered it once. Turn in now and get your head down. It'll pass.'

The hunted expression eased at the extraordinary confession of his captain, and Kydd sent him away before his messmates could do much with his hammock.

That these petty fooleries must concern the captain of a mighty ship-of-the-line with far greater worries was aggravating. His primary duty was to the ship, to bring her to full fighting trim in the shortest possible time. Within three or four days he would be making his number with the commander-in-chief, then taking his place in the line-of-battle, no more to decide *Thunderer*'s day. With a rush of feeling he realised he had only this handful of time to bring her to a level of effectiveness that could see her a trustworthy part of the fleet.

He would start tomorrow. Sail, guns, evolutions.

It wouldn't be easy. He knew nothing about the ship he

was commanding, what was possible, what was asking too much – of *Thunderer* and his men. He had to know all the little foibles and eccentricities that his ship possessed so that he would not be caught out in the heat of battle. He had to make discovery of these in the few days left to him. Once he knew the weaknesses he could concentrate on them.

Feeling better, he turned in and dropped into a dreamless slumber.

Chapter 18

In the pre-dawn half-light Kydd was jerked awake by a grating discord. A mournful ringing, the knell of hopes and dreams, a sepulchral reminder of mortality – for whom?

Struggling awake he shook his head to clear it and realised it was the bell forward tolling: the mariner's worst fear – fog. A glance from a window confirmed a milky blankness in every direction.

The ship was barely under way. His ornate hanging cabin compass was showing their course as west by south, set to round Ushant later but from now on there would be no certainty in their progress. It wasn't likely that they could end on rocks as they were well mid-channel by now but, in the busiest shipping lane in the world, they could find themselves in a collision course to a homeward-bound merchantman.

On deck Smale was hunched in his foul-weather gear, dewdrops of condensation forming runnels down it. He looked up in relief as Kydd approached. 'Came on just now after the wind veered. And out of soundings, hereabouts,' he added. The usual remedy, to anchor until the fog burned away in the morning sun, was thus not open to them. They must press ahead at some three knots or more merely to keep steerage way on, with the risks this would bring.

The morning-watchmen appeared, padding to their stations in the cold and damp, a savage contrast after their warm hammocks.

'Minute guns, if you please,' Kydd ordered. It would make it hard on the off-going middle-watchmen trying to snatch their rest, but the safety of the ship came first. After an interval the first fo'c'sle swivel barked into the blanketing softness.

The fog wouldn't last. Already, the high royals and topgallants were taking a breeze that, with the sun in an hour or two, would result in a clearing to brilliant sunshine.

Then, almost as a ghostly spectre high in the whiteness, Kydd saw the suggestion of a fore topgallant sail. And, from its perspective, it was ignorant of their presence and cutting across their bows.

'Hard up the helm!' Kydd roared. 'Hard up!'

Painfully slowly, *Thunderer* paid off to leeward, her bowsprit tracking away from the menace, but the unknown ship was under all plain sail and moving fast. Thinking quickly Kydd leaped over to the mizzen course sheets and began throwing off the turns to slacken the sail until relieved by startled seamen. Hopefully the crew on the fo'c'sle would think to flat out jibs and staysails to form a rotating lever to help her around faster. It seemed to work – they were going to make it!

But in the other ship the lookouts woke up and screamed their alarm aft. In a panic of fear the wheel was put hard over to the wrong side. The end was inevitable, a long drawn-out colliding bow to bow, thankfully at a fine angle but the noise and bedlam were overwhelming. A rending, cracking and splintering gave way to a visceral thumping and deep twanging as rigging caught.

Thunderer was close-hauled and had been struck on her weather side with sails and gear sagging to leeward. Mercifully, little damage was done but the nameless merchant jack was going large downwind: she had suffered more, her canvas ripped, ropes stranded and trailing.

Thunderer tore free from the assault and fell off to leeward. Kydd rapped out the orders to douse sail, then rounded on Smale. 'A boat in the water, with Mr Briggs and half a dozen marines. Now!' he barked at the flustered lieutenant.

'Sir, they won't need rescuing, they're—'

'Do it!' snarled Kydd.

The merchant ship was now dead in the water, drifting slowly ahead. It gave him plenty of time to do what he planned.

'I'll thank you to discover our hurts while I'm away, Mr Roscoe,' Kydd ordered the newly arrived first lieutenant.

'Away? You're thinking to board that merchantman?'

'I am.'

Kydd buckled on his sword, clapped on his gold-laced cocked hat and got aboard after Briggs. With his coxswain, Boxall, at the tiller they headed for the mutilated vessel.

Kydd snatched a glimpse of the outside of *Thunderer* as they passed. She looked half in ruin but he knew appearances could deceive. Small damage and disorder in the extraordinarily complex tracery of lines that was a square-rigger's gear might look calamitous but could quickly be put right by a skilled crew.

The merchantman, a fair-sized general cargo vessel with no flag to be seen, was in a worse state but her spars still held. Her name was *Success of Bristol* and there was little doubt of her nationality. Eventually a rope ladder unrolled and Kydd hauled himself up, seething with anger and resentment.

'The master?' he roared, unmoved by the disorder and ruin on deck.

A figure approached, picking his way through the tangle of debris. 'Youlden, barque *Success o' Bristol*, Tilbury in spices.' The man was sullen and defensive, desiccated by long tropic service.

'Captain Sir Thomas Kydd, His Majesty's Ship *Thunderer*.' He paused to let it sink in. 'Mr Youlden. You'll know why I've come,' Kydd said, his voice tight.

'You were athwart my bows as I couldn't do aught to stop it.'

'Under full sail in a fog? And helm orders all ahoo when we're sighted at last? I won't argue, let your owners do that. You'll sign a deposition as to events and times before I think to leave.' He was conscious that the Royal Marines sergeant in charge had paraded his men at attention in a line behind him.

Youlden mumbled something but Kydd guessed what had happened. Towards the end of his voyage the master had been cracking on into the fog competing for his freight first landing and his lookouts had been few or none. The affidavits from both sides would clear Kydd, and if *Thunderer* was fit to resume her passage, it could safely be left to the Admiralty lawyers to bring justice to the situation.

'The barky's in no danger, I see,' Kydd said, as he was ushered below. All damage was above the waterline and a group of men were beginning the long and disheartening process of hauling in and repairing the ravelled lines while others took in the rags of canvas and brought up more to bend on in their place.

Getting the deposition was not a protracted business, the facts speaking for themselves, and tucking away the signed papers in his coat, Kydd regained the deck.

He looked about, then declared loudly, 'And I'll take a score of your hands, if you please, Mr Youlden.'

There was a concerted rush to the hatchways but the wily sergeant had already posted his men well.

Youlden turned on Kydd in a fury. 'You're pressing men after all this and a six-month voyage from the Indies?'

Kydd nodded, a hard smile playing. After what had happened he had little compunction in stripping the merchantman. 'Mr Briggs?'

It was neatly done. At the collision every seaman had hurried on deck and since had been put to work clearing the raffle. With them prevented from hiding below, Briggs had his pick.

'Let 'em collect their dunnage while Mr Youlden writes me a note-of-hand on the owners for their back wages.'

Chapter 19

The gunroom, Thunderer

'The kind o' guardo move you'd expect from a dandy-prat frigate-built bastard,' the gunner said, licking his burgoo spoon and looking around the mess table. The general consensus was that it was a crying shame on the poor beggars within hours of England after so long at sea and Kydd deserved nothing but scorn for his action.

Craddock kept his opinions to himself. If they hadn't the sense to see that getting the extra hands would make it easier for them he wouldn't be the one to bring it up. Kydd was on deck with the boatswain, who was at work with his mates bringing order to the chaos, and Craddock was taking breakfast in the gunroom with the seamen not in the boatswain's party.

Thunderer had not suffered overmuch in the incident and a morning's splicing and re-reeving, some timber repairs and paintwork fully restored would see them much as they had been.

With the brilliant morning sun came a veering and

strengthening of the wind into the north-west. Impatiently Kydd let them get on with their repairs, and when they were completed he sent the men to dinner an hour early and told Roscoe that he expected the officers on deck for sail-drill with the men. It would rouse their hostility but there was more at stake than their feelings.

He stood by the wheel as men tumbled up from below and took station – Briggs at the fore-mast with the experienced fo'c'slemen, Smale at the main and Mayne at the mizzen and under eye. The breeze was obligingly freshening, the seas were no more than playful and the Channel was opening up to the Atlantic with all the world ahead of them.

It was time to make the ship dance.

First the basics. 'Full and bye,' he ordered. As comfortably close to the wind as she would lie.

A dog-vane fluttered in the weather shrouds and Kydd could see that they were achieving a steady six points by the wind – not bad.

'Heave the log,' he rapped. The midshipmen went into action. One held the rotary log-reel over his head while the other prepared the log-ship, the wooden stop to be streamed. It was hurled into their wake and the shout 'Mark!' went out when the first knot on the line shot past. A sand-glass was turned and the log-line rattled away until the glass had run out. The number of knots that had gone over the taffrail was noted.

'Seven and a whisker,' the master's mate reported.

Kydd sniffed the wind and stowed the information in his memory. 'Luff 'n' touch her,' he called, ordering them to ease the helm until the weather leech of the main topsail began fluttering. *Thunderer* was as close as she could claw to the wind. He peered over the leeward side and saw that the lower-deck gun-ports were still a good four feet above the seething side-wake. So, they could fight to leeward when hard by the wind.

The slight swell and running seas were coming in on the bow. 'Lay over to starboard until the seas come in abeam,' he commanded. Obediently the helmsman eased the wheel until the slap and thump of the waves along their sides became constant. Kydd, balancing on the balls of his feet, sensed the change in the motion of the ship. She sailed on smoothly, not deigning to dip and wallow – she was therefore not crank, reacting with excessive lean and slow recovery to the swell of the waves under her. Neither was she stiff, jerking upright as soon as the swell passed beneath her keel. She would be a good gun platform.

'Put the ship about, if you please,' he told the sailing master. The old ship had docile manners and he was beginning to breathe easier.

Now to where the mettle of his seamen mattered. They moved mechanically, carefully, with none of the egoistic leaping of the frigate sailor.

The shouts rang out: 'Ease down the helm!'; 'Helm's a-lee!'; 'Rise tacks and sheets!' and then a satisfied 'Mainsail haul!' and finally 'Let go and haul' and on to the new tack.

Kydd timed it: twelve minutes in all. If the breeze had picked up there was every chance she could make it in ten and never a foot of sternboard. It was more than adequate and even compared favourably with *Tyger*. The drill, however, had been suspiciously faultless. Was it the result of so many empty exercises of a fleet on blockade?

'I'll have the courses taken in and tops'ls with two reefs.' This was more or less as would be needed when closing in on the enemy for a gun duel or desperately easing the strain on masts damaged by enemy fire. His timepiece still out, Kydd consulted it, glancing up every so often to see the men racing up the shrouds and crowding into the tops. He waited until the midshipmen messengers hurried to report their masts as completed. Suspiciously, they arrived within seconds of each other, and the times were woeful. Was this because the order was unusual in a fleet and therefore not practised?

'Not as I'd say a prize showing,' he muttered to Roscoe, who recoiled and looked away.

'Now let's get the reefs out and courses set in half the time,' Kydd said briskly. 'Carry on.'

This time he didn't concentrate his attention on the watch but kept his eyes on the men.

The fore topsail was handed and reef points let fly in a fine show, but then the men stayed where they were, out on the yard. The main topmen were slower and they, too, came to a stop. Then the mizzen – the least skilled in the ship and accordingly kept aft under eye. And when they had laboriously completed it was as if a starting gun had fired. On all three masts there was a disciplined scramble as the topmen laid into the tops and, as one, the shrouds became black with men as they made the deck together.

'What the . . . what the devil's this about?' Kydd exclaimed in amazement to Roscoe.

'I thought myself it was rather well done,' was the tight reply.

Kydd grimaced: the performance was just that, a pretty and spectacular circus trick designed to make the ship look smart and prove how it was working faultlessly together. 'Rubbish!' he snorted, consulting his watch. 'I've never seen slower times. What's the meaning of it, sir?'

Roscoe drew himself up. 'These men have done their best,' he ground out. 'And you're obliged to admit, they all touched deck again within seconds, first and last. Do you really expect—'

'I expect to loose sail under fire or stress of weather in the smallest possible time, not entertain the crowd.' Kydd was conscious their raised words were reaching many ears but didn't care. 'We do it again, but frigate-fashion.'

The features of his first lieutenant were pinched and dangerous. He was responsible to the captain for the manning and rating of the men aloft and Kydd's words were a condemnation.

'Be damned to it!' he burst out. 'You're going to cripple this ship with your small-ship ways. These men at least know exactly what's expected of them and do it. Now you're—'

'*L'tenant Roscoe!*' Kydd blared. 'Go to my cabin and wait on me there – *this instant, sir.*'

In the appalled silence he caught Smale's eye and rapped, 'You have the deck, Mr Smale. I won't be long.'

Chapter 20

Roscoe stood in the centre of the cabin, his face white but resolute.

Kydd didn't waste time. 'Sir, what I heard on my own quarterdeck just now I might choose to consider an insult before witnesses. And prejudicial to the provisions of the Articles of War relating to the conduct of an officer to his superior. Pray give me reason why I shouldn't seek court-martial on you?'

Leaving no time for a reply he went on, 'I've suffered all the provocation I need to have you confined to your cabin until such times as we join the fleet, there to be removed. You'll be broke, sir.'

There was no change in the tense, defiant features.

Kydd felt a moment of hesitation: the man was in other ways a good officer, who cared for his men. 'Before I do, Mr Roscoe, I ask you one last time. Why in Hades do you behave towards me in this manner?'

For a long moment there was nothing. And then Roscoe looked away, clearly struggling. Something was riding him, a personal animus that went beyond his resentment of a frigate captain.

Kydd waited patiently but the defences remained up, the unyielding obstinacy still plain. He wavered, at the very edge of making the order.

'I must apologise to you, Sir Thomas, if it appears I'm wanting in conduct to your principles. I shall endeavour to improve my behaviour.' The voice was a monotone, under great self-control.

Kydd drew in a ragged breath. It was barely enough but could he take the gamble of keeping him, at the risk of his remaining a focus of disaffection in the ship?

He let out the breath slowly. 'You've just three days to renew my confidence in you as my first lieutenant. Fail me and you're finished, Mr Roscoe. Understood?'

'Sir.'

'Then we'll return and continue with our little exercise.'

'Sir.'

The first two marks of respect he could remember from him. Was this a turning point?

On deck no one had moved an inch. Men still clutched ropes, tailed on tackles and stood in orderly groups, stolidly waiting.

Kydd strode out and stopped by the helm. 'Hale aft all the mast officers and their warrant officers,' he demanded. He waited until they had presented themselves, then began, in a friendly voice, 'The first l'tenant has been good enough to explain to me how sail-handling has until now been conducted in *Thunderer*. As you know, I come from frigates and I'm used to a different way of doing things. A faster way.'

He could tell by their expressions that hackles had risen but gave a boyish grin and continued, 'But I can give you a smart turn-out all the same.'

What they wanted were the regimented movements that resulted in a synchronised mast-by-mast sequence ending with a mass return to the deck. They were achieving it, but by the device of taking their time from the mizzen. Consequently all three masts were held back by the speed of the slowest.

'Sir. The mizzen is going as quick as it may,' Mayne blurted. 'I don't think we can—'

'This is nothing to do with the mizzen, sir. We change our objectives. Frigate-fashion, we put times before appearances and in doing so retain our smartness.'

Briggs looked puzzled. 'How is this, Sir Thomas? I've served in single-deckers and never a care given to mast times or evolutions by the book.'

'Then do learn how it's done in a crack frigate. This will be carried through by *you*, gentlemen.'

He saw he had their attention now – and, out of the corner of his eye, Roscoe's.

'At the next drill each of you will observe along the yards to determine the most able topmen in action aloft. The object is to put them out at the yardarm for any manoeuvre. The slower go to the bunt. We shall do more than a few exercises and between each you'll refine your positioning on each yard until you have your fastest crew. Clear?'

There were slow nods, so he went on: 'And this is not all. Then we run the drills several more times and each yard is timed. At the end the first lieutenant, from these, will evenly distribute the best crews across all three masts. This way you'll get them naturally finishing and getting off the yard and on deck together. Compree?'

This time there were smiles of understanding.

He had lied: this was not how it was done in any crack frigate he had known. In a frigate an officer *knew* his men for he could be leading them, without much warning, into a boarding or stealthily on a hand-to-hand cutting-out

expedition and needed to be aware of their qualities intim-
ately. To distribute their seaman-like talents evenly was a
trivial task.

'Oh – and allow to the people that their captain believes
their hard labour is deserving of reward. It's to be a double
grog at supper.'

'Knows his nauticals, then.'

The boatswain nodded in acknowledgement. 'None o'
your strut-noddy fancy ways, Nobby.'

'Aye. An' I knows why.'

'What's that, then, Nobby?'

'Cos he's a foul-weather jack. Can see it in the cut o' his
jib. He doesn't want t' be laid by the lee in a blow by a parcel
of landmen.'

The carpenter slapped down his leather blackjack. 'Not
as I sees it,' he said definitively.

'Tell us, why don't ye, Lofty?'

Craddock set aside his book to listen to the carpenter, a
long-serving standing officer through several captains and
years of service.

'You should know. Different ships, different long-splices
– some owners come down hard on sail, others for gunnery.
You're safe wi' yer iron, Nobby – he's a salt-horse sailin' man.'

Opie sank his drink and gave a satisfied smile. 'Um. Nice
touch of him, the tots. Many wouldn't give a toss about
what it takes to fist a sail.'

'Bribes.'

'No, Lofty, don't reckon on this one needin' to do that.'

'Doesn't have to. He's not goin' to be in *Thunderer* fer long,
mates. He's in thick with the Prince o' Wales an' his crew
who won't stand to see him out o' hail for long. Just putting
in time for his admiral's flag.'

'Heard he's a fightin' seaman – Spain, the Med, Java, all over,' Opie said uneasily.

'O' course ye has,' the gunner replied forcefully. 'Any small powder gets burned, it's in all the papers, a proper noise. I'll believe it when m' peepers tell me.'

Craddock couldn't help it. 'In his last ship they called him "Tom Cutlass" and no doubts as to his mettle with a fat purse of prize money for all hands after the last voyage.'

'Bull, tell yon Pedro that we don't need 'im to put his oar in. We makes up our own mind.'

Chapter 21

It must be all around the ship by now, Kydd mused. He and Roscoe were not getting along and there were no guesses as to who would be first to suffer. The first lieutenant was always strictly polite, still speaking few words but punctilious with at least one 'sir' in each utterance. After a while its near artificial expression grated on Kydd but he realised its purpose: evidence. In any future court-martial the question 'How did you address Sir Thomas?' would be answered with a factual reply that he'd rendered marks of respect always.

Whatever the state below decks, one thing was plain. At this time it would be disastrous to invite Craddock to share his cabin in companionship. It would be seen as the formation of factions with Craddock, as his man, in the midst of them all. Kydd would have to endure his solitude for now. He could only hope that the man would take care of himself in the meantime.

The trick with the sail-handling the previous day was easy enough with those not living daily at the edge of imminent action, but in a few minutes the bell would strike the forenoon watch when the entire ship's company would turn to for exercise at the great guns. There were no bluffs or short-cuts in gun-handling, and it would be a hard day for all.

Luscombe entered with Kydd's action rig – a near thread-bare coat with the minimum of gold lace that would very soon be smeared with powder residue, and old-fashioned breeches but with fine silk stockings in stout shoes against wounding. And his fighting sword. He caught sight of the lad's features and his heart wrung. Dark pits around the eyes, listless movements and avoidance of Kydd's gaze.

'Are the beggars not leaving you alone, Josiah?' he asked kindly, deliberately choosing to use his forename. 'I'll have 'em keel-hauled!' But Kydd couldn't do a thing about it and the young man's tormentors would know it.

'It's not just the names, it's the jokes,' he said miserably. 'Y'see, I can't understand them and they fall about laughing.'

Common seamen were continually with their shipmates, their messmates, and very soon they'd get to know a raw new friend and take him in hand. Luscombe didn't have that asset: theirs was not his society of equals. Instead he was in with the idlers, the stewards, servants and suchlike, and his world was half theirs and half that of the potentate in his palace.

The firm double knock. 'Both watches of the hands mustered. Sir.'

'Thank you, Mr Roscoe. I shall be on deck presently.'

He had moments to detach himself from one distressing problem to concentrate on the larger issue at hand. Should he reach out to the crew, who would have to fight for him, in a stirring speech, trying to make himself heard to six-hundred-odd men on a blowing deck in a seaway, or limit it to the principals to pass on as they pleased? Or begin without ceremony or notice the savage and brutal ballet that was gun-play in a man-o'-war?

They'd had warning enough. He'd made plain his views on the primacy of gunnery in a warship at last night's dinner, but then only the officers had been present. It was the seamen at the guns he needed to inspire, smashing in the broadsides to fight the ship for him.

They were by their guns when he emerged on deck. In their hundreds, a battleship at quarters, but with expressions varying from boredom to glassy-eyed indifference.

Kydd was no stranger to thirty-two-pounders, the biggest great guns afloat, as carried by first-rates like *Victory*. He'd served his time at them as a young pressed man, and the drill he'd learned then was deeply ingrained.

'Officers at quarters, lay aft,' he ordered those who, during action, were stationed on the gun-decks fore and aft. Under them strove the lesser mortals, the master's mates, midshipmen, quarter-gunners.

In pithy, down-to-earth terms Kydd laid down what he wanted: two entire decks of guns working together to make a species of hell for the enemy such that *Thunderer* must inevitably prevail. Speed, coolness under fire, care and attention to the safety of the ship, with cross-training to ensure a gun would not be put out of action by a key member of the gun-crew made a casualty.

The first concern was to take measure of the gun-crews, their performance at standard gun drill.

He took out his watch and gave the order.

Harsh shouts rang out and the men bent to their task in a methodical flourish, but wielding their implements sloppily, rammers of one gun tangling with spongers of the adjacent. Consequently those on the gun-tackle of a 'fired' gun interfered with the neighbouring gun running out.

It was a dreadful display of incompetence. These men had

obviously not exercised together for some time. They were simply going through the motions.

'Cease fire.'

Almost lost for words, Kydd hesitated. All thought of timings was irrelevant – this performance was not even half decent. It had been sham firing, of course, imaginary round-shot and powder cartridges used. Would they do better in the din and blood of a genuine action?

'Mr Roscoe, when was the last gun practice?'

'Um, I believe the last Friday of the month previous. Sir.'

'And the last live firing exercise?'

'I – I cannot readily recall, sir. I can ask the gunner if you wish.'

Kydd bit his lip. 'The last engagement with the enemy at which *Thunderer* burned powder?'

'Oh, er, that must have been the hostility off Rochefort, in deterring a sortie putting to sea.'

'When was that, pray?'

'About two years ago, or was it nearer to three? Sir.'

No wonder it was such an abominable showing. In the same period *Tyger* had been in furious action more than half a dozen times at least.

It was no excuse, and Lyell should have countered it with imaginative exercising, competition and rewards. This was a mere grudging byplay, the main attention going to smartness and appearances.

'I shan't conceal it, sir,' Kydd told him sorrowfully, 'this greatly disappoints me. And we shall do something about it. I want the officers, assisted by their warrant officers, to observe closely the guns being served, to take particular written note of those of each crew who gets out of the way of others.'

He hoped he could bring about the same kind of even distribution of talent as in the sail-handling. It would be painful, breaking up gun-crews and their comfortable relationship with each other, but greater issues were at stake. And in both cases the priceless side benefit would be the officers' acquisition of a close familiarity with their men, their capabilities, weaknesses, peculiarities.

'Sir?'

'I'm interested in the ones spry enough to make good gun-handlers, ignoring the rest getting in the way.' It was obvious to him that this was a sign of superior agility and alertness. It seemed not to his first lieutenant.

'Quarter-gunners are now responsible for their gun-captains,' he continued. Those were the petty officers in close charge of every four guns and the most experienced gunners. 'Should they see any failing in their duty they're to rate the second gun-captain in his place without the necessity of consulting the officer of his division.'

Their duty would be read as not only competence at the gun-lock but, more importantly, power of command in their crew.

Once a quarter-gunner had a list of the better ones they would be put to the more skilled tasks: manipulating the rammer, the wad and cartridge, the shot. The remainder would be condemned to the brute labour of the tackle falls each side of the gun, which were used to run out the three tons of iron after reloading inboard.

And, finally, the timings would be used to show up the more successful gun-crews and those who were weaker, a continual process as crews were refined to a point at which Kydd was satisfied that an elite was emerging. To earn distinction and public incentives, these men would then be set to instruct the rest of the gun-deck on how it was done.

116

If only he had *Tyger*'s gunner's mate Toby Stirk aboard to take them by the scruff!

Impatient to be started, he set the larboard side guns to three firing cycles under the mocking eye of the starboard crews. It was a shambles as the quarter-gunners came down hard on the gun-captains, who in turn bullied their crews, but the process was beginning and Kydd left them to it. They would exercise all forenoon and again in the first dog-watch. By tomorrow he'd have his list and the laborious upward path to skill-at-arms with the great guns would begin.

Chapter 22

The gunroom

Lawlor came below in a foul mood, throwing himself into his chair with a growl. 'He'll be the ruin of a good barky, that scrim-shanking knows-it-all,' he snarled.

'Nobby, he's got his ways, an' it's how they does it in frigates,' the boatswain soothed, ruefully inspecting the bread-barge, now with none of the soft tommy from shore. 'Younker, get us some more,' he snapped at the gunroom boy.

Craddock sighed and laid his book down. 'I'd advise you fall in with Sir Thomas's desires, er, Nobby. He's a habit of dealing harshly with those who cross him. Better for you in the long run.'

Lawlor ignored him and made much of screwing his chair around so his back was towards Craddock, who burned at the insult.

'Lofty, why does we have t' suffer a clerk in the gunroom? Why don't 'e sling his hook with his high-struttin' matey aft?'

'Yeah! Why doesn't ye, Pedro?' the carpenter grunted.

'Because this is my mess,' Craddock replied bluntly, and buried himself in his book.

'Fair enough, mates.' Opie chuckled then looked reflective. 'So we're back wi' the fleet tomorrow. Floggin' up and down until we rot with our ships. Ain't human. I'm missin' m' woman, don't mind tellin' ye.'

'Me as well,' the carpenter said, in a low voice. 'Lives up at Clydeside and I haven't seen m' Mary and the little 'uns in a dog's age. How's it fer you, Nobby?'

'Wife's dead 'n' buried these four years, mate. Lives with the family now.'

Opie glanced across at Craddock and said mildly, 'Y'r lady has t' get used to you bein' at sea for years now. How does she feel about that, Pedro?'

At first Craddock didn't respond, his gaze fixed on the page, then he paled, his grasp on the book near manic.

'Hey, Pedro,' the boatswain said, concerned. 'I didn't mean t' say—'

'I saw my wife and children some months ago burned alive by the French in the Adriatic,' he said quietly, but with an edge of madness. 'And I'm on the ship as the best way I know to afflict the monster Bonaparte. To torment the very coast of France seems a fine enough thing.'

The gunroom was shocked into stillness.

'I think . . . a little sea air is what I need at the moment.' The book fell to the deck as he rose carefully, dignified, and took his leave.

'Harry – how good to see you!' Kydd exclaimed. 'Sit down, old chap – a snorter?'

Craddock eased himself into an armchair with a wry smile. Solitude dure must take a toll on a fine mind like Kydd's. 'Just wanted to see if there's anything I can do for you.'

'Let's not worry about that,' Kydd said happily, then noticed something in Craddock's face. 'You're feeling well, Harry? Are they treating you with respect in the gunroom, the salty devils?'

'I have a question.'

'Fire away, old fellow.' The lines in Kydd's face were easing in the warmth of their meeting again.

'You said before your officers at dinner that I was acting as ship's clerk *in temporarius* only until another be found. Does this mean—'

'Dear chap, believe me when I say you shall have tenure for as long as you desire it,' Kydd answered fervently. 'It was only a device to explain your presence on board.'

Craddock loosened and smiled. 'Then I shall rest content.' The fingers twisted together unconsciously as he went on lightly, 'As I do confess that I find myself not yet ready to take my place among the shore creatures as you'll understand.'

'I do, Harry – I do. I can only apologise deeply for the condition of this ship. It's not what I'd want for my friend to endure.'

'Take no mind on my situation, Thomas. My messmates are a parcel of nature's children only and have no real apprehension of the wider world and its sorry tales of suffering *in extremis*. Or even the ineffable rapture of having one's being cradled in the deep while in the society of those of like mind and character, never to be plagued by the alien beasts of the land.'

Kydd looked at him in awe and affection. This was the friend he so desperately needed to see him through this time of trial. 'Talking of beasts . . .' He hesitated. What he was about to say went across all his years of sea service on the quarterdeck but at the same time it would tell him how far he could go with Craddock.

'Beasts, yes?'

'My precious first lieutenant . . . Harry, believe me when I tell you that a first lieutenant is a priceless fellow whom I must trust with my life and, even more importantly, the ship. It's a sad problem for me.'

Craddock heard him out then answered, 'I rather think that it's not your problem, more the sainted Roscoe's.'

'Yes, but—'

'The problem is his to solve. Inside, he's nursing a canker, a grievance or hatred, but unless he conquers it himself, his future is to be damned. His end in *Thunderer* is inevitable, and once removed under a cloud, his chances of either promotion or another ship are not to be entertained.'

'That's as may be, Harry but what's to do?'

'I believe you're right in the particulars – you're powerless to do anything. He must be the one to move. Your only course is to give him every chance to find a remedy or let Fate take him from the board.'

'He's at root a good hand,' Kydd admitted, 'and if it weren't for his infernals I'd welcome him as premier.' But the three days he had given him to prove himself worthy would soon be up . . .

The gunroom fell silent as Craddock returned. Without comment he saw his book had been carefully placed on the table and he picked it up. Finding his chair still available he settled to resume it.

'Feelin' better, shipmate?' Opie said quietly.

'Thank you, yes.'

'Um, I has a drop o' the right sort as'll cure y'r mullygrubs, Pedro.'

Surprisingly, it was the gunner, his voice now low and gruff. He fumbled in his ditty-bag and, looking about him suspiciously, came out with a bottle.

'That's kind in you, Nobby,' Craddock said politely. 'Just a small one, if you would.'

'Nasty blows topside, this time o' the year,' the carpenter said, with a rumbling sympathy. 'Watch y' don't catch a green sea as you're not expecting, mate.'

'I will.'

'Is there anything we can do fer you, cully?' Opie's compassion was transparent.

Craddock gave a smile of appreciation. 'That's well meant, Bull, and I thank you for it, but time will heal everything, I'm persuaded. For now I feel all a-taunto.'

This brought grins all round.

'Can I ask it, Pedro? How did youse and the captain get alongside each other in the first place?'

'Certainly you may, Lofty. In short, he was on a raiding party on the Balkan shore and . . . and did rescue me from the flames. Since, I flatter myself that I was in some measure of use to him in the article of intelligence as he roamed the Adriatic bringing disaster and ruin to the enemy.'

'In a frigate.'

'Yes, *Tyger* frigate as distinguished herself nobly at Lissa where I had the honour of being present.'

'So it's true, what we heard, that 'twas a right good drubbing?' On blockade, news filtered through slowly.

'It was. That I can assure you – and as well, that Tom Cutlass is your natural-born fighting captain as you'd be proud to own to.'

The gunner looked awkward. 'But – I humbly begs pardon – it doesn't sit s' good with us as he gets in thick with that scowbunkin' crew at the King's court just to get hisself a sail-o'-the-line.'

'Aye,' the carpenter said, his voice rising. 'Specially when it costs a man his own ship.'

'Hold, you ignorant swabs,' Craddock said, in his best seamanlike growl. 'He didn't even want a ship-of-the-line. I tell you, as I'm the nearest thing he's got to a friend, that when he heard he was to take *Thunderer* he nearly wept. You see, he once did a favour for the Prince of Wales who thought he'd be returning it by insisting he gets a bigger ship, more prizes, he thinks.'

'Than a frigate? The loon.'

'Just so, Lofty. Now can you imagine how Captain Kydd feels? All his honours and prize-tickets won in a frigate, to have it taken away, a fast, sweet-lined frigate, with independent cruises for blockading. But he's never going to be cast down. He's going to do his duty and bring *Thunderer* up to the mark as he sees it – frigate fashion.'

There were thoughtful looks before the gunner declared, 'Then we goes for it. Give 'im a chance. Right, mates?'

Chapter 23

U shant could just be made out emerging from the grey murk of mist and drizzle to larboard. A long south-westerly swell from the opposite direction told of a wicked storm far out in the Atlantic. Here, however, winds were sullen and fluky and, given his concerns of his unknown crew, Kydd wasn't going to attempt stunsails to make a quicker passage. In any case the Channel Squadron was just around the corner.

'Stand down, starb'd gun-crews, close up larb'd.'

For the starbowlines there was panting, stretching and rueful flexing, but he noticed that the men had turned to more willing, giving it heart. Also, the larbowlines clapped on to their tackles with real purpose.

Kydd was not about to give away precious hours of practice simply because Admiral Keith's fleet was not far off and they would still be drilling when the flagship hove in sight.

Grimly, he paced the gun-decks, his splendid silver hunter on open display.

The miserable light rain didn't spare the nine-pounder

crews at individual practice on the quarterdeck and fo'c'sle, but where was it decreed that battles were fought only on a fine day?

Quite unexpectedly a man-o'-war slid into view from the lee side of Ushant. It flaunted the red ensign of the commander-in-chief and its challenge was replied to in the correct manner. Kydd ordered the signals master's mate to hoist 'Come within hail,' inwardly exulting in the power he now had to order about the grandest frigate.

Obediently the vessel swung about and glided into their lee, striking sail as she did so. He watched, knowing exactly what was going on – the languid movements deliberately designed to yield sea-room to the massive and less agile 74.

'*Jason*, Captain Everard, sir,' came a blare from a speaking trumpet held by a figure on her quarterdeck, no doubt curious to know who had relieved Lyell at such notice.

'*Thunderer*, Captain Sir Thomas Kydd. Any news?'

'None, the mongseers so shy. If it's news, do you have anything from England, Sir Thomas?'

'Send a boat and you shall have a newspaper or two, Captain. Where are Lord Keith and the fleet?'

'In this breeze? In the Iroise, somewhere between the Vieux Moines and Raz de Sein, Sir Thomas.' That was the age-old fair-weather station, clamped directly across the harbour like a rat trap and about thirty miles distant.

Thunderer would rejoin the fleet in the small hours.

Meanwhile the order went out, 'Hands turn to, part-of-ship, to clean.'

Admiral Keith, a dour Scot of unbending will and probity, would have seen *Thunderer* depart the trimmest and most cared-for ship in the squadron, and would expect her back in the same condition. If it cost Kydd his precious hours at the sails and guns so be it, in this his first appearance before the commander-in-chief.

The Western Squadron of the Channel Fleet was raised later in the afternoon, a straggling line hardly moving in the oily swell and peevish winds. The flagship was nearly hidden behind a slow-drifting curtain of light rain, but when she emerged, glistening and stark in colour, there was a hoist at her mizzen peak halliards.

'Our pennants, sir – "Captain to repair on board".'

There would be no gun salutes, for this would alert the French that the forces opposing them outside had increased, unwise when everything was being done to lure them out.

Thunderer lay off to leeward and Kydd took to his barge.

The 100-gun first-rate *Royal Sovereign* was one of the legendary ships of Trafalgar. She had flown the flag of Admiral Collingwood and had had the honour of being the first ship in action that fateful day. Kydd had vivid memories of seeing her from *L'Aurore*, his first ship as a post-captain. This day, however, he was boarding her a baronet, with fame and honours – and as the captain of a ship-of-the-line that had been at Trafalgar in that same line-of-battle with Collingwood.

He mounted the side-steps, hauling on the beautifully knotted man-rope to the entry-port. It was thrilling to be piped aboard by a full crew of side-boys and lieutenants, each in white gloves in honour of his august rank, only a step below an admiral.

He faced aft and doffed his hat, then acknowledged the group of officers inboard, who stood together while he was relieved of his dripping oilskins. And in the centre waited a slender, long-faced senior officer, with cold, flint-like eyes and hard features: the commander-in-chief, Lord Keith.

This was the admiral who had lifted him from the common

herd as a lieutenant and raised him to commander of his own ship, the brig-sloop *Teazer*. In those fearful days on the eve of invasion when the navy had stood alone against Napoleon, Kydd had served in the white-hot centre of the fight, Keith's Downs Squadron.

He snatched off his hat and bowed. 'Captain Sir Thomas Kydd joining your command, my lord.'

'With *Thunderer* in hand and fit for service?' That well-remembered Scots brogue and cold stare. 'Much the more important to me, sir.'

He followed the admiral aft to his day cabin and took the chair offered him. A long, appraising look and then, 'Ship in good order, ready for what must come?'

'She is, sir.'

'Then it's well with ye.' A tiny icy smile briefly appeared. 'As before you've proved yourself worthy o' my trust – when was it, the year aught one, a lieutenant running afoul of your captain? And turned y'sel' into a first-rank frigate man since.'

'Sir. I can only thank you again for—'

'Which is what I want to talk to ye about.'

'Sir.'

'I've no sense of why their lordships took you out of a crack frigate and pitchforked you into a sail-of-the-line. Some say it was the Prince of Wales interfering on your behalf, but I doubt it. You're a prime frigate driver, Kydd, and it doesn't have much meaning.'

'I can assure you, my lord, that it wasn't myself who—'

'Be that as it may, sir, my advice to you is that you must be prepared to change your ways. More to my sorrow, I've no place for a daring, bold and thrusting captain in my fleet. Before, you made a decision and acted on it to secure prizes by your own efforts. What I want and need is a captain I can rely on to a split yarn in carrying out my orders in the heat of battle, who'll stay the course and suffer grievous enemy fire while stoutly remaining in the line, who'll keep the vessel fighting whatever its wounds.

'The age of Nelson quitting the line is over. We may well be summoned to our duty supreme at any moment and I want no heroes at my expense.'

'I understand you, my lord.'

'Then we shall get along. Now, have you seen service before in these waters?'

'Never at length, sir.'

'A pity for, as ye'd know, this is an iron-bound coast and among the worst to be found anywhere. La Rochelle and to the suth'ard?'

'With Captain Cochrane at the Basque Roads engagement and above the usual sea service off northern Spain.'

'That will do. I will attach you to the Rochefort squadron, Rear Admiral Houghton. At the moment all is quiet and you should not look to much entertainment from Boney but you'll no doubt be informed of the strategic situation by the admiral.'

'Thank you, my lord. It shall be my pleasure to serve under you.'

'Oh – so remiss of me. Before you quit the station for Rochefort do stay and take dinner with us. There's precious little diversion on blockade and I would have you meet your fellow captains.'

Chapter 24

'R ochefort, La Rochelle?' Craddock said lazily, as he took his ease with Kydd in *Thunderer*'s great cabin. 'As I spent a glorious summer there in business before the Revolution. Rochefort and its cheeses, Bordeaux to the south with its claret and, should you need more, Cognac to the east for its *eau de vie*. That the Aquitainians should be caught up in this madness is none of their doing. By the way, how did the dinner go?' He hoisted his glass high and squinted through it in mock concern.

'Such a quantity of naval officers of the highest *éclat*, it would turn the head of the most jaded.' He didn't mention that for the most part the looks cast across the table had been ill-natured and sour, the conversations abrupt and barbed. It didn't take much to realise that the canard of his reaching for influence at court had reached even there.

Thunderer would depart at dawn the next day. Two days more of independence to bring his ship to a full fighting asset.

Kydd remembered a hard-countenanced Captain Houghton

in the old 64 *Tenacious* years ago. Was this the same man and, if so, how would he be as an admiral?

At some two hundred miles southward there were the same baffling breezes and sullen swell. *Thunderer* was not at her best in light airs and, with diminished wind force on her higher sails, she rolled badly with the swell coming abeam. Kydd sent Luscombe away, his seasickness wretched. Others fell into the same miserable existence: gunnery practice was a shadow of what it should have been and, with only a slight breathy wind, sail-handling would have little meaning.

The Rochefort Squadron was at neither of the two rendez-vous, north of the Île de Ré and the estuary of the Gironde, and no cutter or frigate was posted to inform of their where-abouts. There was only one thing Kydd could do: sail up and down between the nominated points and hope to sight them or be spotted by scouting frigates. It was odd: a blockade required that a deterring force be seen to be effective, and there was not a warship in view.

The following day, passing the lighthouse at the tip of the Île de Ré, they came upon four battleships lying at anchor, several frigates and brigs moored further inshore. Challenges exchanged, Kydd brought *Thunderer* to anchor at the end of the line and prepared to make visit.

Houghton's flag was in the centre, in *Pembroke*, not a 100-gun first-rate but a 74, like *Thunderer*. To man and main-tain such giant ships was an expensive and questionable act when a squadron was so small.

Kydd mounted the side-steps to be received with side-boys and pipes in the now accustomed ceremony. He was greeted by *Pembroke*'s captain, who explained that Admiral Houghton was caught up with much work but would nevertheless like to see him.

Pembroke was a newer ship, built and launched with the rise of Bonaparte. Plain and sparing in adornments, she was a creature of war, not peace, and her great cabin seemed a place of frowning rather than ease. Houghton was standing legs abrace, his heavy face tugged into grim lines, the same unsmiling, abrupt manner that had kept the officers of *Tenacious* in humble subjection. But now there was also a marked paunch and sagging jowls.

'Sir Thomas Kydd, *Thunderer* 74, to join, sir.'

There were no decorations or sashes on Houghton's uniform and Kydd had never heard of any action in which he'd distinguished himself.

'You took your time, sir.' There was no sign that Kydd had been remembered, but it had been a long while ago.

'I raised rendezvous in two days from the Brest station, sir. In both I could not make out your squadron.'

'Didn't it cross your mind that we might be just to seaward on an important occasion?' His face was flushed.

'I felt it more in keeping with my orders to remain at the rendezvous, sir.'

'A gross lacking in initiative, sir. I was under the impression that you frigate captains had more backbone, b' God. But, then, could it be that, having laid hands on your ship-of-the-line – by whatever means – you may be inclined to a quiet life?'

Kydd's heart sank. Here was another tainted by Prinny's unfortunate act, however well meant. When *would* he be able to shake it off? 'My elevation to a sail-of-the-line command was not my doing, sir. It was—'

'Damn it all, sir. I will not have the pickerooning style of a frigate in my fleet! You'll act the captain of a ship-of-the-line both in my presence and away. Should you not, I'll see you relieved of your command. Understand?'

Whether it was the assumption of an unfair influence at court or rank jealousy at his successes and fame as a frigate captain, Kydd saw that in Houghton he had a dangerous enemy. One who could bring about his professional ruin. It would only show up the difference between them to remind him that at one point he was a first ship junior officer under him. Kydd had risen swiftly, a knighthood and prize money, and through all the ranks bar Houghton's, while the other man had progressed, but that one step.

'I do, sir,' Kydd replied evenly.

'Then see Flags, sign my order book and get back to your ship. We sail as a squadron tomorrow for fleet exercises.' He regarded Kydd with pursed lips for a space and, with a muttered 'Carry on, Captain,' sat heavily at his desk.

The flag-lieutenant was garrulous but all sympathy. 'His Nibs only made flag earlier this year, and all the world knows it'll be his last appointment, only in post because Essington at the Admiralty owes him a service.'

'I see.'

'Likes to think he's a Nelson but this translates into bullying his squadron when at his copious exercises. Here's your orders, Fighting Instructions and signal codes. Could I suggest, Sir Thomas, you ensure your signal crew gets it by heart?'

'So, not a fighting admiral.'

'You burn powder, you account for it in five ways or you'll be held to the expense.'

'Sociable?'

'In a word – no. Just between we two he's plenty of friends he keeps in his quarter gallery, and every so often he invites one out to make merry, not forgetting to remove the cork first.'

'The other captains?'

'They seem content enough with ship-visiting each other when at anchor. You'll get to know them soon enough.'

He rattled off the names. *Malabar*, *Resolution*, *Asia* and, of course, *Pembroke*. All 74s and a mix of new and old. The captains' names meant nothing but they were the ones he would join in the line-of-battle, placing *Thunderer* where it may, trusting their courage and seamanship to keep the line unbroken.

So, a crabbed and envious admiral, a quiet station and no prospect of action or distinction in these times of stalemate. It was the worst situation for any officer trying to catch the eye of the highest. On the other side of the scale was the certainty that if he stumbled in his command of a ship-of-the-line it would be seized on by his enemies to bring about his public downfall.

The evening gun thumped out from *Pembroke* at the point when Kydd's barge was halfway back. A scurvy move by Houghton: the practice was for each ship to follow this with guard and band of marines paraded as the ensign was lowered. All officers would solemnly face aft and remove their hats in respect. What was he expected to do, being at neither one place nor another?

'Oars!' he growled. The boat glided to a stop and Kydd stood up, faced *Pembroke* and slowly removed his hat, remaining in position until the last faint strains of the band had drifted over the still waters. He would not be found lacking in respect for his superior.

His spirits were low when he returned to *Thunderer*. Under Houghton, all thoughts of a chance at independence, of a personal hammer blow at the enemy, were derisory. He could look forward only to a future in this backwater of animosity and futility, even with his own officers and ship's company.

Craddock was waiting for him and picked up on his mood. 'Not a joyous meeting, I'm sanguine.'

'No.' Kydd looked around for Luscombe. 'Where's that youngster now?' he muttered. 'Had enough time to learn the ropes and so forth, surely.'

'Ah. I meant to see you about that.'

'Why?'

'Because the lad came to me in some misery and distress and asked me for advice he couldn't get from you.'

'Oh?'

'Recollect, Thomas, he comes from a different world, the genteel society of the Devon countryside. His head was no doubt filled with dreams of adventure and prize money with a legendary local sea fighter. Now he's finding that the rations are vile, the company worse and seasickness thrown in free of charge. And no prospects for advancement that the meanest pressed man can hope for. He's bright and well-mannered, holds himself proud and doesn't indulge in profanity. Dear fellow, he doesn't belong in a ship of war.'

Kydd slumped back in his chair. In effect Luscombe was enduring *Thunderer* in much the same way as he was, but without the benison of being able to do something about it, however slight in effect. 'So what should I do for the poor wight?'

Craddock gave a lengthy sigh. 'I cannot conceive of any act you might take that will relieve what ails him. Like your Roscoe, his salvation lies within himself.'

Chapter 25

'Prep, "unmoor", sir,' Mayne, the signals lieutenant, called out smartly. He'd been warned off by Kydd that any slackness in responding to the flagship's hoists due to unfamiliarity with the signal book would have serious consequences.

'Very good. Messenger, let the fo'c'sle know.'

Kydd had their hastily scrawled orders from *Pembroke* to proceed to sea by a cast to larboard when all anchors were signalled a-weigh, leading to a forming up in Order of Sailing on a line of bearing west by north.

Anchors were won more or less together, but *Thunderer* and *Malabar* took more of the cheerful breeze on their beam and, when their anchors broke ground, began drifting to leeward. *Thunderer* was dangerously overlapping and bearing down on the other ship.

All ships had not yet hoisted their 'anchors a-weigh' and therefore no sail could be set without orders. Kydd felt a paralysing inevitability. But then, galvanised, he roared forward, 'Let fly jibs and headsails!' and spinning about ordered, 'Sheet in the driver!'

It gradually stopped the frightful sight of their spearing bowsprit aimed into the belly of *Malabar* but at the cost of setting his ship aback. The only solution was to bring the wind on the opposite side. This sent *Thunderer* back through the forming line, mercifully missing *Asia* and ending up well to weather of the ragged line.

The 'Form order of sailing' hoist was thrown out and jerked down in the 'execute', and the remaining two ships scrabbled to obey. Almost immediately the signal was hoisted again, and with it *Thunderer*'s pennants, and the flat thud of a gun to draw attention of the delinquent to it. Kydd's ship was being held up before the world as laggardly and incompetent.

Inwardly raging he began the difficult and dangerous manoeuvre of taking up parallel with the line before insinuating himself under full sail between *Resolution* and *Asia* in accordance with the Order of Sailing. Before he could complete it, in a maliciously timed act, Houghton required the squadron to execute a 'wear squadron in line', the order for all ships to turn as one off the wind and around to take up on the opposite tack.

It threw out Kydd's meticulous calculations but he saw a way through. To wear a ship needed plenty of searoom in their wide wheel-about but Kydd had *Thunderer* at a sharper angle in his attempt to regain the line and, able to cut across the turning circle, he eased in astern of *Asia* and settled on course as before.

Taking up on the new track, Kydd absorbed the arresting sight of a fleet of ships from the inside. Foaming along in *Asia*'s wake, the ships ahead were all but out of sight, occasionally visible when sagging to leeward but for the most part his view was dominated by the ship ahead's stern of martial plainness.

Further on, *Pembroke* was completely obscured but that was what the repeating frigate *Hyperion* was for, standing well out to windward to read the flagship's signals and hoisting them for all to see. Kydd had more than once performed this office and knew that from the moment battle was joined the flagship would be near hidden in a double measure of rolling gun-smoke and the frigate's purpose gone.

The line-of-battle was a completely different experience and gave meaning to much of what he'd seen from the outside in the several fleet engagements he'd been at in a frigate. He realised what it meant to be part of a fully formed-up fleet. Bucketing along at twice the speed of a running man, he was expected to keep a steady two hundred yards from the ship ahead – a bare three ships' lengths, or forty seconds of travel, with all the inertia of several thousand tons of battleship.

'*Hyperion* from Flag. Squadron, take station line-ahead, one cable.'

When a ponderous ship-of-the-line took whole minutes to bring in sail, the equivalent of the brake on a carriage, this was a fearful demand on seamanship. At first Kydd burned with resentment until a calmer voice told him that not only was the reigning admiral perfectly entitled to order this, to close the line for an impact from an enemy trying to pierce it, but this was precisely what he himself had ordered at Lissa.

'Mr Hobbs,' he called to the sailing master. 'A cable apart. Can we do it?'

'Sir.'

'Carry on, if you please.'

He'd never been in a fleet manoeuvring in such close order, except the informal succession of eager men-o'-war entering the bay at the Nile. But then he'd been a junior signal lieutenant in an old 64 and had had little interest in the technical details of the manoeuvre. Now it was completely different: he was a captain. He watched an elaborate positioning of men on all three masts, tailing on to the braces, the weather tack and sheet of every large sail.

Crisp orders from Hobbs had sails trimmed from forward, coming aft one after the other until he was satisfied. *Thunderer*'s bowsprit unerringly tracked *Asia*'s stern walk as it advanced slowly by yards. No need for sextant angles between mast height and waterline, a single cable's distance was easy enough to judge by eye.

'One cable, sir,' Hobbs said impassively, his seamed countenance immovably fixed on the ship ahead.

It was intimidating, the continual stream of trimming orders forward to aft that kept them in place, and the large number of men involved, but this was how it was done apparently. Why so many? It seemed it was believed that a precise distance apart could be achieved better by many small adjustments, and therefore most of the watch-on-deck would be standing by a line, ready to trim.

Kydd turned and raised his pocket telescope to check on *Malabar*, next astern of them. As far as he could make out she had the same arrangement, and all three ships were scrupulously at their correct distance.

But something in him rebelled. The object was achieved, but was that all? If a desperate encounter was looming, a clash of fleets in a grand way, with nearly all of the ship's company employed at sail-trimming to keep an admiral satisfied, they could not be manning guns or readying weapons. Admittedly the close order of sailing was necessary in certain circumstances but there must be a better way.

In frigates there were occasions without number when a convoy was escorted. Some, like the Baltic convoys, included hundreds of ships by column and row. He'd taken it for granted when as escort he'd closed with them to demand better station-keeping but how actually had they done it? With the whole crew constantly stationed at the lines? No. With crew numbers cut to the bone they all used the same method: a chosen sail, usually a topsail, with one corner led up on the lee side to the tops by a strong purchase. The idea was to spill wind in a controlled manner simply by this one tackle and a small number of men on it.

His mind saw how he could rig *Thunderer*'s fore topsail, leaving all its gear in place so when battle was joined it could readily be cast off. Meanwhile a small party would be all that was necessary to spill wind to the master's order to scrub off speed or ease out to spread more canvas, more speed, in just the same way as the merchant jacks.

Inelegant but effective. He'd do it!

By now he knew Houghton's intention was to make life as difficult as possible for him so, without doubt, he would spring a new manoeuvre shortly. The most complex and intricate had to be setting the squadron to sail large, the winds from directly astern. At this point of sailing there were no weather tacks and sheets because they'd be on neither a larboard nor a starboard tack but in effect both. By the usual method employed he had no other option but to man both sides of every sail, every hand he could find on the end of a line. In his way of doing it, they'd simply rig a similar purchase on the other side of the sail as well.

But that wasn't the worst of it: each ship, apart from the last in line, would be blanketing the next ahead, stealing her wind. It would make for a nightmare of orders rattling out to deal with the fluky wind currents swirling up the line, and the chances of a collision, through inability to manage speed, were that much greater.

By his method, adjustments could be made far more rapidly

— again not so prettily, viewed from outside, but much more safely.

'Mr Hobbs. A word with you, if I may.'

The master didn't argue, simply saying neutrally, 'This then is frigate fashion, sir?'

'No,' Kydd said shortly. 'As they do it in a merchantman.'

At Hobbs's suggestion, in view of the blanketing effect of their own sails, the mizzen topsail would be handed and the main topsail was put to taking the purchases.

As he'd suspected, within the hour *Hyperion* threw out the signal for the squadron to run large.

It worked immediately. Moving forward to the quarterdeck rail to stand by the men at the purchases, Hobbs could see as well their side wake and their next ahead, and quickly developed a system of hand signals to control their wind-spilling and hauling.

And for the first time in a long while Kydd gave a long, slow smile.

Hardly had the squadron come to moor at the end of the day than 'all captains' was demanded from the flagship.

'A fair day's work,' Houghton said gruffly, 'were it not for the abominable display of attempted station-keeping by one of you.' His pompous and carefully enunciated speech spoke of his having visited his friends not very long before.

'I won't name the ship concerned but you all will have seen her lubberly exhibition of man-hauling her canvas about in an ungainly and grossly unprofessional manner. Such ignorance of elementary fleet manoeuvres has no place in the Rochefort Squadron, I must with pain point out.'

No one caught Kydd's eye. In career terms it was better to fall in with the admiral than stand with Kydd, no matter the justice of the cause.

'As a consequence we shall repeat the manoeuvres tomorrow. I trust I shall see a marked improvement or I shall be compelled to take strong measures in the case of any unable to stay with the squadron in its motions.'

There was little more to discuss. Houghton had had his petty triumphs and the captains left the great cabin, visibly relieved.

Chapter 26

They congregated on *Pembroke*'s quarterdeck while they waited for their boats, chatting amiably about everything except the day's events.

The urbane and polished Devenish of *Malabar* came over to Kydd, the only one of them to do so, and murmured something he couldn't catch, then paused and said more loudly, 'And I'd consider it an honour to entertain the victor of Lissa tonight, Sir Thomas.'

Kydd was still boiling with rage and knew he'd be a poor guest. 'Thank you, no,' he said unsteadily. 'Too much work.'

Devenish looked at him curiously then courteously took his leave when *Thunderer*'s boat was announced.

The pull back was conducted in silence, the boat's crew quailing under Kydd's black expression. When back aboard he strode viciously to his cabin and flopped into his chair. He needed a whisky badly and roared for Luscombe. There was no response and Kydd swore under his breath. Where's that useless galley skulker?' he spluttered. Something would have to be done, no matter the lad was having a hard time settling in.

Then he noticed one of the doors to the stern walk ajar. And on a small table near it a piece of paper. Crossly Kydd got up and retrieved it.

To Captain Sir Thomas Kydd, Bart.

Sir. I am truely sorry for my actions of this day. It is not becuse of you, dear Sir Thomas. It is that i made my own mistak to go on a ship. I haite and lothe the sea and some of the saylers who think it funy to tawnt me so. This is why i leave Thunderer for a beter place. Dont worry of me, wherevr I go will be a happier lyfe for me. I pray, do give my humbal presnts to Lady Kydd and it is my last wish that you shuld prosper and be victorius alwyas.
Josiah Luscombe
Capts servant, HMS Thunderer.

ps — yr breeches for tomorow are wanting a press but are lade out on yr bed.

Kydd froze. If the tormented soul had done away with himself then the blame was largely his for taking on a young-ster rather than a mature man able to care for himself below decks. His heart wrung with pity.

The door opened noiselessly. 'Dear fellow, I thought you were . . .' Craddock tailed off at Kydd's obvious distress. 'Something has happened?'

'Luscombe. He's gone over the side.'

'What?'

'He's drowned himself out of loathing of his situation.' He handed over the paper.

'Not necessarily. By these words he could have equally, um, left for the land in some way,' he finished lamely.

'The stern walk,' Kydd said abruptly and made for the screen door. On the gallery outside he saw a thin rope tied to the rail that led down to the water. 'You see?'

Craddock peered over. 'Ah. Then from this I deduce that, far from doing away with himself, he had the intention and means to flee the ship. A body bent on self-slaughter would plunge without complications into the deep, and here . . .'

Kydd returned to the cabin. 'Pass the word for the purser's steward,' he snapped.

After some minutes he appeared, puzzled and apprehensive.

'Luscombe is absent from place of duty. Do you and your men search for him – and report to me the state of his berth. Whether his clothing is still in his chest and so forth.'

In a short while the man returned to report there was no sign of Luscombe and his shared chest was empty of his gear.

'You see?' Craddock said, relieved. 'No suicide takes a change of clothes and his small valuables in his last plunge. He's headed for the land, sure enough. He's safe, but this makes him a common deserter, does it not?'

'Hold hard, Harry. He didn't have a boat,' Kydd said, with rising feeling.

Hurrying out on the stern walk he looked again and could picture it all happening. The lad had bundled up his clothes and lowered himself over the side. In the water he had struck out for the nearest land, Île de Ré, only a few hundred yards away. It would seem so close, but it was something no seaman would dare to attempt. The young landman had not realised that the island was off the estuary of the tidal Charente river. Fierce offshore currents were at play whenever the tide was on the make or ebb, and ran parallel to the coast, not directly into the shore.

He would panic, not knowing what was happening. The slight chop Kydd remembered from earlier had seemed to Luscombe like the waves of a storm. His bundle of clothes would become waterlogged, a dead weight, and in his terror he would let them go, splashing out in a muscle-sapping frenzy for the passing shoreline. His maniac efforts would rob him of his strength and the cold remorselessly seize him through his outer layers, insidiously penetrating until only a tiny core of warmth remained.

Somewhere out in the inner estuary he had known his last moments on earth.

Kydd gulped then ran through the cabin to the watch-on-deck. 'Man the cutter, hoist "Man overboard", and alert the first lieutenant.'

He ignored the curious glances and forced his mind to concentrate. The tide was on the flood at the time, and *Thunderer* was still at anchor in the same spot. A free-floating object from here would be carried in a giant spiral even further into the seven-mile width of the Pertuis d'Antioche.

'Boat ahoy! Search on a line of bearing sou'-east b' south.'

Roscoe appeared. 'Man overboard, sir?'

'My servant. Fell when priddying the stern walk. I sent away the cutter.'

Roscoe said nothing and fell back, awaiting events with the others.

In the gathering dusk the cutter was soon lost to sight but ominously reappeared some twenty minutes later. Closer to, Kydd's glass picked out a still shape under a tarpaulin. It brought with it a flood of despair that threatened to choke him.

'No, it's nothin' to do with the younker,' Kydd slurred, slapping down his whisky tumbler, annoyed that Craddock was taking it all so calmly. 'I mean, o' course it has, but why I'm s' down on the world is that it's as if his life was wasted in the same w-way as 'most everything else is wasted in this accursed barky.' He took another pull, taking a fierce glee in the fiery path of the liquor down to his belly.

'Thomas, my dear friend. Do allow that I'm no simkin. I've been witness to all your travails, no matter that I can neither appreciate to the full their foolishness nor do anything about it.'

'Damn r-right you don't know the all of it . . . That's t' say, Harry ol' fish, there's much 'twould not be seemly for you t' know.'

'And at the same time I've seen you take full on each stab of malice, every idiocy – and win. I'm persuaded you've only to stay with it to prevail, dear fellow.'

'B-balderdash! In a sail-o'-the-line on blockade there's nothin' to give me hope I'll e-ever be noticed. Kydd o' the *Tyger* is no more. He's faded from the public eye an' will finish a sad figure nobody remembers.' He hiccuped, staring morosely at his glass.

'Of course not!' Craddock came back strongly. 'This is only a short period before you get an admiral's flag, and then—'

'With Houghton riding me all the time?' Kydd sneered. 'He's going to make damn sure I don't get anywhere near a fair report, an' admirals get made b' seniority an' old age, not even a rousing good battle.'

'Dear chap, you can't just—'

'Can't what? I've done main well in the article of prize cobbs, m' name's still known all over the country. Why not take t' my estate an' my most excellen' wife?'

'This is not what I heard before.'

'Well, you're hearing it now,' Kydd growled. 'I don't fancy t' spend the rest of my life witherin' my soul in pleasing that precious bastard, years o' nothing but—' He broke off, taking a long swig, wiping his mouth afterwards. 'Y' see, I don't need the navy any more. I've run m' course an' I'm ready t' cast anchor ashore.' He chortled as if in memory of something. 'Who was it said, "I'll leave the sea an' carry an oar into the land, an' the first man that asks, 'What's that thing you're carrying?' that's where I'll set up hearth an' home"?'

'That would be Odysseus, I think you'll find.'

'Yes. Him.'

It didn't seem to satisfy.

'Why not—'

Kydd's face crumpled. 'I own before you, m' dear friend, this'n is the worst, the lowest as I've ever been. No e-escape! Even my first luff hates me, an' the ship's company, why, they may be f-fine fellows for all I know, but they're not frigate man-o'-war's men, an' if it comes to a mill with the mongseers where'll they be?'

'At your side!'

Kydd seemed not to hear. 'I had m' dreams before, even as a green l'tenant, thinking about what it'd be, right up there as cap'n of a ship-of-the-line. Now I know an' I don't want it any more.'

'Not want the glorious elevation to the god-hood of captain of a battleship?'

'Don't mock me, Harry.'

'I'm not, dear fellow. But simple observation tells me there's still more you can give to your country. Much more and . . .'

But from the armchair there came only snores.

Chapter 27

'Thick and dry for weighing.'

Kydd glowered. His wounded head did nothing for his mental acuity and he cravenly left the unmooring to Roscoe.

'Flagship – "Proceed in order of sailing",' Mayne called.

It was going to be a repeat exercise of before, as threatened by Houghton, and Kydd was faced with the decision of whether to do it the admiral's way or his own. In a wave of desolation he decided to let them do it any way they wanted to. He was finished with the navy.

After an interminable fussing they stood out for the open sea, back past the shoreline of the Île de Ré, young Luscombe's last sight of land.

The island was set out from the land at an angle, one side Pertuis d'Antioche and La Rochelle, the other Pertuis Breton and shelter against Biscay storms from the south-west. Any sail on one side would be hidden from vessels on the other.

The squadron reached the tip of the island in impeccable line – and were met with a shocking sight. A cloud of French ships not a mile distant was emerging from the other side on the same course and same larboard tack.

Kydd's bitter thoughts fled in an instant. He whipped up his pocket telescope, a beautiful three-draw model finished in mahogany and brass that Persephone had given him.

Concentrating on their manoeuvre the British squadron was slower to respond. The French, under the goading of their flagship, soon manoeuvred themselves into line – four ships-of-the-line and two outer frigates, standing out to sea in the freshening breeze.

Kydd didn't wait for Houghton's order. Cutting through the ecstatic jabber on the upper deck, the marine trumpeter and the pipes of the boatswain's mates sounded together the 'Clear for action'.

'Flag to squadron. "Form line-of-battle, west-nor'-west, distance two cables".'

The shuffling and commotion of the two-cable spacing seemed interminable before *Thunderer* could set about going to quarters and Kydd swore roundly. He was immovably locked into position in the line and could do nothing to alter the outcome. In the meantime the French were making good sailing while their opponents were sorting themselves out. They had not opened fire – at near a mile off they were now pulling ahead.

Kydd's mind took on an icy focus. What were the French doing? Most likely they had sheltered in the Pertuis Breton before the last leg to Rochefort past the Île de Ré, and with the short distance to go had neglected to send out a reconnaissance before leaving. It was their bad luck to choose the same time as the British. Or was it?

It was the greatest wish of a French admiral to successfully break out of blockade to the open sea, to stalk the sea lanes or join with others in ports closer to England to overwhelm the forces there and make invasion a reality. Houghton's foolish insistence on meaningless exercises instead of a blockade with patrols in depth had provided their chance. These four battleships – a very respectable force – were now ignoring the invitation to close action of the English forming up in line-of-battle and were on their way to freedom.

By now it was obvious to all on deck what was going on and the exultation and cheering died away, replaced by resentful looks at the ships streaming ahead.

Houghton, no doubt realising with horror that he would be held accountable for the release of these predators on the world, made an urgent signal.

'Sir – "General chase"!' whooped Mayne, as the order came to abandon the formal line-of-battle and make full-tilt for the enemy by any means.

Kydd seized the moment. 'Luff 'n' touch her!' he bawled. The move to windward took him out of the line at the cost of some way lost. But he'd craftily avoided the fate of the others who had all instinctively put their helm over to the easier leeward and now were trying to avoid each other and the balky winds.

The French would not give up their chance just to oblige the English with a general battle. Their intent was to disappear into the limitless wastes of the Atlantic, lose their pursuers and be free to do as they wished. There was little likelihood that they would turn back on their pursuers.

'Mr Hobbs – I want bowlines on the fore and main course and topsails.' These were lines led from forward that, by means of a bridle, stretched the forward edge of the sail to offer the tightest surface for working to windward.

'Sir, I'll do my best for you, but we never use 'em in the squadron. Y' see—'

'I can guess. You go at the speed of the slowest. Then do

what you can.' Kydd paused, then asked, 'How's her trim this morning?'

'Er, by the stern five inches.' It was the sailing master's job when at anchor to take note of the attitude of the ship in water as stores were consumed. Trimmed by the bow, her deeper forefoot would bite higher to the wind at the cost of delay in putting about; trimmed by the stern gave more manoeuvrability but meant pointing less high into the wind.

There were various devices he could put in train in a frigate to bring about a more bows-down trim, from moving guns forward over the deck to re-stowing the hold. But this was a massive ship-of-the-line and needed *all* the tricks he could think of that he'd used in the long years of running down his prey.

Soon *Thunderer* was foaming along, every sinew taut and straining, well out in front of the rest of the squadron. Hour by hour they drew further ahead and were hauling in on the French.

It was decision time for Kydd: join action when within range to delay the Frenchies' escape, with the risk that they could turn on him? Or track and follow them to discover their destination?

Thunderer was showing her mettle. Ropes thrumming with eagerness, sails flat and hard, the elderly battleship was thrusting forward like a cavalry horse in a charge, bursting through the waves on her weather bow. Eruptions of white sent the spray back aft in stinging, exhilarating succession.

At this rate they would be well up with the French before midday – burning powder before the sun reached its height. Kydd felt the age-old excitement build, now with the added zest that he commanded a ship of real force. He paced up and down with an impatience that was difficult to control after the recent heaviness of his heart.

'May I know what you intend, sir?' Roscoe stood by his side. He was wearing his fighting sword, a plain blued-steel weapon with a standard lion-headed pommel.

'What would you do, sir?' Kydd challenged.

'Fall in astern and follow,' he answered, in a level voice, without hesitation.

'And wait while our friends catch up?' Kydd came back ironically, flicking a glance astern. Houghton's squadron would be out of sight below the horizon in another hour.

'You'll offer combat, then.'

'We'll see. Pipe the men to quarters when the enemy's one mile distant and I'll make inspection. I may tell you that there's every reason to suppose we'll suffer grievously if there's an engagement. All attention should be directed to get the ship in the stoutest possible condition.'

'Aye aye, sir.' Was Roscoe showing spirit, animation, even?

At two bells, with the British squadron now completely out of sight, *Thunderer* went to quarters. In *Tyger* they'd appreciated a pre-battle rousing talk but in this ship, with him days only as her captain, it would be received in suspicion and possibly with contempt. Besides, it wasn't at all certain that there would be a battle, for what could be achieved? On her own *Thunderer* could inflict some damage to one or two ships of the enemy but the rest would plunge scornfully on, the prize of the open sea too alluring.

An hour later, as *Thunderer* closed from astern on the close-knit group of enemy ships the decision was taken out of his hands.

A string of flags mounted the signal halliards of the foremost, larger vessel. Taking Kydd by surprise it was answered by the rearmost two ships-of-the-line, which fell away from their close-hauled line and continued to turn in a wide arc, effectively splitting the line into two. The first continued their dash to seaward but the others were making as if to go after the now disappeared British ships.

What was happening? There was no meaning in the action and Kydd felt the first stirrings of foreboding.

There was not long to wait for the rear two were continuing around in what amounted to a circle and soon they would be as firmly in Kydd's rear as he was with the first division ahead.

Neatly done!

Thunderer was now in the jaws of a professionally sprung trap with no way out.

Kydd forced his mind to an icy calm. The logical thing now was for the foremost French to throw over their helm together to present their starboard broadsides and begin the execution. After their cannonade the rear division would lay out to smash their larboard broadside into *Thunderer*'s unprotected stern, as the first reloaded to continue the pounding.

But Kydd was about to do the unexpected: take the extraordinary risk of putting about to the starboard tack and away in the opposite direction. This was their only chance.

With a crew barely understanding his frigate-fashion methods he had to loose his own broadside. Then force the men in the smoke to abandon their guns and take to the lines to put the ship about while under cruel fire. Something he'd hesitate to do even with the Tygers. At four to one the odds were ridiculous but if this worked . . .

Kydd sent midshipman messengers racing down the deck to the guns with his orders and the strictest instructions for speed when the time came.

The French rear division had nearly completed their circle. Ahead, the first two threw over the wheel and began to heel as they fell off before the wind, in the process bringing their broadside to bear.

Getting in first, Kydd threw *Thunderer* up into the wind and, true to her name, she slammed out a full starboard broadside, the first time he had heard his ship shout in anger. Instantly he roared, 'Hands to 'bout ship!'

Pale-faced seamen leaped to obey the routine orders as the big ship began to turn, so incongruous in the bedlam of combat.

The smoke from *Thunderer*'s two decks of guns was tremendous, towering down on the first two preparing to open up with their own broadside. The barely trained conscript crew was near blinded of their target and their shot went wild, but *Thunderer*'s guns, crashing out their tons' weight of roundshot, lent their assistance to propel her around in the act of putting about.

When the rear division finished their circle they found the previously flying *Thunderer* stopped across their path, daring a collision. Their only recourse was to keep helm on to take them around again, but their guns were manned on the wrong side. Before the crews could cross the deck, Kydd loosed his own larboard broadside into the helplessly careering vessel.

It was breathtaking, only minutes from a doomed encounter to taking up on the new tack and putting distance between them.

A storm of cheering erupted in *Thunderer*, hoarse and unbelieving – but it was not over yet. The quandary still remained: to follow or delay? It was critical for Houghton to put an end to the foray. If Kydd wore around to resume position, without question the French commander would envelop him with his superior numbers.

Out of nothing came a glorious, battle-winning thought. 'Mr Mayne,' Kydd growled.

The signals lieutenant hurried up. 'Make – "Request shore provisions include treacle for thirty men".'

'S-sir?'

'Instantly – at the main, and with the priority pennant.'

'B-but—'

'Now!' Kydd said dangerously.

Thunderer threw out her urgent signal, followed by another at the mizzen – 'Permission for hands to bathe'. There were more but *Thunderer* was now shaping course to sail ahead of the French as they regrouped.

The dilemma had passed from Kydd to the French admiral. Could the whole thing, the absurdly handled main squadron and the remarkably speedy 74, be a larger trap to lure them seaward, to be set upon front and rear by a pair of squadrons acting together, as urgently summoned at that moment by this daring ship?

Napoleon Bonaparte would never forgive the admiral who gave the Royal Navy yet another victory, and that risk was not worth taking simply for a taste of freedom. Without further delay the French hauled their wind and scuttled back in the direction of Rochefort, leaving HMS *Thunderer* victor of the field.

Chapter 28

Aboard Pembroke

'A near thing indeed, sir,' Devenish of *Malabar* said, with feeling. The admiral looked up with an ill-natured frown but Devenish went on strongly, 'As deserves our approbation and respect of Captain Kydd's action, I believe.'

'Rubbish,' growled Houghton. 'It's nonsense to believe four sail-of-the-line would in any wise take flight before a single. Without doubt the enemy saw our advance as the main force and decided on a retreat rather than risk an engagement.'

'But, still, when Sir Thomas—'

'Sir. Know that I take Captain Kydd's action as impulsive and ill-considered, not as befitting the command of a ship-of-the-line, more that of a buccaneer.'

Around the table the senior captains stiffened. They were not fooled by this bluster, and its public airing was in bad taste.

Kydd said nothing. He knew what had been achieved.

The transformation in his ship's company was almost palpable, and to hear the happy buzz from the mess-deck at grog and later the gleeful singing on the fore-deck told of a much different relationship developing. Roscoe had not shared in it, though, keeping out of Kydd's way and excusing himself from the evening's celebratory dinner.

'However, we're not here to debate a brush with the enemy, albeit well intentioned,' Houghton continued. 'It is to take note of a change of my plan for the blockade of Rochefort. Given that the French are daring to sortie in numbers, we shall no longer act as an offshore fleet in deterrent. We will disperse our effort among all their ports, patrols in depth to ensure it cannot happen again.'

His impressive tone did nothing to spark enthusiasm and he continued in evident pique. 'The following ports will be invested by one 74 and attendant sloop. La Rochelle, Rochefort, Bordeaux and Les Sables d'Olonne by *Resolution*, *Malabar*, *Asia* and *Thunderer* respectively. Your orders will detail how the squadron will gather and form line in the event a species of sortie is reported from any one of the above. Questions?'

It was only what was normally done at other blockaded ports and the region was quiet, no longer the powerful naval base it had once been. And the recent break-out attempt had been an unplanned, impromptu sally but it had alarmed Houghton enough to have his futile exercising dropped for the more usual and effective method.

No one had questions, and even if they had, they would not have been answered so they left for their ships.

Kydd knew the area well. With Cochrane he'd been with fireships at the battle of Basque Roads some years ago and remembered the shoals, currents and island forts that infested the coastline. He couldn't put a reason to why his port – Les Sables d'Olonne – was to be noticed. A medieval dried-fish port, tidal and cramped, it was never going to be the lair for a powerful battle squadron. Was this a move by Houghton to keep him from gaining any kind of win?

At least he was, for the moment, independent, and he had the quaint but reliable brig-sloop *Daphne* as his gun-dog to sniff out the game close inshore.

They headed north together, the sloop demurely in *Thunderer*'s wake, until towards evening they made out the low sandy coast of the Vendée and the sheltering headland of La Chaume.

Innocently continuing, Kydd waited until they'd passed out of sight from the shore, then hove to, signalling *Daphne* for a conference.

'Hoskyns, commander.'

The man was elderly but in keeping with his no-doubt foreign-built sloop had character and dignity.

'Welcome to the coast, Commander,' Kydd said easily, aware from his own experiences in the past that his exalted station and decorations might be intimidating.

The older man kept his composure. 'Ah, well, as I've been here nigh on four years, sir.'

'Then you're just the man I need. Our orders are to patrol and invest Les Sables d'Olonne.'

'Sir – why? It's rare good for stockfish and it has an inner harbour, but . . .'

'That these are our orders is all the reason both you and I will get. First I must have a reconnaissance. Is there anything of consequence within? It may be Admiral Houghton has intelligence that he's unwilling to share and inside there's a vessel of significance. The game is all yours, Mr Hoskyns. You have until this time tomorrow to take a peek.' It would be his decision whether to make it by day or night.

Even if he was on detached service, if this was going to

158

be the pattern for the weeks and months that followed it would be a tedious endurance, in effect like the Brest blockade, which had its inshore and offshore divisions with all the excitement belonging to the former. At least he was granted time to get his ship in order.

Daphne returned in due course, her commander somewhat downcast. 'In fine, nothing, Sir Thomas. And fired on for my pains by the heaviest metal they could offer.'

'Nothing?'

'A midshipman with a glass at the main-mast truck saw not a sign of anything three-masted within.' No sail beyond a brig or lugger.

'Then I've no alternative but to send you back, this time on patrol. La Chaume to Pointe de Tanchette until relieved. *Thunderer* will be in the offing at all times. Let me know should you spy anything interesting.'

'Sir. Oh, I did take note o' the guns, where they're sited an' such.' Diffidently, he handed over a folded piece of paper. It was a neatly executed plan of the small bay of d'Olonne with careful notations of the batteries and estimated size of the pieces, with their fields of fire.

'Thank you, Mr Hoskyns. Well spotted, and you're a caution to us all.'

Chapter 29

The sloop leaned to the wind and was away, Kydd shading his eyes as he watched her go. In many ways these were the real heroes of blockade, not the lumbering line-of-battle ships, he reflected. Taking all the dangerous inshore work among the fringing reefs in brutish conditions of endless heaving seas and gales, prey for the men-o'-war that lurked safe in harbour, their endurance and skills were never going to be recognised by the public. Nor would they at any time be crowned with distinction.

Thunderer turned about for a three-mile run north, there to take up her night position. In the morning, under easy sail, she would put about and run down the coast for twelve miles before going about for the return, her passage in accordance with the table of rendezvous drawn up by the sailing master and given to *Daphne*.

The evening breeze was chilly and he went back to his cabin to call for a hot negus and warm togs, then remembered that he didn't have a manservant and therefore neither would supper be waiting. It would have to be the old marine of before and reluctantly he sent for Hare, captain of marines, to require him back. He picked up a copy of the *Gentleman's Magazine* but its earnest articles and long-winded opinion pieces didn't suit his mood and he laid it down.

A small procession arrived: the purser's steward, the marine and Craddock, each bearing some morsel for his supper.

'Harry, old fellow! How thoughtful.'

Kydd opened the wine and they settled back companionably.

The cabin with its discreet sconce lights and Persephone's feminine touches was turning into a snug retreat. But the thought of what was looking more and more likely, the prospect of years of inaction and an undistinguished conclusion to his career, nagged at him.

His dark mood returned.

The morning was equally depressing. Night had turned to a grey, cheerless day, chill and wet with a clamping mist. The wind had backed northerly with a sulky lop to the seas. Kydd knew that this was probably the beginning of a period of dispiriting weather but without the vicious squalls common to these parts.

Hands stood down from their customary dawn quarters but Kydd delayed going to his cabin: there'd probably be no breakfast waiting for him and Craddock was unavailable. The sodden atmosphere of mist and rain was beginning slowly to lift, the leaden curtain receding grudgingly.

He went below and his mind turned to the bad feeling that had developed between the marine, the purser's steward and the nameless cadre of servants, stewards and idlers who had made Luscombe's existence so unbearable. There was little he could do about it.

Disbelieving shouts came from the upper deck, joined by others. Kydd didn't need telling what it was. He raced on deck to see sailors excitedly pointing to starboard at the edge of the wall of mist.

'Oh, sir, I was going to call you, but I wasn't sure.' Briggs was uncharacteristically nervous.

A glimpsed grey shape had appeared shrouded in the mizzle long enough to catch the eye of a lookout. It had three masts, was headed south and as quickly had disappeared.

'We'll go to quarters, Mr Briggs,' Kydd said crisply. 'Let the first lieutenant know – and without drum or trumpet.' If there was something there, no need to announce themselves.

With Britain's command of the sea it was more than likely to be friendly, especially this far out, when the fearful French always clung to the land to move coastwise. Nevertheless, there was no harm in preparing, and it made a good exercise for the ship's company.

Thunderer was closed up well before the white curtains of drizzle finally lifted and a French corvette firmed out of a ghostly silhouette. It sighted them at the same time, not a mile to starboard, shocked, no doubt, to see a British ship-of-the-line appearing, like a nightmare, so close. Within moments, its helm went over, whether to hide in the fast-vanishing grey-white murk or reach for the embrace of the land was not clear.

An exultant roar came from every quarter of the ship. This was surely fitting meat for their Tom Cutlass!

Inconveniently, *Thunderer* was close-hauled to the north and the stranger was going with the wind to the south. Kydd gave the order to wear around and fall in astern of the chase. But the winds were not only in the wrong direction, they were light and fitful. Their sails hung limply wet and disconsolate, and *Thunderer*'s wear about was anything but swift and masterly. In the time it took to reverse course the corvette forged ahead, the gentle winds suiting its finer lines and lighter build.

Cursing under his breath, Kydd knew all eyes were on him to pull something from the same bag of tricks that had earlier seen them leave the squadron behind.

Why was the corvette so far to seaward? Was it making its way to the south by passing outside the blockade cruisers clustered around the ports? By its new course to the east-south-east it was almost certainly going to the nearest sanctuary port – under the guns of Les Sables d'Olonne.

They had to lay it by the tail before it reached its destination: thirty-six-pounders were mounted ashore, which greatly outgunned even a ship-of-the-line. But at this rate they weren't going to overhaul the corvette. It was no use spreading stunsails and the like, for in the fluky breeze the additional speed would be minuscule. Their only hope was for a change in the weather and even then it would chancy.

If they fell in with *Daphne* Kydd could send the smaller sloop to throw herself across the path of the corvette to delay it until he could deal with it but he couldn't find it in him to order such a sacrifice.

Arriving off the small port they found the corvette methodically settling to two anchors off the broad beach. At *Thunderer*'s appearance guns opened up from the shore. The heavy round-shot smashed out, skipping each side of the Frenchman in a show of spite and demonstration that any move against their visitor would be met with a righteous fury.

The corvette was safe and Kydd had to think again. As he considered the options, one thing became clear: he couldn't let it go. For the sake of British shipping at sea on the coast, this dangerous predator must be put down. The victuallers, powder hoys, dispatch cutters, lesser craft, even *Daphne* herself were menaced.

Also, if he left it in peace he would be handing Houghton

a perfect excuse to accuse him of lack of martial spirit, afraid to send his ship-of-the-line even against a paltry corvette. What could he do? Take *Thunderer* in and blow the corvette to flinders? In these light airs she would probably take hours in the approach and by that time would suffer unmercifully from the shore guns, the spoils not worth the bloodshed.

If they waited offshore until a brisk wind blew up, then stormed in under full sail, that would reduce the time exposed to the batteries to an acceptable level. Even if they spent days waiting, were they not ordered to clamp a hold on this very port?

As if on cue, *Daphne* came in sight from the south and together they retired out to sea to plot the future.

'Begging your pardon, Sir Thomas, but it won't do.'

'Mr Hoskyns?' Kydd said in surprise, not used to having his plans dismissed in a manner so out of hand.

'He's only waiting for the tide as will take him through the channel by warp and capstan to the inner harbour.'

'When's high water?'

'Just missed it, sir. I think he'll want to move in at some point tomorrow morning.'

That would give the corvette complete security where it could wait for months, if necessary, and at the first opportunity resume its voyage of destruction.

Chapter 30

Kydd's duty was to clear the seas of these vermin and throttle all movement in and out of his designated blockade port. He was doing that by his presence but every fibre in his being cried out to do something active, a daring frigate-style stroke that would settle it once and for all.

In a ship-of-the-line? With this blashy weather slowing them to a crawl before the massed guns ashore?

The corvette was safe and they knew it. There was no doubt of the eventual outcome: an increasing number of boats were leisurely making their way to shore and into the channel. The colourful coats of officers could be seen plainly, doubtless to set up for a long stay at the town's expense.

Kydd had not much more than hours to make a decision. A cutting-out expedition? As soon as the thought came he dismissed it. Any attempt would be at night, but a half-competent captain would have a welcome of flares and pitiless illumination ready that would give the gunners ashore unmissable targets.

If not a strike by boats, then what? There was no answer

and Kydd stared gloomily into space under the sympathetic gaze of the sloop commander.

In a sudden flash of inspiration he snatched the paper out of his pocket that the officer had so carefully made of the battery sitings. Yes!

'Mr Hoskyns, how reliable are your observations here?' he said urgently.

'Sir. I was with Captain Hurd in the survey of Brest Roads.'

Hurd was the near mythical surveyor of the most challenging coastline to be found anywhere, later hydrographer to the Admiralty.

Kydd thought furiously. 'Commander – I do believe you've just solved our little problem.'

The four boats lay off under oars in the outer darkness, thankful that the moon had not yet risen and the blackness was near complete. On shore the lights of the town twinkled along the seafront, providing an impeccable navigational aid. At one place they were blotted out by the silhouette of the corvette, an even better fix.

They couldn't make a move yet. Hidden somewhere in the black of night, a French row-guard waited to give warning of any hostile approach. They could be anywhere but they'd have to keep within hail of the ship, a hundred yards off or so at most. Meanwhile their duty was to stay quiet and out of sight.

The boats were in two pairs, one to board at the bows, the other at the main-chains, the second of the pair to stand off and fire at the defenders as the first scrambled up. Who should command the assault had been a hard decision. By rights the first lieutenant had claim to the honour but Kydd couldn't allow it. He still had his doubts about Roscoe and especially his qualities of leadership and courage under the most severe conditions of all: mortal combat.

Roscoe had made his demand to lead in the most strenuous terms but Kydd bluntly pointed out that it was not only *his* plan but, without proof of battle reliability on all sides, he must take the responsibility for and leadership of the expedition. Only after Roscoe's near-begging pleas did Kydd realise there was more to it than simple honour and agreed they would share the charge. He would take the main-chains thrust while Roscoe would go over the bows.

In the boats, men crouched, faces and weapons blackened, each one a warrior as attested by his divisional officer. They engaged in the usual pre-combat banter in low whispers. Mayne was beside Kydd on the stern sheets of the long-boat, silent and rigid. The tension was snapping: there was no hiding the fact that in a short time each would be facing the enemy in a fight to the death.

The waiting was hard. Kydd had had his share of desperate occasions but he felt for the younger seamen who'd never had the chance to match themselves against a foe in this way.

'Sir!' hissed Mayne, his voice a croak. 'Beyond the point – to starboard.'

The lights in a farmstead blinked out then on again. A shadowy presence was moving about close inshore.

Kydd tensed. A gun-flash leaped out in the blackness, the heavy concussion carrying clearly in the night air.

It was *Daphne*, right on time. More savage gunfire erupted, with no response from the shore. She was using the night-time offshore breeze to slash past between the corvette and the beach, firing on the batteries as she went. With no lights showing from the land she was near invisible against the blackness out to sea.

'Ship oars – give way together,' Kydd rasped, 'and stretch out for your lives!'

The sloop was nearing the corvette, now firing furiously on both sides at the shore and enemy ship together.

All hostile eyes were on the sudden irruption – what did it mean? That the batteries were being pounded to give the ship-of-the-line a clear run against the corvette in the morning? Or was it a direct strike against the anchored ship itself? But if the shore batteries turned their guns on *Daphne* they'd lose their carefully sighted-in aiming set up by daylight and be much less of a threat to the boats.

The Thunderers had a chance – the corvette's guard boats would race back to join the defence and their approach would be discovered that much later.

As they neared, the men were beginning to pant and tire, even as they put everything into their strokes. Kydd knew this was because they were out of condition for such extremity of effort. Would they be exhausted at the supreme moment when they must clamber up on deck and face a waiting enemy?

Roscoe would be out there with the same doubts and fears. How would he respond? There was no way of knowing. They would both be on their own as they swarmed aboard, but if he failed, Kydd's party at the other end of the ship would be overwhelmed. Now was not the time for corrosive doubts.

Then the tables were comprehensively turned. The corvette was barely a quarter-mile distant when all along its seaward length flickers of flame appeared, quickly flaring from a suspended incendiary carcass that illuminated the sea for hundreds of yards around.

They'd been discovered and could expect prompt attention from the shore guns.

'Forrard there!' Kydd threw at the midshipman in the foresheets, an indistinct shape in the darkness. Would his other trick answer?

A splutter of sparks and a small lanthorn took life. Enough to read the eight-inch boat compass the youngster held.

'Le Remblai,' Kydd called impatiently.

A quick squint at a paper, then the compass and a young voice piped up, 'Starb'd!'

A boat under oars was an agile creature and quickly laid over to the right, the midshipman industriously noting the angle. 'Well!' he rapped.

The boat resumed its onward rush towards the corvette. Ashore, the sweating gunners slewing their cannon around saw the boat merge with the line of bearing of the corvette. The painstaking observations of *Daphne* were now paying off handsomely. Knowing the exact location of the batteries ashore, Kydd could make his deadly approach along that line of bearing with the target itself in the line of their fire.

Now also rudely illuminated by the carcass, level with them, and using the same trick, was Roscoe's launch. A standing figure in plain sight aft was wildly urging the boat's crew on, aimed unerringly for the beakhead.

As Kydd had guessed, the French officers heading ashore had left the corvette weakly led. No one was there to urge the gunners firing on *Daphne* to cross the deck to attend to the far deadlier threat.

The Thunderers closed in, past the point where the guns ashore could intervene, nearer still. A thin sputter of musketry played fitfully along the line of deck, a waste of powder and shot, given the blackness of the outer gloom.

The carcass flared and sparked, then died to a glow and Kydd's heart leaped. They had a chance!

Cast now in shadows, the seaward side of the corvette,

close to, towered up. The midshipman, at the risk of his life, had tied the lanthorn with its shutters wide open high up the long-boat's mast. In its light the boat thumped into the ship's side below the main-chains. Conscious of the cutter taking position behind them and peering up at the dark figures along the deck-line, Kydd thrust his way towards the bow. When it came within reach he leaped for the little platform that was the chains with its profusion of handholds. He paused, allowing another two seamen to vault up beside him – and for the marines in the cutter to realise what was wanted: ferocious fire upwards, a roar of English cheering, a bedlam of confusion!

Kydd reached for the lower shrouds, then wrenched himself upwards and around the lanyards to land on the enemy deck, his hand scrabbling for his cutlass, grateful for the fighting lanterns the French had provided.

A pike-head stabbed murderously at his face but he was ready and ducked. Grabbing the crude spike, he lunged forward to allow his blade to do its lethal work.

There was a concerted rush towards him but he let his cutlass drop and yanked out his pistols, thrusting them into the faces of his attackers and firing. One flopped down without a sound, the other clutched at his face, falling to his knees, blood spurting between his fingers.

'Thunderers with me!' he roared. With a frantic cheer others crowded on to the deck to stand by him, faced by a wavering line of defenders. This was the climax and finality of the boarding: if they were repulsed it was all over but if the French broke . . .

'At 'em!' he bawled, brandishing his bloodied cutlass and hurling himself forward.

He was not betrayed: in an ear-splitting screech every

man-jack of the boarders threw themselves after him – and the French broke and ran.

'Avast there, the boarders. With me – lay aft!' To the quarterdeck. To haul down the flag. At night the colours could not be seen but the significance of taking control of their display was undeniable.

He raced aft to the diminutive poop deck. By the halliards in the light of a rising moon was a bull of a man, clearly ready to sell his life in defence of his country's flag.

'*À bas le pavillon!*' Kydd bellowed.

The matelot replied immediately with a snarl and flourish at Kydd's face with a heavy, old-fashioned hanger.

It was pathetically noble. The man could be cut down in an instant by a boarding pistol and there was no shame in yielding to a superior enemy, but this fierce-eyed sea-dog was going down fighting.

Kydd gestured to his boarders to lower their weapons. There was no response, the man turned this way and that, threatening, taunting.

'*Laisse tomber ton arme, mon brave,*' Kydd said quietly, which provoked a torrent of execration.

'Drop him, sir?' The Royal Marine corporal with a musket made ready.

'No.' Kydd hadn't the heart to cease the existence of the brave man.

'Jimmy Rounds, sir?' The lower deck 'translation' of *je me rendre* – I surrender.

'Er, not until . . .' Kydd couldn't finish.

'Royal Marines – present!' A dozen muskets rose to settle on the man's breast. Fearlessly he tore open his jacket.

'Hold!' Kydd ordered.

'Go the bastard!' The corporal threw aside his musket and

flung himself bodily at the man, quickly followed by others, pinioning him with the weight of numbers.

Then Roscoe appeared out of the dark, with the rest of the boarders from forward, his sword not yet sheathed and visibly bloodied. He gave a bleak smile. 'You have the ship, sir. And my congratulations upon it.'

Chapter 31

In the wan morning light the three made a satisfying picture. A sleek line-of-battle ship at anchor dwarfing the brig-sloop and the trim corvette that lay between them, not one scarred by war but preparing to set sail in triumph for the squadron and its admiral. Houghton might grind his teeth in frustration but Kydd had shown what a ship-of-the-line under a frigate captain could achieve.

Thunderer was a different vessel. Men swaggered about, now having a tale to tell of desperate doings the next time they were ashore and in company with men of the fleet. How Fighting Tom Cutlass himself had led them in to snatch a live corvette from under the guns of the mongseers without so much as a by-your-leave.

Kydd sat back, musing, as he paused in his dispatch. The men had more than earned his respect, crowding behind him as he hurled himself aboard, fighting like demons but showing mercy where it was deserved. Roscoe had acted in the best traditions of the service, leading his men to victory over the voluted beakhead in the darkness and he now had no doubts about his professional fitness to be his second.

Were it not for the first lieutenant's moody antagonism he would be happy to have him remain in the post. Even so, he wouldn't let this affect the natural justice of what he was saying. He wrote on.

> . . . he at all times manifested that zeal which is so indispensable in the character of a British officer and—

A firm double knock interrupted him.

'Come.'

Roscoe stood on the threshold for a moment, as if reluctant to enter. Face set, he collected himself and approached Kydd at his desk. 'Might we talk, sir?'

'By all means,' Kydd said, sensing a moment had come. When Roscoe had returned on board he'd gone straight to his cabin, which he'd put down to the man's reaction after the one-to-one savagery and bloodshed.

'Sir, I desire to express my regret – my repentance, for my attitude towards you since you took command.' The voice was unnaturally low and constrained.

'Oh?'

'There was a reason, a compelling excuse, if you will, for it.'

'Go on.'

'My family . . . is related to Viscount Carlisle.'

'Yes?' It meant nothing to Kydd.

'Who, some small years ago, we heard was cruelly deprived of the object of his affections by one who deployed despicable means involving the Prince of Wales to gain an ascendancy over her. The name mentioned . . . was yours, Sir Thomas.'

'Charles Pountney.'

'As was before his elevation. You will conceive my feelings then, sir, to be confronted by that very one as our new captain who had achieved his command by the same method, at the cost of a fine man's career and the advancement prospects of all aboard.'

'Mr Roscoe, I've told you before that—'

'Sir. This is to allow before you that my views are changed. These past few days I've been privileged to see not only a master seaman at his craft, but a fighting sailor and true-blooded hero. This has been enough to persuade me that your promotion into *Thunderer* was well considered and entirely upon merit. I cannot believe there are any other reasons for it.'

'Ah, thank you, Mr Roscoe.'

'Therefore I'm obliged to suppose that those who hold otherwise can only be impelled by motives of a more sinister cast.'

'Um, possibly.'

The stiffness fell away and an unexpectedly shy, warm smile spread. 'Which obliges me to say as well that I must acknowledge that Miss Lockwood ended with the right man, Sir Thomas.'

Kydd felt a blush rising.

'Sir, I would that we could reset the clocks and begin our association anew. Would you . . .?'

He held out his hand hesitantly and Kydd hurried around the desk to grasp it in both of his. 'Dear fellow, you had good enough reasons. Consider it so!'

'Oh, and I may have omitted to mention, sir. The wardroom in its collective wisdom have reflected and do conclude that Mr Craddock would indeed prove a worthy and interesting messmate and, for the usual subscription, do invite him to join them.'

'He would be delighted, I'm sure.'

'Just so. Then I must on deck. We've the corvette to fettle for her voyage of prize. Her name's *Volage*, by the way.'

'Do carry on, Mr Roscoe.'

He turned to go, then remembered something. 'Oh, and there's one of the prisoners insisting to see you. A most importunate fellow, making a nuisance of himself and not saying why. Do you wish to indulge him?'

'Send him. It may be important intelligence. And shall we take a brimmer together before supper?'

'I'd like that, sir.'

After Roscoe left, Kydd settled in a chair to marvel at the turn of events. He'd had the feeling that, for an intelligent man like Roscoe, there had to be a deeper reason for his hostility. And now he knew, and there would be a cheerful postscript in his ongoing letter to Persephone.

But before he could begin, a curious Craddock made his appearance. 'Did I see what I saw?' he said, in something like awe. 'Your Mr Roscoe, and he—'

'You did, Harry. And you'll never fathom why.'

Detailed explanations were made and Craddock shook his head in amazement.

'So as of now you're a wardroom-mess member, old fellow. Felicitations on your translation.'

With a knock at the door Briggs looked in apologetically. 'You asked to see the prisoner, sir.'

Raised voices outside tailed off and a slender individual with a sensitive face was escorted in, manacled.

'Won't tell his name or business with you, sir.'

'Very well. Escorts to leave us – and does he really need the irons?'

'Master-at-arms insists on it, sir.'

'Remove them.' Kydd resumed his place at the desk and waited until the man stood free.

'You have some information for me, perhaps?' he prompted.

'You are ze *capitaine de vaisseau*?' he said quietly, in a peculiarly well-modulated tone, the English not at all native.

'I am he,' Kydd said, 'Captain Sir Thomas Kydd.'

'Then I 'ave something to offer you, *mon capitaine*, as will be of much advantage to us both.'

'Carry on.'

'Not wiz zis gentleman. It is private, *n'est-ce pas*?'

Craddock got up to leave but Kydd motioned him down. 'This is my confidential secretary. He will stay to listen to you, sir.'

The man hesitated, glancing once at Craddock then resumed: 'Ees it to occur that I will be *prisonnier de guerre* – ze prisoner of war?'

The man's refined nature was unlike that of any French *matelot* Kydd could bring to mind. 'Your ship was fairly captured. The laws of war must take their course.'

'So I shall be sent to *les pontons*, you say, er, ze hulks.'

'It would seem so. I'm sorry.'

The man's well-kept hands twitched spasmodically. 'Sir. Then I make offer. On board of ze *Volage* I was ze *maître de navire* to Capitaine Delvaille. If you will spare me ze hulks I vill glory to be the same for you, sir.'

'*Maître de navire* – sailing master?' Kydd hazarded.

He looked pained. 'No, sir. You know ze *maître d'hôtel*? Well, *maître de navire* for ze ship. I take care for you in all things.'

'I already have a manservant,' Kydd said abruptly.

'Before ze revolution my family serve an English wine merchant in Bordeaux. We keep ze standards of the *ancien régime*, very 'appy together. I know your English ways an' for your distinguished banquet I can make a gran' affair.'

'I'm sure you could. But a Frenchman aboard an English ship, that's another matter. How can I know you are not an agent of the state, a saboteur who will take any opportunity to harm the ship?'

'In Bordeaux we 'ate Napoleon, we 'ate ze Revolution. It bring us nothin' but ruin and *dépourvu*, um, the bankrupt. We long for zis miserable war to end, the British to come back to their wine houses, an' the good times, they return.'

If this man was who he said he was, a professional in the duties of service, then Kydd would be prepared to take him on even if it meant posting a sentry to follow him every hour of the day.

Craddock leaned forward to speak. 'Dear fellow, may I make contribution?'

'Do so, please.'

'M'sieur, I have done business in your fair town in the old days,' Craddock opened easily. 'I'd be interested to know the name of your English employer. I may remember him.'

'Sir, it was Monseiur Frank Douglas. At La Maison Bleu. His château, of course, in Mérignac, a very fine—'

'The colour of Madame's hair?'

'Ah, I cannot know. She die before I come. Monsieur take comfort with Madame Arnaud. Her hair change all the time but if you want . . .'

Craddock glanced at Kydd and gave a slow nod.

'Then what is your family name, if you please?'

'Sir, ze secret police are everywhere in Bordeaux. If I am discovered to serve an English, zen my family, they will be arrest.'

'This is not a problem,' Kydd said briskly. 'In the Royal Navy we have the custom that those who volunteer, but don't want their name known, are given instead a "purser's name" for the ship's books. No one will ever learn you've been on an English ship.'

In something near a whisper the Frenchman told Craddock his name. Craddock gave a satisfied smile. 'Captain, the name is honourable and has given long service to the English community. If he were known to have betrayed us he would bring shame and disgrace on his family. I believe you may trust him.'

In a gleeful rush of hope Kydd pretended to consider. That he'd already performed duty in the corvette meant that he was no stranger to sea service and needed no coddling. His distinguished bearing would go far in insulating him against the petty vanities of the lower orders aboard – there was no reason he couldn't make a start. Why not at once?

'Very well. A purser's name for our latest volunteer, Mr Craddock?'

It penetrated that the tide had turned in his favour and the man struggled to keep his features composed.

'Er, perhaps Binard? René Binard? An ancient and well-known name in the Vendée, I believe.'

'So how do you like that, M'sieur, er, Binard?'

'*Merci, merci, mille fois merci, mon seigneur!*'

'Then to the details. Mr Craddock here will instruct you in your duties, which will begin immediately. Have you any questions?'

'None, m'lord. Oh – an' when will I meet my staff?'

'Staff?' Kydd asked in astonishment.

'Your pastry chef, *coiffeur, valet de chambre? Les domestiques?*'

'Mr Craddock. Do ensure M'sieur Binard makes acquaintance with the ship's boys and, for now, the officers' cook, who will be told that he might well learn much if he takes on board M'sieur Binard's wise advice.'

After they'd left he resumed his musings in his armchair,

trying to get over his astonishment at the change of fortune that had seen him plucked from the depths of misery to the heights of felicity. Service in a ship-of-the-line from this time forward might well be very different.

Chapter 32

The House of Commons, London

'Order! Order! The witness will be heard,' Speaker Babington bellowed, above the raucous catcalls that filled the hallowed chamber.

The hearing was not proceeding well, the fractious displays of temper doing little to clarify the issue. Yet it was one of the utmost importance: an examination into the effects of the Orders-in-Council that had set the Royal Navy into wholesale blockade of the Continent and Bonaparte into inflicting his Continental System in retaliation.

'I call Robert Hamilton.' The eminent barrister James Stephen, who had famously steered through the anti-slave-trade bill, waited patiently for the uproar to subside to begin his cross-examination.

'Order! I will have order in the house!' Babington repeated, but a cry rang out abruptly from the back-benches, demanding why the prime minister was not in attendance to justify the Orders-in-Council that he himself had authored.

It was an extraordinary request but these were extraordinary times. After a whispered discussion it was decided that a messenger would be sent to Downing Street desiring the presence of the honourable Mr Spencer Perceval at the hearing.

In the crowded lobby the news was received with resignation. Many had congregated outside the chamber in these frenetic times and Peregrine Fookes MP, as a master lobbyist, was used to it.

'You'll know there'll be no answer today, old man,' he replied, an irate Lancashire ironmaster.

The messenger pushed through urgently and disappeared into the evening throng outside.

'His Nibs will be along shortly, you'll find,' Fookes muttered, to a colleague.

A tall figure in brown and yellow appeared at his elbow, his hair dark and curly, his serene blue eyes seeming never to rest on anyone in particular. It was the fellow who'd asked him earlier that day to point out Perceval for him. 'Sir, is it that the prime minister will be coming?'

'Er, yes, Mr, um, Bellingham. He'll have to come through here and you'll get a good view of the fellow, don't worry.'

The man's hand strayed inside his coat as though to scratch at a flea. Fookes shuddered and looked away. Bellingham had some sort of grievance following a failed business venture in Archangel, Russia, of all places, but he'd get no satisfaction from Perceval, who was only holding together the finances of the realm with prodigies of invention.

The ironmaster was having no nonsense, though. There had to be a reckoning – these Orders-in-Council of blockade might be the sharpest blade in the armoury but they cut both ways: there was real hardship in the industrial north, with unsold goods lying about and workers laid off to the mercies of parish relief.

There were raised voices outside. At the door a short, plain-looking gentleman came into view, a distracted frown on his pale, boyish features. His appearance was so nondescript and private that those not knowing him would have been forgiven for failing to recognise the revered yet notorious Spencer Perceval, prime minister and chancellor of the exchequer of the kingdom of Great Britain and Ireland.

The press of lobbyists fell back respectfully to make a lane.

'He's in a hurry, old fellow. You'd be better off catching him as he leaves,' Fookes murmured, annoyed that Bellingham had stepped out to intercept him.

'Are you the prime minister?' he asked calmly.

'I am, but do let me pass, sir. I'm in haste to be done.'

Bellingham pulled his hand from the coat's breast pocket and came out with a short, ugly pistol, which he thrust hard against Perceval's chest and pulled the trigger. There was a sharp flash and blast and Perceval recoiled with a strangled gasp. He dropped to the floor, blood gouting. In a spasm of agony he cried out, then lay still.

Pandemonium erupted. Fookes and others hurried to the fallen man, the sightless eyes paralysing them with horror. Screams and shrieks filled the air as men began running aimlessly, some shouting for meaning of the helplessness they felt. And the man who had done the deed, with the same serenity as before, turned, crossed to a bench and sat down, his smoking pistol still in his hand.

He it was who had assassinated the prime minister of Great Britain.

Spencer Perceval was lifted tenderly by two bystanders, Fookes trailing in the throes of shock, and they took him into the nearby room of the speaker's clerk and laid him on the table.

A passing surgeon was brought in and took less than a minute to pronounce life extinct. All present fell back in frozen horror.

Hammering at Fookes's reason was the overwhelming realisation that at this moment Great Britain's parliament had been decapitated, its leader and figurehead taken, to leave it rudderless, unable to function – or even to exist. He took a long, quavering breath, and made the first contribution to the scrabble for sanity in a world gone mad. 'G-gentlemen, the cabinet must m-meet.'

Outside the news spread wildly, and within the hour Parliament Square was filled with an excited, seething crowd, hundreds swelling to thousands, screaming and hurling insults, lunatic, out of control.

The doors were slammed and a cry rose, 'Cabinet! Cabinet! In the committee room.'

As members of Perceval's cabinet stumbled up they were shown into the room until enough were present and the door locked. The home secretary, Ryder, was Perceval's closest friend, but he was plunged into a paroxysm of helpless weeping, as were several others. Even Lord Eldon, the High Tory lord chancellor and senior minister, was too shocked to continue, and for some time in the stunned atmosphere all were unable to speak.

Then the first tentative conclusions came. In Perceval they had lost not only a prime minister but the chancellor of the exchequer and of the Duchy of Lancaster, as well as leader of the House of Commons, all of whom had to be replaced without delay. Yet no one could conceive of anyone who was constitutionally able to perform this and, with the home secretary still prostrated in grief, none to take it further.

By now the menacing tumult and bedlam outside were

tearing at nerves on edge and grieving turned to fear. What if this was the first act in a Jacobin uprising, paralysing the country until the conspiracy was complete? A link-up with murderous Revolutionaries, deranged Republicans and Levellers? Was a wider plot signalled by the assassination? Were others involved? Given the situation, the under-secretary to the Home Office should be empowered to call out the militia, the volunteers, nothing less.

A breathless Treasury clerk broke in to announce that an attempt to smuggle Bellingham out to Newgate prison had been thwarted by the mob, who showed every inclination to free their hero as a liberator from Tory tyranny. His escorts were still fighting to keep the hostile rabble at bay.

The men about the table stared at each other in dismay. Then at the door appeared the patrician form of the secretary of state for war, the second Earl of Liverpool.

'R-Robert – you're here,' gasped Ryder, through his sobs.

Liverpool took in the hapless sight with a glance and found himself a chair. 'Mr Perceval has been taken from us, this much I've heard. What else do you know?'

In a chorus he was told of the rioting crowds outside, the threat of an imminent uprising and—

'We must have a prime minister – a head of government. To take charge before the mob does.'

'My lord, we know this, but there's no precedent, no constitutional path without we have a general election,' the lord chancellor pontificated.

'There is.'

'Pray do enlighten us.'

'We are the cabinet, the king's ministers. We choose one of our number and desire the Prince Regent to empower him with office.'

*   *   *

'Prime Minister. Might I be among the first to felicitate you on your elevation?' purred Nicholas Vansittart, the new chancellor of the exchequer, as the cabinet sat for the first time.

'As meet and right as it turned out to be,' the home secretary, Viscount Sidmouth, harrumphed.

It had taken three weeks of chaos and confusion, and four others rejected before him, but finally, in despair, the Prince Regent had made his choice and Great Britain now possessed a prime minister.

'Your kind sentiments are noted and now this cabinet is in session,' Lord Liverpool snapped. 'We've a devil of a lot to deal with and not a lot of time to do it in. The first is to secure the kingdom.'

The Horse Guards were ordered from their barracks and the Foot Guards set to clearing the streets. Ringleaders of the mob would face justices of the peace, parish beadles made into special constables and the militia turned out, the watch doubled.

'What is perhaps even graver is the wider issue of foreign involvement,' Liverpool continued. 'For instance, a revolt of the disaffected harnessed by those desiring a revolution.' He stopped, looking suddenly grave and tired. 'Gentlemen, I've had a passing chance to read Mr Perceval's secret papers and what I've seen frightens me.'

'Concerning the external situation of this country?' Castlereagh, foreign secretary, wanted to know.

'I would think so.' Liverpool sighed. 'Much beyond a mere affair of hay-forks and rick-burning, I'd believe.'

'May we know the contents of what you saw?'

'Until I've digested its import, no, you may not.'

'If we are to move on this, my lord, then we—'

'I've already decided the action, sir.'

'Might we understand which?'

186

'As any other sane prime minister will think it with the country *in extremis*.' He looked down the table to the still figure of Melville, the newly appointed first lord of the Admiralty. 'I desire you, sir, to strip the nearer blockading squadrons of any available battleships and concentrate them at Portsmouth where they may best be disposed as the threat develops.'

'Immediately, my lord.'

There was a rustle of relief about the table.

They were in the best possible hands. The navy was being brought home to defend them.

Chapter 33

It made no sense. After a successful action that was going to add to his laurels as the reigning admiral, Houghton had abruptly sent Kydd to report to the commander-in-chief off Brest. Then the mystery deepened. Boarding *Royal Sovereign* in full dress, he'd found that Keith had already quit his flagship for the Admiralty and had left instructions that Kydd would, without a moment's delay, press on to Portsmouth and the Spithead anchorage for orders, no reason given.

Thunderer leaned to the stiff north-westerly, the gunmetal sea moody and restless, but not so far ahead lay the grey headland of St Catherine's Point with its medieval lighthouse. Beyond was the dog-leg past the Isle of Wight and then the great naval anchorage athwart the entrance to Portsmouth.

In the early afternoon Kydd spotted a fleet at anchor, a line of eight 74s that could neither be the Channel Squadron, which was on its station off Brest, nor the Western Squadron, which was at the ready in its home port, Plymouth. What in Heaven's name did all this mean?

His pulse quickened at the obvious explanation: that a

special expedition was being mounted and secrecy was key. But where were the army transports, the victuallers, the necessary frigate escorts? Only 74s?

Just as soon as their anchor had rumbled out, he was in his barge making for the dockyard and the port admiral. As they passed Portsmouth Point the rollicking old town was curiously subdued, no uproarious taverns spilling rioting customers into the narrow alleys. With a fleet manning of many thousands, this was odd.

Disturbed, he landed at the dockyard steps and hurried to the port admiral's office. When he appeared at the anteroom there was more astonishment: neither the admiral nor his flag lieutenant was present, apparently on their way to London. Orders for *Thunderer* were waiting but they instructed him only to come to a twelve-hour notice for sea. No liberty for the hands was to be granted and row-guard and nettings were to be deployed to prevent desertions. No indication as to how long the situation would obtain.

Baffled and annoyed, Kydd returned to his ship and went to his cabin to shift back to sea rig. A pleasant-looking fellow in the comfortable uniform of a post-captain rose from a chair at his appearance.

'*Montagu* 74, Dick Moubray. I do apologise for this intrusion, old chap. Kydd, is it not? Heard much of you in these home waters but didn't know you'd deserted frigates for a battler.'

'It is and I have so. Er, do you have business with me as will throw a bit of light on this ragabash situation?'

Binard noiselessly appeared, a starched napkin over his arm.

'Ah. And I was hoping *you* might.'

'*Thunderer*? We've been on blockade until untimely snatched away and sent here. A snort of sherry?' He nodded to Binard who gave a short bow and left, returning suspiciously quickly with a silver tray and two glasses.

'So you haven't heard.'

'I've only cast anchor this hour, sir.'

'The prime minister is . . . no more.'

'What did you say?' Kydd was incredulous.

'In the lobby of the House of Commons. A pistol shot to the heart by one many rate as a common lunatic. Others shout that it's the work of revolutionaries or such. Whatever the right of it, we're now without a premier and line of authority from the Admiralty.'

It was stunning. Kydd's mind reeled at the implications. The ship of state without a rudder: no decisions could be made, no precautions taken. The future was a bleak unknown.

'So what are we doing here?'

'No idea. Intelligence of a rising by the Irish? Boney up to his scurvy tricks? A break-out from Antwerp or ports east of it?'

They were interrupted by the mate-of-the-watch who reported that the admiral's flag had broken at the dockyard signal tower, signifying his arrival back and this had been quickly followed by an 'All captains'. Kydd could not remember that this signal had ever been made in Portsmouth before.

The nine captains filed into the upper meeting room and sat in a loose gathering. The admiral, Strickland, stood waiting, grim-faced but patient. There were no rolled maps, blackboards, piles of operational orders. This was not a council-of-war.

'You will all have heard of the much-lamented loss of our noble leader, Mr Spencer Perceval. It's thrown the kingdom into an uproar and made all our plans moot.'

After the rustle of comment died away he continued: 'I'm

able to tell you now that we have a new prime minister – and, in fact, a new cabinet who are meeting as I speak.'

'Sir, who—'

'Our new man at the helm is my lord Liverpool, who before was our secretary of state for war. I won't bore you with all the details of his administration but one you'll take notice of. It's Melville – not Nelson's man but his son, the second Viscount Melville. A steady hand on the tiller, you'll grant.'

The group remained silent, watchful.

'So what are we doing here? I will tell you. From various sources on the Continent of Europe we've heard rumours of a shocking and disturbing development. A move by the French to break the stalemate there by amassing an army of colossal and unstoppable size. What it's for and where it's aimed nobody knows, possibly at this stage not even Bonaparte himself, but it's increasingly obvious that it's of serious intent to do us harm. The reason we're summoned here is that, in this time of immense threat, the prime minister has acted instinctively. With an invasion army some twenty times that of the one poised before Trafalgar threatening, he remembered what the Earl St Vincent said at the time and acted accordingly.'

Standing in Parliament, the crusty admiral had intoned grimly, 'This only am I sure upon: I do not say, my lords, that the French will not come. I say only they will not come by sea.'

Strickland continued. 'Yes. When it's clear what mischief Boney is up to we sail instantly to deal with it, which is to say why we lie at Spithead in the highest degree of readiness.'

So that was the reason. Without knowing where the blow was aimed, a significant force was now assembled at Portsmouth, a point halfway along the Channel from where they could proceed either east or west as necessary.

'How long should we expect to be at readiness, sir?' Moubray queried. It was asking a lot – sail bent on in all weathers, seamen at sea watches, keeping up on victuals and water as they were consumed, routine maintenance without entering a dockyard.

'As long as Boney keeps shaking his fist at the world.'

'Sir, it could be considered unreasonable to deny men their liberty ashore,' Kydd said carefully. 'Might we—'

'Captain, you're at twelve hours' readiness. If you can assure me your ship will be fully manned and ready to face the enemy within that time I don't give a fig about your liberty arrangements.'

The older Davis of *Blake* asked, 'Should we sail as a fleet, whose flag will we be under?'

'If you sail it will be as a squadron, part of the Channel Fleet and therefore under the flag of Admiral Keith, who will in any event be leading in *Royal Sovereign*. He will be arriving here presently and will no doubt be plainer in his requirements. Any other questions?'

At first the unusual routine and tension kept *Thunderer* alert and braced but as the days passed so did the feeling that they were a first-rank fighting force about to save England. With only a small number of exercises possible at anchor, no firing drill or mock landings to keep up an edge, and means ashore all spent, it was the dreaded tedium of any lengthy harbour stay.

Kydd was delighted when Persephone arrived. She made herself comfortable in the George, which Kydd pointed out was where Nelson had stayed for his last night before sailing to destiny.

Over a sturdy roast of beef and a decent claret, she told him breathlessly of the riotous chaos breaking out in the street she'd seen with her friend when the news of Perceval's assassination reached Plymouth. With no coaches running, they'd had to take rooms but the drunken revels and boisterous marches had kept them awake the whole night.

No revolution had taken place and the disorder was apparently over now. Kydd feared, however, that this was the beginning of a much worse phase, with Britain stretched to the utmost in a world-spanning war that had reached colossal proportions. He made light of the reason *Thunderer* was in port, telling Persephone of the changes aboard, especially in the first lieutenant. Not wishing to upset her, he mentioned that young Luscombe had swum to shore on realising that he wasn't fitted for a life at sea but that he'd been able to find a replacement in a Monsieur Binard.

'Other ladies of fashion boast a French cook but my fine husband has a French *homme de chambre*,' she noted happily.

He smugly presented her with a conversational bauble by telling her that, after reading the newspaper accounts of Perceval's end, he'd remembered the name Bellingham. A somewhat unhinged Englishman in a Russian gaol when *Tyger* had first visited, Kydd had spoken at length with him, more out of pity than anything else. With female eagerness she demanded he describe the encounter in detail.

The wardroom found no shortage of questions to chew over in their leisurely dinners, the most raised being just what Napoleon Bonaparte was going to do next.

Attack Russia? An outrageous suggestion, Russia being, first, his ally and, second, having done nothing to cause even the voracious Bonaparte, at insane expense, to mount an invasion.

Flood his great army westwards to put down the rebellious Spaniards and their small but impudent English ally in one overwhelming stroke? Possible, but unlikely, for the prize was hardly worth the effort.

It was generally conceded that the most credible was to right the wrong of Trafalgar by throwing the entire gigantic horde in a never-ceasing flood into the south of England, then march on London. That would end the war once and for all and, with Great Britain in chains, the world would be Napoleon's by right of conquest.

This was usually the signal to raise a bumper in a brave and defiant toast of damnation to the Corsican tyrant, which was inevitably followed by a lull of introspective silence.

One evening Briggs changed the subject, reflecting that the recent noisy accusations and calumnies coming from the United States might develop into war. This brought on much merriment at the thought of a vast army of Red Indians falling on the green fields and forests of ancient England to march on the Tower of London.

And what did Briggs think was worth risking their great merchant fleet that carried so much of the world's trade to their very considerable profit? And inviting the ire of a nation with the biggest navy at sea at this time, which was quite capable of landing whole armies? No: however loud their demands, the Americans were not a nation of lunatics.

In the fog of rumour and fear there was only one thing that was to be done: stay where they were and wait.

Chapter 34

The tedium fell away abruptly for Kydd when a note was handed in to the officer-of-the-watch. It was short and to the point, from a Mr Johnstone, who begged an interview with him ashore at the Swan and Compass, concerning a matter of grave importance. There was no indication of the subject but a postscript added that, were it not so urgent a matter, he would have enclosed a covering from one Nicholas Renzi attesting to his bona fides. The mention of his dearest friend was enough for Kydd and he hurried ashore, some instinct telling him to go in plain clothes.

He knew the inn, not far off in Southsea, and soon he was being shown into the snug by a respectful maid.

A man rose noiselessly. His appearance – perfectly anonymous clerkly black, dark eyes a-glitter, like a crow's, in a pallid face, a spare frame almost ascetic – was arresting.

'Charles Johnstone. You may understand I represent the secretary of state for foreign affairs.' The voice was low but dry and elegant.

'You mentioned Mr Renzi.'

'Lord Farndon. He's been so good as to work for us in the past on several concerns of a vexatious nature.'

'Is he in any kind of danger?' Kydd wanted to know.

'No. This meeting is on quite another matter, which I must tell you is of the gravest moment and considerable urgency.'

'We may be interrupted, Mr Johnstone.'

'I don't believe so, Sir Thomas. I have hired the snug for the nonce. Shall we sit by the fire?'

No convivial glasses were summoned, and Kydd felt the stirrings of unease. The man was of the government but not in the public eye or an elected official. Who was he?

'What I have to tell you is to be reckoned secret, not to be discussed with any.'

'Not even my officers? I find that a hard thing for an active captain of a 74.'

'None. Sir, there is a service you may render the Crown for which you are particularly well suited, so much so that your name was put forward as the first I might try.'

'Sir. I'm captain of HMS *Thunderer*, a ship-of-the-line under twelve hours' notice for sea. I cannot see how—'

'Arrangements at the highest level will be made. Do, sir, hear what I have to say.'

'Very well. Fire away, Mr Johnstone.'

'You will have a fair idea of the forces by sea that Bonaparte commands.'

'That he keeps in idleness in port, never to sail against us.'

'There have been developments we've been made aware of that throw your conceiving into considerable doubt.'

'With all due respect I hardly think you in a position to make comment on strategic naval dispositions, sir.'

'Captain, what I can say is that Bonaparte's idleness is a deliberate policy. They are in effect being husbanded against a great enterprise. We in government think it unwise to allow the scale of this accession to strength be known to the general public, and therefore have reported fewer than there actually are.'

'Oh?'

'Let me give you an example. Toulon and lesser ports comprehended by the name. How many ships of what weight of metal do you believe to lie there within?'

'Eighteen – seven of the line and eleven frigates have been sighted. Possibly more we haven't heard about.'

'It will certainly shock you to discover that, from deserters and other sources, we find that there are now one hundred and twenty-one men-o'-war massed in Toulon of which twenty-two are sail-of-the-line. Eleven of these are of 80 guns and above.'

'Above an 80?' That would mean a sore fight for *Thunderer* with her 74.

'As it happens, yes. And even three of 120 guns.' The first-rate *Victory* was only of 100 guns. Remorselessly he concluded, 'And no less than five of 130 guns.' Far bigger than anything the Royal Navy possessed, a truly staggering imbalance and in only one of the ports ringing France.

'Why do we not . . .?' But Kydd couldn't finish, the thought of such menace freezing his words.

'The Admiralty in its anxiety has sent for Admiral Pellew to take command of the Mediterranean fleet and increased the number of his ships as much as they are able, but we're greatly outnumbered.'

Pellew was a renowned fighter but it was a dismaying situation.

'You said husbanded for a great enterprise?'

'Less than one month ago, Bonaparte demanded the expenditure of two millions in the furbishing of a fleet. Sir Thomas, this is no less than the invasion fleet of England, which, since Trafalgar, has not only been kept at the ready but subjected to a continuous building programme.'

'Sir, if you intend to frighten me, you're succeeding.'

'With this we must observe that an army of unknown but vast size is assembling under Bonaparte's personal command. It is of such huge dimensions that it must be employed soon or cause a ruinous drain on his treasury. The collective belief in Lord Liverpool's administration is that its destination cannot be other than England.'

Kydd swallowed. The months before Trafalgar in *Teazer* when he'd been part of the last line of defence against invasion had scarred his memory: at every dawn the last act always poised to occur, the continual near-suicidal attempts on a swarming enemy. Now it was all about to burst on them once more. 'You asked a service.'

'I did. In all this there may be a flaw in the reasoning. Napoleon Bonaparte is an arch deceiver. That we know. If his object is not England but some other, then he may desire to create fear and confusion among us such that we draw in our defences to guard these islands and abandon all else.'

'I see.'

'We need to know, sir. The cabinet has to make terrible decisions bearing on the safety of this realm and must have the truth of the matter. In short, if the invasion fleet is an invention, a cheap mockery made up of imitation craft or such, then we may suspect the last. If it is credible, a sea-going armada truly capable of conveying an army, we must then look to our defences as a dire necessity.'

'Mr Johnstone, have you not spies or their ilk available to do this?'

'Spies are rarely knowledgeable in the maritime arts and cannot be expected to recognise the soundness of a vessel or its equipment for the task. More to the point is the enormity of the decisions to be made. Only if the report stems from an absolutely unimpeachable source will the prime minister feel able to act upon it.'

'Myself.'

'Your name will ensure your intelligence will be received with due reverence, I can assure you, sir.'

In growing horror Kydd realised the implications. 'You wish me to land on the coast of France and satisfy myself as to the particulars? Like a common spy?'

'Not at all.'

Kydd let out his breath in relief.

'The coast before Antwerp instead will be satisfactory for the purpose. If two or three shipyards are sampled it will be enough to tell us if the rest of Bonaparte's invasion fleet is a sham or a deadly threat, for there's no point in producing the actual article in one place and its counterfeit in another.'

'Antwerp, Calais – it's all the same to me, sir. Enemy territory as requires me to act the phantom, the footpad. This is not within my power, sir.'

'Sir Thomas. Your role does not demand you do. You'll be landed privily to be met by the agent who alerted us to the threat. Your only duty is under direction to sight what you're shown to make report later, the entire business to be concluded within a very few days.'

Kydd was under no illusions as to what would happen should he fall into French hands, but a mischievous voice pointed out what a splendid opportunity it would be later to mention casually to Renzi that he'd been involved in just the same kind of furtive mission as he'd undertaken in the past.

'Very well, Mr Johnstone, I'll do it – supposing only that I'm to be satisfied with the details.'

Chapter 35

The smuggling craft bobbed and splashed as it made its way through the short and choppy seas of the Channel, Kydd's instincts in the chill darkness telling him they were coming up with the land, the low, dune-fronted flatlands of Zeeland. There was no other in the lugger beside the man at the tiller and two hands at the sheets. They kept their silence, peering intently ahead into the clamping murk of night.

The choice of a smuggler was inspired: he would know to an inch the coast so they were assured a safe passage. The *douaniers* of the Batavian Republic were as anxious to let past English goods into the Continent as those making the crossing were to supply, and no strict examination of the crew was expected. Kydd was not in uniform: he wore a frayed jacket and wide trousers with a kerchief, the traditional clothing of a common seaman.

He smiled wryly. This was a stretch of coast he knew well: it had figured several times in his past, the first as a lowly master's mate before the ferocious battle of Camperdown, during the long years of blockade and in the first war cruise of *Tyger*.

A quarter-moon dared peep out from beyond the scud, and reluctantly the shoreline was revealed, anonymous, level and fringed with a pale beach. In the minutes before the light died as the moon was obscured again, he noticed a tell-tale well-remembered seamark: some two miles inland a fat church with a spindly, out-of-proportion steeple, Koudekerke. It told him they were up the coast from Flushing, the ancient medieval port set right at the mouth of the Scheldt.

A man forward raised a device like a watering can, a spout lantern, and held it steadily. From high on the Koudekerke steeple a light glimmered in return, on and off, on and off. Kydd knew the routine and felt the boat heel slightly, then head inshore. He scanned the pale beach for sign of movement and saw none but his pulse quickened as the shore neared. It was so different from casually scrutinising on the deck of a heavily armed man-o'-war. The agent had better be waiting or he'd be away again very smartly.

He spotted a twist in the smooth line of beach, hardly noticeable. A small stream ran into the sea from behind a hillock and, sails doused, the craft nosed in and came to a stop by a dilapidated jetty with figures waiting. It was swiftly and economically done, the boat held by a painter forward and rotated to face out to sea again before being hauled in. Low voices sounded in the night and Kydd was gestured impatiently to get out: these men had work to do, passing contraband ashore and into the ruined house beyond.

The tiller-man whispered to him. He was to make his way inland a hundred yards, and behind the dunes he'd find a fisherman's hut where his agent was waiting. Feeling half naked without arms of any kind, he set off and, after trudging across the sand for a short while, he saw the hut, showing a soft light within.

He knocked gently and heard a scraping movement inside.

Then the door slowly opened. An old lady sitting in a chair by the fire, knitting, looked up at him, bemused.

'Um, good evening, Madame,' was all Kydd could think to say, in English.

'*Kom binnen, mijnheer*,' she replied, gesturing inwards.

The door closed behind Kydd, and he swung around to see another woman standing with a large military pistol trained on him.

'Are the oranges yet ripe?' she asked evenly and in perfect English, her eyes never once straying from his.

The part of his mind that had remained cool noted that she was remarkably attractive, with dark looks reminding him of his sister Cecilia. But if he was to avoid an ignominious end the correct response was needed straight away. 'Oh. No, they're not, but, um, the raspberries are.'

She paused fractionally, then lowered the weapon. 'You may call me Anneke.'

'And I am—'

'I need no name. I will call you Piet.'

'Anneke.'

'Listen carefully, Piet. You will do exactly as I tell you, however stupid it seems to you. There are those who long for freedom and there are those who lust for gold, but there is no telling the difference.'

'I understand.'

'Do you? I've been told that you are an adept on ships, not on secret work.' Her tone hid a brittle tremor, which, in a perverse way, comforted Kydd, with its hint of humanity.

'I will do what you ask, Anneke,' Kydd said quietly. 'What is first?'

'The Van Beek shipyard. Now.'

She eased outside, carefully checking, then beckoned him to follow.

Once in the night air she walked briskly along a path until it was crossed by a road. A small calèche was drawn up there, its driver nodding in sleep. They clambered aboard. At Anneke's sharp Dutch he came to and snapped a whip over the patient horse.

There was no talk as they made off down the road but Kydd was uncomfortably aware of her thigh pressing into his in the narrow seating. After an infinity of turns he was relieved to see the glitter of water ahead and the gaunt ribs of a vessel on the stocks against the night sky. Anneke had timed their visit to the hours of darkness when no workmen would be on the site.

'Wait,' she hissed imperiously, jumped down and disappeared into the blackness. She returned with a man and a lantern. 'He says be quick – the *veldwachteren* are out.'

The elderly man clucked in alarm at a strange noise in a field and Kydd's heart jumped. This creeping and dread were not to his liking. Anneke snapped something contemptuous and went to the side door of a large shed, let them in and set a lantern going.

In its ghostly light Kydd saw the outlines of two craft and recognised them immediately from his experiences off Calais. The nearer was a *chaloupe canonnière*, this one sizeable, quite able to mount a twenty-four-pounder on a slide and pound to ruins anything smaller than a frigate. The other, by its Scandinavian lines, was a *crache feu*, the kind of gunboat that had made life so galling for the Royal Navy after the Copenhagen action.

He went up to the slip, managing in the gloom to trip over some loose timbers, which tumbled about with a wooden clatter. The hull was half straked and he bent to smell the new work. It was fir, Baltic pine probably, as far as he could see, straight-grained and prime timber deals. He put his ear to the topmost and tapped sharply. It rang sound and true, not the dull clunk of deadwork.

He called for the lantern and inspected the line of fastenings along its edge. Copper, flush on the outer side and properly secured with roves on the inner. At the bow of the craft, much as he expected, the fay of the planking to the stem was neat and workmanlike.

He drew back and considered. This was no mockery or sham: it was a well turned-out article of the shipwright's art and of new construction.

Outside again, stray light caught shapes in the background. Three, five: these were completed craft lying in a creek, masted and with standing rigging rove. He reached one and looked at it carefully. A Dutch *schuyt*, two-masted, shallow draught and strong, ideal for landing either troops or artillery in quantity on a shingle beach. It, too, was sound and clean-lined, an occasional pale streak revealing recent repair or refurbishment. The rigging was taut, well tarred and, as far as he could tell in the dimness, ready for immediate use.

Bonaparte was not bluffing: if others along the coast were like this then the invasion fleet was a reality and once again England was under threat.

'We can go,' he said. Anneke turned sharply at the tone of his voice.

The older man scuttled away and they returned to the calèche. Anneke urged on the driver and, as her gaze fixed pointedly ahead, the vehicle ground off sharply.

Kydd needed to think. How much evidence should he find before breaking it to Johnstone that a genuine invasion fleet was poised? Was the sample method sufficient? Setting a fleet to sea was much more than the sum of the ships involved. There had to be storehouses crammed with supplies – powder, shot, rations. Should he be looking for these as well to prove the enterprise was on a credible footing?

His thoughts were interrupted when Anneke asked, 'Can you tell me what you think, Piet?'

They were grinding down a featureless, straight road with nothing in sight but Kydd kept his voice low. 'Those are true sea-going craft, well able to do duty in an invasion. If there are others like it, I fear for England.'

She looked at him intently, then patted his knee. 'You English have friends, do not fear.' The hand stayed where it was as the vehicle slewed sharply to the right, down a smaller track and to another shed among others nearby. It came to a stop by the deep shadow of an overhang.

Leaning across her to open the door politely, he was taken by surprise when she threw herself at him, her arms around his neck, her dress wrenched high to reveal a pale flash of her upper thigh in the moonlight. 'Kiss me! Now, you fool!'

Kydd was shocked rigid. She redoubled her passion, writhing in ecstasy and mumbling something between a smother of kisses.

Then he saw what had caused it. A figure materialising from the shadows came to a halt uncertainly, unslinging a musket.

She hastily smoothed down her dress, screaming curses and waving her hands in anger.

Sheepishly, the man resumed his sentry-go in the shadows, but she hurled more insults until he gave a grin and shuffled off into the night.

'I – I . . .' Kydd was lost for words, aware his gentlemanly instincts were at war with the baser ones.

'I believe it safe to enter,' she said primly, adjusting her clothing. 'The time of darkness is passing. We've more to do.'

Let in by another older man, Kydd took his lantern and advanced on the vessel on the stocks. In the dark and confined space it seemed massive. It, too, he recognised: a *praam*, the most dangerous of all. Three-masted, full-rigged and armed like a miniature frigate, it drew so little water that it could go in with the boats and slaughter any opposition. This one was nearly completed and, from the whiff of Baltic resin, he knew it, too, was the genuine article.

He withdrew quickly – he'd seen enough. That she'd been so keen-eyed to spot the *veldwachter* and had known instantly what to do left him in admiration of her.

'Anneke, we must go to another place, not near here. See if they too are building.'

'There is shipbuilding of all kinds along the Scheldt. We are famous for it, Piet.'

'Well, perhaps—'

'I shall find one. There are many in Flushing but it is running in those French bastards.' Kydd flinched to hear her language but it was she who was suffering the occupation.

'The other direction. Six, seven miles north. Westkapelle.'

The calèche turned inland and found the road up the coast, the noise of its passage through villages echoing from quaint Dutch houses looming out of the darkness. Occasionally a splutter of a light showed at a window and a face appeared. Several times a dog barked witlessly. It was not wise to be making a fast run through the night at a time when no one had business to be out, but it was unlikely that any curfew would extend so far into the country.

An argument with the driver appeared to be under way and Kydd asked if there was a problem.

Anneke bit her lip. 'This is not part of the arrangement and he worries that there will be trouble. I have to pay him more.'

206

There was tension in the air as they swung off the road and took a track out to the seaward line of dunes. Kydd's senses detected the barest lifting of the darkness, the quarter-moon beginning to pale. 'We have to go faster,' he said, trying to keep the nervousness out of his voice.

'Not so far, Piet,' she said reassuringly.

They passed through the dunes to a seafront dominated by a line of sheds and slipways behind a high fence. She told the driver to stop where the fence was closest to the sheds, and in the chill of the pre-dawn darkness she got out and ran to the fence. Kydd loped after her.

'This is the biggest boatyard in Westkapelle, but I haven't made agreement with Mr Heemskerk or his brother to come in the night. We have to find our own way in.'

Break into a shipyard?

'Here,' she commanded, pointing to a loose paling. 'Make it bigger.'

Kydd pulled it from the top. It gave, with an appalling *screeeak* into the calm of the night. He did the same with the one next to it, leaving a vertical hole just large enough to squeeze through.

They ran to the shed to find the door unlocked and went hastily inside. They didn't have a lantern and she cast about in the disordered gloom for one. Kydd didn't wait, feeling his way forward until he came up with the bulk of a hull. He didn't care what it was: all he needed to know was if it was ever going to be seaworthy.

The smell was right, the timbers of the outer side of the frames planed smooth. It was a good professional job and he moved towards the bow further inside.

Suddenly he heard her whisper an alarm. Her grip on his arm tightened. A figure at the door held a lantern high and called out a querulous demand. Kydd held still, her grasp fierce.

The figure entered the shed. By now the early light had begun to steal in and there was an angry shout and a determined advance towards them through the work debris.

'Go!' Anneke said, and stumbled away in the opposite direction. Kydd hesitated, then followed. Intelligently, she was making for the bow and as soon as she reached it she hurried down the other side to the open door.

There was a shrieking challenge but they reached it first and ran outside. Frantically searching, Kydd spotted salvation: a gig of sorts drawn up to a dilapidated jetty, probably the watchman's.

The man emerged, screeching incomprehensibly.

'Quick – he's calling the gendarmes!'

A muffled trumpet call came from behind the dunes and distant return shouts. Kydd pushed Anneke into the boat. There were oars and it was the matter of moments to untie the painter and shove off into the creek just as a squad of men burst into view. An officer with them gestured to half of his men who doubled off along the bank.

'He's told them to get another boat and intercept us,' she said, her fears under tight control.

Even with their start, that boat with at least double the men at its oars would outrun them.

Kydd put all he had into pulling and, unused to it after all his years as an officer, was soon panting, his muscles burning. All the while the detachment loped along the bank, effortlessly keeping up in the grey light of daybreak. The end couldn't be far off. To be captured not from the deck of a man-o'-war but a workman's gig would make splendid copy for Boney's newspapers, Kydd grimly reflected.

As he strained to the limits Anneke got to her feet and clambered awkwardly over his oars. Through runnels of sweat and a universe of pain he looked up and saw a *schuyt* putting out to sea past them, its sails lazily sheeting in. Anneke stood erect, shouting and waving the end of a rope.

Answering calls came back. 'To the *schuyt*!' she screamed in excitement to Kydd. 'He's going to tow us to sea!'

Chapter 36

Downing Street, London

A light still shone in the upper rooms of Number Ten, the thin rain giving it a somewhat melancholic cast – or was it the pressing news that Henry Bathurst, the third earl of that ilk, minister of state for war and the colonies, was bringing to the prime minister? He gave a nod to his assistant and they hurried in, their capes and hoods imperturbably taken by the major-domo.

The head footman preceded them up the portrait-hung staircase to the Cabinet Room, his footsteps echoing in the late-night stillness. Bathurst knew that it was always Lord Liverpool's practice diligently to prepare the night before a planned division in the House.

'Oh, it's you, Henry.' Liverpool yawned, pushing away the papers in front of him. 'Now why do I sigh at your appearance, old fellow?'

'Prime Minister. We've word back from Antwerp as you required.'

'The invasion fleet? That was quick work – perhaps too quick? Did your man spend enough time to be sure?'

'Sir. We took the precaution of employing a serving officer of distinction whose judgement in the matter may certainly be relied upon.'

'Oh? Who is that, pray?'

'At his particular request I beg to be excused mentioning his name but I do allow he is a post-captain and bears the honour both of a knighthood and baronetcy.'

'I see. Then what are his conclusions?' Tension had crept into his voice as he waited unblinkingly for the answer.

'It's genuine. By means of random selections he's established that the boat and shipyards between Flushing and Westkapelle are actively building all manner of invasion craft and harbouring the completed articles. Sir, we must accept it as a verity that the invasion fleet exists and is in a condition to put to sea.'

Liverpool slumped back, his expression bleak.

'Not only that, Prime Minister, but it was determined from local sources that the entire Scheldt river is crowded by slipyards that at the moment are engaged in swelling Bonaparte's battle fleets. The number of twenty-four line-of-battleships as nearing completion was mentioned. And there is no reason to suppose it's any different in the Batavian Republic or certainly in France itself.'

'Good God. So it isn't a species of bluff. They really mean it.'

'Or in truth they actually want us to discover the extent of the fleet and its quality in order to oblige us to withdraw our blockade squadrons and other in the defence of the kingdom, giving them a free hand in Russia or to indulge in mischief anywhere. Cheap at the price, I'd say.'

'You're a cynic, Henry. We've always known they never discarded the invasion flotillas after Trafalgar. Why should we be frightened now?'

'Because for the seven years since then they've been steadily building and building. Two million francs laid out this year alone. It must be of an astonishing size by now, Prime Minister.'

'And so you leave me with the choice of whether or not to call an invasion alarm along the lines of what we did in the year five.'

'Yes, Prime Minister.'

Liverpool groaned, holding his head in his hands.

'It truly grieves me to add to your burden, sir.'

'Heaven preserve us. What now?'

'I'm in receipt of hard evidence of the size of Bonaparte's latest army. Sir, I must warn you it greatly exceeds what rumour holds.'

'Well?'

'In excess of some six hundred thousand under arms. Past half a million men from a dozen nations in full marching order. The greatest military horde seen on earth since the time of the ancient Persians, a vast, seething mass of—'

'Yes, yes.' The premier's voice dropped almost to a whisper. 'How sure are you of this? Rumour and hearsay are no substitute for hard intelligence and—'

'The Russians have a man well placed in Paris. He's passed back to his masters copies of the orders-of-battle of the entire army, courtesy their foolish notions of seniority among their field commanders, which demand they have knowledge of what their rivals command. Our man in St Petersburg has, for a suitable fee, passed them on. Do you . . .?'

'No, I leave that kind of thing to you,' Liverpool said, staring down at the table as if it had answers for him.

'It means—'

'I know what it means. A host of such terrifying size can have but one purpose – to crush and extirpate. The question must be – is it to be unleashed on the Russians or Napoleon's greatest foe, England?'

Chapter 37

Boulogne

The skies above were deep blue and almost cloudless, as if they were obeying the wishes of the all-puissant Emperor of the French, Napoleon Bonaparte, for perfect weather on the occasion of a grand review before the massed splendour of his Grande Armée. For miles on either side a horde of eighty thousands was encamped on the high ground overlooking the seaport.

This day a marine pageant was to be mounted in honour of the most powerful man on earth, a parade of the countless craft of the invasion flotilla dedicated to the destruction of Great Britain, displaying their might and numbers before their emperor.

Placed prominently on the heights was the splendid panoply of Bonaparte's campaign headquarters, transported from Paris for the occasion. Princes, grand marshals, the imperial gendarmerie, all summoned to a spectacle of the pomp and majesty at the Emperor's command.

In the largest, most sumptuous tent, the glittering few were gathered, those who rode to war at his side in the army general headquarters, called from all corners of the empire, in a near-blinding display of gold lace, swords of great beauty, cockades and gleaming gold-spurred boots. It was a show, too, of hauteur, pomposity and arrogance, as duke and viscount, baron and marquis paraded their wealth and finery before the military.

On the edge of the throng stood a no longer youthful colonel of engineers, Jean-Baptiste Moreau, summoned imperiously from his post with the eighth division in Prussia to be adjutant commandant in the Imperial General Staff of the greatly swollen Grande Armée. He sipped his champagne, not to his taste so early in the morning but it was essential to appear ardent in the service of the Emperor at this level or risk the ignominy of recall to his old brigade. It was, of course, a heady, glorious sensation to be plucked from the common run of the army and called to service with the Emperor himself. To this very hour he still had no idea why he'd been chosen – was it that lucky bridge-sapping operation at Wagram? He'd never even seen Bonaparte but shortly he would appear before him.

If only Angélique could see him now! His wife had not had an easy time during his progression through the ranks. He'd not gone in for the vainglorious strutting or shameless plundering that got one ahead in these times but she'd always taken pride in him, and his two sons, now at the prestigious St-Cyr military academy, also rejoiced at his promotion.

But he had to admit to unease. The Emperor had carried the nation before him, with his promises of honour and glory for all in a war of conquest and liberation. He'd made good on those, but at the cost of nearly twenty years' continuous warfare that had led to victorious Frenchmen under arms across Europe but also to unknown graves in far-off lands. Why could they not cease the eternal blood-letting, settle down with the spoils of their conquests, and discuss the limits of empire, with England their only remaining opponent?

If the rumours held true, a grand enterprise was afoot, for which an immense army was being brought into being. It could be anything: the Ottomans, the Russians, even the British. Were they extending themselves too far? For any one of those it was not just a matter of conquering but of imposing Gallic civilisation, with laws and taxation that would require a different army: a civil administration watched over by garrisons without number.

A small voice within asked a simple question: Was this aggrandisement for the cause of France or that of yet more *gloire* for Emperor Napoleon Bonaparte?

'*Eh, bien, je n'ai jamais!* If it isn't the little cockerel!'

Moreau swung round and saw, to his delight, his old friend of the years before Austerlitz, Rochambeau. He was in the high-collared blue and silver of an *ingénieur géographe*, a staff officer concerned with maps and topographical advisories.

'Bertrand! How are you? I haven't seen your hide since . . . well, a long time ago. Are you on staff to the Emperor?'

'As of a month ago, brother. And you?'

'New called from Berlin and the corps of engineers – I drink to our reacquaintance.' The champagne tasted better already.

Rochambeau eyed him steadily. 'Have you heard anything of why we're here? A junket called by His Nibs is all very well, and on this scale, but I'd like to know why, if you see what I mean.'

'No idea. I'm still finding my feet.' It was his old friend but he wasn't about to open his mind in these surroundings.

'We'll learn soon enough, I suspect.'

An aide announced that all who were going aboard the Emperor's state barge should now make their way to the quay.

'Isn't that Murat?' Rochambeau surreptitiously indicated a gorgeously apparelled, exquisitely tonsured officer ahead.

'Um, I've never met him.' He had, in earlier times, but never as the King of Naples as he now was. 'Over there – it's got to be Duroc, grand equerry.'

'No, that's Berthier.' Moreau's chief of general staff.

'There's Junot – I know him from the Lisbon folly. And next to him Savary. He's your new Fouché.' Minister of police and a very dangerous man.

It occupied them until, in an easy promenade before the good citizens of Boulogne, they reached the richly decorated barge. It was a large galley of eighty oars, its long deck with raised dais in the stern designed for spectacle with pennons, ornate flags and every kind of ornamentation. On the quay the galaxy of nobles and officers jostled for position: not to be the first to board but the last in order to make an ever grander entrance than the previous. It enabled them both to select an unobtrusive position below the Emperor's throne on its dais, where they settled to wait.

A distant baying of trumpets sounded nearer and the crowds grew frenzied, then, as the Emperor's entourage was glimpsed, subsided into awed whispers. Moreau couldn't see over the enormous tasselled cocked hats of the notables but knew that he'd soon be getting a close view of the man who held the fate of nations in his hands.

With a spreading rustle of bowing, scraping and subdued conversation, he heard the Emperor approach. Suddenly those in front of him parted and drew back. And there, unmistakable in his tricorn worn across, white breeches, a plain dark-green tunic, with a single star, and a grey overcoat against the sea breeze, was Napoleon Bonaparte.

The recognition was like an electric shock, followed by another equally unsettling impression – of fallibility. Moreau saw past the trappings and noted the thinning hair with forelocks curled forward theatrically, the massive head carried low between hunched shoulders and a well-concealed flabbiness. At the same time there was a feral quality about the man – the pale grey eyes piercing mercilessly, the smile with the lips only, the rest a brooding mask – and he was shorter than nearly all of his followers. This was not the heroic Greek god of the painter David, or the majestic figure of his coronation, but a creature of restless energy, his undoubted air of genius and terrifying presence conveying a message of destiny and conviction.

'Get going,' Bonaparte snapped, as soon as he'd finished receiving the inevitable ovations from his throne.

A naval officer in splendid garb coldly shouldered past Moreau to take position at Bonaparte's right hand. 'Rear Admiral Baste, Your Imperial Majesty,' he pronounced. 'Fleet commander of the Boulogne Flotilla.'

Napoleon gave a cursory acknowledgement and impatiently stared ahead at the lines of anchored craft, his lips moving as he counted. 'Two hundred? Where's the rest for which all year I've been shovelling francs into your hands?'

'This is the outer harbour, sire. The inner harbour is resident to twice their number,' the admiral said complacently. 'Safe from storm and tempest – and the impertinence of the English pirates.'

'Take care of them, Baste. I may have need of them very soon.'

'I will, Majesty.'

They reached the first line of invasion craft, moored parallel with the shore in an immaculate line. Bonaparte stood up, his pose haughty and imperious. One hand inside his coat, his gaze far-seeing and commanding, he nodded slowly as they passed the array of might.

'All is well, Baste. They parade like the Old Guard. I like it. But who is that out of line?' His finger pointed impatiently at a vessel at anchor further out to seaward. 'Tell the wretch to fall in with the rest or I'll know the reason why.'

'I beg Your Imperial Majesty's pardon, but . . . but it is not to be commanded, sire. It's a vessel of the Royal Navy that visits on occasion to be awed and intimidated by our great fleet.'

'Comes visiting? Sails in and drops anchor to – to come visiting?' exploded Bonaparte, in a choking rage. '*Merde!* It's not to be borne by any Frenchman and certainly not by me! Get rid of it, Baste! I'll not be gawped at by English sailors!'

'Yes, sire.' Baste bowed low and, snarling under his breath, pushed past. Summoning his boat, he departed hurriedly.

It didn't take long. From the inner harbour sailed a line of the biggest invasion escort vessels: *prames*, three-masted, full-rigged and armed like frigates, seven of them.

'That'll settle the beggar,' Rochambeau chuckled.

Bonaparte drew out his campaign telescope and watched developments grimly.

It soon became clear that the British commander knew his business. As the line of *prames* emerged from the harbour it was into a stiff breeze that was foul for leaving, obliging them to take the same track out. And his chosen anchoring spot just happened to be precisely opposite. Not even bothering to raise anchor, the unknown frigate opened a crushing fire on them, a spring passed to her mooring cable enabling her guns to bear with devastating accuracy.

More French ships were sent out, a bomb vessel and no

less than an additional ten brigs that threw themselves into the fight, knowing all the time their emperor was looking on.

The ominous sound of the guns reached the shore. Through the roiling gun-smoke the sea-fight was visible, a single ship surrounded and blazing away – but still confidently at anchor. For hours into the afternoon it went on until a wounded flotilla made its way back into Boulogne, leaving the frigate still at anchor, apparently without a scratch.

In an unforgiving fury of indignation and frustration, Bonaparte called off the grand review until such time as Rear Admiral Baste saw fit to put down the impudent frigate.

But the next day it was still there. And it now had reinforcements, if only two small brigs and a cutter, together mustering a fire-power barely that of one or two of those ranged against them.

But Admiral Baste, now at sea with *Ville de Lyon* to take personal command, knew his standing with the Emperor was at stake. He had with him another fifteen of all classes of warship, making up an overwhelming twenty-seven men-o'-war sailing to obliterate the impudent English vessel.

Battle was joined early. Napoleon Bonaparte observed from the heights as the bay before him, crowded with sail, erupted into violence. The English frigate, however, gave no ground in its position before him and it soon became clear that Baste's flagship was in trouble. *Ville de Lyon* closed to help it but the game little English brigs snapped at its heels and brought it to a standstill. Almost immediately boats from the frigate put off and, with Bonaparte a helpless and enraged witness, boarded and captured the vessel. Its colours were struck and in minutes the intolerable sight was witnessed of it being unceremoniously taken out to sea and away.

Bonaparte lowered his telescope and for a long and awful space, he gazed after it and at the scene of shattered, still smoking wrecks drifting in with the tide. No-one dared a comment as he turned on his heel and stalked away, his face like stone.

Chapter 38

Paris

The City of Light in springtime was a delight – it was what she had been born for – but Moreau was unable to take joy in her. Bonaparte had stormed back from Boulogne in a foul temper and had not been seen for some days. Today he'd called a conclave of the Army General Staff, implying that decisions had been made.

In the ornamented anteroom Moreau took position, his duty as an adjutant commandant to escort the Emperor into the inner military council at ten thirty precisely. Standing by the door were two others, Grand Marshal Montand of Mecklenburg and his deputy, talking animatedly, clearly excited to meet Bonaparte face to face. Another three stood gravely nearby, cavalry brigadiers and adjutants, too junior to attend the council.

They ignored Moreau with his blue-white engineer signifier. He drew out his watch and consulted it. Another twenty minutes before the Emperor was expected into the chamber – and suddenly he was striding into the anteroom, looking as though to assure himself of an audience.

Snapping to attention all five murmured greeting, but Bonaparte took no notice, a black scowl on his face. He snatched off his hat and thwacked it at his side, irritated, distracted.

'Sire,' said the grand marshal, lightly, 'do we see our chieftain cast down?'

Gazing moodily into space, Bonaparte made no reply.

'As it's not granted to mere mortals to command the Fates—'

'Cease your babbling, Montand. If you knew the worries of state I have on my back you'd spare me an hour of peace.'

'My most earnest sympathies, Majesty. The English?' he finished delicately.

'Of course, cretin. While they cowardly hide behind their precious wooden walls instead of fighting it out man-to-man on the good land, like any other self-respecting and honourable nation, we're deprived of the opportunity of uniting the affairs of the world under the one fair polity. Thus I fear we'll be driven to stern measures as will inconvenience if they persist in their intransigence.'

'Should we land on their shores with the Grande Armée they will sing a different tune, I'm persuaded.'

'At a cost!' Bonaparte snarled. 'Which I'm not prepared to pay. There is another course in bringing them to their knees upon which I'm tempted to embark.'

'Sir?'

'To humble the Tsar of Russia before his people and thus isolate Great Britain, who shall be obliged to treat on my terms.'

'Invade Russia?' gobbled Montand. 'Not as if—'

'As if it were not justified?' Bonaparte roared. 'An ally of France, sharing in all the spoils of war that French bayonets have won, and now has broken her sacred oath of alliance which we have faithfully kept? I have every excuse for a chastising, but in this I stay my hand!'

'May we know—'

'My Continental System. The only sure way of bringing the foe to his knees, and they seek to spurn it for the sake of sordid profits! To allow neutrals free access to Russian ports – with false papers. This is the same as inviting British ships to trade openly with the Continent! Above two thousand made port last year alone, an intolerable insult when but a dozen honest French vessels docked.'

'Unforgivable, Majesty,' quavered the grand marshal. Bonaparte, when angry, intimidated, like a lion out of its cage.

'And I will not forgive! Of that you may be assured.'

'Sire?'

'Ah. You would know the mind of an emperor.' He glanced imperiously at them all, one by one, then grunted, 'So. I like what I see. Loyal and true, serving only the state and the people.'

Legs astride and eyes piercing, he went on, 'And you will here learn how a master attends to his trade. I will tell you.'

Moreau kept well out of the circle of admirers, as befitted a senior officer of the Army General Staff shortly to be under Bonaparte's direct orders. But what was happening? Why were these nonentities being brought into secrets of state?

'On the one hand I sweeten the alliance for Tsar Alexander. Should he stay staunch at our side in this matter, he shall have a free hand in recovering the ancient sovereign lands of Russia in Poland and Prussia.' This was greeted by wise nods of understanding.

'And on the other I allow him a glimpse of my golden horde of half a million under arms, the guns, the horses, the powder stockpiles. This I bring within a short distance of the Niemen, the Russian border. It presents Alexander with a conundrum. Should he cast in his lot with the English, suffering beyond endurance the rigours of our trade blockade and the last nation in the civilised world still standing against us? Or receive from us a guarantee of peace, with rich pickings in old Prussia and a withdrawal of our terrifying host, displayed before him, for the trifling act of maintaining the existing alliance in all its provisions?'

'Will he listen, sire?'

'He'd better,' Bonaparte said grimly, seemingly mollified by this recitation of his plans. 'As my demands in this tenor have very lately been sent to him for his prompt and earnest reply.'

A breathless silence fell.

'Alexander, brought within our empire so securely, and consequently being thus humbled, will be of no further use to the English who, exhausted, must sue for terms. And, as you may perceive, my object is gained with no blood spilled in any wise.'

Then in quite another tone he resumed: 'Naturally this privileged information is not to be divulged to any outside this room. I'm sanguine you'll agree the next month will be interesting indeed, citizens.'

Moreau held his breath. He'd been in Headquarters long enough to know that the ways of a Caesar were above those of mere mortals. He clearly wanted these five to know his plans, even in the almost certain knowledge that they'd let them slip in a bragging to their juniors or even to their families.

Why? To put pressure on the players? It mattered little to England that he was making gestures to Alexander. As far as the English were concerned, France and Russia were in an alliance already and maintaining that was no alarming news. To the Tsar, Bonaparte's wishes and intent had always been clear. This was only a pointed reminder. So why . . .?

In a creeping chill he realised the shocking, terrifying reason. It was Bonaparte's secret plan to fall without warning upon Russia with his colossal Grande Armée.

His intention? To eliminate any distraction from the greater objective of putting down his last rival, Great Britain. And to add lustre and glory to the sum of the conquests in his name by conquering the biggest country in the world.

To this end, in the guise of pressuring Alexander with the proximity of his host, he could work up his legions and stores close to the border without triggering a panicked response. And bring on a cataclysm of opposing forces such as the world had never seen.

'Sire, if the Tsar refuses?'

'He won't,' Bonaparte said cuttingly. 'His own people won't allow him to take the wrong side. They've too much to lose.'

Discreetly, Moreau eased out his watch. 'Your Majesty? Time for your conference.'

The council was already in session. In the modest room it was like a busy campaign headquarters. A vast table in the centre was scattered with maps and diagrams, and over-hung with bright lamps, aides and equerries stepping aside in favour of generals, brigadiers and fighting soldiers of every stripe.

Bonaparte entered briskly, acknowledging this one and that, considerately answering the murmured enquiries after his health. This was quite another creature again and Moreau was fascinated: there was no denying that he dominated the room, a focus of all the energy that whirled about him.

'If the grey wolf can find it in him to save his shaggy stories for later, *hein*, Pelleton?' It brought a ripple of laughter about the table, for Napoleon Bonaparte missed nothing and the grey-whiskered major general chortled. It was this intimate knowledge of his men and the camp-fire camaraderie that had made him a leader to follow anywhere.

'So. Our priorities have altered, gentlemen. Lack of time and naval preparation force me to reorder the options before us.' The expressionless faces left no doubt that the real reason for putting aside the employment of the Grande Armée in an invasion of Great Britain was well taken.

His voice dropped to a commanding dictation. 'I've been assembling my host these last weeks for one object and only one object. You'll mark well what it is and act upon it.'

Moreau held his breath.

'This being the mustering of an overwhelming force next to the Russian border in an open display of might, that the Tsar will see what a broken oath will cost him.' He drew himself up, his expression stony. 'To that end I've instructed my ambassador to deliver a note to the Tsar, requiring he stand by the terms of our alliance in return for attractive territorial concessions, a soft demand. I do believe that will be enough.'

Letting the moment hang, he swept his gaze about the room, but in the stillness Moreau heard himself ask steadily, 'Sire, but what if he refuses?'

'Who's that?' Bonaparte asked sharply.

'Jean-Baptiste Moreau, adjutant commandant in the Imperial General Staff engineers.'

'Well asked, *mon brave*. You shall have a rapid answer. And it is that if I get no satisfactory reply, a second note will be given. The hard demand. This will specify that unless the alliance is publicly reaffirmed I shall consider it breached and Russia subject to retaliatory measures.'

'An invasion.'

'Sir, hear again this one word I uttered. *Unless.*' His frown cleared. 'I shall accompany this with a massing of my Grande Armée along his borders to demonstrate to the most ignorant just what it is that's being risked – and, above all, what the empire can do if spurned. The stubborn clique next to Tsar Alexander will realise by this that their bluff is called. No longer can they practise delay in pursuit of sordid profit. They must preserve themselves and their holdings in the only way possible: by resuming the provisions of Tilsit and that directly.' Without waiting for comment he added, 'The strategy needs every one of you to play his part.'

He went to the table and smoothed out the map of Central Europe, then looked up as they crowded around.

'The entire conceit of my note is rendered useless if it's concluded that this is naught but a threatening troop movement. To be credible it must appear to be in earnest. Guns, stores, baggage, supplies for a deep thrust beyond. Therefore I desire that as of this date we act as if an invasion is truly planned. Grand Marshal Berthier has been working hard on this appearance and he has the order of march for each of you. Our focus for the accumulating of war stores is Danzig, the assembly area Prussia and the Duchy of Warsaw.

'The soft demand has been dispatched. Gentlemen, before the hard demand is delivered I want the border from end to end lined with imperial bayonets and artillery, baggage trains and field-kitchens. All to show to the meanest peasant that without question Napoleon Bonaparte stands true to his word.'

Chapter 39

London

'D arling?' Cecilia called softly to her husband, Nicholas
Renzi, Lord Farndon. He was in their town-house
drawing room appreciatively taking in a clever but scurrilous
article in the *Morning Chronicle*. 'I am sorry to disturb you, my
love, but there's a messenger boy outside desires to deliver
his note into your hands directly.' The curiosity in her voice
was barely disguised.

'Oh? Then I'll come.'

It was a single folded note, sealed with a wafer he recognised at once. He tore it open, pulse racing. If this was what
he thought it was, the future could be much more interesting
very quickly. *My club, if it does not inconvenience, my lord*. Yes! It
was signed Congalton and this was a request from the high-
ranking member of the British secret service to see him in
his discreet Whitehall office as soon as possible.

'That's sixpence, m' lord,' the youngster piped, holding
out his hand.

Cecilia supplied the coin but he remained standing there. 'Off you go, then,' she scolded.

'A reply is begged, an' that'll be another sixpence.'

Renzi dashed *Directly* underneath Congalton's scribble and the lad darted off.

'You'll go,' Cecilia said, in a small voice. 'Even after Vienna? You've done enough, Nicholas.'

It was always amazing to Renzi how women with some kind of sixth sense could so easily penetrate the thoughts of their menfolk. 'I'll see what's to do only, my dear.'

Congalton rose respectfully at his desk, a wintry smile playing. 'You are most kind to visit, my lord. Refreshment?'

Renzi politely refused. Not the re-corked civil service dry sherry so early. He took the single visitor's chair and waited.

'Your success in Vienna was much remarked, my lord. In fact, I have it as a surety that the prime minister was well impressed.'

'And I'm persuaded wishes me to repeat the exercise?' Renzi said, with a raised eyebrow.

'Most insistent it is your good self that is employed in the venture, my lord.'

'Shall you now tell me what is contemplated, Mr Congalton?'

'You will have heard the noise occasioned by the discovery of Bonaparte's assembling of a great army on the Continent.'

'Indeed, as with a vast invasion fleet bound for these shores.'

'Yes. Well, we've since received indisputable information that leads us to conclude that the invasion of these islands is no longer Bonaparte's first objective.'

'Russia.'

'Quite.'

An unspeakably vast country ruled by a tiny elite and, in

particular, an autocratic tsar of mystical persuasion and child-like impulses.

'Then do I understand you wish me to call upon the person of the Tsar?'

'I do, my lord.'

Russia – a nation in alliance with Bonaparte, an enemy of Great Britain and with an unreadable complexity of rivalries and interests connected with its bid to be recognised as European. And now threatened by the greatest military power in the world, both reigned over by a despot.

'The government is greatly desirous that the mind of Alexander is known, whether or no he intends to stand against Boney if he invades.'

'Not as if that is a difficult task, in course.'

'As usual, His Majesty's Government has its sources, all of whom are either diplomats or inferior paid intelligence, neither being well placed in the article of trust or insight.'

'It will be gratifying to hear of your scheme to find me on easy terms with the Tsar of all the Russias, that I shall have the honour of achieving where they have signally failed.'

'Then if I satisfy you in the particulars you will agree?'

'Should it prove . . . conceivable. Do share it with me, sir.'

'I have naught to share, my lord. I rather felt that you should create your own situation as it were . . .' Before Renzi could respond Congalton was reaching for his hat and coat. '. . . in the presence of one who should know. A short walk only, my lord. The gentleman concerned may be considered most reliable in matters of discretion and you may speak freely before him.'

The mansion in Belgravia was large and secluded, well away from the din and odours of London. When Congalton showed his card he and Renzi were admitted to be greeted by a genial figure in a colourful crimson velvet jacket and tasselled cap.

'Velcome, my friend!' he exclaimed in a startling bass, advancing to bestow a hug on Congalton, his eyes coolly taking in Renzi as he did so.

'Dimitry, this is Renzi, come to seek your advice upon the usual terms, and this is Count Dimitry Vonskoy, late of Moscow.'

'Honoured,' murmured Vonskoy, with an English handshake. 'Shall we fin' somewhere quiet?' He padded along the hall and entered a drawing room, dismissing the two footmen with an irritable wave. A samovar stood on a side dresser. 'Tea?'

'Kind in you,' Renzi said.

'To what I owe your wisit?' Vonskoy asked, passing him a glass in an ornate silver holder.

'Count Vonskoy is, shall we say, a broker, and lately a gentleman of consequence at the court of the Romanovs,' Congalton explained.

'Until I dismissed the presence,' he said darkly. 'Of zat, nothing more said.'

'Then he is precisely the one who might advise me.'

Vonskoy bowed shortly and listened.

'Should one desire to be close to the Tsar, upon friendly speaking terms as it were, how best to achieve this?'

The eyes opened wide in surprise, followed by a bellow of laughter. 'No one achieves it! Around his person contend not one or ten, but a hundred who seek his favours. An' protection, lands – his gold. Why, is zis what you want?' he said in a fruity chortle.

With a snatched glance at the imperturbable Congalton, Renzi gave a polite smile. 'Yes, it is.'

The laughter ceased as though cut off with a knife. 'Vy?'

'To learn as much as I may about him.' Even to his ears it sounded a thin and unconvincing purpose.

To his surprise, after a keen glance, Vonskoy nodded. 'I accepts that. Come, let us talk together.'

They settled in a pair of huge chintz Oriental armchairs, Congalton nearby.

'You are Englishman. Is not difficult, there are many in Moscow, more in Petersburg. Merchants, money-men, those who make it their business, we Russian do not lack your English baubles.'

Renzi inclined his head attentively.

'But none at court among the boyars.'

'You're saying it is not possible.'

'Not that, Sir Renzi. More difficult. A pity you no scholard – Alexander worship learning, most particular of Europe. An' he will want to quiz you, to discuss and acquire wisdom.'

Congalton harrumphed firmly. 'Ah, but he is, Dimitry. He corresponds with Count Rumford upon the vexing questions of the age in natural philosophy and notably the study of ethnicals in their economic striving related to their culture.'

'Oh, bravo, Sir Renzi. Zis study is much applauded. Ve much desire to know whether our origin the Kievan Rus or is to be a more antique Slavic peoples.' He broke into a smile. 'Which give me idea. You shall go to Moscow, or better, Petersburg, to consult an academician. Lebedev – he will glory in your attention – and that will be your starting point.

'No difficulty about a passport, you may be sure,' he added.

Renzi shifted uncomfortably. It had been years since last he'd done serious work on his opus on the subject. His horizons had immeasurably widened since he'd acceded to the earldom of Farndon and soon afterwards adopted his clandestine lifestyle in service to Congalton and his mysterious masters. But his interest in the field remained and he'd met

234

Rumford several times at the Royal Institution, the proximity of a fecund mind always stimulating.

'The idea has merit, I agree, Count Vonskoy.'

'You shall go to Petersburg an' take lodgings with Lebedev. Write now, Sir Renzi! I will see it get to him the fastest way. Desire you shall visit him to discuss the serfs of Russia, perhaps.'

'Is there not a danger Napoleon will invade?'

'Not a chance,' Vonskoy replied impatiently. 'Even the Corsican tyrant know better than to march against a country of such vastness of size an' uncounted millions. He will make noise but never to go too far.'

Later, as he and Congalton strode back to Whitehall it all seemed possible. A Baltic trader at this time of the year could receive a reply very quickly, and in that time he could immerse himself in his studies again and learn from Vonskoy about life in the Romanov court.

Chapter 40

St Petersburg

What had been a noisome swamp just a single century before was now Russia's proud capital, the seat of the Tsar, with palaces and parks, ornamentation, and grand buildings without number, as part of a sanguinary and enigmatic history of enormous complexity.

As the trading barque eased sheets for the final approach to the docks, Renzi looked out over the low and flat Vasilyevsky Island where his voyage would end. As with all docklands it was a dingy, drab prospect with no promise of the wonders that he knew lay within this Venice of the North. Despite himself, his heart beat faster in anticipation of the compelling aesthetics to be found in a city that had brought the barbarians of Tartary face to face with the civilisation of Europe.

Lines were thrown ashore for warping alongside and Renzi felt in his waistcoat for his precious documents. He was the only passenger on board and he hoped to be dealt with promptly.

The customs officer wordlessly accepted his administration fee and handed him a letter. It was from Lebedev and urged him as soon as he landed to take a *fiacre* to the address shown. Very soon the carriage had left the dock area and was bowling along a fine embankment that looked out on the broad river he knew to be the Neva, with the frontages of imposing buildings along the way. Before the straight road took a sharp curve he was deposited in the inner courtyard of a classically styled but oddly different establishment. It was the Imperial Academy of Sciences, the affable doorman assured him, and, yes, Academician Lebedev was in and expecting him.

Renzi was met by a short, bearded man of mature years with fierce grey eyes. He greeted him fussily in meticulous French and an awkward bear hug. '*Mon cher collègue!*' he cried, holding him at arm's length the better to regard him. 'We are honoured in the extreme by your visit. Come, I will show you to your rooms.'

They were along the hall from Lebedev's own quarters and were comfortable, if somewhat monastic in appointments. Renzi left the servants to arrange them to his requirements while he was welcomed into Lebedev's apartment.

Clearly the domestics of a bachelor, it was snug and warm, dominated by a huge writing desk flanked by ceiling-high bookshelves. A silver bell tinkled, prompting the appearance of a servant.

Lebedev looked at him respectfully. 'A restorative, my lord?'

'Thank you, yes.' Renzi knew what was meant, and when the vodka arrived he downed it in one. 'A fine drop, sir.'

'Pertsovka, my particular favourite, which is with honey and pepper and bison grass.' He leaned forward with intensity and said, 'Tell me, my lord, for I do crave to know, what is your interest in us?'

With a light smile Renzi answered with as much gravity as he could muster. 'My study is in the production of a hypothesis of economic response to stress on resources, as mediated by culture.' He sat back and pondered. 'I've been fortunate in the matter of means and have travelled far in pursuit of my object. As an Englishman the oceans of the world are an open highway to me and the Great South Seas, Constantinople, darkest Africa, all these have furnished me with much material, but I'm persuaded there's a great deal to be learned in Russia, an ancient and oft overlooked land.'

'I fear this is an unfortunate time for you to arrive here. Bonaparte threatens us and has caused much mischief in our ranks, but the Tsar holds staunch and you will be safe in St Petersburg, I believe.'

'Yes, very tiresome. I had hoped to—'

'You shall – you shall!' Lebedev exclaimed earnestly. 'In the morning we will meet my associates and others most curious to see an English lord and member of the great Royal Institution to hear of your travels in far places unknown to them. It will be a distinguished occasion. And then we shall go forth to explore our famed Imperial Library on the Nevsky Prospekt. After that—'

'Academician, pray allow me to make occupation of my quarters and we shall meet at breakfast?'

The man was insatiable. Renzi was accustomed to the frowning silence and defensive flourishing of newspapers in an English gentleman's club at breakfast but Lebedev had found a corner of the academy refectory and was badgering him with questions and opinions even before the day had

238

begun. Only the need for a hurried change into morning dress before the reception was enough to part them.

Who would come? If it was a handful of desiccated scholars only, his mission would be near inconceivable – but just one notable with access to the Tsar would be enough.

The occasion was not formal: if Renzi, Lord Farndon, was not of value or interest the higher-placed could slip away, while if he was, then the same could meet him to take his measure. Thankfully, it meant that probably he was not expected to address the learned throng and therefore could direct conversations as he pleased.

In the large chamber, hung with portraits and with a minstrel's gallery at one end, above a hundred were assembled. Conversations stilled and heads turned curiously as he entered by Lebedev's side. In the middle of the floor the academician proudly stepped forward and declaimed in Russian something that evoked a round of polite applause and an expectant hush.

'Honoured colleagues – peers and associates all,' Renzi replied urbanely, in courtly French. 'It is indeed an honour . . .'

It was received well, his frequent and deliberate references to Count Rumford, the Royal Institution, and his travels provoking admiring looks from some, stony-faced envy from others.

Afterwards there was a press of people towards him. A stiff bow and click of the heels from the president of the Academy of Sciences, a fulsome greeting from the professor of humanities and a brace of enthusiastic young men introduced as student *doktorskaya*. They, and the crush of unnamed others, were not whom he was interested in. It was those who stayed back, biding their time until they could get his undivided attention.

A ridiculously ornamented military officer waited with heavy patience, his hand on his sword, glowering. Next to him, occupied with a scruffy, beady-eyed figure in dress more seen in a past age, a tall, well-dressed individual, whose friendly looks were betrayed by thin lips, gazed at Renzi with disconcerting precision.

Renzi freed himself from his admirers and strolled over to them, by now supplied with the inevitable refreshments. Above the hubbub he learned that the officer was one General Arakcheyev, who needed to know his views on whether the British, not a race of soldiers or known for Continental ambition, would face up to Bonaparte's half-million-strong army. He stalked off at Renzi's innocent ignorance and left him with the dishevelled but intense man, still in conversation with the taller, who broke off when he saw Renzi was free.

'Mikhail Speransky, administrator,' he said, with an elegant bow. 'An honour to meet you, Graf Farndon.'

'Er, yes. Thank you.' This was the powerful and feared courtier that Vonskoy had spoken about, who had the one quality he needed above all others. He was personal assistant to the Tsar.

'You are a scholar about to make exploration of the Russian soul, I've heard.'

Renzi inclined his head politely. 'Fortune has been kind to me as providing for my travels and studies even as I sustain my duties as the Earl of Farndon.' The potted version of his study did not appear to satisfy and he launched into a more rarefied account, which caused the intelligent features to wrinkle in concentration.

'Graf Farndon, I believe your hypothesis has both merit and application in the Russia of these times. I would wish to debate it with you at a more opportune time.'

'It would be my pleasure, Mr Speransky.' He bowed. 'As I can be parted from Academician Lebedev.' It couldn't have been more fortuitous. In fact, it was more than his pathway to the Tsar: it was the chance to wrangle his logic and thesis with a worthy disputant.

It brought a fleeting smile. 'Then perhaps tea when you're free?' He turned and left.

'The most dangerous man in all Tsardom.' It was the untidy individual still remaining.

'I beg your pardon?'

'Karamzin. A historian you won't have heard of, yet not without influence. Yes, there's a devil in Speransky that drives him to an elevation of confidence by the Tsar, and yet at the same time to outlandish and exotic theories of governance of the Russian peoples that betrays this same confidence.'

So. Factions and enemies. As must be the case anywhere. All the more reason to act the disinterested savant.

Lebedev took possession of him once again and in the afternoon they visited Catherine the Great's Imperial Library. This was not among the buildings along the embankment but on the other side of the Neva, in the centre of St Petersburg, not very far from the squares and palaces of the Romanovs. Although it was not yet officially open, he was an honoured guest and given a research alcove of his own in the huge edifice, which he was told contained more than a hundred thousand works of scholarship and learning.

It was a pleasant and stimulating visit but time was pressing. Speransky was the key, and it was with marked relief that he boarded the carriage for his estate and the promised tea. It was out in the country, giving Renzi a chance to take his fill of the sights, even if his mind was racing with both possibilities and dangers.

Would he be credible enough to gain admittance to the person of the Tsar? Inevitably he would be seen as cleaving to the Speransky faction, whom Lebedev had dismissed as trouble-makers of reformist liberals and therefore in the conspicuous minority in this deeply conservative country.

Would it matter? Possibly – but he had to reach the Tsar. And this was his only chance. Without question Speransky was testing him against his reputation for evidence of value and would decide whether or not to take things further with him. It had to be done in this way, and by the time he entered the stately villa he was prepared to fall in with any opinions of Speransky that would help the situation.

'Welcome, Graf Farndon, welcome,' Speransky said heartily, standing in front of the fire in the well-appointed sitting room. 'I do feel gratified at your visit, my lord. If there's anything I might get for you after your journey, do pray let me know.'

He was in a comfortable wine-coloured coat with velvet lapels in the new Romantic fashion taking hold in London. Renzi had taken care with his appearance: as a harmless scholar, his dress was modest, understated, dark, but as an earl the material was costly and elegant.

'Tea?'

After Count Vonskoy's tuition he knew what to do. When Speransky had filled his glass with an intense black brew from the samovar, he reached for a sugar cube, put it between his teeth and drank through it. With a gracious inclination of the head in acknowledgement, Speransky produced a platter of dainty biscuits thick with jam and heavy cream.

Renzi took one and pronounced it good, even if his palate was unused to the assault of sweetness.

'Named after Suvorov, our imperial marshal who put down the Kościuszko uprising,' Speransky mentioned smoothly.

'Oh, do forgive me – I find military matters so tedious in the detail,' Renzi murmured, secretly pleased to have his harmlessness confirmed so early.

'Of course, dear fellow.'

Lebedev had been free with his insights and opinions, and Renzi had already formed his ideas about what drove Speransky. The man was some form of reformer in a liberal mould. In a state so autocratic and diehard traditional, he would find himself very much on the defensive – but Speransky had the Tsar's ear and could keep them at bay indefinitely. Apparently he was a logician and took well to arguments so presented, even if opposed to his.

If he was to get further, Renzi had a single overriding objective: to win over the man by showing he had personal value.

'So your studies have brought you here?' Speransky continued pleasantly.

'Indeed. Would you wish to hear them?'

'Very much indeed, sir.'

As warmly as he could Renzi set out his thesis that common underlying strands of human striving lay beneath the daily challenges of life, hidden by distracting cultural layers. Only by comparing in detail these responses could the strands be made to reveal themselves for use by the governing class.

'You have made progress, Graf Farndon? I'm much taken by the vision of your comparing the natives of the South Seas and the serfs that toil in the fields of Russia. Do tell.'

The interest was genuine but tinged with an element of cynicism. He would have to try harder.

'Sir, much of what I discovered is claimed by politicking animals whose desire is to appear scholarly in their views. Without a reigning hypothesis and data to support it, they tread upon treacherous sands and cannot prove their position. Take, for example, the role of human bondage in the getting of food . . .'

He had the man's interest now and, with persuasive conviction, went on to examine on the one side crucial economic factors and on the other the irrational, affective motivations involved – and how bondage as a method of extracting labour must inevitably fail.

Before he'd finished he could see that he'd succeeded. Possibly because in his heart he believed in what he was saying.

Speransky's eyes glowed and, in his rapt attention, he still held his empty tea-glass. 'Bravo!' he said huskily. 'As I'd give much to be at the address to the academy that will no doubt be asked of you.'

'Then should I now take my leave, Count Speransky?'

'No!' Speransky said hastily. 'No. That is, I rather feel that Alexander – the Tsar, I mean – would be much seized by your work. If I introduced you to him, would you be so good as to attend on His Majesty to discuss it? I can assure you of an intelligent audience.'

Renzi felt a leap of exultation. He'd done it! Speransky had seized on what he had to offer. That which gave him special value. He was going to be flourished before the Tsar as a scholar of distinction who would publicly declare the rightness, grounded in science, of his liberal reforms.

'The Tsar!' Renzi breathed, overcome. 'B-but this is . . .'

'Come, sir. This is only your due in bringing to us the fruits of your enlightened position. I have His Imperial Majesty's particular trust and affection and you may be sure of an audience on my account. He takes a keen concern in the practices of other polities, and to couple this with the rigours of natural philosophy will be most engaging to him, I assure you.'

Chapter 41

It was just a short passage by ferry across the Neva to the South Bank, the heart of St Petersburg. In keeping with his vision of a Venice of the North, Peter the Great had ordained that there would be no bridges, only boats, and in winter, sleighs over the ice. The crossing gave a stunning view of the principal splendours of Russia, but Renzi was distracted.

To have gained the attention of the Tsar at this early stage was miraculous but so much was riding on this first encounter. Every instinct urged that time was running out, that there would be an eruption into war very soon. It was of crucial importance that he let London know his best estimate of Alexander's intentions in that event. Any judgement of the autocrat as a military leader, however, was a task for another.

If he could provoke the Tsar's curiosity he had a chance – but if Vonskoy and Speransky were wrong about his thirst for learning, he'd be ignored and would have no alternative but to return to England empty-handed.

He was jerked back to the present by the spectacle of magnificence the avenues of imperial buildings made: the gold-finished onion-shaped domes of churches, the regular symmetry of the architecture, the simplicity yet grandeur of the stately monuments to one man's purpose. Truly a city of princes. And none was more majestic than the residence of the Tsar, the Winter Palace. Renzi's intellects told him it was in style late Baroque, but in its white and turquoise finished in gold, and contrasting stately yellow stucco walls, there was an alluring emotional component that was purely Russian. Within, it was a glory of the most exquisite ornamentation on walls of every colour conceivable, each room furnished in carved elaborature and red velvet. There was nothing remotely like it in the England of George III that Renzi knew of, a sumptuous and exotic feast for the senses.

'My friend,' Speransky murmured, 'at this notice even I cannot command an audience. We shall join others who wait on His Majesty's appearance and I shall then introduce you to him.'

Flanked by bewigged footmen they passed down a passage and entered a day-room resplendent with mirrors, paintings and ormolu. Inside, ladies in the height of fashion, jewelled, with romantic head-dressings, were accompanied by officers in elaborate uniforms and swords. Faces turned in surprise at their entry.

Near the window a lady of splendid maturity was holding court, and at Renzi's appearance conversations fell away. He gave an elegant bow as Speransky introduced him in French. There were disdainful and even hostile expressions on the men, but from several ladies there were bold, appraising looks, languid fluttering of fans doing nothing to hide their naked interest.

'An Englishman?' one of the officers said, in a bored tone. 'Come to tell us how to beat Napoleon?'

Through scattered titters Renzi gave a beatific smile and

in the flowery French of the old regime replied, 'As came to Russia to see whether to admire or merely pity. Lord Farndon, at your service, sir.'

Speransky touched his arm. 'The son of Grand Duke Nikolai, and a soldier of brave heart – in the salons.'

The sound of voices approaching brought tension to the gathering and two guards entered, taking position each side of the door.

Then into the room came the unmistakable form of Alexander, Tsar of Russia.

Instantly everyone made obeisance, ladies held in a deep curtsey, the gentlemen dropping to one knee. Renzi compromised with an elaborate bow as might be expected at the Court of St James.

'Do rise, my people,' the Tsar said, his voice carrying, high-pitched and light. A tall, even boyish figure in pearl-grey plain military uniform with sash and decorations, he carried himself well, statuesque yet delicate, his golden hair slightly balding. He approached the elderly woman, wearing a fortune in pearls, who made to rise from her chair, but Alexander quickly went to her and gently kissed her, exchanging soft words. Renzi was touched at the tenderness he saw in him, unaccountable in a suzerain of Tartary.

He greeted each group politely, exchanging quiet words with this one and that until he arrived before Renzi.

Speransky's bow was familiar, and in return Alexander reached out and patted his arm. 'Well, old fellow, you're bearing up after your fever?' he asked and, without waiting for a reply, his gaze alighted on Renzi.

'Sire, it's with pleasure I'm able to introduce the Earl of Farndon of Great Britain who's journeyed here to make study of our ways.'

'Goodness me, whatever for?' Alexander said, in a benevolent but curious tone. 'In an Englishman I find that singular indeed!'

'He is a well-regarded scholar, Majesty, whose interests do not include the practice of war. At the moment he's engaged in a monumental work of natural philosophy that I would be failing Your Majesty if it were not brought to your attention.'

The Tsar turned to Renzi, who had a fleeting impression of cloudless blue eyes and a soft, near-luminous presence. 'Would you explain it to me, sir?'

Renzi had practised his words until he could deliver their essence in short, pithy phrases leading inexorably from the general to the particular and then a conclusion.

'Fascinating.' Alexander's gaze rested on him for a moment longer. Then he smiled briefly and walked on, leaving Renzi holding his breath in suspense, but it was over, Speransky silently motioning him to remain.

After the Tsar had left, the room burst into excited chatter. 'Well, did I—'

'I cannot say,' replied Speransky, and held his silence.

Before long an imperial functionary entered. The chatter died as he crossed to Speransky, who bent to catch the whispered message.

'I may say that it seems you have succeeded, Lord Farndon. Tsar Alexander begs that if you are at leisure this afternoon you will attend on him to further discuss your hypothesis.'

Accompanied by Speransky, Renzi was ushered into the Tsar's presence, this time in the sanctity and quiet of a private imperial withdrawing room, set about with crimson damask, gilt bronzes and malachite, a fire blazing comfortably. The refreshments were more to Renzi's taste: a brandy of the first rank.

With only the three together, the threads of Renzi's thesis were explored and Renzi found himself warming to the Tsar, his transparent desire for answers, for reasons and causes. If he was guided by a worldly but progressive statesman such as Speransky, who knew what Russia could aspire to?

At one point Speransky excused himself for a short while, leaving them alone together. Almost immediately Alexander turned anxiously to Renzi. 'Tell me, Nikolai, Speransky is a vastly able thinker but he frowns on some of my theorising. For instance, do you not believe the ancients have much to teach us?'

'I do, sire.' What was going on? This was an autocrat of immense powers keeping at bay both the patriciate factions and the peasantry: what need had he of ancient Grecian politicking? And any reasonably educated person could have no quarrel with the precepts of Pythagoras, Hipparchus and the rest.

'You do? Then if we accept their precepts and propositions we do so in full acceptance of their circumstances and conditions?'

'Er, it would seem wise to do so.'

'Yes!' exulted the Tsar. 'As I do! That Achilles dwelled in his tent has deeper meaning, as does Ulysses upon the rock of despair. If we are to aspire to rule in all unassailable logic, then surely we must invoke the same conditions as then.'

Turn Russia into a three-thousand-year-old throwback? He was saved from answer by Speransky's return, but he'd seen what Vonskoy had hinted at – the Tsar's mystic nature, which ruled his thoughts.

Speransky effortlessly took charge of the conversation. 'Ah, yes. We were discussing the role of the land-owning power in the choices facing the tenant?'

The offer, when it came, was both flattering and dangerous. 'It has been most interesting, Nikolai. Regrettably I've a state dinner tonight that Elizabeth accounts important I must attend. I have it in mind to grant you a state apartment here in the Winter Palace for the length of your stay in Russia. For selfish reasons only – that we might spend more time together.'

Chapter 42

Thunderer, *at sea*

At last! The brisk south-westerly, a fine, quartering breeze with the clean tang of brine in it, purged away all the gross humours of the land, carrying Kydd's ship on with a will up-Channel.

The new administration had concluded that the vast host gathering on the Continent was not intended for the invasion of Britain whatever else Bonaparte had in view, and the hastily assembled fleet of defence at Portsmouth was released to go its separate ways.

The situation, however, was grave, unstable and unknowable. The great horde was intended for a purpose that would probably be set in motion very shortly. It was thus considered prudent to strengthen what was now Britain's most vulnerable preserve, the Baltic, and *Thunderer*, with two other ships-of-the-line, was on her way to Admiral Saumarez to reinforce his command. Ahead, *Montagu* was taking the seas spectacularly on the bow. Tucked in astern, the elderly *Blake* made best speed to keep with them as they passed the familiar coastal sea marks.

Kydd and Craddock took their ease for a space in the stern gallery, hearing the swash and roar of the ship's wake below and admiring the soft green of the English countryside as it slipped by. They passed the mass of ships anchored in the Downs waiting for a fair wind, held up by the same south-westerly that was making their own passage so lively. Then it was around the North Foreland, to Sheppey and the Nore.

They didn't linger and, after passing over dispatches and mail to Flag, they made the most of the bracing wind to stand off for the Yarmouth Roads and the convoy assembling for the Baltic. Kydd knew that to land there to replenish cabin stores for himself and the wardroom would be to compete with the hundreds of vessels preparing to sail. Instead he sent away a cutter under sail south to Lowestoft with Binard and a good-sized purse, to be back before sunset.

The convoy-escort commander in his brig-sloop, with responsibility for near six hundred ships, was gratified to have an unchallengeable addition to his force with the three sail-of-the-line. In the Navy way of things, they would be under his command.

It was an uneventful few days across the North Sea and to the dispersal point, Wingo Sound, discreetly to the west of Gothenburg. Kydd saw to his pleasure the noble bulk of *Victory* at the naval anchorage, the flagship of Admiral Saumarez whom he'd known as a young commander in his first ship. 'Mr Roscoe, call away my barge. I'm to make my number, I believe.' He didn't return for some time and that night was invited to a wardroom dinner.

'The admiral was delayed, sir?' enquired Smale, filling Kydd's glass.

'Not as if he meant to,' Kydd came back mildly, raising his glass to admire its lustre. The low evening sun's glitter on the water reflected prettily on the deckhead and was picked up in flares by the mess silverware. 'He was flag when I was a raw commander of my first ship. Caught up in an affair alongshore in Guernsey for which he turned me out of my ship and I went a-privateering.'

It brought gasps of astonishment.

'The occasion not being any culpability of mine, I was able to prove my innocence and was restored. Today he was moved to remark my elevation in the service since, is all.'

'We'd be obliged for details, if you'd confide them, Sir Thomas.' Roscoe could clearly smell a good dit. Sailors told these yarns among themselves in the leisure sea-time together allowed.

'On another occasion, perhaps,' Kydd said, preferring to let it rest until he knew them better.

Briggs murmured politely, 'You've served in the Baltic before, I understand, sir.'

'Yes, and not so long ago.' This was when *Tyger* was part of the urgent need to preserve the critical Baltic trade, closed off by Bonaparte's recent Continental System of economic blockade. In those desperate times the threat to Britain's supply of naval stores alone could have brought down the country. A third major fleet, after the Channel Fleet and Advanced Squadron, was set up to defend it from, among other menaces, the Russian battle fleet lying in Kronstadt ready to pounce on the foreigners to the Baltic.

Kydd had been delayed in his return because he wanted to know from Admiral Saumarez where they stood these days.

The answer had been chilling. At this moment every single nation bordering the Baltic was an enemy, an ally of Napoleon

Bonaparte and therefore must support his Continental System. If together they willed it, England would be on her knees in weeks and out of the war. Or, if Bonaparte exerted his maritime strength, put to sea even some of his many sail-of-the-line, the handful of ships Saumarez commanded would be quickly overcome and the result would be the same.

And was his massing of a colossal army not so far to the south a prelude to an occupation of the Baltic coast end-to-end, designed to bring about the collapse of Britain's presence and trade as Kydd knew it, again with war-losing consequences?

Kydd had come to appreciate that Saumarez was an undisputed master at manipulating, cajoling and threatening in a bizarre conjuring of diplomatic moves that had the Baltic – for now – open and free.

It was extraordinary: Sweden was at war with Great Britain but Saumarez had privately conceded to him that not a shot would be fired in what amounted to a friendly war. Furthermore, they would not be watching as big convoys assembled off Gothenburg and Hanö to convey, like a mill-race, the products of Britain's industrial might into the very heartland of the Continent. In the many trading ports customs officials were bribed, hidden caches of goods were auctioned off, smugglers alerted – in a wholesale circumventing of the Emperor's will.

Other wildly irregular means were found to make the Baltic the fatal wound in the Continental System. At an early stage Saumarez had let it be known that neutral shipping would be afforded a place in the convoys for their protection, on production of their papers. They were forged on a massive scale, but escort commanders and shore authorities alike accepted them with straight faces. Bonaparte's subjects had a taste for the tin pots, cheap lace, crockery, fine linen, machinery and robust clothing that poured out of England's factories and furtively into homes under his subjection. In return, precious supplies of grain, timber, iron ore and hemp made their way back. Even Lloyds of London was hesitant about insuring a vessel for a voyage to the Baltic unless it carried 'simulated papers'.

But the entire system hung on a ramshackle framework that could so easily be upset. If there was a concerted move to stand by obligations under the Continental System – under threat or otherwise – it would all come undone for Saumarez and his conjuring. But at this point there was only one nation in active opposition to the British, faithfully supporting Bonaparte with its geographical situation at the entrance to the Baltic, the Sound, which it had traditionally commanded with passage dues and strict regulation. Since the British Navy had robbed it of the entirety of its navy, Denmark had gamely fallen back on home-built gunboats and brigs to enforce them. They used the craft as best they could, rowing boats against frigates, brigs before ships-of-the-line, in a courageous but doomed fight for honour.

'I do not in the slightest underestimate the Danes. They of all have reason to hate us,' Saumarez had murmured.

Now, glass in hand, Kydd had to make clear to his officers their purpose in these waters, what they faced in coming to the support of the Baltic Fleet and what was the best guess for Bonaparte's next move.

'Where shall we be doing duty do you think, sir?' Roscoe asked.

Saumarez and the majority of his fleet were stationed at the mouth of the Baltic where they could move with dispatch to counter threats either within or outside the landlocked sea. But a substantial number of his ships, including sail-of-the-line, were far inside, keeping unblinking watch on the major naval base of Kronstadt at the other end of the Baltic where Russia maintained its fleet. Leave and diversion were easily found in Gothenburg, a handful of miles under their lee, but not for those on vigil far in.

'I've been led to believe we shall shortly be relieving the Kronstadt guard.'

Long faces appeared around the table. This was no better than the blockade they'd left, with the added disadvantage of the weather as the year moved into autumn and then the winter ice.

The next few days saw *Thunderer* storing for the hostile station she was about to take up but matters were interrupted by a sudden summons from *Victory*.

'Sir Thomas. I fear your joining Admiral Byam Martin off Kronstadt will have to be delayed.'

'Sir?'

'On account of word I've received from Denmark.' Saumarez had a first-class intelligence network and it could be relied upon. 'Which is most disturbing.'

Kydd waited patiently.

'You were at the bombardment of Copenhagen.'

'I was.'

'Where we removed their navy and stores, leaving them nothing.'

'Sir.'

'This makes it near impossible for them to achieve what they most need to do – choke off the Sound to us on the one hand and look to their dependency, Norway, on the other.'

'Dependency?' Kydd asked.

'Union, if you must. All matters such as foreign affairs, trade and so forth are centralised in Copenhagen, and they have a common monarchy – a Danish king. This war with

Bonaparte has been ruinous to the Danes and nothing more so than to their Norwegian brethren, who are now cut off from their governors and trade partner.'

'You mentioned intelligence, sir?'

'Yes. What single thing do you think could, in one, restore the situation for the Danes?'

'Er, an alliance?'

'They already have one – with Napoleon Bonaparte. No, sir. Consider a frigate – a heavy frigate of 42 guns loose on the sea-lanes. Coming upon one of our prodigious convoys guarded only by a gaggle of sloops, they'd be cut to pieces at immense loss in treasure to us. And the opposite – an enemy convoy of military contraband with an untouchable escort that can cross to Norway and plant an unstoppable insurrection in our rear.'

'And there is such a one?'

'There is. The cunning and resourceful Danes have scraped together all the timbers that remain from when we destroyed any of their ships-of-the-line we couldn't take in prize and from it have built a formidable frigate. And it has just left the shipyards, bound for Norway, fully armed and stored for a cruise of plunder and ravage. It must be stopped. Sir Thomas, I want you to hunt it down and destroy it.'

Chapter 43

Kydd knew why Saumarez had chosen him: as a proven frigate warrior he was best able to fathom the reasoning of another of the breed. The choice of *Thunderer*, a ship-of-the-line, was another matter. If he was to run a frigate to earth it wasn't so much a matter of speed or gun-power but the fact that Norway's coast opposite Denmark was a frightful chaos of skerried reefs, inner leads and craggy, rocky islands. They ranged in size from puny to substantial and numbered in the thousands. Not the place for a deep-draught battleship but a measure of how consequential Saumarez believed the frigate's destruction to be.

Their charts were old and unreliable but he'd been given a brig-sloop, *Calypso*, and two unrated gun-brigs, *Podargus* and *Flamer*. They would have less trouble with the shoals, but if they came upon the Dane they'd be comprehensively outclassed.

His information from the flag-lieutenant was clear and concise as far as it went. The frigate's name was *Najaden*. Captained by one Hans Peter Holm, it was manned mostly with Norwegians and was said to be a flyer. It was now heading for the capital of Norway, Christiansand, the base for their privateers and gunboats, which were the only weapons left to the Danes. Accompanied by three brig-sloops it could call on up to twenty-five gunboats, each armed with at least a twenty-four-pounder long gun.

Kydd knew the best outcome of the hunt was a meeting in the open sea where his much larger armament would tell decisively. But Holm would be too astute for that, plying the inner leads among the treacherous reefs and islands between strikes.

Saumarez couldn't afford to keep one of his precious sail-of-the-line out of the fleet indefinitely in a fruitless flogging up and down the hundreds of miles of coast: the way ahead had to be information.

Thunderer raised the untidy scatter of forested islets off Christiansand in an easy westerly and almost immediately sighted sail, two merchant brigs outward bound from the capital.

'Heave 'em to, Mr Roscoe.'

They were a pair of Swedish Pomeranian fish traders lightly disguised as Estonians. Kydd didn't pry too deeply for he wanted something of them far more precious than their prize value.

'Sir,' his first lieutenant reported, 'they said that the Danish frigate arrived three days ago and left again for the north yesterday with three brigs-of-war in company.'

'Where bound?' Kydd asked hopefully.

'Rumour has it that it's gone to join with the gunboats in Arendal.'

A notorious nest of the vermin some forty miles to the north-east. It made a good deal of sense for Holm to keep away from Christiansand, a well-watched seaport. And from Arendal he would be central to the length of Norway's eastern seaboard, an intolerable threat.

'Clap on all sail! I want to be smelling powder before sunset, Mr Hobbs.'

To be on the scent before even they'd arrived – was this too good to be true? Nevertheless the little squadron shaped course resolutely for the north.

Kydd paced impatiently up and down the quarterdeck. He had *Calypso* in the lead, a brig-sloop smaller even than *Teazer*, his first command, but more sizeable than *Podargus* and *Flamer*, the little brigs out on either beam. These were of the same class as the legendary Cochrane's *Speedy*: the admiral had famously said he could walk his quarterdeck with her whole broadside in his pockets. They wouldn't have a chance against *Najaden* but they didn't have to face the big frigate, just keep *Thunderer* informed.

Flamer lagged, taking seas on the bow that others could shoulder aside. *Thunderer* had to bring in sail to compensate, but Kydd did not believe that Holm would be taking the direct route by sea: he'd be threading his way up by the tortuous inner leads and losing time because of it.

They had a chance.

As a lazy evening began to draw in they were at the seaward approaches to Arendal. Two islands loomed, the larger to the right, Merdø, under a mile long of ugly bone-grey rock. Beyond them was an obscure channel barely a couple of hundred yards wide, presumably leading to the inner leads and the harbour.

'We can't enter there,' the sailing master pronounced, with finality. 'Give 'em best, sir.'

Kydd took in the reality of the iron-bound coastline and knew he was right. But as he pondered *Podargus* hauled its wind to come within hail.

'Sir Thomas? I've a man aboard knows these parts. I submit we're best suited to lead us in.'

'Are you sure he can act the pilot?' It was an immense responsibility, and if he was some kind of lower-deck braggart, disaster would be complete. And saying 'lead us in' – it was foolish in the extreme to contemplate taking in a ship-of-the-line.

'He says he's certain, having been this way many times before.'

'Very well,' Kydd said reluctantly. 'But *Calypso* and I will wait for your reconnaissance.'

He'd only met Lieutenant-in-Command Robillard once but had been impressed. With growing concern he watched as the young man eased sheets and brought his ship around and into the narrowing passage. The little sloop had only just cleared Merdø when she sheered violently to one side. A signal jerked excitedly up – 'Enemy in sight'!

At the same time a lookout in *Thunderer*'s foretop shrieked down, '*Deck hoooo!* There's ships a-lying t'other side of the island! I just seen their masts!'

The object of the mission lay out of sight behind the island, a shrewd move by Holm. He was protected by the horrors of rock and shoal that would deter outsiders from entry while leaving him within minutes of putting out, able to fall on a convoy.

What Holm hadn't reckoned on was that the hunters would have a pilot to show the way.

The crump and slam of firing sounded from beyond Merdø. Columns of gun-smoke rose into the air and shot-strike tore the water viciously around the hapless *Podargus*. Ominously, from the island opposite, shore batteries sighted in to cover *Najaden*'s anchorage began to speak.

Kydd knew he couldn't simply give up and sail away, the deadly threat nearly in his hands. Neither could he lie off to wait for it to emerge: an infinity of inner hidden inlets and passages would allow it to make off unseen. 'We go in,' he snapped. 'Take station on *Podargus* – she'll be in the deeper water. As soon as *Najaden* is in sight, give it a starb'd broadside.'

'Sir? There's no room to manoeuvre in there!'

'Get under weigh this minute, sir!'

Thunderer took up ponderously in the fjord-like calm and slid past Merdø, her guns run out, but instead of a clear field of fire they found the enemy frigate near encircled by another three islets.

And *Podargus* was stopped with a very definite list, gone aground in going about to warn *Thunderer*.

'Sir! I see one – no, three – five gunboats to the nor'ard!' From out of the eye of the Arendal passage and almost certainly with more on their way.

And then came a barely perceptible shudder, then another, sharper, and a significant slowing. 'Hard a larb'd!' the master shouted, but it was too late. *Thunderer* was brought up all standing, herself victim of a hidden skerry outcrop.

'Get the sail off her!' Kydd roared, in desperate frustration. Not yet within striking range of *Najaden*, they were motionless, unable to either move forward or retreat. *Flamer* sailed past gamely on her way in to stand by *Podargus*, now under fire from the first gunboats. As long as she could keep clear of the reefs she was a mortal threat to them, moving faster and with carronades and grape-shot. But *Najaden* thundered out her spite on them both.

Furiously Kydd forced his mind to concentrate. Shadows were lengthening as the evening drew to a close but night would bring no relief. Unless he could come up with a plan they stood to be battered to pieces or brought to an inevitable surrender.

Then he had it: as long as Holm thought *Thunderer* was at

his mercy, *Najaden* would take her time to warp out and take position on the big ship's bow to hammer *Thunderer* into oblivion. If he saw that she wasn't helpless under his guns, he'd wish he were somewhere else.

'Mr Roscoe, I want every boat in the water with a line to our bow.'

'We're going to tow off the reef?' the first lieutenant came back incredulously.

'Yes – and no. Go to it, sir!'

In the last of the light, watchers from *Najaden* saw furious activity in the fore-part of *Thunderer*, then boats with towing lines clawing the water directly towards the frigate. It seemed the massive ship-of-the-line was only lightly aground and in a short time would be in position to bring a storming rage of shot to destroy them.

Sometime during the night the frigate slipped away into one of the many inlets or sounds to the inner reaches of the jagged Norwegian coastline, leaving *Thunderer* to ease free on the tide in the early hours of the morning.

Re-grouping in the slop and hurry of the blessed open sea Kydd had much to think on.

Among these craggy archipelagos it was going to be next to impossible to force a conclusion with a man-o'-war that had all the advantages of local knowledge. Unless Robillard's seaman pilot . . . Could this tip the balance back?

'I'll trouble you for your man,' Kydd hailed *Podargus*.

He watched as the seaman warily came over the bulwark, his bag thrown expertly ahead of him.

'Todd, sir. Quartermaster,' he said, touching his hat.

Kydd noted the lines of maturity in his open face, the well-kept sailor's rig that was the mark of the born mariner. 'Come below and tell me something of the coast,' he invited. 'You'll be given a mess but no duties while you're aboard.'

264

It was a revealing talk. Todd had been a merchant seaman earlier, unusually in the coastal trade in a Danish-flag brig that needed to pass through the appropriate leads and inlets in accordance with the weather at the time, a perfect qualification.

Questioned about where Holm would most likely go now, he had no doubts. 'He'll not want to return t' Christiansand with you in the offing and agin this westerly, sir. So he has to go up the coast, taking the inner sound. Once he's in there, he can't get out to sea until he's passed right through – and there with brisker winds offshore you'll be waiting for him.'

This was something like Kydd needed.

With the westerly holding they made good time to seaward of the Hasteinsundet sound and, with sails backed, waited.

Later in the afternoon sail was spotted about to round the end of the outer island. It was *Najaden*.

'You see, sir, he's well aggrieved,' Todd said quietly, next to Kydd on the quarterdeck.

'Yes, well done,' Kydd replied.

'Oh, not that, sir. I meant as it's not what he wanted. He sees us but, in this westerly, can't go back down his bolt-hole. He has to stay out t' sea, and sailing north there's no channel to the inner leads for a dozen or more miles.'

The frigate was doomed.

As it emerged Kydd saw three more warships keeping close company, brig-sloops mounting full-calibre carriage guns, but none that could deter *Thunderer*'s unanswerable might.

The ship was already at quarters, and as they closed in for the kill, a mighty cheer broke out. After so long on dreary blockade they were going to be blooded!

But the canny Danish captain had not finished. The only advantage of a following wind was the ability to select his course with precision and he chose well. To his left were the impassable dour heights of a long island, but all along its outer seaboard was a near continuous necklace of islets. Jagged rock tips protruded from white sea-scars, an ugly roiling of sub-sea menaces all along the sea-cliffs.

Holm could be seen next to the helm, conning his ship directly towards them, not slackening the pace in the slightest. Then, in a masterly show of seamanship, he began threading his way through them, close in up the coast and safe from *Thunderer*.

Kydd looked at Todd who gave a wry smile. 'Can't follow, sir. Not in this'n. What does she draw?'

'Say twenty feet aft.'

A sorrowful shake of the head in response.

All afternoon the English squadron paralleled the Danish a mile or more out to sea. Sooner or later, when the coast cleared of hazard they would have a chance to pounce, but at four, conditions changed.

From astern, with the wind, a white curtain of rain advanced slowly, enveloping the ship in a cold deluge, hissing loudly in the sea and bringing misery to all on deck, but, worse, cutting visibility to yards until they lost sight of *Najaden* and her consorts.

What would Holm do? Would he take in sail and reduce speed in prudence, leaving *Thunderer* to forge ahead and lose him? Or would he take the opportunity to dog-leg to sea for a rapid advance to the next channel inshore? Possibly he'd merely go to anchor, knowing *Thunderer* was standing north and making away.

It was an old saying: 'Long foretold, long past – short notice, soon past.' The rain squall would not go away for some hours.

'Get *Podargus* alongside,' Kydd ordered.

Briefly he told her to remain in the vicinity and, when the

266

squall lifted, look out for *Najaden*. He ordered *Calypso* to stretch out ahead to do the same. *Thunderer* and *Flamer* would go on at best guess for the north.

The rain lasted for another two hours before it thinned and cleared.

Najaden was nowhere in sight.

Kydd had half hoped that the frigate in its hubris would appear wrecked and broken on some craggy reef, but it seemed that Holm was too good a seaman to let that happen. From Todd he discovered that there were channels bearing off each islet, which, while leading to a seaport of sorts, would be a trap for him, a dead-end. With no word from *Podargus* Holm had to be somewhere ahead.

Calypso appeared but with no sighting signal flying. 'Spotted, sir. Three miles south of here, but since vanished.'

'Mr Todd?'

'Can't think why . . . Yes, I can! He's gone to ground, and I know where.'

'Say on.'

'A snug little anchorage, sheltered on all sides an' not seeable from the sea.'

'Go on,' Kydd encouraged.

'We used it to make Vinterstø in the winter and—'

'Show me on the chart.'

It was an insignificant cove off an impossibly narrow waterway to the larger coastwise sound.

In his bones Kydd could feel Holm gloating that no Englishman would know of this hideaway, with its convenient access to the open sea and passing convoys, as he lay low there.

Send in *Calypso* and the others? Against a heavy frigate at rest – they wouldn't last more than minutes. But *Thunderer* . . .

'Todd, draw me a chart – a diagram. Show me everything.'

His heart sank as he studied it closely. A perfect maze, a warren of paths and inlets, sounds and fjords. And basically an impossible situation: *Najaden* and her consorts lay concealed in the tiny harbour of Lyngør to one side of a narrow channel through which *Thunderer* might pass but could never turn and go back. Or manoeuvre to bring guns to bear or any other motions against the enemy.

Kydd looked again. If this was what Holm was able to do every time he was sighted and chased, the hunt could last for ever.

How could he conceivably turn it to advantage, having the knowledge but not the ability to do anything?

He racked his brain. 'What's the depth of water?'

'Main north–south passage near bottomless. Off Lyngør it shallows.'

'And *Najaden* lies there.'

'Sir.'

What he was thinking of was a desperate, even lunatic act but, given the stakes, he'd do it – he'd have to.

'Mr Hobbs,' he told the sailing master. 'I'm going in. Mr Roscoe, gun-crews to their guns, sail trimmers to stand by tacks and sheets.'

'Sir, would it not be better—'

'No, Mr Roscoe.' If it failed he wanted it laid entirely to his account. 'As well, I want a well-secured kedge anchor over the stern.'

When all was ready Kydd took a deep breath. 'Ease her away, if you please.'

The deck fell silent as the rocky grey coast pressed in on them as they slid by, close enough to see the splash of orange lichen and individual details of the dark green northern scrub. And then a quarter-mile past the steep bulk of the final island the Danish frigate and its three brigs burst into view.

'Hard a' starb'd!' Kydd roared. Then, to the tense sail-handlers, 'Let loose and throw off the lines!'

Najaden was taken by surprise, and *Thunderer* was left to complete her manoeuvre.

The sailing master, appalled at where they were going, gripped the rail in despair. 'Sir – we're . . . we're . . .'

The bowsprit of the great ship-of-the-line continued to track around to point accusingly at the frigate.

But it didn't stop there. With loose sail banging and slatting, she continued the turn as though wearing about, her yards seemingly within feet of the rugged stone of the shore.

'Slip the after kedge and stand by!' Kydd bawled, and spun about again for the crowning move.

Roscoe turned to him, his face pale and set but holding back as *Thunderer* completed her turn – and ran her bow ashore in a grinding thud and long drawn-out squeal.

'You . . . you've—'

'Hold your peace, Mr Roscoe,' Kydd said, gazing intently at the angles, for what happened next would either make or break his wild plan.

And it was working! Pinioned by her forefoot, the inertia of the turn kept her stern swinging until she was at right angles to the rocky coastline.

'Kedge – hold her at that!' he bellowed, his voice breaking with the intensity of his feeling. The seamen out of sight below threw on turns and hauled taut, the line thrumming dangerously, but the swing was caught. *Thunderer* eased and stopped. It left her broadside facing precisely the awkwardly placed *Najaden* not two hundred yards distant. Two whole decks of guns, including thirty-two-pounders, the armament of the biggest battleship, was now aimed at the frigate which was helpless and bottled up before them.

They were close enough to see every detail as Kydd stared at its quarterdeck, at the figures who seemed to stand waiting for death. Under such menace surely it would be understandable to strike colours now.

There was no movement but then foolishly, heroically, came a thin cry and the frigate's guns threw out their defiance, knowing full well what the awful response would be.

'Open fire,' Kydd said woodenly. Such courage deserved better than what had to happen now.

Thunderer's guns erupted in a blast of sound that echoed off the rocks, magnifying their rage and making all the more brutish the savagery of the ruin brought on the frigate. Battering to death the sleek creature, destroying the proud command of Holm, the seaman Kydd had come to admire, and leaving in its place a broken, shattered and flame-devoured wreck.

Chapter 44

St Petersburg

Outside the Winter Palace a soft wind rustled leaves and set a loosely fastened window shutter creaking. The profound darkness couldn't have made better conditions for the two figures on the balcony. Quietly cursing, the smaller tried yet another key on the ring but this time, with an oily click, the lock obeyed.

Noiselessly they dropped inside on to the deep carpet and eased the window shut behind them.

'Light!' hissed the smaller. A small dark-lantern was passed and one of its shutters was opened, shedding a dim glow in the large room. Their eyes darted about. It was richly appointed – even in the shadows the glitter of gold took the eye, as did the intricate carved giltwork and mantelpiece ornaments. But these men were not interested in costly gew-gaws; theirs was a stealthy quest for something of far more value: the rumoured evidence of the grossest act of treachery against the Tsar of Russia.

'Here!' one said, crossing quickly to a large ornate writing desk. It was locked but these men were professionals and it took little to force it open. He began swiftly rummaging, glancing at each article by the light of the lantern resting close by, and discarding them as quickly for they knew what they were looking for.

The other went from chair to table, carefully feeling beneath them for concealed packets or clipped papers. Behind pictures and hangings, under porcelain, heavy urns.

'*Chert voz'mi*,' the one at the desk muttered, under his breath. 'If it's not here, where the devil can it be?'

He straightened, catching an ornate vase on a nearby table. It fell, shattering noisily on one of the extended legs.

Both men froze for a long minute.

'Nothing.'

But then a shrill, agitated female voice sounded from the top of the stairs outside. 'Grigor! Grigor! There's someone inside – come quick!'

'We have to get out,' the smaller intruder snapped, slamming shut the desk leaf and making for the window.

'Wait!' the other said, bending to the wastepaper basket under the desk and feeling about in it.

'Leave it – he's no fool, he'd never make that stupid mistake. Drop it – let's go!'

The window opened out but then the door handle began rattling. 'Grigor, here!' the voice on the other side demanded loudly. 'Come here, bring help, you oaf!'

'Get out! Now!'

'Not yet – what's this? Take a look, Vladimir.'

He clutched several crumpled pieces of paper showing without doubt that ciphers had recently been worked on in that room.

'Thank God! We have it.'

Chapter 45

Renzi's apartment the following day

'But, dear fellow, if you do allow that the serfs go free to bestow their vote on any they deem worthy, you'll replace one set of problems with another.'

'To be dealt with in due time.'

'Unhappily that is not a quantity you can command.' Renzi was enjoying a cosy debate with Speransky, an intelligent and cool analyst. 'Without they understand the principles and facts, their choice is worthless. I rather feel a vast programme of education is called for to yield an informed vote, else—'

A thunderous tattoo at the door interrupted him. Before Speransky could answer, it burst open and half a dozen burly uniformed men flooded in, a sneering officer taking position in the centre.

'What's this, Balashov? You dare to—'

'Gosudárstvennyy Ministr Speransky. You have been arrested for crimes of treason and the betrayal of His Imperial Majesty's trust for which you will now answer – if you can.'

'You're insane, Balashov. This is the apartment of our distinguished English guest—'

It was the French of the Imperial Court that was being spoken and Renzi could understand all of what was being said but not its meaning. As far as it made sense, it was something of a coup by one of the many factions opposed to Speransky's reforms that threatened the age-old ancestral power structure. If so, he was caught up in as dangerous a plot as any he'd survived. And Renzi's fate was unconditionally bound up with Speransky's: he was the foreign savant who was giving the legitimacy of learning and natural philosophy to the man's visions.

'What are you trying to say, you idiot?'

The man's face darkened but he went on doggedly: 'You omitted to destroy these.'

He held up the pages of code, snatching them away when Speransky reached for them.

'So, you broke into my study, a flagrant criminal act.'

Renzi saw, however, that his face had gone white, and his voice was unsteady.

'These talk of high things, Speransky, and they're coded to "Toad", an address in Paris we've been watching and believe to be that of the traitorous Talleyrand. What do you say to that?'

'It's not as it appears. Take me to the Tsar. I'll explain only to him.'

'You're a cold-blooded criminal, Speransky. I can't allow that.'

'If you do not, my evil friend, you'll have to explain why you've removed his chief minister from his side without leave from him. You fancy standing before his wrath then, Balashov?'

*   *   *

274

The closed carriage rattled through the empty streets and out into the black and somnolent countryside as the cavalcade clattered on to Tsarskoe Selo, the retreat of the Tsar of Russia. So early in the morning the blustering Balashov was refused admission, Alexander said to be at his morning prayers, so the prisoner and escort, along with Renzi and the others, were left in a small room until after ten.

'Well, Balashov, what is so urgent it demands I abandon my presence before the Almighty?' Alexander snapped, at the chief of police on his knee before him.

'Grave and treasonous charges to be laid against Gosudárstvennyy Ministr Speransky, Your Imperial Majesty.'

Evidence was produced and allegations made, but Speransky remained stubbornly mute until Alexander cut through the stream of spite. 'Speransky, you shall account for it to me personally. Not you, Balashov.'

The two went into the stateroom together, the door firmly shut in the face of the chief of police and his entourage.

Renzi's fears retreated. For as long as Speransky held the Tsar's favour he was safe.

It was more than two hours of tension and boredom before there was movement and then they reappeared. Speransky emerged first, white and shaking. Behind him. Tsar Alexander had, tears in his eyes. He called softly, brokenly, 'Mikhailo Mikhailovitch – this is our farewell!'

Speransky stopped and looked back. Impulsively Alexander went to him, embraced him warmly, and sobbed, 'Once again, farewell!'

They parted and the Tsar fled back into the stateroom.

As if under a spell, the onlookers moved aside as Speransky walked through them, like a condemned man. As he passed Renzi he looked at him and murmured, 'Siberia.'

Balashov rounded genially on his followers. 'Thus do perish all tyrants. Let's drink on that, comrades!'

Departing noisily they disappeared, leaving Renzi alone. He was no longer a threat, just another doddering intellectual who'd lost his audience. With his access to the Tsar now cut short, there was little advantage and much danger if he stayed in Russia. He'd apply for his passport and quit the realm as quickly as he could.

Returning to his apartment he began sorting his belongings ready for the journey, reflecting on the near-criminal carelessness of Speransky in not destroying his workings. And if he had indeed been in correspondence with the wily Talleyrand it could only be for the purpose of undermining Bonaparte and now that was finished. It was a disastrous end to a promising beginning.

A reply to his request for papers to leave arrived within forty-eight hours but not in the form he expected.

'Graf Farndon, His Imperial Majesty desires you should attend him, if you will.' Renzi followed the chamberlain down the passages to the withdrawing room and was ushered in.

Tsar Alexander turned and straightened, clearly distraught.

'Dear Sir Farndon, so good in you to come.' He advanced with both hands outstretched to take Renzi's. 'I do so need a clear and honest mind to join with mine in finding a course through this quagmire of . . . of . . .'

'I understand, Majesty,' Renzi said, with a polite bow.

'Do know that it has been a practice in Russia since the esteemed and revered Pyotr Velikiy – that is to say, the Great – to seek counsel and philosophies from those in eminence in western lands. Should I beg it of you, sir, you will not deny me?'

Renzi held down a leaping exultation: this was more than

276

he had dared hope. 'I shall, sire, with my most sincere endeavours. I pray, however, I might stand excused from discussing matters military or even of diplomacy, in neither of which can I claim a sufficient degree of comprehension in their complexities.'

'You desire to avoid the unreason, the mischances and ill-fortune that follow in their study. That I can understand, my friend.'

'Sir.'

'Then do consider my plight, sir. I'm autocrat and ruler of all the Russias, yet must part with my most trusted adviser. Is this what it must cost me?'

There was nothing Renzi could do for Speransky: the Russian's foolish mistake had brought about his downfall. 'I fear so, Majesty.'

'It was I who told him to make contact with Talleyrand. He is innocent of treason.'

Renzi was momentarily at a loss for words but knew everything now hung on his response. 'Neither are you to blame for your action. A statesman is ruled by his reason, not his emotions, Majesty. You correctly saw that if you continued to lay your trust in one revealed as in communication with a hostile power it would be seen as the act of a weak-minded ruler. For the sake of all Russia, he must be offered up to martyrdom.'

Alexander's eyes glistened. 'You are right. Sir, you are undoubtedly right.'

'And I dare to say you will make his time of exile as comfortable as shall match his past status?'

'Yes, yes. That I can do for him.'

'Then you will have done all that is expected of you, Majesty.'

'Not all. I have no adviser and am presented with a

perplexity no man on earth can support without divine aid. I wish to share it with you, Nikolai.'

'Sire.'

'Not so long ago I made visit to Moscow. There the Patriarch himself stirred me to the bottom of my heart. He pronounced before all in the cathedral that I was the living icon of Russia and the instrument of God on earth. Into my hands was placed the destiny not only of Russia but of creation itself, to be the Almighty's shield and sword. Nikolai, when I stood before the tombs of great men in the Kremlin I was transfigured in heart and soul and for the first time saw this destiny before me.'

He drew himself up, a rosy flush mounting to his cheeks, and in a sublimely expressive gesture, he mimed opening a holy book. 'And that night I read in the Book of Revelation, "And I saw, and beheld a white horse: and he that sat on him had a bow; and a crown was given unto him: and he went forth conquering, and to conquer." My dear friend, I knew those words were meant for me alone. I'd had a dream of setting forth on such a white horse, but only to be set upon by another clad in black and intent on a duel to the death.'

The Tsar paused, his child-like blue eyes lifted in ecstasy. Then he dropped his gaze and, looking directly at Renzi, said gravely, 'Nikolai, by this I know that I'm fated to lead the world on a crusade against the Antichrist who is even now on earth, incarnate.'

Renzi managed to say, 'And you have identified the Antichrist?'

A slight frown passed quickly. Then Alexander replied, without hesitation, 'Of course. It's the Emperor of the French, Napoleon Bonaparte.'

'Yes, sire. But, er, where is your perplexity, pray?'

Just as rapidly the mood of ecstasy passed and the Tsar's

expression turned wooden. 'If I'm to lead the world, will the peasants fight for me?'

'I beg your pardon?'

'Russia is a country of millions. Against such a number none can resist. But only if they follow me. Will they?'

Entirely out of his depth, Renzi was floundering. 'I cannot know that, sire. But it is written that whosoever is of brave heart will never lack for followers.'

'My army commanders – Bagration, Barclay de Tolly, Rostopchin – bicker among themselves for honour and advantage. Some desire peace at any cost to save Russia from the greatest army the world has seen, led by its most victorious general. Others clamour for a surprise first attack on the French to deflect their purpose. What is your view, Nikolai?'

This was far past what Renzi should have been doing, but to retain any kind of presence he had to prove supportive. After all, he reasoned, the Tsar didn't have to take his counsel.

'Majesty. You yourself have said you are to be the Almighty's shield and sword. Not your subordinate generals. You shall be the one to appear at their head to inspire and lead. You shall assume the post of supreme commander and bear the honour and responsibility for the destiny of Russia in accordance with your vision and all shall obey.'

It was without question that if it came to war the autocratic Tsar would in any event trust no one but himself and seize the reins of military power. This provided only a gloss for the move.

Alexander's eyes glowed. 'This is how it must be. You are wise and understanding, Nikolai.'

'Therefore—'

'Therefore my decision is made.'

'May I—'

'Certainly.'

279

Renzi held his breath. In the next moments he would be getting precisely what he needed.

'I shall not move against Napoleon Bonaparte.'

Then it was not going to be war.

'Russia will be defended by the moral rightness of her cause.'

'And if Bonaparte attacks?'

'It will be a fatal mistake. But know that while I shall not be the first to draw the sword, I shall be the last to return it to the scabbard.'

The uneasy peace could yet endure. Without an ill-considered flourish by Russia to provoke war, Bonaparte was not in any position to keep his colossal army in existence indefinitely and must retire for the foreseeable future.

'A wise and thoughtful decision, sire,' Renzi said encouragingly, for with it the world would be spared the appalling spectacle of the slaughter of hordes that would follow any other course.

'You think so? I'm glad, Nikolai. Now, if you'll excuse me, I have an important journey to make. I hope you will be able to accompany me.'

'Of course, Majesty. Er, where will this be?'

'To Vilna,' Alexander said briskly. 'As my forebears have done before me, to seek aid and guidance from the Black Virgin at the Gate of Dawn.'

Renzi sat alone in his apartment. He had no illusions. At the moment he was of use to the Tsar, possibly even a genuine friend. If for any reason he failed him, he would be cast out by the eccentric autocrat as speedily as he'd been taken up. Yet at the moment Renzi was as close to his decision processes as any.

It was time to let London know. But what would he tell

them? That Tsar Alexander was anything but a ferocious barbarian Tartar lord, ready to summon up the unknown millions in Russia's vast interior to fall in a frenzied madness on Bonaparte's army? That instead he had to be reckoned an arch mystic, convinced his holy mission on earth was to rid it of the Antichrist Bonaparte – but not yet?

In answer to his quest to discover whether he would fight or no, there could only be one answer: it depended.

The Tsar would not declare war, that Renzi believed. At the head of an untrained peasant army and facing Napoleon Bonaparte, who had beaten him twice before, all that could be said was that if Bonaparte provoked an aggression he would respond.

The auguries were bleak, and he couldn't see how Great Britain could justify sending troops and wealth into such an apocalyptic unknown future. Now it was his duty to lay out his findings.

He sighed deeply and reached for the materials that would begin the procedure of activating Congalton's network to get out his vital message.

Chapter 46

The border at the Niemen river

The fire crackled and spat as the mess-pot was lifted off and taken away for doling out the contents to the soldiers, leaving the officers to their evening conviviality.

Adjutant Commandant Moreau enjoyed this time of the day, even though he disliked the crudity of mess arrangements while on campaign. Although they were not on the march, this was as much a campaign as any. The Grande Armée, encamped so close to the Russian border, was there to put the fear of God, or more precisely that of Napoleon Bonaparte, into the heart of the Tsar, his army and his people. Its purpose was to bring about a submission before even a shot was fired.

It was something Moreau greatly wished for as he knew the Emperor would not rest until the Tsar and his realm were his. He went along with the posturing, gestures and deceit for that very reason, knowing it was bringing ever more pressure to bear to this end.

The parading of a hundred thousands along this side of

the Niemen river border, drums thundering, bayonets glittering, all the panoply and raw colour of war, was a daily occurrence. Only today the Emperor had made another of his inspections for his strict instructions were that appearances must be as realistic as possible. With spies everywhere it had to be seen that the Grande Armée was ready in every particular or it would be put down as a grand charade, the vast, expensive assembling all for nothing. Any makeshift, and not only the men involved but their commanders would face harsh penalties.

Moreau had taken appropriate steps in his engineering corps to meet the demand, the whole a unit that was war-ready to move out at once. His speciality was the building of bridges, or pontoons as the army liked to call them. His meticulousness was well known: the long carts with the pre-drilled timber lengths also carried bolts and brackets, each keyed to a single position in the finished article, and strictly matched against a check-off list. Each man had an assigned function in the bridge-building, was responsible for his specialised tools and could be challenged for them.

'How much do you reckon this is costing the Emperor?' His friend, Ingénieur Géographe Rochambeau mused, sipping his wine. An unconventional, warm-hearted fellow, he'd done well to reach where he had and was at his best when about him things were at their worst.

'Does it matter? He'll screw it all back from Alexander after our eccentric Tsar comes to his senses.' It didn't escape Moreau's attention that it had been 'costing the Emperor' rather than 'costing the public purse'. His friend took it for granted, just as he did, that the Republic's treasury was in fact the Emperor's property.

'Hmm. Sooner this is over and done with the better I'd

like it. A dash of leave, say six weeks in dear Cavaillon with Marie, and I'm set up for the year. You?'

'I tell you confidentially, Bertrand,' Moreau said, looking over his shoulder, 'this marching back and forth the whole length of the civilised world for near twenty years on end leaves me tired and sick of it. And how we're to show enthusiasm for a crack now at the barbarian world is beyond me.'

'Don't worry, *mon ami*. I heard that Bonaparte sent an emissary to Alexander demanding final satisfaction in the strongest terms. It'll all be over shortly, you'll see.'

The evening drew in, supper was taken and moodily Moreau wandered to where the camp ended above the river and stared over into Russian territory, which was quickly shading into darkness. There were one or two pinpricks of light, but no acres of campfires stretching into the distance as there were on their side where a great army crouched. The population of the Grande Armée exceeded that of most cities in Christendom. It contrasted ominously with his view across the banks where an unearthly stillness spread from the interior of a continent that ranged many thousands of miles into the savage, unknowable east.

He shuddered and turned to go back before the darkness became complete.

There seemed to be some kind of activity, movement – lanterns, torches, raised voices.

'Where have you been, Moreau?' a high aide-de-camp snapped. 'Never mind. Join them in the General Staff pavilion.'

There was an almost palpable tension in the air. Senior officers in every degree of splendour occupied the chairs in front, and the rest, including Moreau and Rochambeau, stood.

'Marshal of the Empire Berthier.'

There was a small delay as the slight figure of Napoleon's

famed chief-of-staff took his place on an improvised dais. Significantly, he was arrayed not in imperial court regalia but in plain campaign dress and appeared ill at ease.

'Gentlemen. This is to acquaint you with the fact that the Imperial Grand Council has met in session with the Emperor.'

An announcement of sorts so soon afterwards implied a momentous outcome, and the assembly settled into watchfulness.

'At which it was decided what must be done to resolve our differences with the Russian Tsar following an unsatisfactory reply to our latest offer of peace.

'For reasons of state – I say again, for reasons of state – it was concluded that we have no other alternative than to make good on our final warning . . . and to launch a punitive strike into Russia.'

For long moments there was utter stillness. Then pandemonium broke out. Shouts punctuated it from all parts while Berthier waited, visibly distressed. He held up his hands for quiet.

A red-faced general in the front row stood up and shouted, 'Whose decision was this, sir, that plunges us into—'

Berthier cut him off coldly: 'Sir, it was the Grand Council in its collective wisdom that reluctantly took judgement so.'

'Madness!'

'His Imperial Majesty has declared that any who refuse to follow the eagles against the enemy will answer for it before the people. Those who do their duty, on the other hand, will share to the full in the plunder from the greatest adventure the Empire of the French has yet seen.'

'When shall we be called to arms?'

'Immediately, sir. While the enemy has not yet thought to bring up his legions to resist us. In short, sir, we launch our enterprise this very night.'

'You cannot mean it, sir!'

'The engineers are to throw up bridges in accordance with their current plans within the hour. The army will step off at four, no later.'

'What is our first objective?'

'A good question. And I will tell you that it is Vilna, in central Courland, where at this moment Tsar Alexander is undergoing a religious ritual of some nature. Our advance will be rapid and devastating, and should an army be thrown out to meet us or the Tsar be encircled, our business will then be concluded.'

'And Vilna is on the road to Moscow.'

Marshal Berthier stayed silent.

In an electrifying pause the news was taken in.

'Gentlemen. Your orders are being prepared at this very moment. Go to your duties and I wish you well for the future . . . whatever it may bring.'

Stunned, Moreau turned to his friend but found words wouldn't come. It seemed Rochambeau had the same difficulty and instead he gripped Moreau's hands wordlessly, then disappeared into the crowd.

The planning, the practice, now it was the reality.

Moreau hurried to his own staff marquee and was besieged by so many he had to take refuge inside.

One by one campfires were doused for night-time rest but under cover of darkness troops were now moving up to the border, concealing themselves in the fringing forest. Their marching packs were stuffed with twenty days' emergency rations of rice, flour and biscuits, as well as the usual campaign impedimenta.

For Moreau it was straightforward enough: pull out the operational order book and detail off the units in sequence as laid down – transports, escorts, stores. A colonel presented himself as the authority who would show him where the crossings were required, and another from a horse artillery regiment announced he was ready to site guns to cover proceedings.

All around there was a ferment of commotion and excitement, hurrying troops and equipment dragged along.

The places had been carefully chosen by Bonaparte himself, an artilleryman by training. One was at the nearer bend in the river, narrowed by the curve. Moreau's experienced eye noted higher ground suitable for mounting the guns to oversee their activity, and access roads existed ready to be extended to serve the crossing. He also saw that where the bend constricted the river flow the water was running faster and a central sandbank would cause trouble. He would take charge there and send a less experienced junior colonel to attend to the existing bridge at Kovno, a small medieval town several miles downstream.

'Well, get on with it!' he roared, at a dithering officer at the pontoons. In hours, tens, hundreds of thousands had to be tramping across their bridges.

He lost no time in taking boat with the *voltigeurs* who would secure the opposite bank, and soon found himself standing in wonder that this dark and still land under his feet was Russia. Where would it all end?

The *vedettes* returned from their reconnaissance with the astonishing news that no Russians opposed them whatsoever: they had achieved the surprise necessary to get the army across and assembled for their march. Moreau whipped his engineers into action and, with the benefit of their weeks of practice and no interference from the enemy, they were able to throw across four bridges before day dawned.

First over was Davout's light cavalry, which spread without pause over the country in a protective shield. Columns of infantry followed and, once across, their bands burst into heart-thumping martial music, their welcome on to Russian soil. In the early hours the figure of the Emperor, in his green redingote and unmistakable plain cocked hat, was seen making the crossing to full-throated roars of '*Vive l'empéreur!*' from the stolidly marching horde.

The endless tramping of his host into Russia had begun.

Chapter 47

The sun, from a tentative appearance at daybreak, strengthened through the morning, beating down on the snaking
lines of humanity that led to the horizon. A pall of dust
hung over them, choking and blinding, the merciless heat
making the march a harsh trial.

Moreau rode at the head of his corps and was soon joined
by Rochambeau falling back to be with him, head bowed and
unspeaking. The Grande Armée's orders were brutally clear:
the Tsar was in Vilna and the deciding battle would take place
before it. A lightning forced march, of the kind that had won
battles and that the Emperor had made famous, had been
commanded.

The punishing pace was telling but those falling out of the
line of march were treated mercilessly as an example while
the columns trudged on, endlessly. Dutch, Polish, Bosnians,
Italians – soldiers from a score or more of nations marching
together at the will of one man and with one objective. The
pitiless sun picked out the breastplates of the cuirassiers, the
fierce helmets of the dragoons, the colours of the lancers
and the red, gold and blue of infantrymen.

On and on, ever deeper into the country, days more before they would sight the spires and churches of Vilna, ever marching, ever hungry and ever thirsty.

'It's too quiet. I don't like it,' Rochambeau said uneasily. They had just passed through a village but there were no sullen inhabitants standing by their doors watching their conquerors march arrogantly by. There was no-one, just a dreary desolation.

'They're terrified by us,' Moreau replied. This was not how it had been on every other occasion he'd been with Bonaparte's advancing armies. It was an uneasy, inexplicable bleakness.

'I heard that we crossed successfully.' There was no joy in his voice.

'Yes. At Tilsit, then two bridges for infantry, supplies and artillery at Grodno, all on their way to join us.' There didn't seem to be much more to say in the face of what was happening – half a million men, a hundred thousand horses, flooding onto the plains of eastern Europe and on into the barbarian east, a colossal movement of humanity.

'Didn't you notice, old fellow?'

'Notice what?'

'All this and we haven't troubled the Tsar by declaring war on him. This is entirely illegal. Should we not go back until we do?'

Once they passed an open field with a scatter of anonymous, untidy bundles – corpses. Who were they? Nameless victims, perhaps hiding in a barn and resisting French foraging parties? A forlorn band who thought to attack the fast-moving column? Even a Russian post flushed out and killed by their dragoons?

At another small township furtive figures darted among the streets but Moreau knew they were looters whose officers had let them loose in return for a cut of the plunder. His lip curled in contempt. By the time the first ten thousand had passed this way they would leave the sad little town picked to the bone, like a carcass left to the buzzards.

The evening bivouac saw little laughter or jollity. Men slept where they fell, and when morning came it was all the sergeants could do to get them on their feet again, to work tortured muscles, to heft knapsacks swollen with plunder, and move out. Relief came when clouds gathered to shroud the sun but this turned into yet more suffering. The distant rumble of thunder developed into a late-summer storm, the sultry heat displaced by squalls. Before long, amid vicious lightning and claps of thunder, a heavy deluge whipped in.

Quickly the dust was laid but in its place the road was turned into a quagmire under the churning from uncountable legions of feet. Supply wagons, guns, baggage trains, all struggled to move forward in the treacherous mud. Disciplined columns became fragmented – and the Grande Armée came to a halt.

The rains continued into the night, guaranteeing miserable sleep, but in the morning the weather improved and once again the marching columns formed up. The sun started to dry the road and, in its fitful appearances, spirits rose. Still the savage, horse-killing pace went on.

Another sprawl of corpses could be seen at the edge of a forest.

'They're ours, Bertrand. How . . .?'

'It's bad, my friend. It means Ivan has finally woken up. Austrians by the look of them. One of our patrols taken by surprise, and I dare say we'll be facing an army very soon. The only question everyone asks is, how many bayonets can they put up?'

That evening, word got around that the Cossacks had been sent to harry and delay them, presumably while the Tsar mustered his army. They were the worst of enemies. Born horsemen from beyond the Don and the Volga, they were hardy, ferocious and knew no fear as they swept in with lances, sabres and carbines to cut off stragglers, working parties and patrols. They used tactics honed by centuries of Tartar warfare on the plains and in the forests, intricate manoeuvres intended to trick and baffle, tire and threaten. A formally constituted military had no ready defence against them.

That night fearful sentries and pickets took position, knowing that out in the darkness those merciless riders were circling, waiting their chance.

And the next day they struck, once, twice and again. Always against detached units, and once, as the Grande Armée passed a sprawl of farmhouse buildings, they recoiled in shock at the sight of the body parts of looters from a Polish regiment hung brazenly on a fence.

Still the punishing advance.

A little before noon the marching columns were brought to a halt. Riders galloped up and down and they were passed by the imperial cavalcade of carriages and escorts. At the lead was the Emperor's legendary six-horse yellow campaign carriage with its turbaned Mameluke bodyguard by the driver; inside Bonaparte was in deep consultation with some general. It pressed on urgently leaving speculation in its wake.

Within the hour orders had been sent back that had Moreau standing at the edge of a river, looking at the smoking ruin of a bridge destroyed by the Russians to delay the advance to Vilna.

He knew what he had to do and waited for the *ingénieur*

géographe to report the best place for a new crossing to be put in place. The Grande Armée was at a standstill until the pontoons were ready, and Bonaparte would be furious at any delay.

Rochambeau had thrashed his horse unmercifully to reach him. 'Upriver, a mile and a half. Bit exposed but I'd think Himself won't thank you to wait for artillery cover.'

Moreau didn't waste time. '*Pontonniers – en avant!*' he bellowed and the ungainly carts left the road one by one for the spot nominated.

It was exposed – flat and with a fast-flowing river but agreeably narrow. Rochambeau was right: he could span it in small hours.

There was no sign of the enemy on the far bank and he sent across boats with their watch-guard, who reported it clear.

In a fever of haste, Moreau dispatched further parties to either side to secure two more crossing points with what escorts he could contrive: it was vital that the Grande Armée faced no bottleneck at the crossing. It left them with little protection for themselves but he'd assurance there was nothing to fear on the other side, and in any case, the covering horse artillery would arrive soon.

The first pontoons were floated and secured. Cross-planking was prepared, doubled in view of the swiftness of the current.

'Dear fellow, do you mind much if I observe at all? I've never really seen a bridge magicked out of thin air,' Rochambeau asked.

'By all means, Bertrand. But do stand aside, dear fellow. These beams can cause a fearful bruise if encountered untoward.'

The pontoon bridge quickly began to take shape.

Then musket shots sounded in a flurry, close, but the danger was on the opposite bank. This was coming from the wrong side.

An ominous drumming of hoof-beats to the left revealed its deadly source: a band of horsemen with swirling scarlet pantaloons and exotic astrakhan busbies, lances lowered in battle position. The fierce glee on their swarthy faces told of one thing. These were Cossacks and their murderous charge was directed squarely at the bridge builders, in particular the loose gathering of officers overseeing them.

They burst through the outer defenders, heavy sabres swinging mercilessly, a bloody swathe leading straight towards Moreau and his group. God knew what Cossacks were doing on this side of the river, and there was nowhere to run, to hide on the flat, cleared area.

Moreau struggled to free his sword toggle to snatch it from its scabbard. The Cossacks thundered nearer, swinging around a small square of infantry in an almost poetic swaying motion that took them past and then, in a tight body, straight for the doomed party. He could see his death in the eyes of the hulking rider of the leading horse who, with a triumphant grimace, lined up his lance for the kill.

Out of nowhere Moreau was struck and sent sprawling to the side. Disoriented, his sword knocked from his hand, he was aware that the light had been briefly interrupted by the great bulk of a galloping animal passing over him. He scrabbled to all-fours and tried to make sense of things.

The horsemen had ridden on, slashing and skewering as they pounded off – but a few feet away an arched body shuddered and dropped to a final stillness. It was Rochambeau. His friend had cannoned him aside and taken the lance in his own body.

Seized by an extremity of grief Moreau fell on the lifeless

body, its mortal warmth not yet faded. He shrieked the unfairness of it all to the uncaring heavens until the tears came to rack him and leave him in an inconsolable huddle. How many more would there be before it ended?

Chapter 48

The Zakret Palace, Vilna

The sentry slowly paced along the ornate gates of the palace, enviously eyeing the bright light of a dozen chandeliers in the ballroom. The gay strains of a Viennese waltz wafted out on the warm night air. The Tsar was in town with his entourage and military council in their splendid uniforms, an irresistible chance for Vilna society to strut its finery and forget the hulking beast that lay across the border.

At this hour, honest citizens had long retired to their beds, but these would see in the dawn. There were worse duties for a private soldier to endure than sentry-go while being entertained by the gaiety of the highest in the land coming and going.

He reached the end of his beat, twirled about in an elaborate turn and began a leisurely return. Suddenly echoing in the empty streets came the strident clatter of a horse being thrashed to its limit. Out from the darkness burst a rider in the uniform of an imperial courier, pulling up at the gate with a crash and a perilous slither on the cobblestones.

'His Imperial Majesty is still here?' he demanded breath-lessly, his horse in a lather and trembling.

'He is.'

'Well, open the gate! I've dispatches of the utmost import-ance for him.'

'Oh? What's to do, then?'

'Get that gate open, you fool!'

The glittering ballroom was alive with colour and noise, animation and spectacle, and when the courier dramatically appeared at the door, travel-worn and wild-eyed, demanding the Tsar, it dissolved into uproar.

Alexander disappeared into an anteroom with the messenger. A little later he hurried to his carriage, pale-faced and flanked by grim military figures, leaving behind a seething frenzy of speculation.

'For those of you not yet aware of it, I'm to tell you that the French tyrant has, without declaring war, launched an attack on Russia.' The Tsar was visibly shaken, pale and emotional, as he faced the army commanders in his headquarters.

'Across the Niemen at Kovno, Grodno, other places. An impossible host thrown into the motherland, which flies like a spear towards us here, Vilna.'

'So . . .'

'He broke his word to me, the sacred word he swore at Tilsit when we—'

'Sire. We must resist. For the sake of our honour, the honour of our country,' Arakcheyev, the hard-featured destroyer of Speransky, declared.

'Yes. Yes. But how?'

'We stand before Vilna with every man and beast that glories in his Russian birthright.'

'No. We do not,' came in the minister of war, Prince

Michael, Barclay de Tolly, known as an intelligent, cunning and forthright field marshal. 'We retire with our army intact.'

'Retreat?'

'We fall back. The advantages are so obvious I refrain from mentioning them.'

'Sir, do so,' the Tsar insisted.

'Sire, at the moment we cannot in any wise stand against the numbers against us. Six hundred thousands, not counting support troops.'

'Two hundred and thirty thousand only, and that from Marshal Bagration himself,' offered another.

'Let us agree to disagree. The numbers are still over-whelming. If we face them in the open we will be defeated, just as at Austerlitz, Eylau, Friedland.'

Alexander winced. 'Agreed. Go on, sir.'

'We're not yet ready to face him – but we will be! We need time to call upon the inexhaustible resources of Russia from far parts to swell our army to a million or more, then fall upon the foul beast.'

Arakcheyev snorted in derision. 'So while we run and hide, Bonaparte will stop his onslaught and wait for us? Never! At the moment he's afoot with his invasion and moving at a cruel pace. What's to stop him if we do not?'

'De Tolly?' Alexander prompted.

'The Corsican would like nothing better than he meets us in battle with our inferior force, enabling him to destroy us piece by piece, army by army. If we waste our being on the battlefield like this, he's won the war and nothing will prevent him becoming conqueror of all Russia. No, Majesty, we must husband our forces until we are ready to face the Antichrist.'

'And meanwhile let him devour us at the speed of a marching army!' Arakcheyev sneered.

De Tolly coolly let him finish. Then, as if delivering

298

a lecture at a military academy, he went on, 'There are other advantages. Bonaparte is even now in extended order, his supply lines hundreds of miles long over bad roads. The further he penetrates, the longer and more vulnerable these become. He has to garrison towns along his route to safeguard them, and this will be at the cost of his numbers. If he goes much further this becomes a serious problem.'

'Since when did Napoleon Bonaparte worry about feeding his troops? He takes what he needs, makes his enemy pay for its own destruction.'

'He does, but in Russia it will be different. We make orderly plans to fall back ahead of him – and when we do, we take all the food, the animals and feedstock with us. What we can't carry off we destroy by fire. By this, every mouthful his army consumes must be brought up over the long weeks by wagon, while we will have all the fresh supplies we could ever need.'

'Are you mad? You want to turn the motherland into one vast wasteland as a deliberate act of war in place of a battle of courage and honour?'

Tsar Alexander held up his hand to speak and they turned to listen to his pronouncement. 'If we offer battle now we will be defeated. This is sure. If we lure the tyrant ever deeper into Russia then I shall have time to raise the nation to defend Holy Mother Russia's sacred soil against him. I have had a vision and this has been told to me as my sacred mission to rid the world of the beast of Revelation and this I shall do, to the very gates of Paris and beyond.'

'Yes, Your Imperial Majesty. Er, the French are advancing on Vilna. What is to be done?'

'Did you not hear me, Marshal Arakcheyev? We fall back. Yield the town to Bonaparte but not its foodstuffs and military stores, its farm animals, grain and so forth.'

'And the people?' a younger general intervened quietly.

'They fall back with us, the sacrifice of their lands and crops a contribution that will rank in honour along with death on the battlefield. This shall include all levels of society, even the nobility, and for time out of mind will stand to their glory.'

Renzi had declined an invitation to the ball, missing Cecilia's presence. In his quarters he woke to the sudden irruption of chaos and disorder and knew instinctively what it was.

He dressed, expecting to be called, and shortly was summoned to the imperial suite.

The Tsar was pacing about his study. Clearly in a tense but elevated mood, he received him absently. There was a sense of disorder, of untidiness that indicated a meeting of many had taken place recently in the room.

'Dear Graf Farndon, you won't have heard the news – I will tell it.'

Renzi was not surprised, the wonder being that the Tsar was. He listened politely, chilled at the speed and ferocity of Bonaparte's advance, however sketchy the details, and knew that the scale, the magnitude of the events, was far beyond his ability to render into some distilled package of wisdom. Yet as he listened he became aware that Alexander had achieved a form of serene dignity, a confidence it seemed was rooted in his sacred calling to deliver his people from the terror falling on them.

Humbly he agreed that, as far as he was concerned, the measures he heard were the only ones possible in the circumstances and that the Tsar should have no fear that he'd chosen the wrong path.

Alexander melted, a beatific smile transforming him. 'And I was greatly troubled that I was being swayed by the arguments of this one or that – but you, standing outside these self-centred cliques, will always tell me true.'

'I will do my best, sire.'

The Tsar, in his exalted mood, looked at him kindly. 'I know you will. A refreshment?'

Renzi agreed. The civilised Alexander would not be offering him vodka.

'When this unpleasantness is at last over, we shall discuss further your thesis on economics relating to national experiences.' Alexander looked sadly at his glass and murmured, 'It's what I'm sure Speransky was fumbling for in all his talk of manumitting the serfs. Poor fellow.'

He finished the cognac reflectively and the moment hung. Then, as though it was just dawning on him, an expression of anxiety turned into one of dread. 'You don't think that . . . My friend, tell me – will they still love me, the common people, I mean, after their only land and possessions are made an ashen wilderness?'

In a frenzy of haste Renzi found his chamber and reached for his concealed materials to begin a message to Congalton. The whole world had changed out of recognition, Alexander with it, so his mission to plumb the Tsar's intentions had to alter. Ironically his task was that much easier. The autocrat's mystic leanings had resulted in a firming of his resolve under the shock of the onslaught and he could safely say that the Tsar of Russia would fight – but only on his own terms, which would not necessarily be those recognisable by Whitehall.

Whether this would answer their need to know if they should come to the support of Russia in any material way, or even with battalions, was another matter, and he wouldn't wish to be the British functionary with the responsibility of deciding. Would this 'wasteland' strategy work against the greatest conqueror seen in centuries?

He finished the cipher in a frantic scribble. Was the chain leading all the way to Congalton still functioning? He forced the tiny roll of paper into the base of the oil-lamp and placed it next to the clock. The Tsar was going to leave Vilna under cover of darkness before dawn on the long journey to St Petersburg, and he had little time to be ready to accompany him.

After five hundred miles or more, through the archaic lands of Courland, Livonia and Estonia, they emerged on the banks of the Neva and went on to the inexpressibly civilised outlines of the Winter Palace and their rest. The Tsar was spirited away by anxious courtiers, and Renzi was left alone to contemplate.

There would be no doubt that, in the time of their slow progress needed to keep the Tsar's flight from Vilna hidden from his subjects, Bonaparte could have changed his objective. He had lost the chance to trap and capture the Tsar so what was his intention now? The news waiting for them in St Petersburg would be of the utmost importance for it could well signal the end – a threat so grave Alexander had no alternative than to treat for peace.

It didn't take long to find out. Bonaparte had not paused for more than days in Vilna and had now moved on, driving a massive column in a swathe a hundred miles wide directly east in a straight line for the border and Holy Mother Russia herself. Could nothing stop the monster?

It was time for Renzi to consider his position. He'd done remarkably well to get so close to the Tsar, a fortunate coincidence of the man's need and the success of his 'scholar' conceit. He had used his position to arrive at conclusions impossible for an outside observer but, with the question he was here to answer rendered moot by events, should he leave, job completed?

Alexander liked him, even needed him for his reassurances. Was now the time to abandon him?

His logic took firm hold. The likelihood of the Tsar's probable fate in the extraordinarily adverse circumstances closing in on him was assassination, exactly what had happened to the three previous tsars in far less menacing contexts. That being so, there was every prospect that Renzi would share that fate, being of the hated tribe of foreigners Alexander openly trusted more than his own. Even if he survived it would be quite impossible to build the same relationship with whoever emerged at the head of the power struggle.

'Graf Farndon?' It was a chamberlain with a message on a silver tray.

Renzi was not surprised to find it was an invitation from Alexander to take tea with him. He knew enough of the Tsar to realise that, if he'd seen fit to make time for him in this whirling chaos of beseeching military and petrified citizens, it implied a crisis had thrown up the need for a hard and immediate decision.

'Ah, my friend,' Alexander opened, readying the samovar and tea-dishes. 'So kind of you to attend on me so directly. Tea?'

'As always, sire, at your service at all times.' The bow was returned formally but it was distracted and traces of exhaustion were not hard to perceive. Slow movements, red-rimmed eyes, a slight slur in the speech.

'Have you heard the news?' the Tsar asked, with false lightness.

'I'm sorry to say I've been resting after our journey, Majesty.' He'd been told for his own safety not under any circumstance to leave his quarters, and without a soul to speak with, the reason for the angry shouts and urgent footsteps in the passages outside had been left to his imagination.

'Of course. Well, the news is not at all good. The beast is pressing on at a ferocious rate, which we can only assume is aimed at nothing less than a violation of the soil of Holy Mother Russia itself. We fall back daily, unable to delay it in any wise.'

Renzi murmured sympathetically and Alexander went on calmly, 'And now we have a new threat, one that I fear will prove final.'

'Sire?'

'The French have Danzig into which they pour their supplies but this is now far in their rear and their lines are sorely extended as they advance. Because of this Bonaparte has detached an entire division under Marshal Macdonald to divert from the order-of-march to make for Riga and the Baltic shore. His orders are to take the port and make it a new bridgehead for supplying the armies as they plunge into Russia. You will understand that—'

'I do, Majesty.'

It was a shrewd and devastating move. In one stroke Napoleon's line of supply would be shortened to just a few days: a flooding river of powder and shot, victuals and clothing, artillery and all the impedimenta of war would reach the invaders wherever they chose to head – St Petersburg or Moscow.

And it made a pathetic mockery of Russia's sacrificial wasteland retreat.

'Riga is under siege at this moment. If not relieved, it will

304

fall and bring catastrophe. I must not allow this to happen but without fighting men I cannot prevent it.'

There was nothing Renzi could say in reply.

'Not two hours ago there was put to me a suggestion that I'd be beholden if you'd hear and make comment.'

'Insofar as my limited abilities allow, sire.'

'Then I shall tell you. In Finland I have men, there in occupation these last two years since I took the country from the Swedes. They are many and in idleness. The suggestion is that should I compound with the Swedish so in some way I can recover these men for defence of their mother country. Except that the Swedes, under Prince Bernadotte, still burn for their humiliation at losing their Finnish territory so recently, and to win their compliance will be hard indeed. But a way has been proposed. If they see fit to comply, we shall not stand in the way of their detaching Norway for themselves from the Danish Crown, the Danes, having their fleet taken by the British, being in no position to defend it.'

'Sir, this—'

'To avoid possible prejudice, I will not tell whose initiative this was, but my desire is for you to tell me if you see any evidence that other motives less than honourable are at play.'

The worst of all worlds. Renzi was expected to make judgement on a strategy of state and a military question. He couldn't for any number of reasons.

'Your Imperial Majesty. I'm but a humble scholar, more comfortable with postulates and hypotheses. Should I make comment, without learning in the field, it would be valueless. I do apologise, but as I told you—'

Alexander held up his hand. 'You did say as much, Nikolai, I do remember.' He sighed, but it was not in despair. 'Yet I'm minded to proceed with it.' He gave a wry smile. 'Just how I'm able to stir those idle diplomats to open negotiations with Sweden in the time we have left to us will be difficult in the extreme. Do go to your rest, my friend, and leave these matters to me.'

'Sire, there is . . .' A tiny thought was taking shape as he spoke.

'Yes, Nikolai?'

'Time is of the essence in this case. I beg you will forgive my bold speaking but it crosses my mind that we have a sovereign solution. Your Majesty, you must meet Bernadotte personally and settle the matter face to face. Immediately.'

'You mean . . .?'

'Sire. Time is to be measured in days. If you go to a town near Sweden and invite the prince to a meeting, I'm certain he will see it in his best interests to come. Is there not a city of consequence in Finland close to Sweden? I seem to recollect—'

'A meeting of princes! A fine notion, Nikolai, and you're thinking of Äbo, directly opposite Stockholm.' The impulsive animation quickly died. 'But then what are we contemplating? From Petersburg to Äbo will take all of three weeks, given the shocking roads, and it will then be too late.'

'Not by road, I beg. By sea a brace of days only.'

'Not possible,' Alexander said sadly. 'The Baltic is alive with privateers and other vermin who would spare nothing to secure the body of the Tsar of Russia. I cannot take the risk.'

Renzi thought quickly. 'Then your conveyance shall be an English man-o'-war. The admiral will see the importance of the mission and will, I'm sure, make provision accordingly. I myself will make the request, sire.'

As soon as it came out, he knew it was asking a lot – possibly too much. His own service in the navy told him that a fleet and its admiral were never at the disposition of any casual outsider, however eminent. He could see a crusty old admiral snorting at the impertinence and reaching for a pen to protest at the gall of it all, then requiring the request be directed to the Admiralty itself.

But if it was spelled out in good round naval phrases, with solid cogent reasons, common sense might well prevail.

A smile tugged at his lips. It might well be that, shortly, some unknown captain would receive orders to transform his vessel from a roving warship into an imperial carriage for the convenience of the Tsar of Russia. Providing, of course, that the Royal Navy still maintained a fleet at this far end of the Baltic and that its patrolling craft were not too distant.

Chapter 49

A shabby *kibitka* waited behind a line of warehouses, its curtains drawn. The patient coachmen kept the horses in check while inside two passengers held themselves in tense readiness.

Renzi's answer had not been long in coming. A report had been made of a British warship coming to anchor out of sight in the St Petersburg roads. Given the state of war that still existed between them it could only be on an official mission and a boat was expected at any moment. If it proved to be what they were hoping for they would be away without delay.

In the feverish atmosphere it was essential that the Tsar left St Petersburg secretively. Onlookers might take the view that he was abandoning the city to its fate and an ugly riot could erupt.

Renzi stepped cautiously out of the carriage to make his way the short distance to the waterfront. A flash of pale sail to the westward resolved by degrees into the familiar lines of a Royal Navy ship's launch under sail, a white ensign and patch of colour in the stern sheets token that an officer was aboard. It was escorted by a pair of harbour craft for the final approach.

At the jetty Renzi waited as the officer in cocked hat and sword mounted the steps and looked about, no doubt expecting a guard and band turned out.

Renzi approached him and, with a bow, introduced himself. 'Lord Farndon in advance of the Tsar of Russia, sir.' The officer looked at him suspiciously for his dress was that of a humble Russian dominie and he was flanked by a pair of hard-faced Slavic keepers. 'And here are my credentials.'

They were taken and studied as the boat's crew looked on with interest.

'Very well, my lord. We are instructed to make known to you that our ship lies ready to convey the Tsar to a destination to be disclosed at a later time. Shall we make arrangements for the imperial progress now?'

'Not at all. His Imperial Majesty is travelling incognito and is anxious to board without delay.' The boat's bowman was still hooked on, watching curiously. 'Do bring the boat close alongside. His Imperial Majesty is no sailor and desires no notice be made of his departure, so I bid you stand fast salutes and piping.'

The lieutenant, a young but hard-eyed individual turned to go but Renzi couldn't help asking, 'What ship, sir?'

'Ah, I do beg your pardon, my lord,' he said, removing his hat. 'My name is Roscoe and I'm first of *Thunderer*, 74.'

Thunderer? A ship he had no knowledge of other than that she'd fought at Trafalgar, but a ship-of-the-line – this was gratifying.

Roscoe gave his orders quietly to the boat's crew as the Tsar, muffled in a cloak, was hustled to the steps and into the boat. 'You will be coming too, Nikolai?'

309

It wasn't what Renzi had in mind but he followed without protest and the boat put off.

'When the Tsar is safely away his retinue will follow,' Renzi informed the lieutenant. Another thirty-odd to victual and accommodate would not please the ship's captain but this was not his concern.

HMS *Thunderer*, a mighty vessel of arrogance and beauty, dominated the anchorage, a towering symbol of Britain's sea power. As they neared her Renzi was struck by her fine appearance: the old-fashioned carvings and stern-gallery well gilded and varnished, the brightwork between the awesome lines of guns, the precisely squared spars. Whoever her captain was, he was running a taut ship and had to be admired for the state of his command.

'Please convey to His, um, Majesty that we will sway him aboard by bosun's chair and I will take a turn around the ship to give them time to rig it.' Apparently Lieutenant Roscoe did not have French enough to explain it.

Renzi passed this on to the Tsar but Alexander was rapt, staring up at the spectacle of this great lion of the seas.

The manoeuvre went well, the all-puissant Romanov Emperor sitting nervously as he was gently hauled up and away. Renzi didn't want to wait for it to return and instead leaped to the side-steps with its man-rope and clambered up just as he had those years before as a naval officer.

He arrived at the bulwark in time to catch the diverting sight of a hastily assembled side-party and the vessel's captain bowing low before the Tsar. A sharp-eyed petty officer saw Renzi come in over the bulwarks and the side-party moved smartly to reassemble in his honour, the captain hesitating before hurrying across to stand at the head of the double line to bow to yet another Russian dignitary.

Kydd straightened – and looked directly into the eyes of his dearest friend. 'Nicholas!' he gasped. 'You – you . . .'

'Dear fellow,' Renzi said, taken quite aback, but with the presence of mind to speak in courtly French in front of the curious side-party. 'Pray do not enquire,' he said rapidly. 'But allow that I present as someone you once knew but find you are mistaken.'

'Oh. Well, welcome aboard *Thunderer*, Mr . . . er, sir.' Kydd spoke in English. 'If you'll accompany me below shall we discuss the Tsar's accommodation arrangements?'

They left the deck and, out of sight, enthusiastically greeted each other.

'Dear fellow—'

'Nicholas, old horse, what—'

Kydd drew up a chair and took in the sight of his friend, obviously in some sort of guise. 'It's as well there's no one aboard from dear old *Tyger* as knows you. May I be told . . .?'

A soft knock and Craddock leaned in. 'Did you wish me to—'

'Come in, old fellow. I think you should hear this. Oh – this is Lord Farndon, whom I've known for many years by the name of Renzi. Nicholas, this is Mr Craddock, my confidential secretary, whom I acquired in the Adriatic in adventurous circumstances. Carry on, please, Nicholas.'

Renzi acknowledged Craddock with a slight bow and continued: 'For my sins I'm a confidant of Tsar Alexander and hated by every right-thinking denizen of the Romanov court. Pray do not enquire of this further – we shall have time enough to talk of it later. For now, I cannot help but remark you have a rattling fine ship in *Thunderer*! It does have to be said, however, that this cabin appears a little less grand than I'd suppose for the captain of a sail-of-the-line.'

'This is the first lieutenant's cabin, Nicholas. Mine is given over to the Tsar while all officers are turned out to have their existence at the after end of the gun-deck behind canvas in favour of his more important followers – such as you, who is now rated gentleman counsellor to the Grand Panjandrum.'

'After the sybaritics of the Winter Palace I would be more than satisfied with a gunroom hammock, if truth be told.'

Kydd grinned and went on, 'I understand this voyage is in some degree one of urgency. I haven't yet a destination and—'

'Äbo to the west, and haste would be welcomed. Just as soon as His Majesty's baggage is aboard.'

During the night *Thunderer* slipped to sea without ceremony or escort, laying course down the Baltic for Äbo a bare two days or so away. With a mountain of baggage struck down in the cable tiers and a dozen Russian nobles endeavouring to deal with their outlandish quarters she leaned to a useful north-easterly and made good time.

Renzi was able to acquaint Kydd of the mission and its reasons, and also give him an idea of how disastrous the campaign was for the Russians. It was hard to credit, but probably by the time they returned to St Petersburg Bonaparte's savage thrust east would have advanced half a thousand miles in just short weeks with no sign of any serious resistance. It was galling to Kydd, for like all the Continental wars of conquest there was little the Navy could do to engage the enemy directly, especially in this case where the immense column marched along, now hundreds of miles inland and ever deeper.

The Tsar was enchanted by his sea venturing and, at his request, strolled about the ship freely, attended by a lieutenant to explain its wonders. When they raised the densely scattered archipelago guarding Äbo from seaward, he seemed sincerely regretful.

It was a charming and at the same time imposing city. Discovering that they were to be blessed with a visit by the Tsar it became a time of festival and celebration, fireworks and gun salutes lighting the sky. The imperial party made their way ashore without lingering but Renzi returned in only an hour. 'Banquets and balls without end. I leave the joys to those who do appreciate such occasions. Should we take our victuals together, brother?'

In years past Kydd had come across Bernadotte as a marshal of the French Empire in command of the army ranged along the border of Denmark during the British bombardment of Copenhagen. In a drama involving the exiled Bourbon king, he had had reason to believe that Bernadotte held no burning loyalty to Bonaparte and he told Renzi so.

'It's as I understand it. You are, of course, referring to the head of state, who should more properly be addressed as Charles John, Crown Prince of Sweden. One who holds honour dear but even more the advancing of his realm I've heard.'

On the following day Bernadotte arrived in his royal yacht to a warm reception from the populace, who had been Swedes until two years before.

It was made clear that Renzi, as a foreigner, was not welcome at the table of the greats in the days to follow so he took to cultivating the confidences of others for his information. Then, on the pretext that he felt the mark of assassins, he declared that while the imperial envoys made much of their lavish and opulent lodgings he himself would sleep aboard ship.

'So how is it progressing, Nicholas? Are they talking together or . . .?'

'Satisfactory indeed. The first words from Bernadotte were

"If Russia falls then Sweden will follow. Therefore we have common cause, do we not?" They thereupon embraced. A pretty scene, you'll agree.'

'And the Norway bait?'

'Do not be so precipitate, old fellow. Bernadotte is a crafty fox and does not want to appear too hungry. We shall see.'

The next night Renzi brought the news that, despite the humiliation of the loss of Finland, Bernadotte might be persuaded to relinquish all claim to the country, allowing Alexander to withdraw his garrisons. It was the 'might be' that brought up short all satisfaction. 'The Norway ploy is too blatant,' Renzi pronounced.

It needed one final push and this was provided by the Tsar – an offer to Bernadotte that should he make attempt to recover Swedish Pomerania, shamefully taken by Bonaparte in a coup, Russia would assist with troops and supplies. There was no prospect at this time that Sweden would attempt to cross the Baltic and confront Bonaparte, but it would serve as a token gesture to rally the waverers behind him.

'So, all is settled, the garrisons released to go to the aid of Riga and a unity of purpose declared. I do believe we may expect to return tomorrow.'

Chapter 50

St Petersburg

Impatiently Alexander stood by Kydd on the quarterdeck as *Thunderer* went to her moorings off the great city. He could not leave until the situation ashore was known. A boat took away an envoy but, by degrees, it became evident that something was not right. When the pinnace returned, it was accompanied ominously by an imperial barge carrying armed soldiers.

The envoy hauled himself aboard and, face set, hurried to the Tsar. 'Your Majesty,' he blurted, 'grave news has been received from your generals. A battle – at Smolensk. It did not necessarily end to our advantage and there are terror and disorder on the streets, which it would be wise to avoid. I cannot give more details in front of the foreigners but if you would return speedily with us it may calm the anxious.'

Renzi shivered but it had nothing to do with the chill of the autumn breeze. Was this a sign of a crumbling of the Russian will to resist? The beginning of the end?

Kydd pulled him aside. 'Nicholas,' he said, his voice thick

with concern, 'you must get away from this madness. Stay aboard and I can give you safe passage out.'

'Nothing would please me more, you may believe.' He glanced across at the Tsar, now to one side and in worried conversation with the envoy. If something serious had taken place he had to know what it was and, crucially, how this affected Alexander in his judgements. Anything less would betray his mission. 'But I have to tell you that I must remain.'

'Then . . . then I can wait no more than a day,' Kydd said, 'as I must have the ship squared away after that scrovy crew leaves. But if you can find out what you have to in that time, I'll be here for you, never fear.'

The Tsar and his retinue were bundled ashore, where carriages were waiting, and a squadron of cavalry to go ahead and clear the way, the fine boulevards and avenues choked with aimless crowds and occasional groups fighting.

At the Winter Palace Alexander disappeared in a throng of gesticulating supplicants. Renzi turned away. He had to discover the situation, but not in this bedlam, and he walked rapidly towards his chambers.

Passing a familiar painting, a painstakingly detailed and florid oil of some past battle a good twelve feet across, he was jerked to a stop. An imposing hulk of a man in elaborate courtly regalia, a magnificent black beard and commanding eyes clutched at his arm. He vaguely recognised him as Count Aleksey Denisov, an ardent patriot.

'Stay, my friend!' he said unsteadily, in a bear-like growl. 'I demand you toast with me to the glories of Russia as must never be forgotten!' The intensity of his words was not affected by a stray hiccup, and he fished a bottle out of his coat with two small glasses and proceeded to fill them.

'*Za nas*,' he commanded, lifting his glass in admiration to the painting, giving Renzi the chance surreptitiously to get rid of the contents of his.

'I would cheerfully drink to Russia in her time of need,' Renzi said softly. 'But why at this moment?'

'Smolensk!' roared Denisov, glaring at him as if he were demented.

'Um, I've been out of the country. What is the news, pray?'

'Hmmph. You'll learn soon enough but I'll tell you.'

First Renzi had to hear of how Smolensk had stood firm against the Mongols and later the Lithuanians, and in the days of the Swedish and Polish wars the city was a byword for staunch loyalty. It was squarely on the road into the heart of Russia and as a result the Tartar Tsar Boris Godunov had made certain the strongest fortress in Russia was built there. Consequently the much-venerated icon of St Luke was safe-guarded within its walls.

How, then, was it possible to yield up the saintly city to the overwhelming forces of Napoleon Bonaparte in accord-ance with the strategy of wasteland retreat?

It wasn't, and Alexander's two army commanders, Barclay de Tolly and Bagration, were told to join together and make a stand.

Within just two days Bonaparte had put both to flight at the cost of some twenty-thousand casualties, an appalling loss. He was now in possession of the proud city, which lay at his feet utterly devastated, bombarded into submission, its inhabitants a mound of corpses, any still alive streaming away in misery and desolation.

There were tears as Denisov explained that Bonaparte's intentions were now open to all. The tyrant had crossed into Russia to defeat the noblest in the land and the highway was wide open to the biggest prize of all – Moscow. What did the future hold for this ancient land of the Rus?

317

Renzi left the man to his maudlin sorrowing and hurried on. He needed to think.

Outside his rooms a stiff-faced military officer waited. 'Graf Farndon, I'm to tell you that His Imperial Majesty in council desires your attendance. This way, if you please.'

No polite greetings or requesting. What did he expect from him, the academic, after this horrific event? And before his council?

He was ushered into a room very different from the Tsar's personal chambers. This was a military headquarters packed with officers, most gathered around a central table covered with maps. At his entrance, they looked up, hostility and resentment on their faces.

Alexander came out from behind them to meet him. Renzi made an elegant bow, but before he could straighten the Tsar spoke. 'Graf Farndon, you will have heard of the . . . adverse circumstance in which we are now placed.'

No one moved.

'Sire, I have,' Renzi said carefully, 'and can only deplore the situation in which Russia finds herself.'

'Yes. May I say before my commanders here assembled that your assistance in the matter of releasing my idle troops in Finland to go to the relief of Riga is handsomely appreciated.'

'Thank you, Your Majesty.'

'Regrettably I've been told that even with these reinforcements the French are pouring in additional divisions. It's considered that Riga cannot hold out for much longer in the face of such numbers.'

Surely they didn't expect him to think of some stratagem to counter the looming disaster, which if it happened would count on the same level as Smolensk.

'Sire, in matters of a military nature I cannot—'

'The council understands that, Graf Farndon.' He looked about significantly. 'It understands too that you are in a unique position to help us.'

Renzi kept silent – however they thought to use him he had to resist. He could not be drawn in, snared in some desperate plan.

'Riga will fall. This is certain, for we've learned in Danzig that a heavy siege train is being prepared that will bring our resistance to an end in a very short time.'

The room was still, every eye on him. What was happening? What did they want, for God's sake?

'Sire. I cannot see how—'

'Your success in obtaining a ship of the British Navy to go to Äbo at such notice is evidence of your authority. We desire you speak with the captain of this great vessel with a view to catching and sinking the armament before it can reach Riga.'

'Majesty,' Renzi stuttered, his breath taken away by the effrontery of the demand. 'For actions of a military nature he does not have the freedom to act. He must have his admiral's approval.'

The Tsar's voice tightened. 'It would go hard for the captain to be seen to refuse a request by the Tsar of Russia, and even harder should it be known that Riga fell for want of his resolve. Do you understand me, Graf Farndon?'

Chapter 51

'Nicholas!' Kydd spluttered, as Renzi came over the bulwark. 'You've come to your senses! You're just in time – but where's your baggage?'

'Brother. We must speak. Your cabin?'

The essence was conveyed in a very few sentences. 'I couldn't argue. They fervently believe I have a mystical power within the sacred Royal Navy and if I don't exercise it it must be from want of respect for the person of the Tsar.'

'I see,' Kydd said, rubbing his chin thoughtfully. 'But if there's so little time I can't make petition to the admiral for a formal sally upon the enemy. If it's to be done, *Thunderer* must do it herself.'

'Dear fellow, I can't ask it of you. To proceed on an act of war without orders will damn you for ever.'

Kydd smiled at his dismay. 'If I did not, on the other hand, I'd be damned equally. Recollect, old horse, we're still at war with Russia, for in these few weeks the politicking is not yet done that will result in an alliance. If the Ruskies desire our help and it's refused, what will this do to the negotiations? As no motion against Bonaparte can ever be deplored by a

320

right-thinking naval officer, a species of distraction is quite in order, I would have thought.'

Renzi gave a lop-sided grin. 'In this I'm only an untutored messenger. Should I return to Alexander to say you will, therefore?'

'You may. The good admiral Byam Martin will understand. He always did prefer the company of captains of active and zealous persuasion and will not suffer blame to attach to my actions.'

'Then do sail on and may good fortune attend always, dear fellow.'

'Thank you, Nicholas. And . . . and do recollect that whatever's to happen in this world gone lunatic,' he said softly, '*Thunderer* will be somewhere in the offing to deliver you.'

After he'd seen Renzi over the side Kydd needed to take a bracing turn around the deck. His breezy assurance that Byam Martin would approve of his unauthorised action now rang a little false in his ears.

An admiral needed to know what was happening in his own domain. If *he* were an admiral he'd be outraged if one of his ship-of-the-line captains took it upon himself to indulge in an act of war on his own initiative, like any common frigate captain on a cruise. This would be depriving the fleet of one of its few heavyweight assets and potentially blocking any higher purpose he had in mind. Kydd's only excuse was the pressing lack of time he had left to intercept the siege train. His only chance to escape a career-finishing censure was to succeed. But how?

Danzig was the point of entry of near the entirety of French war stores and was heavily defended. On the face of it, the only way to get at the quarry was to cruise off the port and intercept the transports on the way to Riga. They would, no doubt, be well escorted, but in a 74-gun ship-of-the-line he could expect to take on several frigates and more. Such an encounter, however, would allow the transports to escape. And, in any case, if the convoy commander was wise, he'd leave at night and they might miss it entirely.

He had to be certain of its destruction. This was too chancy, too uncertain. But what else was there?

He called the first lieutenant to his cabin.

'Come in, Mr Roscoe,' he invited. 'Do sit. I have a difficulty, a challenge, which I'd like to talk over with you. The watering near complete?'

'It is, sir, and . . . and thank you for your confiding in me.'

It took Kydd by surprise, and then he remembered that in *Tyger* he'd thought nothing of chewing over possibilities with his first lieutenant, Bowden. In the navy this was unusual, and he couldn't imagine the previous captain of *Thunderer* unbending to such a degree. Was it that his long relationship with the younger man had allowed him to unburden before him?

To be the sort of first lieutenant Kydd wanted, Roscoe would need to recognise his way and, in so doing, would benefit professionally, like Bowden, as he learned the reasons for decisions, the possibilities, the risks.

'Certainly I shall confide, old fellow. Are you not a prime hand, as we must say, that might be heard?'

'I shall do my best, sir.'

Kydd sat back, considering. 'I'm sure you will. But I'd think it better should we be on, who might say, friendlier terms. I desire you might speak your mind, be plain with me in your views.'

It was asking a lot of the mere lieutenant sitting upright before him, opposite a knighted and famous frigate captain, proven sea predator and known familiarly at the royal court. On the other hand, until he'd lately won Roscoe's respect the man had not been particularly intimidated by his rank and stature, and he suspected that a strong character lay not far beneath. Perhaps it was only necessary to provide a channel of informality and ease of approach to release it.

'Sir.'

'While we're on our own, shall we leave aside the "sirs"?'

'Very well, um, yes.'

'You're Christopher, I believe. What are you to your friends, pray?'

'They call me Kit, actually.'

'So.' Kydd lifted his little silver bell and rang it.

'*Mon capitaine?*' Binard didn't blink an eye but Kydd saw that he'd instantly taken in the relaxed scene.

'What can you suggest as will recruit the strength and sharpen the intellects?'

'Ah. Perhaps *un eau de vie?*'

'Do find us a brace, there's a good fellow. Now, Kit, this is the essence of what's exercising me.'

It was easy enough told: the grave, near catastrophic situation ashore and what hung on their intercepting the siege engines before Riga fell. The touching faith that the Royal Navy would naturally prevail in any contest. The urgency of the whole affair.

'Show me the chart,' was Roscoe's immediate response.

A large-scale Danzig approaches was found, with two merchant rutters in German, while the master looked out some sketches of the harbour made by Sanders, a Royal Navy officer present at the siege of 1807.

They pored over them carefully.

'Forts at the entrance, both sides, sir,' Roscoe murmured, remembering too late his dispensation.

'And a brute of a fortress well inside,' Kydd observed. 'I see that Danzig must be accounted an inland city, served only by the one waterway to the sea. And the town itself sits behind marshland on the coast and high ground all round further in.'

Even then it was obvious that if the siege train was being loaded at the town docks safely within the city walls it would take an entire army to reach it. No wonder Bonaparte had chosen Danzig as the route of his supply train into the interior.

Roscoe shook his head sadly. 'We might only conclude that their siege guns are safe from us while they're inside.'

'So we must take them at sea.'

'As is not at all certain,' Roscoe said quietly. 'They could slip out past us at night, or in mizzling weather, or . . .'

'Yes, Kit. Now you see my dilemma.'

But Roscoe's eyes were on the city plan, his eyes bright, searching. 'There may be . . .'

'Oh? Say on, old fellow.'

'I'd swear this is a canal, at least the stretch downstream from the big fortress to the Baltic itself.'

'And . . .?'

'We can't get at them where they lie, it's too chancy to rely on intercepting at sea, so why not stop 'em here, before they get to sea?'

'Kit, you mean—'

'I do. A ship across the canal, put a stopper on 'em!'

A blockship preventing the siege train ever getting out – it was as good as destruction at sea, and far more certain.

'Hmm. I like it. Let's see if we can come up with something. A canal – this implies it has warping piles. And an even bed – with a limited breadth of passage.'

Animated, Roscoe took it up. 'So – our blockship. We

324

secure the after end to one warping post, let the current take the forrard end out and, when athwart, secure to the other side, blocking navigation.'

'I rather fancy the French will have it free *tout de suite*, dear chap. More permanent would be—'

'Ha! Blow the bottom out of her. No tides in the Baltic, they'll have to get divers down from somewhere.'

'To break it up – this is a job of months. Riga is saved, I believe.'

Kydd inwardly exulted. It seemed he had the kind of first lieutenant he wanted – intelligent, imaginative and one who spoke his mind. What could the future not bring? 'To the details,' he cautioned. 'This ship, how do we get her past the forts and into the channel?'

The bones of the plot quickly took shape. A suitable ship, her hold packed with gunpowder. A small, picked crew. Appearing out of the blue, chased by a bully ship-of-the-line into the protecting arms of the forts, flustered but thankful to have made port. The rest was straightforward enough, the question only remaining of how her crew would be returned safely.

'You'll agree that I shall take the ship in,' Roscoe said firmly.

'In normal circumstances this would be the case,' Kydd replied, equally firmly.

'By the custom of the service a first lieutenant is offered the chance of distinction in these affairs. Do I understand you wish to reserve this to yourself?' The voice had grown tense and obstinate.

'Not at all. I shall be in charge for quite another reason.'

'You haven't trust in me.'

'This is not in question, Kit. The reason is that the matter is dire and, of us both, only I have the experience.'

'Experience?'

'Of touching off a fuse and making away. You see, I was at the Basque Roads leading the fireships.'

The younger man looked dogged. 'As was a great business. This is a trifling task by compare, the mere lighting of some slow-match and retiring. I believe my competence is sufficient for the task.'

Kydd sighed. He saw where this was going. Roscoe knew where honour and repute were to be won, and while service in an active 74 was all very well, the only opportunity for his individuality to come to notice was on very rare occasions. And he probably felt that Kydd had all the acclaim and renown he needed.

If Kydd gave him his chance, how much could he be relied upon?

'Very well, you shall lead.'

There was a flash of feeling – was it triumph? And then Roscoe announced calmly, 'As commander of the ship, and that in full measure.'

'Commander? You shall take her in at the right time, see the fuse is lit and your men leave in good order is all, Kit.'

'If I take charge and responsibility, the ship must be mine. To outfit, man and direct as I see fit for the needs of the operation.'

Kydd paused then responded, 'Agreed. Always providing the overall command stays with me.'

It was an almost unheard-of thing to demand of one's superior. But Kydd could appreciate his motive: that in the heat of the action he wanted to be free to make decisions not bound by the need to consult a superior. Once they got to know more of each other it would be taken as said.

'Shall we then find ourselves a ship to sacrifice?'

They had their pick from the scores of ships lying idle beyond Kronstadt, their trading patterns thrown into confusion by the rapid advance of the French. Roscoe's choice was *Azov*, a stoutly built Archangel trader of about 250 tons, barque-rigged and sound, her ice-strengthened hull not easily taken apart.

As the powder barrels were taken aboard, her manning was addressed. True to his word, Kydd stepped back as Roscoe found his volunteers, midshipmen to topmen, each without resort to coercion or vague promises. Before the day was done he had them aboard *Azov* laying along the gear necessary to turn her into a floating bomb.

And within a very short time the pair of ships had put to sea, bound for Danzig.

Chapter 52

To Roscoe, the time seemed to pass interminably. He was fighting down by turns a fierce need to prove himself before the most prominent and inspiring figure in his life – and the challenge of the fearsome trial that lay ahead.

If he was truthful he'd have to admit that his cool confidence lay in the knowledge that in his entire career he'd never failed, never felt deficient. He'd always succeeded in whatever had been thrown up against him. Yet could this be because he'd never really been tried in the fires? His had been a big-ship calling, and until now he'd always been under eye and never had to act alone.

This time he was in personal charge of the assault and all responsibility lay on his shoulders. And, far from being a matter-of-course cutting-out expedition, this was unorthodox, against great odds, and its significance to the wider war went far beyond its immediate goal.

He was not prey to fears and anxieties but the wait was trying as the flat grey of the north Polish coast made its appearance to the south – or should that be the Duchy of Warsaw, Poland under Bonaparte having ceased to exist?

At ten miles offshore *Azov* came alongside *Thunderer* and all but the skeleton crew transferred to the bigger ship. It had begun!

Sail was spread and the chase started, *Thunderer* giving *Azov* a good start as the gallant little ship made for the safety not so far ahead.

Danzig lay deep into the self-named bay. The charts showed it with a narrow entrance flanked by forts. A south-south-easterly fairway led in that, within half a mile, made a sweeping curve to meet the canal at the main fortress.

Roscoe paced up and down in his borrowed merchant-service rig, the cramped deck space and utilitarian fittings so at odds with a proud man-o'-war. He flicked a glance astern at *Thunderer* and again was struck by the picture of warlike grace and lethal beauty the big 74 made, crowding on sail in her pursuit. Her staysails were cunningly led to spill wind and keep her speed down, not something a soldier in the forts would notice, with her battle ensign brazenly streaming out that would catch every eye.

The low shore firmed, the shadowed presence of wood-land over marshes, a few scattered hamlets. Off to the left, the dumpy grey and red of two forts straddled a narrow entryway, the larger with a lofty flagstaff and a signal tower.

A faint thud and rising powder smoke indicated they'd been noticed – there would be formalities on arrival, from customs to quarantine, and *Azov* was being invited to lie to while the authorities sent a boat. She took no notice, the fierce sight of her pursuer good enough reason to flee on.

A hoist of flags soared up the staff, undoubtedly a demand to reveal her colours, which Roscoe was damned sure he wasn't going to do. His terrified crew had other things to worry about, had they not?

There were buoys, then a series of posts, the beginning of the warping progression.

A flurry of thuds came. The forts were opening up – on the big warship. These were not warning shots: plumes of shot-strike leaped up close by.

The north-westerly was near perfect for Roscoe: they could carry sail right inside, before the fairway curved into the straight reaches of the canal.

More firing erupted, sharper now but aimed at their pursuing menace. It was working!

'Lay along the warp springs, fore 'n' aft!' Roscoe bellowed, the exhilaration of the moment keying him up while he fought for coolness and rationality. Eyeing the first warping stakes ahead, he set in train the 'panic' crew, who raced meaning-lessly up into the rigging. Others hurried along the deck to the fo'c'sle where they excitedly waved on the fort gunners to greater efforts.

Under every rag of canvas they could hang out *Azov* plunged forward into the enfolding embrace of the forts, seething by them as they valiantly drove off the disappointed Englishman, which in a wide sweep made for the open sea and away.

Thankfully, *Azov* doused sail and settled to a more sedate pace, readying to bring up to the warping piles. It would be understood that she would secure to one to yield to a boarding for the formalities but also to spell the crew after their frenzy of deliverance.

For Roscoe it was now critical. The ship should be far enough in that there was no possibility that the wider last section of the fairway would allow the siege train transports to slip past to sea. At the same time they must not be so far in that their final flight could be headed off.

As they slowed his eyes picked out a place – at the begin-ning of the curve to the left, the waterway at its narrowest.

Alerting the after warp spring party, he concentrated on the approach, then tensed. From the opposite direction a heavily laden Dutchman under bare poles was hauling itself along, warping out the last few hundred yards to the sea. The convention in England was for the craft under sail to stand on, the other to haul in to the bank and pause until it was past. Was that how it was done on the Continent? If it wasn't, they would stand revealed at best as a trespasser.

Well before the chosen spot the fat Dutchman stopped and heaved itself in. They were safe but, with a wry grin, Roscoe realised that the unfortunate captain, by correctly observing nautical custom, had just condemned himself to a month or more trapped in the canal.

They eased off as sail came in, gliding in precisely to the correct spot. It was imperative to get the timing right and Roscoe himself took the wheel to nudge the stern quarters against the piles.

'Go!' he hissed. The line was looped over a pile and brought back inboard to the bitts. With a perceptible tug, *Azov* came to rest.

Everything depended on the next few seconds. Roscoe picked an argument with the fo'c'sle crew, who responded with angry shouts and waving arms. A fist flew out and in the next instant the deck was alive with fighting bodies. Imperceptibly at first but with increasing speed the current crowded into the space between ship and bank and *Azov's* bow swung slowly out.

The Dutchman's crew saw what had happened and bawled out angrily at the lubberly sailors. In their mindless scuffling they took no notice until the ship was well across the waterway grounding with a soft bump against the opposite bank, comprehensively blocking the channel.

Now for the final, deadly stroke. The two boats were in

the water on the outward side, out of sight of the Dutch craft. One filled quickly with seamen and put off rapidly, the other lay hooked on while Roscoe raced below. In the gloom of the hold the stacked powder barrels, their copper bands glinting dully, waited patiently to do their work.

A lanthorn hung ready and Roscoe shoved the end of the match hose through the pane until it caught. He blew on it and a reassuring flare came in response. Laying it down carefully, he sprinted for the open air and hurtled into the boat. 'Give way, for your lives!' he panted.

The boat pushed off and the four men pulled like maniacs. On the shore they had seen that something was amiss and several figures gathered, shouting and gesticulating. Roscoe ignored them but first one, then several musket shots were heard, sending up warning splashes ahead of the two boats.

'Stretch out, damn it!' he urged, but a betraying thought tugged at him, becoming more insistent by the minute. By this time the charge should have gone off.

What was going on? How long should he give it? Must he go back and check at the risk of their being caught, unable to get away?

Common self-preservation led one way, duty another. If he left without ensuring *Azov* was sunk in place it could be cleared away quickly and the entire mission would fail.

'The charge hasn't exploded. We have to go back. Hold water larb'd, heavy up starb'd.'

There were disbelieving cries and his hand dropped to his sword. The boat reluctantly swung around and retraced its way back, but not before one of the crew muttered, 'An' if it goes off when we's a-looking?'

All it needed to bring the match to a fizzling stop was a chance imperfection in its composition. And all that was required to bring it to life was a remaining red ember to burn its way slowly past and burst into flame the other side, bringing on a delayed detonation. It could happen in the very next second.

Heart hammering Roscoe swung aboard and treading softly made his way down into the hold. Holding the lanthorn he stared at the deadly grey length of slow-match. Its course could be seen by the canvas tube rendered to ash as the burning fuse crept forward but in the dimness it was hard to see more.

He bent closer, a vision of an imminent explosion beating at him – and then he saw it. The fuse had led past a stanchion, and when laying it down after lighting, he'd not taken this into account. The cord had kinked as it went around.

He knew what he had to do and fumbled for his pocket knife. If he picked the match up it might catch again but he had to take the risk. There was no sudden blaze so with quick, hard slashes he cut it a few inches beyond the kink and threw the remnant nervously behind him, jamming the end of the match into the lanthorn, noting as he did that already the fuse was now near half its length.

It flared and caught. Letting it drop, Roscoe scrambled for fresh air but the boat had pushed off to keep at a safe distance if the worst happened.

Teetering at the edge of the deck for a heartbeat he neatly dived in and as he struck out for the boat the blast and visceral blow of a detonation took him painfully in his stomach, disorienting him. When his wits returned he saw that wreckage blown into the air was small and ragged. The detonation had vented upwards as it had punched its ship-killing spite into the vessel's bottom.

Taken short by the shocking development the firing ashore died away. Now, with their real purpose exposed, they could expect no mercy from the forts between the boats and the sea. They would slew their guns around and, at point-blank range, blast them to flinders.

It was hopeless but the oarsmen threw themselves at their task as the first of the big guns crashed out, narrowly missing them.

Roscoe felt a strange peace. It would be over very soon but at least in his last moments he would know that he'd succeeded in the mission.

Then a heavy rumble sounded out at sea and past the forts. Wonderfully, gloriously close, and under full sail, the over-looked *Thunderer* was blazing out broadsides that took the forts squarely, smashing and splintering stonework in a hell on earth for the gunners, who had the choice of fleeing or being torn apart.

The seamen pulling like lunatics, the boats won clear, and in the blessed freedom of the ocean they were reunited.

'Mr Roscoe,' Kydd said loudly, as he came over the side, 'well done! You and your Thunderers both.'

But then, without a pause, he turned to the sailing master. 'Mr Hobbs, clap on every stitch of canvas we have – I want to make St Petersburg before it falls!'

Chapter 53

St Petersburg

On his way back to the shore Renzi glanced at the dimin-
ishing bulk of *Thunderer*. In her was his closest friend
in this world and he was about to put out into the madness
that was the despairing attempt to save Riga by destroying
the siege train at sea. A near hopeless venture – all brought
about by the end working of his own mission.

By the time he reached his quarters in the Winter Palace
his desolate mood had deepened.

In a stab of harsh reality he began to question what he
was doing there. His purpose was coldly to appraise whether
Alexander would fight or seek peace with a conqueror – in
effect whether Great Britain should trust him enough to
commit troops and gold in the defence of Russia.

He'd achieved the priceless first step of winning Alexander's
confidence and faith, but two things had conspired to make
it near impossible to reach a usable conclusion. The first
was the character of the man: he was a mystic, naïve, distant
from the actuality of what was happening around him.

Nothing could be logically deduced, for he was not logical. Neither could he be relied upon in the article of consistency, often swayed by the arguments of the last he'd spoken to. The future of Russia was in his hands but how he would react was at the moment unfathomable.

The second was the nature of the peril. Bonaparte had confounded all by the speed and savagery of his movements, thrusting with unparalleled fury into the heart of Russia, in days and weeks overturning all notions of conventional war.

After the usual precautions Renzi found his materials and began to prepare a communication to England but failed at the first hurdle. What could he report that wouldn't be affected by the colossal events that even now were rapidly unfolding into uncharted regions? Could he say anything about Alexander that might reliably guide the British government to a course of action? No: therefore not to write anything was better than to offer guesses that could only mislead.

Days passed while, some hundreds of miles to the south, Bonaparte's army raged onward. In the feverish atmosphere of St Petersburg each scrap of news was seized avidly, then interpreted in different ways, but one thing was certain: its course after Smolensk was now undeniably straight as an arrow for the great prize – Moscow.

The Tsar did not call for Renzi. It was known that he'd caused the Black Virgin to be paraded through the streets and had attended the Patriarch's rambling services at the Kazan Cathedral but mostly he hid himself away at Tsarskoe Selo, his private palace in the country. Renzi found his time increasingly taken by Denisov, who inevitably ended his visits with impassioned accounts of the glory days of Russia, the Swedish wars and earlier.

He tried not to think of his dear friend Kydd throwing himself, his ship and his men at his vital objective. What if the transport was escorted by a powerful squadron? Without hesitation Kydd wouldn't flinch and would join battle whatever the odds.

On one afternoon, the same as so many before, Denisov suddenly paused in his story, his eyes wide. There were running footsteps and the door burst open. 'Aleksey – news!' It was a noble Renzi didn't recognise, dishevelled, his tunic unbuttoned as if carelessly thrown on.

Ignoring Renzi, Denisov leaped to his feet. 'Tell!' he demanded.

'A mighty battle as the world has never yet seen! Bagration and de Tolly both made a stand before Moscow!'

'Well, what happened, Pyotr? For God's sake, what happened, man?'

'I – I don't rightly know, but we've a battlefield messenger in the Imperial General Staff telling his story. Shall we go and hear?'

The room was crowded, its calm, lofty splendour out of keeping with the excitement and febrile atmosphere.

'The lieutenant is sore wounded and in with His Imperial Majesty,' was all the news they could get.

Frustration built until someone shouted, 'The stables! A survivor!'

The room emptied quickly as everyone hastened below. In the courtyard by a well a bandaged sergeant stood with a crowd about him. He looked up, startled by the rush of nobly dressed gentlemen.

'You were there?'

'Who won?'

'What was it like, at all?'

They were savagely shouted down by Denisov. 'Let the

337

creature speak, you fools.' When it was quiet he asked the man, 'Where was this battle?'

Forgetting himself, the sergeant answered in Russian, but then went on in crude French, 'Ah, near Borodino, twenty leagues afore Moscow, as please ye, sir.'

'Prince Bagration and Commander-in-chief de Tolly, no?' If it were both, then in and around the little village that day no less than a quarter of a million men had met in murderous combat.

'Yes, sir. Under Field Marshal Kutuzov. They forms up in the morning . . . when was it? On the twenty-sixth.'

'Well, what happened, damn it?'

'Can't rightly say, sir. I'se with L'tenant Borodinsky, galloper to General Ushakov, an' didn't have time to look around, like.' With an injured look the sergeant continued: 'Well, all hell breaks loose on us. Guns s' many it splits the air, fighting so fierce the ground's soaked in blood.'

The listening crowd fell silent as a harrowing tale unfolded in all its terrifying detail. The cruel cold of the pre-dawn when every man slept in the open with his musket, fearing what the day would bring, but with nothing to prepare him for the desperate actuality. A gigantic canvas portraying the hideous sight of line and column hacked into bloody corpses even as they screamed, '*Vive l'empéreur!*' Russian peasantry with pitchforks slaughtered to the last man in desperate, hopeless stands against Bonaparte's veterans. And always the dust and gun-smoke swirling about them in acrid clouds that threw every man into a world of isolation where only the imperative of kill or be killed had any meaning.

As the day went on and ammunition was spent, the fighting descending into animal savagery – screeching soldiers falling on each other with teeth and fists, piteous scenes of heroism and terror, blood and death until darkness came to shroud the scene from the eyes of men. And with the night came the looting – not for the usual pelf but precious food and water, for no supplies had crossed the hell on earth that was Borodino.

And then, mortally tired, their desperate ride for St Petersburg across square miles of corpses.

'Who won, damn you?' Denisov ground.

The sergeant looked pained. 'As I don't rightly know, sir. Difficult t' make out what's going on, all them guns a-roaring together, an' the lieutenant, he won't tell me.'

'We'll get no sense out of this ninny,' Denisov growled derisively. 'Let's wait for this messenger lieutenant.'

But the man stayed with the Tsar and the crowd dispersed. Renzi left Denisov in a frustrated pacing and went back to his quarters – almost an insult of comfort after what he'd heard.

Renzi was under no illusions: the de Tolly strategy of retreat and destruction had worked. That it had been thrown aside in favour of an out-and-out confrontation with Bonaparte was disastrous and he wouldn't be surprised to hear that the carefully hoarded Russian armies had been crushed and scattered, leaving nothing to stand between the Emperor and the soft body of Russia.

For a time St Petersburg was plunged into a nervous ferment, waiting for reliable tidings and then, as Renzi pored over yet another turgid exposition from the Imperial Library, there was an interruption that chilled him to the core.

Gunfire.

Flat thuds that came from the north-west. He jerked upright, straining to hear. Oddly it seemed to be single guns – and sounding at measured intervals. Then the bells began, first one, then a bedlam of sound as every cathedral and church joined in, a frenzy of joy that spread across the city.

Bemused, he sat back. This was a victory celebration. Sometime later, the streets below erupted in cheering and shouts that redoubled in commotion as if something momentous was approaching.

He rang for his servant who appeared, animated with excitement. 'Do pray open the window,' Renzi told him.

Renzi went to the balcony and looked down. It was some kind of military parade with an open carriage bearing a splendidly dressed officer. 'Do you know who that is?' he asked.

'That, sir, is the Field Marshal Kutuzov, victor of Borodino!'

The carriage turned off the street and into the gates of the Winter Palace where it was lost to view. The boulevard was quickly filling with people, wild with jubilation but held back by a line of grenadiers.

Victor? In a fury of impatience Renzi hurried to the Imperial General Staff. The room was in an uproar, packed with the military, the highest in the land, all talking animatedly. It wasn't hard to spot Denisov, loudly arguing with a hard-faced general, and he thrust through to him.

'What's the news?' he asked.

'A victory! We're in possession of a monstrous great victory!'

'Of course you are, but—'

'We have Kutuzov here, as he's left the field o' battle to tell us.'

'Yes, but what news does he bring, Aleksey?'

'When he departed Borodino he left the Russian Army standing proud, still in possession of the field. In the whole day never did he hear a single word of retreat, of yielding. Nikolai, we fought Bonaparte to a standstill. A famous victory that will resound down the centuries!'

'I see.'

'No, you don't, Nikolai! What this means is Bonaparte has been brought to a stand, he can't go further.'

'So—'

'So the devil is stopped in his tracks. He sees he can't get past us. Riga has been preserved to us, so he hasn't easy supplies, and there's only one thing he can do.'

'Yes?'

'He must give up, go home. Russia is saved, Nikolai!' He seized Renzi by the shoulders and hugged him. 'Glory be, and we're saved!'

If indeed Bonaparte's horde had been brought to a bloody halt, the Russians had good reason to be proud.

'My sincerest and deep-felt congratulations,' Renzi said formally, with a respectful bow. 'Shall you be celebrating at all?'

'Ha! Already His Imperial Majesty has decreed three days of official celebrations, beginning with an address to be read out in the Alexander Nevsky Cathedral. We shall not forget this day – ever!'

Renzi left him to his adulation of the victor Kutuzov and, in a daze of impressions and unsatisfied suppositions, he tried to return to his books, but the noise outside did not allow it. Again, there was no call from Alexander and he wondered why, in these momentous times, he hadn't been asked to make comment or pronouncement.

Denisov briefly visited with more details and in the evening Renzi went into the streets to take in the atmosphere.

It was an intoxicating, unforgettable and deeply moving sight as the Russian people gave vent to their feelings. Seething, happy crowds thronged the long avenues, trumpets blaring discordantly, drums thumping boisterously and fireworks swooshing and banging on all sides. Strings of multi-coloured lanterns and illuminations hung in windows for as far as he could see.

And then, by the edge of the water, glittering with reflections and alive with craft hurrying in every direction, he heard his name, faintly but clearly against the laughter and din of crowds. It came from a boat touching at the small sea-wall landing. To his intense pleasure he saw it was a British naval launch, which had to have come from *Thunderer*.

He waved an acknowledgement and hurried over.

'Lord Farndon, sir?' The lieutenant looked greatly relieved.

'It is.'

'The captain has given me instructions that we should without fail convey you this instant to the ship.'

On the way Renzi learned that Kydd's venture had been entirely successful and that no casualties had been sustained.

A beaming Kydd met him as he came aboard and they hastened to the privacy of his cabin.

'A cognac in a bumper, at seeing you spared!' Kydd declared warmly, taking a glass from Binard.

Their tales were exchanged, then Kydd leaned across seriously. 'Nicholas, know that I've to go now to Byam Martin to report myself and I cannot return. You will be coming with me, I beg.'

Renzi sighed, putting down his glass. 'Dear brother, there's nothing I crave more than to leave this madness, but unhappily the business is not yet concluded. Until I can see the tide irrevocably turning, I must not quit this benighted land.'

Kydd slumped back. 'There's nothing I can persuade you to that will see you on the way back to England and Cecilia?'

'No.'

'Then I must depart shortly, Nicholas. After storing and watering. And then . . .'

'I understand. Do not concern yourself on my account, my dear friend. I shall find ways to make my exit, I assure you.'

Chapter 54

In the Winter Palace the celebrations were unending, a vast dinner given in honour of the Tsar, a magnificent ball, parades and salutes without number.

But then, without warning, it turned to ashes. Denisov burst into Renzi's rooms, his eyes wild. 'News – dispatches. I fear it's a calamity!'

Renzi felt a grim foreboding. 'A disaster? What's this, my friend?'

'All I know is that the news is bad, Nikolai – I must go and find out more.'

He was not away long, returning with an expression that told of all that Renzi had feared.

'Nikolai. Prepare yourself. The most terrible thing. That devil on earth has flung us aside. He's secretly outflanked our positions at Borodino and forced us to fall back in disorder. Our hero Prince Bagration has died of his wounds. Nikolai . . . Nikolai . . . it means the road to Moscow is wide open! We're lost! We're lost!' He gulped, his eyes filling.

It was a catastrophe of the first order. Moscow taken and Alexander reduced to treating for terms, Bonaparte dictating the future of the world from the Kremlin, a realignment of interests that left England firmly out in the cold to find peace as she could.

'Stay here, Nikolai. I'll see what further news there is.'

Renzi was left alone with his thoughts. One thing was sure: now he had no choice but to stay and see how the Tsar would handle the end game for his nation. It could all be for nothing: the most likely outcome was an assassination. His duty to the mission, though, was to see it through to the end. Kydd and *Thunderer* would have to leave without him.

A sinister quiet lay over St Petersburg. Renzi stole a peek at the street below. It was deserted, the decorations sadly askew. As dusk drew in, a light drizzle centred each in a soft, sad halo of light.

He couldn't concentrate. Even with the melancholic silence that had descended on St Petersburg the philosophic ruminations of scholars of the last age held no fascination for him. The present times now were too chaotic, leading nowhere.

He heard disturbances below in the wet boulevard, shouts and excitement. And, with growing insistence, a low, haunting chant from powerful masculine voices in unison. He hurried to the window and drew back the heavy curtain carefully. A sizeable crowd had gathered but this was not a dangerous mob. They carried icons, banners, images, and were looking up reverentially, some with hands in a prayerful position, others making the sign of the Cross, still more with candles illuminating their rapt faces. This was no religious parade of the sort he'd seen before. It was a loose, spontaneous expression of some kind.

He rang for his servant. 'What's this below, pray?'

The man turned to him slowly and spoke in a strange hushed tone. 'Sir, the Little Father has spoken to his people and they hear him. They come to offer up their lives to him and to Mother Russia in her time of need.'

Even as he gazed down on them, the multitudes of people outside the Winter Palace were increasing in number, now spilling into the roadway. The chant swelled and broadened, and he watched, captivated. This was the Russian masses, those whom Napoleon Bonaparte was bent on conquering, subduing. It suddenly didn't seem quite so certain. He turned back but was startled by the two figures arrayed in the livery of the Imperial Household who loomed impassively in the doorway.

They said nothing but Renzi knew why they'd come and followed them.

Tsar Alexander was not in the Imperial General Staff, or even in his private drawing room. Renzi was led along a plain, barely lit hallway to a pair of massive doors, embellished with the holy significations of the Russian Orthodox creed. The doors were opened soundlessly and he was ushered inside.

The chapel was illuminated only by a pair of candles, the soft gold touching the churchly objects with an unearthly magnificence, revealing figures kneeling before one standing motionless in what resembled a penitent's robe. It was the Tsar.

To one side Renzi could make out another, clad in costly vestments and wearing a jewel-encrusted ecclesiastical crown, murmuring continuously some beatitude. Nearby an acolyte swung a censer of incense.

'Be welcome, our loyal English companion.' Alexander's voice was low, soft and infinitely serene.

Renzi knelt, like the others.

'I have bid you come that you might hear the words I have to say from my own lips.'

'Sire.'

'Know that in this, our greatest hour of trial, I shall not rest my burdens until Bonaparte, the very sceptre of the Antichrist, is driven from Holy Mother Russia.' His voice had strengthened, risen in spiritual ecstasy. 'In the name of our sacred ancestors I shall stand before him. I shall fight to the last breath of my body and inch of my realm. Know, too, that with my people and nation rising in arms together against the usurping tyrant we shall remain in the forefront of battle until he is hounded from our land and then – as God is my witness – I will keep faith with the crushed and conquered of this world to rid the earth of this foul violator of mankind.'

His eyes, lifted in saintly rapture, dropped to look down on Renzi. 'Is it in your thoughts, my companion and counsellor, to remain by my side while my crusade is done?'

Taken by surprise, Renzi found himself saying into the stillness, 'I shall, if this be Your Majesty's desire.'

For a long moment he thought Alexander had not heard. Then the Tsar said, with a rising intensity, a vehemence that was almost fierce, 'It is not my desire. My wish and my prayer is that, now you have heard my words, noble lord, you will reverently take them to my brother, King George of Great Britain, the only remaining foe to the tyrant left in the field, as witness that Russia will never be vanquished, never yield to the oppressor of humankind. This is the greatest service you can do for Russia, dear friend. Will you swear it?'

'I so swear!' Renzi said, realising as he said it that his sincerity was genuine.

He rose from his knees and, with a profound bow, backed out of the presence.

Outside a bear-like figure took his arm. 'Alexsey,' Renzi murmured.

The man was clearly in thrall to the moment.

'Nikolai. The Little Father has spoken. When you bow before your king and convey his words, do know that they are being retold in the cathedrals, the market-squares, the lowest taverns. They will shout from the pages of newspapers and be written on banners and borne into battle by the common soldier. Nikolai, tell your king that it is not the Tsar only who stands alone before Bonaparte but the soul of Mother Russia – her people!'

'I know, my friend. I can hear them. And therefore I will truthfully say that I myself heard the soul of Russia cry aloud to be avenged.'

In bare hours Renzi was standing on the finely carved stern gallery of *Thunderer*, watching her wake dissipate in the cold grey waters while the coastline of Russia slipped away into the distance. The searing experiences of the last month were slowly rendering into memories that he knew he would take into the remainder of his life.

Russia – a monstrous conundrum. Congalton had said that France was a civilised country ruled by a barbarian, Russia a barbarian land ruled by a monk. So true – but he'd seen only part of the whole and knew there were unfathomable depths to which he'd never been witness. And now it was all over. The climax to this clash of Titans was imminent but its outcome was denied him. He didn't know whether to be thankful or melancholic, but in any event his part was complete. He had enough to state that Tsar Alexander would stand against Bonaparte and that the people of Russia were with him. Whether that led to

Continental-scale slaughter or a grave setback for Bonaparte could not be known at this time.

Kydd moved to his side. 'Nicholas, it would gratify me extremely were I to hear something of your adventures. I have a fine Madeira going a-begging in the telling.'

Chapter 55

The grey bulk of *Aboukir* firmed out of the rain mist at last. With the entire length of the Baltic shore now in thrall to Napoleon Bonaparte, any fleet rendezvous was meaningless and Byam Martin's flagship could have been anywhere along its length. *Thunderer* knew better than to make the traditional thirteen-gun salute. As long ago as Cornwallis, most blockading admirals had seen it as not only a waste of powder but an alert to the enemy of big-ship movements.

Three other sail-of-the-line were in sight, all four under lazy sail, vaguely standing across the Gulf of Finland to some purpose that was not clear to Kydd.

He mounted the side-steps of the flagship to be met by a genial Admiral Byam Martin, who nevertheless seemed grey and drawn beneath his greeting. 'A welcome to ye, Kydd,' he rumbled warmly. 'As I've been desirous of making your acquaintance these weeks past.'

'I do apologise, sir. Delayed in joining by events in Russia – it's all in my report.'

'Let's below an' you can tell me about it.'

Below was really further aft on the same deck, similar to *Thunderer*, but long habit of using the term more appropriate to a single gun-deck marked him out, like Kydd, as a frigate man at heart.

It didn't take long to tell of the Danzig exploit and to receive full support for his action in falling in with the Tsar's call. 'As I'd hope an enterprising officer would behave, you receiving my blessing on your previous conveying of His Russian Nibs to Äbo.'

'Sir, there's a person aboard *Thunderer* of much importance. The Lord Farndon, who's been in clandestine service with the Tsar since before the descent on his country. He fervently desires to return to England and lay before the Foreign Office certain intelligence he's since acquired.'

'I see.' He reflected for a short space. 'Then we can do something about that. After Riga there's nothing of note that I need any kind of fleet for and I've lately a mind to send back some of my sail-of-the-line to Admiral Saumarez as dispensable, he having more of a need, I believe. Can't see why you shan't join 'em as well. No doubt Sir James will then find an aviso cutter on regular visit to England as will convey your man.'

'Thank you, sir.'

'It might be in order to pay a call on Admiral Reynolds at Hanö. He has a hard enough situation.'

'Our convoy collection point.'

'Just so. Well, off you go, dear fellow. No point in moping about.'

With much satisfaction Kydd laid *Thunderer*'s bows to the west and, in the increasingly chill autumn easterlies, made good time to Hanö Bay, flanked by two other sail-of-the-line. Without a naval or other base in the Baltic, this was where convoys from England were escorted, then to disperse under false colours and papers to the many ports within Bonaparte's Continental System. It was also where merchant ships with their vital Baltic cargoes would make their way to assemble into the regular convoys back to various ports in Britain.

With his several ships-of-the-line, the admiral's task was to watch over the immense gathering of wealth that was a several-hundred-ship convoy, as well as to see it on its way through the Great Belt passage and out of the Baltic. A glittering prize for any determined marauding enemy.

But Kydd saw that the two sail-of-the-line at anchor were old and worn out, assigned the station as deterrents, never to storm into line-of-battle as a fleet or even meet an equal on the high seas. The flagship, *St George*, was a 98-gun second rate dating back to before the war. The other, *Defence*, had already aged forty-odd years in her brave fight at Trafalgar.

Admiral Reynolds was affable and clearly felt honoured at Kydd's visit. 'Kind in you, old fellow. You should know, o' course, that the season's over in these parts.'

'Sir?'

'Sir James agrees a date for clearing the Baltic of our shipping well in advance of the winter icing over, since we once lost an entire convoy frozen in by leaving it too late. This is the last of 'em for this year.' He had kindly features, distinguished grey hair adding to a figure of some presence. Kydd recalled that, as the notable frigate captain of *Amazon* at the beginning of the wars, he'd been with Pellew in the celebrated action in the midst of a fierce storm that had ended with a French ship-of-the-line destroyed in the breakers.

'We sail shortly. Care to take passage with us?'

'I'd be honoured,' Kydd murmured. The two that had accompanied him could choose for themselves. Renzi would agree that a day or two's delay in exchange for undoubted security for his intelligence would be acceptable in the circumstances.

After his previous service in the Baltic, Kydd was no stranger to the arcane rituals of convoys. This one was of some hundred and fifty sail, which, while middling in size, at one or two cables spacing, covered the sea from horizon to horizon. Falling in at the rear with the others, *Thunderer* picked up speed and the entire company of ships put to sea. They emerged from behind Hanö island for the run along the south coast of Sweden. Almost immediately they were caught in an ugly cross-sea, the onrush of a powerful swell from the north-east contradicted by an increasing wind-driven bluster from the west-south-west.

Uncomfortably the convoy pressed on, smaller merchant-men falling astern with loss in speed after taking in sail to withstand the blow.

'Can't say as how it's looking so good for us, is my opinion, sir.'

Kydd trusted Hobbs, the sailing master, a steady hand and not given to undue alarm. 'How so?'

The man looked into the eye of the wind and bared his teeth, as though tasting its quality. 'Doesn't do to miscalculate in the Baltic. This snorter comes over from the North Sea t' bully us right enough, where's born some o' the worst seas on the planet. This time o' the year – autumn, like – we can expect evil weather any time.'

Kydd could remember some hard blows in his own service here. The fortunates in massive line-of-battle ships wouldn't find themselves threatened but the hundreds of merchant ships, each effectively on its own in the midst of many, didn't have that comfort and would be battening down and rigging lifelines.

They passed the southern entry to the Sound by

dead-reckoning, the air misty and storm-racked. Then it was tack and tack again to round Gedser Point and relief from the bruising cross-sea, before the last day's run to the enfolding peace of the Great Belt passage.

The final staying about was with Gedser Odde in plain view, the sullen roar of the wind's blast redoubling once around to its weather side, seething seas racing across offshore shoals with no sign of life ashore. And to the south, away from Denmark and not more than twenty-odd miles downwind, was Rostock and the entire length of Bonaparte's hostile Baltic coast.

By now the convoy was losing any semblance of an organised body. Some ships fell off the wind to turn tail for the safety of whence they'd come. Others were in difficulties with torn canvas or splintered spars. Kydd wasn't surprised to see *St George* signal a run for shelter northwards, presumably deep into Nystad Bay.

As if in sympathy the winds eased and, at last able to shed oilskins, Kydd watched the motions of the flagship, determined to moor within easy sight for orders when they came. The bay, though, was shoal-ridden and dangerous. Hobbs shook his head at the sight of whitened humping waters betraying reefs and sandbars not far below the surface.

St George had her best bower anchor run out to its full scope, allowing her to swing and face into the wind's eye and Kydd did likewise at a safe distance off, the two other sail-of-the-line taking position on the side. All round them the convoy loosed their anchors and settled down to ride out the gale, a vast mass of ships in the sweep of the bay, each one bobbing and jibbing uncomfortably to their anchors.

Kydd had endured such before, but never for more than a day or two, and his sympathies were for Renzi, with urgent and vital intelligence locked in his breast, held to a standstill by the run for shelter. Then again, if he'd gone on in a dispatch cutter, he would have been no better off, balked by the same storm.

The day faded into a bleak dusk while the hurts of the ship were taken in hand, and the ship's company given a hot meal. Further off, *St George* hoisted three lanthorns into her maintop for all to be reassured. All around them lights appeared as the convoy waited out the night, but as the last dog-watchmen handed over to the first-watchmen Kydd, in his cabin at supper with Renzi and Craddock, felt a subtle but noticeable change in the ship's heave and snub at her anchor.

Within ten minutes a soaked and red-eyed midshipman-of-the-watch brought a message. 'Mr Briggs's respects an' the wind's backed into the sou'-west an' strengthening.'

In this short time, backing a whole quadrant and from that quarter was bad news, in a trice turning the whole bay into a lee shore. Kydd excused himself and, pulling on his foul-weather gear, hurried out on deck. It was now a flat, streaming blast and a glance at the compass told him it was indeed from the south-west.

'Don't like it, sir. With a bigger fetch it could turn ugly. Clear away second bower?'

Kydd hesitated but only for a moment. 'Compliments to Mr Hobbs and I'd be happy to see him on deck.'

The master had no doubts. 'A change so quick – we're going to a fresh gale afore long.' He sniffed at the wind distrustfully. 'An' anchors aren't all we'll need.'

'Mr Hobbs?'

'We're like to be embayed if this blow shapes more southerly. I'd advise we lay along sail ready to cut 'n' run, sir.'

'Thank you. We'll see how the breeze does in the next hour.'

Over on their bow the three lanthorns in *St George* were a beacon of calm in the gathering darkness. The big three-decker seemed hardly to notice the blow, but the merchant ships pitched and rolled, fretfully brought up to their anchors and simply enduring. *St George* serenely rode it out.

As far as the eye could see the convoy had been transformed into so many lights in the darkness, blinking as their low-slung navigation lamps were obscured by the short steep waves being kicked up. It would be an uncomfortable night, even in *Thunderer*, where the smash and judder of waves were beginning to make themselves felt. Kydd took a last look around before returning to finish his supper.

Craddock's face was a study in seriousness as he cradled his toddy. 'Mr Renzi warns it's as likely to get worse as better.'

'And he'd be right,' Kydd said, allowing Binard to whisk away his dripping oilskin. 'I'd pass a lashing over your cot if I were you.' He would be turning in all-standing, fully dressed to be ready if urgently called on deck, which was looking increasingly likely.

The gale increased remarkably rapidly, the motions of the ship-of-the-line less ponderous, now convulsive, the weighty sequence of creaks and groans along the length of the vessel louder and more insistent. The wind's whistle in the rigging turned into a continuous dull drone and then, quite audible even in the great cabin, rose to a demented organ pitch that clutched at the heart.

It was time to return on deck. It was all Kydd could do to stand upright against the savage blast, made all the more unnerving by the pitch-black darkness and the stinging spray. Briggs appeared out of nowhere, his foul-weather gear streaming and his face red with endurance. 'Barometer dropped three-quarters of an inch this last hour. Can't go on like this,' he shouted into Kydd's ear.

'I've seen worse in the Caribbee,' Kydd yelled back. 'Count on it, it will.'

'Flagship in sight, no signals,' Briggs added formally, as was required of him at the appearance of his captain on deck. He gestured mutely into the murk to leeward. *St George*'s three lights could just be glimpsed through the wild night, but there was little sign of the convoy lights, a few occasional pinpricks appearing and disappearing. The wind-driven spume stung Kydd's eyes as he took it all in.

'Carpenter reports two feet in the well, bosun says anchor holding,' Briggs added. Kydd knew that would be the stolid Opie right forward in the bows, his foot resting on the bar-taut cable to the hawse, feeling for dreaded irregular vibrations and twitches indicating that the three-ton bower anchor was ploughing a furrow in the seabed.

If it did fail he had to decide whether to let go more anchors at the cost of losing them if things got worse and they had to cut them free to make a break under sail to seaward. It would be certain destruction to face any other crisis with empty cables.

The watch on deck was nowhere to be seen. Kydd was not annoyed, for it showed the consideration Briggs had for his men, sending them to shelter in the deck below, on call.

Kydd shuddered in the cold. How long should he keep Briggs company on this awful night?

From somewhere far forward a faint cry cut through the hammering wind blast, the fore-deck lookout loyally singing out hazards. Kydd leaned into the bluster, shielding his eyes and gazed into the wind-torn welter of seas. At first he saw nothing. The three lights in the maintop of *St George* were still there but they had been visible as a threesome spaced along the after end of the top. Now they blended into one as their perspective changed.

It could mean only one thing: *St George* was under way of some kind, no longer anchored. Drifting? Deliberately making for the open sea?

The first was unthinkable. The three-decker had the best ground tackle of them all, massive anchors, twenty-three-inch cables. As for the other, the signal for an emergency break to sea was a blue and a red light simultaneously displayed, their ghostly glare unmistakable. It was unimaginable that their careful and highly experienced admiral would forget to signal his intentions.

Kydd's mind whirled as he tried to wring sense from it. It was impossible to make out anything in the dark chaos of the storm. Their only course of action was to stay as they were until daylight revealed the mystery.

It was a tempest of hideous proportions, the harshest he'd seen in the Baltic, and made all the worse by that sea nightmare – lack of sea-room. In the Caribbean there was a good chance to outfox a hurricane with adroit seamanship, given the distances between islands, but the Baltic was in effect an inland sea with reef-fringed land in all directions.

In the early hours Kydd sensed a lessening of force, or was he deluding himself? There was nothing he could achieve out in the open until daybreak and he left the deck for his cabin, slumped into a chair and drifted into a troubled sleep.

He woke with a start. The motion of the ship was noticeably less but the wicked drone of the winds was still audible. His watch told him that dawn was an hour or so away, but he snatched up his oilskin and made his way to the half-deck.

'Oh, sir. You're awake?' It was Smale, the officer-of-the-deck coming out of the master's cabin, looking dry and rested. Clearly he'd seen no reason why he shouldn't see out the blow in some sort of comfort.

'I am. And you?' Kydd asked pointedly, but at anchor there

was no rule that said an officer had to be on deck as long as he was within immediate call.

There was no way he could go back to sleep in the tension of waiting for dawn, and he passed the time in forced conversation with Smale.

At the first glimmering of daybreak they peered out into the grey murk, rain squalls marching in adding to the chill misery of dawn.

When visibility had reached out to a mile or more, a terrible sight was revealed. The sea was nearly empty, the convoy no more. A thin scatter of merchantmen had miraculously survived, but wrecks could be made out everywhere, dismasted, stranded, sunken.

In the centre of the wretched scene one sight brought gasps of horror. Hard aground, on her beam ends and entirely dismasted in a pitiable wreck, was the hulk of *St George*.

There were men still aboard: a flutter of colour at the stump of her fore-mast, some clinging to her sloping deck as they fought their way along, others struggling to secure gear as the battering seas threw spars and wreckage at her naked hull.

Then, from a makeshift flag-mast, a signal appeared: 'All captains, as convenient', meaning that when the seas had abated enough for boats to reach the wreck they were to go to the flagship. There were something like nine hundred men aboard *St George*, a colossal rescue by boat to contemplate, but the signal implied the admiral was still aboard and taking charge.

For an hour or more Kydd helplessly watched the seas seething in under the lash of the gale until they'd subsided sufficiently to risk the launch, *Thunderer*'s biggest boat. Coming in on the leeward side, *St George*'s entry-port was within easy stepping distance and Kydd was helped up the steeply canted deck by the side-party, soaked but unhurt.

A life-line had been rigged and he hauled himself along to the admiral's cabin spaces aft. Reynolds greeted him warmly, as did Guion, his flag-captain, the austere Atkins of *Defence* with his habitual long face rising to greet him. One or two others murmured a greeting, presumably captains of the lesser craft Kydd had seen converging on the flagship after daylight had exposed the shocking scene.

A table had been wedged into the lower corner and refreshments tastefully laid out, for all the world like a flag-officer's entertainments.

'Gentlemen. I don't have to tell you that *St George* has suffered grievous wounds in the night's gales.'

'Sir, how did it happen at all?' one of the junior captains asked, wide-eyed. 'I mean, a three-decker and—'

'A substantial-sized merchantman was driven athwart my hawse during the night and carried away my best bower.'

'Aye, sir, but—'

'L'tenant, the inshore bottom hereabouts is cobbles.' Small loose rocks, rounded by centuries of rolling together in foul weather and hopelessly slippery. The worst holding for the anchors of big ships.

'When we struck, axes were laid to the masts to ease her pounding but as it stands, our rudder has been beaten off entirely.'

Kydd felt for them: a frightful night of terror and hopeless labour in the cold wildness, relentlessly driving into the shore with who knew what awaiting them. But discipline had held and, in the howling darkness, they'd done what was needed to prevent the ship toppling. 'When shall we begin taking off your ship's company, sir? By boat some nine hundreds will take time and—'

'Thank you, but it will not be necessary.'

'Sir?'

'I intend to refloat *St George*, re-rig with jury masts and complete the voyage.'

This was either madness or inspired, Kydd reflected, but saw the flag-captain, Guion, nodding slowly.

'How can we help, sir?' Atkins asked.

'Stand by me. And I'd be grateful for the loan of your carpenter and his mates.'

'Your rudder, sir. I could have a try at a Pakenham for you,' Kydd offered. Some years ago an enterprising captain had devised a method of providing a rudder where one had been lost or dashed off, using only its remains and ship's stores. The Admiralty had been so taken with the idea that they'd printed out instructions to be issued to every king's ship to be kept for just this moment.

Reynolds gave a twisted smile but then gravely agreed. 'Do so, Sir Thomas. I would be grateful.'

'Jury masts, sir?' Atkins enquired.

'Indeed. Topmasts were struck down before the storm as usual and are to hand. I shall extract our mast stumps and substitute the topmasts, which I'm sanguine will answer.'

Half the size, but if it could be achieved, then canvas could be spread and *St George* would be no longer a dead ship. It was looking possible.

'Getting afloat?'

'The master assures me we are held only by a third of our length. Should we lighten ship, then with every man-o'-war boat a-swim and manned to excess I believe we may succeed in pulling her clear.'

Kydd couldn't help but be carried along by the tide of creative hope. This was what it was to lead and inspire, and his respect for the kindly admiral increased.

'I'm supposing you'll be as surprised as I to learn that, of our convoy of a hundred and fifty, no less than seventy-odd survived the night. I'm sending them on with suitable escort and *Rose* will press on separately to alert Admiral Saumarez as to our disposition. All sail-o'-war save her will remain with me.'

The conference broke up in a far different mood than when it had met, and the captains left with grim purpose to begin the heroic salvage plan.

As he turned to go Kydd remembered Renzi. 'Sir, would it be in order for *Rose* to carry ahead my distinguished guest? He has vital intelligence for their lordships and—'

'Of course, dear fellow. She'll put off at midday when my dispatches are ready.' In a more concerned tone he went on, 'And that Pakenham rudder. I've heard it's a beast to put together – are you sure *Thunderer* can conjure it?'

'She will, sir!'

The gale lessened as quickly as it had struck and work began without delay. Men swarmed over the cruelly dismasted *St George* to start the prodigious labour of extracting the remains.

In *Thunderer* they set about producing a three-ton, seventy-foot rudder that could be mounted securely enough to take another gale. From the depths of Craddock's ship's office the Pakenham screed was found. Just a single sheet printed on both sides but it seemed to satisfy the carpenter, Upcot, who bore it off to sketch out the requisites.

He was back soon. 'Er, sir. Here it says as we has to forge an iron plate t' take the weight, it not havin' your reg'lar pintle and gudgeon a-tall. I can't do it.'

The principle of the Pakenham rudder was robust but the actuality difficult to achieve. The rudder shank would be passed up into the trunking as usual, but instead of being supported by half a dozen pintles rotating in gudgeons bolted to the ship's sternpost it was essentially hung at the top with a massive forged shoulder bolt penetrating the two-foot-square rudder-stock, and bearing on a weighty circular iron plate. A stout tiller-bar inserted into a mortice in the rudder-head and equipped with relieving tackles provided the necessary steering capability.

'Tell the armourer to lay aft,' Kydd snapped. This was Ferne, one of the ship's artisans and seldom seen about the decks, but now about to be central to the action.

'Mr Ferne, please to consult with the carpenter concerning his needs. You and your mates are to turn to, double tides, until the job's under hatches.'

With Roscoe and much of *Thunderer*'s complement away in *St George*, there was plenty of room to spread out the workings of the huge rudder over the quarterdeck while Ferne set up his forge right forward on the fo'c'sle, the acrid stink of his fire soon spreading aft.

Renzi made his farewells and departed in *Rose*, and before the end of the day the convoy had set sail for the north leaving the warships to their exertions.

A bare three days later, all ships put every boat they possessed into the water, double-banked on each thwart, and with a drummer of the Royal Marines embarked to beat time. A ferocious heaving and straining, along with much cursing and heavy sweat, at long last had the great three-decker afloat.

Rapid soundings of her well confirmed there were no serious leaks. The last mast stumps were withdrawn and topmasts lowered into the mast steps.

In *Thunderer* the finished Pakenham rudder was swayed overside with a yardarm stay tackle and floated out to *St George* where it was fitted, to much applause.

Light-headed with exhaustion and relief Kydd kept the

deck until the first canvas was spread in *St George* and, to roars of cheering, the battleship ponderously took up on the starboard tack and headed resolutely for the open sea.

In a stroke of irony, the lessening gale dropped to a light breeze and then a playful zephyr, almost unknown at this time of the year. It was nothing that *Thunderer* and the others couldn't deal with but, burdened with an awkward jury rig, *St George* was in no shape to manoeuvre out of it. Her sails were struck, the remaining anchors tumbled down, and the flagship was once more at a standstill, threatened with the same lee shore.

It was a wicked twist in fortune and Kydd made an instant decision. 'Make to flag: "Prepare to be taken in tow".'

Not waiting for a reply he ordered, 'Mr Roscoe, rouse out a cable, double-bitt it around the mizzen-mast and out through the gun-deck sternports.' If they could get *St George* out to sea there was a good chance that there she could pick up a usable breeze.

The messenger line was taken out by *Thunderer*'s launch. *St George* took it in and hauled away valiantly until the heavy rope made its way in through her hawse to be seized around the fore-mast.

Cautiously Kydd applied small sail until the 74 had taken the first strain, waiting until the signal from the flagship indicated that her anchors were aweigh before spreading more sail until, by inches, the two moved ahead to the accompaniment of a thunderous creaking.

As if on cue, Binard appeared on deck before him, bearing a salver on which was the brave sight of brimming champagne glasses.

'I rather thought this to be your intention,' Craddock said smoothly.

Kydd proposed a toast. 'Gentlemen. To us, *St George*, and

why Boney can never carry the day while the Royal Navy keeps the seas for its own!'

Every officer first raised their glass to the flagship and then to Kydd, whose heart swelled with pride.

'And a double tot to all hands, Mr Roscoe.'

Chapter 56

At a steady five knots the ships passed along the south of Denmark, the tow, the jury rig and the Pakenham rudder holding firm. Ahead, the fearful passage of the torturous reefs and currents of the Great Belt loomed, a hard enough beat at the best of times but for a ship under tow a nightmare.

With *Bellette* going ahead and *Defence* bringing up the rear, *Thunderer* and *St George* won through into the northern entrance to the Baltic, the Kattegat – and blessed open sea. As if at last relenting the wind turned to a brisk south-easterly, fine for the final distance to the commander-in-chief, Saumarez.

The anchorage was crowded with shipping. A convoy was clearly about to depart for England and there was every chance they could be with it.

Rear Admiral Reynolds was quick to report, his barge in the water just as soon as the tow had been cast off and *Thunderer* had found her berth.

Within the hour the captains of *Defence* and *Thunderer* were summoned.

'I've been hearing a little of what you've achieved,

gentlemen,' Saumarez opened. 'Admiral Reynolds speaks in the most handsome terms of your diligence to duty and enterprise. Might I add my own admiration to his that you have been instrumental in preserving for His Majesty a most valuable flagship. Bless you both!'

'As was my bounden duty only, sir, to stay with my admiral,' Atkins protested, in the manner of the crusty traditionalist that he was.

'Yes. Well, as it is I have a problem,' harrumphed Saumarez. 'What to do with *St George*. I will be sailing to England shortly, and patently she's in no fit condition to stay with the fleet. I would think it therefore prudent for her to over-winter here and employ the time gainfully in repairs.'

'Sir, I do protest!' Reynolds spluttered. 'With Boney setting the world upside down Britain needs every ship of force that can—'

'I appreciate your dedication, sir, but this is not to be entertained. Your vessel must be sorely tried in the stranding and I cannot allow her to risk the North Sea as winter approaches.'

'Sir! With shoring in 'tween decks and the Pakenham holding well, I've every hope that—'

'No.'

'With *Thunderer* standing by and—'

Saumarez's brow creased. 'Very well, this I'll grant: a hull survey by three, and if they allow perhaps I'll reconsider.'

Kydd was there when the report came in. Two had misgivings and one allowed that, should the vessel be spared further torments by the weather, she had a chance.

Reynolds was accompanied by Guion, his flag-captain, and in nominal command of *St George*.

'Sir. We have been with the old lady for some years and we know her qualities,' Guion said, adding, 'It's but a three-day sail to Sheerness with a fair wind – as it does today, sir.'

The mild north-easterly was indeed directly fair for England. Saumarez pondered the risk to the injured ship against its restoration to the British fleet. 'Very well. Much against my inclination. Do take *Thunderer* as a precaution and you can have *Defence* as well. I believe I'll send the convoy off with *Hero* without delay and myself sail with the Baltic Fleet separately.'

When *St George* put to sea it was without a tow, the north-easterly almost coming in from astern. Logging a good six knots, she had *Defence* on her weather beam, *Thunderer* under her lee and, with the loyal *Bellette* sloop ranging ahead, the course was set for England.

But first they had to clear the Skaggerak, the seventy-mile-wide route from the Baltic entrance across the north of Denmark and out into the North Sea, before the quick run to the south-west and the dockyards of Sheerness and Chatham.

Kydd had always distrusted the North Sea, let alone at the coming of winter, and made sure the towing cable was faked down on the gun-deck, its lighter messenger line attached ready. Who knew if *St George*, with her awkward jury rig, would need a hand to pull clear of a hazard if the wind fell or even be plucked off a lee shore in a heavy blow?

Through the night the winds stayed fair, and dawn saw them leave the shelter of the Skaggerak passage – but the treacherous weather had not finished with them. The winds began to back more into the west, whipping and moaning, with every indication of turning ugly. By now the squadron had passed some distance down the outer coast of Jutland on its way south.

Hobbs voiced his concerns: 'Better to make an offing while you can, afore you stands to the suth'ard.' Kydd was inclined to agree but sympathised with *St George* in her pressing need to get into dockyard hands, now only a day or so away.

As the light strengthened, so did the wind, backing even further. At this rate they could soon be met with winds foul for their crossing.

St George threw out a signal. 'All ships,' the officer-of-the-watch called, his glass up but wavering in the increasing blow. 'Fleet to return to base.'

Painfully *St George* paid off and took up close-hauled on the larboard tack, heading back up the invisible Jutland coast for the eventual turn to starboard into the Skaggerak. *Defence* took the outer, weather side while *Thunderer* lay to leeward as they clawed their way north, the winds becoming fiercer at a dismaying rate. 'Double reefs in topsails,' Kydd ordered, the viciousness of the driving gale off the open North Sea touching him with a primeval icy foreboding.

St George took in all sail bar her staysails and treble-reefed topsails – a precaution with her weakened jury-rigged top-hamper. Further out to sea *Defence* was conforming, but Kydd's foreboding took on a stark reality when a lookout lashed into the foretop hailed down something and a messenger raced aft.

'Sir – fore lookout reports land all t' leeward!'

In a stab of anguish Kydd knew they had not reached the critical far end of Jutland to allow them to turn and go before the wind to safety. The lookout had seen a continuous line of white where the breakers were thundering on shore and they'd clearly extended out of sight ahead. With the winds from the west it was a dead lee shore and *St George* was at hazard unless she could soon weather the point of Holmen into the Skaggerak.

'Signal – land in sight to loo'ard!' he shouted at the signals messenger by his side. 'Hoist at fore and mizzen both.'

Kydd glanced at the flagship through the stinging spray kicked up from windward. A pale flicker on her deck forward resolved into another staysail being hoisted forward, a balancing staysail at the mizzen. She'd seen and understood the message of the fearful danger to leeward and was trying to add weatherliness without throwing an intolerable strain on her spars. If they carried away it would, without doubt, mean her destruction.

The speed at which the gale had clamped in was shocking, and it was now worse than any Kydd had encountered in this part of the world. He had to look to *Thunderer* too, for she was even closer to the low coast – about ten to a dozen miles off at the lookout's height of eye.

He felt his arm twitched. Hobbs shouted in his ear, 'Sir, I mislikes what I sees, but . . . but if'n I'm not mistaken *St George* is makin' a terrible lot o' leeway.'

This meant that the mighty three-decker was falling downwind on *Thunderer* in her lee position and at the same time adding to her perilous situation relative to Jutland.

'Bear up as will keep us clear.' His duty was to his lee station with respect to the admiral. *Defence*, on the other side, was already taking in sail to slow to stay loyally in his own weather station and was uncomfortably bucketing about.

And now to complicate matters night was coming on, the racing scud overhead looking more lethal, the shriek of wind tearing at the senses.

'Sir.' The sailing master beckoned and they left the half-deck for the shelter of his cabin where he clearly wanted to talk.

'Mr Hobbs?'

'We has a decision t' make, sir.'

'I know.' The 'we' was kindly meant but in reality it was the captain's decision alone. On this larboard tack and with the fearful leeway the flagship was making they were not going to weather the Holmen.

'In this kind o' blow we're not going t' be able to tack about,' Hobbs prompted.

'No.'

'And the Danish coast shoals well out.'

'Yes.' The utterly flat coast, hard-packed sand compacted by centuries of pounding storms, extended underwater well offshore, and could not be detected by sounding in this raging storm.

'We has t' wear about.' Hobbs's voice had an edge of quiet desperation.

He'd made it official. Brought the peril to his captain's attention. If Kydd did nothing about it and the worst happened, if he survived, the subsequent court-martial would be merciless.

On the other hand his orders were plain and direct. He was to maintain the leeward station as *Defence* would the weather and, besides, it was a fundamental rule of naval practice to stay with the admiral in battle or tempest, whatever the conditions.

'The admiral has not signalled to wear,' he said stiffly.

'No, sir, he hasn't. As doesn't mean we shouldn't, being as how it would save the ship.'

And her many hundreds of souls. At the cost of abandoning his admiral, leaving him and his near thousand men to their fate.

'I'll think on it,' was all Kydd could find to say.

A fleeting memory came to him – another place, another storm. *Alexander* and the helpless *Vanguard*: Horatio Nelson driving on shore to his inevitable doom. Ball had stayed with his admiral and, in a feat of magnificent seamanship, had at the last moment got a line across and snatched the ship from certain death in the breakers. Nelson had been saved and a few weeks later had gone on to achieve an immortal victory at the Nile.

Was this what he should be doing, not cravenly fleeing?

Out on deck again the night had come in but with an eerie twist. There was a full moon, not visible behind the flying murk and clouds. But it shone through, permeating the scene with a luminosity, touching everything with a sheen of light, turning the sleeting spray to diamonds, the mist and spume torn from wave-tops into a radiant luminescence – and revealing in piteous detail ships fighting for their lives.

'Anything from *St George*?' Kydd asked hopefully.

Roscoe shook his head. It might well be that no signal flag could survive in this.

'Any sign she's going to wear about?' In this visibility they could easily see if she began the manoeuvre.

'No, sir.'

'Lay along for wearing. Just as soon as she does, we do too and that damn quick.'

'Sir.'

Hobbs looked about, his face drawn and haggard. He knew what it would be to end life cruelly battered to death in a crashing chaos ashore – he'd survived a shipwreck before, Kydd recalled.

'He has to wear!' blurted Smale, perhaps realising for the first time the totality of what was ahead.

'Land to starboard,' reported Briggs. That it was visible from the deck meant it was some five to seven miles off and the space needed to wear was closing to nothing.

Eyes stinging not just from the salt spray, Kydd gazed at the flagship. The kindly Reynolds, what was he going through now? What desperate move was he trying to devise to stave off the death that awaited them all?

A flicker of moon-pale canvas showed at her main, mounting up to be snatched away as if by a giant hand. A last desperate attempt at sail blown to shreds the instant it

371

met the wind. Agonisingly, on the fore-mast, another – with the same result.

He understood immediately. *St George* was trying to wear but could not, her despairing attempts denied her by the wind's blast and her own wounded rigging.

Gulping, Kydd rounded on Hobbs. 'Wear ship, this instant!'

In the brutish savagery of the storm, a few feet of water remaining under her keel and the gale now a demented shriek, *Thunderer* fought her way around, her men like heroes against the foe, her movements frenzied as those of a maddened horse. On one side the spectre of a life-ending catastrophe – and on the other the delirium of continued existence out in the open sea.

Kydd snatched a look beyond *St George*. Was *Defence* going to follow *Thunderer* to wear about to salvation? She could be made out, bucking and rearing – but still close hauled on the larboard tack, if anything closing with the stricken three-decker. As *Thunderer* won around he saw, with an inevitability that was as harsh as the gesture was noble, that her captain was going to stay with his admiral and within a very short while both ships would meet their end.

Guilt pierced him cruelly. If Atkins thought it his duty to stay, what was Kydd doing, fleeing? Then he brought to mind the hopeless attempts in *St George* at showing sail to the storm. Without a shadow of doubt it was the admiral's intention to wear about and, if this was so, Kydd was essentially following his example and unspoken orders and had no need to accuse himself. His had been a successful manoeuvre. *St George's* had not. That *Defence* had chosen the way she had was Atkins's personal decision and had no bearing on his own.

Now safely close-hauled on the starboard tack *Thunderer* stood out to sea, pounding and crashing through the violence to her deliverance . . . while astern the last moments of two great men-o'-war were played out. Mercifully, as if unable to bear the horror of the carnage below, the moonlight dimmed and failed, and they were spared the sight.

Rigid with anguish Kydd saw through his ship winning her way seawards, salvation over death, her destiny reprieve and safe harbour, while under her lee astern life was ending for thousands.

'Nothing we can do, sir,' Roscoe said gravely.

'No,' Kydd choked. 'Nothing.'

Even if they waited for respite and there were survivors, Denmark was the home of the enemy, hostile and resentful after its losses at Copenhagen and would bitterly resist any landings. But they were a sea-people and would treat any survivors well. It only remained for him, with heavy sorrow, to take the news to England of its latest sacrifice to Neptune and the gods of war.

Chapter 57

In just the two days it took to cross the North Sea the storm faded into a spiteful scend and fluky breeze, and they finally raised the brown cliffs of Sheppey in a well-behaved south-westerly. Pennants were hoisted and answered as they passed around Garrison Point and into the dockyard anchorage to pick up moorings, where *Thunderer* went to her rest.

It had to be Sheerness, for it was best connected by telegraph to the Admiralty and Whitehall, and Kydd had news that would shock the kingdom. 'Come on, old man. Let's face it together,' he told Craddock, finding his carefully worded signal. He was grateful to have the level-headed Craddock at his side at this time.

His barge touched at the weed-slimed steps he remembered from another life when he'd mounted them as a mutineer those uncountable years before. A marine guard snapped to attention as he landed, his dress now that of the captain of a battleship, his mission the making of a thousand new widows.

'The port admiral, if you please at your earliest convenience.'

'Admiral Cuthbert,' the lieutenant answered. 'Certainly, sir.'

A plain carriage waited and, with Craddock aboard, they whirled off to the residence, with its red ensign of seniority floating above the doorway and its two sentries.

Cuthbert descended the stairs. 'Be welcome to Sheerness, sir. It's . . .?'

'Sir Thomas Kydd, *Thunderer* 74, with urgent news.'

'Not so urgent you'll refuse a bracer? Do come in, old fellow.'

They entered a comfortable, well-ordered drawing room with nautical ornaments from the seven seas tastefully on show. A fire crackled busily, throwing its warmth even to the corners. 'Now what is this news that exercises you so, Sir Thomas?'

Wordlessly, Kydd handed over his signal. 'I'd be happy to see this sent off by telegraph without delay, sir.'

'Very well.' A small silver bell was rung and a flag-lieutenant appeared, his curiosity barely concealed. 'Flags – get this off instanter, if you will. Replies to me here.'

The admiral was of an age, lines of experience deeply incised, but his manner was pleasant. 'So. From the Baltic?' he said keenly.

'Aye, sir. And the news from there grievous indeed.' To his shame, the tears he'd held back since his helpless witness of events on the Jutland shore now brimmed over.

'Good Lord! I had no idea . . . Helen, a brandy – chop-chop, dear.' His wife hurried in with a generous glass.

They sat together by the fire and Kydd managed an account of the times and a rough estimate of the appalling losses to be expected.

Cuthbert remained silent for a moment, transfixed as if in memory. 'The poor devils,' he breathed. 'Not a chance, but they played it like brave 'uns.'

'It's bad cess ashore as well,' Kydd replied. 'Boney going like smoke and oakum into Russia. I heard that Smolensk was taken, and then a smaller town called Borodino but with a monstrous pile of dead the result. It seems there's nothing between Bonaparte and—'

'Yes, but I think I have later news than you, an aviso cutter taking the northern route around your storm. Seems that it's all over, is all. Bonaparte's prevailed, conquered. He's in Moscow, set it aflame and now has the world at his feet.'

'Then . . .?' Kydd was at a loss. If Bonaparte now had his immense army astride the capital and had burst out of his Continental prison there was little that Britain, with its contemptible little army, could do to stop his final erupting into the rest of the world. It was as near as could be imagined the end of everything.

'That's not all.'

'Sir?'

'The Americans have taken another frigate, damn the rascals. It's not to be borne, the rogues.'

Kydd hunched in gloom and despondency. Since the beginning of the endless French wars in '93 there'd been setbacks and black periods but none where the whole world had been set against them.

'Oh, I'm forgetting.' Cuthbert fumbled in his waistcoat. 'I've a signal addressed to you, *Thunderer*, received only an hour ago. As through Admiral Saumarez, your commander. Saves me passing it on.'

He handed over the paper, a telegraph office form. It had to be urgent, going by this privileged and near-instant means.

Kydd took it, his mind too full of recent events to give it much attention.

It was short and to the point, the originator, Flag, Plymouth.

'Accession to your fleet: one nine-pounder, all trim and a-taunto, in due course admiral's flag.'

What the devil? The port admiral of Plymouth was advising that a nine-pounder unit, presumably a sloop, was being attached to *Thunderer* in the flippant guise of his fleet, but he was at an utter loss as to what the reference to an admiral's flag meant.

'Nothing,' he said heavily, passing it back.

Something in his tone made Cuthbert hesitate. He took the signal and read it, frowned – then brightened.

He grinned. 'Dear fellow! Do believe that in my time I've seen more than a brace of telegraph signals and I've a notion what this one means.'

'Oh?'

'Why, it's perfectly understandable to those with the wit to construe it.'

'May I know what—'

'Certainly. A naval lady of some enterprise has found a way to let her husband know of the arrival of a nine-pound infant set fair to win his admiral's flag in time. Could that in any way mean your own good self, hey?'

As with a midsummer's dawning, Kydd's world transformed. He was a father – he had a son who was his to instruct and guide, to love and cherish. To be a Kydd in the years and decades to come. To—

'As we will wet the younker's head in a bumper. Flags – the biggest bottle of champagne you can find!'

In a haze of undiluted joy Kydd bashfully acknowledged the admiral's full-hearted toast.

But there was a catch in his throat as he thought of those he'd known who were leaving their bones on a desolate Jutland beach, their families never more to see them. The even more immense numbers that were tasting death at the hands of

Bonaparte's hordes to satisfy the greed of a tyrant. And far away, across the Atlantic, the unimaginable spectacle of American frigate victories. The world was convulsed in an apocalyptic ruination and here he was, toasting the entry into it of a tiny scrap of humanity.

He composed himself and raised his glass instinctively to the view out of the old-fashioned mullioned windows. The eternal sea. And by chance his eyes focused on one ship at anchor, sea-worn and storm-battered but holding herself proud – and his mind cleared.

'Gentlemen. To . . . to *Thunderer*.' His voice was husky but he didn't care. 'The ship, as I will be proud and happy, shall take my being into the future, whatever awaits us there.'

'His Majesty's Ship *Thunderer*.'

And the world became another place.

Glossary

abaft	positioned closer to the stern of a ship
barky	affectionate slang for ship
Black Virgin	a painting held in Vilna (Vilnius) of the Virgin Mary in black
Brodie stove	standard stove fitted to British warships
carpenter's wings	space cleared against the ship's side for the carpenter, to enable access for repairs
cat and fish	when the anchor is clear of the water the process of securing it to the ship's side
chaloupe canonnière	single-masted 50-foot gunboat mounting one or two large cannons
cobbs	hard coin of value
Cossack	east Slavic peoples inhabiting the interior plains of Russia
crache feu	gun-brig of Swedish origins mounting up to three large guns
cuirassier	French cavalry with breastplate armour, with sabre and pistols
dandy prat	overly ornamented show-off
dark-lantern	lantern that when alight can have its light obscured or revealed at will
dit	curious naval yarn swapped among seamen
douanier	continental customs official
drubbing	humiliating thrashing
druxy	wood so rotten it squelches to the touch
fay	timber strakes laid and secured on the one below
fiacre	light four-wheel carriage for hire

Great Comet	seen in the sky for nearly a year, it was greatly feared as a portent of doom
guardo	as seen in a harbour guardship, notorious for sharp practices
gudgeon	the receiving hole for the pintle on a rudder, secured to the sternpost
hoy	workaday craft around a dockyard
lady's hole	where the 'lady of the gunroom' keeps his rags and implements
larbowlines	slang for the larboard watch
Leveller	term of abuse for seventeenth-century political belief that all men should be equal
messenger line	a light line tied to a larger to better enable it to be passed across
Mr Vice	form of address to the vice-president of the mess
pendant	normally a line attached to rigging blocks, as opposed to pennant, a form of flag
pintle	a pin fixed to a rudder to insert into the gudgeon that supports its weight
priddy	pretty up
redingote	knee-length frock coat
roves	circular copper devices placed inside a clinker-built boat over the nails
rutters	manual of sailing instructions for foreign seas
schuyt	galliot-rigged barge-like Dutch vessel
sheer	curve of the decks towards the bow and stern
shicer	low trickster
siege train	heavy guns complete with all their gear for operation and deploying
simkin	of low intelligence
spirketting	timber laid fore and aft at the meeting of deck and ship's side
starbowlines	slang for the starboard watch
stay	line used to steady a mast
stonachie	pocketable rope's end used by petty officers to strike laggards
the silent hours	during the night after lights are doused
tie-cleat	one- or two-armed fitting for temporary fastening of ropes
tie-mate	friends who take turns to plait each other's pigtail
vedette	a mounted sentry on patrol
veldwachteren	Dutch country watchmen
voltigeurs	military skirmishers, sharp-shooters
waister	seaman whose station is in the middle of the ship

Author's Note

The year 1812 is dominated by one colossal event that sets all else almost to irrelevance. It's probably the most written-about affair of the entire span of the French wars and at the time held the world in thrall — a Titanic canvas against which I set this tale: Napoleon Bonaparte's invasion of Russia. I could not ignore it, and in my long-standing desire to provide the reader with context and reason for events as they unfold before Kydd, I hope I've given satisfaction. The times were momentous, the stakes epic and the scale monumental, not least of which was the immense size of the horde that flooded across the plains into Russia, in numbers only exceeded by a very few cities on the planet at the time. That Britain was not more closely involved was almost certainly down to the untimely assassination of Perceval, the prime minister, which threw the government into chaos and paralysis.

The book opens with a pivotal event in Kydd's career. Despite his sorrow at losing *Tyger*, the command of a 74-gun ship-of-the-line was no mean achievement for any naval officer. The line-of-battle ship was a real wooden wall in a well-drilled fleet; they were proven battle-winners and Britain's history resounds to their victories. Their sheer magnitude was deeply impressive. A yacht's two-inch deck cleat translates in a 74 to a man-high fitting; her sails all set abroad could be measured in acres; and her guns were each the heft of two or three family cars. And if you stepped aboard it was possible to pace along her decks for miles before repeating yourself. A squadron of sail-of-the-line in line-ahead was a majestic and breathtaking sight, its war-like splendour never to be seen again after the vanquishing of Bonaparte.

The action of Lyngør described in these pages has to be to the undying credit of the Norwegians and Danes, particularly Captain Holm of the *Najaden* who fought against impossible odds to the end, knowing that he commanded the last and only ship of consequence left to the Danish/Norwegian Navy.

On another tack, it's not widely known that Napoleon's invasion fleet was kept fully intact after Trafalgar and, in fact, battle-fleets and invasion craft were still building when overrun just before the end of the war. My own belief is that it was the display of effortless sea supremacy at Boulogne that tipped the scales more towards a gigantic invasion of Russia rather than taking on the thin naval forces around Britain, whose empire in far parts of the globe absorbed most of her maritime resources.

Tsar Alexander was a strange and mystical creature, driven by impulses buried deep in the Russian psyche yet eager to take his country out of its medieval torpor. His fascination with the west led him to trust foreign savants, such as Renzi, in preference to his own faction-ridden and often ignorant tribe. He did, however, become central to the later nation-consuming fight-back against Napoleon and, true to his word, it was he and his peasant legions who marched on to be first at the gates of Paris, to enter as conquerors. The history of our own time would be very different if this all-powerful and autocratic Romanov had held on to the liberal Speransky and adopted his plans for the liberation of the serfs and so forth, almost certainly heading off the bloody revolutions of a century later.

The battle of Borodino is notorious for its savagery and murderous ferocity. Modern research examining artillery dockets of ammunition expended has determined that in the fourteen hours of the battle the average rate of cannon fire was three shots every second. In the square miles of bloodshed, casualties included forty-seven French generals – and it wasn't until May 1813 that the last corpse was finally interred.

The latter part of the book is devoted to the loss of *Defence* and *St George* on the wild shore of Jutland. I freely make confession that the event took place precisely a year earlier in 1811 but, such is its resonance to me of striving and sacrifice, that I felt I must include it before its time-frame receded too far. Events are as close as I can make them to what actually happened, Kydd and *Thunderer* standing in for Captain Pater and the similarly rated *Cressy*. The incident is almost unknown to a general readership, but deserves telling – the magnificent seamanship involved in refloating the flag-ship and getting her under tow for the entire distance out of the Baltic as winter closed in, the jury rig and rudder surviving all but the last and worst gale, the hopeless hours at the end played out so nobly.

What Kydd could not have known until later is that after *St George* unsuccessfully tried to wear she tried that last hope, a club-haul, as described in *Seaflower*. She was desperately unlucky for she overran the anchor and its fluke tore away the Pakenham rudder, leaving them out of control and unable to do anything further to avoid their fate. The two ships went into the crashing surf and by morning it was all over. Just twelve survived of the 865 in *St George* and six from the 560 of *Defence*. Added to the loss with all hands of *Hero*, a sister ship to *Thunderer* who was escort to the convoy and suffered shortly afterwards on the Dutch coast, the navy's toll of dead in this one North Sea hurricane was greater than the entire death roll at Trafalgar.

That night the Danes tried heroically to rescue more but were overwhelmed by the violence of the storm, taking tender care, however, of those who were saved and later repatriating them to England. The next day bodies were so thickly strewn that there was no alternative but to bury them where they lay and, ghoulishly, the local people still call their waterfront *Døde mands klitter* – 'Dead Man's Dunes'. At Thorsminde, where the drama played out, you will find a stone memorial that honours those thousands who perished and a museum filled with artefacts that are still to this day turning up regularly.

Some readers at this point will cry, 'Have you then written Stirk and his shipmates out of the series?' I can say to you that most certainly I have not! In this tale I didn't want to make it easy for our hero in his elevation but in my next book you will be making their reacquaintance . . . with a twist.

As usual, to all those who assisted in the research for this book, I owe a debt of gratitude. My appreciation also goes to my agent, Isobel Dixon; my editor, Oliver Johnson; designer Larry Rostant, for his striking cover; and copy editor Hazel Orme. And last, but by no means least, I make heartfelt recognition of the role of my wife and literary partner, Kathy, who has been at my side for every step of Kydd's journey.